/ DATE DUE # 4

AUG 2 2 1997		
SEP 9 1997		
OCT 3 0 1997		
DEC 3 1997		
JAN 2 0 1998		
FEB 1 0 1998		
FEB 1 8 1998		
MAR 2 3 1998		
MAY 0 6 1998		
JUN 1 1 1998		
0 2 1999		
NOV JUN 1 3 2000		
11/6		
KINDLE COUNTY Series		

DEMCO 38-297

FARRAR
STRAUS
GIROUX

ALSO BY SCOTT TUROW

THE LAWS OF
OUR FATHERS

SCOTT TUROW

THE LAWS OF

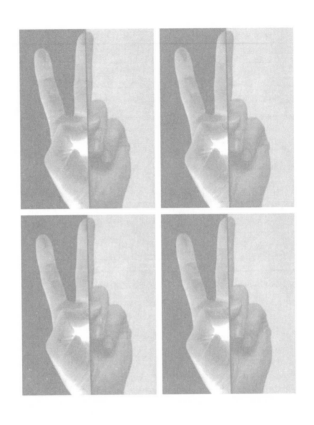

OUR FATHERS

FARRAR STRAUS GIROUX · NEW YORK

Lyrics from "Hey Nineteen," by Walter Becker and Donald Fagen, are quoted with the permission of MCA, Inc.

Lyrics from "I Remember You," by Johnny Mercer and Victor Schertzinger, are quoted with the permission of Famous Music Corp. Copyright © 1942, renewed 1969, by Paramount Music Corp.

A signed first edition of this book has been privately printed by The Franklin Library.

A portion of this book appeared, in slightly different form, in *Playboy* magazine.

LIBRARY OF CONGRESS CATALOGING-IN-PUBLICATION DATA
Turow, Scott.
    The laws of our fathers / Scott Turow. — 1st ed.
        p.   cm.
    ISBN 0-374-18423-2 (alk. paper)
    I. Trials (Murder)—United States—Fiction.   I. Title.
PS3570.U754L3   1996
813'.54—dc20
                                             96-16104
                                                CIP

For Rachel, Gabriel, and Eve

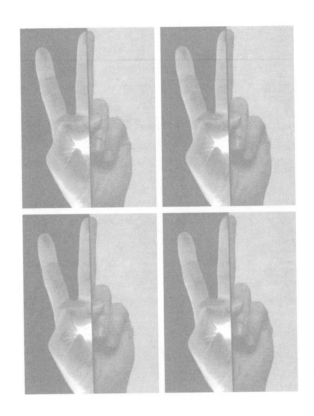

Part One

ACCUSATION

*T*HOSE OF US BORN IN THE YEARS OF BOUNTY *after World War II knew we had a different outlook than earlier generations of Americans. Blinkered by need, they had come of age with narrower commitments—to the glory of God, the glee of acquisition, or the mean little business of survival. But we took seriously the promise of the Declaration of Independence that the birthright of America was not merely life or liberty, but the pursuit of happiness. Personally, as a child, I always assumed that was the point of growing up. So I'd feel better than I did then.*

Which leaves us with the awful doomed inquiry of our middle years, the harpy's voice that whispers in dreams, at sunrise, at those unforeseen instants of drilling isolation: Is this as happy as I will ever be? Do I have the right to just a little more? Or is there nothing better I should hope for?

— MICHAEL FRAIN
"The Survivor's Guide,"
September 7, 1995

September 7, 1995

HARDCORE

Dawn. The air is brackish, although this place is miles from water. The four high-rise towers hulk amid a hardened landscape of brick, of tar and pavement broken by weeds, of crushed Coke cups and candy wrappers, of fly-about newspaper pages. A silvery bedding of broken glass, the remnants of smashed bottles, glitters prettily — one more false promise. It is a time of uncommon quiet. In the night, there are often sounds of life at the extreme: outcries and drunken yells, machines at volume. Sometimes gunfire. The day brings voices, children, the many standabouts, the species at large. Now the wind is up, whistling in the fence links and on the bricks. At the prospect of motion, the man walking this way looks up abruptly, but there is only a dog huddled in a gap between the buildings who, out of some animal instinct, has determined, across the distance of a hundred yards, to have no truck with him. A single used tire sits, inexplicably, on the cracked blacktop of the play yard.

The man, Ordell, is almost thirty-six years old. He still maintains some of his penitentiary build, buffed up, he'd say, although he's been out again four years now. He is dressed simply, black shirt and trousers. No gold. 'Don't wear you no gold when you workin,' he often advises the Unborns, the eight- and nine- and ten-year-old wannabes who trail after him, complimenting his appearance and offering to do him favors, when he arrives here most afternoons. 'Hardcore,' they always goin, 'get you Co-Cola by Ko-rea?' like he don't know they aimin to keep the change.

This morning, Ordell Trent, gang name Hardcore, is alone. The building he approaches, the tallest of the four which comprise the Grace Street Projects, has come over the years to be called by everyone 'the I.V. Tower,' due supposedly to the Roman numerals, but most suspect the label originated with the familiar mockery of the residents practiced by the police, who refer to the building among themselves as the Ivory Tower. The open structures—windows, porches, connecting walkways—are caged in mesh of heavy gauge. Formerly, from the gangways and balconies refuse was sometimes thrown, bricks were tossed down on enemies as in the Middle Ages, drunks and dopeheads stumbled to their death, and several persons were pushed. Around three or four windows you can see the ragged blackening marks of bygone fires and at street level, on the bricks, in rounded letters, the initials of Ordell's gang have been inscribed in phosphorescent colors etched in black: "BSD." Black Saints Disciples. His set—the branch of the gang which Ordell heads—the T–4 Rollers, is often celebrated, too, and some daring members of Gangster Outlaws, a rival organization, have also put their marks here, wallbanging, as it is known. Occasional messages of personal affirmation, quickly sprayed, appear now and then as well. "D'Ron Is Cool." "Lucifer!"

Inside, Ordell nods to security, Chuck, he named, chump rent-a-cop from Kindle County Housing Authority, huddled in a concrete shelter with a small window of bulletproof glass. Chuck gettin half-a-one—fifty dollars—every month from Ordell, and Chuck, he like to love Hardcore, man, see him, Chuck damn well salute. In the entry, the sole illumination is from a Pepsi machine, with a heavy padlock. Every electrical fixture is gone, stolen to sell, or put out by some Saint who prefers to do business in the dark. Bare wires in twisted bunches snake from the walls. The atmosphere is sodden with the bitter reek of hallway filth and broken plumbing. The paint is old; the pipes, exposed overhead, have grown rust stains and mold. The impression is of a bunker—something built to survive the bomb. The floor is concrete, the walls are cinder block. Everything—everything—is marked with gang signs: the Saints' halo, the capped '4' which represents the T-4 Rollers, and names—"D-town," "Mike-o-Mite," "Baby Face," "Priest"—written in school markers or, more often, smoked into the plasterboard or paint with a cigarette lighter.

The elevator, one of them, is working again today and Hardcore rides to 17. The first five floors of this building are more or less deserted now, given up by folks who found even $38.50 a month too high a price for a life where beds had to be placed on the floors to avoid the gunfire, where the safest sleeping was in the bathtub. When he lets himself in, Hardcore hears the old woman's husky breath, clotted by the deteriorations of living, emerging from one of the two back rooms he lets her have.

Ordell has the two front rooms. Where he watches. From up here, he can see the entire operation. Sometimes the po-lice—'Tic-Tac,' as the Saints call the Kindle County Municipal Police Force Tactical Unit—the ones who won't accept Hardcore's money and a few who do, sit down there and watch. They're wondering, he knows. How come this nigger so cool, how come it freeze *up* whenever they on the scene? Because Ordell sees. From here. He got all them tiny gangsters—the youngest gang members—'peepers,' as they're called, rovin, scopin. Any po-lice, any rent-a-cop, any limp DEA, any them mothers truck into them towers, Hardcore gone know. On the street that cuts a perpendicular, there are two three-flats and some tiny gangsters down there on the steps each day, servicing the cars that pull up. They got rock, bottles, crank, sometime pills. Some Top Rank Gangsters, veterans in BSD, they-all slang a couple zones—sell a couple ounces—to they homies every week, be tight, all they need. Not Ordell. He got him houses and ladies, he got a Blazer and a slick BMW 755, shit, he got his gold, but what be fat and all is this thang, what he got goin here—'DJs,' so called, to mix the stuff, and 'scramblers,' who get paid in drugs to make the connections, 'mules' to carry it and move it two times every day from the garages and apartments where it's stored, and his 'artillery,' Honcho, Gorgo, and them, armed motherfuckers so nobody think they can move up on Ordell. Seventy-five people, sometime a hundred, and Hardcore watchin over: Go here, mother, go there, don't get beat by no snitch, don't deal with no narc, don't mess with no rings or gold, see cash, man, do it! *That's* what he wants, somethin happenin, man, every day.

Now, slightly past 6:00, his beeper alerts, vibrating at his hip. Hard-core curses aloud when he inspects the readout: Nile. More whining. "Too late for that shit," he notes to himself. At his voice, the old wom-an's rasping breath briefly ceases. Perhaps she is awake now, listening, pressing at her grey hair, snuffling and clearing her throat in hopes he'll leave. Here in the front room, there is nothing. Two chairs. Old news-papers. The concrete floor holds the sallow glimmer of the early light. The rug was stolen long ago.

This was her apartment, raised her children here, the boy in Rudyard, two boys, Ordell thinks, and some bitch, a silly pipehead selling what she can out on the street. In the pen, the boys come to Jesus and busted out, quit BSD. So Ordell's set moved in here. The old woman was tough. 'You-all go on, shoot and kill me, do whatever you-all like, I ain movin out, this here's my house, I ain givin my house to no bunch of silly-ass hoodlums.'

T-Roc, one of BSD's two heads, Vice-Lord he called—T-Roc told Hardcore straight up, 'Do just like she say, man, fade her.' Hardcore, he put in work for his, done whatever for BSD, be a bar-none Saint and all, but he don't fall to cappin no old lady. He decided leave her stay.

'And I ain gone have no dope-peddlin or whorin or any other gang-banger whatnot in here neither,' she'd said to Ordell.

'We ain doin nothin,' he told her.

'Hmm,' she said.

Now she sleeps. Just then, 6:15 like they been sayin, he sees the ride, some shitbox Chevy a hundred years old, bend the corner on the street far below. Now, Ordell thinks, now we gone tear some shit *up*. He has field glasses but he can see well enough. Bug, just folding the flip-phone back into her jacket, approaches the car. Then she retreats a distance, as she's supposed to do. The cell phone in his pocket makes a throaty sound.

"Yo," he answers. " 'T's up, cuz?"

"Ten-two," Lovinia says. They use radio code, mix it up, make them Tic-Tacs crazy. "Ten-two." Means trouble. Need help. "You hear?" she adds. That Lovinia. Don't never have no respect.

"Stall out, bitch, I hear. And I don't *see* no damn 10–2." On the broad avenue, on Grace Street, there is nothing, cars, white folks driving by fast. Not even foot trade. "I ain't seed nothin. You standin still, bitch, and you best be hittin the wall, man."

"Ain to see, not from where you is, and I ain talkin on this punk-ass telephone neither. Ten. Two." She's gone with that.

Setup, he thinks, as he often thinks. Bug—as Lovinia is known—damn Bug be settin him up. Kan-el, T-Roc, one them, maybe them Goobers—as the Saints call the Gangster Outlaws—one them switched her somehow. He ponders Kan-el and T-Roc, Commandant and Vice-Lord of BSD. They on top, man, but they all the time trippin and shit, worryin is Hardcore on this power thang, man, he gone bust his whole set right out the gang or what? And him running eight zones into the jail every week, so BSD down for theirs, catch his black booty he be gone for-ever. Set him up. "Mmm." He grunts aloud at the thought of it.

But he's on his way. He has a 9-millimeter pistol stored behind the iron grating of the air return and he tucks it in his belt and lets his black silk shirt hang out of his trousers. In the elevator he continues rumbling with his angry thoughts, speaking to himself and wondering if he should have shouted out for Honcho, some of them. Scared, he thinks, scared is what he is and old enough to know it. All them youngsters always puttin down that shit, 'Cain't no nigger fade me,' shit like that, make him laugh. You always scared. Get used to it is all. Gotta be is gotta be.

He has three sons. Dormane—Hardball he called—got two kids of his own, he inside, doing fifteen no-parole on some fool buy-bust, and Rakleed is on these streets, too, and the little one, Del, still too young to know too much of nothing. They mommas, each of them, behind Ordell's back, told those boys the same. 'Don't you be no dope peddler now, don't you be slangin and hangin and bangin, I'll be whompin you backside, you ain never gone be too big for me do you like that.' That's what they sayin. In his own time, Ordell gave each of these boys his answer: 'You got to be somebody. They's bad shit here. With them bad coppers—bad motherfuckers everywhere here. But, man,' he said, 'man, this here what you-all's—you with the people here, you giving them what these poor niggers need, some nickel's worth of happiness white folks and all don't want them havin.'

Walking from the IV Tower, the first stirrings of the day, music and voices, from some windows, wondering is he really gone get himself gauged, Hardcore thinks, as he often does, about his sons. He walks past one of the newer buildings, where the concrete corner has parted, revealing a cheap core of pink foam. In a nearby play area, only one seesaw remains, and on that both seats were long ago shattered by some teen in a random outbreak of destructive will. A milky-eyed drunk is teetering down the block, slept it off somewhere and now looking for home. He has a tatty overcoat and his hat askew, a face of white whiskers, and when he sees Hardcore, he wants to move, get *out* the way, man, and his legs can't let him. Funny. Hardcore calls him "Man" as he passes by. They got they needs, he thinks, wishing he'd told his boys that, too. 'Everybody on these streets, man, these motherfuckers out here is just completely crazy with what they need. This gal she need her check, and this momma be needin to hold her baby, and that old cat need his fix.' Needing. He sometimes thinks he doesn't walk on pavement—he is just moving on top of what everybody needs.

He crosses the boulevard, Grace Street, and starts down Lawrence, a block of ruined three-story apartment buildings, stout as battlements, with flat tarred roofs and limestone blocks placed decoratively amid the dark bricks and as a border above the doorways and at the cornices. The windows are gone in some, boarded up. A raised garden area of railroad ties sits under the windows of 338, the dirt desert dry, even the weeds struggling to survive.

"Yo," Lovinia calls, emerging like a cat from one of her hiding places. This Lovinia, he thinks. God, look-it here at this scrawny bitch, motherfucker are you gone believe it? With this fuzzball stocking cap dragged down over her whole damn head and this grey coat and twill pants. Don't want nobody comin up on her to know she a bitch is what it is, figure they'll shoot her ass or molest her ass or somethin. They better not try neither, she ain't strapped—armed—she know better than that for when Tic-Tac come by, but you bet she got it near here, under the mailbox, or in a hole in one them trees, you mess with her, she gone smoke you ass. Word up. T-Roc, he think Hardcore stone crazy using Bug, but she sharp. She strut up to the cars, she change her whole routine now, she sort of swingin it a lot. 'What you like, man?' Make them say. Anybody she take for Tic-Tac, narco, when they say 'Dope,' she just go, 'Oh, man, I ain sellin *dope*, man, I got somethin sweeter 'n that, man,' like she thinkin they was here to bone.

Now she points to the white Nova at the curb, a hundred feet away. "I done told her, 'Lady, you in the wrong place.'"

"Lady? What kind of motherfuckin lady?"

"Tol' you now, 10–2. He ain come. She come. She be lookin for Or

Dell." Bug smiles then, toward the walk. Lovinia, just a kid and all—fifteen—she love to play.

"Lady," Hardcore repeats a few more times. Damn. He advances on the car. "Lady, this the wrong place for you." Leaning into the darkness of the car, he catches some of her soapy smell and the humid sour scent of his own overheated breath. "You best get out here fast."

"Mr. Trent? I'm June Eddgar." She extends her hand, and then laboriously leaves the car to stand in the bluish morning light. Old. She be fat, too, big and fat. Some kind of hippie or farmer or some such, and her thighs all mashed together in her jeans. She have a plain face and some long lightish brown kinda hair going to grey, kind of lopsided and knit together like it ain't really combed. "I thought we could talk a minute."

"Lady, they ain nothin for you and me to talk about."

"Well, I thought— I'm Nile's mother."

"Told him get hisself here. Didn't tell him send nobody's momma."

"I thought it was better if I came."

"You better go. Thass all. They's some powerful shit may go down here. Word, now. Go on." He steps away, flitting his hand.

"Look, I know them both. I think there's a misunderstanding."

"Only misunderstandin is you stayin here stead of leavin out when I say go. Thass the only misunderstanding we got."

"I really think—"

"Lady, you gone get fucked up bad, you hear? Now jump in you rusty-ass ride." He throws a hand again in disgust and walks away. Lovinia has stepped toward the street, waving.

"Gorgo," she calls, signaling overhead.

"Aw, fuck me, motherfuck," Hardcore says. From the alley across the way, Gorgo has emerged, tearing out on a sturdy black-framed mountain bike. He has a mask on, a blue handkerchief across his face like he some cowboy motherfucker, but looks otherwise like he just goin home to momma, blue pack fixed on his back, red satin jacket, hat turned behind his ear, just a kid, if you don't notice the gat—the gun—held low by his side. A 9. Got his Tec-9. The semiautomatic weapon, from its sheer weight, seems to drag behind as Gorgo rides. Bug keeps on waving, calling out as Gorgo rushes on, but he doesn't see her. He never will, Hardcore knows. You can see Gorgo's eyes at sixty feet now, popped out like some pipehead's, only with him all it is is panic. I gotta do this, Gorgo's thinking, got to do this, man. Hardcore knows. His whole self is shrunken down to a little pea of violent will, so there's no room for anything to tell him no. The gun is up, straight this way, and for one second Ordell sees nothing of it but the small silver *o* and the frightening black space within it, at the end of the muzzle.

"Gorgo!" she calls again, and Hardcore, who has already dropped to the pavement, catches the hem of her coat and drags at it.

"Get yo fool self down," he says, and she comes to him, easy as a leaf falling from a tree, just as the first shots bolt the air. Damn guns always be louder than you expect. The reports come at once, five or six volleys, a rampage of sound. Just that quick. Afterwards, it is the same as always, a moment of awful, cowering stillness—the birds gone from the trees, radios knocked silent, folks in the adjoining buildings stretched out flat along the cold floors, desperate not to stir. Caught up, the pointed scent of gunpowder embitters a sudden breath of wind. A block off, in some silly act of jubilation and relief, Gorgo cries out shrilly and his voice trails down the distance like a ribbon.

Breathe, Ordell thinks, breathe now, nigger. He's amped: his heart is hard with panic. You okay. He talks to himself. You not hurt, stay cool, stay movin. Then he sees the blood spread darkly on the sidewalk.

He has been shot twice before, once when he was sixteen, that was some serious shit, sort of giving face to some dude, and the mother pulled out a .38 and boom, just like it was but a little more downtalk. Now he cool. He's checked his body twice, felt everything. He damn well knowed he was gone get hisself popped and he didn't. But Lovinia has hold of her knee, and she is moaning.

"Happenin, Bug?"

She's crying. Tears well across her smooth face and curl in silvery traces about her mouth.

"It hurt, Hardcore. Man, it hurt *real* bad."

"We gone help you, girlfriend." He crawls closer to her. She is lying on her side, with her knee drawn up halfway. Her hands are covered with blood and it has turned most of the right leg of her twills brown; this close, he can detect the strange animal smell of it. He isn't going to get her to move, he can see that. How'd she go get shot in the damn leg of all places? Ricochet, or some such. Dudes shot in the leg died, too. He'd seen that. Severed femoral artery. Leg might be broke. There was no use shoutin out for any of his people, tiny gangsters or them. Soon as the guns rang out, they sprung.

"That Gorgo. I'm gone fuck that motherfucker up bad." Gorgo is long gone—between the buildings, up an alley, down one more gangway. Somewhere along, the Tec-9 went into the backpack. Now he's just some skinny kid out on his ride. Up above, somewhere, a window screams as it's opened.

"I hope all you goddamn gangbangers be dead, what I hope." The woman's voice carries clearly in the thin morning. "I hope you dead. Look at what you-all done."

"Call the 'mergency, bitch," he shouts.

"I already done that. Po-lice comin. They gone take yo sorry ass down to the jail where it belong, Hardcore."

At his name, he wheels and the window is slammed to, that fast, before he can see. Lovinia is still moaning.

"Gone help you, homegirl," he repeats. The white lady, he sees now, Nile's momma, she layin there, too. They's just blood, blood, all over her head. Half her brownish hair gone and she ain't moving none. Smoked, he thinks. He's seen dead before and knows it for sure.

Bug is all gone to pieces. Some is like that. Them po-lices, Tic-Tacs, they done her like they do, took her, handcuffed her arm over her head all day, walk by her smacking them nightsticks in they palms, she be tight, like it don't bother her none. But now she cryin like a baby, she like something what got broke. She wasn't gonna hold. Nile neither. Specially Nile. His daddy gone be goin on now, *in* his shit. When them Tic-Tacs start in with questions, wasn't nobody gone ride this beef. Gone be *all* fucked up.

"Po-lice comin," he tells Bug. He's going to have to figure something. That damn woman know his name. Tic-Tac be knocking on his door. Call the attorney. Call Attorney Aires, he thinks. Gone have to look after hisself. How it always be.

He stands. The white Nova is messed up. The windows, except the one which was open, are shot through, jagged pieces gone and the remainder a map of silver crazes; the tires on the side that faced Gorgo's onslaught are flattened, causing the car to list. Through one of the steel window supports, there is a single bullet hole, the white paint burned grey about it. Damn him anyway, Hardcore thinks. Damn Nile, fuck everything up.

"Best gimme that shit, girlfriend. You got trouble enough."

She opens her mouth, but cries out as she turns herself to reach.

"Here?" he asks and slips his finger quickly between her tooth and gum to pull out the little foil packet. Goddamn, what he gone catch from her mouth anyway? "This here just some damn drive-by," he tells her. "You hear? Outlaws ridin down. Po-lice gone be askin. Thass what you say. Same as we done said. Just Goobers ridin down on you." He touches her cheek. She wasn't never gone stand up to Tic-Tac. "Posse out," he says. Bye-bye.

"P.O.," she repeats.

He hates it most when he has to run.

September 12, 1995

SONNY

Her Honor, Judge Sonia Klonsky, enters her chambers, burdened with packages and the teeming, solitary feelings of the lunch hour, and finds two police officers in the outer office usually occupied by her minute clerk, Marietta Raines. Both large men, the cops linger over a yellow legal pad, drafting an affidavit to support an arrest warrant. The white one, Lubitsch, is a self-conscious prototype, a body builder who has turned himself into a human landscape, with mountainous shoulders and a neck like a tree stump. He has removed his sport jacket and seated himself at Marietta's desk. As he writes, his partner, Wells, makes sounds over Lubitsch's shoulder to show whether or not he agrees.

Passing by, the judge glances at the face sheet of the warrant which they have already completed for her approval. From the two brown paper sacks she carries, the aromas of a household arise, bread and produce and cardboard, items gathered as she rushed store to store among the little Italian shops that persist on these depleted streets near the Kindle County Central Courthouse. Lunch is the most important hour of the day for Sonny, the only time she is without direct responsibilities to others. She must retrieve Nikki from day care by 5:00, and then begin the hours of feeding, bathing, talking, mothering—her truest labor, in Sonny's mind. Now, with the bags still in her arms, she remains vaguely conscious of six summer nectarines she picked by hand whose cool flawless skin and sensuous cleft woke her unpredictably—comically—to some semblance of longing.

The warrant is for one DeLeel Love, residing at Apartment 9G, 5327 Grace Street, DuSable. On Saturday, September 10, according to the warrant, "Defendant did commit the offense of deviate sexual assault against one Zunita Collins, aged twelve, a minor, in that he engaged in the unconsented and offensive touching of said Zunita Collins's breasts, buttocks, and vagina." Wells points to the defendant's name.

"Guess he's just *Love* all the time," he says. A stout man, Wells smiles too broadly. He has dark, venous gums and snaggle teeth. Lubitsch continues writing, which means he has heard the remark before.

The last time Wells was in here, a month or two ago, he talked to Sonny at length about his son who was competing in the Special Olympics. But the crime—the projects—has brought something rougher to the surface. There are some cops who remind Sonny of her Uncle Moosh, in whose home she lived for extended periods throughout her childhood, men who seem to be the calm center of the world, quietly and confidently sorting good from bad with the cheerful conviction that it is somehow worth the effort. But neither Wells nor Lubitsch is like that. For them you can see that each case, each crime is personal, riling contentious feelings.

In this, of course, they are more like Sonny than she would prefer. In her prior job as a prosecutor, an advocate, it seemed natural to feel this intense connection to every case, to the world's need to punish, to be for the victims and their right to receive whatever poor amends they could. Coming to the bench, she welcomed the prospect of more distance, but instead, she frequently finds herself not merely touched by cases but, in ways that puzzle her, still deeply involved. Occasionally, she is gripped by the anguish of the victims. But most often—too often for comfort—it is the accused, the defendants, poor and always somehow wretched, who remind her in the most secret and fragmentary ways of herself.

The judge lifts a hand to the cops, letting them resume work on their warrant. They are amiable regulars here, particularly welcome because few other persons around this courthouse seem to fully trust her. Most of the clerks, the deputies, the PAs and judges regard Sonny as a foreigner, a former federal prosecutor who was one of a half dozen lawyers of established integrity recruited to the state court bench by a Reform Commission created in the wake of the latest bribery scandal, which enveloped four different courtrooms. Sonny suspects that after only two years on the bench, she is regarded by her colleagues as unqualified to be sitting on felonies, a plum—and demanding—assignment. Certainly she is unwanted here amid people who have been entrusted with each other's secrets for years.

In the interior office of the chambers, the deputy sheriff assigned to the courtroom, Annie Chung, is arranging the array of multicolored paperwork that resulted from the tumultuous status call which Sonny holds each Tuesday morning. At the sight of the judge, Annie rises to relieve her of her packages, taking an instant to peer discreetly into one. Annie has begun night classes at college. She dreams of law school and, Sonny is sure, envisions herself someday in the flowing black raiment of a judge, on the bench, empowered and obeyed. To these hopes there is a heartsore quality, since Annie a few months ago married a sleek, wealthy boy from Hong Kong, far more traditional than she is. At times Sonny sees Annie staring at the wedding and engagement rings on her left hand, admiring them in the light, but with the startled, immobilized air of some discontent she cannot yet name.

"Reporters called," Annie says.

"What about?"

"You god a new case, up for initial appearance at 2:00. Ordell Trent. A.K.A. Hardcore." She has a distinct Chinese accent that softens the r's to the point that they are indistinct. Aw-dell. Hahd-caw. "Murder in the First Degree."

"You caught that one, Judge?" Lubitsch has come to absorb the light in the doorway. "We had that goof in the station this morning. Big-time Saint. That's the one I was tellin you about?" He is speaking to Wells. "Where we got to get over to General? Judge, that case's a doozy."

Sonny shakes her head. Her dark hair is abundant and, as has been the case since college, is worn free to her shoulders. There is now more than a little grey, which in this job is thought to add distinction.

"Fred, come on. Don't backdoor me. I'll hear it from the PA in court."

"Yeah, okay," he says, "but it's a doozy."

"It's a doozy," Sonny says and restrains, in the name of amity, a motion to Annie to close the door. She has taken her chair behind an enormous mahogany desk, which, with its tiered edges, reminds her of a steamship. From the tall old mullioned windows behind her, a grand view of the back reaches of DuSable city recedes. On her desk is a Lucite gavel, three feet long, given to her by her colleagues when she left the United States Attorney's Office. In jest, they had it inscribed *Ms. Justice Klonsky.* There are also pictures of two children, her daughter, Nikki, almost six, and Sam, a knock-kneed boy past twelve, whom she helped raise during the years she was married to his father. Sonny left that man, Charlie, almost three years ago.

"It was on the radio last week," says Annie. "Those damn gangbangers or somethin. Some kind of drive-by shooting? And this lady god in the way. A white lady."

"White?" says Sonny. "Where in the world did this happen?"

Annie reads from the complaint in the court file, prepared by the PAs in Felony Review: 6:30 a.m. September 7. Grace Street again.

"What was she doing at Grace Street?" Sonny asks.

"Maybe she's with Probation? Children's Services? Somethin like that."

"At that hour?" Sonny motions for the complaint. Reminded, she calls out to the officers to be sure they notified Children's Services about Zunita Collins.

"Already got her," Lubitsch answers.

"Got who?" asks Marietta, coming through the door. Returning from lunch, she is still wearing sunglasses and carries a package of her own. Without a word, the two cops rise at once to make way. Marietta Raines is proprietary about every aspect of this courtroom, where she has been the clerk—and procedural ruler—for almost two decades. She throws her purse and packages inside her desk and immediately reads the pages the officers have drawn for the judge's approval.

"Lord!" says Marietta, shaking her head over Zunita Collins. "I don't wanna hear about nobody had a better weekend than me." In a heavy-footed way, Marietta moves into the inner chambers, feigning to remain oblique to the dark look the judge has passed her. With barely a rearward glance, Marietta throws the inner door closed on the two cops still howling over her remark. She has on a long bunchy cotton skirt, summer wear that will outlast the season in this overheated building. Despite their nine months together, Sonny is still not certain whether the woolly Afro Marietta wears is a wig. Rather than further confront her clerk—always a challenge—the judge returns to the murder complaint Annie handed her, the one naming the gangbanger Hardcore.

"Oh my God," says Sonny. "My God. 'June Eddgar'? I know June Eddgar. She's the one who was killed? My God. Her son's a probation officer, isn't he? Nile Eddgar? Remember when he was in here I told you I knew his family?"

Marietta, already familiar with the murder case, nods and with a flawless memory recalls the matter on which Nile appeared last May. Nile, as Sonny remembers that appearance, was tall and poorly groomed; he wore a funky goatee and was far too fidgety to meet her eye. He gave no sign he might have any memory of her from so long ago.

"Oh God," Sonny says again. "June Eddgar. Do I have to disqualify myself?"

"What for?" asks Marietta. "She your girlfriend or somethin? How'd you know her in the first place, Judge? You-all from the same neighborhood?"

"No, no, it was in California. We lived in the same apartment building with the Eddgars. My boyfriend and I. He used to babysit for Nile. This is years ago. Twenty, at least. More. God, what a weird coincidence." She shivers somewhat. It always takes her an instant to recognize what has gripped her so fiercely. Death. Dying. A dozen years ago, she had cancer of the breast, and anything that whispers about her own mortality can seize her with panic. "Nile's father's here, isn't he? In the state legislature? Is that right?"

"State senator." Marietta, who is beholden to her councilman for her job, goes to all the dinners, knows every party figure. "District 39. Far Kindle, Greenwood Counties. Some kind of college professor seem like. And he got some funny name."

"Loyell Eddgar," says Sonny, and all three women laugh. Names, around here, are a never-ending subject. African names, Hispanic names, gang names. Aliases by the dozen. "People just call him Eddgar. At least they used to. I think he was teaching at Easton at one point. That's how he ended up back here. He'd gone there before. When I knew him—in California?—he was a Maoist. God, those were crazy times," adds Sonny and for a moment is held by the turmoil, the conflict of those years. It seems so far away and yet, like so much of life, underlies everything she is doing, like the soil from which all that's planted blooms. And now he's a state senator. 'Wow,' is what she wants to say. Lexicon of that bygone era. Wow. There have been some changes in her lifetime.

"I think June and he split up a long time ago," Sonny adds. "As far as I knew, she didn't even live around here." The details have not really stuck. Her mind is porous when it comes to gossip. She will often make terrible gaffes.

"And which boyfriend is it you was living with?" asks Marietta. "The one who writes the column now?"

Yet another dark look passes from the judge to her clerk, a plump brown woman of middle years who, as ever, makes a determined effort to pay no mind. Within the chambers, when there are no outsiders, there is an odd intimacy among the three women, especially when the conversation turns away from the law to home, men, children — the female realm with its mysterious equality. Yet Marietta knows no proper bounds. The way she puts it! As if Sonny had submitted a curriculum vitae of her love life. 1969–70: Seth Weissman a.k.a. Michael Frain. 1970–72: various gentlemen of the Philippines. 1972–75: long dry spell. 1977–1992: Charles Brace. In truth this is information that Marietta has cobbled together with her own insistent curiosity, which Sonny always feels somewhat powerless to turn aside. Marietta has a husband of sorts, Raymen, but they have their troubles. For Marietta, therefore, this is the question of her life: What happens to love?

"What guy who writes the column?" Annie asks.

"Now haven't you heard that? Judge here used to live with that fella — what's his name, Judge?"

"Marietta, that was in the dark ages. I was a child."

But the usual look of appreciation for Sonny's accomplishments has already come across Annie's tiny face.

"He's in the *Tribune*," Marietta says. "How'd you call it, what he writes, Judge?"

"Lifestyle, I suppose. The sixties survivor point of view."

"Right. You know how funny people can be in what they do."

"I think the column is called 'The Survivor's Guide.' Michael Frain," says Sonny. "He writes under the name of Michael Frain. He's syndicated," she adds and then feels that she's fallen into Marietta's trap and is actually boasting about this boy who came and went from her life before Noah set to sea.

"Oh, I read that," says Annie. "He make me *laugh*. *He* was your boyfriend?"

"Momentarily. But his name isn't really Michael Frain. It's Seth Weissman. Michael Frain is a pen name. The whole thing is somewhat confusing. We knew somebody named Michael Frain at that point. He lived in the building, too."

"With Nile Eddgar and them?"

"Right. Nile and Eddgar and June in one apartment. Seth and me in another. And then Michael Frain. Other people, too, obviously."

"Sounds like some commune," says Marietta, and Sonny cannot contain herself, she laughs aloud. Sometimes Marietta might just as well say it: You white folks are strictly crazy. Yet there was some aspect of happy communalism in those years — young, before the walls were up, the boundaries drawn. Seth's best friend, who was in law school, was always in their apartment, Hobie something, a big, funny guy, black, a wild character.

Annie has looked up from the files and studies the judge, trying to comprehend all of this — the names, the relations. She has delicate looks, her eyes smallish against a broad flange of cheek. Sonny repeats herself.

"Michael wasn't my boyfriend. My boyfriend's name was Seth. He's the one who writes the column. But the pen name he uses is Michael Frain."

Marietta, with a big-city look of mistrust, finally speaks the lingering question. "So what happened to Michael Frain?"

"I haven't the foggiest," says Sonny. "God's Truth. Seth and I were past tense by then." Not that she hasn't wondered. A sudden stab of curiosity sometimes reaches her when she sees the name, the picture at the heading of the column. How did Seth become Michael? Where did Michael go? The questions, even now, make her uneasy.

This talk of Seth, of newspapers, brings Sonny's mind again to June Eddgar and the murder. There will be reporters in the courtroom. A white lady murdered in a drive-by. Mother of a probation officer. A prominent politician's ex. Lubitsch is right. It's a doozy.

"I'd love to keep this case," she says to Marietta. It's not really the attention that excites her. Since all new judges face a yes-no retention vote six years after appointment, the accepted wisdom is to avoid publicity, so that the voters will have no reason to reject you. It's more the past that seems somehow alluring. The unexcavated remains of her own existence. Something back there, perhaps merely her youth, inspires curiosity, the vaguest thrill to think of the distances she's moved.

"Keep it," Marietta answers. "Chief Judge don't like you to transfer cases anyway." The judges—lawyers, pols, bureaucrats by training—are often schemers, inclined to dump demanding or controversial cases on colleagues with less clout. As a result, the Chief, Brendan Tuohey, has erected strict rules. The mere thought of Tuohey and his edicts makes Sonny uneasy. Raised without a father at home, she inevitably finds men of a certain age formidable. And Tuohey, a crafty pol whose probity has long been open to question, has never cared for Sonny or the Reform Commission that forced her into his domain. To her face, he is unfailingly polite, even courtly, but Sandy Stern, Sonny's old friend and occasional mentor, has gone so far as to suggest that Tuohey placed her in the Criminal Division, in spite of her limited judicial experience—a year in the matrimonial division, a few months in the criminal branch courts—in the hope she would fail.

"Well, I have to put something on the record. About knowing June. When's this case up for the bond hearing? Now?"

It's nearly 2:00. There will be no bail, of course. The gang defendants are invariably on probation or parole, and bond, under the law, is not permitted. Sonny asks about Hardcore's probation status and Annie sets off to the outer office to get the answer from Marietta's computer console. Marietta continues racking the files from the morning call on a stainless-steel cart for transport back to the clerk's office.

"Hardcore has himself a probation officer." Lubitsch, having thrown open the door a bit too forcefully, is on the threshold, with Annie beside him. Beaming, virtually luminous with secret knowledge, the policeman engages in a stage pause until Sonny beckons with a hand.

"Nile Eddgar," says Lubitsch. "He's Hardcore's probation officer."

In the corridor outside, between the chambers and the courtrooms, somebody important enough to be disdainful of the peace happens by whistling.

"This gangbanger killed his probation officer's mother in a drive-by?" Sonny asks. "That's a coincidence?"

"That's no coincidence. And no drive-by. Maybe the Saints want to make it look that way. This was a contract killing."

The portent of this is bad: A street gang taking deliberate aim on a probation officer's family. A new battlefront opened in the war on the streets.

"Want to know the rest?" asks Lubitsch, still glowing.

"I'll hear it in court, Fred. I'm going to do your warrant after my motions."

"Whatever you say, Judge," he answers, but cannot restrain one more disbelieving toss of his head. He says yet again, "It's a doozy."

Sonny grabs the black robe from the coat tree behind her desk and zips it halfway. With a certain processional formality, Marietta and Annie hasten before her down the hall into the courtroom. A double doozy. Everyone will want a piece of this case. The Mayor will be on TV, sticking up for law enforcement. An atmosphere of brooding anger will penetrate the courtroom. Sonny, who has not yet endured the storm of a controversial case, becomes conscious somewhere at her center of the troubled qualms of fear.

In the corridor, Marietta's fine alto arrives, so round with pride you would think it's her own name she is singing out. "The Honorable Sonia Klonsky," she can be heard crying, "judge presiding."

Two p.m. bond call. Black men in manacles. The Chief Judge, Brendan Tuohey, sets bail according to a pre-established scale on all cases on which the grand jury returns an indictment. But under state law when a defendant is arrested on the basis of a prosecutor's complaint, he is entitled to a bond hearing before the assigned trial judge. Sonny regards it as one of her saddest duties to deliver the crushing news most of these young men receive, that their liberty, like some item checked at the door, is lost and unlikely soon to be retrieved.

April, Eliot said, is the cruelest month. But if he was looking for the cruelest place, he should have come here, to the Superior Court of Kindle County. A kind of barbarity seems to blow in with the defendants from the bad neighborhoods and mean streets, a grim devastation, a slaughterhouse reek. Here are freely traded the secrets no one wants to hear. At one point last month, there were four different trials ongoing involving mothers or fathers who had murdered their children. This morning Sonny arraigned six gang members who surrounded a recalcitrant twelve-year-old in a housing project stairwell and beat him with a pipe until the brain matter was literally oozing from his skull. These tales of astonishing brutality, of stabbings and rapes, of shootings and stickups, of the inevitable 'crime of the day,' so heinous that, like certain forms of pornography, it seems beyond normal imagining—these are routine, routine, routine, and their meanness is matched only by the system of which she is standard-bearer and emblem, whose clandestine rationale too often seems to Sonny to be to capture, judge, and warehouse the very poor. Every month or so, preparing for a status call, she will go back to the lockup, looking for Annie or the transport deputy, and confront, through the bars, the day's load of prisoners, twelve or fourteen young men. You would expect them to rise up and revolt, but most are quiet, shifting about, smoking their cigarettes. If they dare to look her way at all it is without defiance or, often, hope. They have been humiliated. Tamed.

On the bench, though, sorrow is seldom the predominant emotion. In this atmosphere of loathing and fear she labors on, trying to impose reason where, generally speaking, impulse and emotion have held sway. Murder is the marquee business of this courtroom—gangbangers killing gangbangers; men killing men. They use guns mostly—also knives, bats, razor blades, automobiles, crowbars, and, in one celebrated case, an anvil. The young people kill each other for reasons that are often incomprehensible: because somebody was signifying on the wrong corner; because a jacket was torn. In nine months, she has mastered all the terminology: "ride-by" (shooting on the move); "drive-up" (firing from a stop); "drive-through" (the car is the weapon); "chase-aways" (the enemy flees). The older folks also live in a world from which anger and desperation emanate, as tangible as heat. Yes, men still kill each other over dice games, drugs, and, naturally, who was coveting whose girl. What can you say about a loaded gun in the hand of a spurned and drunken man? On the streets, unrequited love and death go together almost as often as in Shakespeare.

Now the courtroom lingers in the somnolent air of the afternoon. This morning, during the weekly status call, the courtroom and corridor teemed with all the urgent antagonists, the defense lawyers, the cops and prosecutors, the aggravated citizen witnesses, the deputies sullenly transporting the defendants, and those defendants' beleaguered, woebegone women. But now there is a melancholy stillness. Outside the open doors at the rear of the courtroom, a custodian mops the halls in the yellowing light.

Marietta hammers the gavel sharply, and the lawyers and reporters and sheriff's deputies slowly gather themselves to their feet, as Sonny climbs up the four stairs beside the bench, a clean-lined oak affair of faux-Bauhaus design. The senior judges sit in stately palaces in the main building on the third and fourth floors, vast chambers that bespeak the same architectural strategies as cathedrals—the individual dwarfed by the majesty of marble columns and gilt-framed portraiture, by the rococo gewgaws of carved walnut and ceilings vaulting two and a half stories above. These courtrooms in the Central Courthouse Annex were built in the eighties, when D.C. poured what money there was into law enforcement. The room strikes a clanging note of late-century efficiency— bang for the buck. For Sonny, the courtroom feels as intimate as her living room, but like certain children, its glory is not obvious to outsiders. It is a pie-shaped room, broadening back from the bench, rickety public construction, the plasterboard gouged in places, the meal-colored carpet already tearing away in hairy chunks. The jury box and witness stand repeat the stark lines of the bench. Weirdest is the track lighting, reminiscent of a motel lounge, which is positioned over the major players—judge, witness, attorneys—leaving dim spots throughout the windowless courtroom where the lawyers, the bailiff, the clerks tend to retreat in relaxed instants, like actors offstage.

In the wake of the shooting death of a matrimonial court judge several years ago, these courtrooms have been built with a wall of bulletproof glass in front of the spectators' sections. The sound of justice being done is piped back there by way of microphones which seem to pick up the heavy breath of everyone—defendants, lawyers, Sonny herself— in the intervals between words. She looks out there every day, toward the friends, the relatives edging forward on their seats to catch some sight, some news about their loved one in jail overalls. In warning to them, Marietta has taped a hand-lettered sign to their side of the glass:

NO EATING
NO DRINKING
NO VISITING
IN THE LOCKUP
OR THE COURTROOM

Now the dozen reporters who are present resume the leather barrel chairs in the jury box, where they have placed themselves to ensure that they can hear. The amplification system to the region beyond the glass often conks out, and the angled walls make the acoustics unpredictable. The journalists are mostly the hangdog beat reporters, but two of the pretty faces of local TV are present. Stanley Rosenberg, the little ferret from Channel 5, in a $500 blazer—and ratty blue jeans that the camera will not see—scurries to a seat next to a sketch artist he has brought along. In this courthouse, where the judges are elected, the press is inevitably accommodated, especially in the afternoon, when the reporters are all on deadline. Marietta calls first the case about the murder of June Eddgar.

"*People versus Ordell Trent!*" From the lockup, the defendant, a.k.a. Hardcore, is brought into the courtroom in his blue jumpsuit, handcuffs, and ankle chains. With mild alarm, Sonny recognizes the lawyer who comes to stand beside him, Jackson Aires. Aires has fought these wars so long he comes up firing out of instinct—one of those guys who talk the trash he knows his clients want to hear, albeit in a somewhat inanimate fashion, with no real body language to his lament. A worn-out-looking black man of mid-tone complexion, with a pomp of age-whitened African hair, Aires wears an old burgundy sport coat and scuffed bucks. With reporters here, he will put on a hell of a show, demanding bail for his client.

The lawyers state their names and Sonny makes her record: she knew the Eddgar family twenty-five years ago but has had no contact with any of them since, save Nile Eddgar, who may have appeared as a probation officer in this courtroom once. Tommy Molto, deputy supervisor in Homicide, a smallish dumpy-looking lifer who rose close to the top of the PA's office a few administrations back, only to slide back down in the shadow of some disremembered scandal, has appeared for the state, filling in on the initial appearance.

"Mr. Aires, or Mr. Molto, if either of you feels the slightest reservation, I'll be happy to return this case to the Chief Judge for reassignment."

Aires just shakes his head. "No problem, Judge." Molto repeats the same words. She knew the Prosecuting Attorney's Office would have no objection. They have 106 cases in this courtroom. They will have between 98 and 112 cases on her docket every day of the year. They are not about to question her impartiality. Not on the record. The only cavil she will hear, if there is one, will come in the corridors, through the grapevine.

Sonny recites the charges in the complaint. Hardcore looks on alertly. The defendants are usually fazed or anxious, lost to arcana of the courtroom. But Hardcore, burly, dark, with thick eyes, maintains himself with dignity. He knows what is occurring. Innocently, as if she did not know she was sounding a battle alarum, Sonny asks, "Mr. Aires, do you have a motion?" Long-limbed, still lithe-appearing, Jackson Aires uncrosses his arms and edges closer to his microphone that angles up from the oak podium before the bench. To Jackson Aires the criminal law really has no categories, only colors, white and black. He can play the game, talk your talk, cite the precedents, but with no evident belief they control, or even contribute to, the result. To him, every rule, every procedure is simply one more device to delay, by other means, the emancipation of the slaves. Now he looks disconsolately at the rug.

"No motion, Judge."

There is a decided change, a pulse in the atmosphere. The two lawyers look up at her like collared hounds, hoping for understanding. They wish to say no more in front of the reporters, many of whom nonetheless seem to have gleaned the significance of Aires's remark. Stanley Rosenberg, Sonny notes, has slipped over two seats toward Stew Dubinsky from the *Tribune.* Stanley's smooth coiffure holds a spot of courtroom light as he bobs his head, absorbing Dubinsky's interpretation.

"Perhaps counsel should approach," says Sonny. She waves away Suzanne, the court reporter, and meets the lawyers, remaining on the lowest step beside the bench. "What's the deal?" she whispers. "I take it the defendant has made an arrangement with the people?"

Aires looks to Molto. Molto says, "That's correct, Judge. We've worked something out. If the court approves." His Adam's apple does a turn beneath the second chin. He is badly pockmarked. "We're still checking the details, Judge," Molto whispers. "There's a lot to investigate. But if the defendant's story holds, we've agreed to twenty years, Judge."

"On the shooter?" She has raised her voice more than she would like. With day-for-day good time, Hardcore will be out of the penitentiary in a decade. "On this case? With a sheet? He's only doing ten inside?"

"He's not the trigger, Judge. And he's giving us someone else. He was just the broker, Mr. Aires's client. There was someone else who got him to do it."

"The Mayor?"

The two lawyers both laugh, a peculiar outbreak of sound in the courtroom where everyone else is silent in hopes of getting an idea of what is transpiring beside the bench. When she became a judge, Sonny found she had grown much funnier. In the interval, she ponders what Molto is saying. Hardcore has flipped, turned state's evidence, which the gangbangers seldom do. It's an interesting development.

"Look," she says, "when you can talk about the case, you call me.

This is going to require some discussion." Sonny is visited by her re-curring suspicion: they are setting her up. Somebody is—the cops, the prosecutors, the Chief Judge Brendan Tuohey. They are hoping she'll make a noteworthy mistake, so they can run her out of the building. She gathers her robes, ready again to ascend, then thinks to ask if Molto plans to indict Hardcore and his co-defendant together. Molto nods. It will be her case. She will preside at trial, if the threat of Hardcore's testimony does not persuade whoever engineered the murder to plead guilty. Molto speaks up to detain her.

"Judge," he says. His voice has dropped to the very edge of audibility. Even his lips are self-consciously stiffened to defeat the most intrepid of the reporters. "Judge. Just so you know. It's Nile Eddgar. It's no problem for the people. But so you know. Given what you said."

An empty second passes among the three.

"Wait." She's come down the last stair. "Wait. I'm playing catch-up. Let's not be cryptic, Tommy. You're telling me Mr. Aires's client, what-ever, Hardcore, that he's going to testify that his probation officer, Nile Eddgar, conspired with him to plan this killing of Mr. Eddgar's mother?"

Molto looks at length across his shoulder to the reporters before he answers. "More or less," he says. The two lawyers face her without ex-pression, awaiting whatever will come next. Sonny labors an instant with the turmoil. "We haven't picked him up yet," Molto says. "We'll prob-ably get a warrant tomorrow." It's a secret, he's telling her. She nods two or three times, numbed.

After the call, she finds Wells and Lubitsch loitering in the inner office. They've placed the draft on her desk, but Lubitsch winds his head back around toward the courtroom as soon as she appears.

"Average American family, right?" he asks her. "Apple pie, hot dogs, and Chevrolet, right?" This gloating, the usual cop smugness—us and them—is rankling to Sonny. Only yesterday, Fred Lubitsch would have called Nile a player on his side. With a bare inspection, she signs the warrant and lets the officers go.

Marietta slinks in about an hour later, having wheeled the morning files across to the main building. She is curious, naturally, about the goings-on at sidebar and utters a startled, dyspeptic groan upon learning of Molto's news about Nile, but shows little other emotion. Marietta has been around.

"Should I take myself off the case now?" Sonny asks.

"Cause you knew these folks twenty-five years ago? Hell, who they gonna give the case to, Judge? Everybody else sitting in the Criminal Division knows Nile Eddgar better than you now. You're the junior here, Judge. The other judges? They've all had Nile before them a bunch of times, worked with him, believed his testimony under oath. We've only had him in here but once. And plenty of these judges know the father, too. He ran for controller a couple years back, didn't he? He was at all the dinners. 'Sides, Judge. A case like this? Nobody's gonna be happy to see it turn up on their calendar."

Race. That's what she means. The great unmentionable. That's what the case will be about. Black against white. On the street. On the witness stand. In the jury room as well. With the press holding up its magnifying glass throughout. Her colleagues will be convinced that politics, not scruples, led her to dump it. There will be narrow looks in the corridors, colder shoulders. Tuohey, surely, will call.

"I'd like to hear it. Really. Who wouldn't be intrigued to see what's happened to people decades later? But it feels so — close." She pauses, waging battle with her own fierce propriety. Is she *afraid* of something, she wonders suddenly.

"Hell, Judge," says Marietta. "This here's bound to be a jury trial anyway. Defense lawyer's gonna wag his finger and say how this gangster can't be believed, when he's puttin all the blame on someone else. We-all seen that a thousand times. Won't be anything for you to decide, except the sentence. Why don't you wait and see, Judge? See what the parties say? Spell it out for them. Like you done today. If it don't bother none of them, no reason it oughta bother you."

She's still wavering, but the truth is that Nile won't want her on this case. She saw too much of his family, especially his father. Eddgar in those years was dangerous, cunning, a zealot who some claimed had even sponsored murders. Like father, like son. That's the thought Nile will be afraid of. With a wave, Sonny closes the discussion.

"We'll do it your way, Marietta. See what the defendant says. It was twenty-five years ago."

"Sure," says Marietta, and then seemingly takes a second to review in her own mind the twisted, long-attenuated connections Sonny has explained. She turns, then turns back with a vague smile, fixed on a predictable thought. "So your boyfriend went off and got rich and famous and you was young and dumb and let him go?"

"I suppose." Sonny laughs. Marietta has long intimated that Sonny has poor instincts for romance, hinting frequently the judge has not properly renewed her social life.

"And you don't never hear from him or nothing?"

"Not in twenty-five years. We had a strange parting." She smiles a bit, consoling Marietta, if not herself, then catches sight of the clock. "Shit!" She is late for Nikki.

"Shit," she says again and flies about the chamber stuffing papers she must study overnight into her briefcase. She runs down the hall, cursing herself, and feeling a lurking foreboding, as if this lapse with Nikki is symptomatic of a larger error. Dashing across the windowed gangway that connects the Annex to the main courthouse, she wonders again if she is doing something wrong, capitulating to whatever it is—the titillating yen for foregone things and the hope of being master over what once was daunting—that comes with thoughts of the Eddgars and that period in her life. So often in this job there is never a correct decision. Far more frequently than she imagined when she was a law student, or even a practitioner, she chooses, as a judge, the alternative that seems, not right, but simply less wrong. And in some ways, this sense of being maladjusted, in the wrong place, has been a hallmark of her life. She often feels, like those people who believe in astrology, that her life has been driven by mysterious celestial forces. In earlier years, she came and went from things with alarming briskness, leaving men with little warning, passing through three different graduate programs and half a dozen jobs before she landed in law school.

Even now, she is not certain the bench is really right for her. It was an honor, and a convenient exit from the U.S. Attorney's Office, where she had begun to repeat herself. At the most pragmatic level, becoming a judge met the desperate need of a single mother to control her working hours and, almost as important, kept her in the law. She had tired of the battle hymn of practice, the race going always to the aggressive and the shrewd. It had brought out the Sonny she least liked, the child always secretly wounded, and, as she explained to herself in the most secret way, had forced her to accept the world according to men. After Nikki—after Charlie—she wanted to have a working life that depended not on slick maneuvering and sly positions, but which was anchored instead by kindness, which had some feeling connection to what surged through her when she held her child, the emotions she knew, *knew* were truly the best, the rightest things in life. But is the serious-looking dark-haired woman of fading looks, the Sonny she envisions up on the bench, this person scolding and sentencing the vicious and the woe-torn, is that *her*?

She is alone now, racing along in the strange night world of the central courthouse, with its empty corridors and isolated, purposeful habitués: bail bondsmen, police officers. Her high heels resound along the marble. At this hour, arrests are processed here from across the city. A broad young Hispanic woman in a bold ill-fitting print camps with a far-off look on one of the granite benches positioned just outside the bank of metal detectors. She embraces a child of three or four, who faces her, asleep, black ringlets dampened to one side of her face. They are always here: mothers, babies, families exhausted by trouble, waiting in the wasted hope their men will be bailed, acquitted, somehow freed.

Racing by, Sonny smiles in fleeting communion. Stirred by this momentary connection, she finds urgent visions of Nikki beckoning to her again. She foresees the humbling scene which is waiting, Nikki a straggler at Jackie's, and Sonny apologizing, vowing nevermore, even as Jackie insists it's not a problem. It is the sight of Nikki herself that will be worst: already in her coat and backpack, wiping her nose on her coat sleeve, gripping Sonny's hand by the fingers and urging her to suspend apologies and to leave; that little life, ragged with the toil of her own day and the worry of a prolonged separation. Within Sonny, there is always the same recriminating thought: How many times did Zora do this to her? How many thousand? It is startling to find how near at hand the pain remains, still fully memorized, how clear the recollection of the occasions when her mother was gone. Gone to meetings. Gone to organize. Gone to touch someone else with all those grand important yearnings: for freedom. For dignity.

So this is who she is, Her Honor, Judge Sonia Klonsky. The sheer momentum of her passions has her dashing a few steps down the street toward her car. The night has entered that moment of magic dwindling light when the sky almost clamors with drama and perspective drains, so that the buildings, figures, trees, the small circling birds, the Center City looming beyond, seem to stand on top of one another in the reduced proportions of a diorama. Neon promises glow cheaply in the storefronts of the tatty bond emporia across the street: "Bail. Fast. E-Z terms." Gripped by the heartsore cycles of her life, any life, the vexing complications of this case, and the perpetual anguish that seeps like a pollutant into the air around the courthouse, she rushes on. She rushes with high feeling and a sudden silvery fragment of happiness lacing her heart. She is thinking of her child.

September 14, 1995

SETH

When the electronic bolt is disengaged admitting them to the guard desk at the Kindle County Jail, Seth Weissman finds that Hobie Tuttle and he are not the sole civilians. A delivery man from Domino's, a skinny guy everyone calls Kirk, is also there with lunch.

"Yo," he tells the three correctional officers and shoves off, counting his tip. The bolt is shot again, a potent sound of slamming metal, stark as a rifle shot, and Kirk departs. On the door a sheet of bulletproof glass has been mounted, but it is the bars beneath which occupy Seth's attention. They are squared off and thick with rust-resistant paint, a depleted shade of beige which is the color of everything here — the walls, the floor, even the reinforced-steel guard desk.

"Warden's got to clear any press interviews, man." A guard waves his fingers, tainted with pizza grease, over the form Hobie has been filling out.

"Nobody doin any interviews, man," says Hobie.

"Says right here, 'Michael Frain. Profession: Journalist.'" The guard looks from the form to Seth twice, as if to assess whether the description fits.

"No, no, here's what I'm sayin now," says Hobie. "This young fella, your inmate, Nile Eddgar, he asked Mr. Frain here to help him find counsel and he chose me. Okay? So he's part of the attorney visit."

After another go-round the captain is summoned, an erect black man who looks longingly at the pizza but shows the discipline to first finish his business with them. Hobie holds forth with characteristic bluster, and the captain, wary of messing with the press or simply hungry, lets them go. They pass from one brick guardhouse to another. Their wallets are checked in a small tin locker, and another solemn correctional officer pats them down.

Then they are inside, enclosed in a small admitting area. The barred door with its lock, thick as a book, clangs home irrevocably behind them. Hobie takes in the sick look on Seth's face.

"Number 47 said to Number 3," he quips, amused. He is quoting "Jailhouse Rock." *Number 47/said to number 3/You're the cutest jail-bird/I ever did see.* On the way over from the airport, Hobie did a complete head-trip. 'If we get on those catwalks, man, stay on the rail, don't go near the cells, those mean dudes will grab your tie, man, just for a hoot, they'll knot it around the bars and watch you strangle yourself screamin "Help!" You'll keep 'em laughin for a week.' He roared at the thought. Although they are 1,000 miles from Hobie's home in D.C., this is still his world.

Another guard points them along a path through the yard. The jail hulks about them, seven red-brick structures, remnants of the institutional era in American architecture. These buildings could be factories or, these days, schools, especially with the heavy chain link that cages each window. They are set down amid acres of asphalt, the sole greenery the weeds and lichens worn but still persisting in the gaps between the path's paving bricks. At the perimeter, stout walls with freshened mortar joints are topped by nasty whorls of razor wire.

"You think he's okay in here?" Seth asks.

"Might be. Might not be. We're gone know in a minute."

"Oh my," says Seth, "aren't you the hard case? You know, it won't dent your armor, Hobie, if you show just a little concern about your client."

"Lookee here," Hobie says, repeating one of his father's favorite expressions. After twenty-five years in which Hobie, a native mimic, has, at times, taken on the speech patterns of everybody from Timothy Leary to Louis Farrakhan, he now most often sounds like his father, Gurney Tuttle. He has stopped dead, his large briefcase swinging by his side. "Here. You call me up in D.C.—you happen to interrupt my personal life at a truly crucial moment—"

"I.e., watching reruns of *Dallas*."

"Hey, you wanna play the Dozens, or you gonna listen up? I'm tellin you how this was. I was with a really excellent lady, and you hype me up, man. I felt like I was being licked by a goddamn puppy. 'Black brother, you gotta do this, you gotta help this little old Mouseketeer, remember Nile? You're the best I know and so you gotta do it for me.' I mean, am I accurate, so far?"

"Close enough."

"Okay. So I'm here." Bearded, Hobie, in his elegant suit, lectures Seth with a finger raised. "But I follow the lady's advice. You remember Colette? 'Who said you should be happy? Do your work.' That's me, man. I work. I get paid. I don't fall in love with them. Some go out the courtroom door, some don't. I accept all collect calls from the penitentiary. But that's the end of my sympathy gig. Now, you've gone and made it your lifetime hobby to feel sorry for this young man, that's your thing. But don't be layin that on me."

"Hey, he's not my hobby. I've stayed in touch with him, that's all. He's always needed a little help. And besides, how would you feel? Guy reaches me from a pay phone. His mother's dead, the cops are hunting him for something he didn't do, and he can't call his own father for help, since he happens to be one of the twentieth century's leading assholes. That's pretty rugged."

"Hey, brother." Hobie sweeps his hand. "There eight million stories in the naked city. You've had it rugged. Lucy's had it rugged. You-all I feel sorry for. Folks in this place—most times it turns out they made their own trouble."

A guard, sent across to escort them to Department 7, where Nile is housed, has been watching their approach along the mottled bricks.

"Which one of you's the reporter?" he asks. "Come to interview me, man? Shit, somebody ought to. I'm not kidding. I been doing this twenty-three years, going on twenty-four. I seen some unbelievable shit."

The guard, a lanky man, laughs robustly at himself and falls in with them. He seems far too affable for the job. He is chewing a toothpick, which comes out of his mouth at the starting point of each stream of declarations. In the meantime, whooping voices tumble toward them from the fenced area of the jail play yard, where the inmates, hundreds of them, in their blue jumpsuits and slip-ons are shooting hoops or jiving with one another in milling clusters. There are three different courts, games at each net. In two side areas, a number of men are spotting around the weight benches. Seth surveys the population. They are long and short; some are fat; some bristle with prison muscles. A few of the inmates are staring with sullen contempt, while others hang on the chain links and call after them. "Hey, lawyer, lawyer, man, you gotta take my case, man, man, I'm innocent, man, I didn't do nothin." One thing: they are black. At a far remove, beneath one net, the Latinos are at play, and after some searching, Seth finally takes note of a covey of white guys, most of them with shaved scalps and visible tattoos. But here in Kindle County Municipal Jail, decades after the great Southern migrations, the sad facts speak for themselves.

It is easy therefore to spot Nile, at the far side of the yard. He looks fatter than when Seth saw him last, three years ago. On someone of his age, Nile's potbelly seems a confession of weakness. His dun hair is long and matted, and he is smoking a cigarette. He rocks on his soles as he talks with three or four young black men. As always, nothing in Nile's aspect is as you might expect. Where is the grim, broken mood that would be natural, whether he was wrongly accused or enduring the internal upheaval that would follow arranging the murder of his own mother? The tall young man looks, if anything, at home. But that is Nile. Mr. Inappropriate. And besides, as Seth himself knows, of all the great emotions, the least predictable in its effects is grief.

The guard, Eddie, has to call Nile twice. One of the khaki-suited officers opens the locked gate to allow him to emerge.

"Hey," Nile says. He is awkward. He prepares to throw an arm around Seth, then thinks better of it. Seth reintroduces him to Hobie. It's been decades. "Great," Nile says. "Great." He rattles Hobie's hand with ungainly enthusiasm. Even for Seth, it is hard to know where to start. Condolences? Outrage over the circumstances?

"So how are you?" Seth asks. "You handling all of this? How's this been?"

"Hey, he's havin a great time," Eddie answers, "this here is Fun City," and laughs with continuing appreciation for his own humor.

Descriptions appear beyond Nile. Up close, he looks himself, painfully uncertain. Behind his eyes, his spirit always seemed to be skittering about on the ice of suppressed terror. Now he shrugs.

"I worked in here," he says. "I meet most of my clients here the first time. I know the drill."

Eddie has walked them into Department 7. The cinder-block walls and staircases are painted thickly in red gloss. Here the steel doors open with a key, admitting them to the barred foyer, where a number of guards are congregated, two of them women. Beyond a wall of bars lie the tiers, the catwalks, the region of steel where the men are housed. There are dour scents of steamed food and disinfectant. A radio plays; a cell door bangs far above and the metal floors overhead resound with movement. A single window at the far end, half a block away, is the niggardly source of the little natural light. Seth, from here, can see the nearest cells, strung with clotheslines. Postcards and family photos are taped inside the bars, above the little shelves they call the bunks. On one a man with smooth dark limbs lies in his briefs, immobilized by the sorrow of confinement.

As they enter, a prisoner, whose jumpsuit is tied about his waist, revealing an imposing physique, comes to the bars, remonstrating with the guards in an intense ghetto squeal. Seth does not understand much. The man's hair is grown wild, uncombed, untreated, rising up in nubby spears, flecked with nits of lint.

"Get your ass back, Tuflac," someone says to him. "We done told you three times already."

Eddie holds a hand aloft like an amiable host and directs Nile, Hobie, and Seth into a cafeteria which doubles as a visiting area. There are four or five other prisoners meeting with outsiders at various tables spread around the room. One man in a tie is clearly an attorney. The rest are family, girlfriends, making the odd visit on a weekday afternoon.

"Okay, now we need to talk," says Hobie. He points Seth away. "Got to be just Nile and me to protect the privilege."

Inclined to protest, Seth can name no reason, except that he has come halfway across the country from Seattle to facilitate this meeting. He is relegated to one of the small tables bolted to the floor, while Hobie, somewhat triumphantly, directs Nile to the farthest corner. The cafeteria is compact, with glazed brick walls, spotlessly maintained, except for the stains and gang signs tooled into the white laminate tabletops. By terms of the jailhouse, this place is almost cheerful. Daylight, soothing as warm milk, emerges from a bank of barred windows, and three or four vending machines provide a touch of color. At the table nearest Seth, a slick Hispanic man is visiting with his girlfriend or his wife. With teased-up masses of dead-black hair, she has dressed to give him an eyeful—a tight red sleeveless top, cut daringly, and black jeans that make a taut casing for her healthy female bulk. Her eyes are painted so heavily they bring to mind Kabuki. She is up often to get coffee, cigarettes, a Coke. Coming and going, she and her man grab as much of each other as they can, a quick, relentless passing over of hands. They are flouting the rules, but the three or four guards in khaki looking on from their positions of retreat around the room remain impassive. Pleasure, so brief, can be forgiven.

Eddie, with time on his hands too, has approached Seth. "So what-all is it you write?" he asks.

Seth rolls out his standard patter on the column: syndicated nationally, printed here in the *Tribune.*

"Oh yeah, yeah," says Eddie, but it's clear he's never heard of Michael Frain and is mildly disappointed. They both momentarily contemplate this dead end. Casting about for a subject, Seth asks if Nile's encountered any trouble in here.

"Don't seem like. Had him in seg when he come in yesterday, but he asked for general population. Now, if he was over there in Department 2? I call that the Gladiator Wing, y'know, all these cats, nineteen years old, always rumblin and scufflin. But he's all right here. Seems like he's okay with them BSDs. They won't let nobody kick his ass, take his food."

"BSDs?"

"Black Saints Disciples, man. We get kind of familiar in here, you know?" Eddie, freely given to hilarity, laughs once more at his own remark, then rolls his toothpick around his fingertips before going on. "You know, PO, coppers, shit, *guards*—you can be okay with these birds if they know where you comin from. When I started out, I worked on stateside, down in Rudyard? Lot of those officers, they just got a thing with the inmates. Their women come see 'em, guard like to come up, pinch her butt, smile like he got new teeth, and her man sittin on the other side of the glass can't do shit. Now you get you a shank in the back that way. Me? Take no shit, give no shit, man, that's my motto. I got myself in here, I'd be okay, same as Nile. Some them BSDs or GOs—Gangster Outlaws?—they'd cover me. Them gangs pretty much run the show in here anyway. You hear what I'm sayin?"

Seth shakes his head once. He doesn't want to say a thing to slow Eddie down. Seth's decided that the guard was right to start. A column about Eddie and the jail might be a terrific piece.

"Here," says Eddie, lifting onto a chair one leg, decorated along the seam with a line of brown piping. He leans over confidentially now that he has found his subject. "First thing they teach you, first day of training: Institution can only be run with the cooperation of the inmates. These days, we got a problem in here, we find whoever's ranking with the Saints, the Outlaws, we get it straightened out. See? What we want is a peaceful place. You hear? Nobody gettin cut in the shower, no gangbangers making war in the yard, no kind of three inmates waitin to cut off some guard's nuts, like they done down at Rudyard. That's what we want."

"And what do they want?" A man who asks questions for a living, Seth knows from the way Eddie's perpetual verbal momentum suddenly loiters they have reached the good part.

"Them?" Eddie laughs again, more subdued. "Now you ain't gonna write this, right?"

Seth lifts both hands to show he has no paper, no pen—as if it is the furthest thought from his mind. Eddie reverses the chair and takes a seat, his long arms crossed over the back. He has a moon face and a fine smile, in spite of a single missing incisor. His hairline, buzzed short, cuts a scalloped frontier across the back half of his head.

"What these gangsters want is not to have nobody all over them gettin their shit in here."

"Shit?"

"Contraband, let's say. Don't you look at me like that. I'm not sayin anything ain't the truth. Everybody round here will tell you that. See, these gangbangers need that shit. Man, these kids in here, jail, it's like graduation for some of them: this is where the big boys go. Hey, you think I'm kiddin you? I'm not kiddin." Eddie looks back toward Hobie, as if he has some hopes he might be nearby and able to agree. But Hobie and Nile are still engaged. Hobie's briefcase, a smooth pouch of umber-colored Italian leather, is on the table, and Hobie, as usual, is doing the talking. Beside them, each has a small paper cup of coffee, breathing steam. Eddie goes on.

"So when they on the outside, half these young men already thinkin,

What-all this damn gang gonna do for me when I get in there? Gotta be anybody dis you, beat you down, man, gotta be all your gangbanger brothers down for you, kickin ass and shit. Gotta be. Now half these young men, more than half, they in here for narcotics and quite a number come in strung out. Gang's got to provide, see? Some others, you know, they like to get them a little buzz, break up the boredom. Either way, the dope's the gang. Like them ads on TV say: Membership got its privileges. Gives them money. Discipline. Gangs gotta get their shit in here."

"We were searched pretty thoroughly coming in."

"Hell yeah, you better bet we gonna search you, cause this here is a penal institution, man, we ain't gonna *help* nobody break the law. Sheriff's got to run for re-election you know. Mayor do too. But these gangbangers find a way. Shit comes in here, same as the money to pay for it. I mean, that's how it is. Everybody knows that. Kind of works, let's say, to mutual advantage." Eddie smiles again, but on reflection he seems concerned that he may have shown excessive candor, particularly with a reporter. He jams the toothpick, long held between his fingers, back into his mouth and drifts off to his duties.

Kindle County, Seth thinks. Always something dirty doin. Always amazing him. Will he ever escape this place? No. He's wondered that for thirty years and now he knows the answer: No. This is where his dreams are set. In the gloomy winter light, thick as shellac. In the air of childhood, tinted with the oily-smelling smoke and ash of burnt coal. No escaping. He and Lucy have lived everywhere: Seattle, Pawtucket, Boston, Miami, and Seattle again for the last eleven years. But now that his life is up for grabs, now that this lugubrious mid-life mourning period, too prolonged to be called a crisis, has him thinking of fresh starts, he answered yes when the flight attendant asked, "Going home?"

About ten minutes later, Hobie and Nile are done. Nile seems more pensive. Hobie says he'll see him tomorrow and Seth embraces Nile quickly, before he's returned to Eddie's custody. The guard waves good-bye, still laughing.

"Okay, Froggy," says Hobie. "Pluck your magic twanger. Let's blow."

"So?" asks Seth, as soon as they are on their way back across the yard.

" 'So,' what?"

"So what do you think. You going to get him off?"

"Wouldn't really know. I left my crystal ball at home."

"Yeah, but how does the case look?"

"Beats me. I didn't talk to him about it."

"Christ, what the hell *did* you talk about then for forty minutes? O. J.?"

"What I talked to this young fellow, my client, about is none of your business. But what I discuss with every client first time I meet em is my fee."

"Your fee!"

"Hell yes, my fee. I asked you, first thing—didn't I ask you, 'Can he afford a lawyer?' And you told me, 'No problem.' Hell yeah, I talked to him about my fee. I pay alimony to three mean women."

"How much?"

"That's none of your goddamn business, either. I told him what I get, which is one hell of a lot, and he says he can handle it. That's jazz to me. I don't ask em where-all it's coming from. Long as he ain't stickin up my mother. All I care is check comes upfront and clears."

"Jesus," says Seth. "What are you doing out of your coffin in daylight?"

"You wanna hear stories about gettin beat? I'll tell you stories. I had one sumbitch handcuffed his woman to the radiator, just to prove he'd be back with the money soon as we finished in court. And you know what I ended up with? Bill for the fuckin hacksaw."

Seth laughs out loud. Hobie's bullshit is still the best. Reality so seldom intrudes.

"Upfront," Hobie repeats. "In hand. Period. You find him another lawyer that won't do him like that, that lawyer isn't worth having, because he doesn't know shit."

"Nobody said anything about another lawyer. I told you, he wants somebody who isn't from around here, so he's sure they won't be beholden to Eddgar. I promised him he can be damn certain of that with you."

Hobie pauses for reflection, a huge pile of a person, the color of dark oak. As he has grown older, little dark flecks of melanin have appeared around the deep wells of his eyes, and his hairline, while not as sadly reduced as Seth's own, has undergone a mature retreat. Softly styled and salted with errant kinks of grey, his hair combines with the beard and the fine suit to lend a subdued edge to his volatile persona.

"See now, this is what I don't savvy," Hobie says. "Eddgar's no kind of pissed with Nile. He says Nile bolted right after the shooting and is refusing to talk to *him*."

"Where do you get that? Dubinsky?"

"Eddgar. Called me in D.C. last night. The warden told him I was counsel."

"Jesus Christ. Why didn't you *say* you talked to Eddgar?"

"Listen here," says Hobie. He stops again in the midst of his rumbling forward movement. "You know, you have got the *wrong* picture. You got the wrong idea. You know what you are here? You're like the *matchmaker*. What's that word? The shotgun?"

"In Yiddish? The *shadkin?*"

"That's it. You're the *shadkin*. Now, the *shadkin* don't get in bed with the bride and the groom. You want me to represent this young man? Okay, I'm gonna do it. But I can't be discussin every detail with you. I got privileges to protect. You better get straight on that right now. This isn't high school. So don't keep askin me what my client's told me. And don't you talk to Nile about this case anymore either. This is a trial," he says, "this is war. You gotta think four steps ahead. Fourteen. Those prosecutors lay a subpoena on you, I don't want you to have squat you can testify about. This is murder, man. Serious shit." Hobie loves this, Seth knows, the superior knowledge, the strutting around, the gravity of his mission. At least it isn't murder one. The state charged conspiracy to commit second degree. No death penalty. Seth checked himself.

"Well, what did Eddgar want anyhow?"

"Listen to you," says Hobie. "What did I just carry on about?" Yard time is over and the place has regained a sullen air. The inmates are all locked down for the afternoon count, but one or two still call after them from windows high above. "Hey, slick. You lookin good."

"Eddgar's gonna throw Nile's bail," Hobie says finally. "That's what he called about. Says he's willing to put up the family manse—$300,000 worth. I gotta go see him this afternoon. How's that hit you?"

It doesn't sound like Eddgar is what Seth thinks.

"Confused me, too," admits Hobie. "Even Nile was pretty much astounded."

"Maybe Eddgar's developed a conscience. Maybe he's bugged by the ironies of the situation. I mean, have you thought about this? Nile's in jail for murder and Eddgar's been walking the streets for twenty-five years. It's incredible."

"Could be it runs in the blood," says Hobie.

"Oh, that's cute," says Seth. "You're the one who's supposed to think Nile's innocent."

"No, man, no way is that my job. My job is to get him off. Period. I don't know what happened. And if I can avoid it, I don't ask, either. They gotta unburden themselves, or spin a tale, well bless them, then I have to listen. But the game here, man, is can the state prove them guilty? That's all. Whether they did it, or some dude named Maurice did it, you know, I don't worry my little mind."

"He's innocent."

"No, he *told* you he's innocent. There's a whole world of difference."

Half a continent away, Nile, on the pay phone, had issued a nasal denial. 'It's bullshit. They say I paid this guy $10,000 to set this up and it's bullshit, all of it, the $10,000, all of it, it *never* happened.' The fierce desperation of this declaration had been too daunting for Seth to probe, unsure if Nile — or, Seth's darkest fear, the denials — might fall apart. He encourages Hobie now, much as he has bolstered himself in the last few days.

"He's too feckless, Hobie. He's never had the first clue."

"Listen, Jack, you better take yourself a reality pill. No decent prosecutor's gonna go puttin on a piece-of-shit gangbanger to call a white boy a killer without plenty of corroboration. Not even considering that Nile's daddy's a politician in the same damn party as the PA, somebody they'd want to cut any break they could. Get yourself ready, man, cause the state's gonna bring some evidence to that courtroom."

Seth is listening. This is the first he's heard of how Hobie really looks at it. When they were cruising in from the airport, it was old times and new times, the state of the world with Lucy, the latest on Hobie's kids. Now that they're here in the scariest place on earth, Hobie is giving him the logic: Nile's guilty. That's what he's saying. The prosecutors wouldn't have brought the case if they had a choice.

"Well, he's gotta have a *chance*, doesn't he?"

"Seth, man." Hobie stops to face him, his dark eyes bloodshot and direct. It is the rare moment between them, fully sincere. "I'm gonna go full-out. Okay?"

"What about Sonny? Doesn't it help to have a judge who knows him? And you?"

"I don't know her anymore. *You* don't even know her anymore. And I don't know *what* she thinks about Nile and whether that's any good for him a'tall. Besides," Hobie mutters, "she may damn well take herself off this case."

"You mean she might not be the judge?"

"Maybe not. And even if she decides to keep it, could be I make a motion to disqualify her."

"No," says Seth. "Really?"

"Whoa," says Hobie. "Look at you. Damn, I knew you were gonna be like psy-*chotic*, waitin till you see that lady up on the bench. Tell me that ain't so. You're transparent, man. You musta been a store window in a prior life."

Seth laughs. A strange coincidence, he says. Life is full of them.

"All the fucked-up luck," says Hobie. "Honestly," he says, and after further reflection adds, "Shit." He fishes his mouth around as if he might spit. "See, man, you never change. You're still like cr-*azy* with that whole California scene we went through. Nile. Sonny. Eddgar. You won't ever let go of it. You gotta write about it. You gotta think about it. Then you gotta write about it some more. I oughta call you Proust. Honest and truly."

"Everybody's got a youth, Hobie."

"Yeah, well listen here, Proust. You stay away from her till I get this all scoped out. I don't care what damn curiosity you got. I don't want to be decidin it's best for Nile that she preside and have you spook her off this case, cause she sees she's gone be holdin class reunion in her courtroom. Time being, you do like me, man, just lay low, till I can figure out what a good lawyer's supposed to."

"Which is what?"

"How the hell to take advantage of the situation."

They have come close to the admitting area, where they started. The bolts are disengaged and they progress toward the uncloistered light. The lieutenant makes it a point to greet Hobie on the way back through. The black thing. There's a handshake and a riff about the pizza. Then Hobie and Seth are outside, moving toward the last guard shack and the iron gates, meant, apparently, to repel motorized invasion.

"Proust," says Hobie again, archly shaking his head to rub it in a little more. "I'm gone go find you some tea cakes, I swear to God. Help you hold on to all this shit you can't forget."

"Hey, I held on to you, too, so just lighten up." It took some doing. They both know that.

"Oh, yes you did!" says Hobie emphatically, and in his grand comical way grabs Seth suddenly and kisses him on the forehead. Then Hobie throws a burly arm about him and pulls Seth along the walk, celebrating the relief of the free air outside the jailhouse. He laughs hugely and repeats himself. "Oh, yes you did."

Part Two

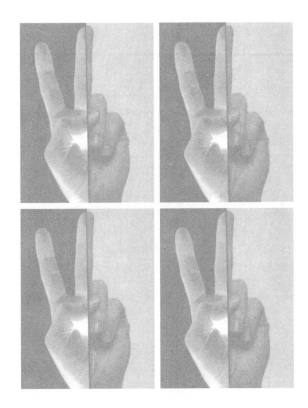

PEOPLE MY AGE ARE HUNG UP ON THE SIXTIES. Everybody knows that and regards it as sort of a problem with us: the generation who won't throw out their bell-bottoms. Whenever something by the Beatles comes on the car radio, my son begins to moan for fear I'm going to sing along. 'But look,' I sometimes want to say, 'all these people said they were going to change things, and things changed: The war. The cruel formalities that disadvantaged minorities or women. People stopped behaving like they'd all been knocked out of the same stamping plant.' These days I say I'm going to stop dropping my underwear on the bathroom floor, and I can't even change that. So naturally I think something special happened in the sixties. Didn't it? Or was it just because I was at that age, between things, when everything was still possible, that time, which in retrospect, doesn't seem to last long?

— MICHAEL FRAIN
"The Survivor's Guide,"
September 4, 1992

MANY YEARS AGO, I LIVED WITH A WOMAN who left graduate school in Philosophy right after she read a remark of Nietzsche's. He'd said: "Every great philosophy [is] the personal confession of its originator, a type of involuntary and unaware memoirs." In light of that observation, I guess my friend decided she was, literally, in the wrong department.

Nietzsche—and, as ever, the woman—were brought to mind recently when I went to a gathering in Washington in which some of the D.C. smarty-pants types, the pundits and pols, were analyzing the primaries and repeating as gospel the adage Tip O'Neill used to like, "All politics are local." But to me that saying has always seemed to be off by an order of magnitude. It's Nietzsche who was on the button. I suspect he'd say, "All politics are personal."

— "The Survivor's Guide,"
March 20, 1992

December 4, 1995

SONNY

My mother was a revolutionary. At least that's what she called herself, although 'visionary' was probably a better word. Guns and bombs and political maneuvering, the cruel mechanics of the war for power, had little hold on her imagination. It was the utopia beyond that inspired her, the promised land where humankind was free of the maiming effects of a hard, material fate. I stood in awe of her whirlwind energies and, in an act of faith of my own, have always kept her soaring hopes at heart. But she and I were never wholly at peace with one another. She was impulsive, a little bit off-kilter—beyond me, in all senses.

With Zora and our differences in mind, I have arrived at the courthouse late. It has been one of those mornings. Nikki would not dress. She lay down when I said stand up, took off her blouse as soon as I had it buttoned, demanded, for no reason detectable to rational inquiry, to wear blue. And when I finally resorted to scolding, she wept, naturally, clutched my hem, and delivered her familiar entreaty: She does not want to go to school. Not today. She wants to stay home. With me. Oh, the agony of Mondays, of parting, of asking Nikki to believe, against the evidence, that she remains for me the center of the world. Someday, I always promise, it will be as she asks. I'll call Marietta with orders to continue every case. But not, of course, today. Today there is duty and compulsion. Nile Eddgar's trial starts. I must go off to my other world, play dress-up and make-believe. And so I begin the week in familiar torment, telling myself I am not my mother, that I am somehow on the road to conquering what remains of her in me.

For both our sakes, I allowed Nikki to skip the car pool and dropped her at school myself. That left me twenty minutes behind our frantic morning schedule. 'Great thing about this job,' one of the old-timers told me when I was sworn in. 'They can't start without you.' Yet I have always regarded a full courtroom waiting for a missing judge as a token of arrogance. I rush through the back door of the courtroom onto the bench, not quite prepared for the scene that greets me. It feels as if both the lights and the heat have been turned up. Beyond the bulletproof divider, the gallery is thick with court buffs and other citizen-onlookers: sickos, retirees, court watchers, and the thoughtfully curious drawn in primal wonder to the act of murder. Within the well of the room, extra deputies in uniform mill idly at the periphery, while the many reporters crowd the limited space available. The jury box must remain empty, awaiting the prospective venire, which will be summoned shortly. Instead, Annie has created a makeshift press gallery, positioning folding chairs on the near side of the yellowish oak panels of the jury box. The best seats, in the front row, have been occupied by three sketch artists, who have laid their pastels at their feet.

As soon as she catches sight of me, Marietta cries out her "Hear ye's," bringing court to order. The room is caught up in the commotion of hundreds of persons shifting to their feet, papers rattling, conversations adjourned in a final buzz.

"*People versus Nile Eddgar*," Marietta cries out, when we all are seated. "For trial." To my surprise, my stomach rebounds with the words. Two of the artists begin work immediately, eyes revolving between their pads and me. On the one earlier occasion I saw a rendering of Judge Sonny on TV — during a heated divorce case — I was disturbed by the severe look the artist gave me, my even-featured face grave with shadow. Surely I'm better-looking and lighter-hearted than that?

Meanwhile, the participants stalk slowly toward the oak podium at the focus of the room: Gina Devore from the State Defender's Office, a sprite in Ann Taylor, accompanied by a burly black man who must be the lawyer from D.C. she said would appear for trial. From the other table advances Tommy Molto, the Homicide supervisor, who has elected to try this case, a rarity for him these days. He too has a companion, Rudy Singh, a slender, inexpressibly beautiful young man with a delicate way and a musical Indian accent, who was assigned to this courtroom only last week to handle more routine matters. Finally, behind all of them, somewhat shyly, stands Nile Eddgar. He is more than six feet, far taller than I remember his father, and looms over both Molto and Gina. When he was last here, for arraignment, his hair was ponytailed and not especially clean. Since then, he's shaved and had a dramatic haircut too, albeit not a particularly becoming one. He looks as if he simply bargained to let the barber cut off half. Charged up by winter static, his brownish hair Christmas-trees about his ears, resembling some hapless Dutch boy's. Nonetheless, as the resident emblem of authority, I'm pleased Nile has made these concessions to respectability, even if off the bench I'd regard the same gestures as silly or conventional.

Back in the lockup, keys are jangling and voices are raised. The transport deputies have been searching desperately for the prisoner, and a peal of relieved laughter sails into the courtroom when they realize he is not in custody but on bail. The lawyers state their name for the record.

"Your Honor," says Gina, "may I introduce Mr. Tuttle from Washington, D.C." Her motion to substitute counsel and Tuttle's appearance form ascend, handed up from Gina to Marietta to me: H. Tariq Tuttle. At arraignment, I allowed the State Defender to stay on the case while Nile attempted to find his own attorney. An out-of-towner is welcome, since that will avoid the sticky conflict issues that might arise if Nile was the probation officer for other clients of his lawyer. I note aloud that Tuttle has a local attorney number, meaning he's admitted to practice in this state.

"Took the bar here, Your Honor, before I moved out to D.C."

"Welcome back, then." I allow the motion, and Gina, tiny and energetic, disembarks at once for the half a dozen other courtrooms where she has cases up. "Mr. Tuttle," I say, "help me with your first name, so I don't mangle it when I introduce you to the jury. Tariq?"

The question startles him. He stares up briefly, then pronounces the name. "It's just on the license, Judge, I don't go by that much anymore. The second syllable's like 'reek.' As in odor."

He smiles at himself. The message is unmistakable: Don't worry, I'm not that way. He's magnificently groomed, a large man of substantial weight, his bulk gracefully draped in a splendid suit of a greenish Italian wool. He is all soft contours, a half-head of Afro hair, roundly sculpted, and a beard trimmed close to a broad cheeky face. He shows the slick courtroom poise of a big-city criminal defense lawyer. This is a man who has stood at many podia, making jokes at his own expense. For the moment, ingratiating himself, he is radiant as the sun. But the worm will surely turn. Between a judge, laboring to rule properly, and the defense lawyer, always criticizing her for the sake of appeal, there is a natural rivalry. The process starts at once.

"If the court please, I have a motion." From beneath his arm, Tuttle slowly removes a newspaper, as if revealing a concealed weapon.

"Before you start, Mr. Tuttle, let me spread one matter of record again." I begin an oration about my past relations with the Eddgar family, but Tuttle shakes his head amiably.

"We're grateful for your sensitivity, Your Honor, but there's no problem. Mr. Eddgar acknowledges his past acquaintance with the court, without objection. As, of course, do I."

"You do?" I ask. I have never been good at hiding my emotions. Instead, since taking this job, I have practiced letting them emerge with a certain confidence, as if I figure it was worth getting to forty-seven to know what I do about myself. Even so, I often find myself undone, as I am now, by the dumb impulsive things that escape me. I am still ruing my lack of control when, unexpectedly, I see what I have missed. Despite my resolve to show presence of mind, I find my mouth has actually fallen open.

It's Hobie. Ho-bie!

"Forgive me, Mr. Tuttle. It's been some time."

"Contact lenses, Judge," he says. "The name. The beard."

"The belly," I hear from near the jury box, a lowered voice that nonetheless carries distinctly in the angled contours of the room. A few of the reporters join in collegial laughter, but it is brought to an immediate conclusion by a single astonishing clack of Annie's gavel on the block she stations on the lower tiers of the bench. You could probably do case studies about what happens when you give a person subjected to a lifetime of ethnic suppression a gavel and a uniform. Annie maintains relentless decorum. She does not permit reading, talking, chewing gum. Even the young gangbangers who come to catch a glimpse of their homies are forced to remove their hats. Now she scalds the offending reporter with a look so furious that he's dropped his face into his hands in shame. Hobie, too, has turned, arms raised imploringly, shaking his head until the man dares to look up again and I recognize Seth Weissman. He scoots himself half-upright on the chair arms, faces me, and mouths, "I'm sorry." I find my jaw slackened again.

It isn't really seeing Seth that's shocking. He's come to mind often enough with thoughts about the case that I'm vaguely prepared for his presence. It's his appearance that stuns me. My first impulse is that he's been sick. But that, I recognize, is my dismal inner urge to pull everyone down to my level. His injury is benign: he's gone bald, a smooth pink dome that nevertheless strikes a note of bathos on a man who used to wear his dishwater hair behind the shoulder. Otherwise, he appears only incrementally reduced by time, thicker in the middle, and still a little too tall for his slender limbs. He has a long, male face, nose-dominated, now more fleshy at the jaw. Gravity has done its work. He has lost color. The same things I would say about myself.

"Mr. Molto," I ask, when I regain myself, "does the court's prior acquaintance with defense counsel have any impact on your position regarding my presiding?"

Molto stands with small nail-bitten hands folded before him, exhibiting his customary impatience. We have been over the issue now half a dozen times.

"None," he says distinctly.

In the meantime, my eyes cheat back to Seth in the jury box. What's he *do*-ing here? I've finally wondered. But the answer seems obvious. A column. About coincidence. And serendipity. He will write about the strange whims of fate, how the figures from his past have reappeared with everyone written into odd new roles, as bizarrely misplaced as the characters in a dream.

"Your Honor," says Tuttle. "My motion? I take it Your Honor saw this morning's *Tribune*?" The news I get generally comes to me on NPR on the three mornings I drive the kindergarten car pool. Sometimes late at night, in moments of supreme indulgence, after Nikki is bedded down, I'll take a glass of wine in the bathtub and turn the pages of the

Tribune or the national edition of *The New York Times*. Most evenings, though, I am too burned out for more than rattled reflections on the day that's passed and the hundreds of tasks undone at home and in court, counted, instead of sheep, as I drift off.

Now as I open the paper that's been handed up, I confront a headline stretching across the top of the front page. STATE: POL'S SON MEANT TO KILL HIM, NOT MOM. *Trial Starts Today*, the kicker reads. The byline is Stew Dubinsky's. Exclusive to the *Trib*. I scan: "Sources close to the investigation . . . murder conspiracy trial of Nile Eddgar starting today . . . Prosecuting Attorney's Office plans to offer evidence that the intended victim of the plot was not the Kindle County Superior Court probation officer's mother, June Eddgar, who was gunned down by gang members on September 7, but his father, State Senator Loyell Eddgar . . . mistake in identity is believed to have occurred when Mrs. Eddgar borrowed her former husband's car that morning."

By now, I've piled a hand on my forehead. God, the calculations that accumulate. Eddgar! I find this news unsettling, most of all perhaps, because in a single stroke it feels far more likely that the strange young man before me may actually be guilty. At last, I nod to Hobie to proceed.

"Your Honor," he begins in a resonant courtroom bass; he grips the podium with both hands. The impression is of some opera star about to hit a booming note. "Your Honor, I have been trying cases for twenty-some years now. And I have seen devilish conduct by prosecutors in that time. I have been sandbagged and backdoored and tricked. But to have leaked this kind of incendiary detail to the press on the day we are trying to pick a jury, knowing that this news concerning a prominent citizen is bound to become a page 1 headline and irreparably prejudice the venire against my client—" Hobie does not finish. He smacks his hand against an extra copy of the paper, which he has held up for illustration, and tosses his large head about in embittered disbelief. He goes on to paint a vivid tableau of dozens of citizens in the jury room in the main building, forming firm impressions of the case even as we speak. Most of them, he predicts, with time on their hands and a peculiar interest in what's occurring in the courthouse today, will have read this one-sided account of the state's evidence in the very papers which, ironically, are provided to them free. His rhetoric is overheated, but I have little doubt he's correct and that most of the potential jurors will have seen this story.

"Your Honor, really," he concludes, "how can this man get a fair trial? I must, I have to, I have no choice but to move to dismiss this indictment." He punctuates his request with a grunt of continuing outrage.

Molto, chubby in his inexpensive charcoal suit, his wiry, thinning hair barely combed, appears somewhat dumbfounded when I call on him for a response.

"Judge Klonsky," he says, "I received no notice of this motion. I came here to pick a jury. I have witnesses subpoenaed. This is the kind of last-minute—"

I decide to save Tommy from himself. "Mr. Molto, let's start from scratch. Is this report fundamentally accurate? Is the state going to contend that it was Nile Eddgar's father who was the actual, intended victim of this crime?"

Tommy takes a deep breath. He looks forlornly to Rudy Singh, who has taken a seat several feet behind Tommy at the prosecution table, where a diminishing circle of light appears on the oak-toned laminate. Eventually, Molto allows his shoulder to drop.

"Basically, that's it," he says. In the courtroom, there is a stir, particularly among the reporters, contending with the fact Dubinsky got it right.

"So I take it, then, that the senior Mr. Eddgar, the defendant's father, Senator Eddgar, will be a witness here?"

Molto grimaces. I'm asking too many questions, as usual.

"We expect him to testify for the people," says Molto. Now there's a real riffle in the press seats. Hard news: PROMINENT DAD TO IMPLICATE KILLER SON. Nearby I hear a bracelet jingling, Annie or Marietta, re-adjusting, caught unawares.

"And as the intended victim, he, too—Senator Eddgar—is without objection to this court presiding? In spite of our prior acquaintance? Have you taken that up with him?"

"Judge, it's not a problem." 'Period,' he seemingly would like to add. Clearly, Tommy has his orders. The mullahs in the PA's office have met and concluded that Tommy should try the case and I should preside. Slowly, I am beginning to recognize that Molto is not especially content with either prospect. I turn my copy of the *Trib* in Tommy's direction.

"Now looking at that headline, Mr. Molto, I can't pretend to be pleased. You know better, the state knows better, than to try a lawsuit in the newspapers, especially when you're aware that the prospective jurors have not yet been admonished about viewing media accounts of this case. Now—"

"Judge, as an officer to the court: I didn't speak to any reporters and I have no knowledge of anyone on our side speaking to reporters, I promise you that."

"Mr. Molto, I'm pleased to have your representation. And I accept it, of course. But you and I are both grown-ups, and we know that someone intent on leaking is not going to send up a flare or call you for permission first."

The reporters find this very amusing. There are a dozen ways this could have happened. Some cop on the case wanted to poison the well, or perhaps it was one of Tommy's superiors. Either way, the police reports appeared in Stew's mailbox in a plain envelope. We'll never know from whom. Behind the reporter's shield law, Dubinsky's source will remain fathomless.

"Judge, the defense had this information," says Tommy. "They had the statements of the witnesses. Our theory is obvious."

The book on Tommy is that he cannot stand down when he should not bother firing, and I lose my patience with him now.

"Look, Mr. Molto, are you suggesting that the defendant would find it helpful to try to pick a jury on the same day the state's theory of the case is detailed on the front page of the *Tribune?*" Molto is mocked by another rollicking burst of spectator laughter, ringing loudest from the press section. "*Res ipsa loquitur,* Mr. Molto. Remember that phrase from law school? The thing speaks for itself. Doesn't it? Again, I'm sure it wasn't you. But you should remind everyone on your side what their obligations are and let them know that if there's a repetition, there will be a hearing." Sallow, still, Molto frowns unconsciously at my rebuke. "For today, I suggest we deal with the situation that confronts us. Do you agree with Mr. Tuttle that I should dismiss the indictment?"

Rudy Singh has come back to stand by Tommy. He whispers urgently, telling him, no doubt, to give up. Fight a different fight.

"No," Tommy says lamely.

"Then what's my alternative, Mr. Molto?"

"Judge, I don't know. We came here this morning prepared to try this case. I think you should do what we always do. Bring the prospective jurors up. *Voir dire* them. Ask them if they've read the paper, and the ones who have, ask if they can put it out of their minds."

Hobie, of course, will have none of this. The problem, he points out, is that it forces the defendant to accept all the risks of juror prejudice created by the state's misconduct in leaking. Instead, Hobie insists again that the indictment must be dismissed. As a young man, he was grandiose and that part of his character clearly has not changed. No defendant subjected to pre-trial publicity—not O. J. Simpson or John Hinckley, who shot the President of the United States on national TV—has ever gotten such relief.

"What if we continue the case?" I finally ask. This is what I have been waiting for Molto to suggest. "In a couple of weeks this story will be forgotten and whatever benefit the state has gotten by virtue of the leak will be dissipated."

"Your Honor," says Tuttle, "leaving aside the personal inconvenience—I've come from D.C., gotten myself settled here—but leaving that aside, Judge, my client has a right to a speedy trial. He wants that speedy trial, and it shouldn't be delayed because of the prosecutors' misconduct."

Smooth, clever, Hobie knows he has the advantage and presses it. Molto, true to courthouse legend, seems determined not to give me—or himself—any help. He again urges questioning the jury pool right now. Singh, with his sleek black hair, stands behind Tommy, with one hand on Molto's jacket sleeve, not completely certain about whether he wants to stand ground with Molto or retreat.

"Gentlemen," I say eventually, "something's got to give. I'm not going to continue the case over the objections of both parties. I'm not going to dismiss the indictment. And I'm not going to allow the prosecution to make an uncombated opening statement in the newspapers and force the defendant to pick a jury out of a pool exposed to that." I stare them down, all three men—Tommy, Hobie, Singh with his large doe eyes—all looking up to me with evident bemusement. Silence, the spectacular silence of two hundred persons rendered mute, veils the courtroom.

Finally, Hobie asks for a moment and strolls off with his client. As Nile listens, the dark dot left by the earring he has removed for the sake of a good impression appears distinctly when he nervously sweeps back his hair. Returning to the podium, Hobie uses his bulk to move Tommy aside.

"There is one alternative which we can offer that would let us get started," Hobie announces. "My client and I are willing to proceed with trial to the court alone."

A current of something—shock, dismay—lights me up. This time, finally, I catch myself and maintain a collected expression.

"Mr. Molto?" I manage. "What's your position on a bench trial?"

"Your Honor," Hobie interjects, "they don't have a right to a position. If you won't do it, the defendant can't make you, we realize that, but this is none of the state's affair."

"You're certainly correct, Mr. Tuttle. But given the disclosures the court has made, I really would not exercise my discretion to accept a bench trial if the state for any reason felt that was not a wise course. Mr. Molto?"

"Judge, all I know is I got up this morning ready to try this case. I agree with Mr. Tuttle. We don't have the right to a position. And if I had a position, and if Your Honor was willing to get on with openings and the witnesses, I'd be very happy." Listening to Tommy insist again on moving ahead, I finally catch the drift. The prosecutors have a problem with their case. They've gummed things back together for right now, but it's going to go from bad to worse with time. Probably one of their witnesses has had a change of heart. Hardcore, perhaps? Someone important.

But does that mean I have to say yes to a bench trial? The older judges always tell you not to rush. They have a dozen sayings: 'There's no stopwatch on the court reporter's transcript.' 'The court of appeals won't reverse for delay of game.' I find myself staring down into the open pages of my bench book. It's an oversized volume, with a red clothbound spine, heavy stock pages lined in green, feathered edges, and a cover clad in rough black Moroccan leather. On the spine, my name has been impressed in gold. In the quaintest of courthouse customs, the book was presented to me when I took the bench, a judge's diary, the place for private notes about each trial. The pages before me are blank, as undetermined as I am.

Decide, I tell myself, as I so often do. In this job, deliberation is respected. Indecision is not. My work, in the end, is simply that, deciding, saying yes or no. But it's hard labor for the natively ambivalent. There's no other job I know of that more reliably reveals the shortcomings of a personality than being a judge. The pettish grow even more short-tempered; the silently injured can become power-mad or abusive. For someone who can spend a tortured moment before the closet, picking a dress, this work can be maddening. I'm supposed to let the conclusions roll forth as if they were natural and predetermined, as if it were as easy as naming my favorite color (blue). But I wait now, as I often do, silently hoping that some alternative, some forceful thought or feeling, will expose itself. The years roll on and life seems like this more and more, that choices don't really exist in the way I thought they would when I was a child and expected the regal power of adulthood to provide clarity and insight. Instead, choice and need seem indistinguishable. In the end, I find myself clutched by the resentment, which I still think of as peculiarly female, of being so often the victim of circumstance and time.

"Mr. Eddgar," I say and call him forward. I explain to Nile what it means to have a bench trial, that I alone will decide whether or not he is guilty, and ask if he's willing to give up his right to a jury.

"That's what we want," he replies. Perhaps because it's the first sound of Nile's voice since the start of these proceedings, the remark takes me aback. What does that mean? 'What we want'? He's going to get it, notwithstanding.

"Trial shall be to the court. What are your thoughts on scheduling, gentlemen?" After discussion, Hobie and Molto decide they're better off spending the balance of the morning on stipulations, hoping to agree about certain facts now that there's no need to educate — or fool — a jury. "If you care to make opening statements, I will hear them immediately after my bond call at 2 p.m." I point to Marietta, seated below me on the first tier of the bench, and tell her to call a recess.

The courtroom springs to life with an urgent buzz. A bench trial! The court buffs and cops and reporters mingle, exchanging speculations as they head into the corridor. I converse with Marietta about discharging the seventy-five citizens who've been summoned as prospective jurors. Then I gather the bench book and the court file. A day at a time, I tell myself. Weary already, I sink down the stairs.

"Judge? Can I talk to you?"

When I look back it's Seth Weissman, hunched somewhat timorously beside the front corner of the bench. A little squeeze of something tightens my heart, but I'm struck principally by the way he's addressed me. It must have been less peculiar to be a judge back in the Age of Manners, or even thirty years ago, when the lines of authority were more absolute. These days the attendant reverence can seem downright inane. People who were grown-ups when I was a child stand a few feet below me and, at their most casual, address me as 'Judge.' To hear it from the first man outside my family who ever said "I love you" raises the implausibility of these customs to dizzying heights.

"Seth," I say. "How are you?"

Something — a sense of the momentousness of time — swims through his expression.

"Bald," he answers, summoning in one word the boy I knew: funny, vulnerable, always willing to accept a helping hand.

I try a straight face that doesn't last. "Is my line 'I hadn't noticed'?"

"I'd settle for 'It's nice to see you.'"

"It is, Seth."

"Good," he says, then hangs midair. "I just wanted to apologize," he says. "You know, the acoustics were kind of startling."

I dispense a forgiving backhand wave. He asks how I am.

"Busy. Crazy with my life like everybody else. But okay. And you, Seth? I can only imagine how proud you are of your success."

He worms around, an aw-shucks routine meant to suggest it's all beyond him. More than ten years ago I first saw a column by Michael Frain. I was sure the name was a coincidence. The Michael I knew could never have become a master of the quick shot or the snappy *bon mot.* Then a year later I saw a picture, which was unmistakably Seth's. What in the world? I thought. How did this happen? Questions whose answers I still want to know.

At times since, I've looked at the somewhat whimsical photo (conveniently cropped just above the brow) and the accompanying columns, wondering about this man with whom I parted company with the usual tangled feelings but no deepening regrets. I liked Seth. I lost him. There were half a dozen others about whom the same might be said, even, if I'm feeling mellow, Charlie. Sometimes — especially when something he writes has struck me funny — I have recalled distinctly the droll delivery of Seth's somewhat monotonous Midwestern voice, in which the glottal *l*'s rasp in a minor speech impediment. At other moments, he can disappoint me. Always the sucker for easy laughs, he is sometimes too quick to flay targets already tattered by public scorn, and he occasionally displays certain ungenerous retrograde political opinions, a former leftist too eager to show he's wised up. At his best, though, he can be quick and penetrating, putting down a line or two that seems to sum up all the world's sadness. Even so, these commonplaces often perplex me. What could have brought that on? I'll wonder. Or even worse, I'll imagine all of it was there in the sweet, funny boy who whirled through my life, and that I overlooked it because I was so busy seeking within myself. Was it? How did I miss it? Where was it hidden? Those questions also linger.

"You were always funny," I tell him. "I didn't realize you were wise."

"You can create a lot of illusions in eight hundred words."

"Oh, you're very good, Seth. Everybody likes what you write. My minute clerk acts as if I used to hang out with Mick Jagger."

"Wait till she hears me sing."

I actually laugh. "Still a smart guy," I say and he seems pleased to find his character so well remembered.

"I've always told Lucy, that's what I want on my gravestone: 'Now what, smartass?'"

With that, the rear door bangs open and Marietta bulls a few steps into the courtroom. She's headed for the bench with a sheaf of draft orders when she catches sight of us and goes completely still. She turns heel abruptly, leaving the courtroom as it was, empty and hushed.

"So I take it I can look forward to a column about all of this?" I ask. My index finger circles toward the courtroom.

"'The Big Chill Meets Perry Mason'?" He laughs at the notion. "Maybe. It's an amazing curiosity, isn't it? Coincidence. Whatever you'd call it. Everybody together? I had to see it."

"I take it from the way you were giving Hobie the business, you're still close with him?"

He laughs about that, too. That's how Seth heard about the case, I suspect, from Hobie, but now that I'm asking questions about the defense lawyer I realize I've probably already let this conversation go further than I should. I offer my hand and tell Seth I'm on my way.

"Is it crazy for me to say let's have a cup of coffee?" he asks.

"Not crazy. But probably inappropriate."

"We don't have to talk about the case."

"We *can't* talk about the case. That's why I'm going to bid you farewell. The case will end. We'll talk then."

"Is there a rule here or something? I'm just asking."

"You could call it a rule. My practice is to make sure that nobody has anything to worry about. I have lawyers in front of me all the time who I know well, but generally, while a trial's ongoing, I don't pass the time with them — or their close friends."

"Sonny, really, I don't have a clue about this case. Honestly. Hobie's got me in an isolation booth."

We both turn abruptly again. Marietta has walked into the empty courtroom once more, using the front entrance this time and arriving purposefully on the other side of the bench. She's a caution: a lot of busy officiousness, shuffling files and humming to herself. Nonetheless, her full, dark eyes slide over this way with foxy calculation and I meet them with a look that sends her back out like mercury.

"Really, Seth, it's wonderful to see you. You seem well. And I look forward to sitting down with you as soon as this case is over, to hear about everything you've been up to."

"How about you?"

I thought we covered this ground already, but I answer that I'm fine.

"Married?"

I hum a bit, not sure when I should simply quit. "I seem to have passed through that phase."

"Kids? Do you have kids?"

"A daughter who just turned six."

Six! He's impressed.

"Late start," I answer. "What about you, Seth? From the column, I think I've counted what, two children?"

A knotted expression tightens his long face as I continue slipping farther away. He tells me that his older child, his daughter, is a college senior. At Easton, he says, his alma mater, an admission that brings forth the same wondering, self-conscious grin.

"Great school," he adds. "Astonishing tuition, but a great education. That's another reason I'm here. I get to see a little more of her."

I nod again and say something polite. How wonderful. I pull open the door.

"It's just," he says and stops. He's stepped nearer.

"What?"

"How many people do you get close to in a life?" he asks. "I feel really badly I lost track of you."

"We'll make amends, Seth. Just not now."

"Sure."

I offer my hand again. He takes it, with a bewildered, defeated look, and holds on just a bit longer than he should before letting go.

A bench trial is still a trial. When it's over the defendant is just as guilty—or not guilty—his prison sentence can be as long. When I was practicing I always felt the same high anxiety at the moment of decision which I did confronting a jury's verdict. But a bench trial is usually conducted without the same atmosphere of flamboyance or chicanery. Frequently, the bench trial is the refuge of the lawyer with a technical defense, an argument too intricate, or offensive, for lay people to freely accept. With a judge as the decision-maker, instead of rubes off the street, the proceedings are usually more understated, even sometimes legalistic.

Nonetheless, there's an alert air in the courtroom this afternoon. The spectators' section remains cheek to jowl, but there's more room in the well of the court, since the journalists have repositioned themselves in the jury box. All sixteen seats are occupied by reporters and sketch artists, while a number of latecomers have helped themselves to chairs from the counsel tables, which Annie has discreetly positioned in the corners of the courtroom, against the glass partition to the spectators' gallery. In the front row, Stew Dubinsky is getting it from two colleagues, who are clearly ribbing him. I can imagine what that's about: Stewie gets more leaks than a plumber. Beside Stew, Seth Weissman sits in his rumpled blazer. The man with a national byline, Seth is clearly a center of attention. In spite of the call to order, one of the TV guys has slunk along the jury rail to shake his hand and pass a word which entertains them both.

Marietta cries out the case name and the three lawyers step forward. Nile lingers closer to the defense table, where two square leather document cases and a banker's box are piled.

"All set?" I ask.

Everyone answers ready for trial. Joint motions to exclude witnesses from the courtroom are granted. I take a breath.

"Opening statements?"

"Your Honor," Hobie says, "I'd like to reserve my opening until after the prosecution has put on their evidence." His motion, a matter of right, is allowed. In one of those untutored gestures of power which I was astounded to find came so naturally to me, I lift my hand to Molto.

"May it please the court," says Tommy, and waits for the courtroom to settle. The other participants now are seated and Tommy has the floor to himself. In the intense light over the podium, his scalp shines amid his sparse hair, held fast by spray.

"Judge, since Mr. Tuttle is going to pass up opening for the moment, I can make this brief. I know you'll want to hear the evidence yourself. So let me just outline what the People will be proving.

"The state will show that the defendant, Nile Eddgar"—Nile has looked up at his name and now uncomfortably meets the prosecutor's glance, as Molto turns. It strikes me that Nile's eyes are the same penetrating marine shade as his father's, but his are fear-beset and seldom still. "We will show that Nile Eddgar was not only a participant in a conspiracy to murder but, in fact, the prime mover. It is a conspiracy that went tragically awry, but a conspiracy to murder nonetheless. What the evidence will show is that Nile Eddgar *asked* his co-indictee, his co-defendant, Ordell Trent, to murder Nile's father, Dr. Loyell Eddgar. Mr. Trent is a member of the Black Saints Disciples, Judge. He is a gang member. He is a drug dealer. He is a repeat felon. And he was Nile Eddgar's friend."

"Ob-jection," says Hobie. I am pleased to see him take the trouble to rise, a gesture of respect the PAs often overlook when there is no jury present. His yellow pad is open before him on the light oval of the counsel table. Behind him, Nile, making his own notes, has looked up, startled. "Guilt by association?" Hobie asks.

"Sustained," I say mildly. A small point. Hobie is merely trying to break Tommy's rhythm. Even Molto recognizes this and accepts the ruling indifferently.

"Nile Eddgar and Mr. Trent, whose gang name is Hardcore, first became acquainted," Molto says, "because Mr. Eddgar—Nile, as I'll call the defendant to distinguish him from his father—Nile was Mr. Trent's probation officer. He was—and I'm sure it's not disputed—Nile Eddgar was a probation officer in this very courthouse. And somehow, and you will hear this from Mr. Trent, he, Hardcore, and Nile developed a personal relationship, a friendship of kinds. And as a result of this close acquaintance, it eventually came to pass that Hardcore also came to know Nile's father, the state senator from the 39th District, Dr. Loyell Eddgar. Dr. Eddgar, who is an ordained minister and a college professor, as well as an elected representative, will testify for the state."

Perhaps he's a Scout leader, too, and also helps old ladies cross the street? I grin privately at Tommy's paean to his witness.

"Dr. Eddgar's acquaintance, Senator Eddgar's acquaintance with Hardcore is complicated and it will be described in the testimony. But suffice it to say, Judge, there were political aspects to it. Senator Eddgar will tell you frankly that politics were involved. At any rate, because Mr. Trent had also met Senator Eddgar, the senator was a frequent subject of discussion between Nile and Mr. Trent, and it came out over time that Nile Eddgar, the defendant, resented his father. He hated his father, Judge.

"Now, the evidence will show, Judge, that one day in September, the week of Labor Day, Nile Eddgar urged Senator Eddgar to meet with Hardcore. Nile told his father Hardcore had something important to discuss with him. And Senator Eddgar agreed to meet. What he did not know was that his son, Nile Eddgar, had promised to pay Hardcore

$25,000 if Hardcore would arrange to murder his father. He did not know that Nile Eddgar had made a $10,000 down payment." Tommy with his notes on yellow sheets looks up at me for the first time. "The People, Judge, will offer in evidence cash, currency that Ordell Trent received from Nile Eddgar on which Nile Eddgar's fingerprints have been identified."

News. Movement in the jury box. In the bench book, I make my first note: "Prints?" The harsh sibilance of whispers continues throughout the courtroom, and is brought to an immediate conclusion by another walloping smack of Annie's gavel. She scans the space with a menacing look. Tommy, in the meantime, has paused and wiggles his shoulders about, appreciatively absorbing the impact he has made.

"Indeed, Judge, Mr. Trent's testimony about this will be corroborated not only by fingerprint evidence but by telephone records showing a long pattern of communication between Nile Eddgar and him, including a page to Mr. Trent twenty minutes before this murder took place.

"And you will hear the details of this murder plan, not only from Ordell Trent, from Hardcore, but from a young female gang member, a juvenile named Lovinia Campbell. Ms. Campbell, Judge, is fifteen years old, and you, Judge, you will hear evidence that Hardcore told her that at Nile Eddgar's request—"

Hobie has again taken his feet. "Objection."

"Grounds?"

"That is most emphatically *not* what the evidence will show. Mr. Molto's engaged in argument."

"Overruled. I wouldn't know if it's argument or not. Mr. Molto, I'm sure you recall your obligation to merely describe the evidence." I smile, a gesture which Tommy finds momentarily confusing. Hobie resumes his seat, satisfied that he has tagged the issue.

"Ms. Campbell will tell you that Hardcore described the plan to her. A plan in which the evidence will show"—he turns briefly toward Hobie—"Nile Eddgar's name was in fact mentioned. The plan, Judge, was for Ms. Campbell, a member of Hardcore's narcotics operation, to meet Senator Eddgar. She would be there when Senator Eddgar drove up to the agreed spot. As the car approached, she would make a cell phone call giving a code word. And then she would greet Senator Eddgar. She would tell him she was going to get Hardcore. And she would exit that area. And as Senator Eddgar waited in his white Chevy Nova, a rider on a bicycle would come around the corner and sweep Senator Eddgar's car with gunfire from an automatic weapon. Ms.

Campbell would then approach the car, ostensibly to aid Senator Eddgar, to see if he was alive, and in reaching over the body, Ms. Campbell, according to the plan, would plant a packet of drugs in Senator Eddgar's hand. And the story afterwards would be that Senator Eddgar was a white drug buyer, that his visits to the area were for drug reasons, not political reasons, and that he was killed randomly, in a drive-by shooting by a rival gang." Tommy waits again to let the details, the horror, the cleverness of these calculations sink in. He knows it sounds right. The bicycle has become the murder wagon of today — maneuverable where cop cars cannot go, easily ditched behind a bush, and not identified by license plates.

"That was the plan, Judge. It did not work out. Senator Eddgar was not able to make it that morning. Other commitments in the statehouse had come up. And unfortunately, Judge, Mrs. Eddgar was here. She lives in Marston, Wisconsin, Judge. Lived. But although Dr. Eddgar and she divorced many years ago they remained close and she was here visiting him and her son. She came to the Tri-Cities often to do that, Judge, she was often in the county, and on this morning Senator Eddgar, when he was called away to his other business, he and the decedent, he and Mrs. Eddgar agreed that she would drive down to Grace Street. As I said, Judge, Senator Eddgar's acquaintance with Mr. Trent had political aspects and he did not want to offend Mr. Trent by missing this meeting. He could not reach him by phone and so June Eddgar agreed to go down and apologize in person for the senator.

"And so she went, Judge," says Tommy, "and so she died. The evidence will show that when June Eddgar arrived in the area, when they realized that it was her in the car, not her husband, everyone — Lovinia Campbell and Ordell Trent — they tried to get her to leave quickly, but it was too late, Judge, to stop this plan that Nile Eddgar had put in motion. The zip bike came and it arrived too fast for the rider to see Ms. Campbell's signals to stop. Ms. Campbell was shot herself, Judge. And June Eddgar was killed. And I'm sure, Judge — it really isn't disputed — that Mr. Tuttle will tell you that Nile Eddgar didn't intend to kill Mrs. Eddgar. Indeed, Judge, we'll offer a statement he made to the community service officer who came to inform him of his mother's death, in which Nile Eddgar all but admitted he intended to kill his father instead."

"Objection!" Hobie booms. Both arms are raised. " 'All but admitted'? Your Honor, that's argument, clearly argument. Defendant did no such thing."

I strike Molto's comment.

"Sorry, Judge," he says before I can reprimand him further. Molto's tiny, darting eyes shy away, knowing he was caught. "The point, Judge, is we acknowledge that the defendant has lost his mother, Judge, which undoubtedly has caused him some anguish and some grief. But that, as you know, is no excuse in the eyes of the law."

With this, my attention falls again to Nile. I felt a momentary kinship with him this morning as I arrived on the bench, thinking about my mother and a childhood lived in the shadow of political commitments. But I'm struck now by a more distant perspective: Nile is simply odd. For the moment, he is occupied with his notepad. Defense lawyers often try to find a focus point like this for their clients, knowing that they are best off showing no reactions at all to the proceedings. But my sense of Nile is that he's beyond the grasp of any plan or discipline. There is an abiding ungainliness about him. He's potbellied, and when he walks, he moves from the balls of his feet, in a loafing, dopey Alley Oop gait. Indeed, for someone who made his living in these courtrooms, he appears remarkably baffled. When he stood before me this morning, his head bobbed about like a barnyard hen's, and he is clearly uncomfortable in his go-to-court clothes. His tie knot is too large and askew, and his shirt collar will not stay in place. Yet Nile is my riddle to solve. What did he do? What did he intend? The most basic tasks in judging, they seem in this case frightening and enormous. Molto is winding up.

"What the evidence will show is that Nile Eddgar planned to murder, took substantial steps in furtherance of that plan, and that a murder resulted. That is the People's evidence, Judge. And once you have heard it, we expect you to find the People have proved beyond a reasonable doubt that the defendant Nile Eddgar is guilty as charged of conspiracy to commit murder." Tommy nods to me politely, convinced he has done a good job, which he has.

Meanwhile, in the jury box, another conspiracy is afoot. Several of the journalists are huddled, trying in hasty whispers to reach their usual consensus about the parts of Molto's presentation which are newsworthy. By striking this accord they ensure that no editor can complain that his reporter was scooped or missed the mark in her story. I can imagine what they're asking one another: What do you think about this stuff about the father and the gang guy having some political deal? What about the fingerprints on the money? I wonder myself. I make a few more notes.

"Again, Mr. Tuttle, the defendant will reserve?"

Hobie nods from his chair, then stands and nods again. We agree to begin the evidence tomorrow. Molto promises to have a witness to fill a couple of morning hours before my Tuesday motion call commences. With that agreed, Annie smacks the gavel once again. The first day of the trial of Nile Eddgar is over.

"See you got to renewing acquaintances," Marietta says as I pass through her small office outside my chambers. The space here is subsumed by her desk, shiny mahogany and nearly as large as mine, which angles into the room to allow for a small matching filing cabinet. Beside the blotter, pictures of her children and grandkids repose in a Lucite frame, under a brass lamp. A fake philodendron, bedded on woolly hummocks of sphagnum moss, rests on one corner of the desk, next to a tiny plastic Christmas tree, one foot high, mold-formed with icicles and candy canes, which has been added in the last week. On her blotter, Marietta has propped a tiny portable TV, on which the screen, no larger than a compact, moves with color. She listens to the soaps throughout the day when she is here, literally with one ear, a black wire running from the set and disappearing amid the dense dark curls on her left side. We have not spoken since she burst into the courtroom this morning, but the calculating sidewards glance she briefly permits in my direction is enough to establish the subject.

"Really, Marietta," I say. "All that running in and out—what was that supposed to be about?"

"I just needed some files, Judge," she answers. "I meant to tell you I seen him out there, only how you arrived so late, Judge, there wasn't any chance." With mention of my tardiness, Marietta's full brown eyes again rise adroitly, retaking the advantage. "Looks like you got to old times anyway."

"It wasn't old times, Marietta. It was very brief. He apologized for heckling Tuttle and I explained that I can't really talk with him now."

She's astounded. "You-all gotta *talk*," she says.

"Marietta, he's close to Hobie. They've been best friends since child-hood."

"Lord, Judge. 'Knows the defense lawyer.' There's no rule like that. Judge, that happens all the time. Everybody in this building knows everybody else. They're all cousins and husbands and girlfriends and boyfriends." Being technical, she's right, of course. But in this case I'm already walking on eggshells. And ethics are hardly what Marietta has in mind. I see how this is. Marietta's constructed the entire drama in her head. It's just like the sudsy fare on her TV. Some Rhett Butler rides back onto the scene explaining he's been a prisoner for the last twenty-five years.

"Marietta, you've got the wrong picture. He's married. He's been married forever. I know his wife, too, by the way. She was also in California."

Shaking her head emphatically, Marietta insists I'm wrong.

"Marietta, I read the column every day. He talks about his wife all the time. He mentioned Lucy to me this morning."

"Nn-uh," says Marietta. "*People* or one of them — I think he's getting divorced, I read."

"I'm sure it was *The Star*, Marietta. Maybe *The Enquirer*. Right after the articles about the two-headed baby or George Bush contracting AIDS."

Stung, Marietta pouches her lips and returns her eyes to the TV. Feeling both provoked and rueful, I creep across the threshold into my chambers.

"You gone end up with a cop," she says in a low voice behind me.

"What?"

"You heard me. I see it comin. I've been around this courthouse twenty-five years, Judge. I've seen half a dozen gals just like you, can't be bothered no way, and every time it's some cop, just don't take no for an answer." She begins her list. Jan Fagin, from the State Appellate Defenders, and Marcie Lowe, the PA. I feel like screaming. Some people, many people, manage cordial relationships with their staff that don't include advice to the lovelorn. Whatever happened to boundaries? But I'm far past the point where I can cut this off with Marietta. I have spent too many hours eagerly soaking up the tales of Raymen's latest infidelity to restrict our intimacies now.

Even as I am ready to rebuke Marietta, some image of Lubitsch rears up, one of those dark mountainous men, like Charlie, who I always thought in former years was my destiny, and I'm paralyzed by fear, the very stuff of superstition, that this will prove to be one of those dumb, chance remarks that in some way, as yet unknown to science, becomes fate. When I discovered boys, or vice versa, when my acne passed and late in high school I found myself suddenly attractive to males, one of the things that shocked me was that I liked so much to be embraced, surrounded. The men I envisioned were all dark and large. Even if they were, in fact, somewhat fair and bony, like Seth, that was how I saw them—one more reason I was doomed by Charlie.

"Marietta, you're pushing my buttons."

"I'm just sayin, Judge."

"That's enough saying for the moment. All right?"

Her jaw rotates in discontent, but she nods in a way. We've had this row a hundred times. Contentious by nature, I cut to the quick: Does she think a woman needs a man to have a meaningful life? Arguing this point, we stand across the chasms of social class. The feminist verities I regard as fixed as the rules of physics do not seem to apply on Marietta's side of the divide. As she lectures me, Marietta's round forms—the full circular do, her soft figure—plump up with disdain. 'Oh, I heard all of that, Judge. But are you really sayin you'd mind if some fella just loved every inch of your skin?'

It's more complicated than that, I always answer. I escaped from my marriage with no lasting disdain for men. In fact, before Nikki was born and I became so often soothed by the succor of other mothers—their helping hands, their reassurance—I had secret moments when I suspected I was one of those women who is more comfortable with males, with their badinage and rivalries. Even now, I wonder if it wasn't some of that which carried me into the law and the roughhouse of trial practice.

Yet, in some ways, I haven't begun to think of myself as divorced. Not that I feel the remotest connection to Charlie. But I cannot willingly take up the striving and the anxiety that sometimes go with being unattached. Riding the bus into the Center City, I observe with almost scientific distance the younger females who are single and still so focused on the details: the eyeliner and the base just right, the hair combed and piled and sprayed with sculptural precision, the hem, the seams, these women who you know look through the stores for clothes for at least an hour a day and are still in every sense presenting themselves. It's such a relief to be uninvolved with that, not because you've sworn some oath, to which you cling in the unreasoning way of religious faith, that a woman shouldn't let herself be judged on that basis (a credo which, after all, hasn't persuaded these young women), but because you're at another stage, another place, a different plane, where your connections are known, fixed, where you're not, like these girls, some atom waiting to be part of a molecule. Done with Charlie, I'm nonetheless unwilling to go back to that, like some upsetting grudge that has finally been forgotten.

Besides, I've found the idea of being a single mother and dating mutually exclusive. Assuming I had time to meet a man, when would I see him? The evenings and the weekends are all I have with Nikki. My few halfhearted efforts have generally been guilt-racked and uncomfortable. Living without sex, which never seemed an especially inviting or necessary prospect, is frankly far easier than I imagined. I am moved to old-fashioned thoughts—that abstinence must be easier for women than men. Still, at moments, especially on the bus, when I am often at close quarters with strangers, there are instants of longing that have the profound purity of music.

"Let's talk about tomorrow, Marietta. What have you been doing with the call?"

She checks the computer screen. If we start early, at 9 a.m., we'll get a couple of hours of testimony before I have to go on to the mid-week status call. Although I hear bail motions and other emergencies each day, routine matters—sentencings, progress calls, arraignments, guilty pleas—are scheduled on Tuesdays, in the morning or afternoons, so that trials can proceed on other days without constant interruptions.

"I think Molto's got a custody comin over," she adds. "That little girl—one who was supposed to put the drugs or something."

"Tommy made a good opening," I tell her. Marietta makes a face. "Tommy's not your style?"

"He's one of those trippin-over-his-own-feet-type guys. Like this morning. What good did all that do him?" The leak to the *Trib*, she means, not just a low stunt, but a stupid one, since I was so unlikely to let him get away with it. Clearly, Marietta does not believe for a second Tommy was not Dubinsky's source. "Besides," she adds, then thinks better of whatever she was going to say. Marietta, who intervenes cheerfully in my personal life without invitation, is too much of a pro to express herself on pending cases. I invite her to go on, but even at that, she seems to take a moment to choose her words.

"Judge, he's sayin the boy was tryin to kill his father. Wasn't it the father, Judge, who posted Nile's bail? Wasn't that in the court file? We had a long bail report and then there wasn't any motion filed, cause the father put up his house. Remember?" I hadn't until now. "What kind of sense does that make, Judge?" asks Marietta. "Have his son try to kill him, then pay to get him out? Most folks think awhile 'fore they do that. That boy killed his momma and the father had him on bail in twenty-four hours. Why'd he be doing that?"

Because he doesn't think Nile's guilty. That's the logical answer, I suppose, but I keep that to myself and respond, more circumspectly, that perhaps we'll hear about this from the defense.

"What'd you make of Hobie, by the way?" I ask. "Smooth, huh?"

"Oh, he's hot stuff, that one. Butter wouldn't melt in his mouth. Now, how'd this go, Judge? You know him, too?"

"Him, too." I shake my head once in bleak wonder.

"Rich boy, idn't he?"

"Hobie? Richer than I was." That's rich in America: someone who has more money than you. His father, if I recollect, owned a pharmacy.

"I can tell," says Marietta, "I can tell every damn time. Feet don't even touch the ground. He's marchin round that courtroom. 'How you doin, girl?' Like he gave a good goddamn how I ever done. Just hopin nobody notice what kind of good time he's havin when he gets up in court, talkin like he's white." She nods to cement that judgment. I think what I always think: God, they can be hard on each other. "And you ain't seen him in years either, Judge?"

"No, you know how that is, Marietta. Once you give up the guy, you tend to lose his friends, too."

A second passes. "And why exactly was it you give the guy up, Judge? He do you bad? Must have been somethin like that if you haven't been talkin for twenty-five years." Her eyes train on the glowing screen, but we both know we have arrived once more at Marietta's favorite subject. Wary of hurting her again, I toss my head vaguely. "Wasn't the other way, was it?" she asks.

"No, Marietta. Not really." *Was* it? For a second I am faint with fear, until the past again returns to focus. "No, the main thing, Marietta, is that Seth more or less dropped out of sight. And I went into the Peace Corps. The last I heard from him, there was something about being kidnapped."

"Kidnapped!" This declaration startles Annie, who has just entered the outer office. The keys on her broad black belt clink as she steals a few steps ahead, surveying the situation. "Yeah, 'kidnapped,'" says Marietta, and humpfs to herself. "Judge, I hear better'n that every Friday night."

"It wasn't like that, Marietta. It's a crazy story. And I never knew much of it." I look somewhat helplessly toward each of them, feeling suddenly vulnerable to the strange arc of my life. The two women, both dependent on my moods, watch me carefully. Time, I think. My God, time.

"We were young," I say.

1969-70

SETH

When I was twenty-three and in the midst of crazy times, I arranged for my own kidnapping. I was not actually abducted. It was a ruse of kinds, but in the aftermath my life was sadly changed. One man was dead and I had taken another name. In the years since, I have always felt I had been stolen from myself.

It was 1970, still the height of 'the sixties,' that period when America was in the midst of war and tumult. The combat raged not only in Vietnam but here, at home, where young people like me who opposed U.S. involvement were openly regarded as enemies of the government and our way of life. This role pleased me in many ways, but it gave my existence a persistent renegade air.

By April of 1970, I had received my draft notice and was being forced to choose between conscription — and the likelihood of a tour of duty in the jungles of Vietnam — or exile in Canada. Each course seemed unbearable. My opposition to the war was unyielding. On the other hand, I was an only child, weighed down by my parents' many claims on me. Even 1,900 miles away from them and my home in Kindle County, I felt them close — a hot breath from behind — a phenomenon that left me alternately infuriated or resigned. They were camp survivors who had met in Auschwitz after their families — her husband, his wife and child — had perished. My father was almost seventy now, still robust, still full of his subtle commanding powers, but bound for decline. Even more troubling was my mother, a fretful person who seemed to sustain herself by clutching me close. When I was a child, a sensation of my mother's pain was always turning near my heart, and I had grown up feeling an unwavering duty not to add further to her suffering. My departure with my girlfriend for California the prior fall had prostrated her with grief. Actual exile, as my father never tired of reminding me, would revive for her — for both of them — unbearable horrors.

Faced with the pressure of sorting this out, I allowed the other relations in my life to collapse. I fell out badly with my best friend since childhood, Hobie Tuttle, who was a first-year law student in the Bay Area. But my greatest agony, as is usually the case, came from love. The spring before, in 1969, I had fallen helplessly for a young woman — strong, dark, and beautiful — named Sonia Klonsky, whom I had met on an overnight bus trip from Kindle County to D.C., heading for one of the first of the Student Mobilization Committee's marches on Washington. At the time, we were both college seniors on the verge of graduation, she from the U. in the city and I from stuffy, renowned Easton College. With her striking dark looks, set amid a stormy abundance of jet hair, her long-waisted, full-busted proportions, and, most important, her air of frank seriousness about herself, Sonny was dazzling to me.

I had never been in love. In fact, I had never been a notable success with women. My bleak outlook and sardonic manner made me somewhat fashionable, I guess, but under the strain of sustained female attention, I tended to come off as simply weird. My relationships all petered out after a few weeks. So my passion for Sonny was a great shock — the heat of it, the puppyish desire to be near, the amazing news that human loneliness, which I took as an elemental condition, could vanish like the reagents in a test tube. My mind and heart spun crazily on the magic of details: We were both left-handed. We both knew the words to every cut on *Happy Jack.* When we were alone, she called me "Baby." The news that I held a spot in the life of someone so fiercely intelligent, so beautiful, so surely destined to make her mark upon the world, clapped home three times a day with the breathtaking impact of divine revelation.

This devotion, the stuff of legends, would have been perfect, had it been better received. Sonny enjoyed my company, my idiosyncratic humor, my headlong commitment to what she thought was right, my unruly, experimental side. But she forbade all talk of love. In September 1969 she prepared to leave for the Bay Area, where she had been accepted at Miller Damon Senior University in an accelerated, interdisciplinary Ph.D. program known as Modern Critical Thought and Philosophy. I moped around until she finally suggested I come with her to California, a step I'd already secretly contemplated, given Hobie's destination for the same locale.

"Because you need a ride?" I was always trying to trap her.

"Seth."

"No, seriously, man. What'll we be, roommates?"

"We'll be 'living together.' " Dangerous words then for a man and a woman, full of a subversive appeal I could never reject. So we had driven west in my yellow VW Bug, in a two-car caravan with Hobie and his young girlfriend, Lucy McMartin. Big and good-looking, smooth-talking and funny, Hobie was a hit with many women, and Lucy had dropped out of her sophomore year at Easton to follow him. Lucy was cute in a Betty Boop way, a little freckle-faced white girl, narrowly made, always clothed in stylish items culled from secondhand stores—leather vests and a short-billed cap like the ones the Beatles wore in *Help!* Hobie found Lucy pliant, sweet-natured, and bright, if chronically naïve, but she was generally overwhelmed by Hobie and his lunatic manner. Behind her back, we called her 'Groovy,' since that was her automatic reply to any inquiry from 'How do you do?' to discussion of the Tet Offensive.

Entering the town of Damon, California, was much like crossing a national border. Beyond the campus environs dwelled men who looked as if they had gotten their haircuts in pencil sharpeners and women in girdles, but here along Damon's main drag, Campus Boulevard, the culture of the young flourished in a tumbling bazaar atmosphere. The town's transient elements—students and street freaks, hippies, home runaways, and communards—now far outnumbered the indigenous residents, the faculty families, and various grumpy Latinos who had watched as Campus Boul sprawled, surrounding the bookstores and student hangouts and mercados with head shops, candle stores, and the new 'boutiques' vending tie-dyed dresses and garments of macramé. The traffic, thick at all hours with touring gawkers, staggered by, while street performers—mimes and bongo drummers and gentle pipers—did their things, and the Damonites, in leisure suits and floral granny gowns, strolled the avenue among the soiled barefoot hippies, each one inevitably accompanied by a mongrel dog leashed on a piece of string. On the building sides, the trisected peace sign was spray-painted, while harsher words praised the NLF in Vietnam, and Huey Newton, then in jail for supposedly killing a police officer. Appearing often amidst the graffiti in Day-Glo shades was a round-lettered injunction which simply urged, "Be Free." Arriving with Sonny, I found all of this, the commotion, the array, the slogans inspiring; I could feel the life of my generation—historical, dynamic, epochal—like a rush flowing through my arms. This was the bold new world, its shape as yet uncertain, but sure to be better than the one our parents had given us.

On the first weekend in town, Hobie led us to Dionysus '69, the theater-of-assault piece, in which cast members mingled naked with the audience. The next night it was Fillmore West, a teeming environment of maximum amplification, sweat, and drug deals, where amoeba-like colored visuals swarmed on enormous projector screens, and various rock maniacs cruised about with a hipper-than-thou air. Hobie, particularly, loved the Bay Area scene: so many wiggy new things to dig, so many new drugs to take. First citizen of the counterculture, he wore shirts mottled with balls of color the size of grapefruits, bell-bottoms bigger than his shoes, and tinted aviator shades. He'd also grown a large globe Afro, somewhat reluctantly, since he'd been at constant odds with the Black Power types at Easton, who called him a Tom for rooming with a white guy.

Hobie and I had grown up together in University Park, the only neighborhood in the Tri-Cities anybody might have called cosmopolitan and probably one of the few in America which, during the years of our childhood, could pass as integrated. Blacks had arrived in U. Park during the Civil War, brought by the Underground Railroad, and were quickly isolated through the device of four public parks laid out around the small area where they resided. But beginning in the 1930s it gradually became acceptable for Negroes of sufficient stature—doctors, dentists, lawyers, certain entrepreneurs—to settle on the white sides of the park. This depressed land values somewhat, and my father, always in relentless pursuit of a bargain, could not resist. Thus, I moved in down the street from Hobie Tuttle. As youngsters, we had little contact; Hobie went to Catholic elementary school and, always large, was known as something of a bully. It was only in junior high that we suddenly found each other. He was someone else who openly admitted having weird thoughts about science, girls, his parents.

In high school, we went through phases together. For a while, we were beatniks, appearing each day in berets and shades and black turtlenecks and calling each other 'Daddy-o.' We spent weekend nights in the paneled basement of Hobie's home, eating pizza, listening to Mort Sahl and Tom Lehrer records, and debating the philosophical issues of male adolescence, such as whether vaginas, like snowflakes, were each unique. In college, we'd become mildly notorious on the Easton campus as performers. During rush week, we did our own minstrel show, a Negro and a Jew, pining together in Jolson-faces before a picture of the honey-haired homecoming queen—Muffy or Buffy or Betty—crooning Bing's old tune: 'I'm dreaming of a'—

Hobie: 'White'

Seth: 'Christian.'

We thought we were hysterical. Both Lucy and Sonny had met the inevitable measure, proving tolerant of our strange riffs. The apartment Sonny and I found in Damon was only a block from them.

So we arrived, and in less than a year I had been handed over to doom. I look back at that young man with his hand-tooled-leather headband, his Sergeant Pepper mustache, the froth of mid-shoulder blondish hair which my father in his correct Viennese accent never tired of comparing to Jesus's and feel weak with shame. In spite of my degree from a fancy, famous Midwestern university, I was largely aimless. For a year or two in college I'd had thoughts that Hobie and I would become a comedy act, but I was simply not funny enough; these days I was talking about writing underground movies and had broken all records for repeat watchings of *Jules et Jim* and the films of Jean-Luc Godard. For the most part, I saw the draft as having rudely barricaded my way, but at moments, especially when I was stoned, I would recognize how large and undifferentiated my universe seemed, how lost I was inside myself. I was liable to fall under the influence of any strong suggestion, acting at moments with no more forethought than a person trying on hats. I knew only a few things for certain: That I was in love. That I wanted the world to be better than it was. Yet my passions seemed powerful enough to light the planet. And now that the earth is somewhat dimmer, I look back with a solitary heart, limp not merely with regret, but also with longing.

Sonny had her fellowship and I supported myself with hand-to-mouth measures typical of the era, food stamps, and a variety of odd jobs. I sold *The Good Times* out on Campus Boul and was eventually re-cruited to distribute a rival publication called *After Dark*, basically a skin mag, whose cover each week featured a blurry color separation of an unclothed full-busted beauty whose smoky look smoldered above the fold in the vending machines where I placed the papers. My principal occupation, however, turned out to be baby-sitting for a six-year-old named Nile Eddgar. His parents lived in the same apartment building as Sonny and I, a brown-shingled Victorian with a round bulb extension at one end that rose three floors to a roof pointed like a wimple. The inner construction was shabby—the usual marked walls and devastated carpeting of a typical student slum—but our apartment had an ample kitchen and many nifty Victorian touches, including a raised pattern in the plaster.

I'd found my job with Nile purely by accident. The day we moved in, I knocked on the door to the single upstairs flat, looking for a ham-mer, and was greeted by Nile's father, Loyell Eddgar, whose movie-star looks undoubtedly contributed to his charisma. He was a slighter, shorter version of Bruce Jenner, an Olympic athlete of the day, with the same long, lank hair smoothly groomed, and a similar Barbie doll handsome-ness. I was struck by his eyes, a remarkable limpid blue, which gave him the pale haunted gaze of a mystic. Eddgar, however, had none of a jock's relaxed way—he was rigid as someone taking an electrical shock. As I explained what I needed, he stood his ground in the threshold and clearly would have slammed the door on me had it not been for a mild Southern voice behind him. A pleasant-looking woman in jeans and a chambray shirt approached, her stiff, bronze hair ponytailed, her mea-sured smile reflecting self-control and excellent breeding.

"Will you sit?" June Eddgar asked, as soon as we'd made our intro-ductions. As it turned out, this was a job offer, rather than an effort to improve on Eddgar's congeniality. June explained that both she and her husband, a theology professor at Damon, worked full-time. Their former baby-sitter, our neighbor downstairs, Michael Frain, had quit unexpectedly only the day before in order to supervise a lab in the Applied Research Center. She was, frankly, desperate and hoped I could step in with Nile, after school and on some evenings.

The notion of me as a baby-sitter seemed slightly preposterous. I had no younger siblings and naturally thought of it as girls' work. On the other hand, I was without any means of support at that point, which meant, even halfway across the country, I felt myself vulnerable to my father and his perpetual craziness about money. He was an economist, one of the first of the money-supply experts, whose lifework—his very consciousness—was given over to money, which, as a result, was the frequent terrain of our many conflicts.

Only after I accepted June's offer did I find out what I had gotten myself into. "Oh, lad. You're a flippin employee of the chairman of One Hundred Flowers," I was informed that night by Sonny's departmental adviser, Graeme Florry. We were at the first of what I quickly came to regard as dreadful events, the departmental party, where the grad students chattered brightly and sized each other up. Graeme, a tall ruddy Englishman with a blond pageboy, wore a skinny Jacob's beard fringing his jaw and narrow yellow-tinted granny glasses suggestive of some psychedelic orientation. I had no idea what he meant by One Hundred Flowers or why he seemed so agitated.

"Ask the FBI, mate, Damon security, the town police. Know One Hundred Flowers well, I reckon. Refer to themselves as a 'revolutionary council,' I believe. The Black Panthers. White Panthers. Weathermen. PLP. The Brown Berets. Everybody, love. The Red Mountain Tribe. Honkies for Huey. Each little root and seed group, all the various head cases who begin nodding vigorously when anyone starts talking about taking up weapons. A treacherous fellow, that one. Believe me. Ordered an execution last year. Did you know that? Word from some poor devil who was involved. God, I hope you're not with the FBI."

I assured him I wasn't. Graeme took another belt of his whiskey to still his concerns.

"Someone from the Panthers they took for an informant. Coppers found him in a ditch down by the Bay. Injected the poor chap with heroin, forcibly, tucked a wee bit of powder in his pocket so the police would think it was a junkie overdose. Not give a bloody damn. Which they didn't."

Graeme briefly sketched Eddgar's history. He was the scion of Southern planters—his grandfather had been raised with slaves—a background of gentility and greed which Eddgar freely acknowledged and regularly denounced. He was an ordained minister and, until he had tenure, had been a promising professor in the School of Divinity, with a scholarly interest in comparing the teachings of the Gospels to Marxist doctrine. But after freedom riding and lunch-counter sit-ins in the mid-sixties, he had begun adhering more to Chairman Mao's *Little Red Book* than the Scriptures. Through his radical organization, Eddgar was suspected of inspiring riots the prior spring, when separate groups of black and white students occupying university buildings had been ejected by a phalanx of city cops, culminating in the wounding of a university guard who had been shot from across the main quad.

In those first days, Sonny heard the same things about the Eddgars— that they had taken part in planning the prison breakout at Soledad, that a faction in the faculty senate wanted to expel Eddgar from the university—and she repeatedly urged me to quit. Sonny herself was a red diaper baby, daughter of a labor organizer named Zora Klonsky, who briefly, during World War II, had served as president of a Kindle County pipefitters local. I viewed Zora more prosaically, as the only real-live Commie I'd ever met, and—in utter privacy—a serious nut. But whatever her sanity, Zora was a unionist. She'd broken factory windows but never staged a prison breakout, never fired a gun. The Eddgars were too much for Sonny.

"They're into very heavy stuff," Sonny warned. I was unconcerned. For one thing, I had learned that first day, as June was vetting me, that both the Eddgars were Easton graduates, fugitive Southerners who'd endured four years of Midwestern winters. I sentimentally assumed that made for a bond that would keep me safe. Beyond that, I was intrigued. Given the dismal results produced by the political process the year be-fore—the police riot outside the Democratic convention; Richard Nix-on's election and his subsequent refusal to bring the war to a close— many people on the left argued that it was time to move beyond civil protests to militant action. In Manhattan, bombs had decimated the Armed Forces induction station on Whitehall Street and the criminal courts building. SDS, the most prominent left-wing organization on many campuses, had splintered over the issue of violence, and in the fall of '69, the surviving Weatherman faction staged the Days of Rage in Chicago, in which dozens of rads ransacked the streets, smashing auto windows with case-hardened chains and going hand to hand with police. In Southern California, Juanita Rice, the daughter of a promi-nent industrialist and Republican fund-raiser, was grabbed at gunpoint out of her high school by some cadre called the Liberation Army, who held her for ransom. I regarded these actions as counterproductive and extreme, but I couldn't stifle a spark of excitement at the notion of reshaping the world from scratch. Amid my sense of wandering, dangling, the Eddgars seemed to represent reality, life, the thing I still felt was waiting to start.

Over the years I've wondered of course why it didn't work out between Sonny and me. The times? Did I frighten her with all my crazy passions? Did I cling? Insight, like some sweet inspiration, remains temptingly beyond reach. But somehow living together was hard. The carrying through. The day to day. Neither of us really had the remotest idea how to be with someone else. Sonny's mother, Zora, hadn't lived with a man while Sonny was alive, and from an early age I'd known that my parents' high-strung, suffocated relationship was something I did not want to duplicate. As a result, virtually everything between us was definitional: who did the wash, who made the social plans, how clean to keep the apartment. We fought about it all.

And some of what emerged couldn't be dismissed as mere adjustment. I regarded the girl I'd been dating as the most 'together' person I knew, thoroughly and enviably adult. Sonny was poised and rigorously logical in all circumstances, while maintaining a warm, frank manner. She was quick to laugh at jokes, if poorer at making them, easy with strangers, kind to street people and their dogs. My principal contribution to her, so far as I figured, was to add a combustible element to a life that was a little too confined by deliberation.

Yet living with her, I found Sonny full of mysterious, molten emotions that seemed to defy both her understanding and mine. She was inclined to manic spells, isolated periods of zombie-like staring, as well as adolescent attachments: writers, classmates, clothes that were one week's passion and then were never spoken of again. And she was touchy. Criticisms from professors about papers, or even their disagreement with a remark she offered in class, could make her funky and combative with me. Listening to her at those loathsome departmental parties, I was struck eventually by the way she presented herself as largely *sui generis*—never any mention of a hometown, or of a childhood in which her father, Jack Klonsky, secretary of the bargehandlers' local, had died in a dockside accident before she was two and in which she thereafter had been traded back and forth to the household of her Aunt Henrietta while Zora traveled and organized. Like a sculpture, Sonny presented no apparent access to her interior space. Desperate for any handhold, I would sometimes study her class notes when she was not around, or inspect the marginalia in the books she read, the passages she highlighted. What was I to make of that exclamation point? What insight made her write 'I see'?

On no subject was she more confusing than school. At times, she was preoccupied by her department and its hothouse politics, the arch proclamations of her young adviser, Graeme Florry, and the complicated realms of thought she was required to master for her classes. Then periods would set in in which she declared it all a waste of time. Philosophy was only about words, she'd say, or she'd repeat an observation of Nietzsche's disparaging the philosophic enterprise. In the catchword of the day, philosophy was no longer 'relevant.' For Aristotle, philosophy and science were one and the same. Now, she said, there were a thousand other fields of study, from psychology to physics, that we depended on to tell us more about the truth.

"It's real things, doing things I admire," she told me, "not ideas about them. That's what I'm trying to say. I can't live like this, talking about imaginary categories or making more of them than they really are."

Often enough, as a means of encouraging her, I asked her to digest her reading for me, like a mother bird chewing and feeding this heavy stuff to me in lightweight bits. In order to speed the degree process, Modern Critical Thought required all students to complete a dissertation proposal by the end of the first term, which meant the work began at once at a furious pace. Sonny's emerging thesis concerned a philosopher named Brentano, who taught that consciousness was, at root, images shorn of all abstractions. Sonny was going to treat him as the unsuspected bridge between the depth psychologists, like Freud, and existentialists such as Sartre. In this connection, she was rereading the nineteenth-century German philosophers. One of her passing fixations was a term—from Nietzsche, I think—*traumhaft*, a sense that all beliefs—religion, love, the golden rule—were but a dream with no provable justification in morality or science. Our lives, Nietzsche claimed, our customs, were really no more than rote learning. We were, he said, actually afloat within sensation and otherwise unanchored, free but terrified, like the moonbound astronauts had been when they left their capsules and stood in space.

"Get it?" she asked. It was a Sunday afternoon, and we were, as was often the case on Sundays, in bed. It was our time of refuge before the forced march of the week began again. Sonny did not dress all day. We ate brunch and sometimes even dinner on the Goodwill mattress on the floor. In alternating periods, we went through the paper and screwed. When she dozed, I took up the sections she'd been reading. In the afternoons, Sonny moved on to her assigned texts.

"Heavy," I answered. "Very heavy. But bullshit."

"Why is it bullshit, baby?"

"Cause that's not how it is. Not for me. I mean all this raging volcanic shit, I feel? Everything's connected to everything else. The draft. My parents. The war. You. I'm not floating. Not hardly. Are you?"

There was a round window, like a porthole, in our bedroom. Its existence had seemed a typically pointless Victorian frill until a night, a week ago, when the full moon had appeared there and filled the room with light so ghostly but intense I'd found it difficult to sleep. Lost in reflection, Sonny looked in that direction now.

"That's what I feel," she said. "A lot."

"*Traumhaft?*"

"*Traumhaft.* There are times when I wonder. Do you know Descartes? Sometimes I wonder about everybody else. Like Descartes did. How do I know *they're* not in my imagination? How do I know for sure there's anything besides me? And even so, I wonder if I can really reach what's outside of me. There seems such a terrible abyss. Even between what I feel and what I can say about it. I can't—"

"What?"

"Get out? Does that make sense?" She scrutinized me with her searing, dark-eyed look. "Am I too weird?"

"Not compared to me."

"No. Really."

"For-real," I answered. "Listen, I'm here. I promise, man." I took her hand. "This is here," I said and fell upon her.

Sex was often the answer. It remains the most intensely physical relationship I've known. Words were the instruments of critical scrutiny to Sonny and talk, therefore, was as dangerous as a game of mumbly-peg. In bed, she was somehow freer to give what remained often inaccessible. She was a willing participant in most of the experiments I concocted from a lifetime of unsatisfied fantasies: feathers and vegetable scrubbers; a large red dildo that briefly entered our lives. Our favorite was a tantric exercise we called The Touching Game. Naked and stoned, we faced each other in the dark, our eyes closed, legs folded yoga-like. The rules allowed us to touch with fingertips only—our bodies could not meet. No brushing knees, no kisses. And the genitals were out of bounds; they could not be caressed until some aching point when it became irresistible. Instead, we drifted our hands across each other for endless periods. I shivered when she stroked the skin behind my knee, my toe tops. We would fall, for long pieces of time, into the quivering zone above each other's lips, out of our minds with drugs and sensation, our mouths a breath apart as we trembled on the vapor of each other, of our beings.

In the Eddgars' apartment, the hot-blooded personalities of the revolution came and went: the Progressive Laborites in their workingman's twills; the leader of the Campus Employees Collective, Martin Kellett, with his sloppy redheaded ringlets; and, of course, the famous Black Panthers from Oakland, turned out in shades and berets and their three-buttoned coats of shining treated leather. The most prominent of the Panthers was Eldridge Cleaver. More often, he was represented by Cleveland Marsh, equally famous in Damon, where he had been a college football star. Currently the Panther Party's Minister of Justice, Cleveland was a hulking guy with a terrifying, insolent look. He was a classmate of Hobie's in the entering law school class, and Hobie, a notorious sucker for celebrities, was forever rushing into the hall whenever Cleveland appeared, the better to fortify their minimal "Hey, man" relationship.

The members of One Hundred Flowers appeared at the Eddgars' for meetings or occasionally arrived individually at odd hours to whisper with Eddgar on the back porch about some intrigue too sensitive for the telephone. Eddgar was obsessed with security. He assumed, probably correctly, that his organization and he were the constant targets of intelligence gathering and infiltration. That was why he'd removed Nile from a local baby-sitting co-op years before and barred me from his home the day we met. Once daily, the Eddgars swept the apartment for bugs. June used a device called a Private Sentry which looked like a voltmeter with a lightbulb attached, and Eddgar backstopped her, plugging a microphone into an AM–FM radio and his TV set. He chattered constantly—usually sayings from *The Little Red Book*—playing the channel knob across the UHF band or the full radio spectrum, awaiting any telltale feedback.

According to the rumors about him always circulating on campus, Eddgar was careful never to issue any revolutionary directives on his own. Even the most treacherous orders—to kill the snitch in Oakland or to aid the Soledad breakout—supposedly had been delivered to One Hundred Flowers through the month of June.

Coming and going with Nile or visiting with June to discuss his care, I now and then caught glimpses of the One Hundred Flowers meetings. The revolutionaries engaged in fierce doctrinal disputes, addressing each other as 'Comrade' and invoking the names of Gramsci, Fanon, Sorel, Rosa Luxemburg, and Bakunin, arguing about Lin Piao and China's role in Biafra. Meanwhile, June would slip off with different members to ride around the blocks in someone's car, where communications could take place securely. Before these ride-arounds, June and the passenger would search one another for recording devices, passing their hands across each other's bodies so casually that conversations were not interrupted.

The only time Eddgar's security concerns yielded was with regard to Nile's baby-sitting arrangements. June called Nile a 'troubled sleeper' and insisted he be put down each evening in his own bed. I could tell the Eddgars had quarreled about this, but June apparently felt I was trustworthy and I stayed in their apartment, alone with Nile, on the nights the Eddgars were out with their 'cells,' or affinity groups. Eddgar kept a deliberate distance from me, to be sure, I guess, that I didn't learn too much.

In truth, Eddgar didn't have casual dealings with many people in Damon. He gave his lectures and spoke at public rallies; he carried on passionately at the faculty senate, delivering speeches which appeared to have been borrowed in tone and, worse, in length from Fidel Castro. Otherwise, he was remote. It was something of a privilege if he made any gesture of recognition when I saw him around the theology department. I was going there regularly in the mornings for meetings of the Damon chapter of the Student Mobilization Committee to End the War, which was coordinating local planning for various nationwide demonstrations that took place that fall.

Early in November, I was there mimeographing observations on draft resistance when the machine broke. I sputtered and wrestled with a reluctant gasket, until someone edged in behind me and extended a hand. When I looked back, I found Eddgar. On good behavior at the department, he wore a plaid shirt and contrasting knit tie, and looked almost raffish. Under one arm, he carried papers for the class he was about to meet. He accepted my gratitude without comment, but took an instant to look over the mimeo, still slopped across the machine's canister in a reeking puddle of toner. He could not have made out much reading backwards, but he seemed to get enough and turned away with a wee, telling smile, which, to my credit, irritated me.

"It's not funny, man," I said. "Okay, you don't agree, but it's not funny."

I could tell I had struck a note Eddgar never expected. He lifted a pale hand in a remote gesture of compromise.

"I don't dismiss good intentions, Seth." He smiled tautly as he quoted Mao: " 'Whoever sides with the revolutionary people is a revolutionary.' "

"But you don't think that's enough, right? Good intentions?"

He reared back and observed me at length. "Seth," he said finally, "you sound like you're trying to involve me in an argument you're havin with yourself." I sensed instantly he was right. This kind of susceptibility, as I was to learn, never passed Eddgar's notice, and he took a step closer now. "I understand you, Seth," he said quietly, "I believe I do. I've seen you here, toing and froing with these Mobilization folk. I see what you're doin. And I confess I've thought of myself. I think of all those high-hope little mimeos and prayer sheets we used to turn out in church basements in Mississippi. I'd say that you bring to mind all the passions of a young Christian activist, if you were a Christian."

I think Eddgar was making one of his rare efforts at being humorous. Perhaps he knew that I thought of myself as quite a card and was trying to meet me on my own terms. But the remark had an unsettling undertone. I was never much at ease, to start with, when someone else mentioned I was Jewish. It called up my parents' lifelong warnings that my gentile acquaintances would never let me forget this difference. Inwardly, I looked forward to a new world where the need for such self-consciousness would be erased. Besides, Eddgar knew little about me, and it seemed to reveal the abiding attitudes of a small-town Southern boy that he kept this detail in mind. He frowned deeply at himself and remarked that what he'd said had not come out right at all. We hung there, both afraid of the implications were we to part. The vacuum made me bolder.

"What happened?" I said then. "I mean to the young Christian activist. Why did he change?" At the age of twenty-two, the news of how lives turned out the way they did gripped me like a thriller.

"What happened?" Eddgar asked himself. He walked as he thought and I followed him into an open courtyard. Although it was fall in the land I came from, Miller Damon was lush with blooming vines and flowering cactuses and ivies with shiny leaves that climbed the sand-stone-colored bricks of the low buildings with their terra-cotta roofs. The sheer abundance of the place was still strange to me. Tall eucalyptus trees with hairy, peeling trunks formed a jungle line at the edge of campus, their aromatic leaves mentholating any breeze. At the back of the campus toward the Bay, the brass-colored hills burned to acres of straw, broken now and then by solitary live oaks, each lonely tree looking as if it had been placed there to accommodate a hanging.

"Teaching happened," Eddgar answered at last. "Scholarship. Mostly, however, I would be inclined to say Mississippi. That was the intervening force." He seemed mildly amazed, recollecting the person he now so clearly renounced.

"Did you lose your faith?" I asked this casually, as someone who's never believed much, but I saw from his astonished expression I couldn't have pried more deeply if I'd asked what went on in bed between June and him. We walked on for some time along the single diamonds of Carrara marble that had been laid out beneath a columned esplanade.

"Every semester," he said at last, "there's a student who by the second or third class becomes confident that he or she has got me. 'How can you claim?' this student will say, 'how can you claim that Christianity, which hallows the life of the spirit, has any common ground with Marxism, which recognizes *only* a material world?' But that isn't what Marxism teaches. Do you think Che isn't spiritual? That Mao or Marx didn't believe in—indeed revere—the life of the spirit? The Marxist believes that the spirit can only find expression in this material world, and in Mississippi, slowly, I came to understand that point of view.

"Slowly, I say. On the night that the Civil Rights Act passed in 1964— on that night, I felt *ecstatic*. I felt that years, decades of goodhearted efforts had been vindicated, that the world was finally changed. And, you know, two years later, I went back to Mississippi and there was not a thing different for those folks. Lord knows, I didn't have to go to Mississippi to see that. I could have walked down the road from my father's house and seen the people who have been cutting black tobacco in his fields for generations. But I had to go to Mississippi to *see* it, if you understand me, and I saw. The same little shacks. The same laundry on the line. The barefoot kids, bathin in big tin tubs. No runnin water, save what came up from the ground. Same ten hours in the field, twelve bits an hour. Still wasn't a school for them within ten miles. Oh, there was some talk of change when I asked. But I had to wonder.

"And I wrestled with myself. I struggled. Viewing that squalor, I would look at those babies, those precious babies, and wonder, 'How do I say to you, after all this work, after this great triumph, how can I say to you that it will be no better in your lifetime? How do I, where do I, derive the right to tell you to wait?'

"You see, I couldn't really comfort myself with hopes for future generations, because that meant accepting *her* misery, the misery of the child I saw now. And I couldn't agree to the sop of the religious, *heaven*," he said with mild contempt, "the poor received in glory, because after all, after *all*, it was not just the Kingdom of Heaven that Jesus said the meek would have—he said they would inherit this earth. Was he merely taunting them? So that was the question, you see: How do I temporize with this generation? With any one child? What mandate of law, of God—where in anyone's teachings, Christ's or Marx's or Adam Smith's, where does it explain how a government derives the moral authority to tell the poor to languish in squalor, to wait and wait for the earth that is theirs while it is consumed by the rich? What happened to me, Seth, was that my faith, or my conscience, or my moral sensibility, told me there is no logic to this life but revolution." His dramatic eyes were wide and pale as a wolf's. I was never of anything but two minds about Eddgar. I always recognized how theatrical he was. But as he finished his tale of ardor and personal pain, as he headed off alone beneath the arches of the esplanade, I was barely breathing.

Near three-thirty each day, chubby little Nile Eddgar limped home from first grade and became my responsibility. June had chopped Nile's straight brown hair into a bowl-shaped do à la the Little Rascals, but it would have been a stretch to call him 'cute.' He was an unsmiling, slow-moving soul, a turbulence of shirttails, smudged cheeks, and dirty fingernails. After devouring a snack his mother had left. Nile languished, child of the revolution, in front of my television. His parents prohibited TV and had gone so far as to get rid of their set, but somehow I found myself powerless to keep Nile from the dials. He would sit entranced, stroking one of the few toys he was allowed, Babu, a handsome bear with a pelt of shiny synthetic fur. I seldom interested Nile in the list of kid-time activities June had suggested—the park, the library, projects from school. He seemed to have no friends, partly because Eddgar, wary of government snoopers, didn't allow visits with families he hadn't approved. Instead, Nile moped around, telling me often how much better he liked Michael Frain, the physics graduate student who lived next door to Sonny and me and who had been Nile's sitter for the last two years. Frequently Nile would sneak away and hide in Michael's apartment, waiting for him to come home, at which point Nile would follow Michael around, resisting my efforts to recapture him.

I found Nile's relationship with Michael humiliating. I knew I was a pretty lousy baby-sitter. I was quick to regard myself as wounded by my childhood, yet I had little memory for a kid's preoccupations, while Michael, who was mute, virtually flash-frozen, with adults, could fall with Nile into the rhythms of children's play. I'd find them in a treehouse in the back yard, or in the park, making funny noises and ugly faces at each other as they twisted around a jungle gym, engaged in games where the rules changed moment by moment. 'Let's say I'm the guy who wants the treasure, no, you're the bad guy, okay then we're both the good guys, and these other guys . . . No, wait.'

Michael had come from a small town in Idaho, and he had about him the arid, silent mystery of those high, empty plains. Michael spoke slowly and only after considerable reflection in a voice with a hee-haw monotone that climbed uphill at the end of every sentence. He had a bit of a stammer, too, so that you had to wonder if perhaps he'd been taunted into silence at home or in school. His looks, I was told, were a little like mine — tall and thin with a prominent nose — but he had a fragility I never saw in myself. His head appeared delicate as a china bowl, his skin drawn tightly across his skull, with the wiggly purplish trace of a prominent vein near his temple. Grown long in blondish dreadlocks, his hair was already receding.

I initially viewed Michael as a hapless turkey, with his slipstick hanging from a plastic holster on his belt. But he eventually sifted his way into our life. I found him uncommonly generous. Michael filled in with Nile when he could, and also helped me keep up a preposterous fiction I'd created for my mother that Sonny and I were living in different apartments. The idea of me cohabiting with a woman was much too much for my mother. In her Old World view, marriage would have been morally required, an impossible thought both because Sonny was not Jewish and because it would represent one more rending of the strong fabric that bound me to her. Instead, I'd had a second phone installed in our apartment which I alone answered when my parents called. With Michael's permission, I gave my mother his address and thumbed through his mail each day for her letters.

Nonetheless, what drew Sonny and me to Michael most strongly was probably our stomachs. He could cook, a skill we each decidedly lacked. With the wok, Michael was a master. He could tell the temperature of hot oil within a few degrees, by dropping a scallion on the surface and watching it wither. Since it was often my job to give Nile dinner, and Nile always craved Michael's company, the four of us often ate together. I shopped. Michael was the chef. Sonny did the dishes. We pooled our student food stamps for costs and also fished scraps out of the Eddgars' refrigerator. On the weekends, we were frequently joined by Hobie and Lucy. She was a terrific cook herself and would add exotic touches — cilantro and peppers she'd found in the mercados along Mission Street, or watercress which she'd discovered growing wild beside the golf course in Golden Gate Park.

Michael also began to join us for something we called 'Doobie Hour.' In college, Hobie and I had always ended the day together, passing a joint with dormmates, and we'd more or less kept the custom alive in Damon. In our living room, amid the tattered, used furnishings, we'd all watch an 11:30 p.m. rebroadcast of Walter Cronkite that followed the local news. We smoked or drank wine, making smug remarks in reply to Nixon or Agnew or Melvin Laird when they appeared on the TV screen. Michael would pass on the j, but always seemed to enjoy Hobie's and my late-hour riffs.

Usually during those first months in California, when the news was over, I became the entertainment, reciting weird little sci-fi fantasies that ventilated my grim obsessions and which I liked to pretend could be turned into movies. There was one about a fakir who somehow lost his ability to walk across hot coals; another about a heartless mercenary from Vietnam who became the ruler of a South Seas nation and met a chilling end when the natives saw through his magic. One night Michael told us how the universe was expanding but might someday reach its limit, contracting like a rubber band. According to Einsteinian theory, this would cause time to run in reverse. I spent a number of nights thereafter spinning out tales about this inverted universe in which effect preceded cause, where people at birth sprang out of their graves like tulips and grew ever younger, where you knew the lessons of life before you'd had the experience, and where you perished while your parents were at the height of passion. Michael was especially amused by my freewheeling improvisations on the principles of physics.

He spent most of his time at the Miller Damon Applied Research Center — the ARC — which was located in the elephant-toed hills south of the campus. Within its walls, elite scientists conducted experiments in high-energy physics, including many projects sponsored by the Defense Department in hopes of aiding in the war. According to various reports, these included efforts to miniaturize nuclear devices, to perfect laser-guidance systems for mortar shells and bombs and — the innovation that was bruited about most often on campus — the battlefield use of microwaves. This would allow the army to stop trying to rout the NLF from their networks of tunnels, dangerous, often lethal duty loathed by our servicemen. Instead, grunts could just point a portable device and cook the gooks alive. These ghoulish rumors were never denied, and as a result the facility was the target of repeated demonstrations. Marchers stormed up the road and were regularly rebuffed by phalanxes of university security police in helmets and shields.

"Hey, man," said Hobie one night during Doobie Hour, "this stuff about roasting slopes in the tunnels — is that for real?"

"That's classified," Michael said immediately, a response which deadened the room. He finally tipped a shoulder. "I'm doing a little work in there. Just a little. In one of the labs. Everything is need-to-know. But there's a lot of unusual microwave research. You hear stuff."

"Evil," Hobie muttered. "What about you, dude?" Hobie asked. "Is your shit classified?"

"That's classified," answered Michael, in what passed from him as outrageous humor.

As guardian of the counterculture, Hobie was always suspicious of straights and he was sure now he was on to Michael. "You think Eddgar knows he's got a fascist scientist around his boy?" Hobie asked as soon as Michael left. "Did you hear him? 'That's classified.' What could he be doing that's classified? You think he's studying the peace process? I'll bet Eddgar isn't hip to it." Hobie hooted. He ridiculed political involvements and Eddgar therefore presented an especially tempting target. Hobie's father, Gurney Tuttle, was on the executive board of the Kindle County NAACP, and throughout high school and the early years of college, I was arm-in-arm with him and Hobie's mother, Loretta, at marches and demonstrations for open housing, for passage of the Civil Rights Act, during those sweet, inspired days when we believed the right laws would bring down every barrier. Hobie made fun of us all. His concern was the inner realm. He read *The Tibetan Book of the Dead* and *Nightwood* and the novels of Hermann Hesse. He listened to Charles Mingus records, and took incredible quantities and varieties of dope. Hobie's credo was that thought was culture and culture was the vice that contained us all. Anything conventional, any activity people had tried before, whether it was sit-ins or, even, revolution, was hopeless, a dreary repetition of the limitations of the past.

"Michael's a good head," I answered.

Lucy, who disliked no one, spoke up for him too. He was an Aquarius, she said. It was a compliment, though I didn't know why. She'd found a job at a kiosk on Fisherman's Wharf, drawing astrological charts, an activity she viewed with Delphic seriousness and which Hobie, to her face, treated as laughable.

"He's just quiet," said Sonny.

"Quiet?" asked Hobie. "Sometimes when I'm with him, man, I feel like I'm in a Bergman movie."

Much as I wanted to defend Michael, there was no denying the cryptic element. He was a ham operator and had three or four radios, big clunky boxes in his apartment. This activity was what had first led him to speculate about wave motion and energy, the unseen realm of the furthest spectrum of light. When he was ten, Michael's mother had died. He never spoke about that, but I often imagined him as a boy in his small Idaho town, lonely, half-orphaned, sitting up at night, spinning the dials and listening to the jits and jots of Morse code, the static-scratched voices in other languages. Typically, he was only a listener; he sent no messages of his own. He said he had tried it once or twice, but he was never quick enough with the snappy lingo of the airwaves. On occasion when I was searching for Nile, I'd knock on Michael's door and, getting no response, let myself in, only to find Michael sitting there with his headset, mystically absorbed by these unseen lives and the flickers of sound they emitted from almost as far off as heaven.

On our side of the Bay, Friday, November 14, 1969, was warm and clear. The National Student Mobilization Committee had scheduled local demonstrations across the country, hoping to spark interest in the massive marches set to take place the next day in San Francisco and Washington, D.C. My own interest in stopping the war was growing increasingly personal and desperate. Throughout the fall, I'd endured a series of dismal phone calls from home in which my mother in her heavy accent read the latest bad news from my draft board. First my application for conscientious-objector status was denied; then I was ordered to report for a pre-induction physical. In response, I talked about leaving the country, and my mother, two thousand miles away, wept. Grabbing the phone, my father would order me to cease discussing such insane plans. The two of us always ended up screaming.

It's probably useless trying to explain the passions of one era to another. I can say now, as a sign of mature detachment and openness to reason, that my views about Vietnam might even have been wrong. But I do not mean it. They were formed then with the hardness of diamonds and not even the surface can really be scratched. I carried few images of Vietnam with me. I did not see its overgrown humid beauty, its mountain verdure, or the casual depravity of drugged-out troops fragging lieutenants or having debased encounters with former peasant girls, now sexual zombies in the meaty trading places of the cities. For me it was the vaguer, close-up view of the nightly news: sweating grunts streaked by camouflage paint, tensely stalking among the oversized leaves of the tropical Asian forests; huts in flames and black-garbed peasant mothers running with their bald-headed babies as strafing raised dust along the earth. The wrong of Vietnam was not on the ground but in the air — in principle, far more than in particulars. I envisioned a black heart, a jungle enshrouded in permanent night, where conscience and reason did not even make the skittering light of tracers in the air. I did not deceive myself: the rage of that era was not simply about whose prediction of the future of Southeast Asia was accurate, or the issue of an indigenous people's right to control their nation, or even the debate about whether Ho Chi Minh was more noble than the U.S.-sponsored thugs. In my own mind, in my own bones, the war protest represented an entire generation in combat against the rigid views of our parents, especially about the roles of men — about the need for males to be warriors, patriots, conformists, unblinking followers of aging generals and other elders. The furious issue was what would happen to all of us, parents and children, if the laws of our fathers were forgotten.

On November 14, about five thousand people surged up the dry road from campus, boiling dust on our way to the Applied Research Center. We larked in the warm air, flaunting banners and chanting slogans. "One. Two. Three. Four. We don't want this fucking war." "Withdraw, Nixon, like your father should have." "Drop acid, not bombs." Although she was burdened by her classes, Sonny was with me. Women's liberation notwithstanding, the war had a special gender inequality, since only men were being drafted. The watchword of the day was 'Girls say yes to boys who say no.' I always felt the moment I'd won Sonny the prior spring was when I'd confided that I was serious about going to Canada, a step she'd pledged to support.

A lawsuit had forced the university to permit us onto the grounds of the ARC, and its iron gates, tipped in spears of gold, were thrown open. A cast of thousands, we marched on the winding asphalt road past the precise lawns and hedges, up to a wide concrete plaza that fronted the Research Center. The building, ordinarily unseen except from a distance, loomed there like Oz. It was a futurist design with large fluted pillars of sand-colored stucco and vast windows protected from the sun by a cantilevered overhang. Between the building and the crowd, the Damon Security Corps positioned themselves in three even rows. In the middle ground, a single square fountain issued a segmented spray that piddled on brainlessly, wavering in an occasional light wind. The cops wore white reflective patrol belts angled across their chests, the better to recognize each other in a melee, and riot helmets whose Plexiglas visors were raised like the lids on welders' masks. Long batons were holstered at their sides, and a large plastic shield rested at the feet of each officer, like an obedient dog.

The turnout was far larger than any of us on the Mobilization Committee had foreseen. The weather, a welcome relief from a recent chilly spell, made it a good day to cut classes. I rarely admitted to myself the extent to which demonstrating had become sport for people my age. A generation that had lived secondhand through the television set seemed to find a special thrill in the live spectacle. But the political climate was also provocative. In the aftermath of the Moratorium Day in October, in which campuses and many businesses around the country had shut down, Richard Nixon had delivered a defiant speech announcing that a 'silent majority' of Americans supported his refusal to withdraw from Vietnam. The ugliness of the war Nixon wanted to maintain had been underscored by reports this week of a young lieutenant, William Laws Calley, detained at Fort Benning on suspicion of having slaughtered five hundred Vietnamese villagers.

As music played, the crowd assembled on the ARC's vast lawn. Sonny and I lay toward the rear on a large beach towel. Behind us, people threw Frisbees for their dogs, while the usual contingent from the National Organization for Marijuana Legalization lofted smoke upwind where the telltale aroma breathed down on the security forces, who were powerless to abandon their posts.

Near 3:30, the speeches began. The Moratorium demonstrations were intended to show the breadth of opposition to the war, and representatives of all the participating organizations briefly spoke: church groups, faculty committees, union representatives, businessmen against the war, women's liberationists, browns and blacks, students of all stripes, from rads to McCloskey Republicans. In this pantheon, One Hundred Flowers had been included, notwithstanding objections that their agenda was not peace. As a makeshift stage, the speakers had mounted a sign for the ARC, a large concrete block perhaps six feet high, and near the end of the afternoon Loyell Eddgar appeared there. The various entities that comprised One Hundred Flowers had identified themselves with red arm sashes decorated with Chinese characters. As Eddgar was announced, a number of them forced themselves through the crowd toward the front. About sixty members of the Progressive Labor Party went by close to where Sonny and I were sitting. They were all in their khakis, and rushed forward, heads bowed, hands on the shoulders of the person ahead, the tails of their arm sashes turned at the same precise angle. They chanted:

> Mao is red
> Red's Supreme
> Mao will smash
> the war machine.

I had never heard Eddgar speak before and my impression at first was that I was experiencing some trick of perspective, seeing from a distance someone I'd known only at close range. Here was this lean figure dressed simply in a button-down shirt and chinos that might have been left over from his college years. His thick, dark hair was lustrous with sweat, and the tendons and muscles in his neck and jaw stood out as he spoke. But gradually I realized he was in fact someone else. Standing on the concrete block, projecting his voice through a bullhorn which amplified both his breathing and the click of the machine going on and off, Eddgar was transformed by revolutionary passion. In the spirit of the cultural revolution, he called for the destruction of all elites.

"We must make this university a place that improves the world rather than destroys it. We do not need to study how to cook our enemies. We must study how to feed the poor, and help them feed themselves. We must stop educating the children of the ruling class, to the exclusion of the black, the brown, the red and yellow people who come into our classrooms more often to clean the desks than to sit behind them as students."

Led by One Hundred Flowers members who were still pushing to the front, the crowd began greeting Eddgar's well-timed pauses with choruses of "Right on!"

"We must take the power to make the decisions about *our* lives from people who care only about *theirs*," Eddgar cried. "We must, as Mao taught, 'Make trouble, fail; make trouble again, fail again . . . till their doom.'"

Suddenly, somewhere near the front, a woman cried out—a shocking, terrified sound. Something was happening. We all knew it. "This isn't good," Sonny said and pulled me to my feet. Around us, everyone was rising.

Eddgar, who had been silent for a moment, screamed another quotation into the bullhorn: "'It is good we are attacked by the enemy, since it proves we have drawn a clear line of demarcation between the enemy and ourselves.'"

I saw the first rock in the air then, traveling a long arc toward the enormous panes of the front windows of the building. The closed environment, the riot-clothed coppers, the university's sullen, entrenched battlefield atmosphere agitated me enough that an abandoned, heart-sprung piece of me probably soared in flight with that stone. But the thinking part was already in agony. The window seemed to drop out at once. A waterfall of glass crashed down on the cops, who reacted immediately. They claimed afterwards there'd been some further attack, but I know I saw batons swinging then. There was intense confusion, high-pitched screaming, fierce buffeting as people fled.

From the rear, where Sonny and I were, the deterioration near the stage had a remote quality for a moment. We could see the crowd peeling back in rows twenty or thirty deep as the line of cops fell upon them. Then suddenly, the ripples of panicked movement were nearby, then around us—molten faces and piercing voices and hair flying about. The earth jumped with the pounding of the mob. Some people held their ground momentarily to throw rocks and cans, but Sonny and I ran. As I reached the road back to the gates, a young woman stumbled to the asphalt right next to me and I helped her up. There was an open gash across her forehead, amid a throbbing welt. Blood ran on her face and was already crusted in her hair. She wiped at it tentatively and cried aloud when she saw her hand, then she ran along, clearly afraid of being struck again. You could feel from the surging, wild movement of the crowd that the cops were still coming, still swinging.

For a moment, as we all rushed toward the gates, the panic seemed to have receded. I had lost Sonny somewhere and I stood on the tarred drive, yelling her name, answered with the cries of a dozen people like me attempting to find someone from whom they'd been separated.

Then, without warning, another hysterical chorus rose up. With the second volley, I recognized the screaming sound of the canisters in the air. The little smoky trails, innocuous-appearing at a distance, dissolved as they rose from the ground, but the students knew enough to take flight with a new, maddened intensity. At the bottom of the hill, I could see people climbing the iron fence, and the spikes rocking at other points as the crowd massed against it. Overhead, the birds who had tasted the tear gas shrieked, flying crazy circles, mad with pain.

Near the gate, it was a horrible scene. I saw a woman with her head trapped against a concrete post, entirely unable to move for an instant until she suddenly disappeared. Beyond the gates, people rushed on, screaming and crying, shouting threats against the police. Once I was on the gravel road, I turned back again, searching the grieved, dirt-streaked faces for Sonny. As they flowed past, I noticed a few who some-how had had the foresight to soak washcloths, which were now stuffed into their mouths to abate the effects of the gas. There were even three or four people, each dressed in the PLP khakis, who wore rubber gas masks. As she came by, one woman pried off the green-monster face of her mask and, improbably, kissed me. It was Lucy.

"We're with Cleveland. We were. I don't know where he and Hobie are." She looked in all directions.

"Cleveland Marsh?" Hobie's law-school classmate. I wouldn't have expected a Panther leader at a peace march — or Hobie, for that matter. Lucy kissed me again and ran on, swept into the current of the moving crowd.

I waited another ten minutes or so, hoping to see Sonny. The wind changed direction then and I ended up catching a mouthful of gas. In full flight, I took off toward the campus. I went to the spot where I'd parked the Bug, but Sonny wasn't there. After some time, I moved on, figuring she could drive home. It turned out she was far ahead and had left the car for me.

Unaware of that, I walked on, reassuring myself that Sonny was okay and hoping to see her on the way. Beyond the bright lights of Campus Boul, the night had closed softly on the streets of stucco apartment buildings, in their soft, reflective shades, and the little tile-roofed homes. Away from the commotion, the panic, I could feel my heart. My shoul-der ached for reasons I could not recollect. It was turning cool quickly and you could feel the fog coming, thickening the air, even though it was not yet visible. I was sick to my stomach from the gas, and my eyes now smarted considerably. I knew enough not to rub them, and so I walked along in the cool night streaming tears that I wiped gingerly on my sleeve.

When I reached our building, I heard some kind of shuffling—fast steps, a voice, something furtive. My impression was that it was more than one person. I drew back with an arm raised and yelled out, "Who is that?"

Eddgar stepped out then from beneath the exterior wooden stairwell which served as a fire escape. He remained in the shadow, beyond the path of light from the fixture over the entry. He was breathing heavily. A rill of sweat glistened on his temple. And he had lost his shirt along the way. He wore only a colored T, and he looked more slender than I might have guessed. He had run from somewhere. Somewhere he was not supposed to be, I thought. I figured he had run to get ahead of the police. So that he could say he was at home. He must have come through the alleys, afraid that the coppers were keeping surveillance on the cars of One Hundred Flowers members, or that he could not move fast enough in the heavy traffic.

"Seth," he said. He seemed unusually full of himself, his face lifted up somewhat daringly toward the light. "It's all right," he said over his shoulder. Then he faced me and in silent instruction nodded toward the stairs. I walked up slowly to the landing outside our apartment, but I knew I'd never make myself go inside. I turned back to watch.

Below me, Eddgar knocked on the shingles as some kind of signal and two people came around the building side—Martin Kellett, the campus union leader, in his heavy motorcycle boots, and a pale, thin person I thought was a woman. She had fly-about dishwater hair and wore an open flannel shirt. She and Kellett carried a rolled stretcher, like something from Scout camp, a canvas sheet suspended between two poles. Eddgar stepped aside then, and they crouched beneath the wooden stairwell. Kellett spoke consolingly to someone. "All right, Rory. Just cool there, comrade. Here we go." A man cried out then, and Kellett and the woman emerged bent from the black space beneath the stairwell. A man lay on the stretcher. Even in the minimal light, I could see that his foot was turned at an inhuman angle. "We're boogying," Kellett said to Eddgar. "Truck'll be in back."

Eddgar moved off with them. The gate slammed and the latch clinked thickly home. I heard the hoarse rumble of the truck come near, and the explosion of gravel as it tore off again. Then, in the borrowed light, Eddgar reappeared. He caught sight of me on the stairs and trudged up slowly.

"He broke his leg," he said.

I knew better than to ask how. Something had happened. Something bad. Something Damon Security would want to know about. But what bothered me most was the way Eddgar cupped my shoulder and headed on, without troubling himself to look back. He knew he had nothing to fear from me.

December 5, 1995

REPORT AND EVALUATION OF PRETRIAL SERVICES
ON NILE EDDGAR

Subject: Nile T. Eddgar
Judge: Klonsky
Charges: Violation of Sections 3 and 76610 of Revised States Statutes
(Conspiracy to Commit Murder)

At the request of his counsel, Subject was referred to Pre-Trial Services (hereinafter PTS) for evaluation and recommendation regarding Subject's fitness to be admitted to bail pending trial. Because of Subject's employment with the Kindle County Probation Office (KCPO), this matter was referred to the undersigned in Greenwood County Probation Office, which is not acquainted with Subject.

On Tuesdays, when Cindy Holman drives—I should probably say 'manages'—the kindergarten car pool, Nikki and I are always prompt. Arriving early, I had time to indulge a moment's curiosity and pulled the PTS report, which Marietta mentioned last night, from the court file. It had remained there unread after Eddgar posted Nile's bail, one more copious summation of information and energy made irrelevant by the swift course of courthouse events.

GENERAL OBSERVATIONS: *Subject was interviewed at Kindle County Jail (KCJ) on September 13, 1995, in the presence of State Defender, Gina Devore. Subject is presently attempting to retain private counsel, but signed Form 4446—PTS Waiver of Rights—in order to allow his new lawyer to file a motion for reduction of bond.*

Subject is a white male, aged 31 years old. He is 6 feet 1 inch tall and weighs 245 pounds. He appears alert and was cooperative throughout the interview. He describes his health as good. Subject was observed smoking cigarettes, which he says give him a chronic bronchial condition. A routine intake urine screen at KCJ was negative for the presence of opiates and other narcotics. Trace amounts of tetrahydrocannabinol (THC) were reported, after Subject's interview, suggesting possible marijuana use.

EDUCATION: *Subject attended college intermittently until three years ago. He claims an A.A. from Kindle County Community College (confirmed) and lists sufficient credit hours in social work–related areas for his Bachelor's Degree. A B.A. has not been awarded due to his failure to complete required courses in science. Subject claims a twelfth-grade diploma from Easton Lab School (confirmed).*

EMPLOYMENT: *Subject has been employed for almost two years as a probation officer with the Kindle County Probation Department (KCPD). Subject's duties generally involve him in overseeing the activities of clients who have been released from the penitentiary and* whose sentence by the Court included a period of supervised release or probation. Subject monitors family adjustment, employment, attendance in chemical dependence programs, etc. His salary is $38,000 p.a. Previous employment was sporadic as Subject was completing his education. (See above)

Subject's KCPD personnel file, which was reviewed by the undersigned, shows that Subject has generally had good evaluations. His written work product is frequently late, causing complaints from certain judges, but he relates well to clients. One supervisor stated that Subject is sometimes too sympathetic and "buys the [b.s.]." In his first year of employment, Subject was placed on review status due to failure to appear for work on three occasions within a month. His attendance has been regular since.

Joseph Tamara, head of KCPD, states that Subject is presently on administrative leave. He will receive his salary but will not be allowed to work while the instant charges are pending. If acquitted of all charges, Tamara says, Subject would be entitled to return to work.

FAMILY HISTORY/BACKGROUND: Subject is unmarried. Since taking his position with KCPD, he has maintained a residence at 2343 Duhaney (confirmed) in DuSable. Subject acknowledges that he continues to spend weekends and many nights during the week with his father in Greenwood County.

Subject states that he was born in Damon, California, November 19, 1963. His father was a university professor; his mother worked outside the home in various capacities.

In 1971, his parents separated and subsequently Subject moved with his mother to Marston, Wisconsin. Subject's mother remarried, Dr. William Chaikos, a doctor of veterinary medicine, in 1975. She divorced Dr. Chaikos in 1979 and, according to subject, chose thereafter to use the surname 'Eddgar' in deference to her son.

Subject admits that in Wisconsin his social adjustment was poor in school and that he did not get along with his stepfather or two stepsiblings when his mother remarried. Subject's father (see below) states that his ex-wife was having problems of substance abuse throughout this period. Therefore, at the age of 13, Subject moved to Greenwood County to reside with his father who had become a professor at Easton University. Subject says that he continued to do poorly in school and had other troubles. (See below.) He moved back and forth on a number of occasions between his father's home and his mother's in Wisconsin.

Subject's father, State Senator Loyell Eddgar, was also interviewed by phone on September 13. Dr. Eddgar characterizes his son as highly intelligent but not well motivated. He says he had to encourage Nile to finish his education. He says that in spite of troubles in school, Nile maintained a stable relationship with both parents. While Sen. Eddgar acknowledges that Nile has experienced various adjustment problems, the senator says that since joining KCPD his son has been productive and seemingly more content. Sen. Eddgar helped Nile secure his present position. Sen. Eddgar refused to discuss details of the instant offense at the request of the Kindle County Prosecuting Attorney's Office (KCPAO).

Subject's mother, June Eddgar, was not available for interview, as she is deceased as a result of the crime with which Subject is presently charged.

CRIMINAL HISTORY: Kindle County Unified Police Force records, FBI, NADDIS reports were requested. All are negative. During interview, Subject admits that while a juvenile he was the Subject of two station adjustments for shoplifting, and one for destruction of wildlife. Subject adds that it was this experience which first interested him in becoming a probation officer.

FINANCIAL: Subject's counsel states that Subject will attempt, through new counsel, to make arrangements to post an adequate bail. He will report directly to the Court on his resources at the time of the bond hearing.

CONCLUSION: PTS concludes that Subject is an appropriate candidate for bail. While subject is charged with a very serious offense for which a grand jury has found probable cause exists, he has lifelong ties to the community, no history of violent crime, and no adult criminal record.

> Maria Guzman Tomar
> Chief, Pre-Trial Services
> Greenwood County Probation Office
> 18 September 1995

'Subject,' I think, is always an appropriate candidate for bail. PTS is a holdover from CETA, a job-training program staffed by persons who are barely beyond the point of poverty themselves. Their sympathies are freely engaged by the prisoners; PTS's message, sometimes barely lettered, is usually the same as Moses': Let my people go. The length of this report—three pages—and the speed with which it was prepared—a week—are a tribute to the political sensitivities of this matter and the suburban caseload in Greenwood County. Here in Kindle, we are often a month awaiting a single paragraph. It's not clear whether Ms. Tomar didn't hear that Nile made bail or decided it was politically advisable to complete her report anyway. But clearly she had no inkling Eddgar would come through for Nile. Why did he, then?

"We-all are ready, Judge," says Marietta, peeking in from the back door of the chambers.

In the courtroom, we get off to a fractious start. Tommy told Hobie the first witness would be Lovinia Campbell, the young homegirl who ended up as another victim of the shooting, but Molto says the transport deputies have failed to deliver her, as they often do. Hobie thinks this is simply an excuse to turn the tables on him.

"Mr. Tuttle," I say, "I have to tell you this happens all the time." Annie is always on the phone complaining about the jail's failure to deliver the prisoners we need. Somehow there is never any keeping track. A thousand inmates go back and forth each day, walked over into the basement of this building down the tunnel that ties the jail to the courthouse. Somebody bonds out. Somebody else never arrived from the police station where he was first arrested. And in a system in which everything—bail, jail housing, sentencing—go harder on repeat offenders, it is a daily occurrence to discover that a defendant has not given his true name. Often the intake fingerprint comparison done at McGrath Hall, Police Force headquarters, will reveal that a defendant has a rap sheet with four or five different aliases. Kamal Smith is Keeval Sharp, Kevin Sharp, and Sharpstuff. Aggravated by all of this, Annie's English is apt to fall apart. 'Today, dis mawnin, you send me wrong Ortiz. I need Angel Ortiz. Numbah, six oh six, faw faw fi'. Tree times now we ged wrong Ortiz. Is not right. Ged me right one. Please!'

"Your Honor," Hobie says, "I think they're not prepared to put on the witness. I think she's giving them trouble."

"Judge," answers Molto, "there wasn't any trouble until she met Mr. Tuttle. And we'll be happy to put her on, but she's not here. Maybe the transport deputies dropped the ball, maybe our office did, but she didn't arrive from Juvenile Hall. We can't change that now. We have some stips to read and another witness on the way over. That's all we can do."

"Mr. Tuttle, are you unprepared for the witness the state intends to call?"

"I'm all right," he answers casually.

"Well then, what's your point?"

He shrugs as if he doesn't know and without more discussion retreats to counsel table, fiddling with his pad and pretending not to notice my irritated glance. A few feet away, Molto and Singh confer. Is Lovinia Tommy's problem? Is she the reason he was so eager to get started? Was he hoping to keep her in line? That's what it sounds like.

After some shuffling at the prosecution table, Rudy Singh arrives at the podium. His limp grey suit is far too light for the season.

"We have reached stipulations, if the court please," he announces. Rudy has a musical voice and pretentious manner. He is darker by a shade than Hobie, slender, with heavy black brows and perfect features. He strikes me as one of those spoiled, pretty-boy princes who seem to be produced by every ethnic group around the world.

Rudy reads what has been agreed into the record. Essentially, the police pathologist's report has been accepted. June Eddgar died of multiple gunshot wounds to the head. Blood gases and the lung tissues indicate death was immediate. Various details regarding the state of her digestion, and facts reported by the officers on the scene lead the pathologist to opine that the time of death was between 6:15 a.m. and 7:00 a.m. on September 7. Mrs. Eddgar, according to the pathologist, was looking straight into the path of the gunfire when she was struck.

"So stipulated," Hobie intones.

"The People and the defendant, Nile Eddgar, further stipulate that the remains examined by Dr. Russell were in fact those of June LaValle Eddgar, date of birth March 21, 1933."

"So stipulated." We have a murder case. A victim dead of violent means.

Next, Rudy reads a summary of an array of telephone toll records. In the era of computers and multiple area codes, the phone company maintains magnetic media recording every call from every number. These summaries show that in August and early September Nile seldom let twenty-four hours pass without calling a pager number. The testimony, no doubt, will be that the pager was Hardcore's. It was dialed repeatedly from Nile's apartment and office, and his father's home on several evenings and weekends.

After that, Rudy recites the parties' agreement about the fingerprint expert's report. One of the shell casings recovered from the scene shows a partial print from Gordon Huffington, a.k.a. Gorgo. Huffington has not been available for any current comparisons.

"He's a fugitive?" I ask. "Huffington?"

Singh looks to Tommy, then Hobie, before responding. Hobie waves a hand to show he could not care less if Rudy answers.

"Yes, Yaw On-ah," Rudy replies.

"And the state's theory is that he's the shooter?"

Again, there's a pause. Molto gets to his feet, his small mouth shriveled by chagrin about my frequent questions.

"It wasn't covered in openings," I explain. "I'm just trying to get my bearings."

"He's the alleged member of the conspiracy who fired the shots," Tommy answers. "And he's at large."

I nod. But there is a hole in the state's case. The actual killer is unaccounted for. That's bound to provide room for the defense.

Singh resumes reading. He allows his voice a flourish meant to inform me that we've reached a point of drama. People's Group Exhibit 1 consists of Exhibits 1A and 1B. Exhibit 1A is a plastic bag. Singh holds it aloft, displaying a long blue plastic sleeve resembling the wrapper from my Sunday newspaper. Group Exhibit 1B consists of 177 pieces of United States currency, 23 hundred-dollar bills and 154 fifty-dollar bills. Like the blue bag, the bills are encased in thick plasticine and sealed with heavy tape, which is inscribed in red with the repeated word "Evidence." When received by the lab, the bills in 1B were bound by a single common latex band and were contained in Exhibit 1A, the blue bag. Eighty-nine bills from Exhibit 1B were submitted for fingerprint examination: the top and bottom bills of the stack—a $100 bill and a fifty—and 87 bills chosen at random, each one identified in the stipulation by serial numbers.

Rudy's reading continues monotonously. The stipulation discusses points of comparison and ridge details, and goes on at particular length about the so-called Superglue Method, involving cyanoacrylate, which was used to develop prints on the plastic bag. But there is no missing what's significant: Nile's fingerprints were identified on the two outer bills of the stack of money, and his prints, as well as Hardcore's, were also discovered on the blue plastic bag in which the money was wrapped.

As a prosecutor, it took me years to learn I was almost always better off with a stipulation. It avoided the hundred ways witnesses fail—memory lapse or slip of the tongue, the fatal, blurted remark on cross-examination. Especially without a jury, Tommy is probably doing exactly what he should. But he's also allowing Hobie to make the best of the situation, by underplaying highly damaging testimony. What excuse, after all, is there for a probation officer to be exchanging large bills with one of his clients? Even the reporters, minutely whispering at the onset of Rudy's recitation, gradually quiet as the details about the fingerprints emerge. Everyone in the courtroom now knows the case has passed beyond the stage of accusation. No matter how dryly delivered, the state has offered real evidence against Nile Eddgar.

As its first witness, the prosecution calls Detective Lieutenant Lewis Montague of Area 7 Homicide, who supervised the case investigation. When his testimony is complete, Montague will be in and out of the courtroom to assist the prosecutors—contacting witnesses, retrieving exhibits. He's the cop on the case. Questioned by Rudy Singh, in an orderly and energetic way, Montague describes what confronted him on the morning of September 7—uniforms, yellow tape, ambulances, and cruisers. Photos are produced. Pictures of the body are passed up to me. I thumb through them and write down the exhibit numbers. There is no face, just mess. Grim, I think. But it's not June. It occurs to me after the fourth or fifth eight-by-eleven I may be reacting to the fact she gained so much weight. In the scramble of papers already heaped here on my leather blotter, I find the path report. Seventy-seven kilograms! I am mortified for June's sake. The woman I knew had an enviable adult sensuousness, on which she clearly counted, even in the midst of the revolution.

"Did you examine the victim?" Rudy asks.

"We waited for the PP." Police pathologist. Montague bothers himself with a glance my way and adds, confidentially, "She was off-line, Judge. Clearly." Dead, in other words. The cops are always at their toughest when the subject is dying. They have a thousand euphemisms. 'Giving the Q sign' is the one that occasionally makes me suppress a smirk. It means the decedent was found with her tongue hanging out of the corner of her mouth.

"And did you, Detective, have occasion to make observation of a young woman who was subsequently identified as Lovinia Campbell?"

"Ms. Campbell was on the pavement at the time I arrived, about fifty feet from Mrs. Eddgar. A paramedics team which was on scene was preparing to remove her."

Montague details her position. A photo of a bloodstain is offered, then a schematic line drawing of the street. Montague makes an X and a Y to indicate the positions of Lovinia and June Eddgar. The testimony is crisp, dispassionate. Montague describes the work of other officers whom he supervised. Evidence techs went over the interior of the vehicle. They found June's purse and dusted it for prints, then inventoried the contents. A uniformed officer called in the plate on the Nova and received a report that the car was registered to Loyell Eddgar in the town of Easton. Finally, Montague says he directed a canvass of the neighborhood. After the results were reported to him, he instructed Homicide investigators to attempt to locate an individual.

"And what was the name of that individual?" asks Rudy, tiptoeing past the hearsay rule.

"Ordell Trent."

"And was Ordell Trent identified by any other name?"

"Hardcore," says Montague. "That's his gangster tag."

"And calling your attention, sir, to September 11, 1995, four days later, did you have occasion to meet with Hardcore?"

"I met him that day, at Area 7."

"And who else if anyone was present?"

"His lawyer. Jackson Aires."

"And did you receive anything that day from Hardcore?" Rudy has gone back to the prosecution table and fishes in the cardboard box where the state stores its exhibits. On the white carton, the prosecutors have written the case name, *People v. Eddgar,* and in letters big enough for a street sign—and certainly for a jury to have noticed—CONSP. MURDER. Rudy again holds up People's Group Exhibit 1, the $10,000 on which Nile's fingerprints were found. Montague says he received the money from Hardcore, initialed it, and submitted it for fingerprint examination.

"And what, if you please, was the result of that examination, Lieutenant?"

Rankled, Hobie takes his feet. "Your Honor, I already stipulated. What's this about?"

"Yaw On-ah," answers Rudy majestically, "I am merely trying to establish the process of Lieutenant Montague's investigation." He is, in fact, attempting to emphasize his best evidence, which is why Hobie accepted the stipulation in the first place. I sustain the objection and Singh is done.

Montague turns his head minutely, awaiting Hobie. Sitting below me a few feet away, Lew Montague is a picture of repose. He wears a blue blazer and a shirt pilled at the collar. His long black hair is smoothly combed. He seems thickened by experience, by his years of scraping blood and guts off the streets near the projects. In the witness chair, he sits almost limply. Montague has been crossed and recrossed once a week for at least a decade and has fully mastered the body language of credibility. He will maintain his calm. His voice will never rise. His answers will be brief. A cop like Montague, a true expert on the stand, could convict virtually anyone he chooses, support the theory of phlogiston or the burning of witches at the stake.

"Just a few questions, Detective," says Hobie. He is in another gorgeous suit; his beard is trimmed and his fingernails sparkle with clear polish. He starts toward Montague and then, seemingly struck by something, retreats. He takes the plastic bags containing the currency, People's Exhibit 1, from Rudy's hand. The band of Hobie's watch, a huge hunk of gold, comes briefly into view from beneath his French cuffs.

"Now when you sent this money here to the state police lab, did you happen to ask them to test for anything besides fingerprints?"

Montague frowns barely. He catches Hobie's drift at once. My friend Sandy Stern has often told me that a defense lawyer is like a person feeling along a wall, looking for a light switch in the dark. Hobie, apparently, is in search of procedural defects, hoping the state performed scientific tests about which they failed to advise him. There is always the vague hope, even in the era of the Rehnquist court, that a defendant can be set free, not because he is innocent, but because the state has been unfair.

"No," Montague answers to the question about other tests.

"So you didn't test to see if there were, perhaps, traces of blood on this money?"

"No."

"You didn't attempt to see if there was, for instance, any evidence of gunpowder?"

"Gunpowder?" Montague contains himself. "No."

"Could you have run those tests?"

"I saw no reason to."

"You could have, though?"

"Sure."

"Could you do it now?"

"No," says Montague. "No, wait. Yes, you could. I was going to say no, because the money was treated with ninhydrin"—the stinky purple print-developing agent—"but we only sent half of it. The lab—" Montague lifts a hand, but it is the soured mouth that says it all.

"The lab sometimes loses track of things?"

"Yuh," says Montague, happy to say no more.

Hobie nods gravely, as if this were a major concession. I'm not surprised to find that Hobie is a bit of a courtroom con artist. As a young man, he was always so emphatic, even when he was out of his mind or ill informed. His initial inquiries of Montague predictably reveal a sort of high-wire style, asking another question because he asked the first one, letting his ego roam free in the thin air of the courtroom. As a trial lawyer, I always felt stifled. I was never one of these great performers. I was more Tommy's style, just somebody who got the job done, but as a result I was not inclined to the kinds of blunders that seem the inevitable consequence of Hobie's free-association manner.

"Now this fellow Ordell — Hardcore," Hobie says, changing subjects, "you indicated he was known to you as a gang member. Which gang was that?"

"You mean what gang he belongs to? At Tower IV at Grace Street, they tend to be Black Saints Disciples. Most are jumped–in to a set called the T–4 Rollers."

"And is Hardcore a leader in that gang?"

"Counselor, a gang isn't organized like the police department or a corporation. You know, who's in charge can vary from day to day, depending on who they think is cool — who shot, who robbed, who busted on the Goobers. Candidly, that's not my thing. They kill each other, I learn what I have to. Otherwise, you know—" He lifts a hand with a glistening ruby ring on the smallest finger and doesn't bother with the rest. Montague is from the Joe Friday school: Just the facts. The kind of stuff Hobie is asking about is for sociologists or reporters, people who think there are motives worth understanding beyond plain meanness. Worst of all, the questions imply that Montague has an abstract interest in people whom, truth be told, he largely despises. In reaction, he casts a wayward glance at the prosecutors. Molto, in his frumpy suit, throws an elbow in Rudy's side and Rudy takes his feet, even as Tommy continues whispering what it is he ought to say.

"Judge, these answers are calling for hearsay and speculation from the witness. Detective Montague is not a gang member."

"This is background on Hardcore?" I ask Hobie, and he nods eagerly, pleased I've gotten the point. I overrule the objection. The defense is entitled to show that the state's main witness did not arrive in the courtroom fresh from finishing school. At the prosecution table, Tommy shrugs off my ruling. He merely wanted to assuage Montague, who apparently was feeling beleaguered.

Granted some latitude, Hobie rephrases his last question, asking Montague to describe the leadership structure of BSD, as he understands it. Montague reacts as he did before, rolling his mouth about with mild distaste.

"Again, counsel, these folks don't give us an organizational chart. This particular bunch," says Montague, "have some relationship to another gang, called the Night Saints. There were some arrests and convictions, say, a dozen years ago. And this is sort of what you could call the surviving organization, although it's much bigger by now."

"And how big is that, Lieutenant?"

"Jeez." Montague directs a few stray hairs back into the black mass shining under the strong courtroom lights. "From what I've seen, the Force estimates, they place membership in BSD at five, six thousand." A murmur from the press section follows this news. Glancing over there, I am mildly startled by Seth Weissman, whom I hadn't noticed yet today. He has his arms laid across the chairs on either side, and he is fixed on me, somewhat disconcertingly. Having caught my eye, he issues a smile of greeting, which I return vaguely. Really! I think, although I am not certain if I mean to criticize him or me.

"And is Hardcore in charge of all six thousand?"

"Not as I get it. You know, the head of the Night Saints was a three-timer name of Melvin White, who was known on the street as Harukan. One of his sons now—who's called Harukan-el—son of Harukan, I guess—anyway, Kan-el is supposedly the head of the organization. But he's been in the state penitentiary at Rudyard for many years. So there's a Jeffrey Wilson, Jeff T-Roc, who is usually acknowledged as the top dog in BSD. Or so I understand."

"And am I correct that this Kan-el is eligible for parole?"

"Supervised release. Parole by another name. That's what I hear. As I remember, he's been up twice. You know, he applies, he gets turned down. He's not a favored candidate, let's say."

"There's some opposition from the law-enforcement community?"

"Some," says Montague dryly.

"Judge," interjects Tommy, "what's the relevance of any of this?" I tell Molto that I want to hear objections only from the lawyer who questioned the witness, meaning Singh, then direct Hobie to explain his line of inquiry. He says he's only trying to establish where Hardcore fits in the organization in relation to Kan-el and T-Roc.

"Then ask that question," I tell Hobie.

"Under them somewhere," answers Montague, when Hobie does. "Core's what they refer to as a 'shot-caller' or 'caller.' He runs the T–4 set."

"Was he over this Ms. Campbell, this young lady who got herself shot?"

"So I understand." Montague, although visibly unruffled, cannot resist an addition. "You've seen her more recently than I have." At that, Hobie comes to a complete stop. Every trial lawyer has his way. Hobie moves. He's big and seems to try to occupy the entire courtroom as a way of guaranteeing attention. He careers between the tables, slides up on the witness, nodding his dark, bearded face over his shoulder as he retreats. He's effective, too. Sloppy at moments, as when he groped with the money. But cagey and stylish. Now he takes full advantage of Montague's lapse by staring the witness down before moving to strike the last remark. I grant the motion and he goes on to another subject.

"Now, Detective, Mr. Singh asked you a couple of questions about the investigation you conducted on September 7 following Ms. Eddgar's murder. Remember?"

"That I had a canvass done?"

"Right. When you canvassed that neighborhood, no officer reported to you that anybody'd mentioned the name of Nile Eddgar, did they?"

"Not that I remember."

"They mentioned Hardcore, right?"

"Right."

"But not Nile?"

"No."

"Then there was this Lovinia Campbell. This young lady on the sidewalk? What's she called in the gang?"

"Bug," says Montague.

"Bug. Did you speak with her?"

"Very briefly."

"And did you ask Bug what had happened there?"

"I did."

"And did Bug tell you that Nile Eddgar had conspired to murder his father, or his mother, or anybody else?"

Tommy prods Singh, who objects that this is hearsay. I overrule. The state opened up the subject of which suspects were named at the scene.

"No, she didn't," Montague answers, somewhat wearily.

"As a matter of fact, Lieutenant, what she said was this whole thing was a drive-by shooting and Ms. Eddgar had got herself caught in the crossfire—isn't that what Bug said?"

"I suppose that's what she said. You know, she was in shock."

" 'In shock'? Is that your *medical* opinion, Detective?"

Tommy's on his feet. "Judge, he's arguing with the witness."

"If anything, I think the witness is arguing with him, Mr. Molto. And I believe this is Mr. Singh's witness, and even in a bench trial, I told you, I don't want to be tag-teamed." I nod to Hobie to proceed.

"The fact here, Lieutenant, is that this Lovinia—Bug—didn't mention Nile Eddgar in any way that day, isn't that so?"

"She mentioned Nile a few days later when she talked to Officer Fred Lubitsch at General Hospital." In exasperation, Hobie wilts. The question was what she said on September 7. In his worn blazer, Montague stares at Hobie hotly. There's no doubt anymore that Lovinia Campbell is the state's problem or that Montague blames Hobie for their trouble. In theory, a defense lawyer is entitled to interview any prosecution witness, but usually when the witness has made a deal with the state, her own lawyer will discourage her from cooperating with the defendant. It keeps the prosecutors happy and avoids the jeopardy that might arise from contradicting what she told the state. Somehow, though, Hobie slipped past Bug's counsel, or even got her help, and the cops and prosecutors don't like it. I'm sure now this is why Hobie brought up Lovinia's name this morning—so I'd have the picture if Montague acted up.

"Come on, Detective," I say, striking his last answer again. Montague makes a face and composes himself. In the meantime, I jot a note: 'Lubitsch!' No wonder Fred knew the case was a doozy.

"Bug didn't mention Nile that day," Montague finally says when the court reporter rereads Hobie's last question.

"Truth is," says Hobie, "when you were there at the scene—what you heard was basically just this: Hardcore and a drive-by, right?"

Hobie leers a bit, daring Montague to disagree in the face of my warnings. The detective blinks first, then answers, "Right."

"Now, from there, Lieutenant, you had a community service officer— Kratzus?" Hobie's looking for the police report on the defense table.

"Kratzus," says Montague.

"Kratzus went to tell Nile about his mother's death. And you took yourself over to see Senator Eddgar to find out how come Ms. Eddgar'd been driving his car, right?"

"Right."

"And you eventually found Senator Eddgar at his home in Green-wood County?"

"True."

"Where he told you a big fat lie, right?"

"Objection!" Both prosecutors are on their feet.

"Your Honor," says Hobie innocently, "it's right here in Montague's report. He says—"

"Judge!" screams Tommy. "Judge, Senator Eddgar isn't on the stand. When he testifies," says Tommy, "he'll explain this encounter with the police. It has nothing to do with Lieutenant Montague's direct."

Tommy's right, of course, but I can't help briefly wondering what Eddgar lied about. Which is why Hobie did this. Very clever. He always was. I tell him he's too far afield for the time being and he lays the report beside Nile on the light-oak defense table. Nile, with his bedrag-gled haircut and errant mood, has observed most of this morning's pro-ceedings with his mouth slightly parted, as if he's largely amazed this is taking place.

"All right," says Hobie. "Here's the point: On September 7, in terms of your investigation, Lieutenant, the big thing was to find Hardcore, wasn't it?"

"I don't know about the 'big thing.' I don't know what that means. I wanted to find him, I can say yes to that." Montague's dark eyes steal toward me, to be sure I've noted how accommodating he's become in the face of my rebuke.

"And did you find him?"

"Eventually. Word was on the street, and on September 11, he came into Area 7 for questioning."

"With his lawyer, wasn't it? Mr. Jackson Aires? That was your testi-mony on direct?"

"That was my testimony."

"And did you talk to Mr. Aires before you saw Hardcore?"

"I had a number of conversations with Mr. Aires that morning."

"You and Aires talked about what-all Hardcore might say if he turned himself in and what kind of a deal he could get, right?"

"Yep. That's how it went," says Montague in a tone meant to remind Hobie that's how it's always done.

"And without going through all of it word for word, the nitty-gritty here is that Attorney Aires let you know that Hardcore was willing to say this whole killing, the entire thing, had been the idea of his pro-bation officer, Nile Eddgar? Right?"

"Close enough."

"And that was pretty interesting to you, wasn't it?"

" 'Interesting'?"

"You knew June Eddgar's murder was all over the news?"

"I don't know. Personally, I don't read the papers much." From Lew Montague, a hard-boned cynic, I tend to credit this assertion more than I might from some. With his rough-complected face, bare of expression, he seems to be without enthusiasm for much. You catch criminals because it's better than letting them go. I doubt he nurtures, even in his dreams, thoughts of a more perfect world.

"It was an important case," Hobie suggests.

"They're all important, counsel."

"Oh, are they, Detective? You knew the PA's office would be willing to make Hardcore a pretty sweet deal if he put it on Nile Eddgar, didn't you? Son of a prominent politician? Everybody'd get their names in the paper. Folks in the PA's office don't mind that, do they?"

Tommy jerks Rudy to his feet to object, but Montague, shaking his head throughout the question, is answering already.

"You got the wrong picture, counsel. Molto approved the deal," says Montague. "On his own say-so. And I don't think his bosses liked it very much. Couple of them seemed like they'd rather the whole case just went away."

In his chair, Molto sags a bit. Eager to score, Montague has spoken out of school. We all know now why Tommy is stuck trying this case. He got ahead of the office pols and they're making him carry his own water.

"So it was Molto who wanted his name in the paper?" asks Hobie.

Rudy comes to his feet again. His teak-colored hand is poised to note his objection, but Montague is headstrong and again keeps talking.

"He wanted to do what was right," Montague answers. "My captain and me brought Molto the case. None of us thought your client should get away with this."

"*You* wanted the deal," says Hobie.

"I wanted the deal," says Montague, more or less acknowledging what Hobie said to start. Hobie knows better than to ask what made Montague so eager, realizing that would elicit a lyric to Hardcore's credibility. Besides, to the courthouse veterans in this room, Montague's motives are obvious anyway. The downfall of the mighty always tickles the police, who generally see themselves as unappreciated vassals keeping the world safe for the airheads on top.

"Okay," says Hobie, "okay, but here's my point." With the concession he wanted, he's striding about, full of excitement. "You were willing to make this deal with Hardcore, even though your investigation had given you no reason a'tall to think Nile Eddgar was involved in this crime."

"I wouldn't say that," answers Montague coolly.

Hobie freezes with his back to the witness. Struggling toward his predetermined point of arrival, it takes him a moment to absorb what Montague has said.

"You suspected Nile Eddgar? By September 11 you were looking at him?"

"What *I* thought? Yeah, I'd say I was."

Hobie's cross, the big windup he had planned—showing that nothing until Hardcore's appearance implicated Nile—has been derailed. I'd caught his drift, which was that the whole investigation was shaped to fit Hardcore's information. He was suggesting that the prosecutors and cops, hungry for the excitement of a heater case, had been less skeptical than they should have about what Hardcore was saying.

"You suspected Nile Eddgar," Hobie repeats. "Why? Because he'd talked to a community service officer when he came to tell him his mother was dead? You weren't there for that, were you?"

"I heard about it."

"And that's why you suspected him?"

"In part." Montague is even now and confident. He is sitting a little straighter in his chair, while Hobie is blundering. He has lost all form, propounding two or three questions at once, quarreling with Montague and forgetting to lead him. Hobie's like a terrier hanging on to a trouser cuff and getting kicked each time.

"And what was the other part?" asks Hobie. "You didn't hear anything from Lovinia Campbell, right? Or on the canvass?"

"We'd talked to his father."

"His father! The senator?"

"That's right."

"So it was what his *father* told you that made Nile a suspect?"

"Basically," says Montague. "Yes."

And just that quickly something happens in the courtroom. It's like that extraordinary instant in the theater when an actor comes through the curtain to take her bow, and the character she has been for hours suddenly has been shed like some second skin. Hobie, too, is someone else. He lifts his face to a refractory angle, and briefly allows a cryptic, constricted smile across his lips, like a lizard darting through the sun.

He's apparently gotten just the answer he wanted, and scared me badly in the process, because I was taken in like Montague, like everybody else. Hobie ponders the witness one more moment, then looks straight to me and says serenely, "Nothing more."

Once each month, as a matter of solemn commitment, I have lunch or dinner with my friend Gwendolyn Ries, without our kids. She is a large cheerful woman, emphatic by nature, one of those people who proudly regards herself as an element of the life force. She wears too much perfume, too much makeup, too much jewelry; there's a reddish wash in her hair too bright to call 'henna.' She appears today in gaucho pants and a woolen vest of South American weave, bedecked with matte-gold buttons in the shape of lizards.

Since the birth of her son, Avi, eight years ago, Gwen, a radiologist, has worked four days a week. Today, she has taken the morning to herself for shopping, long her favorite pastime, and dashes from the taxi into the restaurant, arms abounding with bags full of gold and silver boxes. We have met at Gil's, a renowned spot, and surely the best meal near the courthouse. Years ago, this place was known as Gil's Men's Bar, and it retains an Old World atmosphere, with its splendid century-old interior. The vast room is a gorgeous wooden box, the wainscoting, the floors, the tables, the paneled ceiling, all hewn of quarter-sawn oak, heavily grained and varnished, accented by various polished brass fittings and great cast-iron chandeliers suspended on heavy chains from the high ceiling. One of the only real perks of judicial life is that I can always get seated here. As soon as Gwen arrives, she and I are swept past the long line of lawyers and other courthouse regulars crowded behind a red velvet rope to one of the many square tables for two aligned in dual rows at the center of the restaurant. For the sake of privacy, the abutting tables are separated by handsome partitions of yellowish wood, into which some clever craftsman long ago burned graceful images of German mountain scenes. The brusque waiters, in black cutaway coats, and the busy patrons speak at volume. With its solid surfaces, Gil's is a cascade of noise.

Gwen opens every box. I admire each item, even though we both know I wouldn't wear most of the exotic clothing if it were given to me free. We are long accustomed to our differences, which I alternately cherish or, in some moods, tolerate with the self-conscious discipline of one who at the age of forty-seven still feels she is learning how to be a friend. I've never had a full complement of close relationships. My mother, always battling landlords and principals, jumped from apartment to apartment, enrolling me in a different grade school every fall; and as a grown-up, I've taken my own bumpy twisting path, forever leaving folks behind as I've gone through my changes. Naturally, there are colleagues and acquaintances. I think I'm regarded as amiable, candid, maybe even charming. I'm welcome in lots of places. Judicial power, like a beacon, draws invitations to zillions of functions, bar affairs, political dinners, law-school dos. And although I was an only child, I have a semblance of family life, through my cousin Eddie, the oldest son of my Aunt Hen and Uncle Moosh, who has always treated me as an honorary sib. I talk to him or his wife, Gretchen, every week, and Nikki and I are with them and their five kids for every holiday.

But, admittedly, it's been hard for me to connect. For this reason, I have found the alliances of motherhood a sweet relief. Is it only my imagination, or are women better to each other at this point in life? It seems as if we all learned some crucial secret in the delivery room about nurturance and kindness. My neighbor Marta Stern, Sandy's daughter and a lawyer herself, who is now at home with two young daughters, has become a special friend. There are a couple of others.

But I go back in time only with Gwen, whom I have known since high school. She was upbeat, alert, one of those loud, effusive, laughing girls I so admired, someone who seemed to have a promising relationship with every person at East Kewahnee High. I felt greatly honored by her friendship, and for years contrived not to notice that I was never invited to her home. Eventually, through other kids who were her neighbors, I learned that her mother was in the final stages of MS. There were a few occasions, after we started to drive, when I'd borrowed my uncle's Valiant and dropped Gwen off, that I glimpsed Mrs. Ries through the window. She was enfeebled by disease, with stricken hands and dirty matted hair and a harrowed look as she sat in her chair, a blanket folded precisely over her knees. The contrast with Gwendolyn was extraordinary. And I can remember taking note of Gwen's slow stride across the lawn as she approached her home, a girl inclined to run on most occasions. I could see her posture take on the weight of knowing that at the center of her world lay trouble no one else could share and which she could not escape. And I remember seeing exactly what we had in common, since during those years I hoped, always— secretly and eternally—no one would know I was the daughter of Zora Klonsky, gadfly and loudmouth, a person whom only I understood, a woman notorious in the early sixties in the Tri-Cities for her conduct at a city council meeting where she had punched a right-wing city councilman opposed to water fluoridation.

"Shit," says Gwen now, as we near the end of our meal. From beneath the brightly striped flap of her vest, she grabs her beeper off her belt and makes a face at the readout. The hospital. She disappears to find a phone. We have spent most of lunch, as always, gabbing about our kids. We're the two oldest moms in U. Lab Lower School and both on our own. Nikki is a kindergartner; Avi's in second grade. I worry that Mrs. Loughery, a benign soul who talks to grown-ups in the same brain-dead singsong in which she speaks to the children, is not challenging enough for Nikki. She was born just on the wrong side of the deadline and seems a little ahead of herself, able to read simple sentences, to add sums in her head. Gwen told me to ease up, Nikki and Virginia Loughery both are doing well, advice I'm somberly pondering when I'm drawn to voices on the other side of the panel at my right: two men who, I realize quite suddenly, are talking about my case. One just said distinctly, "Molto."

"Why's it wrong?" the first asks.

"It's wrong. I'm telling you it's wrong. This bird, around the courthouse they call him Mold-o. I'm not kidding. Talk about a guy who walked through the metal detector too often."

"He's doing all right," the first man says. "He did all right yesterday." The voices are familiar. Lawyers, I guess. It has to be. I think the first one, who I've heard often, tried a case before me. A good guy. Very good. A flush of positive feeling is the sole retrieval when I send the summons to memory.

"Eh," says the second one. "Room temperature IQ. Molto—Jesus, he was nearly disbarred back in the eighties. Were you ever around here when Nico Della Guardia was the PA? Molto was sitting at the right hand of God then. I think he used to write Nico's papers in high school. So when Nico wins, Tommy gets to be Queen for a Day. And the two of them fucked up some murder case to a fare-thee-well. God, I can't even remember what it was." I hear knuckles rapping on the table. "Sabich," the man says.

"Who?"

"Too hard to explain. But there was this implication they'd doctored the evidence. So, you know, the baying hounds of the press ran Nico out of office. With help. Plenty of help. He'd gotten crosswise of the Mayor in the meantime. And Molto they sent out for hanging with BAD.

Bar Admissions and Discipline. And it's a typical BAD investigation. Four months, six months, eight months, ten months. Two years. Nothing happens. So he's still here. Still a deputy PA. Poor mutt. What else is the son of a bitch gonna do for a living? His name is shit on the street. All he can do is keep cashing that green check. That's Molto. Now you tell me. Is this the guy you send to court to win one for the Gipper? I think not. He's sleepwalking up there. He's a beaten dog. I checked my file. He hasn't tried a case in three years. He's just a bitter little man waiting to collect a county pension."

"So what are you saying?"

"I'm saying it's wired. Didn't you hear that cop today? The PA and his cronies want to see this thing go in the dumper. They sent this poor hump Molto up there cause he'd get lost looking for the men's room."

"Jesus, Dubinsky," the first man says. Stew Dubinsky! The *Tribune* courthouse reporter, the man to whom the prosecution leaked yesterday's story about Eddgar being the murder target. I feel an immediate impulse to leave. I shouldn't listen to discussions of this case, let alone from someone who could turn my eavesdropping into a *cause célèbre*. But I see no unoccupied tables nearby and there's still half a piece of sole on Gwendolyn's plate. Besides, she'd kill me if I left all her new treasures unattended. Instead, I look straight forward with an impassive expression, but the voices, raised in the raucous lunchtime atmosphere, remain disturbingly clear on my side of the panel.

"Jesus," the first man repeats. " 'Wired.' Doesn't anybody ever tell you you're paranoid?"

"All the time," Stew answers. "That's how come I know they're part of the plot."

"Christ. Go watch *JFK* again." Whoever this is has Stewart's number. He's always snooping around the courthouse and implying in his stories that the true facts have been concealed in an obscure conspiracy of silence. "How's your salad?" Stew's friend asks.

"Shit," Dubinsky says. "This isn't food. Why'd I let you order for me? Spinach and spring water. I feel like I'm a fucking elf."

"You don't look like an elf, so just keep chewing." Stew has pretty much lost the battle. His belly has the dimensions of a late-term pregnancy, and his face is swaddled in chin. This has to be an old pal to be freely giving Stew the business about his physique. "So what'd you think today?" this man asks. "How'd you like that business at the end about Eddgar?"

"Six point zero for Artistic Impression. Zero point zero on substance."

"How's that?"

"You don't watch these alley cats day in and day out like I do. It's standard defense melodrama. Letting rabbits loose in the courtroom. Eddgar's the big name so Hobie figures he'll raise the most dust that way. But it's a smoke screen. Take it from me. I know what I'm talking about on this one."

On reflection, my assessment has not been much different. The craft was impressive, but it's hardly a shock that the target of the murder scheme had things to say that drew suspicion to Nile. The other man maintains his doubts. Hobie, he says, seemed to have a point.

"Listen, why ask me what he was doing?" says Stew. "Talk to Hobie."

"I keep telling you, he won't say anything to me about this case. Not word one. I came two thousand miles and I'm sitting in the Hotel Gresham at night playing computer games."

It's Seth! With Dubinsky? How interesting. In the midst of my spying, I hear within a discordant note, a fugitive thought calling for later reflection.

"You know," Dubinsky says, "you call me suspicious—"

"I called you 'paranoid.' "

" 'Paranoid,' fine. But look at you. You think Eddgar's Darth Vader's misplaced twin. His constituents admire the guy."

"Shit," answers Seth, "talk about the American electorate. I think about Eddgar in the State Senate and I can't believe we're not on *Twilight Zone.*"

Dubinsky recounts Eddgar's emergence in local politics more than a dozen years ago. Eddgar had become a green. He forged a coalition of anti-capitalists, ecologists, and animal-rights supporters. When a large cosmetics company made a grant to one of the labs at the university, Eddgar led demonstrations.

"College kids didn't want rabbits to die to make eyeliner. Christ, they didn't even wear makeup," says Dubinsky. "After that, he gets elected to the City Council in Easton first, then mayor. Then a State Senate seat opens up. He ran for controller two years ago. Nearly won."

"Don't people know about him? His history?" Seth asks.

"Hey, you know, you've given me the heads-up. I've done the articles. Twice, in fact. But being a former radical is very—what?"

"Trendy?"

"It makes him trustworthy in a certain way. I think that's what it is. It goes to show he has a commitment to reform. And besides, Eddgar never burnt down anything around here. Christ, everybody was crazy in the sixties. And it's not like he's representing Orange County anyway. His district's a college town and some East Kindle housing projects. Lincoln would lose that district if he ran as a Republican."

"I can't imagine that guy backslapping and glad-handing, though."

"No, no. He's shit on a stick. These big dos, everybody breathing on each other, looking for the biggest ring to kiss, I see him half the time, shrinking against the wallpaper, nibbling his lip. But you know, he's a professor. People figure he's a dead fuck anyway."

"How about a woman? He ever show up with a companion?" A moment passes. Perhaps there's an expression of discomfort from Dubinsky, long divorced, as I remember. His own social life is probably far from scintillating, but Seth persists. "Any talk?" he asks.

"Ah shit," says Stew, "people talk, they don't talk. Nothing really. I don't know—boys, girls, pygmies. Christ, he's old. He's sixty-what? Five. Sixty-five, sixty-seven. I'd guess he's retired in that department."

"Yeah," says Seth. "I was just curious. Did you ever reach out for June?"

"Sure. Remember? During the election? When he ran for controller. You gave me that tip. I dug her up. She's in this little burg in Wisconsin?"

"Right."

"Told her I wanted to talk about Eddgar. And I get the oh-fuck five-minute pause. And then she says, 'I'm too old to remember that.' Friendly enough otherwise. Ready to tell me anything I didn't want to know. She sounded like an old drunk. You know, ditzy middle-aged dame, chasing every butterfly dancing through her brain. Afterwards, I get a call from Eddgar's flack. I'm 'delving into his personal life.' I'm like 'Fuck-you, give-me-a-break. This guy's got secrets he wants to keep, let him join the CIA.'"

"He's got secrets," Seth says, somewhat ponderously.

"So you keep telling me. But say what you want, maybe he was a bigger jag-off than Captain Hook, but he's gotten it done now. Christ, he gets awards. The whosycallit. Women," he says.

"The League of Women Voters?"

"Exactly. Twice. Best legislator. Bleeding Heart of the Year. The century. You get him in the statehouse? He's in his element, he's high. You should feature this bird in his office, with four phones ringing and the staff people running in and out, the pols, the interest group people coming by to smooch his derriere. I mean, this is the guy. Manipulating. Plotting. The other side of it, you know—Getting elected? Making them love him? I think he really hates campaigning. But the back doors? The back rooms? The deals. The doing. We're talking high, *high* on that stuff. And he gets his shit through. We got a new juvenile-justice scheme. He's got a program now where the state pays 250 bucks to poor kids who finish high school. College Preparation Awards, he calls it. Day care. Mental health care. And you know, he's czar of penal reform, prisons. Any warden sees him coming, they start moaning, he's all the time in their faces: Job training! Job training!"

Just as Dubinsky on the other side of the partition explodes in laughter at a joke he's made — probably the most inappropriate remark I've heard yet — Gwendolyn reappears. I rise at once and greet her some feet from the table.

"Are you done?" I ask.

She wants coffee and I suggest the bar.

"What's wrong with the table?"

I raise a finger to my lips. We bear her packages into Gil's noted barroom, where the lawyers and law enforcers mix each week in a burly Friday-evening scene. It's another gorgeous room, if somewhat dimmer, centered on the oak bar, where carved pillars and vines surround a beveled mirror that runs forty feet above the whiskey bottles. We pile the shopping bags along the brass boot rail below and hike ourselves onto the stools. My explanation to Gwen about the occupants of the table adjoining ours is briefly interrupted when our heavy-browed Greek waiter bursts in, certain we ditched the check.

"You mean the columnist?" asks Gwen. "Your old squeeze? He's around now, too?" Gwendolyn's inquired once or twice about the case, because of the articles in the paper, but she's heard nothing of these events. "Ooh," she says, "how cinematic. What's he look like?" She elevates herself on the stool in hopes of seeing over the stained-glass divider to the restaurant. Gwendolyn has a bold attitude toward romance and, particularly, sex. She's made love to colleagues in the Doctors' Lounge. Privately, I regard this as unconvincing feminist bravado, particularly since I've followed her counsel on a few occasions in the last year or so and each time found the experience alien and sad. She's been married three times, most recently to an Israeli doc several years younger than she, whom she was training. She met him, had his child, and booted him out the door in a whirlwind period of eighteen months.

"He looks like he's approaching fifty, the same as I do," I answer now.

"Don't be dour, dear."

"Sorry. I'm a little sensitive. Marietta's giving me the business again. She's just biting her nails until I take up with him."

Gwen rolls her eyes. "You're the only woman I know who got divorced and still has to put up with a mother-in-law."

I laugh heartily. It's too true. And Charlie's mother was easygoing, a delight.

"It's crazy," I say. "This is complicated enough. Just sitting on this case, I feel like I'm Humpty-Dumpty ready to fall off the wall." Above the demitasse from which she's drinking an espresso, Gwendolyn's reddish face narrows.

"How did you end up in this position in the first place? One way or the other, won't somebody say your decision is based on how you feel about this boy or his family?"

I explain the circumstances. I was free to keep the case if I wanted to. The week before the trial, I even took the precaution of describing my predicament to Brendan Tuohey, the Chief Judge. The thought of me in a ticklish situation seemed to spark some brief delight beneath the crafty veneer of his narrow rosy face, but he was reassuring. 'You're the right judge, Sonny,' he told me. 'You know the saying: "If you can't tell the difference between your job and your friends, you don't deserve either." Comes with the robes, you know. Besides, if you don't sit, no one in the Criminal Division will want to. Then the Supreme Court will make me pay the bill to bring in someone aw-ful.' He regaled me with a long story about the extravagant expenses the court incurred when the Supreme Court designated an upstate judge named Farrell Smedley to sit on the fraud trial of Marcelino Bolcarro, the former Mayor's brother. 'Did you know, Sonny, that man never met a lobster he didn't like? I finally asked him, "Don't you ever get a taste for ground beef?" And the poor dumb backwoods s.o.b., he looked at me, I thought he was simply gonna cry. "Li'l Abner," they called him behind his back.' Tuohey went off shaking his head.

"But why did you?" Gwen asks.

"What?"

"Want it? The case? It sounds so messy."

"Nostalgia?"

"You're not nostalgic. I don't know anybody who was happier to grow up. You quake when I mention high school. You barely remembered me." This, of course, is an exaggeration, but I did lose track of Gwen, like so many others. Then in 1983, I took a routine mammogram. In one of those strange twists, the radiologist at Bethesda who read the film was Gwendolyn. She showed up at my house in person, took my hand, wept when I wept after the biopsy, and promised we would arrive together on the other side of the experience, as we have. Another part of the past I don't much care to remember.

"I don't know," I say. "Do you know anybody our age who doesn't look back at that time without feeling they did something amazing, like going off to the Crusades?" I've often heard recollections of Gwendolyn's experiences in Madison. She performed nude onstage in rock musicals and still relishes the memory.

"You know what it is?" Gwen points a long nail at me, manicured in a persimmon shade. "It's Zora. You're working something out with Zora."

"I'm always working something out with Zora. I'm working something out with Zora when I send Nikki to school in the morning."

She shrugs. I do as well, but Gwendolyn has exerted her customary power to upset me. I bundle her into a taxi, feeling low, feeling again that I'm careening about as the captive of mysterious forces and that I blundered taking this case. Everyone else knows something—about me, or the case, or what will happen with it—which has completely eluded me. Dubinsky had his own sarcastic prediction, the last thing I overheard from the next table. He was talking about Eddgar's role as a legislative advocate of penal reform.

'Eddgar's in those prisons twice a month, looking them over and giving the wardens hell,' Stew said. Then his laughter, sharply nasal, always somehow derisive, pealed forth, loud even on the other side of the partition. He'd amused himself greatly with a thought.

'Now he can go on Sundays, too,' Dubinsky said.

Fall, 1969

SETH

Jolted by the million marchers who'd gathered on the Mall on November 15 to protest the war, Congress enacted the draft lottery system the next week. Now, instead of years of continuing jeopardy, eligible men would confront only a single night when their fate would be decided. Some would go; some would be free. I recognized the lottery for what it was, an ignoble effort to divide and demobilize the young. But privately I was near jubilation. All but certain to be drafted days before, I now had a chance to escape.

The lottery was conducted on December 2, at 5 p.m. our time. We watched in our apartment. Hobie and Lucy were there. So was Michael.

Sonny sat next to me, holding my hand. The local news yielded to Walter Cronkite and a live feed from Washington. It looked like my imagination of a court-martial — a bunch of old men up on a platform. A congressman pulled the first little capsule from the rotating drum. A date, September 14, was read aloud by an elderly colonel and posted on a board behind him. The point of the lottery was to place every day of the year in a random order, which would, in turn, become the sequence in which young men would be called. If you were born on September 14, you'd be drafted first. On the other hand, if Hobie's birthday or mine was pulled above a certain number — 200, we figured, given the many deferments in University Park — we'd be free.

Members of President Nixon's Selective Service Youth Advisory Board grabbed the remaining little bullets from the drum. They were draft-age men with haircuts which revealed their ears, work-within-the-system types whom I despised. One of them drew my birthday, March 12. It was the fifteenth number selected. I would get a draft notice by April at the latest.

"Luck of the Irish," I said, but the joke was bad and my tone was worse. Somehow I'd gotten to my feet. From behind, Sonny wrapped both arms around my chest, just to hold on. "I am fucked," I told her. There was no counter.

The local newscast resumed, with the numbers from D.C. scrolled along the bottom of the screen. I watched stupefied, trying to envision my future and hating everything in America. In Hartford, two students were on trial for criminal libel for publishing an obscene cartoon of Nixon in the college paper. Mark Rudd and the Weathermen had been indicted in Chicago for the Days of Rage. And the saga of Juanita Rice, currently riveting California, was continuing. The girl was the object of occasional sightings across the state, while her captors issued various communiqués demanding five evenings of national TV time. Since it had occurred, the Rice kidnapping had been of irrational concern to my mother. Having heard about my radical acquaintances in the building, she convinced herself they might kidnap me, too. It was, I suppose, some kind of coping mechanism, a danger she could reasonably dismiss — unlike Vietnam.

In the meantime, Hobie sat silently before the TV, watching the numbers roll. Hobie was as intent on avoiding Nam as I was, but he had a different approach. He swore he would show up for his induction physical in a dress. He was going to claim to have had homosexual relations with every prominent black Communist from Patrice Lumumba to Gus

Hall. He also sometimes attached his leg to a concrete cinder block and pulley, hoping to aggravate a high-school football injury. Now, once the numbers passed 275, we knew he would not have to go through any of those antics. Inconsolably jealous, I nonetheless roused myself to kiss him on the forehead.

"Luck of the Irish," Hobie said. He did not hit until after 300. The last one to go was Michael at 342 — and him with a 1–Y. Even though he had grown up mowing and baling, Michael had been exempted from the draft for hay fever and asthma. It did not seem fair, but very little at that moment did.

My mother and father had viewed the lottery with almost pitiably high hopes. They did not find the courage to call until the following afternoon. It was 6:01 p.m. Central Time, the very minute long distance rates went down. No matter how extreme the circumstances, my father would never violate his personal dogma about money.

When my parents phoned on Sundays, my father and I barely spoke. He made a few correct inquiries regarding my health or the California weather, then passed the phone to my mother, who painfully elaborated a list of questions I knew she had been assembling all week. With a rush of constricted feeling, I would visualize the two of them, my mother holding a ball of Kleenex, her fingers touching her mouth, my father close enough to overhear, but with his head in a paper to show he did not have much interest. But this was a moment of confrontation with his renegade son, a challenge from which my father never retreated.

"I believe this decision is unwarranted," he said at last, when I told him I had no choice now about Canada. "There are alternatives."

"Such as?"

"I have the name of a doctor. He is conversant apparently with all the regulations."

"Oh great. I'm going to bribe some MD to find something wrong with me. Is that the idea?"

"The idea is this man feels as you do and will assist you."

"Oh sure. What other ideas have you got?" I imagined that my mother had rushed him straight to the phone as soon as he came in from work, still in his heavy wool suit. Beside him stood his briefcase, which, as a child, I had improbably associated with a cowboy's saddle bags.

"I have talked with Harold Blossman. He tells me his son has joined the Naval Reserve. There is some period of training, then you are free to go on your way. Write movies, whatever."

"And what happens if you get called up?"

"Called up?"

"You know, they activate your unit. Then when you run away they call it treason."

"Apparently that is rare."

"And if it happens?"

"Then you confront the matter at that time, Seth. Dear God, you cannot make plans for the rest of your life concerning a matter of this sort."

This talk of compromise, difficult to counter, tended to terrify me. In my passionate disapproval of the war, I had found one thing—perhaps the only thing—which I knew to be right and which was thoroughly mine. To believe so strongly and not to act on it, to capitulate to my parents' needs, was to condemn myself to a murk in which I'd never find my own outline.

"I'm against this. You don't understand. I'm against this war machine. I *want* to resist. I don't want to just skate through so that some Puerto Rican kid from the North End can go die for me. I don't want to pretend I'll serve and let them torture me in basic training and then run away if they're going to ship me out to Nam. It's another form of involuntary servitude, to go fight the war that the defense contractors want. There is one alternative."

"This is not an alternative."

"Dad, this is the kind of thing that has to be fought. I would think you'd understand that." I knew this was a vain argument. My father and I agreed that there were lessons in history, but not about who was who. He scoffed at the parallels I drew between our national government and Germany in the thirties. It was the students at Columbia whom my father compared to the beer-hall *putsch*; the Panthers, in his eyes, were the brownshirts with berets.

"Your mother would feel that her life had come to nothing," he finally said. "You should have some feeling for her. I do not need to remind you." As I had gotten older, my conflicts with my father were all supposedly conducted for her sake. What he wanted, did not want, was never purportedly in his own behalf. He was her spokesman, her defender. I begged him not to start with that.

"And Hobie?" my father asked. "What will he do? Will he run away with you?" My father and Hobie always had a peculiar kinship, on some weird wavelength of their own. My father had the usual Viennese snob's appreciation for high intellect, and he listened to Hobie's smart remarks with a dry, approving smile he never found for me. When I told him that Hobie had pulled a high number, he sounded relieved. "So you will take this step alone," he pointed out. "And when is that?"

"I don't know. Not for a while."

"I see. We can hope then for your better senses, can we not?"

I did not answer. Sonny had come in by then and she stood tensely listening to the conclusion of my conversation. I looked to her as I cradled the phone.

" 'Zere are alterna-tifs,' " I said, mocking my father's accent. I had made fun of both my parents this way all my life, even to their faces, never quite focusing on why this teasing was acceptable to them. Yet it was always vital to my parents that I be genuinely American, fully at home here — and secure. They spoke English whenever I was around, and had even given me a name which to my enduring puzzlement neither of them could correctly pronounce. I was 'Set' in my mother's Czech accent, 'Sess' to my father. This passionate desire of theirs that I fit in was my sole avenue of escape in a home where my father's humorless correctness and my mother's anxieties left me little other refuge. My claim that something was 'American' — cap guns, when I was six; watching too much TV; my irregular sense of humor — almost invariably caused them to yield. Which, in large part, was why so much seemed to be at stake in my decision to leave the United States.

"Did he have any new ideas?" Sonny asked.

"Zip," I responded. In truth, there were other courses that fit my moral regimen. I could go underground. False IDs — especially a social security number — were needed, but it was really life on the run, with the constant anxiety of apprehension, that seemed impossible to me. There was also the more noble alternative of accepting prosecution. Brad Kolaric, a fellow I knew at Easton, had done it and was now in the federal penitentiary at Terre Haute. But the prison butt-fuck stories kept me up at night, and I didn't feel my government should be imprisoning me for its errors. Exile seemed my only alternative.

"Maybe I can trade myself for Juanita Rice. Maybe the Gypsies would kidnap me. Carry me away with them. My mother always told me how they snatch children."

Sonny had heard the same from her Aunt Hen.

"You think they have an age limit?" I asked.

"They might."

"Shit. I thought I had the solution. *They* could take me to Canada." I looked at Sonny. "It's such a down," I told her.

"There's no answer, baby."

"Kidnapping," I said.

Sonny gave me a melancholy smile. "I don't think so."

"Hey, look, I know what bothers me. It's not Canada really. It's deserting them. That's the way they see it. If they knew I was safe in a real nice country but being held against my will—" I shot out a hand: smooth sailing. More than the government, what I needed to escape was my parents' unspoken condemnation—that I would dare forget what was never to be forgotten.

No doubt, that night I dreamt about the numbers. Frail figures, they turned up in my dreams throughout my childhood, usually appearing to my horror somewhere on my body: under a trouser cuff, in the center of my forehead when I caught sight of myself in a mirror. Unlike my father, who wore long sleeves on all occasions, even in the mug of summer, who, so far as I can recall, never swam in public—unlike him, my mother made no exceptional efforts to hide the blue-green characters tattooed on her forearm, a few inches above her wrist. The marks, so distinct, were always remarkable to me—ineradicable and vaguely disfiguring, but dear and special because they were so identifiably hers. I can recall more than one occasion when I was very young when I wet a finger from my mouth and with no objection from her tried to wipe the numerals away. When I asked what they were, she said simply—always—'Those? Those are numbers.' And when I wrote numbers—scribbles, really—on myself in pen, she walked me to the sink at once.

As I learned to read, I remember noticing that the figures were peculiarly formed—hand-drawn in a style that struck me as foreign. There were tails of some sort on the fives and a dash across the middle of the seven. And around this age I began, at last, in some awful unspeaking way, to associate the numbers with that large, indescribable horror, that dark fog that lay somewhere in the past which was always the subject of silent allusion in my parents' home.

My father never allowed any talk about the camps. If something appeared on TV, he watched it with unwavering silent attention. But he made no mention on his own and would discourage my mother with stark looks. And yet the few images I saw—of the naked skeletal bodies, the cyanotic corpses stacked and so profoundly without life—endured as specters. They lived with me inalterably, part of the high tension of my household, which had an atmosphere at all times like a tautened instrument string waiting to be plucked.

Much of what I knew came from what I'd read—almost unconsciously—or what my mother eventually told me. I learned the few details I was allowed in my teens and largely in answer to my own ceaseless question to her: What was wrong with him, this man, my father? The stories I was told, in the barest strokes, were so alien to the secure envelope of University Park—its streets canopied by elderly elms, its confident persistent values and enduring social ethos of calm, intellectual debate—that I was truly years in absorbing them, some kind of titration of my own experience that took place in infinitesimal measure like medication being dripped by IV, tear by tear into the blood. And even so they remain to me the very quintessence of horror: how my mother's husband had disappeared from her for good, as they were sorted by gender in one of Birkenau's lines. How my father's six-year-old boy was shot dead right before him at Buchenwald. The inhuman work. Meals of boiled grass. The unfathomable nature of what it means to have survived this utter blackness.

I rigidly avoided any conscious thought of my parents as the victims of any of those barbarities, and never took account of the mark their experience had made on me. Sonny had shipped literally hundreds of books from home. I had taken only four or five: *The Diary of Anne Frank; The Rise and Fall of the Third Reich.* Talcott Parsons; Alan Bullock's biography of Hitler. A few lonely volumes, they stood together on the lee end of one shelf amid the board-and-cinder-block bookcases erected along every free wall of our flat in Damon. Even seeing them side by side, I had absolutely no sense of what connected them. They were simply great books to me, consumed in college in hours of isolated reprieve from life's furies. I did not see any relationship between my parents' past and my political passions. I didn't recognize the futile deal I'd silently negotiated with myself: that if the world could be reformed, made right, if I *knew* there could never be another Holocaust, I would be free of the burdens they had placed upon me. It was all invisible to me. Instead, during those years, I had an unexplained phobia which filled me with so much racing panic that I was always forced to leave the room whenever I saw scenes in cowboy movies of cattle being branded.

In the aftermath of the melee at the ARC, demonstrators—consistently reported to be wearing the red arm sash of One Hundred Flowers members—had rampaged on campus. Windows in most of the buildings on the main quadrangle were smashed and glass vials of sheep's blood were splashed on the buff bricks. A smoke bomb was hurled through a basement window into Ryerson, the main undergraduate library. It was closed for four days and hundreds of thousands of volumes were removed to protect them from the lingering stench. Another bomb had been dropped down the chimney of the headquarters of the Damon Security Corps. According to reports, the bomber had slipped in his haste and cascaded off the tile roof, thudding to the ground, feet first, right outside the police station windows. The cops claimed he had been gathered up by other armbanded rads, who carried him away, his foot, or ankle, or lower leg severely injured. Emergency rooms throughout the Bay Area had been combed, but the bomber was not identified.

On campus and on the Boul the talk for days afterwards focused on how it all went wrong. The campus police announced that Eddgar was under investigation for inciting to riot and claimed that his boisterous, singing quotation from *The Little Red Book* was the cue for the rocks to fly. But I spoke to dozens of people who had been at the head of the crowd and were certain the cops had struck first, clubbing a woman whose dog had innocently approached the police line. Pressed, most of these witnesses admitted they had merely seen her bloodied face. No one seemed to recall the batons falling on her. Some said she wore a One Hundred Flowers sash, and others were clear she hadn't. The woman could not be found. Eddgar calmly denied any role in the provocation.

"How foolish do you think I am, Seth?" he asked when I finally attempted to talk to him about it the following week. "Do you really believe the faculty apparatchiks? The administration's theories—why, they're actually amusing. I'm not fooling. They paint me as the arch manipulator, the grand schemer with control over scores of lumpen rebels. And yet they want to claim I would stand in public and issue signals to a mob? Does that sound like a well-conceived attempt to subvert anyone but myself?"

I knew that this speech was rehearsed, that it had been given a dozen times already. Only last week, I had heard Eddgar quote Sun-tzu to June. 'War is deception,' he had said. Eddgar never explained—nor did I dare ask—how the smoke bomber, with his broken leg, arrived under our stairwell. But I wanted to believe him when he denied orchestrating violence.

Sonny was far more skeptical. We quarreled about Eddgar all the time.

"At least he's not like the head cases out on Campus Boul saying, 'How can I make the world better for me?' " I explained to her one night. "He doesn't say, 'Let's change everything, but make sure there's still plenty of LSD and lots of cool James Bond movies and someone to do my cleaning.' What I think is that he's said to himself, 'If I was poor, if I was dispossessed, if I was, you know, like Fanon says, one of the wretched of the earth, how would I react? If I had these smarts, what would I do? Would I put up with this crap for an instant?' And he's being honest when he says the answer is no. He'd want to smash everything that kept him from being equal and free."

"And you agree with him?"

"'Agree'? No. Not completely. But I mean, I'm more with him than against him. 'Whoever sides with the revolutionary people is a revolutionary.' Right?" I smiled puckishly and Sonny made a face. "Christ," I said, "why do I have to explain this to you. You're the one who was raised as a Commie."

"I wasn't 'raised as a Commie.' It's not like being a Baptist, baby. My mother belonged to the Party. Not me. And that doesn't make her the same kind of Stalinist zealot Eddgar is. He'd think she's a Trotskyist."

Sonny always stuck up fiercely for her mother. During her term as president of her pipefitters' local, during World War II, Zora had appeared on the cover of *Life*—Wendy the Welder—with her acetylene torch glimmering like the Lamp of Liberty on the lowered visor of her mask. She was famous then. But because she was a Communist, and female, she was hounded from leadership and, eventually, from the union once the men came back. At the height of the McCarthy years, Zora had packed canned goods and blankets in two suitcases, expecting the army any day to take Sonny and her to the camps.

Sonny was cheerfully tolerant of her mother's eccentricities. Zora tended to call out of the blue and would keep Sonny on the phone forever. She would sit locked in the bedroom, even when we had guests in the apartment or people waiting elsewhere. By habit, Sonny never disagreed with her. She was silent. Zora talked.

"So what did she say?"

"Not much."

"In an hour and a half?"

Sonny shook her head. It went beyond her power to explain. "You know her."

I didn't really. I had met Zora on only a few occasions. She was a tiny woman, not more than five feet, if that, always smoking Chesterfields. She had one walleye and heavy glasses and barely filled out her shirtwaist dress. I recall being impressed by the strings of muscles in her forearms. A tough bird, you'd say. The few times Sonny brought me by, Zora had not directed a single word to me, including hello. Instead, she soon launched into an account for Sonny's benefit of some recent outrage she had suffered — unemployment, landlord troubles, a union steward who had become a management whore. Small and quick, racing back and forth, Zora reminded me of a hamster in a cage. She screamed, spat words, raged her hands through the air, as she rambled at enormous speed and volume.

Sonny tirelessly consoled Zora. She sent her money whenever she could afford to and also maintained communications with Zora's enormous Polish family — the Milkowskis — with whom Zora, generally, was not on speaking terms. I took Zora with her wild look, erratic manner, and self-centered habits as clearly out of her mind. But this, I quickly learned, was not a view I was free to share.

Late one night the meeting of one of Eddgar's collectives ended upstairs, while Sonny and I were in the rack, stoned and amorous. In order to confound the Damon police surveillance, the rads would head out from Eddgar's in all directions, and three or four of them came clomping down the back stairs in their work boots, passing right next to our open window. We ceased grinding, waiting for the loud voices to drift off into the thin night. One of the last remarks I heard was someone trying to be brassy, boasting about the oinkers he was going to off on the day the rev came. Drifting on the dope, I found myself pondering the question that life in Eddgar's midst was gradually forcing on me.

"Do you think there's going to be a revolution?" I asked. "I mean, really?"

Beneath me, Sonny groaned. "Of course not."

"Oh."

"Seth, I mean — baby, I grew up with this. It's a crazy discussion. If there was no revolution in the United States in the 1930s, when 15 percent of the workforce was unemployed, how could it ever happen now?"

I repeated, somewhat experimentally, what I'd heard Eddgar say about raising the consciousness of the working class. "These guys on the assembly lines who think they love George Wallace? They're like avoiding the despair of their own lives."

"Seth, these are the people my mother has been organizing all her life. I've listened to Zora explain to them that they don't recognize their despair, and they've run her out of town."

"That's Zora."

Beneath me, Sonny slid her hips back so that I was suddenly on my own. "What does that mean?"

I knew I was on tender ground, but somehow I felt provoked, probably by her callousness toward my own screwy hopes.

"It means, you know, no offense, but your mother can come across as a little weird."

"Meaning?"

" 'Meaning?' Jesus, don't be dense, goddamn it. I mean, maybe all these working joes are like rejecting Zora, not what she's saying."

The light went on then, a painful brightness. Sonny, whose warmth seldom left her, was cold as stone.

"Not my mother," she said.

I shielded my eyes. "Okay."

"Never."

"I get it."

She flipped the light off and turned her back on me.

"Sonny."

She shirked my hand.

Eventually I slept, but about an hour along I woke. Some sense, perhaps just waiting for my bearings, told me not to move too quickly. Gradually I became aware of Sonny beside me, breathing heavily, jolting with small tremors. After a number of minutes, I realized that her hands were beneath her waist, finishing off what I'd begun. I lay there in the dark, absolutely still, not knowing what to do, whether it would be too humiliating if I intervened—or if, as I suspected, that was not even desired. Instead, I listened, as her breath slowly rose, reaching its summit and briefly ceasing as she thrilled to her own touch, and then resuming softly as she disappeared into sleep.

Hobie's newfound alliance with Cleveland Marsh, which had uncharacteristically brought both of them to the ARC demonstration, had begun one night in the fall when Hobie was at our apartment for dinner. Heading up the stairs to a meeting at the Eddgars', Cleveland had caught sight of Hobie in our doorway, where he was lurking as usual in hopes of passing a word with his illustrious classmate. In his black turtleneck and shades, Cleveland drifted past, then thought better of something and, a few steps above, extended a finger Hobie's way. A .45-caliber cartridge, sleekly jacketed in copper, swung like an amulet around his neck.

"Hey, Blood," he said. "We got a kind of study thing we might be doin in Contracts. You know? Maybe you be up for that?"

Personally, I was somewhat unsettled by my passing contacts with Cleveland. Not because he was manifestly angry. Leaving aside Hobie, every young black person I knew seemed perpetually pissed off, an attitude which required little explanation in 1969, a year after Martin Luther King had been gunned down, and one in every eight Americans had voted for George Wallace for President. But I'd grown up around black folks; I'd marched, I'd held hands; I'd dated black girls. I knew the churches and the preaching; the dance steps; the hierarchies of the black middle class. I knew what was different and what wasn't. Cleveland was the first black person I'd encountered who unrepentantly refused to look beyond the color of my skin. He viewed me with the sinister, unfeeling look you'd save for a snake.

Nonetheless, Hobie was thrilled by Cleveland's comradeship. Cleveland had grown up in Marin City, the housing project at the foot of the Golden Gate, and had become an all–West Coast Conference running back for Damon. In the spring of 1968, he had made the national news shows repeatedly, first when he announced that he had joined the Panthers, and then when he was admitted to Damon Law School amid protests from faculty and alumni, who objected either to his political views or to his qualifications. Hobie regarded anyone who'd been on television as if they descended from a higher realm. In this, I suppose, he took after his father, Gurney, who had a treasured row of celebrity photos above his soda fountain, featuring baseball stars, jazz musicians, and boxers. Besides, Hobie's relationship with Cleveland soon took on a predictable dimension. Shortly after the ARC demonstration, Hobie arrived for Doobie Hour with a small bundle which he opened as soon as Michael was gone for the night.

"Called co-caine," he told Sonny and me, as he spilled a small white rock out of a test tube onto a pocket mirror. Sonny was always too earnest to really enjoy drugs of any kind. She described the near-ruination of Sigmund Freud's medical career when he'd unwittingly addicted patients to this miracle substance, and left the room in disgust. But with Hobie my watchword was to try anything once. Overall, I wasn't impressed.

"It's groovy," said Lucy. "Except the straw. Everybody's nose? That's gross."

"Where do you come into this stuff?" I asked Hobie.

"Panthers are into some awesome shit," he said, as he was sniffling and wheeling his head about to absorb the rush. "This here, man, this is a far-out form of political fund-raising. They've got a dude, man, he's stamping out acid in tabs with the big B on them? Wrapped in the little bubbles of cellophane? Aspirin all the way, when you look at it. Outta-sight operation."

"Hobie even went to Cleveland's house," said Lucy. "He's got like *kids*. It was all weird and everything. Did you tell Seth? There are *all* these guns? And—"

With his huge hand, Hobie had taken hold of her knee. His eyes flashed at me somewhat tentatively.

"That whole scene, they're freaky paranoid, you know. 'Safe houses.' All that shit. Fucking *I Spy*, or something. You know the rap: I'm righteous and I'm a brother, but anybody else, nothin bout nothin. I had to swear by the Zulu gods." He smiled at himself. It took me a second to understand he was saying he wasn't going to talk about it. Hobie and I generally had no secrets, particularly when it came to his exploits. But Cleveland remained a touchy subject.

Late one afternoon, shortly after the turn of the year, Hobie rang the bell and stood downstairs in his green army-surplus poncho. The rains had come then, occasional chill downpours, but more often drizzle and heavy fog, nasty stuff that felt like a cold hand gripping my bones. The blue flame in the space heater in our hall was never off.

"Okay you drive?" Hobie yelled up. We were going to play basketball on campus. As we were walking among the puddles toward my car, I glimpsed Hobie's old Dodge Dart, springshot and rustworn, off in a corner of the gravel lot. The car had the old push-button automatic and half a psychedelic paint job, both front fenders whorled in color. I asked what was wrong with it.

"Nothing. I just got some stuff in there."

Hobie had an uncharacteristic poor-mouth expression and I pushed past his hand to inspect. The car was full of oozing burlap sacks, piled on the front and back seats. Hobie, who'd followed, pointed to the sky and told me it was raining.

"Hobie, don't be a douche bag. What is this, the Magical Mystery Tour? What the hell do you have back here, man?"

"Sandbags."

"Sandbags?"

"Suckers are heavy, too. Wudn't even sure Nellybelle was gonna make it up the hill on Shattuck." Nellybelle was his car, named after Roy Rogers's sidekick's jeep.

"You get the lowdown from Noah? Are we havin another flood?"

"It's just a favor, man. That's all. I was rappin with Cleveland a little after Contracts yesterday, and he asked when I was comin this way to hang with you. So he's like, well do I mind any stoppin at an auto-supply place—tells me where a couple are—pick up a can of battery acid and twenty sandbags. Gives me the money and all. Weird, right? Said just leave the car unlocked. Somebody'd get it."

"Eddgar?" Cleveland didn't know anyone else in the building.

"Man, I didn't ask. It's just a favor. Dude does for me. I do for him."

"Hobie, you better watch your ass."

He hooted at that, particularly coming from me, Eddgar's admiring employee. "Come on. Battery acid and sandbags? Gimme a break, Jack. Why should I be gettin uptight about that?"

"Well, what are they doing with it?"

Hobie shrugged. "Only thing I could figure is like winter travel. You know, Gurney's always topping off his battery and throwing a few sandbags in the trunk around this time of year. But it's gonna be a hell of a climate change for California, if that's what he's getting ready for."

"Maybe he got an advance forecast from the Weathermen."

We larked around for a moment with the notion. What a gas if the Weathermen really knew something about the weather. Or, better yet, could change it. Talk about making trouble.

When we came back later, I was careful, at Hobie's instruction, not to pull in next to his car. Instead, I watched him cross the lot. It was still raining. Inside, he turned my way and rolled down the window so I could see him as he mouthed a single word: "Gone."

One Wednesday afternoon in January, I walked into Michael Frain's apartment, calling for Nile, and found Michael in bed with June Eddgar. It was around 4 p.m. Down on campus at another Student Mobilization Committee meeting, I'd been pierced by a sudden fear June had forgotten I was off today, and that Nile, as a result, would have no one looking after him. Shouting the little boy's name, I'd rushed through all the places in the building he was likely to be. From the bedroom, I was sure I'd heard Michael answer, "In here."

When I pushed open the door, June was sitting up in the bed, with the sheet drawn across her chest and her other hand pinching the bridge of her nose. Lying beside her, Michael was turned away from me. I could see nothing but his skinny shoulders and the pale bald spot among his longish dreadlock curls. But even at that I recognized him. It was, after all, his apartment.

I said exactly one word, "Whoops," and turned completely around. I ransacked myself for some idea of what to do next and finally, foolishly, called Nile's name again.

"We said, 'He's not here,'" June answered behind me. She was in the doorway now, unclothed. She confronted me flatfooted, utterly confident of herself, as I took in what she unflinchingly revealed—limbs of trim strength, the dark female triangle, a tummy barely sloping and withered by childbirth, her daring uncompromising nature. Released from her ponytail, her bronze hair fell to her shoulders. "Nile's with Eddgar," she added, clearly aware of the boldness of speaking her husband's name in these circumstances. That said, June closed the door.

June had always seemed elusive to me. Campus legends painted her as a revolutionary drone, fully governed by Eddgar and the requirements of doctrine. There were astounding rumors—that at Eddgar's demand she'd slept with the entire Panther leadership council in Oakland; that she'd taken wild risks smuggling in weapons for the Marin County jail breakout. But to me that picture never seemed quite right. She rarely passed a mirror without a prudent look at the fine figure she saw there, straightening her collar, patting a stray ringlet back into place, still a bit the Southern cotillion queen. June's training at Easton was in theater, although, in the spirit of the cultural revolution, she now worked on the line in a salmon-canning plant in the East Bay. Yet at moments she continued to exude a star's enigmatic domineering air. She was forever laying a hand on my elbow and somehow getting me to do favors—run to the store, throw wash into the dryer—although we both knew these errands weren't part of my job. Even Eddgar, at moments, seemed wary of her. Now and then I saw them in the kitchen, hip to hip, debating in low voices beneath an old console radio playing to foil any wiretap. Eddgar watched her tensely lest something be missed at his expense, his lean jaw set, his focus unblinking.

The dimensions of the Eddgars' relationship, always unclear to me, now seemed unfathomable. But no one else, it turned out, was as shaken by my discovery as I was. Sonny, when I told her later that afternoon, actually laughed.

"You mean this isn't like the shock of the century?" I demanded of her. "You don't find it perverted? Don't look at me that way. It's weird, man. She's a mother, for crying out loud. She's fifteen years older than him. I mean—" I couldn't find the words.

"God, are you uptight." I was always unnerved that Sonny's sophistication about sexual matters was so much greater than mine. Most girls I'd grown up with fretted obsessively about their virginity, but Zora was a freethinker and in late adolescence Sonny seemed to have found welcome solace in the attentions of men.

"Uptight?" I asked. "I mean, what about Eddgar?"

"What about him? Maybe he doesn't care. Maybe he likes it."

"*Edd*-gar?" There were many disciples of free love in Damon, but it was hard to imagine Eddgar as one of them. "Think about this. I bet she's the one who convinced Eddgar they can trust Michael. You know. Even though he's hooked into Applied Research and that whole thing? I'll bet she did."

"So?"

"So, it's like her revolutionary movement is all in the hips."

I debated for a few days about whether to mention what I'd seen to Hobie and Lucy. He was a menace with secrets, especially when he could use them against someone, like Eddgar, whom he wanted to cut down to size. But the gossip was too sensational to keep to myself and I finally shared it at Doobie Hour. It turned out both of them already knew.

Lucy nodded stoically. "It's sad for him, really," she answered. "For Michael?" Over time, Lucy had succeeded far more than the rest of us in drawing Michael out. No one ever disliked Lucy; she was too passionately sincere. Men, especially, seemed to pour their hearts out to her, stirred by the way her tiny brimming brown eyes, her entire being, seemed given over to whatever they had to say. For Michael, so ill at ease, this avid, unquestioning interest must have been especially welcome. Lucy and he usually cooked together, on the weekends. The rest of us did the scutwork while they toiled happily in the kitchen, murmuring to each other like children. Lucy let cheerful talk pour from herself with the natural forward motion of a fresh running spring. It hadn't occurred to me, until now, that there'd been anything confessional about their discussions.

"He wants her to leave Eddgar," Lucy explained.

"Le-ave?" I'd envisioned this relationship as no more than a dalliance.

"I mean, her thing with Eddgar is a nothing. *Noth*-ing," she repeated, with an emphasis that suggested sex. "Not since Nile," she added. The intimacy of this detail threw me for a loop. I suspected at once that June—or Michael—was simply inventing excuses.

"What sense does that make?" I asked. "Why's she stick with the guy?"

Lucy hitched her slender shoulders. "She told Michael he's like the greatest actor she ever met."

"Actor?" I'd heard similar remarks about Eddgar regularly—that he was a chameleon, a phony. But I hardly expected that from June.

"It was a compliment, I think," Lucy said. "You know, like a great actor makes Shakespeare even greater? Or maybe, he's at his best on-stage?"

"That dude doesn't even know who he is if he's not onstage," said Hobie, who'd been listening with his joint from his usual outpost on the rug.

I was unsettled by all of this. Neither Michael nor June ever spoke a word to me about their affair, but I felt the silence we all maintained made us—me, in particular—conspirators against Eddgar, even, possibly, Nile. The whole arrangement suggested things about love, the world of women and men, that I didn't understand, or perhaps even wish to know. After that, I was always uneasy whenever Michael and June were together, pretending to be indifferent to one another.

"From what I hear, Graeme's parties are really wild," Sonny told me as we approached the little Victorian coach house in the city where Graeme was living. It was late January, near the end of the semester. I could see that Sonny had weighed saying anything at all. I was carrying a half-gallon jug of wine in a paper bag and she was wearing a black shawl and a floor-length skirt made from an old American flag. Her hair, freshly washed, lifted in the city winds. I thought what I always thought, that she was gorgeous. "We'll just see, okay? But I may not want to stay long."

"He's your buddy." I'd thought it was sporting of me to come in the first place, but Graeme had promised it would not be the usual departmental party, with people talking about Foucault as if he were an intimate. Sonny found Graeme endlessly intriguing. He was ironic and complex, and egalitarian in manner, and she admired his innovative if grandiose structuralist theories. Graeme claimed that the Western societies were in the midst of altering the *episteme*—the ultimate generative structure from which all thought in the culture devolved, a kind of girdle on the brain that loosened and changed shape only at critical historical moments, one of which was now.

"Sonny!" Graeme cried, as we came through the door. He was lit already. Both arms were aloft, a clipped roach in one hand glowing amid a twirl of fragrant smoke. He came crashing down upon her in a stifling embrace and, without a glance at me, swept her into the living room and the midst of the dense, gabbling party crowd.

I realized gradually that Graeme had been honest in a way. This party was nothing like ones we ordinarily went to. An expectant, high-voltage energy charged the air and the crowd was far more funky-looking than the Damon contingent—leggy sinuous women with miniskirts and ironed hair, men in beads. Plangent sitar ragas groaned from speakers hidden amid the deep human undergrowth in the room.

That night people seldom spoke of politics—the war or Loyell Eddgar—which were the staples of university conversation. Here there was only one topic and frequent references to bacchic adventures that had occurred before. The guests tirelessly discussed open relationships, always concluding that anyone who refused to take part was not simply unhip but somehow dangerous. A girl whom I encountered while I was putting down our coats uttered the Weatherman dogma that one purpose of the revolution was to destroy monogamy.

This young woman, named Dagmar, remained by me most of the evening. She was a student of Graeme's, a junior in one of his undergraduate courses. Dagmar was blond, with a cheeky face and imposing breasts, barely concealed by a stretch top she wore braless. It did not occur to me until later that Graeme might have inspired her role as my escort, or distraction.

Whenever I tried to find a sight line to Sonny, she seemed unapproachable. There were always a dozen people around Graeme. His long form and whitish pageboy remained bent over Sonny, his arm loitering about her shoulder. At one point, I broke free to offer to fetch Sonny a drink. There were mescal and tequila available, and a tremendous amount of dope. In the first instant she glanced over, Sonny seemed somewhat startled to see me, then reached for my hand in a way that seemed so paltry and apologetic that I fled back to Dagmar immediately.

Near midnight, virtually at the stroke of the hour, a group of men and women stalked through the living room entirely unclothed, the dark pubic regions and swinging parts shocking and incongruous as the clink and chatter of the party went on. A moment later, someone switched off most of the lights.

"Are you ready?" Dagmar asked.

"For what?"

"For what's happening. Come on, Seth. Be mellow. Don't hassle it." She touched the heavy buckle on my jeans, and I jolted back protectively. Dagmar took this response antagonistically. She eyed me fiercely and tended to herself. Her little miniskirt slid to the floor, then she unsnapped the body stocking and peeled that off too. She was revealed at instants by the oscillating shadows of a lava lamp. Drunk and stoned, besotted by the evening, I found it hard to deal with the cruel edge of this invitation. Dagmar's breasts were very large but tiny-nippled, blued by a heavy network of veins. We confronted each other without speaking, then she moved off with an insolent toss of her soiled blond hair. I heard the determined thud as she pounded up the stairs.

I careered through the first floor. Sonny and Graeme were gone. Forlornly, I considered the staircase up to the bedrooms. Utterly bewildered about what I might do next, I headed up. In Graeme's bedroom, I was relieved to see no sign of Sonny. But most of the group which had capered naked around the living room were there, six or seven men and women, applying body paint freely to one another with their hands. One fellow had sprouted an impressive hard-on, which a young lady was obligingly swirling in a kind of Day-Glo green from a squeeze bottle. Two other groups were engaged in various states of intercourse. On the waterbed, three people, two men and a woman, were entwined, a nest of butts and legs, in what I took to be a post-coital trance, while below, on the semi-privacy of the shag rug, another couple was grinding away. The guy, who was on top, had a belly so huge it looked almost as if there were a foreign object between him and the woman beneath him. When she turned my way, I recognized Dagmar. She gave me a vaporous smile and lifted one hand, still pudgy with baby fat, even as she jolted with the fat man's emphatic thrusts. I thought she was waving and timidly waved back; I realized then she had been beckoning me inside.

"On the bus or off the bus, m'boy." Graeme had caught me by the elbow. He was in an improbable getup, dressed only in briefs and dark elastic socks attached to calf garters. A few errant hairs grew amid the spots on his sternum. He tried to edge me from the door, but I was too spaced-out to move. The room stank with cat pee, and I noticed only now shadowy forms within the waterbed mattress which I recognized as goldfish. Graeme was gone momentarily. When he returned, Sonny spoke behind me.

"Come here, baby." She stood down the narrow hall, which was yellowed by a Chinese paper shade that covered the single bulb. If anything, she appeared prim and collected in her flag skirt.

"One of those girls asked me to sleep with her." I was well enough out of it that this struck me as some kind of explanation of my conduct.

" 'Women.' Which one?"

I turned back to the bedroom to point, but the door was closed now and Graeme was gone.

"Did you?"

"Hell no." I was slow. "What about you and Graeme?" I asked.

She seemed to shake her head.

We found Sonny's shawl bundled in another room downstairs, and left in silence. I stood still suddenly on the walk outside, my face to the stars and the dank city night. It was like the touch of a cold towel, a sobering relief after the spoiled, smoky air of the cottage.

"God," I said, "what a dildo I am. This guy invited us to this party fourteen times, and I never flashed on what he was up to."

"Referring to what?"

"Referring to the fact that in your case he's got his own ideas about conquering the mind-body dichotomy."

She said nothing.

"You sure you didn't sleep with him?"

"No. I said no."

"But you thought about it?"

"You're hassling me, Seth." She plunged down the walk and I slowly followed, the noise and music of the party dwindling. "Am I supposed to be against it?" she asked. "Am I supposed to think it would be immoral or bad? I didn't *feel* like it. He's old. He's strange. It's not my bag. Okay?"

"Yeah, but I mean, I'm trying to figure out where we stand here."

"Here's where we stand, baby. I live with you. I sleep in the same bed with you. You want a chastity belt, too? You want to have the key?" Like most conversations that started out about the way we felt, this one was quickly wandering toward the safer grounds of politics, where the doctrines were previously determined and where Sonny could nimbly foreclose any genuine discussion.

"But I mean, look," I said lamely, "I love you."

"*Why* do you always say that?"

"How about because I do?"

"What does it mean?"

"Mean? It means I think you're keen. It means the biggest trip in the galaxy is hanging out with you. It means what it always means."

"It scares me. You're twenty-two years old. You don't know what you're saying."

"Okay, so you're gonna head-fuck me, right? *You* tell *me* what *I* feel."

Silence. I was not satisfied, naturally, to have won the round.

"So here's the deal, right? I love you and you don't love me."

"Oh, Seth. Not again. This is a drag." Her arms went limp, allowing her shawl to lie half on the sidewalk as we stood beneath a streetlamp. Our voices were strangely resonant in the sudden isolation of the street, where small single-story houses stair-stepped the hill.

"It's the truth. I mean really, man. What is this, you and me? Entertainment?"

"It's life, Seth. It's living. I mean, I enjoy you. I care about you. It's better being with you. Usually." She walked on then. She stopped in a moment when she found more words. "Seth, you drive me crazy to say I love you, because you can't say it to yourself."

"Oh yeah, great," I said. "Great. I'm like incredibly glad you told me. Now I can save all the bread I was gonna spend on that trip to Esalen."

"Seth, you don't see this. Sometimes, it feels like you want so much of me that you'd like to be me." She nodded sharply, certain that she'd scored. I caught her by the arm as she turned to surge ahead.

"So what," I said suddenly. "So what? Let's say that's true. At least I know what I admire. You're the most together, the sanest—"

"That!" she screamed, "that's the problem. You don't know the first thing about me. I'm an imaginary person to you."

"Jesus," I said. "What are you talking about? I've like fucking *studied* you. I've listened to your batty old mother. I've met her friends. Your aunt. I've read your high-school yearbooks. I try to wheedle any story I can about your childhood. And you think I'm missing the point? Here's the problem, lady. You're *afraid* I'll know you. You don't want anybody to discover the shit you don't want to know yourself."

"What a load," she said. She twisted in agonized disbelief. We were done then. She was the first one to the car and I half expected her to leave me. Instead, we puttered across the Bay Bridge in silence, the only noise the little engine of the Bug, which, at high r.p.m.'s, uttered a sound as if change were twirling through its carburetor. I turned on the radio finally—KSAN—where, naturally enough, they were playing a clever, larking piano arrangement of "What Is This Thing Called Love?"

December 6, 1995

SONNY

In the same short-sleeved blue coveralls worn by the male prisoners, Lovinia Campbell is escorted by the transport deputies from the lockup and walks alone to the stand with a loose, disaffected ease. She is a thin, dark girl, with perfect skin and prominent eyes. No wonder she is called Bug, except the name belittles her beauty. She has the exotic, assertive looks of some of today's fashion models, big-featured and proud to be more than merely cute, although this young woman seems largely unaware of her striking appearance.

Questioned by Tommy, whose heavy grey suit looks as if it had been stuffed in a drawer overnight, the girl says she is fifteen years old, sixteen soon. When Molto asks, she looks to the courtroom ceiling to recall her precise birthdate. Her hands are in her lap and her shoulders are rounded protectively as she sits in the witness chair. Her voice is small.

"And where do you presently reside?" Tommy asks. "Where do you live?"

"Sometime I stay by my momma."

"No, I meant right now. Are you in the Juvenile Hall?"

"Uh-huh. In juvie."

"And how long have you been there? Since September?"

"Uh-huh," says Lovinia. "Since I be out the horspital." She scratches her nose and watches Tommy alertly, her mouth barely parted, sitting forward slightly to hear the next question. It is not Tommy, however, who speaks.

"Your Honor," says Hobie. Basso profundo. His hands, in more courtroom opera, are lifted imploringly. "If Mr. Molto can't bring out the witness's residence without leading, we may as well just administer the oath to him."

"All right, Mr. Tuttle." Hobie knows Tommy has a tough road here and is serving notice that he will not let him travel easy. I remind Tommy not to ask his witness questions which suggest their answer and Tommy nods resignedly. He and Lovinia move falteringly through the details of her bargain with the state. She has acknowledged responsibility—a guilty plea, in juvenile terms—for conspiracy to murder and been adjudicated delinquent. She will be in juvenile facilities until she turns eighteen. She will not, however, be tried as an adult, will not even have a criminal record when she emerges. It's a great deal, a point which Hobie is bound to emphasize on cross. Tommy turns then to BSD, eliciting Bug's gang name, her set, her acquaintance with Ordell Trent.

"And what was your relationship to Hardcore in terms of BSD?"

"Core no kin to me," she answers. "Only BSD sides me is my brother, Clyde, and he downstate." 'Downstate' is one of many euphemisms for the maximum-security prison at Rudyard.

"No," says Tommy, "no, what did you do for Hardcore in the gang?"

Recognizing her mistake, Lovinia's eyes plunge to her shoes. "Kinda like scramblin," she answers softly.

"What does that mean?"

"Sell."

"Sell what?"

"Mostly smoke and crank. Sometimes blow." Crack and speed, occasionally powder cocaine.

"You mean you sell dope for Hardcore?"

"Leading," says Hobie, as Lovinia says yes.

"As long as he's clarifying previous answers, I'll allow it."

Tommy nods. One for his side.

"And do you sell for Hardcore in any particular location?"

"Round T–4. Mostly by Grace Street and Lawrence."

"Across from the IV Tower?"

"Kinda there, uh-huh."

"All right," says Tommy. Feeling somewhat steadier, he leaves the prosecutor's table and travels a few steps along the carpeting.

"Now, Ms. Campbell, do you know a man named Nile Eddgar?"

"Uh-huh," she says. She gets a smile, this girl, this accomplice to murder, and is at once her age, happy, even a little silly. She looks askance. "I be knowin Nile for a long time."

"And do you see him in the courtroom? Point him out please and say what he's wearing." Although all eyes in the courtroom are already turning toward him, Nile, in another of his odd moments, seems un-selfconsciously merry. He has turned himself fully about in his black bucket swivel chair, his worn cowboy boots—cowboy boots!—planted on the carpet. He sports an absolutely foolish grin, as if this young woman were here to entertain him. Lovinia is not quite able to meet his eye, even as she lifts her hand.

"He over there, by the big fella," Bug says. This description of Hobie brings down the courtroom. The laughter resounds, even from me. Caught by the outburst while her slender arm is still midair, Bug once more drops her head abjectly. Like most of the homegirls, she wears a plastered mass of straightened hair, dulled wisps, stiff as a hedgehog's, that go in one direction, another shiny patch of bangs shellacked in place with spray. The Afro, the do of liberation, is long gone, one more forgotten fashion of the disrespected past.

"Ms. Campbell," I say, "he *is* a big fella. You didn't say anything wrong."

Hobie stands grandly. "I'll stipulate to that, Your Honor. Bigger than I should be."

Lovinia nods, somewhat mollified by all this reassurance. She is, as so many of these children turn out to be, a nice kid, without much protection at the core.

Tommy resumes. "Now how do you know Nile?"

"He round," she says, "he hangin."

"Around where?"

"IV Tower," she says.

"When did you first see him around the IV Tower?"

She rolls her eyes again to the ceiling and guesses it was about March.

"And how often after March did you see Nile around? Once a week? Twice?" asks Tommy.

"Seem like."

"Judge Klonsky," says Hobie, "he's leading."

Tommy tries again, asking simply, "How often?" Bug can't really say. Tommy's eyes close briefly. He says something to Rudy, seated just beneath him, and Rudy shrugs. I imagine they're debating whether to go after her, to remind her that she said something different before. But that is always the last resort for the state. Once they attack the witnesses they've called, they're admitting they have no direct road to the truth. Tommy decides to venture on.

"And did Nile tend to be with anyone when you saw him?"

"Seem like he kickin it with Hardcore."

"He was with Hardcore?"

Something darts through her expression and her eyes flash away, perhaps toward the defense table.

"You know, seem like he be checkin out lotsa different cuzes," she adds.

Tommy frowns. He leans down and confers with Rudy once more, then opens a file folder on the prosecution table and stares into it for a moment.

"Ms. Campbell, do you recollect ever characterizing Nile as, quote, 'Hardcore's road dog'?"

Lovinia passes off the question with a vague gesture.

"Isn't a road dog a best friend?" Tommy insists.

"Don't know nothing bout no road dog," says Lovinia.

At the table, Rudy waves his long slender hand. Move on, he's saying. It's a small point, and she already gave the answer Tommy wanted before. But Molto stares darkly at Lovinia another second before accepting his younger colleague's guidance.

"Let me call your attention, Ms. Campbell, to September 6, 1995. Do you remember having a conversation with Hardcore?"

Hobie makes a standard hearsay objection. He and Molto debate at length whether a preliminary showing of a conspiracy has been made, but given Nile's fingerprints on the money, I rule in the end for the state.

"Do you remember that talk with Hardcore?" Tommy asks, starting again.

"Kinda," she answers.

"Kinda," Tommy says. He raises his eyes to God. He's strolling now. "Where did you speak to Hardcore?"

"Seem like in the crib on 17."

"In an apartment on the seventeenth floor of the IV Tower?"

"Uh-huh."

"And what did Hardcore tell you?"

"Said next a.m., real early, man, we was gone ride down on some dude on my corner."

"What kind of dude? Did he describe the dude you were going to ride down on?"

"White dude."

"He said your set was going to ride down on a white dude?"

"Uh-huh."

"Did he say who the white dude was?"

"Said somethin bout some kin to Nile, seem like."

"What kin? Did he say what relation the white dude was to Nile?"

She tosses her head around uncertainly. Across the courtroom, Molto is still, his lips drawn into his mouth. He knows for sure now. She is going to do it to him. Rudy knows, too. He has already picked up the file folder Molto had before. When Tommy gets back to the table, he takes it from Rudy and snaps it open.

"Ms. Campbell," he says. "Do you recall talking to police officers on September 12? And September 14? And September 29? Do you remember that?"

"Seems like I be talkin to the po-lice *all* the time."

"Do you remember on September 12 that you spoke to officers Fred Lubitsch and Salem Wells at Kindle County General? And on September 14, you were released and you spoke to them at the intake area of the juvenile home? And you saw them there again on September 29? Do you recall all of that?"

Her shoulders rise and fall in mild resignation.

"And do you recall saying on each of those occasions that Core said you were going to ride down on Nile's father?"

"Maybe I say it be some kinda kin *like* his father." In this brief interchange, Lovinia's youth has left her. The girl shamed by the courtroom laughter and intimidated by the setting has disappeared. Her street mask is on now. She sits straight in her chair.

"Ms. Campbell, didn't you meet with Mr. Tuttle two weeks ago?"
Hobie rises immediately. "Your Honor, what's the insinuation here?"
"You'll have to let me hear the question to know."

"And wasn't it only after meeting with Mr. Tuttle that you suddenly began to say that you couldn't recollect which kin of Nile's it was Core said you were going to ride down on?"

"Can't only say but what I 'member. You done tol' me that a bunch of times," she says to Tommy.

"I ask you again: Didn't you tell Officer Lubitsch repeatedly that Hardcore said you were going to ride down on Nile's father?" Tommy has rolled up the police reports in one hand and he brandishes them for a second. He has shown her those reports often by now. There have been a dozen impassioned sessions in the little attorney interview rooms at Juvenile Hall, with their barred windows and peeling radiators. In menacing tones, he's reminded her what the cops say she told them and he's put it to her: she flips him, her deal's out the window, she'll be tried as an adult, do murder time, maybe even some perjury time, too. Molto waits, while the unspoken memory of these threats is summoned.

"I don't hardly 'member," says Lovinia. "Might be I been sayin that."

"Okay," Tommy says. He's finally getting somewhere. He straightens his coat and finds his notes. "Did Hardcore tell you *who* was going to ride down on Nile's father?"

"Objection to 'Nile's father,' " says Hobie. "We still don't have such testimony."

"Overruled." Hobie's being a pest. Judging from the opening, the state has plenty of proof that Eddgar was the intended target. But Hobie, I surmise, messed with Lovinia's testimony on this point anyway, just to throw down roadblocks for the prosecutors. I still can't quite make up my mind about Hobie. He's already done some memorable things: the way he snuck up on Montague or courted Lovinia here. But there doesn't seem to be any overall purpose or strategy. Stew said it yesterday: it's all diversionary tactics. For all his craft, I see Hobie as another charming courtroom blowhard, ad-libbing and always onstage, more interested in causing a constant commotion than conducting a symphony.

"Gorgo, he said. Said some white dude gone roll up and be askin after Hardcore. And how it be, I'm s'pose to say I'm gone go get Core, then I'm s'pose to shout out for Gorgo instead."

"How were you supposed to shout out?"

"On my flip."

"You had a cell phone for the dope business?"

"Uh-huh."

"And what was the number?"

She gives it.

"And after you called Gorgo, what were you supposed to do?"

"Jam," she says.

"Get out of there?"

"Uh-huh. Leave out."

"And was there a further plan? Were you supposed to do anything else?"

"Uh-huh," she says. "After they done burned a cap in him and all, then Core say like I oughta get back up to the car and put a seam on him."

"And by 'a seam' you mean a little foil packet of narcotics?"

"Uh-huh," she says. "Blow." Cocaine.

"And did Hardcore tell you that the idea was to make it look like this white man had been killed in a drive-by while he was buying blow?"

"Objection. Leading."

Caught, Tommy slumps a bit. Lovinia continues on her own.

"Hardcore, he like, 'Gone be like GOs come bustin up while this dude was coppin.' "

"Were you supposed to tell the police that? That this was done by the Gangster Outlaws?"

"Uh-huh."

Pleased with himself, Tommy struts back to Rudy, who reminds him of one further question.

"And by 'busting up' and 'riding by' and 'capping,' did you understand that Hardcore was telling you this white dude was going to be murdered by gunfire?"

"Uh-huh."

"All right now, Ms. Campbell, now after Hardcore had explained all of this to you, did you have any further conversation with him, there in the crib on 17?"

"No, sir. Not so I 'member."

Tommy breathes once, sharply, through his nose. "Did you ask him why it was necessary to kill this relation of Nile's?"

She shakes her head, with far more vigor than she has mustered until now.

"Didn't he tell you he was doing this killing for Nile?"

"Objection!" Hobie lumbers to his feet. "Objection, Your Honor! There is no good-faith basis even to *ask* that question." He raised the same point—at similar volume—during Molto's opening. Tommy is looking back at Hobie with awful hatred. His view is obvious: Hobie suborned her. At a point so critical, I decide to take over. I lean down toward Bug.

"Did you hear Mr. Molto, Ms. Campbell? He says Hardcore told you he was doing this for Nile. Did he say that?"

"Nn-uh," says Lovinia. "I ain never be sayin nothin gainst Nile."

The courtroom is at a standstill. Tommy's witness has gone over the border. Prepared for this, Molto is resolute.

"Did you not state on September 14 to Officer Lubitsch, and here I quote, 'I asked Hardcore why we had to be doing like this with Nile's father and he answered, quote, "We all are doin it on account of Nile." ' Did you say that?"

"Nn-uh," says Lovinia.

"Do you recognize this statement?" Tommy approaches her, flourishing the papers like a flag.

"I din't write that. That ain my writing."

"That's Officer Lubitsch's writing, isn't it? And didn't he write down your words exactly as you spoke? And didn't you then sign this statement? Isn't that your signature right here?"

"That be what I wrote, just here, my name. I din't write none the rest."

"Isn't this your signature under all these words?"

"That just be my name."

"And right before your name, it says, 'I sign this statement freely and voluntarily, under no coercion of any kind, and swear that the foregoing is true and correct.' "

"I don't hardly understand that," says Lovinia, her beautiful dark eyes quite wide. Buckwheat could hardly improve on her performance.

"And, Ms. Campbell, wasn't it only after your meeting with Mr. Tuttle that you suddenly disavowed this portion of your statement, where you said that Hardcore told you this was being done for Nile?"

"I don't understand what you saying now neither."

"I'm saying you're lying."

"Nn-uh," says Lovinia. "This here, what I be sayin now, this the swore truth. And I ain never been sayin nothin gainst Nile."

"Didn't you say again yesterday, Ms. Campbell, in the presence of

Mr. Singh and Detective Montague and myself, when I met with you at the Juvenile Hall, didn't you in fact say *again* that you now recalled Hardcore saying this was being done on account of Nile?"

"Is that when you-all was trippin on me, how I tricked on you and I was gone away for M–1?" Murder one.

Tommy stands still in the middle of the courtroom with his eyes closed. The trial lawyer's bad dream: major witness giddyap and gone. At the defense table, Hobie is making notes madly. Behind him, his goofy client remains fixed on the girl with the same erratic grin. Bug, in this idle moment, becomes aware of Nile's attention and again looks toward her shoes.

"Lunch?" I ask Molto.

With evident gratitude, he nods.

Annie knocks her gavel once to announce the recess and the spectators rise, voices racing with the trial's first taste of excitement. I stay on the bench to write a few more notes in the bench book about Bug, not certain yet what I think of her or the way the attorneys have dueled over her testimony. Marietta appears with the files on two new custodies, both State Defender cases. They are scheduled for bond hearings at 2 p.m., but Gina Devore has grabbed Rudy Singh in the hopes of doing them now. She has a suppression hearing before Judge Noland this afternoon. I oblige Gina, and the keys rattle and doors clank as the transport deputies head back to retrieve the prisoners.

We immediately reach the Crime of the Day. Rogita Robbins slouches out of the lockup, small and overweight, with orangish hair and many black marks on her face. I am almost sick listening to a description of this case. Rogita and her man, Fedell, are Gangster Outlaws from Fielder's Green. They had a date with their homegirl, Tawnya, who was safekeeping the night's entertainment, multiple doses of dust. When they arrived at Tawnya's apartment, Fedell found both Tawnya and their PCP gone, and in reprisal exorcised his fury by sodomizing Tawnya's children, a boy eight and a girl nine. Fedell was apprehended months ago. Nailed on DNA and fingerprints, he pled out for sixty years before Judge Simone, whose call I inherited when he transferred to Chancery. Rogita has been at large, and was taken into custody on a shoplift. She will probably not deal, Gina and Rudy explain, since the state is light on her. The PAs have only the boy and girl to testify against Rogita. A mother of two, Rogita aided Fedell by holding both children down.

"A million full cash," I say.

Gina looks at me. $100,000 would keep Rogita behind bars.

"Full," I repeat.

She gives her wavy high-school hairdo a churlish toss, but I doubt if we changed places the ruling would be different. I like Gina. She's a tiny, athletic woman, a gymnast at one point, if memory serves. It's always impressive to see her, barely five feet, even in her big high heels, standing in the lockup, reading out her clients, who hulk over her. Yet last month she cried in my chambers. She'd spent hours she didn't have cobbling together bail for Timfony Washington, a decent young man being held for setting fire to the back porch of his girl's apartment. Gina talked the contractor who employed Tim as a laborer into making a $1,500 cash advance on some overdue workmen's compensation benefits and, late Friday, handed the money to Timfony's mother and sisters with instructions to post bond at the jail at 8 a.m. Monday morning. Instead, it was gone after the weekend—spent, stolen, disappeared, you could guess whatever you liked based on the four or five different stories the family told. In the jailhouse, Timfony accused Gina of ripping him off, and became so abusive he had to be restrained.

By the time we are done, the courtroom is largely empty. A few stragglers, elderly buffs with no place to rush to, are gossiping behind the glass, while Seth has remained at the near end of the jury box. He's preoccupied, looking toward his lap, his hands moving furtively. Idling on the question that finally came home to me after overhearing Dubinsky and him yesterday, I drift his way.

"What in the world?" I ask, when I first see the needle in his left hand. Then I realize he's sewing a button back on his sport coat. He's made a terrible hash of it. Thread is going everywhere. It looks less like a button than a leak.

"You can see why I gave up a career in surgery." He bites off the thread between his teeth. "I thought we weren't talking," he says.

"We're not."

"Ah."

"There's just one question I've been meaning to ask you."

"I figured you would. The answer is, I truly don't know. That's straight up." His eyes, a dense, greenish-grey, narrow mysteriously. I haven't a clue what he means. "Forget it," he says. "I need some work on my Carnak routine." He raises a hand, inviting my question.

"I couldn't help noticing you sitting here every day with Stew Dubinsky. I wondered how well you know him."

"Stew? Only since kindergarten. We all grew up in U. Park together."

"All of you? You mean Stew and Hobie and you?" I didn't have the remotest idea how I was going to broach this subject as I moseyed over, but I've done a decent-enough job. I sound casually curious. Life is full of these funny little connections.

"Hobie wasn't there in grade school. He went to St. Bernard's?"

"St. Bernard's," I say, simply to fill airtime. When I was in fourth grade, my mother made the first of her periodic out-of-town journeys, living for three months in North Carolina while she attempted to organize a stamping plant. In the interval my Aunt Hen put me in St. Rita's down the block. I was already developing, well ahead of everyone else, and my skin had become awful. I was delighted by the uniform and the opportunity to look like all the other girls. By comparison, the discipline, the catechism, the nuns smacking their rulers on the desktops seemed unimportant. When Zora came back, though, she had a fit. *Catholic* school? Had Henrietta lost her mind? "Hobie's Catholic?" I ask, still being somewhat diversionary.

"Just his mother, but Loretta's pretty religious. He got a full dose. I remember, when I was first getting to know him, in sixth grade we had this phe*nom*enal argument because he refused to believe his parents had intercourse in order to conceive him." Seth laughs at the memory. "I actually made him cry."

"But you guys all went to high school together, you and Hobie and Stew?"

"U. High," he says, "in the fabled days when U high was a question, not a place."

A little buzz passes through me, the naughty satisfaction of the old prosecutor vindicating her suspicions. Stew and Hobie are old pals. Hoping to remain unobtrusive, I smile at Seth's joke.

"If you stick around for Narcotics Court," I say, "you'll find those days aren't over. I live in the neighborhood. They have undercover cops in the high school now."

"Yeah," he says. "That's a good column, you know. I write it three times a year. Being the first generation to take a dose of our own medicine. 'Listen, kids, Daddy really didn't mean what he was saying about sex, drugs, and rock 'n' roll.' "

"And turn down the record player when I speak to you."

"The CD player."

"The CD. So, thanks," I say.

"That's it? Jeez, don't run away. So what's the deal with Stew?"

"Nothing to talk about. Something struck me while I was on the bench." He'll mention my question to Stew, I know, even perhaps to Hobie. Which is fine. If it's what I fear, then I want them to realize I'm on to them.

"No, really," Seth says. "Take the load off your feet. Tell me what I've missed in the last twenty-five years. Anything dramatic?"

The courtroom is empty now and quiet. One of the stout Polish cleaners, friendly, mute, and virtually analphabetic in English, is emptying the trash can behind the bench.

"I don't think of my life as dramatic, Seth. Anything but. What about you? You're the one who's rich and famous. What's dramatic with you?"

"I'm not famous. Not really. I may not even be that rich pretty soon." His eyes, his face draw in somewhat with the discomfort underlying this cryptic declaration, then he disciplines himself to look straight at me. "Lucy and I are separated," he says.

Sorry, I say. The only thing you can.

"Yeah, well," he answers. "Life. Love. The big city. We've been talking about getting back together. I think we will. But it's been a pretty rough patch." He sighs at the thought. I should have known better than to argue with Marietta. She always has a faultless grip on facts.

"Is she well? Lucy?"

He nods. "I think so. She still looks like she's fifteen. There are days I'd say she acts that way, too, but then again there's twenty-five years with me, so she's got her excuse." The joke does not seem to elevate his mood. "So you live in U. Park?" he asks. "You know, my father's still there."

"Your *fa*-ther? God, my memory really must be going. I have this picture of him as elderly twenty-five years ago."

"He was. He's ancient now. Don't bother looking for a nicer word. Ninety-three. Visibly failing. Still going to the office a couple of times a week. And still full of shit."

That was a difficult relationship, Seth and his father. The old man was cold, unyielding. A Holocaust survivor. He had endured, but was hardly unharmed.

"And your mom?" I ask.

"Gone. She died in a home. Advanced Alzheimer's. Terrible thing. It's just a body in a bed."

"Oh, that's right." I tap my forehead. "That was a number of columns, wasn't it?"

"Columns? Hell. That was two years of treatment."

He's funny, he always was funny, a sweet, vulnerable boy, unusually in touch for a male of his era with the fact he was needy. Irresistibly, mysteriously, I find, still standing above him, that I've touched him on the shoulder. He asks, of course, about Zora, and I answer with the sad news: passed too. I hope my delivery is stoical and mature, but there is still a throb, an inner outcry whenever I am forced to acknowledge this.

"She died of lung cancer four years ago."

He winces. "God. I remember the cigarettes. Chesterfields, right? Cancer," he says.

"I had cancer myself," I tell him. "You asked what was dramatic. I suppose that was."

"No shit," he says, "cancer?"

"It was shit, but I'm not kidding."

"Lung cancer?"

"No, no. Breast. I had a breast removed, almost twelve years ago." I never impart this information, especially to a man, in a mood of complete neutrality. In some minute way, I always feel as if I'm issuing a warning, an attitude that persists even though I took my retirement money when I left the federal government and, with Gwendolyn's relentless encouragement, used it for a reconstruction. I had terrible conflict about this. I *hate* the idea of apologizing for being sick. And I'd adjusted. On Saturdays, I'd walk around without even bothering to stuff the other side of my bra. Then I became single again. And it was easier for Nikki. She'd begun to notice and I was always concerned about explaining it to her. Even the little ones are so quick to peek into the void. And what reassurance can I really give her?

Seth says the right things, mentions everyone he knows who's doing well, cites the recovery statistics with which he's familiar. He's clearly pained at the thought of what I went through.

"Was chemo as bad as they say?" he asks.

"I didn't have chemo. I was lucky. There were no lymph nodes. And I still wanted to try to have a baby. It was radiation. A lot of radiation. It was pretty terrible. But I hated the surgery more. It just seems so barbaric. Cutting off a piece of you? The whole experience made me crazy. It was a little disappointing. I thought I was mature enough to weather anything."

"No such illusions here." He's raised a finger. "We're all as crazy as we used to be, Sonny. There are just fewer opportunities to show it."

That line I like. My laughter bounces off the empty pews. Standing over Seth, in my robe, I feel some echo of the usual relations of the courtroom, where so many men look up toward me, hoping for clemency of some kind. Seth also wants something. I can feel that much. I've noticed him once or twice, resting his chin atop his hand on the urethaned oak railing of the jury box, his expression as he watches me so stupid, beamish, and—face it—adolescent that I find my heart surge in a combination of shock and dismay as I turn away. It is, all in all, an odd grown-up he's turned out to be. His feelings seem slightly beyond his full control, like a dripping nose. I like him, though. I'm pleased to find he's maintained some basic appeal. It would be horrifying to think I'd wasted my time with him, too, particularly since I've long since reached that conclusion about Charlie.

"Before?" he asks. "I thought you wanted to know what happened to Michael Frain. When you said you had a question? I figured you had to ask eventually."

"*Can* I ask?"

"I gave you my answer." He said he didn't know.

"Well, is that all there is to it, Seth? I've always thought it was a bizarre choice for a pen name."

"It's a story," he answers. "I'll tell you one day."

"And you never hear from him?"

"I doubt he's alive." He says this in a morose, deadened tone that spells trouble to me.

"Okay," I say and lift a hand in farewell.

"Are you really going to avoid me as long as this trial lasts?"

"I intend to try."

When I wave again, he catches my fingers, and with his other hand taps once on my knuckles, a tiny gesture affirming some lingering contact. I take it that way, with a laconic smile, and turn at once, where, to my misfortune, I confront Marietta, who has just come through the back entrance to the courtroom. Chief Judge Tuohey's chambers are on the phone, she says, counting noses for a judges' meeting later today. I take the call at my desk and assure Wanda, the judge's officious secretary, that I'll be along.

By the time I'm done, Marietta has resumed her standard lunch-hour posture at her desk in the outer office, attention fixed on a minute TV held on her lap, while she eats a sandwich off the brown sack in which she brought it. The metal band between her headphones glints amid her bushy curls, and disregarded crumbs dandruff her full bosom and the nubbly brownish tweed of her sweater. Nonetheless, I become aware, through the open doorway, of her droopy eyes drifting toward me in assessment.

"Not a word," I tell her.

She remains silent only a few seconds. "Folks never do forget bein in love," she says suddenly, as if to herself.

"Oh, give it a rest, Marietta." I scowl at her from twenty feet. She turns away, but her jaw is set as if to show she's standing her ground. "It wasn't love," I say, "not for me." She actually grimaces slightly. I'm blaspheming. But over time my understanding has become surprisingly clear. "He adored me," I explain, "and the ugly truth is I loved *that*." I never felt more splendid, more admired, than in those months I spent with Seth. But his attention was draining because it was so needy. Seth was like a nosebleed. So close, too close. Life with him was always on the verge of turning suffocating.

"Well, I thought you two wasn't talking," Marietta offers in her defense.

Annie has just come in and quietly takes the straight-backed chair in the corner of Marietta's office. She is carrying a school text and demurely finishing an apple.

"I had to ask him about something." I explain to them that I found out Hobie and Dubinsky have been friends since high school.

"So?" asks Marietta.

So it means the notion Molto offered two days ago which I scoffed at is actually possible: Hobie could have been the source of the very leak for which he blasted the state on the first day of the trial, the story revealing that Eddgar was the target of the shooting. I've caught both women's attention with this idea. Marietta lays her earphones down. Annie is quick to accept that there is a conspiracy afoot.

"That Dubinsky," she says. "He is bad. He is a snake." She recalls an incident two or three years ago, during the *Termolli* trial, in which an oil executive and his mistress were charged with killing his wife. The judge, Simon Norfolk, found Dubinsky with an ear up on the jury-room door, during deliberations. Norfolk stuck Stew in the lockup for several

hours for contempt, before the *Trib*'s lawyers arrived in flotilla screaming about the First Amendment.

"Yeah," says Marietta, "but you asked the right question, Judge, the
other day. What's the defense get out of leaking this? It don't make any
sense for them."

In reply, Annie speaks up softly. "Maybe for the bench trial?" she
asks. That's what's occurred to me, too.

"Think about this, Marietta," I say. "Tommy's hair's on fire—he has
to get started, because he's hoping to keep Lovinia corralled. Hobie
knows it, since he's the one who's been causing the problem with her.
So he pushes his story into the paper, screams bloody murder about
how he can't get an impartial jury, and then magnanimously takes a
bench so we can get started, realizing that normally I'd be reluctant to
do it in a case where I know so many of the players. Remember that
remark of Nile's when I admonished him on the jury waiver? 'That's
what we want.' "

"Ooh," says Annie and makes a face. "Ooh. That is sneaky."

"What *I* can't figure out is what he thinks he gets out of a bench."

Marietta laughs. "Judge, I'm not picking on you or teasing you or
nothing but, Judge, you know, there's lots of defense lawyers who work
in this courthouse might have said to him, 'You get a bench with her,
you got a pretty good deal.' That's fact, Judge."

In this building, the judges who were once PAs are expected to exhibit
the loyalty of a Marine to their former office. Many think of being a
prosecutor here as akin to combat experience, each courtroom another
theater in a war zone, civilization versus barbarians. After my weekly
call, I've heard supervisors ask the courtroom PA for a "body count,"
referring to the number of guilty pleas. But the rhetoric I grew up with
in the federal courts was constitutional not military: I still think about
rights, about inviolable first principles in the dealings between individ-
uals and the state. The defense lawyers regard me as a natural ally—
and Marietta as a turncoat.

She stands, her skirt another pleated brownish print that spreads about
her amply, and tosses her empty soda can into the trash, then shoots
me a hard look, reaffirming her message. Hobie did this because he
thinks I'm more likely than a jury to acquit Nile. Who'd be more sympathetic to Nile, twelve coldhearted folks off the street or me, somebody
who knew Nile as a boy and, better yet, who knows firsthand the gripes
of a child who lived through the revolution at home? That's the bet

Hobie took. I'm here because I'm Zora's daughter. Always. Inescapably. Just as Gwen said yesterday. Marietta goes off, unable to restrain a slight toss of her head in unending amazement at what I miss.

The trial resumes with bickering. Hobie wants to have lab work performed on the money the state introduced yesterday. He cites Montague's acknowledgment that the bills had not been tested for blood, for example, or gunpowder. Rudy objects for the state.

"Yaw On-uh, such tests are to be puhfawmed befaw thee trial."

"I made some calls," says Hobie. "I can have the tests done in twenty-four hours. Montague admitted the state doesn't need the bills they didn't submit to the lab. What's the harm?"

"What's the relevance?" asks Tommy. "Even if there's gunpowder or blood on the money, so what?"

"Well then," says Hobie, "the state will have to explain how it got there."

"Talk about a fishing expedition!"

Tommy's right. But I allow the motion. It's harmless, and the accepted wisdom in this job is to let the defendant have his meaningless victories. It shows evenhandedness to the court of appeals.

The state completes its examination of Lovinia uneventfully. With unsettling calm, Bug describes the shooting on September 7: the approach of June's car, her call to Gorgo, and then, when a woman, not a man, rolled down the window to the Nova, summoning Hardcore. The woman and she were alone for about five minutes.

"Did you have a conversation with the woman?"

"She askin, can she talk to Or-dell." Messing with Hardcore's given name, Bug pauses to smile. Hardcore came up fast, she says, and the woman and he conversed momentarily. Then Gorgo swung out of the alley. "I got wounded," she says, with the composure of a soldier.

Having survived the last of this examination, Tommy retreats to the prosecution table with a glum look, awaiting whatever will happen next. Hobie rises for cross.

"Bug," he says. In his fine suit, a rich grey nailhead which I would bet is part cashmere, Hobie strolls around the courtroom, hands in his pockets. 'Bug,' he called her. No pretending they're unacquainted. "Let me ask you a few questions about this shooting. You say you didn't hear what Hardcore told this lady?"

"Nn-uh. Seem like they trippin with each other."

"Some kind of argument?"

"Seem like."

"Did she leave the area?"

"No how. She standin there, you know, out the car, gone on with Core."

"And then Gorgo came and fired. Now, when that happened, where was Hardcore?"

"Come by me."

"He'd come over by you, leaving Ms. Eddgar at her car. Right?"

"Yes, sir," she says.

At the easel, Hobie has raised the street schematic, People's 3, where Montague made his X's and Y's to show the location of the bodies. Now he is indicating that Lovinia had stepped into the street about fifty feet from June Eddgar's vehicle and that Core was near Bug.

"And what did he do?"

"Seem like he tryin to get me down."

"Before Gorgo shot?"

"Seem like. It was all, man, that scene go down like ninety, man. Fast."

"But it seemed as if Hardcore was trying to get you down, as if he knew Gorgo was going to be shooting?"

"Cuz got his T–9 out there, gone look like blastin." Everybody laughs.

"But did you see Hardcore trying to stop Gorgo?"

"He behind me, man."

"Well, Bug, do you remember hearing or seeing Hardcore do anything to stop Gorgo?"

She eyes Hobie narrowly. Whatever her disaffection with the prosecution, her loyalty to Hardcore remains supreme.

"Can't be tellin you that," she says.

"But *you* were trying to stop Gorgo, weren't you?"

"Yes, sir."

"And he shot anyway?"

"Shot me."

"You've said. Now did Hardcore get shot?"

"Nn-uh."

"He ducked in time?"

"Got down by them cars."

"Okay." Hobie lifts his face to consider her, the equivalent of a musical caesura. It's not completely clear if he's really suggesting something or simply wandering the way he does. The mystery of this unannounced defense briefly lingers, like smoke, in the courtroom air. Then Hobie glances at his notes, shifting subjects.

"Now, Bug, Mr. Molto, Tommy over here, talked to you about some of the things that Hardcore said to you. Let me ask you this first: Whatever Hardcore says, does he always tell you the word?"

"No, sir."

"He's not always truthful with you?"

"Not hardly. Like be what kind of mood he in. Sometime, man, he get off, he just woofin." Her emphatic delivery sets off a volley of hearty laughter.

"And Mr. Molto said that yesterday you told him and the police officers and Mr. Singh that Core said on September 6 that this killing was being done on account of Nile. Remember Molto saying that?"

"They all was gettin heavy on me."

"Were they angry?"

"Hoo-ee," answers Bug and inspires more chuckling. She's beginning to like it, to play a little to her audience. "They was deep," she says.

"But let's make one thing clear, Bug. When you say Hardcore was doing something 'on account of' someone else, does that mean he was doing it *for* that person?"

The question, unfortunately for Hobie, confuses her. She looks all around the courtroom, searching for clues. Then she subsides to being what she is, a kid.

"Maybe, kinda like that. Folks be saying lot of stuff, you know."

Stung, caught for the first time, Hobie tries again. "But it could mean something different?"

"Objection," says Tommy. "Asked and answered."

"Here, let's make this very clear," says Hobie. He has perched on the defense table and leans there, like a teacher against a blackboard. He raises both hands. "Very clear, Bug. Hardcore *never* told you he was doing this 'on account of Nile,' did he?"

"No, sir. I ain never be sayin nothin gainst Nile."

"But you did talk with the po-lice?"

"Too much," she says sadly.

"Too much," he repeats. "You don't really remember what you told the police one time or the next? That how it is?"

Her narrow shoulders turn.

"You have to answer yes or no," he tells her.

"Seem like I kinda be sayin what they say."

"Is that what happened yesterday? These men were angry and

telling you what you'd said before and saying you were going to go to the penitentiary if you didn't say it again?"

"Uh-huh," she says. "Molto and them, he sayin, Tell the truth." 'Troof,' she says, "then he start in readin from them reports, sayin I don't say it here, I a lie, I gone have do time on the hot one." Murder one.

Everybody in the well of this courtroom has witnessed similar scenes. What's interesting, though, is that Hobie's backtracking. Despite Tommy's accusations, Bug went further on direct than Hobie wanted. He knows I'm not likely to accept Bug's testimony that she never said what's in the signed statement she gave Lubitsch at the hospital.

"So let's go back to how this started," says Hobie. "Now, Mr. Molto asked you about this deal that your lawyer in the guardian's office made for you with the state? You remember that? That was a good deal for you, wasn't it?"

"Whole lot better than M–1." More light laughter ripples through the room.

"I just wanna be sure Judge Klonsky understands how you felt about the deal you made." He looks up to be sure he has my attention, seldom a problem for Hobie in any courtroom, I'd bet.

"Now, you told Mr. Molto where you were living when you were arrested. Sometime with your momma, is that what you said?"

"I stay by my momma some. Sometime by my auntie, too, or some my homegirls."

"And has your momma been to see you while you've been inside?"

"Nn-uh," says Lovinia. "We ain been talkin none. Might be she don' even know where I is, seem like. Might be she done booked." Lovinia shrugs, with an effort at sullen indifference that still somewhat betrays her. I've learned this much: these children know. From the comparisons to the TV, to the billboards, from the expression on our faces. They know they are the measure by which even the desperate give thanks they don't have less.

"You and she don't get on?"

"She just some smokehead bitch, you know. All she be." Bug's eyes slide sideways. The softness in Bug is gone now. Although spoken quietly, this last declaration escapes her with venom. Hobie, wisely, lets the moment linger, so that I am accosted yet again with a clear vision of the life of the poor. This is the sanest, noblest legacy of being Zora Klonsky's daughter and I freely indulge it, pondering what it really means not to have. It's not the lack of luxury, the stuff we all know we can comfortably endure—driving a rusted beater, or having to eat p.b.

& j. on your sandwich instead of smoked turkey and Boursin. And it's not just the lack of esteem, the sense of having finished second, which sometimes briefly grips me when I bump into friends from law school who chose the plummy, thin-air life of corporate firms and allow themselves crowing references to trips to Tuscany and Aruba, to 'second places' up in Skageon, to the kinds of delicious excess Nikki and I will never see. 'Poor' means what it probably has meant to Lovinia's mother—competing with the children for the little that is left, these drippy-nosed kids begging dollars for stupid trifles, a bag of chips, a Coke, when you need that six bucks in your pocketbook so bad, for just a little fun on Friday night. And they just keep up with it, Can-I? Can-I? Can-I, so that you want to bust them for asking, again and again, what you hear as only one terrible question: Who do you really love, yourself or me?

"You've done a piece of time in juvie before, haven't you?" Hobie asks. "A couple of weeks for selling dope last year?"

"Uh-huh."

"And when you went on selling dope, you knew there was a good chance you'd be goin back, right?"

Her slim shoulders move loosely again. "Seem like nobody has a forever run."

"So your deal with Mr. Molto sounded all right to you?"

"Yeah," she says, "all right." Hobie nods. He's moving again, more slowly. This is the most artful he's been. A roof, three meals, a place where she belongs—Lovinia has plenty of reason to like juvie.

"And when was the first time somebody from the state talked to you about a deal? Was it when Detective Lubitsch came to see you on September 12?" Hobie motions irritably at Nile for copies of the police reports. Still somewhat hypnotic, Nile wakes himself and fumbles awkwardly in the large carton of materials.

"Oh yeah. He was rappin to me. Gone make me a good deal."

"Had you been knowin Lubitsch for a while?"

"He in Tic-Tac. He done gaffled me twice."

"Arrested you?"

"Uh-huh."

"And had he done right by you, Bug?"

She gives him a complex expression suggesting the amount that can't be freely communicated in these circumstances. "He ain beat on me or nothin," she says, inspiring more laughter.

"He's better than some, right?"

"Word," she answers.

"And you were in the hospital, on September 12? That's where Lubitsch came to see you, right?"

"Uh-huh," says Bug, "on accounta I been shot."

"On Account Of you'd been shot," says Hobie slowly, throwing his watery, dark eyes my way again. "And did you have a fever?"

"Fever? Uh-huh."

"You getting pain medication?"

"Seem like they givin me all kindsa stuff."

"And the po-lice questioned you anyway?"

"Uh-huh."

"Did you have a lawyer?"

"No, sir."

"Was your momma round?" asks Hobie.

"No how."

"They bring a youth officer?"

"I don't know who-all they was there. Ain no one said that."

"So Lubitsch came to see you. And he said they could make you a deal? Is that what he said?"

"Yeah, if I spill. You know, all bout how this lady got faded and shit." Lovinia's eyes dart toward me and she murmurs, "Sorry."

"And did you tell him at first, when he asked, what had happened?"

"Nn-uhh. Say I don't know nothin. Just some Goobers comin through."

"But eventually you said something different, didn't you? Mr. Molto's read some of the statements?"

"Seem like I have to," she says.

"Seems like you had to," says Hobie. He knows just where we're going; he's fully the master of this child. I had this happen to me on one or two occasions when I was a prosecutor, and it was agony, sitting there as the defense lawyer waltzed my witness to any destination she or he chose. It brought to mind those mournful country/western tunes, where the singer wails about watching his date at the big dance go home with someone else. "I want to ask you about that, but first tell me this, Bug. Before you changed what you said, did Detective Lubitsch tell you that Core had been talking to the po-lice?"

"Uh-huh. Told me he gone state and all how he been goin on."

"They told you he was a state witness now. And did they tell you everything he'd been saying about this crime?"

"Uh-huh. Seem like."

Again, Hobie looks my way. He's scoring quickly now, and wants to be certain it's all getting posted.

"Now, Lovinia, let's talk about the gang, BSD. When did you get courted-in?" He's asking when she became a member, using the gang talk smartly, not just to make it easier for her, but to acknowledge again that he's spent time with Bug.

"I be claimin mine a long time."

"Years?"

"Five years at least."

"Okay. Where do you stand? You still a Tiny G or you a full homegirl now?"

"Homegirl," she says.

"But Hardcore, he's Top Rank, isn't he?"

She nods once, cautious again about the gang and its workings.

"If he says go sell dope at Grace and Lawrence, you do that, right?"

"Most times," she says.

"If he says somebody's got to be beat down, do you say no?"

"No, sir."

"Have you ever given some homegirl a beat down because Hardcore said so?"

She freezes a bit here, looks away before answering. "Once. Little girl name Tray Weevil. They was lotsa us. She been doin crazy stuff."

"Okay. Have you ever gotten busy with someone because Hardcore said so?"

She does not like this subject, sex, at all. She looks straight at the lockup door from which she emerged. Hobie has finally gone too far with her.

"Don' know bout that," she answers finally, her eyes still nowhere in the room.

"Okay, but you follow Hardcore's lead, don't you?"

"He Top Rank," she says.

"And so when Lubitsch said that Hardcore was cooperating and told you what Hardcore said, you repeated exactly what they said Hardcore had, didn't you?"

"Seem like." Over at the prosecution table, Tommy has taken to flipping his pen in the air and catching it, a jury-trial trick meant to distract me. I'd call him on it, but after twenty years, it's principally second nature for Tommy and it's obvious he's too furious over what's going on between Bug and Hobie to be thinking clearly about much. It's all baloney as far as he's concerned, crap Hobie made up which she's parroting. But even Tommy recognizes the significance. Lovinia's statements to the police mean nothing if she was merely echoing what she knew Core had said.

"They told you they'd make you a deal, they'd let you stay in juvie, if you said what Hardcore said?"

"Pretty much."

"You had no choice, did you?"

"No, sir. Specially since I messed up on the lie box."

Hobie stands still, viewing her with half a face. "Are you saying they gave you a lie detector?"

"Uh-huh."

"There in the hospital on September 12?"

"Right where I was layin there in bed."

Hobie looks to me. "Your Honor, I need a sidebar."

Tommy and Rudy drag themselves over. "I don't know anything about it," Molto says. His eyes close briefly. He sighs, in pain.

"Judge, if there's a polygraph, I'm entitled to the report. I'm entitled to explore this. Your Honor, this is a clear discovery violation." I have my doubts about Hobie's claim of surprise. He's interviewed Bug too thoroughly to have missed this. I suspect his outrage is theatrical. But he has a point. "Judge Klonsky, I might have grounds here to suppress her testimony."

"Yeah, right," says Tommy. "I'll join in that motion." The four of us actually laugh. The moment of candor is becoming to Molto.

"What do you want?" I ask Hobie.

"The report."

"There is no report," Molto repeats.

"Then I want the examiner," says Hobie. "We can't complete her testimony without knowing what this is about."

I take two steps up so I can see Bug on the witness stand and ask her who gave her the polygraph.

"Lubish," she says to my astonishment. Molto's skimpy eyebrows have also jumped up his face.

"Fred Lubitsch can't do a box," says Molto. Rudy cuts in and draws Tommy away. They whisper heatedly, leaving Hobie and me looking at each other in order to give the prosecutors some privacy. As the silence lingers, I finally ask Hobie if he's married.

"Not now, Judge. Three-time loser," he says. "I'm in solitary." He emits a brave laugh, then regains a sober expression. Somehow, in this scrap of conversation, I see a clear resemblance to Seth, not simply in the news of foundering marriages, but in the attitude: the gloomy eyes, the dark fog of things that did not go well. Having had such high hopes for the world, are we the unhappiest adult generation yet? Hobie tells me he has two daughters, the older one a junior at Yale. Singh and Molto return then.

"We'll have Lubitsch here in the morning," Molto announces.

"We'll recess now?"

The lawyers agree. From the witness stand, the transport deputies remove Lovinia, who, despite his fixed gaze, his silly smile, still will not look at Nile.

Winter, 1970

S E T H

The early months of 1970 were terrible. We were in California's first season, whatever it's called. The acacias had bloomed; the purple ice plants flowered beside the freeways. But everyone I knew was miserable.

The Eddgars' household was in turmoil. The Faculty Senate voted to conduct hearings beginning April 1 to determine whether Eddgar should be expelled for inciting to riot at the ARC. The role of martyr suited Eddgar well. Anger, sacrifice, discipline — all his favorite attributes were called for. His public appearances were characterized by an intense nervy excitement. He stridently denounced the university's case against him as hokum, designed to stifle dissent. But at home, his mood was more ambiguous. He worried out loud about snitches. June was even gloomier, clearly depressed by what the authorities were about to dish out. She took to quoting from various Greek dramas she'd played in at college.

I stayed busy with Nile and had also advanced somewhat at *After Dark*. I now swept the office and was also getting up at 5:00 four mornings a week to fill the vending machines around the Bay Area. The publisher of *After Dark* was a potbellied, bald-headed guy in polyester pants named Harley Minx. I liked Harley and found him somewhat touching in his frank desperation to experience the life of lust imagined in his paper. In idle moments in the office, I'd recounted some of my Doobie Hour fantasies to him and Harley had persuaded me to write a couple down. He decided to run them as a sort of serialized comic strip, each tale stretching over three or four issues and accompanied by R. Crumb–like cartoon panels. The column was called "Movie Trips," and except for Harley's warm support drew virtually no attention. However, the sight of my words in print was dizzying.

The initial serial concerned a leader named A.B.1 and his son, I.B.2, and was set in the year 2170. By then, I suggested, medicine would have scored its ultimate triumph, allowing humans to live forever. As a result, the earth and the habitable planets would become a reeking over-populated mess. Procreation was allowed solely with governmental license, and then only if one member of the parenting couple agreed that twenty-one years later she or he would die. In my story, A.B.1, a man of some importance, decided that he could not keep that bargain, and so he set about pursuing the only alternative allowed under the law—sacrificing his child. At the end of the first installment, A.B.1 convinced I.B.2 to join the Fortieth SkyFighters, knowing that danger and even death often accosted the members of the galactic militia.

"This is like a parable or something," Lucy said, when I brought the first edition home to Doobie Hour.

"Something," I answered. Sonny put the paper down sadly, her eyes, when they found mine, flooded with shared misery.

"What happens to the son?" she asked.

"We'll find out soon."

By now, I was in an endgame with my draft board, employing every gambit in a last-chance hope that a sudden breakthrough in the Paris peace talks would allow Nixon to end the war. I had filed for reconsideration of my CO and contested the results of my physical. When all that failed, I could transfer my induction to Oakland. That would provide me a few extra weeks. But the point—which never left me, even when I was driving my delivery route or laughing with Sonny—was that I was going. I was gone. When I received my draft notice, I would point the Bug north. That could be late April at best. I had gathered maps from all the motor clubs. I had spoken with the resisters' organization. At the border, I would say I was entering for a visit. Then I would stay. I knew a guy who knew a guy. He'd hire me for day wages at a nursery outside Vancouver. I would be digging and planting as long as the war lasted. After that, who knew? Often, I was wild with anger. The thought of abandoning the U.S.—its crazy turbulence, into which I felt woven like a fiber—of giving up my friends, my food, my music, of being unable to visit my parents as they aged, was horrible. I remained somewhat startled that the remote world of political abstractions was actually going to alter my life. But I could not back down. I had refused to come home over the holidays, knowing that my parents would create unbearable scenes, wheedling and demanding I change my plans. My ability to withstand their pleas to see me seemed to persuade them for the first time that I was actually going to take this step.

Sonny was in her own crisis. Her dissertation proposal was due by the first of March. She would emerge from long hours in the library, bedraggled and bleak, describing her situation as hopeless, claiming to lack both ideas and interest. Her eyes were circled and ink smudges spotted the sides of her hands and the cuffs of her shapeless fisherman's sweater. Two or three times a week, I propped her up with lengthy pep talks, reminding her how brilliant and promising she was. But she rarely seemed convinced. In February, she requested an extension. And then two days later, to my astonishment, she simply quit. Reading the letter she wrote to Graeme resigning her fellowship, I felt short of air. I followed her around the apartment, arguing.

"You get this stuff. Husserl. Heidegger. I watch you and I can see all the little lights blinking on the Univac." I made twinkling gestures with my fingers until she actually smiled.

"That's what I've realized," she said. "I'm here because I get it, because I'm good at it. But that's not a reason to do something. This isn't me."

She was in the living room, shelving her books, tidying up a portion of her life that was now declared past.

"So what's you?" I asked finally.

She shook her head and looked vacantly at our secondhand furniture. We had an imitation Persian rug of magenta Belgian cotton that ran when we spilled water on it; an old brown tweed Hide-A-Bed which required two people to move; and a wing chair and hassock, on both of which the floral print upholstery had split, allowing the ticking to emerge through the strands of fiber in a herniated bulge. Against the walls stood the ramparted bookcases.

"I want to travel. Go other places. Be somewhere else."

"How about Canada?" I asked.

She appeared tempted to smile, but withheld it for my sake, realizing I was earnest. "I could," she allowed. We were both silent. "I could," she repeated. "I could do a lot of things, Seth."

When I asked for examples, she removed an informational packet on the Peace Corps from her canvas book sack, a glossy brochure she'd picked up on campus. It featured a radiant, full-cheeked young woman on the cover amid a splash of red white and blue. Even I saw some slight resemblance to Sonny.

"I probably wouldn't even get in," Sonny said. "You know the story: It's Kennedy's program so Nixon's cutting the funding. But I think it would be far-out to go somewhere that was completely new, *undeveloped*. Unknown. I think about it, I don't know—I feel optimistic." She was clutching her hands near her heart.

"For what? What in the hell is this supposed to accomplish?"

"It's different, baby. I want to see what's different. To explore. Get out. Move out. Expand. I don't have to justify that. You understand."

"Yeah, right." I mocked her: "Do your own thing, man. You know, you're worse than me. I can't sort all this shit out. But I admit it. I feel it jerking me one way, then the other. I can't even figure where you're at. You're *traumhaft*. You're in Surf City. I listen to you: 'This option. That option.' It's almost like it scares you to actually move ahead with your life."

"So what if it does? God, Seth, it's all this middle-class junk with you."

"Oh, fuck that noise. You think it's bad to be committed to something? I don't."

"I don't think it is either, Seth. But I can't be committed just because I think it's a good idea."

We were in the bedroom by now, with its porthole window and glossy yellow enamel on the fleur-de-lis patterns in the walls. The heater spurted up out in the hall. I crumbled sadly on the bed.

"I mean, really," I said after another silence in which neither of us had the bravery to look at the other. "What about us? Don't you think about it?"

"God, baby, I have. I have. Of course, I have. But it's not a thinking thing. I have to *feel* that it's right. To go up there—I might, but it's such an enormous step. For me. It means I'm following you. It means it's your stuff, not my stuff. It means I'm in purgatory, because you are. There are so many problems. I just have to work it through. You understand. I know you do."

I couldn't believe it. The Future. The dread spot where my life fell apart. I was finally there.

A couple of weeks after New Year's, the phone rang in the middle of the night. Waking, I first thought something must have happened to one of my parents. But it was the line they didn't use that was ringing. Lucy was on the other end, asking me to come over, her voice shrill with distress.

"Bad trip," she explained. "Really bad."

I'd never known Hobie to bum out. Senior year, he was heavy into hallucinogens—LSD, psilocybin, magic mushrooms. He loved to borrow a motorcycle and cruise the wooded hills of Greenwood County. I went along once and had a peak experience, my spirit seeming to flood out of me, crystallizing in the treetops of the oaks, where it shimmered magically as the undersides of the leaves spun in the wind. But for the most part I stayed away from acid, wary of confronting my own spooks.

When I reached their apartment on Grand Street in Damon, I found Lucy cowering behind the door, shooing away their dog, a large cream-colored husky named Mighty White. Hobie's late-term cramming had left the apartment looking as if a twister had hit. Throughout college, Hobie had indulged Gurney, his father, in a pharmacist's predictable dream that his son would go to medical school. Those of us who knew Hobie well realized his only interest was in getting his hands on his own prescription pad. In the end, he chose law school both to pacify his parents and because he'd heard the only required work was a single exam in each course. He didn't want to waste his time on papers and midterms just to get drafted. But now that the lottery had freed him, he had to learn something about law fast. The first exams were a few days away. His casebooks and notes were thrown all over the living room, and the place reeked of cigarettes, a habit he took up at the end of each semester, asking all his friends to save, from their flights home over the holidays, the little four-packs that the airlines handed out with meals. I'd seen this routine many times at Easton: Hobie begging every guy in the dorm for notes on the classes he'd cut, the texts he'd never bought. Ultimately, he always made the Dean's List, with grades higher than mine.

At the moment, Hobie sat across the room on the sofa, a secondhand piece with rolled arms and a campy countrified floral pattern. He was sobbing. His cheeks shone and his arms hung loose between his knees. At the same time, he remained fixed on the TV, which, pursuant to the needs of his lifestyle, was positioned only a few steps from him. An old movie was running. Hepburn and Tracy.

Lucy explained that Hobie was enduring the results of playing chemistry lab with his own head: he had dropped some acid and taken a noseful of Cleveland's snow as a garnish.

"He's been crazy," she said. "Throwing stuff? Screaming?"

"Have we got like a theme?"

"You'll hear." She rolled her eyes in a rare show of exasperation.

Near the sofa, a picture of Hobie's family was smashed in its frame. An ashtray had been emptied. I sat down next to him carefully. He was wearing a T-shirt of his own design, which he had produced and marketed at Easton—an anatomically perfect heart and lungs brightly serigraphed above a black legend which read "Be My Transplant."

"So, Mr. Gordon, any sign of the evil emperor Ming?" In his eyes, you could see my question lost like quicksilver in some crack in his brain. Somehow it was always a gas for me when Hobie was fucked up and I was straight, making me, for a brief interval, the master in our tangled relationship. "So like what's flipping across the screen, dude, got you so unhappy?"

"Hey, man, you know." Blasted by the drugs, he was softer, deprived of his usual hard-shell hipness. His round face was puffed up by tears.

"Are you in-body?" I asked. Hobie had experienced reliable sensations two or three times during acid trips of being someone else: a fourteenth-century woman in Avignon who worked on the weaving of one of the Papal tapestries, and a Nepalese peasant named Prithvi Pradyumna, whose life each day, treading behind his oxen, was consumed with unrelenting bitter anguish that his brother, rather than he, had been permitted to become a monk. His eyes flickered up now.

"It's all bad," he told me.

"You mean the dope. What are we saying?"

"Dope? Huh? It's dope. It's everything. It's being skulled and crazy. It's *all* the dope."

I agreed: he did too much. I told him that. Immediately, he began to rage at me.

"No! You know why I been stoned for five years, man? You know?" He thundered to his feet abruptly and loomed over me. "I've been killing the pain, boy! I've been ignoring the facts! Did you know that?"

"No."

"Did you *know* that?" he screamed with his substantial arms outstretched. Lucy peeked in from the kitchen. Now that I had arrived, she had given way. She was crying, her face a mess of melted liner. "Man, there is something I ain't never wanted to tell myself. And you know what it is? Do you *know* what it is?"

"No."

"He doesn't *know* what it is," Hobie bellowed to the ceiling. Up there, he had glued one of his casebooks with a note reading 'Law is a natural high' dangling from a corner. He faced me so suddenly that I flinched. "I'm a *black* man," he declared and briefly descended into a terrible grief-strained spasm of tears. "Do you know what it means to be a black man? Do you know?"

Growing up in my father's home, I'd felt a special sense for the brute pain of oppression. I began to remind Hobie of my efforts, the meetings, the marches I'd made with his parents. It only infuriated him.

"*Don't* tell me about that! You think cause you went marching up and down the street askin people not to be so mean, I have to send you a fucking thank-you note? What'd that ever do, man? That was nothing more than a walk in the fresh air." Hobie kicked the coffee table, a miserable piece of cheap wood with a scarred veneer, so that it jumped against my knees.

"I know the world's fucked up, man. But it's changing. It's *changed,* for Chrissake. Twenty years from now, man, there isn't going to be a slum left in this country. Poor Negroes—"

"Blacks! *Blacks,* man."

It was Hobie's dad, Gurney, in his avuncular way, who'd taught me one day in his drugstore when I was seven to say 'Negro' rather than 'colored.'

"Right, blacks. Blacks, poor blacks are like immigrants who got off the boat in 1964. They're newly arrived. You think they won't jump into the melting pot, too? They'll stop speaking dialect, they'll—"

"'*Di*-alect'? Man, that's our language. That's our culture. Shit! You know, I just can't talk to you about this." Both Lucy and the dog cringed by the wall as Hobie strode from the room. In time, I found him on the back porch, a rickety wooden construction off the kitchen, where the floor was reinforced to hold a washer. He was ripping wet laundry out of the machine. He picked up three or four items, slinging them without aiming across the bright kitchen. A shirt stuck to the refrigerator. A sock hung on the clock. A pair of jeans hit the yellow wall with a moist thwack and after a time crawled down to the floor, leaving a glistening trail. He reared up in fury when he saw me again.

"America is a nation conceived in original sin and that sin is slavery!"

"Oh, stop it," I said. "Stop trying to bend my mind with how bad the Negro people have had it. I get it, okay? And they aren't the only ones who have suffered."

"You tell me who's had it worse?"

"Who? Oh, fuck you, Jack. Man, I wouldn't even be standing here—"

"Oh, that. That! Except the whole fucking white world got its little act together, man, and kicked Adolf Hitler's ass. Now, let's lookee here, over in the U.S. of A., man: We got lynchings and rapings and burnings. We got KKKs and White Citizens Councils and Orval Faubus. We got Bull Conner lettin his hound dogs loose on black teenagers who just want to sit at a *lunch* counter, have a sandwich, man. And did all them European leaders say, 'We got us another threat to civilization'? Don't tell me, man. I've already heard it a thousand times: that's different."

"It is different. Even slavery isn't annihilation."

From her corner, Lucy said it was all terrible and asked why it mattered which was worse. Neither of us was paying any attention.

"Our slavery never ended," Hobie said. "We will never be anything here but slaves or the children of slaves. Never! There is no forgetting." Standing over the machine, he was virtually hyperventilating.

"You and I never remembered."

"Bullshit!" he screamed.

"Hobie, you're tripping."

Somehow this was the worst thing I had said yet. He took fierce hold of my shirt. As I was trying to break away, I ended up getting butted hard by his forehead. My lip bled freely. Lucy brought me a cloth and ice and I sat at the kitchen table, attending to myself. Hobie did not seem to notice. He came back in my direction, still screaming.

"This Is Not a Fucking Trip! This Is My Fucking Life!"

Afterwards, replaying the conversation for Sonny, what shocked me, as much as Hobie's anger, was the instinctive speed with which I had seized my parents' experience as my own. I'd been indignant that Hobie, of all people, would forget the solemn moral claims of my heritage.

Our relationship was never fully repaired. I knew Hobie better than to expect an apology, but he made no amends of any kind. His appearances at Doobie Hour became infrequent and Lucy often arrived without him. We simply let time pass. The night of my birthday, March 12, we tried it again. The four of us went out to a little Vietnamese restaurant Hobie had found in San Francisco. It was a hole in the wall on Van Ness, specializing in spring rolls and savory soups. Catholics, the owners had dolled up the little place for Mardi Gras with boughs of gilt leaves.

"Three great cuisines, man," Hobie pronounced. "Chinese. Indian. French. And only one place they've met. We're bombing the finest fucking cooks in the world."

Lucy wore sparkles in her hair for the occasion and had brought sequined pinwheels for each of us. Sonny gave me a copy of *Abbey Road*. We all drank Chinese beer. Hobie said it was the best high he'd had since he'd given up cocaine. I—and especially Sonny—were pleased by that news.

"No lie, man," Hobie said. "I'm totally checked out of this white-is-right bag."

Against the counsel of an inner voice, I asked what he meant.

"The American thing, man. White men have been destroying people of color around the globe since the sixteenth century, taking their countries, killing them, or making them slaves. The war in Vietnam and the war on the U.S. plains, man—same damn thing. You think it's just coincidental that those grunts in Nam call NLF territory 'Indian Country'? Think it's an accident we dropped the A-bomb on the yellow folks in Japan and not the whites in Germany? And now, man, if one planet ain't enough, now you-all gonna colonize the fucking moon." These imperialist designs, Hobie said, were betrayed everywhere, not merely in the gross manifestations, as in Vietnam, but in the seemingly innocuous items of daily life. Hobie was now convinced that refined sugar was the product of a ruthless oligopoly, the subjugators of Cuba and Hawaii, who had purified their product in order to addict children, while appealing to the basic racist subtext of American life by turning a brown commodity white. The same was true of cocaine. "White," said Hobie. "Purity, propriety, cleanliness, and stature. This country's got white-is-right on the brain. Look at all those dudes going to work every day in white shirts, washing their hands in Ivory soap. Think about it, man," he demanded. "*Think* about it."

I studied him for quite some time, then told him he was mouthing Black Panther bullshit. He became incredibly provoked.

"They are powerful black men!" he shouted. "Can't you dig? The Panthers are exactly what America has not wanted to see for four hundred years, man. They are African males, with their great big guns, not runnin, not hidin, sayin, Stick 'em up, motherfucker, I want what's mine."

"You're fucked," I said. "You're out of your gourd."

"Man," Hobie told me, "you can't even see me anymore. If I'm not just some cute Negro with a bunch of amusing things to say, you can't cope. Let's go," he told Lucy and stalked out.

I sat there an instant, unhappy with myself. I briefly looked to Sonny and Lucy for consolation, but I finally followed him out. On the crowded street of low dun-colored buildings, Hobie stood on the walk, observing the streaming traffic mounting the hills of Van Ness. One of the aboriginal fern bars was down on the corner.

"If I've been talking down to what you believe, then I'm really sorry," I told him. "I've got my own thing right at the moment. But I get it. You know. I'm with you. I've always been with you."

"You won't be there forever, man. Nobody white's gonna be there forever."

"How's that?"

"This country's for you, man. It's *for* you."

"It is, huh? That's why I have to run away from it?"

"Oh, you know. Time passes."

I couldn't believe it. I swore at him.

"Okay," he said. "I'm just saying how it is. I know you're against things right now. Cause right now they're gonna draft your ass."

"Right and you're a disinterested philosopher. You care about the oppression of people of color because you're a Negro — or black, whatever word it is this week."

"But here it is, man." He pounded on his palm. "Twenty years from now, you'll be rich and fat and white — and I'll still be a Negro, or whatever it is that week."

"And I'll be a fucking Canadian."

I understood all right. It was clear now. We had been through college, we had been through everything. We had been children, we had played intense boy-games, football on cold afternoons, wrestling where he always was pinning me, sitting on my throat or bloodying my nose. We'd done junior high school who-loves-who, showed each other our pubic hair when it started to grow in. In high school we'd made friends with Weird John Savio, who took us driving on the frontage road behind the highway in his mother's three-speed Fairlane, which he ran at 110 miles per hour until the engine smoked. In college, we stayed up all night at least twice a week, drawing anyone we liked into our discussions about Occam's razor and various proofs for the existence of God, pondering the implications if it turned out that it was actually life on earth that was really Hell. We secretly knew we were the instigators of Easton's legendary freshman-sophomore water fight. We'd done heavy doses of cannabis and Benzedrine hoping to bend our minds about what Einstein had meant when he postulated that matter equaled time. We had been through everything. But we were not going to get through this.

I turned into a nag, worrying at Sonny: Come with. In my anxiety, she glimmered like a treasured object. I needed love's comfort, a body to hold, her to believe in. If she would come, I could go.

Sonny continued to toy with the idea. I could tell she wanted to think of herself as valiant and right-thinking. But she took a job waiting tables at Robson's, a ham-and-egger on Campus Boul, and proceeded with her Peace Corps application. As time grew short, I insisted on personalizing things. The real issue, I told her again and again, was her commitment to me. She'd sit in the living room with her eyes closed, trying to endure my stupidity.

"Seth, it's not how I feel about *you* that matters. I'm twenty-two. If I was thirty-two, if I was forty-two and we were together, that would be one thing. But I want a life. My own life. I've never lied to you. Or led you on. Have I?"

"Sonny, I don't have any choices now."

"I know, baby, and that's what makes it hard. Because what you're doing is important. And I support it. But thinking it through, I've spent hours, days—And look, how is this any different than if you were doing something else that was important—if you got into grad school somewhere or found a great job someplace? Suppose somebody offered you a job in Hollywood, writing movies? You'd go. Right? Would you expect me to jump up and follow you?"

Most of these discussions ended up as fights—bitter, accusatory. Without Hobie, I felt bereft, especially as my parents grew more frantic. One night late in March, Sonny and I arrived home from a movie on campus to hear the second phone ringing in our apartment. It was my mother, no doubt hoping to twist my innards. She was beleaguering me, calling almost daily, either to implore me to come home to visit them or to see if magically I had divined some alternative to going to Canada.

"Oh man." I was in no mood.

"Call them back," Sonny suggested. But I went to the phone. It was, instead, my father. There were few pleasantries. He got to the point.

"Your mother has informed me that if you carry through with this plan to emigrate, she feels we have no choice but to follow you wherever you settle."

For quite some time neither of us said anything further. It seemed preposterous. My parents never vacationed, never left Kindle County, travel for them long before having lost any association with pleasure.

"You're kidding."

"Deadly serious," he said.

"She's crazy," I finally managed.

"We share an opinion," my father replied. My mother, no doubt, was standing nearby, a hand poised dubiously near her mouth as she listened.

"Have you tried to talk her out of this?"

"Repeatedly."

"You're not coming, are you?"

"Me? My business, as you know, is here. At my age the possibility of starting again in another city—let alone another country—is unthinkable." Retirement was unmentionable. Without an income stream, my father would feel cut off from his vital source.

"So?"

"Your mother is determined."

"She wouldn't go without you. Who would take care of her?"

My father did not answer at first. "I do not know precisely what she envisions. Her son, of course, will be nearby."

A sound of pure agony escaped me. "Will she talk to me?"

He spoke to her momentarily, then informed me sternly, "No. There are no discussions. This is, you see, a decided matter. *Punkt.*"

I was reeling, but crawling through me was the unlikely sensation of some sympathy for my father. He sounded collected, almost cheerfully so, but if she left, I knew he would sink into the clutches of his own peculiarities, afraid to venture beyond home, spooked by wrath and paranoia.

"Seth, I hope this goes to illustrate—" My father could not continue. His voice shook, with either rage or the humiliation of having to prevail upon me. But eventually he forced himself to finish. "I hope you will reconsider."

I waited quite some time, but told him at last what I always did: I had no choice.

"This is not a plan," he cried. "This is madness. You have no concept what you are doing. How will you support yourself?" my father asked, always to him the foremost question. "You cannot provide for yourself, let alone two people."

"She's not coming," I said. "You know she's not coming."

"On the contrary," he said. "Can you not see what is happening?" Of course, gradually, I could. For more than thirty years my mother had accepted my father's stiff personality, his thousand rules, as the price of his assurance he would safeguard her and me. Now, if he could not honor that compact, she considered herself the victim of a fraud. There was no use talking to her about the damage in her own life, because that was beside the point. She had long since agreed to an existence where she had ceased craving satisfaction in her own right, as if that only invited further terror. Her credo was simple: My child is my country. My duty. My life. She had survived solely so as not to abandon the future. No matter how ghastly it seemed, I knew she would follow me. While that reality crept over me, my father went on with his denunciations.

"Do you know what it is to be a penniless immigrant with no means in a country that is not your own? I have some idea. War is not the only thing in life that is intensely unpleasant, Seth. I will say to you what I have said to your mother: If you choose this course, if you cross this border, do not expect to receive aid from me."

"I know better than that, Dad. Believe me."

"You know better about everything, Seth."

"I will *never* ask you for money." We had now reached the absolute core of what was between us. "Underline: never. Do you hear me?" He did not. He had already hung up.

Someone said that money is the root of all evil. For my father it was far more than that. Originally a professor of economics at the U., he eventually became a consultant to banks and brokerage houses, one of the first of the nation's money supply experts. As a result, I heard the theoretical justifications throughout my life: how money is the medium through which everybody competes for what they want—the more you want something, the more you'll pay. It's emotion made tangible, or comparable at least, a sort of river Ganges of life into which all desires somehow pour. A perfect theory, I suppose, ignoring things like how much everybody has to start with, or what the songwriter had in mind when he declared that the best things in life are free. But at least it recognizes that if you want money, you really want something else. What my father wanted, though, was never clear to me.

His name was Bernhard and thus he was frequently confused with Bernard Weissman, a Kindle County developer of vast wealth who owned the Morgan Towers in DuSable and several of the largest shopping malls in the country. 'No, I am the poor Weissman,' my father would always say, in a tone which, given his modulated manner, struck me as ridiculously abject. I knew that he was doing well—this came from the comments of his business acquaintances whom we met on the street—but he made no admission of the fact and seemed to die inside any time he had to spend a dollar.

In college, a group of us in the dorm used to conduct Legendary Cheap Contests, exploring a strange common ground in which we matched, competitively, the miserliness of our parents. My main rivals were other ethnic sons, Slavs and Greeks, although there was one Yankee who was usually in the race. But I always won. My father took the cake. Our dormmates roared as I told the stories: How my father, rather than replace the evergreens in front of our simple hip-roofed bungalow, colored them with green spray paint after they died one particularly harsh winter. How my father would return merchandise to stores, two or three years after purchase, when a button broke, a collar frayed, and haggle for some partial refund of the original price. How my father would keep important clients, bankers, waiting, so he could go buy a case of toilet tissue on sale. How my father late at night could be found refolding the brown lunch bags that I brought home from school, per his instructions, balled in my coat pocket. How my father put a timer on the bathroom light because as a little boy I often forgot to turn it out, with the result that I was frequently left terrified, still sitting on the can as the room went black.

Yet it wasn't the lack of possessions but the atmosphere that mattered most. My father wasn't motivated by a spiritual disdain for material things; he felt none of the pleasure of people of little means, who enjoy the few things they can afford. There was a tight-fisted compulsive quality to my father's refusal to spend, a kind of death grip he held on the household against which I always chafed, and which had led to our most wrenching prior dispute at Christmas time in 1963.

In my household, there was never really a holiday season at any point in the year. In Vienna, my father had been raised as a freethinker. He identified himself as a Jew and was ever on alert for anti-Semitism, which he found pervasive, but even after his wartime experiences — perhaps because of them — he disdained all form of religious practice. That was not true of my mother. Having lost everyone who mattered in the camps, having seen everything precious destroyed, she clung fervently to the customs, albeit in a fairly unobtrusive way, since she preferred no disputes with my father. She bought kosher meats, did not mix milk and dairy, and lit candles on Friday nights. On holidays, she celebrated in muted fashion — a polite Pesach Seder and a Yom Kippur fast. My father went to work. For her sake, I was given a religious education at Temple Beth Shalom, where professors from the U. sent their kids.

At Hanukkah, we lit the menorah, and my father and she gave *gelt* — not the foil-wrapped chocolate coins but real money. In my father's eyes this was a gift with meaning. The closest we came to any other form of seasonal celebration was driving down the snowy streets on Christmas Eve to admire the lighted decorations of our gentile neighbors. My father, of course, approved of any form of entertainment which did not require spending money, and the lights always thrilled me: the brightness, the festivity, the whole season of free-spending and openhanded generosity.

At any rate, the year before I turned sixteen, I took the $10 bill my father had given me for Hanukkah and on impulse bought a four-foot aluminum Christmas tree. I made the purchase at a local five-and-dime and had the tree set up on its green wood base before either of my parents saw it. In shock, my mother stood before the tree, which was mounted on a small end table in my bedroom, a bit like an altar, and remonstrated with me in each of the four languages she spoke.

Consciously, I had persuaded myself that because he was not observant, my father would not mind the tree. Of course, he was in my room within instants of arriving home. He was a person of medium size — my height comes from my mother's people, and I think that neither of us could get used to the fact that I was already two or three inches taller than he was. He was one of those bald-headed men who lets the hair on one side grow long and pastes it across his scalp. He wore metal-framed glasses and a heavy woolen suit, three pieces. He rocked on his toes.

"I see," my father said, in his heavy accent. With his talent for the most prosaic, he added, "This is how you spend the money we give to you?"

"I thought it was a gift." I was lying on my bed reading. "A gift means a person buys what he likes."

"No," said my father staring up at the Christmas tree. He shook his head ponderously. "No gifts for this."

The next day when I returned from school, the Christmas tree was gone. Neither of them ever offered an explanation. And my father never willingly gave me another dollar. The idea, I suppose, was that I was first required to make some amends. But that I refused to do. I know, in retrospect, how they saw what I'd done. Not simply a rejection. But an act of emotional vandalism. I ignored their pain, no doubt. But I took no pleasure in it. My concern was myself. I wanted to break out of the lightlessness, the dead air, the suffering and silence of my parents' home. I wanted to stake my claim to a life where every moment is not shrouded by the memory of the most terrible deeds and to ask them, I suppose, to recognize that desire in me, to give me their blessing to be different from them in that fundamental respect. But this was not a destiny either of them had ever envisioned for me, and such permission, as it turned out, was never to be granted.

After that, I had board and shelter in my parents' home. Otherwise, I provided for myself. I had a collection of odd jobs after school and over the summers: hardware-store clerk, busboy, fry cook. My mother was always tucking $20 in my pocket when my father was not around, but she did not dare confront him. In college, I financed my tuition with a federally subsidized loan. To embarrass my father, I went to his bank, where they knew how wealthy he was, and when I'd saved enough money for a car, I bought a Volkswagen, the Hitler-mobile, knowing it would drive him wild. But in time, I realized that given impossible choices, I had lost anyway. I had indulged my father in his fundamental selfishness. And I never removed the restraint of their expectations. My mother never lifted her prayerful gaze from me, never stopped fussing over me or begging me in a million silent ways to redeem her life. I was never free. And the weight of all of that fell over me again now in the wake of my father's call.

As Sonny watched, I replaced the phone. I sat first, then lay down fully on the rug. My hands were over my face.

"Oh, kidnap me," I cried, "kidnap me, kidnap me. Somebody kidnap me."

When I opened my eyes, Eddgar was across the living room on the threshold of the open front door. Ironically, he held money—a few bills—rolled in his hand. He had come down to pay me for the week. Unspeaking, he watched me lying there in agony, his perfect, mad eyes unblinking, intent.

"What did you mean?" Eddgar asked me the next night. "Kidnap you?" June and he had just returned from another long evening with their lawyers. A number of attorneys from the ACLU and Damon Law School had come forward to mount Eddgar's defense, joining the old standbys, renowned lefties, who'd been defending the Panthers for years. I had the sense there were sharp divisions in the legal team over tactics, about whether the forthcoming hearing should be conducted to make a political statement or to save Eddgar's job. Arriving home, the Eddgars often appeared wrung out and at odds with each other. Scrutinizing me now, Eddgar already looked exhausted, so dark beneath the eyes he might have been bruised.

I'd often explained my differences with my parents to June and I was in no mood to go over the subject now. But Eddgar's look lingered. I sensed, as I often had, the special reprieve for Eddgar in moving about in someone else's life.

"So if someone wanted to kidnap you, you'd go?" he asked.

"I don't think they'd believe it."

"I would think not," June said. She was drinking bourbon and smoking. Sitting at the sofa's edge, she flicked ashes from the end of the cigarette more often than necessary, flipping her thumbnail against the filter. For whatever reason—practicing perhaps for the demeanor she'd affect in the hearing room—she'd taken on more of a subdued, girlish appearance, a bit of the homespun country gal. Her hair was pulled back and secured with bright rings of yarn. She wore a little sundress, and the length of her smooth legs, without hose, glowed as she sat there. Leaning toward the ashtray, she jerked a bit on her hem, in response to my inspection. "They'd certainly have suspicions," she said.

Eddgar held his jaw. A sign might as well have lit up on his chest, reading, I am scheming.

"What if there was ransom?" he asked. "Can your father afford it?"

"Afford it? Sure. He could probably afford a lot. But knowing my father, he wouldn't pay it."

June laughed. "Seth, you remind me of Eddgar when you carry on about your father." Eddgar's father was a physician by training, but he made his living as a tobacco planter. If you could credit their descriptions, he was a man of ruthless temper, rigid, unforgiving, a hard-shell Christian more excited by the damnation of the wicked than the eternal grace of the saved. June and Eddgar both referred to him in an act of academic derision as 'The Mind of the South.'

For the moment, Eddgar ignored June, struck by my prediction that my father would refuse any ransom request. He threw up his hands.

"Then you're free!" For an alarming, split-brained instant, my liberty seemed to dwell in the tender field between Eddgar's open palms. Then the dreary misery of a better-known reality reclaimed me.

"Well, then he'd pay it to spite me."

They both laughed again. Clapping her hands to her thighs, June said she was exhausted and I headed down. Kidnapping. I laughed at the thought. Outside, as I neared the foot of the wooden stairwell, I heard Eddgar speak my name. He'd come out to the landing above, and stood in the intense beam of the floodlight.

"Would they call the FBI?" he asked quietly.

"My parents?" I was startled he was still on the subject, but I shook my head. Given their history, my parents were terrified by encounters with the police. I had been in the car on more than one occasion when even a routine traffic stop had crashed my father into disorder and panic. His hands shook so fiercely he could not hand the copper his license, and it required half an hour at the curbside afterwards for him to regain his tenuous hold on the present. There was no prospect he—or my mother—would ever involve law enforcement. "No chance," I told Eddgar.

Standing a floor above me, he smiled. Amid the mounting anxieties of his own situation, this notion had become a diversion. He tapped a single index finger on his temple to show that he was going to keep it in mind.

Four days after I received my draft notice, Sonny told me she was moving out. It was the middle of April.

"It's no good, Seth," she said. "I have to do it. We're going to end up hating each other." We were fighting all the time, bloody battles in which I spoke of love and she of independence.

"So you'll desert me now, rather than later?"

Sonny shivered to show she was exerting self-control. She had to make the point, she said. The 'point' was never specified, but I understood. I couldn't have her. I was on my own. If she remained in the apartment, I'd keep hoping, keep putting off departure, instead of facing what was now inevitable.

"I have to find something else, anyway," Sonny said. "I can't afford the rent here by myself."

"Where will you go?"

She hitched a shoulder as if she hadn't thought about it much. "I'll stay with Graeme for a while. He's been trying to find someone to take a room."

This was a hammer blow, worse than mere desertion. He'd be in her bed within a week, I realized, if he hadn't been already.

"Not what I think, right?"

"It isn't," she said. "And it's none of your business anyway."

We went at it again, of course.

In the end, I helped her move. It was just as easy for me to load a few boxes every morning into the Bug. I mailed her books to her aunt's from the post office. The other items I dropped outside Graeme's door as I was on my way to *After Dark*. I watched her disappear from the apartment in stages, like something melting.

On the last morning, a Monday, we filled the Bug and put on the portable rack to load the roof. Even so, a couple of boxes remained that I'd have to drop off later. Then I drove Sonny across the Bay Bridge, out of sunshine and into the fog. She hugged me on the street, although I refused to return any visible sign of affection. So this is how it is, I thought, this is how it turns out. An epic moment in my own life, which I would always recount—how could it simply be happening, like any other moment in the ever-present is? There was only fog, carried like smoke on the ocean winds, and seagulls whose hoarse cry could be heard even though they were lost from sight. I noticed, marking him for life, a slender bearded fellow in bell-bottomed trousers and a V-neck sweater moving down the steep hill in the usual heavy-footed way, his weight back to the heels. I had a sudden vision that I'd accost him on another street someday: I saw you when I said goodbye.

"Call me," she said. "All the time. Promise I'll see you before you go." I took her hands from my face and studied them — broad sturdy hands sculpted with working grace. I figured I would leave for Canada by the end of the week. My draft board had obliged me in my last tactical move by transferring the site of my induction to Oakland. May 4 was the day, but there was no point in waiting now.

"People don't just walk out of each other's lives," I said. I wasn't sure if this was a protest or a response.

"It's just another phase, baby. We're both going to survive. And nobody says it's forever." Sonny often talked vaguely of getting together again in the future — after the Peace Corps, after I was able to come home. This notion — the hopes it raised and my certainty that it was cruelly false — brought the unwanted impact of a sob halfway through my throat every time the subject came up.

"Thank you."

"For what?"

For uttering enough intolerable bullshit, I had been about to say, that I actually had some desire to leave. But I had no control over myself and the words emerged hollowly. By accident, I'd found the note I wanted to strike.

"Just thanks. I love you. It's been a gas."

I drove away. I had always known, I told myself. Some shockproof, inner apparatus, a black box near the heart that invariably registered what was true, had never lost account of the fundamental facts: she did not care for me, not in the abandoned, soaring way I cared for her. I'd known but trudged on anyway, dumb and hopeful, and now I was paying the price. Was there anything in life more painful than that inequality? A few blocks on, suffering miserably, I stopped the car across from the enormous rolling park near Mission Dolores. I knew I was back to where I'd started, to the unendurable agony of the young. I could not have put words to it then, but through time I can make out that inner cry: Who will love me for myself? Whose love will let me know myself? I looked at the palm trees rising starkly above the median while I wept.

December 7, 1995

SONNY

"The testimony is irrelevant," says Molto, standing before the bench.

This guy. He has an unerring capacity to aggravate me.

"Mr. Molto, you're the one who offered to bring in Tactical Officer Lubitsch. We had a discussion at sidebar and, as I recall, you ended it by volunteering."

"Judge, we've had time to think. There was no polygraph. So there's no discovery violation. And the testimony is irrelevant."

"Mr. Molto, we've had sworn testimony that there *was* a polygraph, and if the witness is mistaken, I'd think the prosecution would be delighted to establish that fact." I turn to Hobie, who's beside Rudy. "Mr. Tuttle, do you still want to explore this area?"

Mum to this point, Hobie offers nothing but a solemn nod.

"Call the witness."

"Judge—"

"Enough, Mr. Molto."

Tommy starts away, then wheels back. "By the way, Judge, this business of not turning over scientific reports? He told us yesterday—" Tommy uses a finger to indicate Hobie; he's too aggravated to speak his name. "He told us he was going to test that money for blood or gunpowder and have a report this morning."

Hobie cuts him short, avoiding a diversion. "There's no gunpowder, there's no blood. I'll give them the money back right now."

"There's your answer, Mr. Molto. No gunpowder, no blood. Who's putting on Lubitsch? It's your motion, Mr. Tuttle."

Tommy, with his dark, beaten-up face, stares at me, sulkily. He's been doing this twenty years, but he still can't roll with the punches.

"We'll call him, Judge," says Tommy. "This will take one second." He motions to Rudy.

Fred rolls in, spoiling macho attitude. He's wearing his cowboy boots and a huge silver buckle on his jeans, an open-necked print shirt, and a tweed sport coat. Word is he was really something when he was younger, always looking for it on the street, with that imposing physique that strains his uniform and a challenging eye. Among the State Defenders the rep lingers that he's a hitter, a cop who'll smack an arrested defendant around. But Marietta, the unimpeachable source, says he's different since he married. His wife, Angela, is another body builder, whom he first encountered at one of those contests where they oil themselves up and pose. She was a champion, famous in those circles, and Lubitsch boasts about her now and then in an openly admiring way I find endearing. They have one child. Like Marietta, I regard him as one of those people who has improved with age.

"Hey, Judge," he says when he arrives before the bench. A bit too familiar.

"Do you swear to tell the truth?" I answer.

Fred's testified here before. Given the cultural limitations of police testimony—every defendant has received his Miranda rights, even though few do these days; every cop has seen whatever his partner has observed—Fred strikes me as more or less a truth-teller, less freewheeling than some others. As he takes the stand, I notice he has his reports rolled up in one hand.

Tommy waits for Lubitsch to settle himself, then Molto positions himself right before the bench. He goes for dramatic effect. A single question. Not even state your name. He lifts a reddened, nail-bitten hand.

"Officer Lubitsch, on September 12, 1995, or any other date, did you use a polygraph machine on Lovinia Campbell, either at Kindle County General Hospital or elsewhere?"

"No, sir," he says.

Tommy heads back to the prosecution table. "Excuse the witness," he says over his shoulder.

I smile at the gambit. This is, in all phases, a game which two must play.

"Mr. Tuttle, do you want cross?"

Hobie sits in his chair for quite some time, studying Lubitsch. His lips are rolled into his mouth, virtually lost in the grey-shot muff of beard. He's stumped. For the first time since these proceedings began, he does not rise to address a witness.

"Ms. Campbell testified she had a polygraph. Did you know that, Officer?"

"I heard that."

"And she's lying?"

"She isn't right, I know that much."

"She's lying?"

"Objection," says Tommy from his seat. He's fussing with his pad, but he reels off a number of valid exceptions to Hobie's question. Asked and answered. Calls for an improper opinion. Hobie stares at Lubitsch.

"Are you saying, Officer, maybe the witness made a mistake?"

"It might be."

"She misperceived something?"

"Maybe."

The courtroom is still. Hobie finally stands, taking the time to secure the front flap of his double-breasted suit jacket, a chalk stripe of soft grey wool.

"Did she *think* she was getting a polygraph?" Molto objects to Lubitsch testifying to Lovinia's thoughts. Hobie rephrases : "Did someone *tell* her they were going to give her a polygraph?"

"Yes, sir, that coulda happened."

"And who was 'they'? Who told her she was going on the box?"

Lubitsch wiggles a bit in his swivel chair. "I believe I did."

"I see. But you didn't actually do it?"

"No."

"But she changed her story anyway? I mean, that's what happened, right? This girl was tellin you one thing when you got there and something else when you left?"

"Sometimes with these people—" Fred stops. "With an offender sometimes—" He wipes his mouth with both fingers. "An experienced officer, sometimes I think I know pretty well when someone's giving me a line."

"Yes?"

"We don't always want to take them down to the Hall for the box."

"The lie box?"

"Right. Here we couldn't. She's laying there with tubes coming out of everywhere."

"So what did you do, Officer?"

"We tell them we're giving them a box, only we don't."

"You created that impression?"

"That's it."

"And how did you do that?"

"We put something on her head."

"What?"

"Something we borrowed from one of the nurses."

"What?"

"That strap-like, you know, for the heart test?"

"EKG?"

"Right."

"And you put that around her head? So you could test what she was thinking?"

Lubitsch doesn't answer. His eyes roll up to Hobie and fix him with a dark look meant for the street.

"And was it just the pressure strap? Was that the entire apparatus?"

"No. It had a piece of telephone cord attached."

"Attached to what?"

"The thing on her head."

"And what else?"

"A machine." Lubitsch looks hard at Hobie. Obviously there's no point. "A copying machine."

"A photocopying machine?"

"Right. We borrowed that from the nurses, too."

"Then what did you do?"

"Asked a question."

"And?"

Lubitsch shrugs. "Then we pressed a button on the machine."

"For what?"

"The answer."

"You get the answer from the machine?"

"That's what we say."

"Is that what you said to Bug?"

"Right."

Hobie doesn't speak. Instead, he simply beckons for more with the back of his hand.

"See, we put a piece of paper in the machine before we start. Okay? Then when we press the button, it comes out and we show it to her. Okay?"

"And what was written on the piece of paper?"

" 'She's lying.' " There is laughter, of course, a rippling chorus loudest from the jury box.

"So you had this young woman sitting there with a rubber strap on her head and a piece of telephone wire that was attached to a Xerox machine, and then you pressed a button and it produced a piece of paper that said she's lying and you showed that to her, right?"

"Right."

"And she believed it?"

"Because she was lying."

Hobie looks to me, without even bothering to voice the objection. I strike Lubitsch's last answer and Hobie expels a magnificent sigh of disgust as he walks back to the defense table, winding his head. Cops.

"Are we done?" I ask.

Hobie argues vociferously that Lovinia's testimony has to be suppressed. He calls the police "deceptive" and "exploitative," as if the Supreme Court hadn't long ago decided to tolerate such conduct in the name of effective law enforcement. When Molto comes to the podium to respond, I greet Tommy with a dour look. He was running changes on me this morning. One of the iron rules of my courtroom, especially for the prosecutors, is that you pay the price when you mess with the judge. The PAs will run you over if you let them, and as a woman, I feel the need to be particularly firm. I'm frosty enough with Tommy to scare him. But I deny the motion in the end. No right of Nile's was violated by what the police did to Lovinia. Bug, especially as a juvenile, would have a pretty strong argument that the statements she made to Lubitsch and Wells can't be used against her. In fact, now that I think about it, I see how Hobie persuaded Bug—and her lawyer—that she could ignore Molto's threats to throw out Bug's deal if she came off her prior statements. Given this monkey business, there's no way Tommy could risk re-prosecution, since Bug might walk completely. Hobie, the pro, does not miss a beat when I rule.

"In the alternative, Your Honor," he says, "I'd like to make the officer's testimony part of my case. So I don't have to recall him."

Relieved, Molto ventures no objection, but says in that case he'd like to ask a few more questions of his own. He stands at the prosecution table.

"Officer Lubitsch, after Ms. Campbell admitted she was lying—"

"Objection. *He* told her she was lying."

"Rephrase the question."

"After this mock-polygraph," says Tommy, "Ms. Campbell made a statement, correct? And is it fully set forth in your report?"

Lubitsch testifies that each of his reports is an accurate rendition of what Lovinia said.

"And returning to September 12 in the hospital, did you ever tell Ms. Campbell what Hardcore had previously told the police?"

"I didn't know *what* Hardcore had said. It wasn't my case. Montague asked me to talk to Bug because I knew her. That's all. She told me a story, we did our lie-box thing, and she made her statement."

"You didn't tell her what Hardcore said?"

"Nope. That's not my s.o.p."

Tommy nods. He's just made up a great deal of ground. Sorting through it all, the critical issue in evaluating Bug's testimony is whether what she said to the cops in the first place was true. I could believe she told them what they wanted to hear, not so much because she seems easily cowed—even at fifteen she isn't—but because she's clever enough to deal that way. But if Bug didn't know what Core had said, there's only one way, realistically, her sworn statements to Lubitsch could match Hardcore's version of events: because that's what happened out on the street. At least, that's the way I add it up. Tommy does, too. He's gone back to his seat with an unbecoming little swagger, enjoying the fact that he's finally put Hobie in his place.

In his chair, Hobie again is taking his time, his lips gummed over each other, staring at Lubitsch once more, puzzling something through.

"Officer, did you figure on testifying in this trial?" he asks suddenly.

"Huh?" answers Lubitsch.

"Did you have it in mind as this trial was coming up that you'd end up as a witness?"

"I don't know. I thought I might."

"You did?" Hobie pushes through the mess of papers on the table. "You weren't on the state's witness list."

Lubitsch has an uncomfortable moment. His eyes briefly close, lizard-like.

"I saw Montague at Area 7 last week. He said the witness might be doing a spin, and if she did, I was going to have to come stand behind my paper."

"Just a warning."

"That's all."

"You didn't go review your reports at that point?"

"No. I kind of live a day at a time, counsel. I woulda thought she was too smart to flip, but you live and learn." That's meant as a jibe. He's clearly had an earful about how Hobie led the girl astray.

"And how did you find out you were going to have to come testify today?"

"When I come on the job at eight, at roll call, I got a message: phone Montague."

"You didn't spend the day yesterday getting ready to testify?"

"I'm off Wednesdays. I was putting up Sheetrock, if you want to know."

"And when you reached Montague today, did he explain why you were gonna be needed in court this morning?"

"I don't know," says Lubitsch, vamping. "Sort of."

"Sort of," says Hobie. "Well, at some point today did someone — Molto, Montague, Mr. Singh — did one of them explain that Lovinia had testified that in persuading her to change her story, you'd told her what Hardcore had to say?"

"I heard that."

"And you realized, didn't you, that it would help the state if you could testify that didn't happen?"

"Nobody told me what to say."

"I understand, Officer. But you've been around a lot of trials, haven't you? And you recognize the significance of your testimony that you didn't tell Bug, don't you?"

Lubitsch's eyes cheat just a trifle in my direction. I get the feeling that in somebody else's courtroom Fred might try a line, a dodge.

"I have the picture generally."

"Now, Officer, I want to hand you a copy of your report of September 12, marked as Defendant's Exhibit 1, and I'm gonna ask you to read out loud the part where it says you didn't tell Lovinia Campbell what Hardcore had said."

Lubitsch sits a minute, staring outward. He has that look again: stop fucking with me. He bothers only with a bare glance at the report, which Hobie has laid on the rail of the witness box. He does not even touch it.

"It's not there."

"It's not there," says Hobie. "So this is just something you remember?"

"I said it's not my s.o.p."

"It's not your standard operating procedure to tell one witness what another witness has said, correct?"

"Exactly."

"And that's why you say you didn't tell Bug?"

"I say I didn't tell her that, cause I don't have any recollection that anything like that ever happened. That's why I say it."

"Okay," says Hobie. "You don't have any recollection." He's moving around again. By now, I know it's a bad sign for the state when Hobie starts roaming. If I were the prosecutor, preparing a witness for cross, I'd tell him, 'Watch out. If Tuttle starts moving, that means he has you on a roll.' But Lubitsch doesn't know that and sits there, with his bulk and his attitude, still thinking he's doing okay. "And it's fair to say, isn't it, that you haven't had a lot of time to review the reports or to get it firm in your mind exactly what went on in your interviews of young Miss Lovinia?"

"I remember what happened, counsel."

Hobie scratches his cheek. He is doing his best to remain mild, if not genial, in the face of Fred's hostility. Someone—Dubinsky, probably—has told him Lubitsch is a regular here, something of a favorite of mine.

"Well, let's talk about your visit to Bug's hospital room on September 12. You say Montague asked you to go over there because you know her, correct?"

"Not like we're pals. I arrested her twice."

"But you had a good relationship with her as a result?"

" 'Good relationship'? I don't know what that means." He's reared back, then subsides a bit, aware perhaps of how contrary he's becoming. "I'm not trying to be cute, counsel, but you'd say we had a professional relationship. She knew I'd be professional with her. The first time where she got cracked, we sort of caught them in the act—I mean, when we, you know Tactical, when we get in the area, this operation of BSD, they're very good at rolling things up. But this time I saw some car tearing off and Bug and me had a little foot race and I grabbed hold of her and I told her how it was and she was cooperative."

"You 'told her how it was'?"

"Usually, when these kids are out selling small stuff, usually they'll keep it up in their mouth. The seams. So they can swallow it if the Man comes on them. It's not enough to kill them. So they swallow. And I grabbed Bug and told her if she tried to swallow I'd have to choke her, or pump her stomach, and for her just to spit it out and she did."

"And you made friends," says Hobie. The delivery is droll, not quite disparaging, just enough to bring out the sad ridiculousness of the entire situation. He derives uproarious laughter from everyone, including me. Yet there is a homely truth here. There are probably two hundred kids in T-4 with whom Lubitsch and Wells have this kind of relationship. They know their mommas and cousins, their gang standing, maybe even in a remote way how they're doing in school. They treat them with some feeling. Fred has reason to be riled and he treats Hobie to an acid look.

"I didn't ride her, okay? It was a thousand feet of a housing project. I could have charged her as an adult. I didn't. We did it as a juvie beef, she did some home time, she got out."

"You were fair."

"I try to be," says Lubitsch and hitches his massive neck.

"And knowing you had been kinda fair to her in the past, Montague asked you to see her in the hospital?"

"That's the picture."

"And you went with your partner—" Hobie starts through the reports.

"Wells."

"You and Wells went and you told her to roll, to make a deal, didn't you?"

"That I remember."

"And she told you what you took for a lie, namely that the shooting of Ms. Eddgar was just a drive-by by a rival street gang."

"That's what she said."

"Are there drive-bys in that neighborhood?"

"Plenty."

"But you were confident she was fibbing?"

"Lying was my impression."

"Even though this girl was more or less in your debt? Even though she'd been kind of cooperative with you before, you didn't believe her?"

Lubitsch permits himself a slight wise-guy smile. Grow up, he'd like to say.

"I didn't."

"You remember why in particular?"

Lubitsch looks to the ceiling. "Didn't hit me right."

"Could it be," says Hobie slowly, "that Montague had already told you what Hardcore had said?" Hobie stops to watch Fred. This is where he wins or loses. Lubitsch takes a breath and once more lets his eyes rise in reverie. He teeters an instant on the brink of denial. But now the events have begun to come back to me. That was the day Wells and he were in my chambers calling the case a doozy. Fred said he was going to General. And he was gloating, because he knew all about it by then. He *knew* Hardcore had made Nile a suspect. 'Fred,' I want to say, 'for Chrissake, Fred.' Instead, with little conscious intention, I clear my throat. His eyes hit mine. The pupils seem to enlarge in that half-instant, he shrinks back in his seat, and it comes to him just as it has come to me. He almost nods, as if his obligation to tell the truth arises as a matter of personal allegiance.

"That makes sense," he says.

"Do you remember that?"

"It rings a bell."

"So you knew Hardcore had turned. And that you were going to this girl for corroboration, right?"

Lubitsch takes a long time to make sure there aren't any snares before he agrees.

"Now Hardcore's in the gang, in BSD? Hardcore's what they call Top Rank, correct?"

"So I understand."

"The younger ones carry out his orders?"

"They sell his dope. Yeah, he's important. What's the point?" asks Lubitsch, clearly out of sorts, as many coppers become when they lose control of the situation. Hobie takes advantage to move a few steps closer.

"Here's the point, Officer. Do you know of witnesses in gang cases being threatened and in fact even hurt or killed?"

"I've heard of it."

"Often?"

"Probably."

"And in your experience isn't that even more likely to occur when someone is offering testimony against a gang leader?"

Lubitsch sees the point then. He ponders what is coming next before saying simply, "Yes."

"Now, Officer, recognizing you came here on short notice, recognizing you didn't have much chance to look at your reports or to think about the events of September 12, recognizing that you *ordinarily* wouldn't tell a witness what another witness said, recognizing all of that, I ask you if it wouldn't have been a whole lot easier to get a homegirl to roll if she knew her shot-caller had already done the same thing, and if she wasn't going to hurt him by talking?"

Lubitsch's shoulders are sunk down and he is stewing in all of it, getting caught by this defense lawyer and having to tell him the truth. Again, his eyes, almost involuntarily, move in my direction before he answers.

"That makes sense."

"And in order to convince her, you'd have *had* to reveal the details of what he had said. You'd want her to be sure you already knew the story she was going to tell you, right?"

"I would have told her, I guess, some things. I'd have tried to hold back a little, you know, for a test. But I'd have to give her enough for her to know he'd turned over."

"And if she says one of the things you revealed to her was that Hardcore had accused Nile of engineering the shooting of his father, you can't, as you sit here today, you can't say that's wrong, can you?"

Lubitsch actually makes a face. He winces in reflection. He waits one more second, his full weight taken on both ponderous forearms, which rest on the witness box.

"I can't completely remember. All right? That's the truth. She could be right, she could be wrong."

"She could be right?" asks Hobie.

Lubitsch doesn't bother to respond. At the prosecution table, Molto is unconsciously probing his temple, staring vacantly at the oak rods that are mounted on the wall in front of him to baffle sound. Hobie has the center of the courtroom to himself. He smiles circumspectly at the witness, careful not to show Lubitsch up for telling the truth. But we all know he's had another high moment of lawyerly achievement. Bug's statements to the police now have to be regarded as no more than a loyal imitation of Hardcore. Core himself may prove a persuasive witness. There may be good corroboration for him, or other evidence of Nile's guilt. But for the moment, Hobie's done his job. Lovinia Campbell is gone from the state's case.

In the sheriff's office there are dressing rooms and showers. Basic fare. Rusted lockers, concrete floors, the reek of disinfectant. The judges, who have free access, refer to this area in irony as The Club. As a former cancer patient who has read all of the studies about the ancillary routes to health, I skip lunch at least twice a week and, in a raveled sweatshirt and leggings of spandex — time-defying miracle fiber of the nineties — lumber off from the courthouse down Cushing Boulevard for forty minutes of intermittent power-walking and jogging. Rosario, the gatekeeper at the Judges' Entrance, a tiny fellow in the blue sheriff deputy's uniform, speeds me on my way, with his standard farewell. "Go get em, Judge." When I return, he will sweep the door aside and say, 'Welcome to Fen-tasy Island.' I have never been certain if he is mocking himself or the eerie atmosphere of the courthouse, where we are always rubbing shoulders with people whom, in other circumstances, you would cross the street to avoid — boys who shout too loud, who strut about with an abject, thuggish glower, surrounded by menace like a dark halo. The federal building was full of officious clerks and marshals, pumped up with the majesty of the United States. But in the Kindle County Courthouse there is a humble geniality among the lawyers, the deputies, the clerks, a quiet need to reassure ourselves that we belong together to a community of decent folk.

I race along with Mahler on my headset, my heart kicking as I twist down the pavement to avoid the jurors, attorneys, and families on their way to lunch. A couple of the lawyers, whose names I don't recall or never knew, wave to me in an eager way as I shoot by. "Hiya, Your Honor." It's one of the last decent days of the year. The light is weakening and dismal winter clouds, heavy as quilting, move randomly from remote quarters of the sky to momentarily darken the day with the awesome suddenness of a primitive curse. But the sun returns periodically and the air is bearable, pushing 40. Soon Mother Nature will prove she is at heart an angry witch. Winter in the Middle West. You're never quite ready.

Not far from the exit, I hear my name, "Sonny," more or less yodeled, carried to me on the sharp wind. Pushing back the earphones, I expect to greet another judge, but it is, instead, Seth, trotting to catch up. "Oh, for Chrissake," I mutter beneath my breath. I'm the one who started this yesterday, who crossed the moat, but this is starting to feel like junior high school. In the same blue sport coat and scuffed shoes he's worn each day, Seth arrives with a self-aggrandizing smile. The fringe of hair above his ears, going colorless, is fluffed up by the wind.

"I was afraid I missed you. Your secretary, Marian? She said you'd come out here."

"Marietta?" Slow death, I think, Chinese tortures—I am *truly* going to kill her. I stand there, jogging in place, toe dancing in my Sauconys and sweatshirt, and give him my loftiest judicial manner, all walls. "What can I do for you, Seth?" He draws back, with a wet-eyed, wounded look that seems somehow typical of him these days.

"I'm holding you up," he says at last. "Come on, I'll run with you." He moves a few paces ahead and motions for me to join him. In his street shoes and blazer, he leads the way along the avenue with a practiced gait. "I'm only going to bother you for a second. I just wanted you to know something. You asked me yesterday about Hobie and Dubinsky? And I thought about that all night. And I think I get it? I think I know why you asked?"

"Forget it, Seth." I see what's coming. He had dinner with Hobie and they planned a response. Seth's here as a guided missile. This is just the reason I vowed to have nothing to do with him. "We're not having this discussion."

"No, I want you to understand. I don't know what Hobie's doing. I love him, but take it from me, Hobie T. Tuttle can be a treacherous fellow. So whatever he cooked up, it's with Stew, not me. I'm not part of it. Hobie and Nile, neither of them are even talking to me. Okay? That's all."

"That's enough." One more line, one more word, and I'll have to do something, stop and shout for the police. But he allows me to proceed in silence, galloping heavy-footed down the walk. We have reached Homer Park, which boasts a circular tarred walkway. In times past, the Park District was a notorious tub of grease, with patronage jobs and no-bid contracts, the haven for no-nose politicians like Toots Nuccio, who sometimes carried his tommy gun to city council meetings in his clarinet case. These days, as the city grows poorer, so do the parks. The programs that brightened my life as a child, the crafts classes and summer camps, are gone. Even routine maintenance has failed. In this park, for reasons I have never figured out, the trees have all been topped. They ring the tarmac path like amputees, barkless, knotted. The lawn, dying in the early winter, is bare in many patches, strewn with trash and leaves. It is a safe haven though in the daylight hours. Latino moms in their cloth coats wheel their bundled babies. Pedestrians bound for Center City cross the park to transfer bus lines. Like a river running through a canyon, U.S. 843, with its thrum and fumes, is a block away and 200 feet down.

As Seth remains beside me, easily keeping pace, I am engaged in reassessment. 'Hobie T. Tuttle can be treacherous.' 'He and Dubinsky cooked something up.' It's hard to imagine Seth as Hobie's emissary and bringing those messages. I'm even briefly tempted to ask what he thinks Hobie's up to, but better sense prevails. With Seth, I have to maintain a firm grip.

"Jesus, it's cold out here." He's attempting to ease the silence with a joke and rubs the open expanse of his scalp. "No natural protection," he says.

"Seth, am I supposed to feel sorry for you because you're bald?"

"Going," he says. "Going bald. Forehead-challenged."

"Let me tell you the truth, Seth. A woman after forty has to worry about everything. Top to bottom. Her chest sagging. The onset of menopause. Bones going soft. If she's had kids, her back end isn't likely to fit the jeans from twenty years ago, and maybe her bladder's weak, too. So it doesn't really break my heart that men go bald. In fact—and I'm not usually like this—I'm *glad* they have something to worry about. And to top it off, the truth is I don't think it looks all that bad. It makes a guy appear mature, which, frankly, is a rare quality in a lot of men. So I'm not sorry for you, Seth."

"Holy smokes," he says. "What's got you so cranky?"

"Come on, Seth. You're following me down the street, on one of my two free hours in the week. And frankly, every time I talk to you, there's this lament. As if I'm supposed to pity you, when the fact is I've got a job to do. Which I've already explained."

Oddly, he does not offer the defenses I would have expected. "Right," he says instead and his eyes fall to his shoes. I realize suddenly—guiltily—that I've been trying to drive him off by picking a fight. His face, in the interval, remains buffeted by strong feeling.

"My son died," he says then. "You asked what was dramatic for me. Yesterday? That was dramatic."

He has tried, it seems, to strike the tone of historical distance we maintained about our lives a day ago. But the edges of his voice do not hold up. I stop at once while he flies on another twenty paces, so completely unable to look at me that it's that long before he notices I'm not beside him. We've reached the tarred oval and he trudges back to me, against the backdrop of the tortured amputee elms, his posture withered by the questions he knows are coming next.

How long ago? I ask. Almost two years, he answers.

"My God. Was he sick? Was he chronic?"

"He was just a little boy. Seven years old. I mean, kind of a difficult little boy if I'm completely honest. He died in a traffic accident." He waits a moment and searches the pewter sky for the sun, where the dark accumulation of clouds has temporarily milked the daylight of everything vital. "I was driving."

"Oh God."

"It wasn't my fault. That's what everybody says. This guy was drunk— just out of his mind, four times the legal limit, and he ran a light. He hit a curb and came careening right at us. I saw him, you know, maybe out of the corner of my eye, I was trying to move the car forward, it had started forward, but he had the angle on us. It like sheared the car in half. One second I'm sitting there telling Isaac to mind his fingers in his nose, and— Afterwards, the one thing I was grateful for was that I didn't have to hear him scream, and yet, Jesus, how can your child *die* without even making a sound?"

By now, my arms have closed around my sides to cope with the rampant pain. I try a few words of consolation, but his palm rises at once, and I realize this must be one of the worst parts, listening to people grope for words, in hopes of expressing an agony so much his, not theirs. Even then, I can't help saying the same thing again and again. I'm sorry. So sorry.

"I had no idea, Seth. Your life seems so exposed in your column. There hasn't been a word, has there?"

"I hate talking about it. I'm rotten with self-pity, as it is. You see it. Everybody sees it. I'm just a running sore."

I find I have taken his hand. Sweat has trailed down beneath his watchband and the sleeve of his dress shirt. His other hand is against the bridge of his nose, in an effort at self-control.

"And the guy who hit you? Is he in prison?" Dumb question, I think at once, stupid, trying to press the whole thing within my own horizons, because the thought of what he's been through so frightens me.

"Oh, sure. He got fifteen years. He had a record, a big record. Some poor fucked-up black guy. Stolen car. The whole shot. He pled guilty. I never even had to look at him again. Lucy went to court for the sentencing. I guess she cried and carried on. I just—I mean, what's the point? I never think about him, the guy. I think, you know, if I'd moved faster, if I'd pressed the accelerator harder. If, if, if." He scans the park. A thirteen-year-old, hat on backwards and smoking a cigarette, whizzes by us on roller blades. "We're going to freeze out here," he says. He starts to jog then and I follow, walking fast. He slows to keep my pace.

"And Lucy? Is Lucy crazy with it? Is she—"

"She's crazy. Not that I'm in any position to talk. We're both out of our minds. But in different ways." This is what's between Lucy and him, I realize. It must be. We travel half the oval without words, but he can tell what I've been thinking. "It's not like she blames me," he says. "At least, not the way I blame myself. But like this? Running? Six months ago, we started jogging together before dinner. We'd take the dog. We bought these lights you wear on your elbows? We had matching suits. But how can you enjoy it? You can't. You think this is not how our life is supposed to be. We're supposed to be at home. We're supposed to be tied down. We're supposed to be yelling at Isaac to turn off the TV, to start on his homework. It's not bitter with us. We just can't find a way to move on."

"I wouldn't imagine Lucy knows how to be bitter."

"Not a clue."

"Still incredibly good-natured?"

"Incredibly."

"I assume she found a career beyond astrology?"

"Yeah. But she still believes in it. And reincarnation. And ethical shopping. And the music of the spheres. You'd call her New Age." He marvels at her with a toss of his head. For the past year, he says, Lucy has been the director of a local soup kitchen in Seattle. He draws an ironic picture of her, on a first-name basis with all the losers, junkies, drunks, and nuts to whom she extends a helping hand. Lucy is a person of boundless generosity, a collector of strays, mother to anyone in need, whether it's a bird with a crippled wing, her beautician who needed English lessons, or their cleaning lady, for whose eldest daughter Lucy, by dint of an eight-month crusade, won admission to Bellingham Country Day, where Seth's own children were not accepted.

"Do I sound like I resent this?" Seth asks.

"Maybe," I answer.

"Then I'm striking the wrong note. I'm amazed—that her heart goes out so fully to people she barely knows, while I'm always in this muddle, trying to find a way to feel enough for the people I'm supposed to care about."

"I hope it works out for you, Seth."

"I do, too. It's a mess now. You've been through it. The friends. The house. I mean, all of a sudden nothing belongs to you anymore. Stuff that was yours forever. People see you coming and they have this look on their face like you goosed them. I'm glad to be out of there for a while."

Charlie's pals were at the U. Ray Napue was acerbic, terribly funny about everyone but himself. Carter Melk, another poet, was gentle but wordless. I miss both of them, but not the university, with its intense, secret rivalries, reminiscent of a medieval court.

"So what did your chump do?" he asks.

"Charlie? Why's he a 'chump'?"

"He let you go, didn't he?"

"I left him. Finally. We took turns over the years. But I got the last curtain."

Charlie! something within me shrieks. The thought of him remains impossible. It's like some trauma I can never fully recall—a bad fall, a beating. With Charlie, what I can't recollect is what I ever saw in him. I remember as a fact, like the capitals of the fifty states, that for many years I felt under his spell. But he was a cad. Autocratic. Self-absorbed. I reestablish that point a hundred times each day. This morning, waking up, I had a clear memory of how often I was scratched by his toenails in bed at night. No matter how reasoned my appeal, he refused to cut them.

"And what did he do?"

"You mean to irritate me?"

"No. That's a short list, right? Guys are so predictable: he didn't love you enough, he didn't pay enough attention, he got hung up on some-one else."

"Right, right, and right," I say.

"No, how'd he make money? Doctor, lawyer, Indian chief?"

"A poet."

"No way."

"It's true. He didn't make *much* money. He's got a teaching appoint-ment at a university near Cincinnati now. But there was a long period while we were together when he refused to teach. He had a feud at the English department. He was a mailman then." We've made a full circuit of the walk. Three blocks from the courthouse and the depleted south rim of the Center City, the lower shapes of a struggling residential area rise up: mercados, taverns, shingle-sided frame houses, the wonderful gilded church spire of the Serbian church, notched like a key to the gates of heaven.

"So he hooked up with a rich lawyer, huh?"

I laugh at the idea. "No, Charlie never approved of my legal career. Rules. Forms. Those are the kinds of particulars he always thought were trivial. 'The detritus of living.' That's from one of his poems. Even when I was a prosecutor, he didn't see the point of what I was doing."

"He wanted the guilty to go free?"

"I think he just would have preferred to banish them. Ship them all elsewhere. Make it go away. That was Charlie's usual approach to a problem."

I had always thought I saw life more or less Charlie's way and was shocked to discover that the law was the sort of thing for which I had some gift. A few times in my last term of law school, I went to court. I was working with the State Defenders Office, allowed under local procedure to stand up in court on little misdemeanor cases. Once, afterwards, I went to the food store from the courthouse, and there as I was looking at the shining clustered heads of a pint of blackberries, I realized that what I had been doing a few minutes before, my ease in addressing a judge, begging mercy for the wretched and the weak, was quite beyond Charlie, who was anguished with words, not merely in his poems, but even in contemplating what might be spoken in his classroom to eighteen-year-olds who for the most part wanted no more wisdom from him than some surefire way to get through English I. Somehow this thought of our relative abilities had never come to me in precisely that fashion. I was accustomed, in fact, to thinking of Charlie as possessed of something empyrean and magical, the stuff, if not of genius, at least of art, but now, in the grocery, I suddenly took heart from my moment at the rostrum, from my exchange of sharp words with the grubby prosecutor and the dutiful wag of the judge's head, granting my forlorn client a generous sentence of ninety days' probation. And the thought had followed then, part of an inevitable sequence, that in a certain worldly way I was stronger than Charlie, I was hardier, the better survivor. And all that seemed remarkable was how unsurprising it was; I had known this always, and none of it, I recognized, had occurred unwillingly.

"Was *your* breakup bitter?" Seth asks.

I just make a sound at the recollection. Across the oval, I recognize another runner, Linda Larsen, Judge Bailey's clerk, and I wave.

"I'm bitter about Charlie. But not my marriage. I'm actually beginning to see it as a useful phase for both of us. It got Charlie away from Rebecca. His first wife. No one should be stuck with Rebecca. And it got me through my illness. He proposed to me when I had no hair from the radiation."

"You had no hair and he had a wife?"

"Exactly."

"Modern," he says.

"Post-modern," I answer. "Sometimes, when I'm in the dumps about it, I wonder of course."

"About what?"

"About whether I meant to leave Charlie all along. You know, did I always know my marriage was doomed?"

He appears confused.

"I mean my mother," I say. "Okay? I was raised by this woman alone. And here I am doing the same thing. And I wonder if I didn't feel a certain destiny there. The older I get, the more like her I'm afraid I am."

"You're nothing like her, Sonny. Nothing." Even as we continue moving, he reaches across and grips my wrist urgently, much as I gripped his. His green eyes are enlarged. "She was cra-zy."

As if pierced by an airborne spear, I am suddenly revisited by the pain of that—remembering how weird everybody thought Zora was. I could never stand to say it to myself, that Zora was not ordinary, not right. Tiny, walleyed from a childhood accident with firecrackers, she spoke with urgency and volume, always regaling me with memorized quotations from writers of leftist spirit, Walt Whitman through Maud Gonne, and free-association gossip about figures from the labor movement. She was on a thousand obscure quests. She prowled junk shops and used-book stores seeking treasures—apothecary bottles, button boxes, squared-off paperclips with little wire curlicues, writings that were lost: a rare translation of Rubén Darío's *Songs of Life and Spirit*; George Eliot's *Felix Holt, the Radical*. She always addressed me in lavishly endearing terms—'my precious darling,' 'my treasure'—and at the best moments—often!—it was true. To be the object of all of Zora's galvanic passion was to stand at the center of the world. But there were other times when she was, in the perfect phrase, carried away.

She once lost me in the maelstrom she provoked at a local PTA meeting, where she had appeared to rail against the inclusion of the words 'under God' in the Pledge of Allegiance. In that era, when men didn't baby-sit and working women were not expected to spend their earnings on child care, I was often in tow, at organizing meetings, steering-committee debates. I played with dolls beneath the dining-room tables and was comforted with nickel Cokes, while my mother and the others furiously argued doctrine and smoked unfiltered cigarettes. But on this night Zora was not among friends. Instead, alone but for me, she confronted the neighborhood of lunch-pail tradesmen in which she'd been raised in Kewahnee. I was a thin, dark child in my cousin's cast-off cardigan and skirt, clutching a rag doll and some hem of my mother's apparel. Zora gestured wildly, her unraveled voice emerging with expectorant pops at ear-splitting volume as she screamed into a microphone. Ultimately, she was hated from the room: 'Get out, you little Polack nut. You godless Commie bitch. Go back to Moscow.' Amid the brandished fists, the agitated throng, I was suddenly alone, pushed along, but uncertain Zora had even noticed I was missing. The moment went on and on. I stood there shrieking, Mommy! Then I was retrieved, almost absentmindedly, snatched up by Zora as she turned heel to reply to someone with foul-mouthed invective.

That's what Seth and I saw in each other, though neither of us knew it then. We both had come of age with parents who weren't in the swing, exiles from the mainstream.

"Tell me about your daughter," he says eventually. That is always pure pleasure. We talk at length. Her costumes. Her moods. The glories of kindergarten. Heading back, we cross the arc of the concrete overpass above the highway and jog through the little Italian neighborhood, where there are still bakeries with dark awnings and sub shops with a crucifix or Sacred Heart over the tables. At this hour, the row of restaurants—Jenna's, Mama Sesta's—are full of a bustling pack of lawyers and courthouse employees. A few tables will remain occupied by men and women who, by whatever whim of fortune, can drink the afternoon away. A grey-haired man, wearing a short-sleeve shirt despite the cold, stands on the walk before his tiny home, suspiciously eyeing everyone and enjoying a cigarette.

A few doors down, there is a wonderful greengrocery, Molinari's. In this season, Jocko has beautifully pyramided the citrus. Space heaters glow, running on extension cords right out here on the street. We each buy mountain water and a gorgeous Granny Smith apple.

"Jesus, look at me," says Seth as we leave the store. His shirt is soaked through and even his sport coat is dampened in a semicircle beneath one arm. He'll have to return to the Hotel Gresham, he says, turn his jacket over to the concierge. We walk back toward the courthouse.

"You sound awfully heroic about everything," he says. "It's got to be tough. The divorce, the cancer. Single mom. You're pretty resolute."

"The divorce," I say, "was a necessity. And Nikki is my joy. Being sick was terrible, but I think I've pretty much left it behind. Every six months or so, I have nightmares, and then there are a few hours when I'm back to scratch. But most days I'm—what did you say? Resolute? Resolved. Not heroic. What I'm gladdest of—proud of—is that I didn't become the disease. You know that starts in the hospital. They act as if you don't have a name. They identify you by the procedure. 'You're a mastectomy.' 'You're a colostomy.' It's so easy to think that this illness that's threatening your life *is* your life. And I got past that. I had my baby. I took this job. Eventually, you say it happened," she says. "Bad things happen. Cancer or divorce. They happen. You know?" I mean it, I believe it. And yet the stress of these cataclysms still rebounds. I must have learned more about myself later than most human beings. The last dozen years, the point when my friends from college seemed to have a collection of habits and chosen reflexes they called a life— for me the same period has been like a bombing run, one explosive surprise after another. Getting sick. Getting back together with Charlie. Finishing law school. A baby. Divorce. The bench. When? I wonder, considering it all, when, when will I come to rest, be in a place of comfort, or at least repose?

"Bad things happen," Seth repeats, and I recognize only now what was contained in his observation about being resolute. I feel unconscionably dull, even though my aching for him continues to engird me, as if my rib cage had been irradiated.

"It takes a long time, Seth."

"People say." He catches my eye. He's heard it all. I begin to apologize, but he interrupts. "I wasn't going to mention it," he says. "I really hate—"

"Oh, Seth. I just—" It would break my heart to think that any old friend, any person who had so much of my life might isolate himself with something like this. And what is it that looms up so large? Life, I'd say. To my amazement, I find, although I'm not a teary person by nature, that I am suddenly crying. He briefly throws an arm around me and I dry my nose on the sweatshirt sleeve from which various threads are hanging. Blessedly for both of us, we are behind the courthouse again, where we started.

"So you got your exercise," he says for lack of anything else. I can only smile. "Do you ever bring Nikki down here? I'd love to see her."

It's an innocent request, but like all else at the moment, it knocks my heart around, thinking about what the sight of friends' kids must be to him, both the torment and the reassurance.

"Come by sometime. When you visit your father. It's 338 Grove."

"It would make the trip worthwhile. Almost," he says. He looks at me. "You better think about it."

"It'll be okay. You're on good behavior and so am I."

"Maybe this weekend?"

"We're in and out both days."

"Whenever."

I hug him quickly. Half a foot shorter than he is, I face him. I know now I was right when he initially stood up in the courtroom and I thought I detected depletion of some kind. Wreckage. Pain. At the Judges' Entrance, I leave him with a slogan of our foregone times.

"You're a good man, Charlie Brown."

April 1970

SETH

Eddgar's expulsion hearings before the Faculty Senate commenced in the third week of April. Sessions ran from 4:00 in the afternoon to 10:00 at night, so faculty members could attend without interrupting their classes. After each evening's adjournment, the Eddgars and their lawyers met for a lengthy planning session, arguing about strategy, gathering information about coming witnesses. Eddgar and June seldom arrived home before two or three in the morning, only a couple of hours before I had to get up to begin distributing *After Dark* to the coin boxes. As a result, I began putting Nile to bed on the living-room sofa in my apartment. Roiled up by my imminent flight to Canada and my breakup with Sonny, I was not sleeping soundly and usually heard one of his parents steal in to retrieve him.

My life in those weeks felt dismal, stillborn, lost. I could not figure out why I had gone on working, why I had not left yet, except that it didn't seem I could take any substantial step in such a shattered state. My induction remained a couple of weeks off, on May 4. Michael, Nile, and I continued to eat dinner each night, but they were sorry gatherings, silent except for the TV which Nile watched. I felt Sonny's absence acutely, and Michael, even for Michael, was remote. He claimed his lab was preoccupying him, but I sensed his affair with June had moved to a critical new stage. Those days each of them seemed tense in the other's presence.

After Nile was asleep, I would lie on the mattress on our bedroom floor—where I now slept alone—my transistor clutched to my ear as I listened to the hearing sessions being broadcast on campus radio at Eddgar's demand. It reminded me of when I was seven or eight and used to lie beneath the blankets at home with the volume on my radio reduced to a secretive hush, listening to the Trappers baseball games in what I now unexpectedly regarded as happier times.

The case against Eddgar depended principally on evidence gathered by the campus police. For all the talk of snitches, none had come forward. Nor did they appear to be needed. The cops had photographs. They showed the PLP members in their gas masks. And in the picture that became more or less the signature of the case, the mystery woman, the girl who'd shrieked and disappeared, was portrayed emerging from the crowd. One moment, she was unmarked. Then her hand was at her face. Streaks of dark blood were shown running from her crown, but, said the faculty prosecutor, something was dropping from her hand. A vial? She was identified from mug shots as Laura Lancey, an employee at Bayside Packers, the canning plant where June worked. As Eddgar's lawyers pointed out, none of this proved she was not beaten; none of this implicated Eddgar, even if it was assumed that Eddgar was acquainted with the young woman, which he emphatically denied. But the sequence of photos—the university produced the numbered contact sheets—showed Eddgar looking twice across his right shoulder, behind himself to the area of the broad pea-gravel plaza where Laura Lancey eventually emerged. As if he knew something was going to happen there. Eddgar's lawyers claimed the negatives had been reversed.

In the café discussions on Campus Boul, there were few testimonials to Eddgar's character. No one supposed he was above violence or lying about it afterwards. He was, after all, a revolutionary, dedicated to undermining bourgeois institutions. But if the university was held to the standards of the system it wanted to defend, its evidence seemed flimsy. Eddgar's speech was just that, a speech. The faculty prosecutor tried to establish that Eddgar had been on campus, aiding the rioters. Two cops claimed they had glimpsed Eddgar, supposedly helping the fellow who tumbled from the police station roof, but they admitted being several hundred feet away at the time. The police had also retrieved a shirt from a trash container on campus. It had a One Hundred Flowers armband tied on one sleeve and the pointillistic remnants of what the prosecutor claimed were Eddgar's initials printed in the collar years before when he still sent his shirts to the Chinese laundry. The ironies of this bit of evidence were not lost on anyone.

I knew Eddgar was guilty. Until the hearing, I'd never bothered squarely facing that, but the recognition settled on me with barely a ripple of surprise. But I found myself vaguely hopeful that he would get off anyway, even though I still wasn't sure I was on his side. In my present mood, though, I was sympathetic to anybody forced to confront harsh authority.

Over the months, Nile and I had found our own rhythm. Sometimes we drew on the sidewalk with chalk, sometimes he let me play a snarling man who could not reach him when he threw things down at me from the treehouse. He still preferred to watch TV in my apartment, but he favored me with questions now and then, provoked by what he was seeing. Why was the boy mad at the girl on account of the other girl? Sometimes he called on me to confirm the lessons his father relentlessly taught him.

"Commercials are just big lies, right?"

"A lot of them."

"They just want you to buy stuff. They're just greedy, right?"

"Maybe they think what they're selling will help you, man."

"They're greedy," Nile repeated. Greed was a sin that Eddgar, especially, furiously denounced. "They don't want to help the peoples. They don't care about the peoples." His eyes lit in space, fixing on some troubled judgment about the world and, perhaps, himself.

Despite June's persistent efforts to shelter him, Eddgar's expulsion hearings inevitably took a toll on Nile as well.

"We're moving," Nile told me one night in April. "Did you know we're getting another house somewhere else?"

I tried to be encouraging and suggested that might not be the case.

"June says." His head bobbed emphatically. "Are you getting another house with us?"

At June's insistence, I made only the vaguest references to my plans. She believed he couldn't handle my departure, particularly with their own situation so unsettled, a judgment that seemed well supported by Nile's surprisingly morose response when Sonny had moved out. Sonny had spent time with Nile only at meals, but she was always kind to him and from the start she had been far better attuned to his moods than I was. Back in the winter, I'd complained about the way Nile seemed to disappear into the TV, immune to any other distraction.

'Don't you see he's depressed?' she had answered. She was seated, legs akimbo, on our bed, surrounded by books like tribute.

'Depressed? He's a kid. What's he got to be depressed about?'

'Weren't you depressed as a child? Isn't that what you're always talking about?'

'I was terrified, man. I'm not sure that's depressed. Why? Were you depressed?'

She shrugged and turned a page, intent. But some impulse escaped her.

'I mean, baby,' she said, 'you have to look at that house. Think what that's like: to be the child of a revolutionary, someone who's always spouting off about these visions of what's bigger and more important than anything or anyone, including you.'

'You mean Nile's got like sibling rivalry with Chairman Mao?' I was, as usual, greatly entertained by myself and could not understand Sonny's sizzling, vexed expression, or why she turned back to her books so bitterly.

Yet she was right. Nile was one of those kids for whom growing up just seemed to be hard. He was always in scrapes of one kind or another at school and often perceived himself as the victim of terrible physical ailments. Any cut, no matter how microscopic, inspired prolonged weeping. He sometimes wore as many as six adhesive strips on his limbs.

One night in the fall, when I was alone with him, I had heard Nile padding to the john. I was startled because he had never gotten up before. He had stripped off his clothes and stood shivering. He wore only a huge diaper which lapped gigantically around him.

'I'm wet,' he said, hardly a necessary announcement. The smell was strong. I washed him, as he quivered, his eyes, dark like his mother's, heavy with sleep.

'Tell my mom I go'd,' he said.

During the hearings, I covered my sofa in a plastic sheet and assured Nile that I was unconcerned about accidents. With my departure at hand, I didn't care if the place reeked. Throughout the months June had never addressed the subject with me. She never told me what to do to help, or confessed that this was why she'd insisted Nile sleep in his own bed. It was one more secret of their household, which, like the rest of what I knew, I was expected to maintain in silence.

The night Eddgar finished his testimony, he showed up to collect Nile. I had heard every word on the campus radio and thought he had done a fine job in his own behalf. He denied any intention of inciting to riot, said he'd never met Laura Lancey, and claimed he had returned to his apartment as soon as the demonstration at the ARC turned to violence. He had no role, he said, in the ensuing melee on campus. He sounded equable, the soul of reason. I suspected that much of what he said was true—that he had been careful never to meet Laura Lancey. But his voice did not betray him in any way, even in the moments that I knew he was uttering unvarnished lies. On cross-examination the prosecutor contented himself with the text of Eddgar's many classroom lectures and public speeches.

'In addressing a group, have you ever repeated the saying "Political power grows out of the barrel of a gun"?'

'Of course, I have. That's a matter of theory.'

'You have called for armed struggle, for violence?'

'At the proper time.'

'And who is it who decides the time, Dr. Eddgar?'

The defense lawyer objected, and eventually the senate president cut off questioning.

I told him now I thought it had gone well.

"To no avail," he answered. "The end is a foregone conclusion. I must admit that was always one of my favorite theological puzzles. Why did Jesus say what he did on the cross? You know the part I'm referring to? About his father forsaking him? Hadn't the poor fool known what was coming? Did his father send him down here with no warning? What kind of relationship did they have, any old way?" He laughed in his usual quiet fashion when something amused him alone.

I asked about the closing arguments, scheduled for tomorrow, but Eddgar appeared uninterested. His eyes fell to the two cardboard boxes of Sonny's belongings she'd left behind. I'm sure he assumed they were mine.

"When will you go?" he asked.

"Next week." This was the second week in a row that I'd said that. At times, I feared I would never propel myself, that I'd wait until some ugly vortex—the FBI or secret military dragoons—sucked me down to a blackish fate. For the moment, though, I used the hearings as my excuse. I would go as soon as the Eddgars were settled again.

"And your parents—are they still hounding you?" he asked.

"Relentlessly." My mother had taken money—her own funds, her *knipple*, saved out of the household money—and bought an open ticket to Vancouver. My father said she had also packed a suitcase. There was only one in the house I knew of, a brown lacquered valise hard as an insect shell, and I imagined it now poised by the front door.

"Perhaps you should rethink being kidnapped."

We laughed. I had, at moments, returned to the idea. It gave me a vicious thrill to imagine my father pinioned that way—between his child and his money. An antique theme. Midas came to mind, although I tended to think more about Jack Benny, one of my father's favorites, and his famous bit where a robber with a gun and a mask accosts Jack.

'Your money or your life,' the robber demands, and Jack, after a splendid long take, answers, 'I'm thinking, I'm thinking.'

Driving my delivery route, turning things over obsessively, like rolling dice, I thought I could measure the true probabilities. Each time, I pushed my imagination further along the train of likely events. My father was too shrewd not to sense the ruse. Of course. He'd see it was far too convenient. Far too coincidental. But my mother would never rouse herself to disbelief—no matter how unlikely the threat to my well-being. She would cry. She would pull on the sleeves of her dress, fumble with her hands, follow him about, crying all the time, begging him in German, shrieking and beleaguering him. He would give in. He would part with the money, suspecting all along that I had exacted a price to leave him in peace.

"It's like I said a while ago: he'd pay in the end and I'd be no better off than I was to start. It's not really workable."

"Oh, there's always a way. It's only details," Eddgar added, as if particulars were not the stuff of life.

I was seated in the living-room armchair, picking at the threadbare patch where the ticking showed through.

"You don't honestly think I should do this, man, do you?"

"Seth, what I think you should do is join the armed struggle. But I'm not so foolish as to believe that's likely to occur right now." He'd picked up Nile's stuffed animal and his blanket and he put them down now on the sofa, where the boy still slept, oblivious to our hushed conversation. "May I tell you a story? This is the worst story I know. The worst. I hate even to think about it. But I have a point to make."

He sat down on a milk crate we used as a coffee table and paused to hike each of his pants legs, his preparations deepening the mood.

"When I was fourteen years old," Eddgar said, "I went with my father to the Overlook Valley Hunt Club. What it is in the life of the South — what it is that when there are so many as six prosperous white families in a 50-square-mile region they will organize themselves in either a hunt club or a country club or some similar pastoral enterprise, what it is I have never fully explained to myself, but my father, like his father, was a member of this club, and on Saturday afternoons, as his week was at an end and he prepared himself for our Sabbath on Sunday, he would adjourn to this club and drink Tennessee whiskey until the sun had set and my father was drunk as a lord. I was terribly embarrassed to see my father in that condition — he took a high red color, bright as a geranium, and it was also an unscrupled breach of his own religious principles for which he never made one word of apology. I hated to go with him, but I was raised in the kind of family where you simply said, 'Yes, Daddy,' when something was required and so I went along on many a Saturday, becoming, I suppose, educated in a tradition which I'm sure he expected me to take up as my own, listenin to large men with the characteristic names — Bear and Dog Head and Billy Ray — drinking bourbon with mint and sugar water, telling about critters they had shot and women they had known. All right?" he asked.

With this story, Eddgar was at home — in every sense. His lexicon had changed and his accent deepened. He had told the tale many times, I knew, practiced it, but Eddgar held me as he always did. I nodded quickly for him to go on.

"Well, the tiny little town of Overlook was near the club and you had to drive directly through it to get back to my father's plantation. It was like most little Southern towns: white and colored patches separated by the railroad tracks; not so much as a streetlight yet because we hadn't gotten Rural Electrification. And one evening when my father had drunk himself silly, turned red as those dirt roads, just absolutely radiating the heat of drink, he came flyin round the corner and plowed smack into the front of some old shivering heap that was stopped politely at a sign there in the colored section. I must say this wreck shook up both my daddy and me. He bounced his head against the windshield and took a good lick there, and began spouting a skinny little stream of blood that ran down into his eyes, but finally we collected ourselves and looked out to see some poor Negro man climbing out the door of *his* car, a rural fellow in a checkered shirt and soiled overalls, who considered the mess that had been made of his Ford. Its entire front end was stove in, completely limp and useless, except for this little white-hot hiss of steam shooting out like some starving cousin of Old Faithful.

"Now by whatever principle of misfortune that was then operating in Overlook, there was not another witness on that street, not another soul besides this man and my daddy and me who'd seen my father come tearing round that corner, as if the devil himself were in pursuit. And my father got out of his car and he came up to this man—not someone I knew, just some poor terrified black fellow—and my father looked at him and he pointed to his head and he said, 'Nigger, you see what you done? Now you got one minute to get some of those other boys out here and get this car of your'n outta my way, or I'm gonna be callin Bill Clayburgh and I'm gonna have him run you in.'

"Well, I suppose I should have been used to that. I can't tell you how my father treated the sharecroppers. When I was a boy, there was one fellow who had accidentally killed a cow, and my father and Billy Clayburgh, the sheriff, and some other white men hog-tied that fellow and held him under the river until he admitted killing that cow and agreed to let the price of that cow be taken out of the pitiful sum that was called his wages. But this wasn't the plantation, this was town, where my father was, as a general matter, better behaved. But I guess his true colors, so to speak, were showing. And he looked that poor man up and down, up and down, that poor black man who stood there wondering, Can this really be happening, can this white man just shoot around a corner, drunk enough that you can smell it standing five foot away, and make a total wreck out of my car that I worked so hard for and give me not a penny's recompense? Can he do that, or is there some small particle of goodness in this world that will prevent that? And then he looked past my father and caught sight of me in the front seat. His eyes loitered on mine. It wasn't a plaintive look, cause this man knew better than that and he was surely too proud to beg. He just looked and kind of asked me in a way, You too? You gonna do this too? Is this here going on and on? I knew what he wanted and so did my daddy, and he just said, 'Don't you look at him, he seen the same as I have.' And I said not a word.

"Well, that fellow didn't have any choice then and soon enough the man did what my daddy told him. He went in and out of some of the little houses, with their tarpaper sides, and collected some of his kin, some friends from out of a store up on the next corner, and by and by they came out and pushed the car out of the way and we left there. And my father, he wasn't done, he rolled his window down and said, 'Don't you niggers let this happen again neither.'

"And I say this is the worst story I know, because I just watched. I was fourteen years old. But I knew right from wrong. I knew brute authority from justice. And I spoke not a word. Not because my heart didn't ache to do it. But because I lacked the courage. I hadn't planned my escape well enough in my mind. I hadn't yet prepared the path to my own freedom. Oh, I wept my eyes out that night and the nights following. And my resolve grew. And I swore to myself that whatever happened, I would never tie my tongue out of fear of my father or anyone else who was doing what I knew to be plain wickedness. In the years since, I have often heard my father say he raised his worst enemy in his own home, and I take pleasure when I hear him saying that. Because however else I judge myself, I think at least I've kept my word."

He looked up to be sure he had my attention. The voice of a neighbor's TV drifted through the apartment, a commercial for a fast-food chain that seemed boldly inappropriate.

"Now I don't know a thing about you and your father, Seth. But let me tell you this much: Free yourself. If you are going to do something as dramatic as running away from your country and allowing some grand jury to indict you and the FBI to hunt for you coast to coast—make sure that it's not for nothing and that you are free on your own terms. If you can't make my revolution, then make your own revolution. Make the revolution you can—and triumph at it. That's what I say."

He lifted up his sleeping boy and barely brought his lips to Nile's brow, while his eyes remained on me, knowing that as ever he'd made a deep impression.

Eddgar was expelled the next day, April 30. More than three-quarters of the faculty voted in favor. Jeering members of One Hundred Flowers were dragged off by Damon's finest as they stood with placards, heckling the president of the university when he returned home from the meeting. Eddgar addressed the cameras of virtually every California television station. Freedom of speech and thought, he said—the supposed cardinal values of university life—had been exposed, he said, as a fiction, a sham, a quilted coverlet masking the iron face of political rigor and reactionary values.

In spite of the high drama, Eddgar's story did not remain at the top of the news. By 11 p.m., when Michael and I took our places in the bedroom where I'd moved the TV set in deference to Nile's sleep, the lead item was Richard Nixon's address to the nation earlier in the evening. I had read that the speech was coming, but like everyone else never anticipated the content. Now Nixon announced he was sending U.S. soldiers into the Cambodian Fish Hook to rout out North Vietnamese supplies and troops, and also bombing their supply routes in Laos. The screen filled with Nixon's shadowy, humorless mug as the President, in one of his Orwellian fabrications, assured the nation that the war was not expanding.

"Can you believe this?" I asked Michael, who replied with a limp shrug. The newsreader ran on to other matters—Eddgar's expulsion; the news that the judge at the Kopechne inquest had questioned Edward Kennedy's veracity; suspicion that Juanita Rice and her captors had robbed another bank in West L.A. Michael eventually slipped out, saying he was sleepy, while I continued fulminating. After all Nixon's talk about how the war was winding down, he was invading another nation. After all the protests, the marches, the mobilized dissent—after all *my* pain—Nixon was still in the spell of the generals and his ingrained paranoia. He was refusing to bow to the Commies as always, struggling to win a war he could only lose, killing young men for the ego and profit of old ones, and proving, as if he meant to, the correctness of those who had contended all along that only far more dramatic measures would breed change.

Within the hour, I heard voices blaring behind the apartment. Out on Campus Boul, protesters had commandeered the microphone at a drive-thru fast-food restaurant and were exclaiming, in the amplified voice, "*Dick* Nixon! *Dick* Nixon!" Another group was in the middle of the street, bringing traffic to a skidding halt and chorusing back something similar about Spiro Agnew. I hung through the open window. At top volume, I screamed right along—*Dick* Nixon—yelling until Nile woke and my throat felt so raw I imagined it might be bloody.

With the news the following morning, I came to believe that I'd been briefly wrested from sleep by the boom of what I took for a storm. That remains my memory—a single vague concussive pock bouncing off the clouds. I'm still not certain.

I was in the shower just after five, when I heard footsteps thundering up the stairs—a determined pounding, oblivious of the hour. There was a single phenomenal bang overhead, which seemed to shake the building, and then, I was sure, shouting. I opened the front door of the apartment and saw three Damon coppers on the landing. They were in full battle gear, helmets and shiny boots and bulletproof vests. They had their riot batons drawn. One of them saw me and said, "Get back inside." I had only a towel around my waist, but even half-naked I found that my reflexive regard for high authority had fled.

"Go fuck yourself," I replied. It was a sign of how my sense was failing. He reared back as if he had been struck, lifting his baton from his side.

There were shouts above, and footfalls again shook the wooden stairwell so hard I could feel them. With his arms cuffed from behind, Eddgar was pushed down the steps with a cop at each side.

"What the hell?" I asked.

I thought Eddgar smiled as he went by. His dark hair was tousled and he wore pants but no shoes and socks. The three cops, including the one who was prepared to hit me, took off to clear the way. They wrestled Eddgar down the stairs and threw him in the back of a squad car parked below whose noisy radio voice I'd heard but hadn't really noted. When I looked up, June stood a few feet in front of her threshold in her long white night shift, clutching Nile, who wore solely his large diaper. Only now he began to cry. Behind them, I could see the door of the apartment, smashed off the hinges and split; fresh wood was revealed in the rent, as with a lightning-struck tree.

"What in God's name?" I brought them into my apartment. June was shaking. I dressed Nile and laid him down on my sofa. The diaper, of course, was soaked. I spent a great deal of time soothing him, and June soon joined me. Apparently, he had not seen most of it, but Nile was awake as his father had been cuffed and hustled out. June and I kept assuring him that Eddgar was all right. Finally, he accepted our advice and with little warning went back to sleep. June and I sat in the kitchen, drinking tea and whispering.

"They just broke in?"

"They said they had an arrest warrant. I never saw it." She lit a cigarette. In an act of hapless modesty, she had thrown an old green knitted shawl over herself before leaving her apartment. She sat in my kitchen in her cotton nightdress, clutching her bare arms.

"For what? What are they busting him for?"

She pondered her cigarette. "The bomb," she said. "Last night. About 1:00 in the morning actually—the ARC was bombed. The whole west wing of the building was destroyed. Most of the labs over there." She described the explosion scene, dust and bricks blown a quarter of a mile.

I asked about injuries.

"The building was—" she said and stopped. "You'd think the building would be empty. They're saying—" June faltered again. "Someone was in his lab late. One of the profs. He's hospitalized. They claim he lost his hand, an arm."

"Oh God. And they arrested Eddgar for it?"

"This is what it's going to be like. Now. I keep telling him that. This is what the faculty did. This is what they've intended. They've stripped away the last vestiges—the last protective plumage of class membership. This is going to happen again and again. Any occasion. Any excuse. It doesn't matter how careful we are. You understand that, don't you?" She leaned toward me with rare directness and grasped my hand. Over time, my relationship with June had acquired a subtle confidential air, beginning, I guess, the day I saw her in all her glory on Michael's threshold. On nights she was home before Eddgar, she poured herself two fingers of bourbon, an indulgence she occasionally allowed herself, particularly outside his presence, and talked to me about her household. With the tumbler in hand, she could emit a languorous air, taking all her weight on her heels, an elbow laid on the kitchen countertop. Sometimes she worried out loud about Nile—his social adjustment, his reading. Occasionally there were candid remarks about Eddgar, issued as her eye rose to meet mine above her glass, which I knew I was expected to maintain in strictest privacy. For me, she was a bit of a confidante, as well. I told her about my parents and of course, as I did with everyone else I knew, poured out my anguish to her about my breakup with

Sonny. But she spoke to me now as I imagined she talked to someone else, someone who knew her far better than I did.

"We have to get out of here," June said, "I keep telling him that. He won't listen, he doesn't care, he thinks he's prepared for what's coming. He *wants* it to happen to him. He still believes that suffering is good for the soul. He's still wound up in so many crazy ideas. I keep telling him to think about Nile. And he keeps asking me if I don't love the revolution, repeating that a child can't be harmed by the truth." She stubbed out the cigarette emphatically. She massaged her neck and wondered aloud if she should have a drink to collect herself, and then concluded that it would be better not to get started, the day would be difficult enough.

With her own thoughts, she stood and strolled barefoot about the apartment. The tassels of the shawl were brought close to her mouth. I was struck how Eddgar's enigma loomed even to June, more unfathomable than these strange events. She paused before the empty bookcases along the walls, relics of Sonny's departure. The thought of my troubles apparently provided a respite from her own.

"How's the heart?" she asked.

"A mess." During the days, I had taken to repeatedly playing on my phonograph a terrible overproduced version of "You Keep Me Hangin' On," by Vanilla Fudge. With the music at 10, I screamed along with the mounting clamor of cymbals and the whining guitars. Everyone for three blocks must have known I was in agony.

"Have you spoken?"

"She calls. To make me crazy. Every other night." Sonny was being responsible, not abandoning the cripple, making me vow that I'd see her before I left. They were brief thwarted conversations in which I pivoted between rage and terrible longing.

"There is surely nothing like young love," said June dolefully. I spent an instant trying to imagine the Eddgars at this stage, as young lovers, still on the threshold with each other. What he saw in her seemed clear to me: one of those bold girls, a rebel beneath the veneer of genteel manners. He was wedding courage. A man could never have too much of that on his own. But why did she choose him? Eddgar was going to be a preacher then, and she a preacher's wife. She had to know she wasn't one for the country club, the cotillions, or the teas. Why him? Why Eddgar? His commitments, I thought, they must have shone with the power of the sun. She must have had some tussle with herself. She must have thought she was going to purify herself in the fiery forge of Eddgar's faith. Idle guesses, but they came to me with the mettle of conviction. She had finally settled again at the small table beside her teacup and lit another cigarette.

"I still don't understand what gives with the cops?" I said. "How could they blame Eddgar? After last night?" I told her about what had happened on Campus Boul. More than a hundred people had gathered before the Damon cops had moved everyone along. "People are really pissed now. Really pissed. It could have been anybody, right?"

"Right," June said dully. Her eye did not meet mine. Instead, she looked through a ring of smoke. "Look. It's all ridiculous. They know he's covered. They don't care. They'd know he'd *have* to be covered. Let them assume what they like. Whatever they like. After all of this, could he possibly be that careless? He was with his lawyers until almost three last night. The same men who are going to bail him out can alibi him. But they don't care." She touched the shawl to her eyes. "They're probably going to come back for me soon. I should count myself lucky they didn't take me now. Will you look after Nile?"

"Of course, but that's not going to happen." I tried to comfort her, but she was convinced she was in peril, that Eddgar and she were now the targets of unreasoning oppression. "Were you with the lawyers, too?" I asked her.

"Most of the time. I left about midnight."

The bomb, she had said, was at 1:00. Her eyes lit on mine and then deflected a bit.

"And?" I asked.

"What?"

"Can you account for yourself?" I sounded stiff enough to be my father.

"If it comes to that," she answered, and then canted her head vaguely across the kitchen, indicating the wall that adjoined Michael's place. She closed her eyes momentarily, smote by some new pain that crimped her mouth. "You might as well know," she said. "He was quite upset. Quite. He didn't take this news very well. He's appalled. Completely appalled. His life is in those labs. He could have been there. He knows this man." She dropped her head into her hands. When she lifted her face, worn by worry, she looked right at me. "He thinks he was betrayed," she said.

On the way to work, I joined the little dribble of gawkers who had already come up the road to the ARC. The iron gates were drawn closed and you could see that the police were out and ready to cordon off the road farther down toward campus. I was astonished that at 6 a.m., in the weak light of sunrise, I was not the sole spectator. Cars were parked along the gravel road and we all stood, twenty or thirty of us, with our hands to the bars, as if we were at the zoo. The others seemed to be people who had driven down from the city and the bedroom burbs of Alameda to see what a bomb really does.

What it did in this case was to gouge up a substantial crater in which the scattered rubble of the building was heaped—bricks, glass, plaster, pieces of pipe, the odd randomly intact remnants of walls and floor tile. Hours later, there was still an impression of dust in the air. An entire projecting wing of the building was gone. It looked like the remains after the wrecking ball. A latticework of iron supports between the walls and floors was revealed at points, while a lone beam, corkscrewed by the force, protruded from the portion of the building that was standing, along with twisted piping and a single strand of black wire, balled up like a kink of hair where the walls were torn away. The fractioned remains of the third floor—risers, subfloor, three blown-out windows, and a piece of a lab table—hung midair at a 40-degree angle. And the roof was torn off, even where the walls looked sound, so that the building reminded you of a bald-headed man. Out on the lawn of the facility, a yellow tape barrier had been stretched. Beside me, a portly, grey-haired man, with a plaid shirt and plastic pocket protector, pointed out to his wife a chunk of brick, resting on the lawn, which needed to be mowed.

I was late for work, but unconcerned. My final day would be tomorrow. I'd taken my transistor, and on the hour, I stopped wherever I was along my delivery route to listen to news. Nixon's speech had brought a turbulent reaction on campuses across the country. At Ohio State University, one hundred students had been arrested, three wounded and seventy more injured in an angry confrontation with National Guardsmen, who had shot at them with rubber bullets to break up an antiwar demonstration. Twenty thousand people were expected in New Haven to rally in support of Bobby Seale, the co-chairman of the Black Panther Party, who was on trial there along with twenty other Panthers, charged with conspiring to murder a snitch named Alex Rackley. But the accounts of the ARC bombing dominated the local news. The injured physicist was in surgery at the Damon Medical Center, and the radio reports said more than ten people had been taken in for questioning.

Listening to the accounts, I felt vaguely vindicated, almost cheerful. The world was being made to pay for its madness. I was in the city, in Noe Valley, filling a coin box on 18th Street, when I heard a report that shrunk my innards in panic. FBI, ATF, and police experts, sifting the debris at the ARC, had come up with a number of items that they believed had been used to prepare the device. Included were the scorched remains of a single can of battery acid.

I had no idea what to do about Hobie. We had not spoken in weeks. I told myself again and again that he wasn't involved, that it was a stupid coincidence, but of course I could not accept that. On my way home, near three, I stopped at Graeme's. I'd brought along the last of Sonny's boxes. I had been determined simply to leave them by the door, but now she was the only person I could think of to give me cool counsel about Hobie. I rang the bell a number of times. The sky was clear, the day thin and cool, and various bright blooms struggled toward the sunshine in the large garden that fronted Graeme's coach house.

"Sahib." Graham opened the door and rubbed his eyes. He had been sleeping. He was in his American briefs. "You wish?"

"I'd like a word with Sonny."

"Klonsky? Haven't seen her all week, mate. More. The gypsy moth that one. Here and there. Waiting tables down at Robson's. Two shifts. Trying to raise a treasury for her departure. Peace Corps thing seems ready to commence. Going to the Philippines, she is."

She'd shared the news with me during her last call.

"Colorful locale, I suppose," said Graeme. "Whole gambit's a bit unclear to me, I must say. In a dither, really. Beneath the cool exterior. My estimate, at least."

As much as I hated him, it was consoling to hear a judgment so close to mine. Over time, I'd begun to take Graeme's measure. He played a sort of showboat Brit, more English than the Queen. He made few accommodations to the American vocabulary, and uttered Anglicisms whenever he could, as if he remained convinced that the War of Independence had not been decided on cultural merit. At moments, his voice trilled in his Oxford accent; at other times he sounded like a Cockney chimney sweep. He had more shapes than Caliban, a man for all moments, who placed himself above American culture and who, I see now, would have run for hiding if anyone mentioned returning to his homeland. He savored American freedom, and the transposition he'd made to a realm where no one thought the less of his middle-class accent.

"Step in, Kemo Sabe. Neighbor-types get their knickers in a knot when I go traipsing about in my johnnies." He offered me coffee or tiger's milk, but I went no farther than the foyer to drop Sonny's things. Without the exotic party scene, the house was appealing, small but lovely, with marks of money and intellect that reminded me of University Park: simple sofas and large paintings on the walls bristling with emotion, many Mexican artifacts, and rugs thrown down at angles. The tasteful furnishings struck a false note against the sybaritic life Graeme led here. I expected the odor of fucking to linger like traces from a litter box.

He mentioned the bombing, naturally. University people today were speaking of little else. On Campus Boul in the morning, a trio of hippies, lit up on crystal meth, were rambling up and down the walks, crooning that the rev had begun.

"I heard they like found a can of battery acid at the scene. Any idea, man, what that's about?"

"Battery acid," repeated Graeme. He hadn't heard that. "Not too surprising, I'd say. Chemical name sulfuric acid. One of your principal ingredients in nitroglycerine, which every anarchist and revo knows can be mixed with paraffin, guncotton, a few other items to make plastique." He nodded, satisfied as always with his vast learning.

"What about sandbags?" I asked. "They wouldn't have anything to do with this, right?"

"*Au contraire*, laddie. When you've got your high-powered explosive ready to go, you direct it by tamping. Create an aperture for the explosive force. Sandbags the best, apparently. Well-placed sandbag very important to effective bombing, so they say." Graeme scratched his nose. I could not move now. Hobie, I thought. Oh Jesus, Hobie. Graeme was watching me carefully.

"Any little bugger we hold near and dear involved with this battery acid and sandbags?" he asked. Graeme's revolution was made in the bedroom, where the persons present could become a universe without rules, where their conduct could be as uniquely personal as it is within a dream. Otherwise, he preferred peace. As he'd made clear since I met him, he didn't approve of the Eddgars.

"It was just a story I heard, Graeme."

"That so, love? Plenty of stories about. Bloody place is fucking rife with rumor, I'd say. Mythopoesy at work. Psychedelic era, what? Hard to tell fantasy from reality all round. Wouldn't give you twopence for most of what people say." He eyed me coolly—contemptuously. "Jolly good moment to step forward, I'd think. Sell out or watch out, that'd be my advice. Sides have been chosen, love. Best recognize that."

I wasn't sure if he was trying to wring information from me or do me a favor. He passed me a penetrating look, clearly meant in warning, and then nodded his whitish pageboy toward the door. He said he'd tell Sonny I'd come by.

By the time I got home from work, near four, Eddgar had been released. As it turned out, the Damon town police had rounded up the usual suspects—every rad they could find from One Hundred Flowers. Kellett, Eddgar, Cleveland Marsh. Six or seven others. Members of Eddgar's organization had stood vigil outside the police station most of the day, shouting slogans; I felt some momentary guilt that I had not joined them. Around 2:00, Eddgar's lawyers had filed a petition in court, and the police, rather than undergo the hearing, had released him and most of the others. They told Eddgar and the reporters that he remained a suspect. The only one who was still in custody was Cleveland. When they'd picked him up, they'd found four pounds of cocaine and more than one thousand cellophane-wrapped hits of LSD in his apartment. He would be charged with felonies. As Eddgar told me about all of this, I had another anxious thought of Hobie. I knew better than to ask Eddgar about Hobie's role, since revolutionary discipline would prohibit acknowledging anything, but I felt sick with the notion of the phone call I might have to make to Gurney Tuttle.

Near dinner, I went next door to see Michael. He was sitting in the dark in an old easy chair. He wore only blue jeans. His long feet and sinewy chest were bare. As June had suggested, he was shattered.

"You okay?"

He lifted a hand to the light. His eyes were red, swimming in sorrow. His head was crushed back in the chair, matted against his own goldish dreadlocks.

"What a horrible day," he said. It occurred to me that he must have been sitting in that spot for hours. I'd always understood that Michael viewed himself as a neutralist. He cared for Nile; he adored physics. I had no doubt he was in love with June. In all of this, he belonged to a higher, more ephemeral realm, one where a simple purity of feeling was acceptable. Now he'd been injected, against his will, into the rough-hewn world of politics. I felt, of course, enormous kinship for him, as another soul mauled by love.

"You want to talk about it?" I asked.

He shook his head no. Throughout the day, I had pondered how much June was admitting when she told me Michael felt betrayed. I had been sure just a moment before that she was telling me Eddgar and she were blameless. But as I turned over June's spare remarks, trying to collect their logic, I'd seen that as usual there'd been more said than I'd recognized. Near midnight she'd left Eddgar's meeting to be with Michael. That had to have been by design, by prearrangement. And as a result, he was out of the labs, otherwise occupied at the moment of impact. Neither I—nor he—could presume that was accidental. Standing in his bare apartment, I gave him what comfort I could.

"Look, I mean, thinking about it—" I lowered my voice. "She protected you, man," I said. "She did protect you."

He planted the heel of his palm squarely in the middle of his face and began to cry again. The physicist who had been injured was named Patrick Langlois—a Quebecer. He had lost almost all of his right hand. His thumb remained, some ghoulish vestige attached to a fragment of his arm. Even the dry descriptions on the news had been sickening. Michael must have known him well.

From Lucy's remarks, I took it that Michael spoke to June of love, commitment, life together. Yet in imagining their relations, I doubted June was interested in any of that. She was merely seeking some fugitive reprieve in a region of pure feeling, of silence, beyond the territory of doctrine. And a part of Michael must have accepted those terms, even welcomed them. That was his truest dwelling place anyhow. But now he was left to wonder about motivations. What idle comments of his had been passed back through One Hundred Flowers to the slick commandos who brought their plastique and detonators in the dark? What if he hadn't gotten June's message? What if he'd decided to work late, enjoying, as he often did, the hours when he had the vast laboratory to himself? He had to wonder about Eddgar as well. Was he accomplishing revolution or some blow against his wife's lover? Nonetheless, I could guess what the worst part was for him. That June knew. Knew and had bowed to Eddgar's will. In the most telling, the most graphic way, she had demonstrated to everyone her ultimate loyalties. Whatever hopes June had raised in Michael, she could not have more clearly chosen Eddgar over him. She had spoken advisedly. He felt betrayed.

"Dinner, or you want to skip it?"

"Skip it," he answered.

"Look, I'm next door if you just want to hang out, man."

As it happened, June asked if I'd mind Nile while Eddgar and she took a ride. That meant they would talk in the safety of the car, circling the streets for hours, checking the rearview and hatching plans. Nile and I played War and Crazy 8s most of the night.

"Where'd the pigs take Eddgar?" Nile asked.

"To the station." We went over it again and again.

"But they don't arreck children, do they?"

"Absolutely not. Nobody can arrest a child. And Eddgar's fine. Isn't he fine?"

"He's mad. Cause the judge said he could go. When I'm growed up I'm going to be a police."

"You are?"

"Then I can arreck the right people."

"Look, Eddgar's okay. He's fine, right? Doesn't he seem fine?"

"I wouldn't arreck Eddgar!" Nile was instantly overcome with tears. The mere thought of Eddgar often seemed to upset Nile. There was never a spanking; Eddgar seldom yelled. But as a father, he could not keep from being himself, always preaching, teaching, always correcting Nile, moving on to the next lesson as soon as the last one was acknowledged.

At Christmas, I had witnessed an awful scene when Eddgar had attempted to convince Nile to donate one of his few toys, a stuffed pig, to a poor people's collective in East Oakland. The pig was soiled and pilled, not recognizable as much more than an oblong lump the color of your gums, and Nile seldom looked at it now that he had Babu, his handsome stuffed bear, with its pelt of shiny synthetic fur. But when Eddgar explained his plans for the pig, Nile held fast to it, wailing, while Eddgar in his tireless intent way held on too, reasoning implacably with his son about other children who had no toys at all.

'I want it,' Nile replied. 'I want it.' Nile hauled on the pig, and lay back. Finally, with a small pop and a scatter in the sunlight of some dusty filament, the pig suffered the amputation of a leg. Eddgar considered this at length. Eventually, he handed the bigger piece to Nile, then went to the boy's room and removed Babu. Eddgar held the bear far overhead, well out of reach, as he headed to the door.

'This is what the poor children are getting now,' Eddgar announced, his long forehead knotted by a fury that I had seldom witnessed, even when he was inciting on campus. Nile hadn't dared to get back to his feet. He made no sound at all until his father was gone out the door, at which point the boy wailed unbearably. Decimated herself, June fell to her knees and held him in her arms, pietà-like, the two of them crippled by grief.

Now, with his sudden tears about Eddgar, Nile crawled into my arms. He was usually inconsolable—likely to throw tantrums and shirk a comforting hand. Instead, he accepted my embrace and clung. He would not climb down and fell off to sleep. For reasons beyond explaining, it touched me terribly that amid all my troubles—fears for my future, guilt about Hobie, my heartbreak over Sonny—Nile had found this moment to finally regard me with trust. In the dark, I curled myself about the small body, holding his fingers, rough with grime, while I absorbed the fullness of my desire to protect him and the whispered promise of a young life.

Women came and went in my dreams, vague figures with whom I became enmeshed, and whose yearnings I somehow could not tell from my own. I was in the midst of some vivid tableau in which one of us was being desperately pursued, but I could not tell who was following whom. I opened my eyes and June Eddgar sat on my bed. Her hand was on my chest, softly circling, prodding.

"Are you awake?" she whispered. "Seth?" I knew this was not the first time she had said my name.

I sat up. I slept nude and I gathered the sheet, aware suddenly of the stiffness below of a urinary erection. Even when I wakened, June remained comfortably beside me.

I asked where Nile was.

"Upstairs. I took him up hours ago. I've just been lying awake, pondering something. I have to talk to you, Seth. I want you to hear me out." She hiked herself up on the bed and came just a smidgen closer. She wore a cotton night shift and the loose weight of her breasts trembled when she moved. "We need money," she said. "Real money."

I reached beside the bedside for the lamp, careful to hold the sheet and conscious that I'd probably exposed my backside anyway. June sat, unblinking, her hair loose as it had been the day I saw her at Michael's. Her tongue briefly touched her lips while she waited for me to shield my eyes and let the pain of dilation pass. Somehow it struck me that all the years she—any child—spent looking in a mirror, wondering what she would look like as an adult, at her prime—that was how June looked now. Her pretty face had the substance of maturity, the weight of intelligence and purpose. I looked at her as a human being who, unlike me, had finished the journey to whatever it was she was to become. I had no doubt she shared that judgment.

"This money is important," she said. "Very important. We have to get Cleveland out. Soon."

"Is this the bomb?"

"Seth," she said severely. It was the same tone that escaped her against her will now and again when she was scolding Nile. She took a moment to counsel with herself. "There are rumors—you understand, this may all be counter-intelligence by the Damon pigs, everything I'm saying may be, so please bear that in mind—but we've heard rumors that Cleveland is talking. That he's started giving them little things, hoping to get his bond reduced. I don't believe it. But with Eldridge in Algeria there have been a lot of rifts within the Panthers. A lot of internal commotion. And we think it's possible. We've sent his mother to see him. And a lawyer. He's going to have plenty of folks at visitors' hours all weekend. But it's best for all concerned to get him out as soon as possible. Certainly by next week. We have to bail him and get him out of their hands, before he's blabbing his fool head off. Do you hear me?"

"Okay."

"There are many people who have an enormous amount at stake. Not only our people. All right? There are many people, people who haven't really— One of your good friends."

My heart constricted again into a tiny knot at the thought of Hobie.

"Seth, there's no use explaining. No point and no good use of it. But things will work out. I'm sure they will work out. If we can get this money."

I asked how much.

"Thousands. Ten thousand minimum. Fifteen would be better." She measured my astonishment "Now listen." She sat forward and smoothed her hand again across my chest to subdue me. The confident way she touched me lit, not wholly to my liking, the spark of some unruly thrill. "Now hear me out. I've been thinking. And it's a question, I suppose— It's two birds with one stone. I wondered if you would possibly reconsider this plan, this idea we discussed."

She waited until I was the first to speak the word. "Kidnapping?"

She nodded only once, as if there was a caution against speech.

"Jesus," I said.

"It seems to make so much sense from your side."

"I know, but—" The thought of scamming my father, from which I naturally recoiled, also seemed, in some moods, to imbue me momentarily with a wild lightheartedness. There was no doubt he deserved as much. Nonetheless, I shook my head. "I can't torture them. Especially not my mother."

"I think we can work out what concerns you, I truly do. If you felt satisfied that could be avoided—I know how odd this is," she said, "but it seems clear you're going to have to do something drastic. You only have a couple of days." The fourth of May, when I was scheduled for induction, was Monday. "If they knew you were safe, Seth, your well-being was assured, but they had to leave you be, let you go, that would be the best for you now, wouldn't it? Am I right about that?"

I didn't answer, fearful of what I was getting myself into.

"Will you think about this? Please? But there isn't a lot of time."

"I understand. I have to get my head around this one."

We looked at each other.

"I mean," I said, "you guys. I mean, Eddgar and you." I swallowed. "And Nile. I mean you're all in trouble now. Right? Real trouble?"

"Seth—" She stopped. "If Cleveland—" She stopped again. "Right," she said. "Real trouble." She looked into my eyes with purpose. I noticed only now that she had gripped me by both shoulders. There were many young men in June Eddgar's life. I knew that then. She might as well have said it. I had no idea what difference it made; nothing was going to happen between us. But some bond was forged nonetheless, if only because a fragment of me was briefly waked to the reality that other women besides Sonny existed. June padded out, barefoot, her shift clinging to her as she departed, having made a moment when, improbably, desire seemed to be the only real thing in the world.

December 8, 1995

SONNY

Friday morning, before we start, I detain the lawyers to talk about our schedule. The prosecution case will probably take another couple of days. We concluded yesterday with Molto doing a tiresome redirect of Lovinia, reading her snippets of her statements which she claimed not to remember. Following that, Rudy examined Maybelle Downey, an older woman who had witnessed June's shooting from a tenement across from the projects and who confirmed the same outward events Lovinia described. Now Tommy gives me the order of his remaining witnesses. Al Kratzus, the community service officer who told Nile his mother had been murdered, will be first today; after him, Hardcore; by Monday we'll reach Eddgar. Following him, the People will rest. The PA's strategy, apparently, is to buttress Hardcore's credibility by showing that his account coincides with that of witnesses—white people—whose version is largely beyond doubt.

"The defense case, if there is to be one, will start by Wednesday?" I'm informing Hobie, who receives the news impassively. "And what are your plans, Mr. Tuttle? In terms of time? Not committing the defendant to offer evidence, of course, just projecting for my benefit."

"Two days."

"So we'll argue at the end of next week perhaps, or the following Monday?"

The three lawyers before the podium all nod. I will have to decide soon after—a disturbing prospect. The case remains murky. Why did this murder happen? I think suddenly. Frowning, I wave the lawyers away from the bench. Molto repeats the same gesture to Singh, who goes off to summon the next witness.

Aloysius Kratzus, a corpulent, white-haired, thick-necked police veteran fiddles a bit as he sits on the stand. Kratzus has the mark of a guy who went to Community Relations willingly, one of those coppers who started out to be a hero and ended up as a bureaucrat. No one gets shot in Community Relations. No one works graveyard. You dispense bad news, you visit schools, you read press releases over the phone, you front for the Force at funerals and ribbon cuttings. It's either a dead end or a comfortable retirement, depending on how you view things. Al Kratzus seems to like it just fine.

Rudy goes through Kratzus's rank and background and eventually reaches the morning of September 7. He had just come on, Kratzus says, 8 a.m., when he received a call. On his desk, you can envision the coffee and pastry in the white bag from the doughnut shop.

"I spoke with Detective Lieutenant Montague."

"And, Sergeant, was Lieutenant Montague making any orders or requests of you?"

"Montague said he was at a crime scene. White female, approximate age sixty to sixty-five, dead of multiple gunshot wounds. She was found outside a vehicle which was registered to her ex-husband. Montague was going with another dick to talk with the husband. In the meantime, there's a health insurance card in her purse, shows a Nile Eddgar as next of kin. Somebody says he's a PO. Montague expects press will get this in a beat or two and he wants me to get over pronto to this Nile, so we tell him before he turns on the radio or TV and hears it that way."

The entire answer is hearsay. Hobie has stroked his beard throughout, waiting for anything objectionable, and has apparently decided to let it pass.

"And did you oblige the lieutenant?" Rudy asks, in his funny, high-blown way. Rudy had three years of English public school before landing here. His father is one of those Indians with advanced degrees, never able to put them to use in any country. The family, Marietta says, has a liquor store on the East Bank.

"He give me the address, and along with Officer Vic Addison, I proceeded there. It was here in the city." 'The city' means DuSable. Al Kratzus is one of those neighborhood guys, like my Uncle Moosh, who remember when this was still three little burgs, not, as the world now sees it, a single megalopolis. In those days, there were still intense rivalries among the Tri-Cities. At eighty, Moosh still discusses the fierce games that were once played in the bitter weather of late December between the public high-school football champs from Kewahnee, Moreland, and DuSable, and a single representative from the Catholic leagues.

Tommy is waving at his colleague. Rudy bends so Molto can whisper his suggestion.

"Yes," says Rudy out loud. "And in asking you to take on this assignment, sir, did Montague give any indication at that time that Nile Eddgar was a suspect?"

Hobie objects, but he pursued the issue of when and why Montague began to regard Nile as a suspect. I overrule.

"We're service, you know?" says Kratzus. "In CR, we're not on the case. Our job is the public. If somebody's a suspect, Montague would assign one of his people."

"Did you in fact see Nile Eddgar?"

"We did. Addison and I went to his apartment." Kratzus sighs, minorly disgusted with the state of his memory later in life, and checks his pocket for the report, then fishes a stout finger there again to locate his readers. "2343 Duhaney."

"And what time was it?"

"It was after 8 a.m., closer to 8:30. I was afraid at that hour we mighta missed him, but he was there. We had to pound awhile, but he come to the door. I identified my office. Somewhere in there we had to ask him to turn down the music actually, then I asked was he a relation to June Eddgar, he says he's the son, and I told him I was very sad—" Kratzus's hand does two forward flips. Et cetera, he means. "And I give him the news. All what Montague told me. Just that one-liner, you know, that she'd been shot dead down at Grace Street."

"And did he have any reaction that you were able to observe?"

"Pretty doggone strange," says Kratzus.

"Oh, object!" Hobie loudly declares and shimmies his entire upper body in disapproval.

I strike the answer and direct Kratzus to tell the court precisely what the defendant said and did. He takes in my instruction slowly. There are plenty of police officers, bureaucrats, departmental politicos who get through thirty years on the Force with barely half a dozen court appearances. Kratzus seems like one of them.

"He give us a look. First off, it's a look. Kind of, you know, 'Wait a minute.' Not so much he doesn't believe it as it doesn't make sense."

"Your Honor," says Hobie.

"Mr. Tuttle, I'm going to accord the testimony the weight I feel it deserves."

Kratzus has turned himself around in the witness chair to face me, too stiff and bulky to do so with ease, but eager to address me almost conversationally. His powder-blue coat bunches up thickly and the unbarbered fuzz of hairs on the back of his neck shows up, the filaments refracting the courtroom lights. He goes on explaining to me, notwithstanding the objection.

"I do this a lot, Judge. All kind of circumstances. Little old ladies dyin in bed. Suicides. Car wrecks. And people respond different. I'm the first to tell you that. But this was strange."

"Sergeant," I say, "just stick with the outward behavior. What he said, what he did. How did he appear?"

"You know, Judge, it's the glazed look, his mouth is hangin open. Then he's gonna talk, then he doesn't. Finally, he takes himself and sits down on his sofa and says, 'My *father* was supposed to be goin over there.' Like he's explaining something. And that's it. For maybe ten seconds. Then suddenly, he starts in to cry."

Rudy takes over again. "Did you have further conversation, Sergeant, after he declared, 'My *father* was supposed to go over there'?" Good prosecutorial question, driving home the critical line of testimony.

"We did. We told him where the remains would be and how they could be claimed. We give him a card with the PP's number." The Police Pathologist's. "He was pretty shook up by then, so we left."

"And following the interview, what did you do?"

"Back to the Hall. I left a message in voice mail for Montague, I needed to speak with him ASAP."

"And in your ordinary practice, would you be wanting to speak to the investigating detective?"

"Object," says Hobie again tiredly. He doesn't bother to rise. The body language suggests another silly excess by the PAs. Hobie's objections have been well timed and usually on point, so that by now I've developed a reflex that he's correct. But I recognize this time he's trying to gull me.

"No, I'll hear this."

"Generally, we have no need. You know, maybe I'll leave a message, 'We done like you asked,' I'll send up a 5-sheet"—a police report, named long ago in the days when there were five layers, with carbons—"but you know, most times they got no need to hear from us."

"So what if anything motivated your call to the lieutenant?"

"Judge," implores Hobie.

"I'll sustain now." But the point is made: Old plowhorse or not, Kratzus thought the kid was wrong. He was taking something off him and knew Montague ought to get a detective out to see Nile, find out what the hell he meant that his father was supposed to have been there.

Rudy sits. I nod to Hobie for his cross.

"Just a few questions," he begins. It's more than that, but he accomplishes little. Kratzus admits he's seen lots of strange reactions when he's imparted news of a loved one's death. And Hobie combats the implication of Rudy's question about the time of the visit, which suggested that Nile was late for work and might have been waiting at home for a call, by pointing out that loud music was on, which would have made it hard to hear the phone.

"And you say that you're not sent out to speak with suspects, right?"

"Not generally."

"And who was it Montague was going to talk to?"

"The father," says Kratzus. Catching the drift, he adds, "Cause it was his car. You figure he'd know what she was doin down there."

"Okay," says Hobie, unwilling to press the point. A few questions later he terminates the cross. Significantly, he does not dispute the accuracy of Kratzus's memory. That means Kratzus wrote a report that day, and that his partner, Addison, will back him up. Kratzus, with his bulk, heads out the doors of the courtroom, but stops at the prosecution table to shake hands. He did a good job.

Aside from the fingerprints on the money, this is the best piece of evidence the state has offered yet. One statement. One line. Yet it has a clear impact: Nile expected Eddgar to be there; Nile expressed surprise not that there had been a shooting but only who its victim was. The first questions anyone, no matter how shocked, normally would ask are, Who shot her? Why? How could this have happened? I have my eyes closed, letting the proof work its way down through the emotional latticework. My reaction creates a lingering moment of gravity that grips the entire courtroom. When I look up, both prosecutors are watching me tensely.

I call the lunch recess then, but don't get out the door. By the time I've conferred briefly with Marietta about the 2:00 call, Molto is in front of the bench. Hobie, typically, has found a way to disrupt Molto's calm. Tommy is livid, red up to his hairline. Hobie has presented Tommy with defense exhibits: Nile's 1994 tax return, his 1995 wage records, his bankbooks, his checking account statements. Molto waves all these documents about and finally lays them before me.

"Judge, we should have received these documents *before* trial."

"What's the point of them?" I ask.

"I don't care what the point is, really. He's not supposed to be producing exhibits now. And he won't say what the point is. We've asked him six times."

"Mr. Tuttle?"

"Really, Your Honor," he says, with a sweet little smile.

"Are you declining to say?"

"No, I'll say. I'll say. I'd have thought it would be obvious to these prosecutors. But I guess not. The point, Your Honor, is that there is not a cash withdrawal exceeding $300 in all of 1995, which is not surprising, since my client's savings never were greater than $3,200." Nile didn't have the money to pay Hardcore, not $10,000 cash, that's the point.

Tommy explodes again. Sandbagging, he calls it. Which is exactly what it is. Tommy goes on at high volume, ignoring Singh's efforts to soothe him.

"Mr. Tuttle," I say, "I can't see how you could have failed to think about these records before."

"Your Honor, what about *them?*" He points. "Really, Judge Klonsky. Here they are, planning to put a witness on the stand to claim my client paid him $10,000 in cash, and they haven't bothered asking themselves where the money came from? It's not a secret my client files tax returns or has a bank account. They should have thought of this, too. And the defense discovery response notified them we might put in these records."

Hobie hands up a boilerplate filing the State Defenders use in every case, but he's got a point. 'Bank records' and 'tax records' are mentioned as possible defense exhibits, along with forty or fifty other categories of documentary evidence, everything from pathologists' studies to ballistics reports. Molto, scattershot, never pressed for details and Hobie waited in the weeds. The lawyering life, I think.

"All right. Mr. Tuttle, I want you to do a better job getting things to the state. Go through this discovery response and before the weekend produce *any* exhibits you might use. This is the last surprise, do you hear me? Given the state's lack of diligence in demanding production, I'm not going to exclude. But I won't be so generous next time."

At my ruling, Tommy groans out loud. Singh attempts to drag off Molto, who, in spite of his soft, unathletic shape, has struck a bantam pose in the well of the courtroom, facing Hobie like he's spoiling for a fight. Tommy is still too furious to see that he's been outflanked again by Hobie. The good trial lawyer always wants the state's best evidence quickly forgotten. Instead of mulling over Kratzus's direct, I'm now heading off to lunch asking myself where Nile could have gotten the money he supposedly gave Hardcore. Did he borrow it? Steal it? Hobie's right. Molto should have thought of this. Then again, Nile's fingerprints are on the money. That will be Tommy's answer in the end: it happened. The devil finds a way. It happened.

As the courtroom comes back to life, I remain a minute on the bench, assessing all of this, then find, as I gather my things, I'm facing the jury box again. Seth, once more, is waiting for me to take note of him there. By now, there is a rhythm to this, as if he knows I'll only have time to acknowledge him at the end of the session. Yesterday afternoon, I was somewhat alarmed to find him gone. I didn't know if it was the sweaty mess he'd made of his sport coat or, as I suspected, the heavy load of what we'd been discussing which kept him from returning. I was un-settled myself. *To lose a child!* The thought came hurtling at me all night. We never remember that even a century ago, this shroud, this burden, was commonplace. Talk about improving our quality of life!

But Seth looks all right now. He greets me with a chipper little smile and then a wink. Like all his gestures this week, it's slightly forward but too well-meant to do any real harm. Hello, he's saying. I'm here now,

I'm okay. We're friends. And to my mild amazement, I find, before I've had time to think better of it, I've winked back.

"Ordell Trent!" Small, sallow, mussed as the weekend approaches, Tommy Molto bleats the name when I tell the prosecution to call its next witness, as we settle in after lunch.

"Ordell Trent!" Annie repeats. The name rolls on twice more, the transport deputy at the door shouting to a colleague in the rear, the second one yelling into the cage for Ordell to bring himself to the door. The keys jangle. Through the wall we hear the solid rumble of the lockup door sliding back, and the second deputy loudly warning one of the leftovers from the just-concluded bond call to stand away. Then, after a lingering moment, Hardcore steps into the courtroom. He has been here before, when he entered a guilty plea in late September. But I knew less about him then. Now, like a lion emerging from a cave, Ordell briefly blinks away the harsh fluorescence and serenely takes in a room full of persons somewhat terrified by what they've heard about him. Behold: the killer.

"Mr. Trent." I point him to the witness stand. His hands are cuffed, and one of the deputies approaches to release him. Then Hardcore, somewhat stout, hugely muscled across the chest, slopes toward me, with sufficient assurance to make it a mildly uncomfortable moment.

"Do you swear to tell the truth, the whole truth, and nothing but the truth?"

"Sure do." He drops his hand and settles in the witness chair.

Tommy is at the podium. His brief preparatory cough resounds through the courtroom, over which a deliberative stillness has fallen. Even Nile, in a blue blazer today, appears sufficiently focused to be taken as tense.

Hardcore states his name and present residence in the KCJ, Kindle County Jail.

"Are you known by any other name?"

"Gangster tag." He rolls out the word: "Hardcore."

"Why don't you spell it for the reporter?" Tommy suggests.

"Oh, now," says Hardcore. "Get spelled any number of ways. H, a, r, d, k, o, r, p, s. Thass one I seen." On the walls. He probably never has cause to write it himself. An odd thought: this name, this word, does not have a parallel existence in the world of letters—it's like some sub-subatomic particle that exists only in physicists' calculations. Gang life is out there somewhere, an intense physical reality with no tie to a more refined realm of symbols.

On the stand, Hardcore looks determinedly relaxed, slumping a bit. In the gallery, amid the faces, I'm sure there are many T-4 Rollers, come to see Core. As a result, he will not allow himself to appear awed. The truth of gang life is that many are primarily hangers-on, gawkers, lookouts, the adoring masses through whom the true thugs promote their name. In other words, as it often is with kids: one bad actor and ten who think he's cool.

Hardcore is well rehearsed and far more cooperative than Bug. Tommy leads him along carefully. The prosecutors' strategy is apparent. As with Lovinia, they have made, quite literally, no effort to dress up Hardcore. He sits here in the sheriff's-department's blue coveralls, an ever-present reminder of his guilty plea and his acknowledged complicity in the crime. Like Bug, Core's clearly been told to be himself. He talks the same language he speaks outside. Tommy wants me to remember at all moments that this is the murdering hoodlum whom Nile Eddgar took up with as a friend.

Consistent with this plan, the first thing Tommy brings out is Core's lengthy juvenile record and his two earlier felony convictions as an adult, both for distribution of narcotics. His initial penitentiary sentence, at the age of nineteen, was for three years. His second—for possession of fourteen ounces of cocaine recovered from a car he was driving—was ten years, no parole. He got out four years ago. Like Lovinia, Hardcore has made an impressive deal in exchange for his testimony: twenty years for conspiracy to murder, which will amount to ten years inside. The criminal justice system recognizes the same rule as accountants: first in, first out. The flipper has to be rewarded.

"Now prior to your present incarceration, Mr. Trent, what was your profession?"

"Gangster," he answers.

"Were you a member of any criminal organization?"

"BSD," he says, "be for me." A familiar slogan. Hardcore amuses himself. The sandy scratchings of a goatee frame his mouth and his large teeth have a yellowish cast when he smiles.

"What was your position in BSD?"

"Top Rank."

"Were you one of the leaders of the gang, one of the shot-callers?"

"S'pose so."

"Who is above you?"

"J. T-Roc. Kan-el."

Tommy identifies them by name.

"And how, sir, did you make a living prior to your incarceration?"

"Slanging."

"Slanging?"

"Slanging dope." 'Hanging, banging, and slanging' is the motto of gang life. In that street doggerel, slang, which originally meant to talk the talk, now is the term for selling drugs—a telling change.

"What kind of dope did you slang?"

"Mostly crack. Some wire." Wire is another name for speed.

"Anything else?"

"Oh yeah," says Hardcore mildly. Core, who is yet to be sentenced and not eager to make himself look any worse, is sluggish with his responses, but Tommy persists and forces him to admit he also sold PCP, methadone, rock cocaine, heroin, and some stolen prescription drugs. He had an organization, he says, of at least ten people working for him, which included Lovinia.

"And do you know Nile Eddgar?"

His face broadened with surly amusement, Core's thick eyes find the defendant. Hobie nudges his client and Nile, with one hand on the chair arm, as if he needs a boost, rises for the formal courtroom identification. Core continues smiling after pointing him out. Nile takes his seat, face averted, cowed and shaken, while Hardcore continues to smile.

"How did you come to know the defendant?"

"He my PO."

"Your probation officer?"

"He keepin his eye on me for the court." Parole has been abolished in this state in most instances. Instead, narcotics offenses and certain other crimes carry a period of supervised release.

"How long has he been your PO?"

"Seem like a year nearly. Had me couple others."

"And how often did you see Nile?"

"Oh, you know, up the top, once a month."

"And where did you see him?"

"T-4."

"And what was the reason for his visit?"

"You know, man. Kinda check me out."

"Eventually, did you begin to see him more often?"

"Yeah, how it come down, man got to be PO for a whole damn bunch of T-4's."

"He was assigned to be PO to other members of the T–4 Roller set of the Black Saints Disciples?"

"Right," says Core.

"Do you know how that came about?"

"Seem like he think be kinda slammin, kickin it with us."

I sustain Hobie's objection to the witness testifying about the defendant's state of mind. Tommy tries it again.

"Did he tell you he'd asked for the assignment?"

Hardcore actually appears to ponder. "Yeah, man, cause how it were, I 'member him comin out one day—"

"When?" asks Tommy.

"Say like December, and you know, I'm like, 'Dang, bo, you gettin in my shit, seein you mo than bad weather.'

"And he sayin like lot them POs don't wanna get with it at the IV Tower, get they asses shot and shit, and he like, he don't mind none. You know, so he goin, 'Gimme they-all, they down by me.'"

"That's what he said? That he told other officers he'd accept the files because he didn't mind coming to the IV Tower?"

"Uh-huh. You know he got Winky, Crouch, Warbone, Handman, Turkey Swoop. Together, Tommy and Hardcore try, with only limited success, to bring out the names of the remaining members whom Nile supervised. "Dang," says Core, "what that cuz be named?" Tommy lets it go.

Closer to me than he has been before, Hardcore, I note, is no child. He looks to be in his mid-thirties, but all youth is gone from him. His face is closed-down and tough, the black, wide, rheumy eyes slow-moving, his look always insolent. What the guards privately—and out of no small measure of fear—call jailhouse trash. When he lifts a hand to scratch his cheek, I see that his nails have grown long and that each is capped by an amber section perhaps three-quarters of an inch, adding the insinuation of a strange, random element in his character.

"And once he assumed this role, how often was Nile at the Tower?"

"Most days, seem like."

"And what was the nature of your relationship?"

"We ain gettin tight or nothin, but I be knowin the dude. He cool and all. Like to be hangin most the time."

"What do you mean by hanging?"

"You know, man, down by them doorways, hangin with the homies, hearin the hoot. Laughin, you know. Just hangin and all."

"Did he require you to fill out monthly probation reports?"

Hardcore smiles and lets a hand blow by. Not so he remembers. "And over time, did you ever meet any members of his family?"

"Uh-huh," says Core.

"Who was that?"

"Met his daddy."

"Senator Loyell Eddgar?"

"Loyell, huh? That his name?" Hardcore draws in his cheeks. White folks.

"And how did that meeting take place?"

"Well, see now, thass a tale." In the witness chair, Core laughs and rearranges himself, crossing a leg to tell his story. "Seem like one day, you know, man, we by them benches by the Tower, and I'm rappin to Nile, cause, you know, got to be cool with the PO, right? And we get with it, I be like, 'Yo, that DOC, man,' "—Department of Corrections— " 'they damn ornery with our cuz Kan-el, man, they stepped on his release twice, man, and he done his time, man, that's just bitch-ass cold, they just steppin on him cause they know he tip-top BSD, cause he down for his, ain counta no tickets or nothin he done in there, can't be, cause ain nobody gone say shit bout him, even if he done it. You hear what I'm sayin?'

"And so Nile, he like, 'You-all oughta best be talkin with my daddy, you and you homes.'

"And I like, 'Who-all you daddy?'

" 'Oh, man, nigger, my daddy he be it, he got power, Jack, he a senator and shit, he done got me my job.' "

Tommy interrupts. "Nile told you that? That the Senator had gotten him his job?" With this nugget, Tommy slides his eyes at the reporters in the jury box.

"Yeah, he gone on *all* bout his daddy. Say, 'Man, he on some committee or shit, them DOC they gotta listen up on him, he get on them, it be all over. Y'all oughta meet him. No lie. Maybe dude can help you out some.' He be goin like that."

"And did you agree to meet the Senator?"

"You know, not up the top, but Nile, man, he be, you know, you say persistent. Got to be a thang, you know. 'You-all wanna get with my daddy? My daddy and all wanna get with you.'

"So one time, man, I kickin with T-Roc and we fall to this thang, how my PO sky-up bout we oughta get with his daddy, help out cuz Kan-el. And T-Roc, he like, 'Might be fat, could be fat, we kickin some serious shit here.'

"So I say to Nile, 'Yo, okay, we get it on with you daddy.' "

"And did you finally meet Senator Eddgar?"

"Sure enough."

"When?"

"May. Seem like about then cause it gettin to be warm, you know?"

"And where did this meeting take place?"

Gazing downward, Hardcore laughs, again his mind full of the scene. "See now, man, we done a lot fussin bout that, cause T-Roc, you know, he ain tight with too many white folks, and you know, Nile was buzzin me how his daddy so busy and shit. So we got it finally, we gone meet in T-Roc's SEL?"

"You met in Jeff T-Roc's Mercedes, is that correct?" Tommy again briefly faces the press gallery. Like the customs dogs who smell drugs through steel casings, the reporters are on alert now. Here it comes. Scandal. A politician in the back seat of a limousine with street-gang leaders. One of those memorable courthouse stories—people in odd places, doing things no one could imagine. Through his fussy courtroom manner, Molto is unable to contain a discordant element: distaste for Eddgar. The senator may be the state's witness, but the prosecutor holds him and his antics in low regard.

"And where was the car located when you met?"

"North End, man, can't remember quite 'xactly, some corner."

"And how long did the meeting last?"

"Say, bout half hour or so."

"And who was present?"

"Nile, me, T-Roc, and the daddy."

"Senator Eddgar?"

"Yeah, him," answers Core, with a brief scowl. He does not like Eddgar either.

"And can you tell us what was said?"

Core hoots, scoffing somewhat at the memory. "Man, we was thinkin, we gone get Kan-el *out*. And this dude, the daddy, he all like whacked or somethin. He like, you know, got his own program, man. We goin, 'Yo, we-all, we got do this thang here, get Kan-el flyin.'

"And he like, 'Oh me, no no, we best be organizin this shit and all.' I mean it was powerful, way he went on."

"Was it Senator Eddgar's idea that BSD would be the basis for a political organization?"

"That's what I'm sayin here."

"And how did you and T-Roc react?"

"T-Roc? After some ticks, this motherfucker, the daddy, he just *up* on himself, man, and T shoot me kind of a look, he like to posse out. He *all* ready to book, then he come and get it, he in his own car. Kinda funny," Core adds and once more displays that ample smile. "Anyways, they get theyself out pretty soon there, and T-Roc, he be like, 'Can you believe this limp mother?' Man, he was burned. He was deep."

"And did you speak with Nile?"

"Oh yeah. Yeah, yeah."

"When and where?"

"Next time he come round T–4. In that next week there. I like to wail on Nile. 'That all's just a psych, man, that motherfucker just playin us, man.'

"And Nile, he kind of, you know, shrug and all. 'That how he be. He play you.'

"I say, 'I ain down for that, no motherfucker play me, daddy or no. Got to stall out on that shit, man. I go head up any motherfucker, man, do me like that. I'd cap that motherfucker soon as look at him.' I, you know, be goin like that."

"And what, if anything, did Nile say?"

"Well, you know, he kind of like *lookin*, like he just ain gone believe nobody be ravin on his daddy like that. And I'm like, 'Fuck you, motherfucker, fuck you up, too, you want.' I'm trippin and all."

At intervals, I've had some instinct to curb Hardcore's language. This is still a courtroom, to which the public is invited. But he is too natural, too forceful a storyteller in his own mode to bear much interruption. Even Hobie, who until this moment has had the star turn here, seems to have no urge to slow him down. Core, quite evidently, is enjoying himself. Over the months I've been sitting in Criminal, I've been struck by how often a simple, childish desire for attention accounts for the presence of many of these young people. Most of these kids grow up feeling utterly disregarded — by fathers who departed, by mothers who are overwhelmed, by teachers with unmanageable classrooms, by a world in which they learn, from the TV set and the rap of the street, they do not count for much. Crime gathers for them, if only momentarily, an impressive audience: the judge who sentences, the lawyer who visits, the cops who hunt them — even the victim who, for an endless terrified moment on the street, could not discount them.

"And following this exchange in which you informed Nile you were angry with his father, did you have any other conversation with Nile about Senator Eddgar?"

"Nah," says Core, and freezes Tommy. "Not first. Then, you know, one day, might even be a month gone by, we all just kickin round T–4 and he come up on me, and he, like first thing, he a'ks me, 'Yo, like, you really cool with that shit, how you fade my daddy?'

"So I be thinkin, Oh, you done it now, nigger, this PO, he gone get in yo face how you rippin on his daddy. 'I's just talkin shit,' I say, and soon as I done said it, I can see, you know, like he busted."

"Disappointed?" asks Tommy.

"Right," says Hardcore, "right. So maybe two weeks later, man, I like, 'So how is it, dude, you really be wantin me to smoke you daddy?'

"And he say like that, 'Yeah, I do.' "

"Who's he?" Tommy asks. "Who were you talking to?"

"Nile."

"The defendant?"

"Yeah, right."

Nile, when I look, has his chin at Hobie's shoulder. He is speaking to him with greater animation than he's shown at any point until now. Hobie is nodding emphatically, as his expensive pen races across the yellow pad.

"And where were you? When you had this talk? Who was around?"

"Just me and him. You know how it is, when he come down round T–4, I's sort of, you know, gettin him back to his 'mobile, so he don't get jacked or nothing."

"So you were escorting him down the street near T–4 to his car?"

" 'Xactly," says Core. 'He like, 'I give you $25,000, you fade him.'

"And I go like, 'Yo, you bent, man.'

" 'Uh-uh,' he say, 'hell I am anyhow, I mean what I say, you do it.'

"I like, 'Man, motherfucker, I see you motherfuckin money, we gone know you mean that you behind it.'

"Whoa! Dude not down with that. He were burnin, ready to tear *it* up. I ain never seed him like that, man. He get up in my face.

" 'I know you here slanging dope and shit, Hardcore. You think I don't know? Put you nigger-ass back in the Yard any time I say. You under paper as it is, Core. I pull you down whenever I like. Man, don't be trippin wit' me now. This here yo idea from the jump.'

" 'No way, motherfucker, this nigger ain but goin on.'

"We trippin on that some, who say do it, but I seen he stomp-down on this, and I ain takin no ride."

"You agreed to do it, rather than have him revoke your release?"

"Say I gone think on it some. And you know, then, every time I see the dude, he on me, 'You gone do this, nigger, or ain you? Thought you was some bad-ass Top Rank gangbangin motherfucker, but you just some bitch-ass sissy like all them elderly niggers down the corner by Best Way Liquor with they forty zones of Colt.' He on me all the time."

Tommy stands a moment and frowns at his witness, clearly afraid that Hardcore, caught up in his performance, has gone straight over the top.

"Did you finally agree to kill Senator Eddgar?"

"Ain never finally agreed, till one day he come up, he got that newspaper bag." Core points, and from the prosecution table, Tommy retrieves People's 1, the money and the blue newspaper bag in which it was wrapped. "He gimme that."

"Where were you?"

"T-4. On Grace Street. He by his ride, ain't even got hisself out. He just come up by there and tell Bug, 'Go fetch Core.' And I come on down, there he be, and he hand me that-there through the window. Say, 'I give you the rest when you done it.' "

"When was this?"

"August. Hot."

"And what did you say?"

"I say, 'Motherfucker, you fixin for me to do this?' "

"He be like, 'Uh-huh, I am.' "

"So I figure, well, okay, then gone have to get wit' it, otherwise he gone pull my paper sure enough."

Tommy finishes laying an evidentiary foundation for the money. Hardcore says he took the bag to the home of Doreen McTaney, the mother of his son Dormane, and left it there until after the killing. He identifies his initials, next to Montague's on the evidence tag. With the money and the plastic bag now fully tied to the defendant and the crime, Molto moves for admission of the exhibits.

"Any objection?" I ask Hobie.

He purses his lips. "Can I reserve for cross?" Hobie knows every trick. Having no basis to keep the money out of evidence, he wants to delay its admission in the hope that in the welter of last-minute details, the prosecutors will forget to reoffer the proof. Across his shoulder, Tommy tosses an irked look. By now he expects Hobie to be difficult. I admit the money, subject to cross, and Tommy picks up the thread with Core, whom he asks about preparations for the killing.

"Got with Gorgo and them. Tell Gorgo get him a good clean

spout"—'a clean spout' would be a weapon that would not trace—"we got us to put in some work. Then I went rappin to Dooley Bug."

"Is that Lovinia Campbell?"

"Uh-huh."

"What did you tell her?"

Probably to keep Core from getting rolling again, Hobie objects for lack of foundation, meaning that Core has not said precisely when, where, and with whom the conversation took place. Tommy starts to explain, but Core has been around enough courtrooms to understand and interrupts.

"This here's day before we done it. Up the IV Tower. Just me and her." He looks toward Hobie and sneers: Think what you think, motherfucker, but I ain dumb. I doubt, however, anyone here has made the mistake of questioning Core's smarts.

"And what did you tell her?"

"Put it down to her. Whole scene, you know."

"What did you tell her specifically about Nile?"

"Nile and me, we fixin to gauge his daddy."

"What did she say?"

"Oh, you know. 'Why-all we gotta be doin like that?' That kinda shit."

"And you said?"

" 'Yo, freeze up, ho. You just be working here.' " The unvarnished accuracy and vehemence with which Core recalls his response provokes momentary laughter in the courtroom. Core smiles, as if he had fully calculated his audience's reaction in advance.

"Did Bug know Nile?"

"Hell yeah, she know Nile. Lotsa time he come round, she be rappin to him. He like her caseworker or some such. She kickin on them benches wit' him, rap for hours seem like. She know him good."

Tommy glances my way, just to be sure I've registered that: Nile was nice to Lovinia, she'd want to protect him.

The remainder of the direct is somewhat anticlimactic. Core explains the plan, how Lovinia called him when June showed up. When he gets to the point where June was shot, Core winds his head around sorrowfully over the mistake.

"And when was the last time you spoke to Nile Eddgar?"

"Morning all this comin down. He beep when I's fixin to leave out, so I give him a shout off the pay phone down there in T–4, say all this cool." Tommy takes hold of the computer records from Nile's phone and directs Core's attention to the call to his pager at 6:03 a.m. Core affirms this is the page which he answered from the pay phone outside the IV Tower. Then Tommy cleverly uses the various stipulated phone records to review the entire direct. 'Was this call on May 14 around the time you agreed to meet Senator Eddgar? Was this call on August 7 around the time you agreed to kill him?'

When he's done, it's near 4:30 and we adjourn. The transport deputies cuff Core to walk him back. His lawyer, Jackson Aires, who has watched the proceedings from a folding chair just inside the Plexiglas partition, approaches Core at the lockup door and rests a hand on his shoulder as they consult, nodding emphatically, telling Core he's done well. Hobie has gathered up his boxes quickly, and pushes Nile, who is still gesticulating toward Hardcore, out of the courtroom. Tommy and Rudy—and Montague, who's entered to help haul things downstairs—are lingering at the prosecution table, smiling among themselves. They've had their ups and downs but the week has ended well. The reporters have disappeared, as if by magic, all racing to beat deadline with today's spicy item: "A convicted gang leader testified today that the plot to murder Senator Loyell Eddgar began when gang leaders angrily rebuffed Eddgar's efforts to turn the Black Saints Disciples into a political organization."

A weird story, but it has the eerie resonance of a tale too odd to be untrue. In the subdued clamor of the spectators' departure, I sit still on the bench, gripping my pen and staring at the pages of the bench book, which are covered with the hurried notes I've made today. The critical line from Kratzus—'My *father* was supposed to be goin over there'—is underscored at the top of the upper left-hand side. Considering it all, an omen bounds home in me: I'm going to find Nile Eddgar guilty.

Nikki loves costumes. She imagines herself with stylish dos and beaded gowns. I took to heart my mother's distaste for glamour and am always alarmed. Where does Nikki get these ideas? I wonder. Is this the penalty for working, for not being at her side twenty-four hours a day? When I pick her up from day care tonight, she is wearing plastic high heels on the wrong feet and a crown.

"I'm getting married!" she squeals.

Married! my heart shrieks, but I take her in with kisses, knowing that this instant when we're reconnected for the weekend is, in ways, the point toward which I've been journeying all week.

"We have stew for dinner. Just the way you like it."

"No peas?" she asks.

"Not one."

When Nikki was born, I decided I would become organized. I would cook meals in advance and freeze them, like my friend Grace Tomazek. I would keep extensive grocery lists so that I would no longer have to go to the store three times each day. I would start shopping from catalogues for clothes, and buy a season ahead so I was not desperate when the weather changed. I would sign up for Moms and Tots on Saturdays. Finally an adult, I would have a life reflecting forethought rather than waning moods and windblown caprice. I wanted this with desperate, almost unbearable longing, as the sign of some gathering of myself, as an affirmation of the capacity of any person to make her life a bit more bearable.

And I succeeded, after a fashion. Oh, of course, I become preoccupied—with the cases before me, with one feud or another with Charlie, with the madness in Bosnia or a memory of my mother that has not visited me in years, anything that catches me on the spike of passion and ends up making me seem, especially to myself, unfocused, even scatterbrained. But for the most part, I have made my life less a momentary adventure. Nikki and I have a routine. There *are* meals in the freezer, which I, generally speaking, remember to defrost. The lunch bag is packed. Amid the whirl of single-mom responsibilities, I often feel like one of those little old ladies, Old World ethnics dressed all in black, wobbling around like a top about to fall. On occasion, I'm undermined by uncertainty about myself. A few months back, as I was listening to the discordant screech of Avi, Gwendolyn's son, sawing away at his Suzuki violin, I was jarred by panic. What was I going to *do* about music lessons? I'd never even *thought* of it. I called piano teachers all night. Lately, I've felt pangs because Nikki knows nothing of religion. But it happens, all of it. My life has what planning always seemed to imply: a center, weight, substance. Love.

Love. I've been so lucky! I think all the time. Not in the ordinary outward sense that people have in mind with that phrase. Because, after all, I've had my pratfalls and distractions, my own tough patches, sickness and divorce, the ordinary major miseries of an ordinary existence. But I'm so lucky to have Nikki, to have someone to love, unambiguously and durably, someone for whom my love will never falter. Love, whatever it means, has otherwise been an unreliable thing in my life. With my mother. With men. In my younger years, it made no sense to me that one word referred to sexual relations and your family. You have to get older for all of that to cohere, to understand it comes down to the same thing, intensity, connection, commitment, some Mecca toward which your soul can always pray.

After dinner, a bath. Nikki frolics, inventing games with Barbie dolls who, except for the moments of their evening drowning, dwell on the tub side in consummate nudity, despairing, no doubt, over the sad fate of their plastic hair, which Nikki's repeated stylings have left a mass of ratted knots.

"I like Jenna better than Marie," says Nikki, "but they're both black."

Once again, panic is forestalled. Teach. Always teach.

"You know, Nikki, whether someone is nice has nothing to do with the color of their skin. You're nice from the inside, not the outside."

She pouts, she bugs her eyes. "Mommy, I know *that.*" Some propositions are obvious, even to a six-year-old.

Eventually, I extract her from the tub. Already, I find myself longing for the baby who has only recently disappeared, the three- and four-year-old with her winsome malapropisms. 'It's gark outside.' 'Hum on' for 'come on.' Now she sometimes seems a being of unknown origins, with tastes and even physical attributes I've never encountered in myself or even Charlie. Where does she get these fingers, I wonder as I'm toweling her dry, which look tallowy as melting party candles?

"Have I told you how wonderful you are?" I ask, kneeling beside Nikki's bed.

"No," Nikki answers at once, as she does each evening.

"Well, you're wonderful. You're the most wonderful person I know. Have I told you how much I love you?"

"No," she answers, squirming shamefaced against my chest.

"I love you more than anything in the world."

I cuddle her until she sleeps, an indulgence I should not permit, but it's a precious moment, again the simplest atom, nucleus, and particle. Asleep, Nikki is soft and smells sweetly of her shampoo.

Afterwards, in the quiet house, I lounge in the living room. A glass of white wine is spun experimentally by the stem between my fingertips. At long last, I reach the glorious moment when I remove my pantyhose. Now, after the parade of the day is over, I find out what has stuck, before it grows into something new in the hothouse of dreams. Night sounds rise up from the city: wind against the gutters, passing cars, teens a block away exuberant with their mischief. Above the painted brick fireplace a Modigliani hangs, a narrow-faced girl in whose inscrutable pose I have always recognized something of myself. While Charlie lived here, I spent hours staring at that painting, since I was loath to move around while the poet was in the throes of creation. From Charlie's study in the extra bedroom, the strong blue smoke of his hand-rolled cigarettes would penetrate the room. He used tobacco brands you saw in Westerns—Bugler and Flag—and could dip his thick fingers into the pouches and line a paper without ever looking up from the page. His concentration as he wrote was fabulous. He wouldn't have heard The Bomb. But he demanded that the house be still, and so until he finished—and God knew when that would be—I would work out here with a cup of tea, cringing if the cup even rang on the saucer, love's zombie, an unhappy refugee in my own home.

And with this memory, as the fretting of the work week recedes, as the courtroom with its tentacles of repulsion and fear falls behind me, I am arrowed by the terrible humbling poignance of the simplest truth. I'm busy, fly-about, overburdened. True enough. But I know this secret, too: In the marrow of the bone, where blood is made and beliefs are gathered, I'm hungry for the intimate company of other humans. I am lonely. And it is not merely a symptom of divorce. There were years, years married to Charlie, when I felt like this, wondering, as I still do, how long it will go on.

And then unpredictably—stealthy as a thief—the line that went by in passing days ago returns, haloed with all the urgent sincerity with which it was spoken.

'How many people,' Seth asked, 'how many people do you get close to in a life?'

May 2, 1970

S E T H

I did not sleep further after June's visit. It was 3:30 by then and I lay awake, telling myself no, then yes, telling myself it was crazy and wrong, and then that it was right for just that reason. Near 5:00, when I was going to leave, I called Hobie's. Lucy's voice was slurred with sleep.

"He's not here," she whispered.

Hobie kept luxurious hours. He read all night and had not attended a morning class throughout college. I was sure that Lucy, pliant as ever, was under instructions to tell me he wasn't there, but when I challenged her, a tide of distress rose through her voice.

"He hasn't spent the night here *all* week," she cried, then went quiet.

She said I could leave a message at Cleveland's. "If anyone picks up the phone," she added.

I tried to think. "How you hanging?" I asked eventually.

"Shitty."

That required no explanation. I told her I needed to see her, to say goodbye if nothing else, and we agreed to meet on Polk Street, where Lucy had an appointment that afternoon. After work, I crawled through the Saturday traffic, in an uneven mood. I had just made my farewells at *After Dark*. My days as a sci-fi columnist—the only line of work I'd ever felt any pride in—were now at an end. I'd hugged Harley Minx. He gave me a guidebook to Vancouver. Then I'd gone out the swinging back doors, with their rubber bumpers to protect against the damage done by the hand trucks, and left one more portion of my life behind me, knowing it was nothing I'd have chosen to do.

Polk Street was the usual florid scene. Hell's Angels, drag queens in cheap dresses, and leather cowpokes all paraded on the avenue, while shoppers ran between the cafés and exotics stores. A white-haired woman in a tight sweater stood on a corner with a pure white cockatoo on her shoulder.

At the sight of Lucy, I brought the car to a squealing halt. She stood on the corner, looking dazedly into the sun, searching for me perhaps.

Blood was streaming down her cheeks.

I leaned out the window, waving and yelling, and finally drew to the curb. By the time I'd pushed her through the passenger door, horns were sounding in a rough chorus behind me in the traffic. In my side-view, I saw a cop approaching and I jerked the Bug into the street, strangely frightened by the thought of an encounter with the police.

"Jesus," I said, "Jesus. What's going down? What happened to you?" I asked if she wanted to go to the hospital. She had popped her contacts into her open palms and sat with her head thrown back.

"I do it all the time," she said. "I forget I have my lenses in. I cry and then I rub my eyes and it cuts something. Just on the surface of the eyeball. I'll be all right. Oh God," she said and began to cry again. The tears, now a milder pink, streaked her face. I drove around and finally parked up on Russian Hill.

She had seen an herbalist, someone she had heard about, a hippie with a tiny third-story shop.

"For what?"

She faltered. "My skin." Lucy was freckled but her complexion was otherwise unblemished.

"Your skin? What do you have, like a rash?"

She rolled her eyes at my dullness. One of her contacts was in her mouth, for cleaning, and she had to spit it out before she could speak.

"Two weeks ago Hobie got rid of the dog? He took it out to Campus Boul and tied it to a parking sign? He said he wasn't going to live with a big white animal." She peered, waiting for me to understand. "I heard they have something you chew? You know? For maybe a month? It like works gradually. It makes your skin darker. It like dyes you? It's pigment or something. I don't know. Anyway, the guy didn't have it. He said he'd heard of it, but he didn't have it and wasn't sure where I could get it. And I just came out of there, I had this feeling like 'Oh, man, it's never going to work.' I mean, my whole life is falling apart, Seth. What am I going to do?"

My reaction, of course, was that it was crazy. She had tiny prom-queen features—she'd look like a brown white–person, like someone who'd overdone it with Man-Tan. But she was obviously beyond the point of practicality. That Lucy's love, her need for Hobie was that large touched me. It was such a dispiriting contrast to the way Sonny had responded to me.

I asked again about Hobie. She had no idea where he'd gone. She thought he'd been with Cleveland, but she'd called the police station and he hadn't been arrested. He had been appearing at home sporadically for weeks now, seemingly arriving only in order to tell her that he couldn't keep living with a white girl. The implication, which Lucy refused to acknowledge, was that he was coming back to find out if she'd left.

"What's he doing? Where do you think he is?" I asked.

"I don't know. He still goes to school, but after that?"

"What about this bomb? At the ARC? Did he have anything to do with that?"

She turned quickly to the window. She said nothing at first.

"You know about that stuff, right?" she asked. "That he bought?"

"Right." The battery acid and sandbags. I knew about that stuff.

"I think he kind of figured out what it was for. Eventually. I mean, nobody told him. He just sort of added things up. I don't know, Seth. He didn't say much."

"But he didn't plant the bomb, did he? He didn't help plan?"

"Hobie? No. God, no. He couldn't have, could he?"

I reconsidered June's warning. Perhaps she merely meant that if the dominoes fell, Hobie would be in trouble. One arrest would lead to another. I had some powerful vision of Hobie, but it left me as bitter as I was concerned. In the interval, Lucy had started crying once more.

"God, Seth," she said again, "what am I going to do?"

Lucy was raised in what used to be called a 'broken home.' Her parents had divorced when she was three. Her father, a well-known lawyer, sent lots of money but appeared infrequently. Her mother was a sort of airy socialite: a martini in one hand, a cigarette in the other, and usually a man nearby to light it. Lucy had come of age in an atmosphere of unfaltering politeness, which as a child left her baffled about whether the air of restraint she always sensed was refinement or indifference. As a teen, she'd tried to find out. She'd run away to a macrobiotic commune in Vermont when she was sixteen. Then, when she was supposed to have been back on track, she took up with Hobie. Lucy told her mother all about her boyfriend, except that he was black, news which my mother-in-law absorbed at once when she came home early one evening during a holiday break and found them fucking away in one of the living-room wing chairs, Lucy's slender freckled legs wrapped around Hobie's medium-brown behind.

In college, as a freshman, Lucy depended on Hobie helplessly. He picked her courses, approved her dresses, gave her books to read. And he relished her slavish attentions. Then every two or three months he would do her wrong. Some girl would take an interest and Hobie would disappear to her dorm room, often for days. Lucy would hang out with me, go to coffee, and beat me at two-handed bridge with an ease I found baffling, since I had not yet recognized the brainpower obscured behind her self-doubts. For the most part, however, she would simply pine incredibly until Hobie returned. There was even one occasion when she stood outside the dormitory where Hobie and the new girl had repaired and moaned for him, a gesture which Hobie was frank enough to admit he had found quite stimulating. Somehow Lucy never seemed to give a thought to saying enough was enough. She groaned even now at the thought of losing him.

"Look, my place will be empty in a few days. Why don't you move in there?"

"God," she said, "God, I don't want to be a-*lone*, Seth." The one word, 'alone,' emerged in a tone I sometimes heard in the singing in temple during the High Holidays. An age-old lament, a permanent misery. I held her.

"Then move in today. You'll have company until Monday. That's my induction date. I have to take off for the great North then." The recollection of June, their plan, the kidnapping recurred. A percussive feeling radiated through me as it had at many moments since the bombing of the ARC. I felt unmoored. The Eddgars' power seemed dominating, because they alone pointed unhesitatingly in a known direction.

"Maybe I'll come, too," Lucy said. "To Canada?"

"Sure," I said. There was nothing else to say, but she took note of my tone, dead of enthusiasm. She stared desolately out the window, trying not to cry. Suddenly, I took hold of Lucy and spoke to her largely as I had spoken to myself since the morning.

"Look. You've got to leave it behind. We both do. All of it. Hobie. Everything else. Everything is changing. *Every*-thing. It's like what we wanted and now we're getting it, and it's happened, and whether it's good or bad, we have to go with it. We just have to go with it." I gripped her shoulders, much as June had gripped mine, and peered into Lucy's small, bright eyes, hoping to see there some sign, some spark, so that I would know I'd persuaded her and, therefore, myself.

I called my father at work. He was there six days a week, reliably. Although it was Saturday, he never departed before 5:00.

"Dad, you haven't gotten any goofy calls or anything, have you, from some guys out here?"

I heard him calculating, drumming. A symphony soughed faintly from a small console radio he kept behind his desk.

"Calls? You refer to what, Seth?"

"There are some guys here. Nuts. I've seen them around the building. I don't know who they are or what they are. Somebody says they're witches."

"Vitches!" Back in Kindle County, my father was astounded by such a thing.

"I don't know. Satanists. They call themselves the Dark Revolution. You can't believe the goofballs out here, Dad. Jesus. One of these guys has got an Afro that's literally dyed the colors of the spectrum. I'm not kidding. Red hair, blue hair, *purple* hair. For—real."

My father grunted in disbelief.

"Anyway, a guy I know pretty well, he came to me yesterday, strictly on the q.t., and he says these guys, the Dark Revolution guys, have been talking about holding me for ransom because I'm Bernard Weissman's son."

"Oh, for God's sake," said my father. Fur Gott sake. "For God's sake. Have you explained?"

"Sure, I explained. 'Not that Weissman. No relation of any kind.' I said it all. But I'm not sure this other guy believed me. I just wondered. He said they'd had this plan for like a long time, you know? And they got nervous or something because they heard I'm about to leave? I thought maybe they were going to do something. I don't know."

"Have you contacted the police?"

"The police? What'll they do?"

"The police will do what the police do. Investigate. Look into matters."

"Pa, Jesus—if they investigated every person in Damon, California, who said weird things, they'd work from dawn to dusk and never finish going down Campus Boul. That's all I have to do is piss these guys off. The thing for me is just to collect my crap and get out of the country."

After a pause, my father said, "That is no solution."

June sat watching me, near the phone. She was close enough to whisper. She held a notepad and a pen, but she had not added a word yet. Instead, she was faintly smiling. I was well past the dialogue we'd rehearsed, flying free, and feeling a distinct glee in secretly holding the upper hand on my father.

"Look, let's not fight about this. I'll call you in a couple of days."

"Seth, I want your word that we will have a further discussion before you take any ultimate steps. I expect such a promise."

"Yeah, I promise. But something has to happen by Monday. Look, Pa. Don't say anything to Mama, okay?"

He snorted. Of course not. In her state. Ransom demands. That is the last thing she needs to hear. "It would be straight to the asylum," he said.

"That was great," said June, as she took the phone. "What?"

My father's last remark about the asylum was like a stab wound.

"We've talked about this," June said. "Your safety will never be in doubt. They'll know you're safe at every moment. It will simply be a question of your release."

The insanity of this, the debased frantic nature of everything, inside me and elsewhere, swam over me. Eddgar came down to my apartment in a few minutes. It was just as everyone said: he was never present when anything of consequence occurred. June related all the plans. Eddgar sat beside her, brittle as glass, the muscles popping up along his jaw. Occasionally, when something required discussion, the two of them left the room.

"Everything's all right," June said. He nodded remotely, so that even now you could not say for certain he knew what she was talking about.

Out on the landing, there were footsteps, a heavy thump, before a piffling knock on the door. Eddgar had wheeled with alarm, but when he threw the door back, Lucy was there, whipping her hair out of her eyes and sniffling. She wore her backpack. A huge green duffel, stuffed oozingly, slumped over the threshold. Her pillow was beneath her arm. She considered the three of us, seeming to hold her ground.

"I'm coming to Canada," she told me.

"WE HAVE YOUR SON," the note read. As in the movies, the message was a collage of letters clipped out of the newspaper and pasted on the page. The words had been surprisingly easy to find. A Sears ad in the *Chronicle* proclaimed, "WE HAVE YOUR SIZE! Sale on Friday." June had stood over the opened pages. She said, "Fate."

It was Saturday night. Lucy was downstairs with Nile; Eddgar, of course, was nowhere to be seen. Assembling the package, June wore yellow rubber gloves. She and Eddgar were deadly earnest about precautions, even though I continued to explain that my parents would never contact the authorities.

"Control the random element," she said. When June finished, she headed off for Railway Express. Sent by air, the package, a small white gift box, would be delivered to my father's office on Monday before noon. Within, he'd find the note and the mezuzah I had received from our congregation at my bar mitzvah. It was a tiny silver cylinder, emblazoned with a Star of David, containing a parchment scroll on which were written the words Deuteronomy required all Jews to speak each day. I wore it mindlessly, regarding it as an implement of fashion, a Jewish equalizer, so that in gym I would have neckwear like the gentile guys who wore St. Christopher's medals and crosses. Yet it didn't seem strange that my parents would recognize this as emblematic of me. That thought, unexpected, was the only tweaking of genuine feelings I experienced. I handed the mezuzah to June with the disembodied emotions that had accompanied much of what I'd done lately. Once again, I was undergoing something momentous, but time just passed, things just happened. *Traumhaft.* When the word came to mind, I suddenly beamed. June looked at me oddly, but did not wait to ask if I was having second thoughts.

"So he comes back yesterday," Lucy explained to Michael at dinner on Sunday night, "and he just starts packing. I mean, Jesus. 'Where's my dashiki? Where's my pic.' He's running all over. That's all he's saying. And I'm like, 'Hobie, what's going on here, talk to me, honey,' and it's like I'm not even there. I'm following him around—" She couldn't bear more. She started crying. It was nothing to notice by now. She had been crying constantly for twenty-four hours.

"He said, 'You better get out of here, too. The shit's coming down now and it ain't too funky.'"

"What did that mean?" I'd heard the story too many times, but in each telling there was something new. "Cops?"

She had no idea. "He was in this like for-real sweat? He kept running to the window? And I'm trying to ask him about, you know, us— Honestly. He looked at *me*? Like I was flipped out completely. Like, who could bother. And I'm like, 'Jesus, Hobie, where am I supposed to go, what am I supposed to do?' And it's—" Weeping, she couldn't find words to relay his indifference.

"Where is he?" Michael asked. "Does he know where you are?" She flapped both arms uselessly. Michael, for his part, was somewhat better. He still looked desolate and bleary, but he appeared more contained.

"I don't know. Sort of. I told him, 'I think I'll help Seth get up to Canada.'" She looked at me. "Do you think he'll call?"

"No," I said. "I don't." I was well past the point of humoring her. It would be some drive north—honking geese and a blubbering hippie. Not that I wouldn't have welcomed the chance to see Hobie before I left tomorrow. Except for the grimy twisted bit between the Eddgars and my father—the direst secret, they warned, which I would have been far too ashamed to share anyway—my plans remained more or less as they'd been. The Eddgars would collect the ransom; I would leave.

Michael and Lucy and I were drinking wine, supposedly celebrating my last night before becoming a fugitive of the state. We'd lit a candle, stuck in a Chianti bottle, and picked at a crab and a big sourdough bread that Lucy had bought the day before, preparing for a sentimental reunion with Hobie. Our conversation never got much beyond Lucy's tortured recollection of how those plans went awry. Somehow the subject offered heartsore reminders to each of us of the failures of romance.

"What a trio we are," I said suddenly. There was a bedtime story I had read a dozen times to Nile. One animal's blind, one's deaf, another can't speak. They find each other and thrive. They form a band. But I always closed the book thinking, What a wretched depleted community. I couldn't help myself. I laughed out loud. "Love's wasted remains."

Michael received my remark with his worn, silent smile and cleaned his plate.

By the time the late news came on, Lucy was asleep on the sofa. I tried once or twice to revive her, to share my amazement over what was taking place. On Saturday, at the New Haven rally in support of Bobby Seale, demonstration leaders had called for a national student strike to protest the war. Nixon had denounced the campus radicals as "bums" but the idea of a strike was spreading. Eleven college newspapers across the country—including the ones at Princeton, Sarah Lawrence, and Damon—had endorsed the plan.

In Cambodia, on the other hand, the invading U.S. troops were finding few signs of a North Vietnamese presence.

As a base of "operations," as they called it, June had selected the Campus Travel Motel, located down on the east side of Damon, where Campus Boul met the highway. From there our business would be done and my departure made. I was supposed to meet June there around noon on Monday.

That morning, I went upstairs to see Nile off for school. "Shake," I said. He grabbed my thumb handover-style, an obedient trainee in the rev. June had begged me not to say goodbye to him. She couldn't endure a scene. I explained only that I was taking a trip and wouldn't be around after school. "I'm going to send you lots of postcards."

"I like candy," Nile said, somewhat solemnly, as if I didn't know.

I pitched my bags into the Bug and drove down to Robson's. I had seen Sonny's little white waitress outfit in the closet, the stiff apron and white shoes inspiring a few half-humorous overtures about playing nurse. But it was disconcerting to see her dressed that way. It made it seem as if years had passed, instead of a few weeks. Her hair was bundled back into a net, and a little white cap, a crepe tiara, sat atop her like some nesting bird. She lit up when she saw me push through the door, so that unruly emotions suddenly overcame me as I drew up to her at the old lunch counter.

"D day." I shoved my hands into the pockets of my jeans, for lack of anything else to do.

"I know." She'd been counting of course. "I was afraid you'd gone already. I wish you'd let me call. Gus, I'm going outside."

Behind the lunch counter, Gus wiped a hand on his greasy apron and nodded without other comment. He was sucking the last from a cigarette. She grabbed her jacket off a peg in the back and walked me out the rear through the commotion of the kitchen. The floor was red concrete and grimy. "Right back," she yelled in response to someone's protest, and clanked through the back grate into the alley. The refuse of the restaurant—melon husks and thick freezer bags from french fries—was piled beside the Dumpster, rotting fragrantly in the sun. Down one doorway, a cat sprawled on its back on a wooden step, waving its paw in the sunshine in a moment of feline languor, invulnerable and relaxed, seeming to enjoy some memory buried in the DNA of its foregone glory as a tiger.

Once we were alone, Sonny came up and hugged me, held on just to be close, as if there weren't any time or differences between us. The feel of her body, so familiar, crushed me in a vise of difficult emotion.

"You waited to the last minute," she said.

"Yeah, I've been jailbait for about an hour. There's some recruiting officer looking at my name on a list, checking the traffic reports for the highway, and hoping like hell he doesn't have to fill out all the goddamn paperwork." Amid all the uncertainties of the moment, this decision still felt inalterably correct.

We talked about the Peace Corps. Her designation had come through with unexpected speed. She'd be leaving for Manila within the next month. Her assignment was at a family-planning center in the north part of the country. She spoke without notable enthusiasm. It was already a particular place, a job. Signing up, she'd envisioned the bush, the jungle, contact with timeless, indigenous cultures. But the descriptions of the center brought to mind those teeming Asian cities—Bombay, Bangkok: desperation, debasement, filth, an entire population longing for the corruption of the rich. For the time being, she seemed less certain that in journeying ten thousand miles she was going to find adventure or truth, whatever it was she thought she'd miss hanging out with me.

"It'll be great," I said.

"I hope so. Graeme is quoting Horace: 'They change their clime, but not their minds . . . who rush across the sea.'" She shrugged, somewhat melancholic. She had on white tights and clunky white Earth shoes. Her coat, probably Graeme's, a black jeans jacket, covered her hands.

"Guess what?" I said, "Groovy's hitting the road with me."

"Really?"

"She and Hobie are splitsville. You know, she's being a pal. Moral support. That kind of thing."

"Right, moral support," said Sonny. "She's been wanting to get next to you forever."

"Bullshit."

"Hey, women can tell this stuff."

It was making her happy, I knew. This kind of flirting. Pretending I already had a happy, separate life.

"I'm just a ride, Sonny."

"What about your parents?"

"I think I've worked it out," I said stoically. She had lived with me too long, however, not to register the change of tempo. I was helpless as she measured me with one of her dark, searching looks. She understood more about me, I realized, than I'd ever really figured out about her.

"Are you up to something, baby?"

"Something," I answered. It was calling me 'baby' that did it. I had planned to be remote, to guard absolutely the secret, as the Eddgars insisted. With Lucy, for example, I had said we were leaving from the motel in case the army recruiters came looking for me, a silly fiction, since by every account there would be no hunt for me for weeks, until my name was reported to the FBI.

"Cross your heart?" I asked.

She stood back, wary already.

"I'm being kidnapped." I smirked, in spite of the sick breach that opened in me at the mere thought of the next step.

"Kidnapped?" She zeroed in quickly. "What does that mean? What are you telling them?"

"Don't ask," I said. "You wouldn't believe it."

She grabbed my sleeve. "Is Hobie involved with this?"

"Forget it. It's cool, really. It's a bit of a mad stunt, but it's safe for everyone. Just keep it to yourself, okay?" Now that she had hold of me, she did not let go. She came close again.

"Seth, don't go crazy on me."

"It's the times," I said. "It's in the air." I didn't say a word of blame about her, but we both knew.

"God," she said, "why do I feel so terrible? Have I been really lousy to you?"

"The end could have been better. But it's like the stories I make up. It's usually the case."

"I like your stories," she said, nestled against me.

Here we were again, like that cry lost in the fog: I want to be with you; I can't. I had no understanding of what tethered her inside herself, only that she was straining against it, and that, however faintly, I was not completely without hope.

"Twenty-five years from now you may feel real bad about this."

"I feel real bad now." She took a deep breath. "Call me as soon as you're safe. You promise?"

"For sure."

"I want to know just where you are."

"In case you change your mind?"

She smiled faintly.

"It's not too late," I said.

"I know." It was the closest she had been yet.

"I'll be waiting." I walked on that observation. I had my movie dream that I'd hear her racing up from behind. But she didn't. Not yet. I turned to check, to wave. The best I got was that she lingered amid the garbage cans in a patch of sun, and tapped the spot over her heart.

At 10 a.m. precisely, we placed the call to my father's office. The terror that raveled his voice was extraordinary. I realized again how close it lurked beneath the surface of his life.

"Oh my God, Seth."

"Dad, I'm all right. Really, I'm all right."

"Where are you?"

"I can't tell you. They're right here. It's been a little wild."

"Okay, that's enough," June said, beside me, loud enough to be heard. The motel room was dismal, clean but otherwise on its last legs. It must originally have been war construction, a barracks perhaps. The walls were clad at half-height in plastic sandalwood-colored paneling, presumably to hide the gouges. June had drawn the heavy green drapes.

"They understand that they have the wrong guy," I told my father. "I mean, they do now. I finally got them to take me over to the library this morning. I showed them Bernard Weissman in *Who's Who*. And your biography in *American Economists*. It took a while to find something that had your son's name."

"They have let you go?"

"Not exactly."

"Okay," said June. "So he's alive. He's breathing. He's fine." She'd grabbed the phone. Her voice was hoarsened in a way that nearly made me laugh. After all her talk of Drama School, I had expected an inspired performance—something Method, wholly unique. Instead, she seemed simply to have borrowed the manner of the gritty radio dramas—*The Shadow* or *Johnny Dollar*—which were still on the air when I was a boy. But she'd correctly calculated the effect. This was, after all, real life, where the overdone suggested someone sinisterly bent beyond normal restraint. My father was terrified.

"Who is this?" he cried. I was poised, not far from the earpiece.

"This is me. This is the Dark Revolution. This is the voice of the truth. Okay? Next time I call, I'm going to tell you what you can do to make us let him go. First thing, you have to listen to the rules. And obey the rules. Rule One: No phone calls over one minute. And your minute is up right now. Bye-bye."

After she'd clapped down the phone, my father must have sat in his office for some time, perhaps checking his own pulse until he could reestablish his normally orderly thoughts. Perhaps he stared at his coarse, pallid face reflected on the glass of one of his diplomas or citations. Certainly, as always, he talked to himself. The world, he thought, had ceased being a reasoning place. People roamed like beasts, seized by unpredictable emotion, giving vent to wretched fantasy. Waking or sleeping—daylight was the only membrane that separated him now from the turbulence of dreams. But a fragment of him must have been contented and serene. He had spent so many years preparing himself. He had always known he would see it all again.

June called back in fifteen minutes to tell him they wanted ransom.

"You have money. You can pay."

"I am a university professor. I am a poor man." I heard that cunning tone I'd listened to at store counters a thousand times, as he criticized quality, the price, hoping for some edge with which to bargain. With a bitter smile, I had predicted exactly what he would do. And even so, something in me crumbled. There was no hope. "What am I to pay? How? You understand. I am not that Weissman." He went on that way another instant before she interrupted.

"You want to know where your son is now? You have any neighbors with a dog? That's where your son is. He has a dog's choke collar around his throat. It's attached to the fucking wall. His hands are manacled. So are his feet. He sits when we say, he stands when we say. He gets to pee every four hours. Maybe we'll let him go next year. Maybe the year after. I don't care. Dog food's cheap. Do you understand me? Now it's your choice. If that's what you want, you just have to say it. That's Rule Number Two. You tell me what you want. Do you want that? You want us to treat your son like some mangy, flea-ridden, shedding, dogshit-shitting dog we'll do that. You just say. Is that what you'd like? I want to hear you say that. Come on. Follow the rules."

I had never heard my father cry before. He emitted a stifled wheeze, then his voice shattered. I bent over completely and covered my head.

"I want $20,000. That's all. Just twenty. We went into this figuring $2 million. It's fucked up, okay, but we have expenses. This whole fucked-up operation wasn't cheap. We have mouths to feed. We have a lot of people who are a lot of disappointed. Okay? And we need time to make some nice new plans. Now either you help us with that or we won't be helping you. Okay? That's a rule too. Dig?"

He was crying too hard to answer.

"No police, FBI, kiddie cops. Pinkertons. No one. Okay? We set the conditions," said June. She nodded as she held the receiver in the wan light of the cheap lamp. I had sunk to one of the beds and could no longer hear him. "You pay this sum and he's free. Subject to conditions: We don't get caught. This never happened. That's how it goes. I don't trust you, you don't trust me. So we set the conditions."

What conditions? he must have asked.

"Next call." June smacked down the phone. She closed her eyes to grab hold of herself, to find her real life, before she looked down at me.

"It's going fine," she said.

December 9, 1995

SONNY

The home in which Nikki and I live is a narrow, rehabbed graystone in University Park. The contractor carved a garage out of the cellar and laid a downsloping drive that floods in the winter thaw. Beneath the limestone ledges of the tall double-hung windows of the upper floors, wrought-iron flower boxes hold fall geraniums, now withered in their terra-cotta pots. Charlie and I paid too much for this place and I will never get what I need if we sell, a step I often contemplate. The suburbs on the East Bank, with their stable, well-funded public schools, and quiet tree-lined streets, seem tempting. At least a quarter of the families of the children who started in Nikki's nursery-school program are gone to that safer world, but whenever I contemplate the move, I hear Zora. 'The suburbs!' she used to exclaim. 'Better a lobotomy.'

This morning, Saturday, is crowded. Nikki demands a pancake breakfast and then time with her cartoons. I have to get the car into the shop; it's leaking oil again, a shimmering, gunmetal puddle on the garage floor. Walking home from Boyce's Repair, both of us are grumpy. I fret about how to handle the working woman's travail of Saturday grocery shopping without a car, while Nikki fears we'll miss Sam, Charlie's son by his first marriage, who is coming by to take his little sister to the Drees Center for a production of *The Princess and the Pea*.

I often say that I had more anxiety about parting from Sam than Charlie. From infancy, Sam was with us every weekend. He is a special kid, even more so to me, because he proved to be the one human being on earth who finally reassured me I would check out okay as a mother. Sam's own mom, Rebecca, is high-strung and still scorns me a decade later as a homewrecker. Once Charlie left, I was positive she'd never allow Sam back into my home. But Sam tolerated no change. He calls Nikki at least once each week and bikes over from his mother's house, a few blocks away, most Saturday afternoons. He lets himself in, sits while I run errands. He makes them snacks. They play at the computer. I find them, both agape before the screen, Nikki seated on one of his knees.

It's all a mystery. How could a crabbed soul like Rebecca have raised a boy like this? He is funny and brilliant, with the heart of a hero. He plays the piano with passion. He acts in plays. At twelve, he is full of feeling and, not so incidentally, pain. After all, he is Rebecca's son, she of the shrewish moods and damaging tongue. Worse, he's been deserted by Charlie. He seems to cling to Nikki because they are joined, not merely by blood, but by circumstance, not just the gene load Charlie left behind, but the longing. Sam, I often think, has decided to heal himself by being a better man to Nikki than his father has been to both of them.

Today, he arrives in a winter parka he can no longer comfortably close. Charlie, a former wrestler, is huge — not so much tall as broad — and Sam is already headed for size. He's an athletic boy, far less awkward than many his age, although he has that stretched-out look of early adolescence. He is dark and very handsome and innocently pleased by his fine looks. He has begun to carry a comb, to look for himself in any mirror we pass.

I open the door to see them off and amazingly encounter Seth Weissman across the threshold, just lifting his hand to the bell. Like me, he's dressed in jeans and wears a fur-collared leather bombardier's jacket and a broad-brimmed Australian hat. He seems to be one of those bald-headed men with a lot of snappy headgear. A mistake, if you ask me, since it's just more shocking when they remove the cap.

"Nikki, this is a friend of mine, Mr. Weissman. And this is Nikki's brother, Sam." I loosen the furry hood so Seth can appreciate her in full glory. Seth praises her beauty and is careful also to give a moment to Sam. Wordstruck, the two of us watch the children go. Rapt in conversation, they pass the row of rehabbed town homes, many handsomely trimmed out with Christmas lights. Nikki, as usual, picks up a stick and drags it musically along the line of wrought-iron fences.

"They say you just teach them to leave you," I finally remark. "From the first step."

"But you never leave them," he replies. His eyes shoot downward and I spend a moment damning my tongue, then step inside to grab my loden coat. Although I invite him into the entry, he will not cross the threshold.

"I've accomplished my mission," he says. "She's gorgeous. Besides, I have to go to my father's. Deal with the crisis of the day. His car was stolen. All these years, I ragged him for driving around in a 1973 Caprice, and now apparently the damn thing's a vintage item."

I confess I wouldn't mind if somebody stole my minivan and left me with the insurance money to buy a car that didn't require a standing appointment at the mechanic's.

"Do you need a ride anywhere?" he asks.

"I'm just going to the Green Earth." As a stopgap, I'll buy what I can carry. One night this week, I'll find a sitter so I can do the mammoth shopping trip even a family of two requires. These days, I'm always amazed how many people are in the store at 11 p.m.

"Up Fourth? Isn't that on the way to my father's? Come on." He's politely insistent and I don't know whether to say no. In his car, a rented Camry, Seth talks nervously, filling airtime, as if I might not notice that my resolve keeps breaking down. He points out sights around U. Park: Phillips Playground, where he learned to play basketball and tennis; St. Bernard's, Hobie's grade school, an uninspired graystone hulk occupying a quarter of a block.

The parking lot at the store is thronged. There is a line seven or eight cars long waiting to enter, and a melee of shoppers weaving with their stainless-steel carts across the asphalt. We are stuck on U. Ave. as first one, then half a dozen horns bray behind us. Seth holds up a hand as I'm about to get out.

"You think you could stand my father for a minute? I wouldn't mind stopping here myself. I'm pretty sick of room service. Then I could drive you home. You won't need to schlep the bags."

I can shop for the week this way, saving a later trip, hours that will be precious. And I'm somewhat intrigued to see old Mr. Weissman, the iron lion of our youth.

"This is bribery," I tell Seth, as we drive off. We laugh, but I'm not fully at ease. I set the limits for my own comfort, so what's the difference? But I know the best judges seldom change their rulings. If they're wrong, a higher court can tell them. There's a lesson in that.

Seth's father lives in what I've always referred to in my own mind as a 'Kindle County bungalow.' I've never seen similar houses anywhere else, a one-story toadstool of a structure, brown brick, with a hip roof and the stained glass and deco features characteristic of the twenties, when literally thousands of these homes were built throughout the Tri-Cities, blocks of them radiating about a central neighborhood core of churches, schools, shops. They were the Kindle equivalent of row houses, places where working folks with steady jobs could raise their families. The heavy oak front door, darkly varnished, sporting a wrought-iron knocker and a small barred window, opens to reveal a tall young woman. She's dressed in the with-it fashions that inevitably make me feel old: an unstructured vest, a flowing print skirt of autumnal colors, black anklets folded over combat-style boots, revealing the visible down of her unshaved legs. Seth clutches her at once.

"I didn't think we'd catch you," he says.

"I was just on my way. I'm meeting Phil at the museum."

"Stay a minute to say hi." Seth introduces his daughter, Sarah, a senior at Easton.

"Judge Klonsky," Seth says, which I instantly correct to "Sonny."

Sarah is tall, with the glowing fresh-wrapped beauty of the young. Her spare form gives the impression that she's not long past the coltish phase taller girls endure, a distressing period when you're not sure how far your hand is from your shoulder, when you've got four inches on all the boys. Her brownish hair, full of tones, is worn loose to her shoulders. Behind her, the living room of the old house is dim. There is a worn Oriental, heavy raw silk drapes of a long-dated greenish hue, and older, threadbare furnishings in Chippendale style. I was here once or twice twenty-five years ago, and although I have little memory for such things,

I'm relatively certain not a detail has been altered. Sarah has thrown her coat on and her backpack.

"He heard the bell. He's expecting you. He wants you to call the police again."

"Christ," says Seth and glumly asks how his father is doing.

"Etzi-ketzi," she answers. "I got groceries. And I put the bills together."

"You're great. This child is a saint," Seth tells me. "He doesn't deserve you."

"Why do you always say that?"

"Truth is a defense. Isn't that right?" he asks me. "That's what they say in the newsroom."

"It depends on the charges," I answer.

Sarah's narrow mouth purses. "He's an old man." She kisses her father. "Be nice," Sarah warns him, and is gone, with a backward flick of her long hair over the shoulder of her parka. When the thought strikes me, I can't contain a smile.

"What?" he asks. I shake my head, but Seth persists until I answer.

"She has your hair," I say.

"Whoa! Talk about 'Be nice.' "

We're still laughing when the front clapper knocks. Sarah has returned to say that a police car just pulled up. Seth asks Sarah to keep me company. I urge her to go on, but Sarah is a first kid, at ease with the gestures of adulthood, and seems happy to remain. As Seth heads out, she asks about our plans.

"Plans?" I explain how I ended up on this roundabout path to the grocery store.

"Oh." She bites her lip cutely. "I think I got the wrong idea. I think I misunderstood something my Uncle Hobie said the other night." Sarah circles a finger in the dark air of the old house. "You guys aren't an item, right?"

"Your father and I?" I laugh out loud, but see how the confusion arose. "We dated," I put it demurely, "years and years ago, before your parents got together."

"Oh," says Sarah once more, a faint smile this time. "I think I'm just basically stressed-out about my parents. It's way weird," says Sarah, "when you have to think of your parents like your friends."

I assume at first she means that Seth and Lucy are somehow too familiar with her. Nikki is only six, but I worry already that I'll be like many of my contemporaries, Peter Pans, so fully defined, in the generational mode, as opponents of authority that they have been utterly unable to play a firm role with their kids. I grew up with that. Even when I was eight or nine, Zora treated me like a pal. I thought it was wonderful — to call her by her first name, to hear about her troubles. Yet in my twenties, I began to feel cheated. There was a turn in the road others were making that I couldn't manage. But it dawns on me eventually that Sarah is speaking of something different: Seth and Lucy regretfully face the same indeterminacy as people in their twenties.

"Do you know my mom?" she asks.

Years ago, I explain.

"I bet she was the same. She's very earnest, you know, incredibly sincere. And my dad's always there saying funny things under his breath. They're very cool together. It's so, so strange to think of them apart." She looks off to a middling distance, trying to measure her own confusion about these facts, the ripples of misery and dislocation that have imponderably followed her brother's death.

When Seth returns, he says the police are guessing it's some joyriding kid and the car will turn up. Sarah hugs her father and, on the strength of a moment's intimacies, hugs me, too, before departing. After disappearing briefly, Seth leads me to a small room right off the living room, where old Mr. Weissman is seated before an immense rolltop of antique vintage, covered with teetering ramparts of yellowed papers. He appears to have summoned himself to the task of greeting a stranger, his old face raised alertly. His age-hoared hair is sparse and his eyes are dulled and somewhat out of focus, but he has maintained the same rigid, judgmental look I recollect. He is dressed in clothing forty years old if a day, a thin-lapeled grey worsted suit snowed at the shoulders with dandruff, worn over a yellow cardigan. A skinny old tie is knotted askew and his shirt has grown far too large for him at the collar.

"Do you remember Sonny, Pa?" Seth tries. California. Long ago. The old man cannot sort through it. He thinks Seth is referring to a recent trip and, in any event, I clearly made too little impact to be recalled.

"And where is Hobie?" the old man asks. It is a strong Viennese accent: Und vere is Hobie?

"He'll come again, Pa. He was here the other day, remember? He's got his hands full. He's trying a case. Sarah's set the bills out here for you. You can look through them, pay them if you like. I wanted to talk to you about the car. The police are looking for it."

"The police? You spoke with the police?"

"They were just here. I talked to the cop. Very nice guy. He's got it under control."

"You talked? Why didn't I talk?"

"I took care of it."

"No, no. This is my automobile. I should be speaking with the police." Wiss ze police.

"I took care of it."

"Uh-huh," says the old man unpleasantly. He spins a bit in an old oak swivel chair and looks about for something. In a corner, on a metal card table, a black-and-white TV with rabbit ears blinks with shadowy figures. The room, with curtains drawn, is unaired, vaguely unpleasant. There are lingering stale scents, boiled foods, the kind of Middle European odors I smelled in my aunt's Polish home. A frail, spotted hand has risen and the old man smiles bitterly. "You think I am so stupid?"

"Stupid?"

"You think I don't understand? I want the car."

"They're looking, Pa."

"Oh yes, looking." He snorts. A single elderly finger remains cocked at his son. "I want the car." I vont ze car.

The light of some recognition suddenly pales Seth. "You think I have the car?" He turns briefly, helplessly, to me. He's still bent at the waist, addressing his father.

"Ahhhhh. Very innocent. It was you, no, saying I shouldn't drife?"

"Pa. That's everyone. I said it. Lucy said it. Sarah said it. Christ, Pa, the cops have said it. Ninety-three-year-old people are a hazard behind the wheel."

"No, no," he says, "this is you who took the car. There was no policeman. This is you."

"Pa, I wish I were that clever."

"Oh yes. This is a trick. You are always playing tricks. You want my things."

"Oh, Pa."

"Always you want my things. You think I don't know? You think I am stupid. I am not stupid. I want this car." The old man pivots away, his mouth and hands move in aimless, elderly agitation.

"Pa."

"Go."

"Pa."

"Go vay, go." His papery hand flutters. "Right now, I want the car.

Right now! Right now!" His cracked voice mounts, and Seth finds my sleeve and pulls me through the house. At the end of the front walk, he stands in the sharp air, wobbling his head in disbelief. Huge elderly trees, bare in winter, rise in the parkway above the line of cars at the curb.

"It's funny, right?" he asks. "It's like a sitcom."

"Not quite."

He lifts his face to the sky, eternity, and breathes. "God," he says. "I never stay more than ten minutes. It's always something."

I rest a hand lightly on his back. "Your daughter is lovely." It is, as I hoped, the right note, the proper salve.

"The greatest," he answers. "I'm weak with pride whenever I'm with her. It's sinful."

"That's hardly a sin."

"She's the best. She's perfect." When he glances up, a broken look still rides across his eyes. "I get no credit. Everything sane and decent in her comes from Lucy."

"I'm sure that's not the case."

"Right, she has my hair."

"Oh, come on."

"Maybe. Mother's compassion, father's intensity. Child as the crucible of each parent's neuroses. Did you read that book?"

"*Pathways to Madness*? She hardly seems crazy."

"I probably have the wrong book. Isaac was crazy. He was *my* child." Seth shakes his head miserably and, only now feeling the chill, closes his coat. Heaving a final sigh, he mentions the store.

We drive a block or two in silence. On University, the neighborhood's main artery, the Saturday traffic is clotted. Seth swings wide to avoid a man in a yellow tie, who is frantically waving at a taxi. With Christmas nearing, the streets teem with shoppers—students, teachers, the neighborhood denizens—all feeling buoyed by U. Park's cosmopolitan air and the upbeat atmosphere of the onrushing holidays. They are visiting the small, bright stores which are adorned with green fringes of Christmas frippery or blinking lights. Behind the wheel, Seth, in his broad hat, studies the road pensively. Eventually, he apologizes again for making me witness that scene.

"Oh come on, Seth. Who better than an old friend?" I try to sound lighthearted, but I'm shaken myself. Parents and children. It never ends.

"Did you lose friends when you got sick?" he asks.

"Some. I probably had fewer to start than I'd have liked. But there were a couple of people who made me wonder if they thought cancer was contagious."

"Yeah," he says and ponders. "That's how it is. It turns out there's only so much of your shit some of your friends can take. Damaged, you're no use to them. I can name six guys who never were the same with me again because I cried in front of them after Isaac." He glances my way. "What happens to us as we get older?"

I can't answer that.

"I'm sorry I wasn't around," he says. "When you got sick? I'm loyal."

I recognize this as a substantial truth, part of what has pulled on me. Seth is loyal. Reliable. No question of that.

"That's me and Hobie," he says. "That's one thing we've finally mastered. Loyalty. Hanging in. I've seen him through three divorces and fourteen religions, and he's seen me through Isaac. All my shit."

"You're lucky," I say, and he is quick to agree.

"Crazy as he is, I'm lucky to have him."

"Is he still as big a lunatic in private?"

"Holy smokes," answers Seth and lets his head reel at the notion.

"He doesn't bring it to court. I'll bet he's got a marvelous practice."

"I guess. But you look at his ability, his education—he should be on track to become Chief Justice of the United States. And instead, he's just bumping along. He's literally been through six law partnerships. Large, small. There's always somebody big-time who's pissed and blackballing him from some honor. You know," he says, "I look around, at this age, I keep seeing the same thing. There were all these brilliant, talented people I knew in my twenties and thirties who were going to do amazing things in the world when they got the right break. And thank God, a lot of them have. But there are other people who got the chance but couldn't get over themselves. You know what I mean? They can't project whatever they've got into the world, because they're forty-eight years old and still dealing with their own shit."

"That's me," I say. My frankness for a moment startles us both. "It is," I repeat.

"How's that you? You're a judge. You're a big *macher*."

"Not in the law world. I'm a public employee. I'm an upper-middle-level bureaucrat. I'm not making $300,000 a year. I'm not a factor to deal with politically. I'm not even sure the powers-that-be won't maneuver me out of this job. There are lawyers who'd tell you I've dead-ended, that I've settled for less."

"I don't believe that," he says.

Nonetheless, that's my view of myself: not a power, not a star, no more than halfway to what might have been my destiny, if I didn't need to spend so much time coping with myself. When I was younger, I believed that the middle ground was a deadly morass. That you had to reach. Not to the greatest heights. But to some slight elevation, beyond the doomed grey middle. Maybe Zora inspired that. But I quit believing that somewhere, probably in the midst of illness, and surely with motherhood, when I made a commitment to the female sector of the yin and the yang. I point Seth toward the store, a block away, and try to remind myself that once we've parted, I'll be harrowed by doubt if I continue these candid reflections on my judicial career.

"And why's Hobie so crazy?" I ask. "Was it his family?"

"Hobie? It's DSM 3.004."

"What's that?"

"A shitty personality." As always, he absorbs my laughter appreciatively. "No, I thought his family was great. His father, man—I'd lie in bed at night and just die wishing his father could have been mine."

"What about all the dope he took? Is that part of it?"

"I think I wouldn't be so quick to use the past tense. And I think in Hobie's case, it's a symptom, not a cause. No, whenever I ask myself what gives with him, I come back to the obvious: being a black man in America. I think Hobie feels like a person without a country. He doesn't fully belong to anybody. I think he's honest enough to see himself as elite. Super education. Big income. But there's still the black thing of not being fully accepted, and dealing with how vulnerable that makes you.

"I always remember the same incident. When we were in eighth grade, we played touch football with some big jerk named Kirk Truhane, who, one day, sort of out of the blue, called Hobie a nigger. You know, Hobie was big, he was rough, and he knocked Truhane down on the gravel. And Truhane gets up and comes out with this *word*. And I mean, I remember thinking, God, this can't have happened, what do I do now? He was my best friend by then. At first I kept playing, even after Hobie left, but finally my conscience got to me, and I walked off too, and I found him around the school building bawling his eyes out. And he just kept repeating the same thing: 'It hurts my feelings.' In any other circumstance, Hobie probably would have beat the snot out of Kirk Truhane. But that one word sapped his strength. It destroyed him—to know he couldn't get beyond that label.

"And I really think that's how it is. Family? Sure. First and foremost.

But history changes people, too. Doesn't it? I mean historical forces—your place, your society, its rules, its institutions. That's what politics is about, isn't it? Trying to get the foot of history off the throat of people? Let them be what they can. I know, as a concept, it can be a crutch. That's why so many people want to be victims today. So they don't have to accept the burden of being raised without historical calamity—without war or famine. They want an excuse for the fact they're still not happy. But there's a reality, too. Your time and its circumstances can thwart you. They can make you crazy—subtly, the way they've crazed Hobie. Or big-time, the way history crazed my father. Maybe Zora, too. I mean, I've always thought," he says, as he slides the car into a space in the grocery lot and faces me with a look of measured daring, "I've always thought history was one of the things that came between us."

Green Earth is a health-food superstore, a virtual supermarket, baking beneath the usual blast of high-powered light. Banners and signs, adorned at the corners with silver Christmas bells, stretch aloft, noting freshness and nutrition data. Seth, never without his pointed observations, the trait that gives him something to say in print three times a week, characterizes Green Earth as a tumorous version of the little macrobiotic places on Campus Boul in Damon where we'd argue about Adelle Davis and the health effects of refined sugar. This is another column he's written too many times, he says: the selling of the revolution. Music went commercial first. But capitalism has sucked up every element, clothing, language, absorbing the style but not the message. Now everyone can be hip, for a price.

The store is in the usual weekend turmoil. We have to queue just to get the featured items off the shelves. In their cold-weather wear, the students and grandpas and city moms trail through the aisles. Seth and I separate to shop. He returns with apples, dried fruit, spring water, peanut butter, little treats for the life of the man in the hotel suite. Surveying what's in my basket, he correctly guesses that I'm a vegetarian. Since my illness, I explain. Nikki occasionally asks for meat, which I willingly provide—it's not a fetish—but the two of us generally subsist on pastas. God has never made a six-year-old who didn't enjoy noodles. He briefly recalls some of Sarah's dietary obsessions fifteen years ago. Noodles and baked beans.

"I never asked what she's doing in school."

"Sarah? You ready?" he asks. "Jewish studies." Another of those moments: I've let my jaw drop. "She's doing an honors thesis on feminist reworkings of the liturgy. Whether we ought to say 'God of our fathers' or 'of our fathers and mothers' or 'parents' or 'ancestors.' Tradition, authority, and gender in a religious context. Interesting," he adds.

"Did you become observant, Seth?"

"It's Lucy," he answers. At the time of their marriage, Lucy promised Seth's mother she would make a Jewish home. She converted and by now has been president of their congregation, not once but twice. Four years ago, he says, she had a bat mitzvah.

"And how do you handle that?" I ask.

"With ambivalence. You know, you get older. You're more aware of the people before you, acknowledging them and what they cared about—and died for. The Holocaust is bigger to me every year, especially now that my mom is gone. I actually raised funds for the museum. But the ritual leaves me cold. They don't even catch glimpses of me in the synagogue. Lucy and Sarah always say they're praying for me. Sometimes I feel like one of those sixteenth-century Catholics who lined up other people to do their time in Purgatory. But I'm proud of Sarah. I'm glad she's serious about important things." We nudge the carts along. Seth circles his jaw as his face mobilizes beneath some transitory discomfort. "I'm not sure I've got her approval at the moment, but she knows she has mine."

"I'm sure she approves, Seth. Of both of you. She just sounds concerned. It's a hard situation for her, too."

He cranes about to eyeball me. "How did that come up?"

"Oh." I shovel the items from my cart onto the moving belt. The checker is a young Asian man. Off-duty, he wears rings through his nose and eyebrows. Nikki cannot control herself and squeals whenever we see him on the street. "Basically, when she asked if we were involved."

"Us? Oh Lord. This is the child whose maturity I've been bragging about?" He grimaces and looks away to a shelf beside the cash register, crammed with the same dumb trash tabloids and ladies' mags I see in the poison supermarket.

"She seemed to have misunderstood something Hobie said."

"Oh. I know what that was. He was giving me gas the other night when we had dinner with Sarah. Guy stuff. Hobie said every time he looks around the courtroom, he wonders if I'm here to watch the trial or the judge." His eyes cross mine bashfully, meaningfully, and then, as shyly as if it were actual contact, he looks away—a rabbit darting back into its hole. It's reminiscent of the moment we had pulling in here when he spoke of history.

We pay separately and wheel one cart through the small lot, back into the winter air, which is sharpening as the hour of darkness nears. The sun is a pale disk in the soiled white sky. Between us a deliberative silence has persisted, more uncomfortable as the seconds mount.

"Can I ask, Seth?" I say suddenly. "Why *are* you here?"

He is slinging packages into the trunk and gives me a brief sidewise look.

"Acute psychological need," he answers. He smiles to put me off, then thinks better of it and turns my way. "Look, I'm here for lots of reasons. This trial—it's like the star over Bethlehem. It's a weird conjunction of the planets. I'm concerned or interested in every person involved—Nile, Hobie, Eddgar, and, God knows, you. I mean, if that's what you're asking, yes, Hobie's right. I've thought about you a lot, Sonny. I always have. If that doesn't sound too drippy."

We've reached a Rubicon. I see it and feel something frantic swimming through my eyes. Seth takes this in, his pale face rummaged by dashed feelings, then moves off toward the driver's side door. We ride halfway to my house without a word spoken.

"Say something," he finally tells me.

"I would, if I could think of anything to say."

"Is it bad that I'm still hung up on you?" he asks.

"Not 'bad.'"

"Shocking?"

"Probably. Surprising, anyway."

"Because you're not still hung up on me?"

"Because life goes on, Seth. It's the past. Before the dinosaurs. I have more recent mistakes to dwell on."

We arrive home at just the right moment. Nikki and her brother are coming down the block. I stand on the stoop in my green coat waving, and both kids rush to join me. Sam and Nikki re-enact a number of scenes from the play, repeating the lines perfectly; it's clear they have been doing this all the way home. Then Sam kisses his sister and me and grabs his bike, which has been locked to one of the iron gate posts. Seth, in the meantime, comes up the walk with the last of my groceries in his arms. Waking to him again, I am deeply struck by his presence. I find myself thinking he has aged well, although that makes no sense. His eyes are lively and deep, there is strength across the brow, but time has thickened his skin, taken something from his looks. In ten more years, his face will be waddled and lumpy. But it's substance, I feel, some sense of the weight of the life he's lived. A good person. Again, a strong sensation of his pain grips me, and with it something regretful and self-accusatory. I was unkind just now. At the store.

"Look, Seth. Why don't you stay and let me make some of these groceries into dinner?"

"No, no," he says. "I have some stuff to write."

"I mean it. I promise it's healthy and it won't be room service."

"Don't take pity on me, Sonny. You warned us both about that the other day."

"No, Seth, no. I want to know you. I do. We're going past each other. And we shouldn't. Stay. Tell Nikki what a newspaper is like." I step down off the stoop to take the last packages from him. "Let's be at peace, Seth."

He flaps his arms. Fine, peace. Whatever that means.

My house has the crisp look of newer construction, everything painted white to expand the rooms. The entry and living area rise to a cathedral ceiling and skylights that spill, even in this dim season, the welcome tonic of interior light; it glistens on the peachy-colored floors of bleached birch. The furnishings are spare—Charlie got the couch, for instance—but the shelves and walls are crowded with art collected over our years. African masks, Native American pots, posters by abstractionists and moderns. Laughing, Seth steps over the blocks and bright toys that litter the living room. He remembers this phase, he says, when some lost plastic piece of something was always turning up underfoot.

Now that Sam has departed, Nikki suddenly turns shy. In the kitchen, as I shelve the groceries, she clings to my thigh and flirts from that zone of safety. She has a somewhat old-fashioned hairdo, a ponytail and bangs. Seth remarks on her eyes—brilliant and intelligent, he says, like her mother's.

"Can you make a beard?" Nikki asks.

"Make a beard?" asks Seth.

"Charlie has a beard."

"Ah." He kneels and lets her stroke his shaved cheek. She accepts him quickly after that. He lifts her to the top shelves to put the canned goods in the dark, oak cabinets. Eventually tired of this, Nikki tries to lure me into a game of checkers.

"Nikki, I need to start dinner."

"I'll start," says Seth. "Give me an assignment."

"Nikki, what if you play checkers with Seth?"

Seth cajoles. He's a veteran. He'll teach her secret moves. They lay the board out on the living-room floor. Nikki is voluble, enthusiastic, and like all six-year-olds plays to win. I hear them as I run the tap.

"Don't go there," Seth counsels. He shows her his moves in advance. Even so, Nikki must take a number of moves back before Seth is defeated. They play Topple next, a game Seth does not know, which involves balancing plastic pieces on a stand.

"Know what?" she asks. "I have a loose tooth."

"No! So early?"

"Feel. That one. Isn't it loose?"

"Maybe." I come out of the kitchen to warn Seth with a roll of my eyes. Nikki and I repeat this exercise each night. Six wants to be seven and fifty wants to be forty. When are we happy as we are?

"Next to it," she says. "Try that."

He has the same lack of success.

"No!" Nikki shrieks and throws herself down on the floor and rolls back to him like a puppy, more or less propelling herself into his arms. She grabs both his cheeks, something she does to Charlie.

I return to the kitchen, trying not to find this performance alarming. My little girl, shy and generally collected, is rocketed into hilarity by the attentions of an adult male, exhibiting all the charm she can muster. When I come into the living room to announce dinner, Nikki has seated Seth on the ledge of the hearth and is singing the numbers from the Holiday Festival, humming through the words she has forgotten. He applauds wildly.

"Dinner. Dinner. Wash up."

In the bathroom, from the toilet, Nikki eyes me. "Do boys have to wipe?"

"Sometimes yes, sometimes no." Yet again, I outline the circumstances. "Some things are important," I tell Seth, when I find him waiting mirthfully outside the door.

My Aunt Henrietta, Zora's sister, insists that Nikki is the image of me. She means to praise both of us, but the observation concerns me. When her will-of-the-wisp father phones on Mondays or Tuesdays to apologize for missing the call he is supposed to make Sunday at noon, Nikki consoles him. 'That's okay, Daddy,' she will say, 'you didn't mean to.' But within, beneath, what is occurring? I played the cheerful child into adolescence—amusing, even, able to adapt to everybody else. It was only in my thirties, while I was in law school, that I began to wonder about the savage part of me, so often kindled in debate. I worry now that Nikki rages too in ways yet to reach the surface.

In the kitchen, removing the cannelloni from the Pyrex dish in a sudden rush of steam, I stave off familiar guilt. There was no choice. With Charlie. And I grew up, didn't I? I muddled through, a little nuts about men, especially in my teens, but I'm centered, I'm normal. And Nikki has a father. Something. A picture. A phone call. And yet a sense of failure always freezes me to absolute zero at the center when I realize that my daughter dwells with the same pain that burned through my childhood. For years, I went through spells in which I persuaded myself that my mother's account of Jack Klonsky's death on the Kewahnee docks was one of those well-intended lies about provenance told in fairy tales—like what they said to Sleeping Beauty to keep her from knowing she was really a princess. I, too, was secretly some other man's daughter. These fantasies took me on strange internal journeys. For many months, I suspected my father was a labor leader named Mike Mercer, a congenial potbellied black man, a friend of Zora's. He had five children of his own, but I believed my parentage was hidden so no one knew I was a Negro.

More often, I imagined my father as someone distant, barely known, some man of majestic importance who would arrive one day and care for me passionately. I envisaged this unknown man as the father on *Father Knows Best*. A striking, dashing, normal person. An American. Did I realize as a little girl how much Zora would have abhorred that image? But he was what I craved, a wise, gentle, omnipotent figure, whose faults all righted themselves within half an hour and whose love for his daughters, especially, was as simple and encompassing as his occasional chaste embrace. In contemplating all of this, I feel, as I often do, horribly sorry for both Nikki and myself.

Seth lavishes praise on the meal. "Who says people can't change?" he asks puckishly. Nikki remains too excited to eat. To interest her, he shows her a trick he did with his children, turning his cannelloni into a dachshund. "Kennel-oni," he calls it, earning a groan from each of us.

"I want a puppy," Nikki tells him, as she often, futilely, tells me. I explain that is one over my limit: the thought of housebreaking is impossible when I'm still celebrating the end of diapers. Seth recounts coming home one night when Isaac was little to find Lucy attempting to train their puppy. She was outside, with her skirt hiked up, squatting over the gravel of the dog run and relieving herself. The dog and Isaac, noses at the screen of the back door, both looked on bewildered. Caught in this compromising pose Lucy remained there, laughing in delight at this amazing, oddball family intimacy.

Nikki finds his story spectacularly funny. "She was going like a dog? Mom, she was going like a dog." She gets off her chair to play out the scene and is far too keyed up to sit down when I demand that. After several efforts to restore calm, I take her to the den and turn on a video. Better a zombie than a creature ricocheting off the walls.

"I should have thought of that," says Seth, when I return.

"Fortunately, it's winter. Otherwise, we'd be on our way outside for a reenactment." Seth follows me into the snug kitchen, where I put another helping on his plate. "It's a great story. Lucy sounds adorable."

"That's what everybody says: 'Lucy's adorable.' "

I take a beat. "What does her husband say, Seth?"

"Oh." He groans. "You don't need to hear me complain about Lucy. Believe me, not every eccentricity is lovable. I mean, I never got used to living with somebody who actually cared about whether the dishes 'matched' the wallpaper in the breakfast room." He spreads his fingers to make the quotation marks in the air. "Even the constant good cheer can seem over a couple of decades like a prolonged form of lying. But on a scale of goodness, 1 to 10, bearing in mind the kind of crumbs many human beings are, Lucy's way up there. Nine point five and rising."

"That doesn't sound too bad, Seth. I'm not sure even Charlie's *mother* would give him more than a seven. On a good day."

"Yeah, but Lucy's not the point. Not by herself. It's us together."

"Because of your son?"

"That's part of it. A big part. What confounds me is that I know that if he hadn't died—Isaac?—we'd be together. The deal, whatever it is that I made, that we made, would seem okay. But when a child passes— It's the most mysterious thing, but the love, I don't know, it can go, too. We've had wildly different ways of coping. She's become this ridiculous, fucking mystic. She's studying Kabbalah, she's into dybbuks. It's very Catholic, frankly, even though the words are Hebrew. And there's this young rabbi—I mean, I don't think anything's going on exactly, and I'm not the one to throw the first stone anyway. But we're a million miles apart. And even if we somehow get over that, I still have to face my own stuff."

"Which is?"

"Well, why did you leave what's-his-name?"

"Charlie? Basically, I realized that growing up as Zora's daughter I had developed this way of capitulating to difficult people, allowing them to run wild while I tried to be sensible. And Charlie demonstrated that there could be too much of that, even for me. Especially once I found out there was a coed named Brandy."

"Okay, so you said, Well, *I* can do better. And you showed him the door. I think that's why most people quit on a marriage. They wake up and think, I'm a better person than that. I can be more sensible. More generous. I can be less fucked up if I give myself another start. Sometimes they're kidding themselves. But sometimes, a lot of times, they're not. And that's really the issue for me. With Lucy. I dwell on what's never been right between us. I mean, Lucy and I, we've always had this"—he's looking for the word—"game? Discussion? Usually it was comic relief during an argument. But we'd ask one another: What if you met someone who was perfect? Who was The Person. What if you met *that* person?"

"You still have to say everything, don't you, Seth?"

"I'm better."

I doubt it. "So what's the rest of the story?"

"The answers would change. Both our answers. Sometimes when we were pissed we'd say 'I'd run away.' We'd say we'd have an affair. That's what we said most of the time—you know, that's where there was permission, if it was *that* perfect. Sometimes we'd say it wasn't worth the risk to our family. But we never kidded each other enough to say, That's you, that person, that perfect person, that's you for me. Never. Not even for a minute."

To absorb this, I have taken a seat on one of the dark oak spindle chairs at the tiny kitchen table where Nikki and I have most of our meals—breakfast cereals and evening noodles. I don't believe in that anymore, the perfect person. That's exactly who I thought Charlie was, dark and massive, quixotic, full of the impulsiveness I grew up thinking was rightfully a man's. He was all that stuff, The Other. It made me wet between the legs and agonized the rest of the time. I will never succumb to it again. But somehow as Seth finishes this confession something passes in his look—that timorous, exploring gaze I got a couple times at the food store—and I react at once.

"Don't, Seth."

"Don't what?"

"Don't start. Or be difficult. Or pretend."

" 'Pretend'? "

"That's exactly the right word. Don't kid yourself. Don't act as if we had the greatest thing since Troilus and Cressida, or that we had some destiny that was thwarted. That's not the way I remember it."

He makes a face, and pushes his plate aside. "Why are you giving me such a hard time?"

"Why? Because you're sitting around mooning. And it's disconcerting."

"So let me have my fucked-up life and my perverted little fantasies, all right? This isn't bail. I don't need your permission."

"Don't talk to me like that, goddamn it."

"How do you think I should talk to you?" he asks. "Look, you want me to be honest? This is honest: I was crazy about you. And I never thought we got to the end of where we were going, before all that historical junk intervened. Would it have been great? I don't know. Maybe we would have fought World War III. But would it have been different than what I went on to? You bet your life. And you know, just at the moment, I can't help thinking about that."

"So?"

"So," he says, "in my head, I figure it'd be neat to be around you a little. See what happens. Time or not, I just don't think people change that much at the core, Sonny. That's where I'm at. But if you tell me to take a powder, I'll do it. I'll feel bad and all that shit, but I accept the risk. But you've started this twice now and somewhere along we're going to have to mention you. You keep acting like you're powerless here," he says, "like all the choices are mine. Where do you fit in, Sonny? What do you do, if you can't talk me out of this?"

We're back to the parking lot, although I can't for the life of me see how we got here. Staring at Seth in the still kitchen, my eyes feel childish and large. I blink.

Nikki, perfect child, arrives at that moment to save me. She holds Spark, a stuffed puppy, by a single, bedraggled paw. She is rubbing her eyes and whiny. She should have a bath, but the thrill of Seth seems to have left her weary and she mewls at the thought.

"A book and bed," I say.

"You read." Nikki points to Seth. Exhausted, she seems to have forgotten his name, everything but the fact that she's in love with him.

From her bedroom, their voices tumble down the stairs. In the living room, I open *The Nation,* but do not even see the page. To speak and be heard; to hear and understand. How much more do we want? So much of this is welcome—why then do I resist? Atop the stairs, Seth tells Nikki good night.

"You know what?" Nikki asks, delaying his departure now by any means. "My teacher, Mrs. Schultz? She's almost fifty years old and she still can't whistle."

Seth whistles a few bars of "Goodnight, Irene," then I'm summoned for the final rituals. We pass on the stairs with contained smiles, measuring our mutual enjoyment of my child. He says he will wait to say goodbye, and is down there, in his coat, slumped over and twirling his hat, as he waits beside the staircase on the old country bench which Nikki and I will shortly be using to pull on our boots, when the snow flies.

"You made an enormous impression," I tell him.

"Hey," he says, "one out of two."

"Seth, it's not like that."

"How is it?"

I heave a weary breath. "Confusing," I answer, and know it's the most honest thing I've offered yet. He tips his head philosophically, then zips his coat. He thanks me for dinner and sings Nikki's praises again, before I finally, thankfully, move him to the door.

"I'm not trying to drive you crazy," he says there.

"Yes, you are," I answer. "You always have. But it's endearing." I extend my hand, but it's a false gesture, far too distant for where we are now. We hold in the abrupt evening quiet of the small house, the whir of the appliances rising from the kitchen, amid a sudden sense of the tender space between us dwindling.

"Do it," he says to me.

"What?"

"Kiss me."

"*Kiss* you?" I laugh out loud.

But he closes on me, as in the movies. I have offered my cheek, but he straightens my face with a single finger and puts his lips on mine. The shock of being this close to a man is one of presence and of longing. Everything kicks in, mobile with sensation—heart and breasts, hips and fingertips. An extraordinary parched ache reaches far down into me so it is all I can muster to hold back a groan. His hand in the moment of embrace has roamed to the small of my back. I step away, and we stand for just an instant with our foreheads touching. I take hold of both his hands.

"Let's sort this out after the trial."

"Listen, that trial won't change anything."

"It'll make this a lot of easier for me. I'll see you afterwards." I turn his shoulder toward the doorway.

When he is gone, my brow rests against the sleek varnish of the front door, chill with the cold outside. Madness, I think again. *What* is in my mind? Is it only because I feel so sorry for him? I hang Nikki's coat on the peg beside the threshold, I turn the bolt. It's because I *know*, I think suddenly. Know that whatever sentiment he nurtures, he is not really here for me. Know that he is wounded and recovering. That his life is circling. That he will be here, then gone. Know that—yes—and isn't this one of those sick truths we always know best about ourselves?—it will be safe.

December 11, 1995

"Mr. Trent," Hobie says with somewhat sinister distinctness. He appears restored by a weekend's rest. He's had a crisp-looking haircut and lost the haggardness of a week on trial, the reddened, jumpy eyes, the runnels of sleeplessness. He strides to the center of the room to confront Core, who is still settling himself on the witness stand.

"Cuz," answers Hardcore. A wayward note of black-on-black contempt. Hobie momentarily addresses him in silence, chin elevated, seeing how it is.

I have already passed an hour this morning with the attorneys in a lengthy chambers conference. Hardcore's lawyer, Jackson Aires, played stalking horse for the prosecution. He asked to limit Hobie's cross, claiming that Core should not be forced to incriminate himself about matters that go beyond his guilty plea in this case. In reply, Hobie railed about his client's constitutional right to fully confront the witness. To avoid poisoning myself with an endless rundown of Hardcore's grossest misdeeds, I ruled that the episodes would be taken up one by one during cross. Each event will be portrayed in generalized terms, and Aires and the trial lawyers then can argue about its relevance.

Aires now sits tensely at the edge of a folding chair, set about six feet behind the prosecution table against the low oak partition that runs beneath the screen of bulletproof glass. Well past sixty, Jackson, in his familiar burgundy sport coat, remains a figure of grace and ease, a long loose-jointed African-descended male with that snowball pomp above his forehead and a manner reflecting thoroughgoing contentment with his own views. In chambers, the discussion between Hobie and him became heated, due in no small measure to the fact, which eventually emerged, that Aires is one of Hobie's father's oldest friends and even employed Hobie for one summer during law school. Jackson, who has never encountered an advantage he was unwilling to use in a courtroom, repeatedly referred to Hobie as "young Tuttle" and told him more than once he had no idea what he was talking about.

Perhaps it is the stress of performing before his old mentor, or the procedure I've insisted on, which has altered the order in which Hobie wanted to proceed, but he seems flatfooted almost from the start of his examination. The cross does not go well.

"You made a sweet deal with the prosecution, didn't you?" he begins. Hobie batters Core with various examples of how much worse things could have gone for him. As part of the plea agreement, the prosecution agreed not to charge Core with any of the narcotics offenses he committed daily. In the upside-down world of contemporary criminal law, a murder conviction often carries a lesser penalty in real terms than a drug crime, for which both parole and good time have been essentially abolished in this state. Core would do eighteen years if the same stretch was for selling dope. And had the prosecutors contrived one of their far-fetched arguments linking June's death to a narcotics transaction, they would have been obliged by statute to seek the death penalty.

Well rehearsed, Core admits matter-of-factly that flipping on Nile dramatically improved his sentence. More important, as Hobie teases out the details of the plea agreement, the inferences somehow turn against him. In one of those spontaneous audience reactions characteristic of the courtroom, we all seem to recognize together that Core's credibility is actually enhanced by the deal he's made. A hang-tough gangbanger like Hardcore would go back to the penitentiary only because he had no other choice. Someone was going to burn him, if he didn't cop out first. And logically the person Core feared could only be Nile. After messing up, killing June, the mother Nile presumably loved, instead of Eddgar, the father he apparently hated, Core recognized a high likelihood that Nile, in grief or rage, would eventually roll over on him. That's how I add it up. I find myself somewhat shocked, much as I was on Friday, by the mounting nuances pointing toward Nile's guilt.

"Some women sold their bodies to buy your crack, didn't they?" Hobie asks, pointing out the gravity of what Core's gotten away with. "Some folks stole?" Hardcore quarrels at points—he didn't tell nobody to steal—but acknowledges what he must in a well-schooled tone that insists, correctly, that none of this is news. Often when I sit up here, I attempt to imagine the outlaw existence of the hardened young people who come before me: getting up each morning with no real conviction that you're going to end the day intact. Someone may shoot you; you may have to slap-up some homie who has a knife you didn't see, or the Goobers may come by, slippin, and gauge you at sixty feet. Creature things must dominate. Heat and cold. Sex. Intoxication. Each moment is a struggle to maintain dominance or at least power—downtalking everyone around you, exerting strength, sometimes cruelly. And making no real plans. A vague shape to tomorrow, and no thought at all of a month, let alone a year. Survive. Make do. Life as impulse. And why not?

Having accomplished little thus far, Hobie reaches deeper. He leers across the podium and asks, "Now, Mr. Trent, would you mind telling us how many other people you've killed?"

Aires and both prosecutors leap up, all of them shouting objections. This is the kind of question we were arguing about in chambers.

"Is this for credibility, Mr. Tuttle?" I ask. He shakes his head yes and I shake my head no. "I don't think it's necessary. Mr. Trent has admitted he's a murderer for hire. Whether it's one murder or twenty, that acknowledgement of that sort of conduct gives me an adequate window on his character. I'll sustain the objection."

Hobie, unfailingly respectful of my rulings until now, can't keep himself from raveling up his lips in pique. He repeats his bitter complaints about interference with Nile's constitutional rights to confront the witness. For the first time, he is clearly setting me up for appeal and even goes so far as to move for a mistrial—a claim that my ruling is so unfair, he'd rather start the trial again from scratch. It's routine defense hysterics—a sort of exclamation point for his objections—and I respond with a single word: "Denied."

Listening to this byplay, Hardcore displays a japing smile. For Core, this is head-up, street stuff, dude on dude, the kind of strife he's always known. He thinks he's winning. Studying him, I notice a teardrop etched beneath the corner of his right eye. He is dark enough that the tattoo barely shows, but it means he's killed with his own hands. There is probably not a Top Rank gangster out there who has not shot or knifed someone. Yet despite my glib assurances to Hobie, the sight—the reality—remains disquieting.

Hobie's next sortie is a series of questions about the crimes for which Core was arrested, but not convicted, as both a juvenile and an adult. I let Hobie explore a charge of deviate sexual assault that arose when Core, early in his career with BSD, lured a whore into a Grace Street apartment, beat her, and made her service dozens of young men, each of whom, under this arrangement, paid him instead of her. But as Hobie attempts to thumb through the catalogue of Hardcore's earlier thuggery—everything from truancy to zip-gun stickups—I begin to see the point of Aires's and the prosecutors' vehement objections. It's unfair to force Core to acknowledge much of this conduct, which has little to do with his honesty. Jackson Aires comes from his seat in back and stands before the bench to argue.

"Judge, I was the lawyer there for Trent here on all these cases," Jackson says, "and I can tell the court, Judge, there was somethin wrong with each of them." On Core's rap sheet there are twenty-two arrests which Jackson somehow beat. Sometimes he filed motions to suppress, or objected successfully on technical grounds like venue; more often— if the rumors are true—he agreed that the $1,500 pocket money Hardcore had when he was booked in Area 7 could be forgotten if certain incriminating details disappeared as well from the collective memory of the police. In Jackson's view, there's no reason black gangsters shouldn't take advantage of the same devices white ones have always employed. He'll admit that to you straight up, in the confidence of a barroom or a corridor, with a stern, humorless look daring you to tell him he's wrong.

By the time we return from the morning recess, a dazed air has come over the courtroom. The spectators' benches, thick at 9 a.m. with those awaiting a cross which the papers promised would produce theatrics, now have thinned. Hobie continues to look poised, but I know, having been there, that he spent the last ten minutes telling himself he is going to have to get Core now or, surely, lose.

"Let's talk about the shooting," he says, ambling toward the door to the lockup. "It was your homeboy, Gorgo, who actually gunned down Ms. Eddgar, right?"

"Sure 'nough," Core answers. You would not call his demeanor mournful.

"And have the po-lice asked you to help them find Gorgo?"

Core thinks about it and shrugs. "Cuz hit the wall, man. Ain no tellin where that mother gone."

"Well, help me, Hardcore, I'd think you'd want to find Gorgo. Isn't he one more person who could tell the police whether or not what you're saying is true?"

Molto objects that the question is argumentative, which it is, but given the constraints I've already imposed on the cross, I allow it.

"He ain goin 'gainst me," Hardcore says with a faint smile. It's not clear if Core is asserting the truthfulness of his testimony or a reality of gang life. "Sides, man," he adds, "nigger don't want to be found, you know? He ain just run from the po-lice neither. I git my dogs on that motherfucker, time I done, he be rankin out." Begging for mercy. Core, feeling friskier as the cross goes on, ends his answer with another sneer in Hobie's direction. There is a scratchy something between them, a contest that goes beyond the courtroom. Bold and unruly, Core seems to assert at every pass that he's the real black man, poor, raised without refuge, full of the rightful indignation of the oppressed. Hobie, in Core's view, is a fake, someone who doesn't know the real deal, a challenge to which Hobie seems oddly vulnerable. That, perhaps, is what's sapped some of his strength.

"You're pretty angry with Gorgo?"

"Word," answers Hardcore, and at the further thought of Gorgo gives his head a disgusted shake.

"Because he shot Ms. Eddgar while you were standing there, right? You and Bug? And that's how you got in trouble?"

"I stand behind that," says Core.

Turning away from the witness, I see Hobie smile fleetingly for the first time. Has he got something?

"Now, how close to Ms. Eddgar was Gorgo on this bicycle when he shot her?"

With his long nail, Hardcore describes the distance between Hobie and him. Close enough to kill. Core grins tautly at the thought. Hobie, catching the drift, smiles too.

"He could see it was a woman, couldn't he?"

Molto objects that Core can't testify to what Gorgo could see.

"Fair enough," Hobie says. "*You* could see it was a woman when you were twelve feet from her, couldn't you?"

"I ain dumb like he is."

Hobie absorbs that. Core fences well.

"Well, Bug was waving to Gorgo?"

"Thass right."

"Trying to stop him?"

"Thass right."

"But you didn't wave?"

"Naw."

"You didn't shout to him?"

"Uh-uh."

"You hit the pavement?"

"Thass right."

Hobie has approached Core gradually. Now he dares to touch the front rail of the witness stand.

"You *knew* he wasn't going to stop, didn't you?"

"Shee-it, man." Showily, Core waves the back of his hand inches from Hobie's nose. "Listen how you get up on yo'self! Look that bitch-made nigger in the eye, man, you gone see that fool straight down to shoot. I like to seen that plenty."

"Sir, you *knew* Gorgo was going to shoot anyway, didn't you, even though it was a woman standing there, and as a result you hit the pavement?"

"I already answered that damn question."

"Judge," says Tommy, belatedly. I sustain the objection and Hobie retreats to his notes to seek another subject, once again short of success. Naturally, I've gotten the point—but it baffles me, as it has when Hobie's prowled this ground before. What earthly good does it do Nile, even if June, rather than Eddgar, was the target?

"Senator Eddgar," says Hobie. "Let's talk about him. You had one meeting with the Senator, is that your testimony?"

"Seem like one."

"Seems like? One or more than one?"

"In my lid, man, you know I got one."

"It could be more?"

Core shirks it off. Hobie fixes him with a look, but decides, after an instant's reflection, not to pursue it.

"Now, Hardcore, to you, to T-Roc, this idea of getting Kan-el out of prison—that was very important, wasn't it?"

"Down for mine, man," he says. "Stomp down." The credo. The gang, he means. Everything for the gang.

"And that's why you agreed to meet with the Senator. Am I right? Because getting Kan-el out, that's a thang with you. Right?"

"You with it, cuz," he answers, and adds a quick simpering smile, mocking Hobie for trying to take up his lingo.

"And you told us, I believe, that when you found Senator Eddgar had this idea that BSD could become a political organization you were real angry—'deep'?"

"Man, what he were stressin, man, that shit ain real."

Hobie nods, mulling as he strolls. Then he turns back abruptly and asks in a smaller voice, "So why'd you think Senator Eddgar was coming down there?"

Core for an instant is dead silent. I see him look to Aires.

"Nile sayin get with his daddy. Thass all."

"That's all? Let's set the scene, Core. We got two gangbangers. Top Rank. Black men. Both convicted felons, right? And we have an important white politician, chairman of the Senate Committee on Criminal Justice, who drives all the way down to the North End of DuSable and climbs in the back of a limousine with the likes of you-all, knowing you want nothing more in the world than to get your homie, Kan-el, out of Rudyard penitentiary. Now I ask you again, Hardcore, what did you think he was coming for? What did you think he was going to get out of this?"

Core stares, motionless, feral. Hobie's finally got him.

"Huh?" asks Hobie. "You and T-Roc had this one checked out, didn't you?"

Core just shakes his head.

"You went there thinking you were going to bribe Senator Eddgar, didn't you?"

Aires unfurls his lanky form from his folding chair and raises his hand tentatively. "Judge," he says, "I have to be heard." Suddenly—in one of those light-switch moments—it's clear what Jackson's doing here. He's not just protecting Hardcore. He's looking after T-Roc, Kan-el, his entire client base in BSD. I wave Aires to his seat and Hobie asks me to have the court reporter read the question back.

"No way," says Core. "You trippin."

Hobie's nostrils flare in a sudden disbelieving exhalation. It's the first moment in which I know for certain Hardcore has been caught lying. Core and Aires have covered this one. If Hardcore acknowledged a conspiracy to commit bribery, T-Roc's supervised release would be in jeopardy. Worse, Core would have dimed out his own, not the way to commence a ten-year stay at Rudyard.

"So are you telling us, Hardcore, that you never offered or received any money directly or indirectly through Senator Eddgar? Is that what you're saying? Do you understand what I'm asking?"

"Nigger, I understand you fine."

Hobie stands with paralytic stillness. The sole movement—an involuntary one—is the tip of his tongue sneaking forth between his teeth. The word, of course. The entire gulf of black life, that heritage of disrespect, stands between them for a moment.

"Read the question back," he tells the court reporter, finally, without taking his eyes from Hardcore. It's my job to issue that instruction, but under the circumstances I do not intervene, just nod to Suzanne.

"No money, nothin," Core says, "ain nothin like that."

"Nothing like that," Hobie says. Standing over his notes at the podium, he takes a few more seconds to collect himself, shifts his shoulder, and rebuttons his handsome, green-toned Italian suit. Over in the jury box, in the journalistic dog pound, there is a steady murmur. Bribery! This case is too much, something great each day. I see Dubinsky and Stuart Rosenberg huddled together, but turn away abruptly when I sense Seth trying to catch my eye.

"Now, Hardcore, most of what you're saying about Nile—there's no kind of record of it, is there?"

"Record? What kind of damn record, man? I ain no DJ up here, man. Record," he huffs.

"No documents. Nothing to prove what you're saying is true. For instance, this phone call you say you made to Nile the morning of the murder, after he beeped you. There's no record of that, is there? Not so far as you know?" The state has already stipulated to this. Hobie's on safe ground.

"They's the money, man," says Core.

"Right," says Hobie. "The money. That's the only thing backing up your testimony, right?"

Hobie's correct, but it's an argument not a question and I sustain the prosecutors' objection.

"Well, haven't the prosecutors told you, Hardcore, how important that money is?"

"Money be money, man. Make the world go round."

"I think that's love," Hobie says, over his shoulder. He's moving again, on the prowl, working his hands, his fancy alligator loafers scudding across the worn courtroom carpeting. "You understood that bag of money you delivered to the prosecutors—you knew it was the key to corroborating your testimony, didn't you? You couldn't have gotten your sweet deal without the money to back you up, right?"

"Yo, man, chill. That wasn't no thang, man, cause I had the damn money, okay?"

"Oh, you had money," says Hobie. "How much money, Hardcore, did you make every day slanging dope—$5,000?"

Core equivocates. He doesn't know.

"Two thousand?"

Hardcore shakes his head.

"How many people did you say you had working for you? Did you say it was five? Wasn't it more like seventy-five?"

"Oh, no, man, no way. You sky-up."

"I am? Let's talk about your cars, Core." Hobie takes him through it all. Jewelry. Houses. Women he supports. Hobie has the police reports from the Force narcotics unit—informant information and occasional surveillance. Core is clearly spending hundreds of thousands of dollars a year.

"Core, you have $10,000 cash dope money sitting around any day of the week, don't you?"

Aires is sitting forward alertly now. Hardcore, sensing he's being trapped again, flares up.

"Look, nigger, he gimme the money, Jack, so just get behind it."

Hobie again comes to a complete halt. His eyes briefly flicker my way. Which is all the invitation I need.

"Mr. Trent, the next time you address Mr. Tuttle in that manner, I'm going to hold you in contempt. Do you want to talk to Mr. Aires?"

"That's all right, Judge." Standing again, Jackson waves the back of his hand in a schoolmarmish way at his client. "You behave," he says across the well of the courtroom.

On the stand, Core lowers his head and mutters to himself. I make out a few words. "Buster, man." It's Hobie whom he's referring to. A drag, he means. Hobie goes back to the prosecution table for People's Group Exhibit 1, the money, divided in two clear envelopes, and the plastic newspaper bag it supposedly was delivered in.

"So it's your testimony that Nile Eddgar gave you this bag and $10,000 in late August this year?"

"They fingerprints, man." Core snidely smiles.

"That didn't surprise you, did it?"

"Ain surprise, man, cause I knowed who dogged me the money."

"But you expected the money and the bag to have prints on it, didn't you?"

Core shrugs. "Maybe."

"Sure you did. You kept this money safe, didn't you? You didn't even take it out of the bag, did you? Isn't that what you said?"

"Straight down."

"You didn't spend any of it, did you?"

"Nope."

"You had other money to spend, right?"

"Right."

"You didn't let this get mixed up with any of your other money, did you?"

"Yo, you hear what I'm sayin? That the money he give me, man." Core's been instructed. By Aires. By Tommy. The money's the case. He knows he can't come off it, not an inch.

"You kept this bag secure because you knew if something went wrong, you'd have a way to give up Nile? That you'd have his prints. That you'd have this to hand over to the po-lice. Right? Isn't that how it was?"

Hardcore considers the implications of the question at length. The weird yellowish fingernails, recalling some Chinese mandarin, appear as he scratches the incomplete goatee, and I see his eyes again drifting to Jackson. There's a trade-off here for Core. By acknowledging these nasty calculations he can explain why he had the cash to back up what he was saying. But in admitting he was prepared from the start to give up Nile, he's confirming the central tenet of the defense. Worse, perhaps, he's dissing his own character. The bangers, wild with the ravages of wounded ego, can rarely endure that. Yet across the courtroom Jackson's chin drops no more than a quarter of an inch, and Hardcore gets it.

"Could be," he says at last. Hobie tries not to look as if he was hurt by the response.

"Sure. You had that thought, didn't you? 'If I have this bag, if I have his prints, I have Nile? I'm always going to have something to give the laws, if worse comes to worse?' "

He shrugs.

"Yes? Is the answer yes?"

"Yessss," hisses Core.

"It isn't the case, is it, Hardcore, that you took this bag and a few bills that Nile had handled and put $10,000 of your dope money in here and made up this whole story, is it?"

Core's head rifles back. He snorts, "Get over yo'self, man. Just get over it."

At the podium Hobie evens his stack of notes and closes his folder. He rests an elbow there.

"Now, Hardcore, I'm going to do something no good trial lawyer is supposed to do. I'm going to let you explain, all right, man? I'm going to be fairer to you than you've been to Nile."

In the moment of suspense, Molto fails to object to Hobie's rhetorical flourish. Purposefully, Hobie strides up to the witness box, holding the three exhibits, People's 1: the blue bag and the two packages of bills. Facing Core, Hobie makes another long, melancholy inspection of him.

"Now, I want you to look at Judge Klonsky, and I want you to tell her why, if this is the $10,000 Nile Eddgar gave you in August, if this is the money you kept safe, if this is the money you never took out of this bag, tell the judge why the West Side Forensic Laboratory says there's a high concentration of cocaine residue on nearly all of these bills?"

Molto, Singh both erupt. Tommy screams, "Oh my God!" and is halfway to the bench before I even catch sight of him. He's bellowing.

"Objection, objection, objection, Judge! Judge, I'm supposed to get the results. You said, Judge, that the People were to get the lab results. I never got those results. Judge, what is this? What *is* this?"

I find I have my hand on my forehead again. Hobie has remained before the witness, holding out the second package, the one which he sent to the lab, but he has turned my way with a sheepish, little-boy face.

"Your Honor, I didn't know if I was going to use it."

"Judge! Oh my God, Judge," yells Tommy. I point to Singh, ten feet behind Molto, and suggest Rudy calm him.

"Mr. Tuttle, am I supposed to believe that? The discovery rules are clear. And my order was clearer."

"Judge Klonsky, they knew I was having the money tested. You allowed it."

"Judge!" screams Tommy. "I asked him for the results. I was standing right there."

"And I told you," Hobie says. "No blood. You mentioned blood. They didn't find blood. You mentioned gunpowder. They didn't find gunpowder. That's what you asked."

"Oh, Mr. Tuttle," I say.

"What?" he asks, as if he didn't know.

Rudy, who's kept his wits, comes to the bench and moves to strike the question and exclude the lab results. I order a ten-minute recess and direct Hobie to turn over his lab report. Molto and Rudy are given permission to consult the witness. I broil a moment in rage. Lord, Hobie is a scoundrel! There are certain defense lawyers who become rogues with their clients, enjoying a commando existence, striking from the borderland beyond the rules. It's the one part of their job I knew I could never handle. What did Seth say about Hobie? He could have been more. Instead, he's just another courtroom tomcat. From the defense table, where he's sorted through the banker's box to find the chemist's report, Hobie approaches the bench with my copy. I hold my head aloft, unafraid to convey my dim judgment of him. A musing, philosophical look crosses his features in reply.

Nonetheless, I have to deal with the facts. In chambers, I study the lab report. Eighty-eight items of U.S. currency from People's Group Exhibit 1B, each identified by serial number, were examined first by washing, then by testing the residue with a mass spectrometer. Every item showed the presence of cocaine hydrochloride, with the residue on each bill weighing between 390 and 860 micrograms. No question, this is the result Hobie hoped for from the outset. It's why he wanted the bills tested. And he calculated well. The law, like everything else, plays its own game of ends and means. With warrantless searches, if dope is discovered the courts always think of an exigent circumstance justifying the intrusion. And Hobie's excursion beyond the rules has also produced its own excuse: Hardcore lied. Hobie caught him, he proved it. No one, even these days, would exalt procedural regularity over a defendant's right to combat prosecution perjury. When the finger-wagging is over, I will not exclude the lab report. And, when my anger subsides, I'll take in more fully what I already sense: that the state case, which hinges on the money, has been badly damaged. At a deeper level,

I remain stuck on the question of motive. There's no reason Core on his own would want to kill Loyell Eddgar—or June, for that matter. It's likely Nile was involved somehow. But it may never be clearer than that. Hobie has taken a giant step toward raising a reasonable doubt.

When we reassemble, Molto urgently renews the state's motion to exclude the lab report. Cocaine traces have rubbed off dope money onto most of the currency in the U.S. by now, he claims. That's true enough, but Hobie's chemist said the concentrations he identified were between fifty and one hundred times incidental levels.

"I'll reserve ruling," I reply, "until the report is offered in the defense case." Hobie plays his part, wailing in anguish, as if he takes my threat seriously. Perhaps he does, but shamefaced groveling is part of the standard routine of the courtroom rascal. I offer the prosecution the chance to reopen their examination of Hardcore. They've had a few minutes together to account for the heavy cocaine residue on money Core claimed was never outside the plastic bag, but as Hobie anticipated, they have not been able to come up with much.

"Man, you know," says Hardcore, when Tommy asks him to explain, "could be I had some shit in that drawer over by Doreen's. Sides, man, I can't be figurin what-all Nile be doin when he kickin.'"

Tommy nods, as if those responses were fully satisfactory, and concludes. Hobie stands at the defense table, for brief recross.

"You know you make a urine drop when you come into the jail, don't you?"

"Uh-huh."

"And do you know that Nile's drop was clean for cocaine?"

Objection sustained. But Hobie's point is made. Both lawyers say they have nothing further and I call the luncheon recess. I stand on the bench, but on second thought motion to Suzanne, the court reporter, to remain.

"I want to say one thing, Mr. Tuttle. On the record. Any further violations of the rules of discovery and there will be two consequences." I count off the warnings on my fingers. "First, Mr. Molto won't even have to bother with a motion to exclude. I don't care if the Pope is here as a character witness for your client, if he hasn't been disclosed to the prosecution, his testimony won't be heard in this courtroom. And second, there will be severe sanctions for you personally. And I'm not kidding."

Hobie's whole substantial upper body sways obediently. "Yes, Your

Honor," he repeats. I stare him down, even as he continues mumbling reassurances.

"What do we have next?" I ask Molto. "After lunch?"

He blinks, taken aback that in the confusion of the morning I've forgotten.

"The Senator," he answers.

Typically me. Most feared is last remembered.

In the meantime, the transport deputies in their brown uniforms have approached the witness stand to return Hardcore to the lockup. One of them, Giosetti, a large man with an unbarbered mass of grey hair, motions him down. Core rises to full height and, looming there, takes another instant to glower in the direction of the defense. Hobie catches him at it and, poised by the paper-strewn table, answers him with an unwavering humorless look. It's not so much personal triumph Hobie communicates as a lesson, a declaration of faith: My way is better. Don't you see, it's better? The moment goes on. In the end it's Hardcore, streetside master of a ruthless look of primal malevolence, who, with the excuse of the deputy's beckoning hand, turns away.

Marietta's TV is held fast before her as I enter her office. The grey glow of her noontime soap is broadcast on her cheeks, but her eyes nonetheless veer toward me an instant.

"What?"

She does not bother with an answer, but hands me a small striped gift box, with a note attached. Back at my desk, I open the envelope first.

```
Sonny—
Thanks again for dinner. I'd say more, but I don't want to
break the rules.
    I thought Nikki might enjoy these things. I hope they'll
hold her for the time being. Please tell her that meeting her
was the nicest thing that's happened to me in weeks. (I mean
it!)
                                                        Seth
P.S. The cops found my father's car. It was parked around the
corner. There was no damage and the doors were locked. The cops
interviewed a neighbor who knows my dad and said she saw him
```

park in that spot three days ago. She's sure the car hasn't
been moved. Apparently, he just got confused.

  I guess I'm going to have to do something.

    Seth. Like a blinkered pony, I've stifled an urge to glance at the jury
box all morning. Even so, in this solitary environment, the thought of
him forces up the warring feelings that have visited me occasionally for
two days now, the adolescent zing of romance, and a stubborn dread
verging on doom. Saturday night I found myself numbed by the madness of being kissed. I sat in the living room, in the pure white light of
a long-armed halogen lamp, attempting to read. Every ten minutes or
so I found my fingertips on my lips, from which I promptly removed
them.

    Inside the box Seth has dropped off, there's a large plastic tooth the
size of an apple. It opens at the top, and within it are a number of dime-
store items: those wind-up teeth that chatter and bounce along the ta-
bletop, and a crude set of false buck teeth, like the ones on which Jerry
Lewis based a career. Nikki will be thrilled.

    'Where'd that guy go to?' she asked on Sunday morning, as if it made
any sense at all to think he might still be around.

    'He went home, silly. Did you like him?'

    The whole head moved, the dark bangs fluttering. She bit her lip and
did not speak momentarily, attempting to cope with the reality that he'd
left her behind. 'He should make a beard,' she finally told me.

    Maybe he should. I amuse myself with the thought of facial hair, last
refuge of the balding. But sobriety returns quickly. I reach the same
conclusion every time I think this through. Just let it go. That's adult
life, isn't it? Small eruptions of insanity, and a regathering of forces for
the long march of responsibility. Rereading Seth's note, I shake my head
over his father, then I repack Nikki's gift. I use the back door so I can
avoid Marietta on my way out for lunch.

All of us—Hobie and Seth and me—have been warped by time. Balder,
fatter, altered in a way. But recognizable. The sight of Loyell Eddgar is
shocking. I've seen photos in the paper on occasion, but they must have
been taken more than a decade ago, when Eddgar first struck out on
his career in local politics. Not for a moment had it occurred to me
that he is now in his late sixties. His hair, naturally, is shorter, thinned,

and preponderantly grey. He has gained, over the years, thirty or forty pounds and his posture is reduced. Eddgar, whom I never imagined softened, is softer.

He stands before the bench now, waiting for instructions. His mere appearance is intensely dramatic, the father his son purportedly meant to kill. The reporters are on alert; the gallery again is SRO. Behind the bulletproof pane, the anxious, curious faces seem as remote as figures on TV. Back by the doors, Annie has stationed another sheriff's deputy to keep order, directing the standees left and right, to make sure there is still an open lane for egress. Even Jackson Aires has returned, his duty done but his curiosity apparently high. He sits in one of the front-row seats generally saved for representatives of the PA's office.

Eddgar stands on the worn greyish carpet at the foot of the bench, ill at ease as the focal point of lurid interest. A paper he has carried up with him is clutched in both hands. He is a smallish, stout man in a wool sport jacket. No one will be surprised when he answers that he was once a professor. He nods to me in a brief lapse into familiarity.

"Dr. Eddgar," I say aloud. Marietta then cries out her "Hear ye's," and I motion Eddgar to the stand. He takes a seat and extends his face to the microphone. He smiles tentatively in my direction, as if he holds some hope for protection. He's ready. Administering the oath, I take note of the eyes, still an astonishing blue.

"I swear," he answers firmly and opens the button on his sport jacket when he sits again.

"Mr. Molto," I say, "you may proceed."

Tommy pouts when he stands. He does not look at his witness. The tone of the first few questions reconfirms my previous impression: Eddgar and Tommy, both zealots at heart, do not care much for each other. They are formal with one another, which ironically makes the direct especially crisp. It lends Tommy an element of cool control, something ordinarily lacking in his presentation.

"How are you employed?"

"I am the elected representative from the 39th state senatorial district."

"Do you have any other employment?"

"I have an adjunct appointment as a professor of divinity at Easton University."

Eddgar describes his district, which comprehends the campus environs at Easton and an area of public housing, one of the first scattered sites plunked down on the border of Kindle and Greenwood Counties years ago on a former military base. He has been elected now to seven consecutive two-year terms and is the chair of the Senate Committee on Criminal Justice. Funding requests for police and prisons pass through his committee, as well as certain appointments in the Department of Corrections. Four years ago, he won the nomination of the state Democratic Farmers & Union Party for state controller but lost the general election.

After quite a bit of this, we finally reach the first crescendo. "Sir," Molto asks, "are you acquainted with the defendant in this case, Mr. Nile Eddgar?"

"I am."

"How do you know him?"

"He is my son." Eddgar does not make it through the answer. His composure, perfect to this point, vanishes as a quaver surrounds the last word. A sound, more hiccup than sob, erupts, though it may not be audible anywhere but up here on the bench. Eddgar braces himself on the front rail of the witness box. The courtroom is still, as we wait for him to recover.

"Do you see your son here this morning?" Tommy asks, turning to Hobie. After Hobie's stunt this morning the two are in the fullest throes of trial hatred, a state of mind fully akin to the one in which men at war shoot each other. Tommy wants Hobie to spare Eddgar the discomfort of having to point out Nile for the record. Instead, Hobie pretends to be busy in the big white cardboard banker's box on the defense table and never looks Tommy's way. He murmurs something to Nile, though, and Nile once more props himself on the arms of his leather bucket chair and begins to rise. He could not look any guiltier if he tried. He cannot even bring his eyes toward his father. He stares directly at the oak baffles on the wall in front of him. Eddgar attempts to lift his hand and instead covers his mouth. He begins to cry out loud. Throughout the courtroom, it feels as if no one can even breathe.

"Record will reflect identification," I say coldly, gazing hard at Hobie. Has he lost his mind? How does this help? A man who misses nothing in the courtroom—he can probably tell you the level of the corner water cooler and how many steps from the lockup door to the witness stand—he continues feigning obliviousness, while his client, visibly whitened, crumbles back into his seat at Hobie's side. On the stand, Eddgar has his handkerchief out and pats his eyes. Tommy puts a few questions to him about Nile's upbringing, then changes subjects.

"Do you know a man named Ordell Trent?" he asks.

"I do."

"How did you meet him?"

"I was introduced to him by Nile."

"And how did that take place?"

"I asked Nile to make the introduction."

"Can you explain why?"

"Objection."

"If it's a conversation with the defendant, I'll allow it. Is this something you told Nile, Dr. Eddgar?"

"In various forms over the years. And we certainly discussed it after the meeting. Definitely."

"Go ahead," I say.

"Basically, I believed that street gangs, like Hardcore's, have done something no one else has, namely organize the poor community. And if that organization could be put to positive uses — particularly expressing the political will of the poor community — instead of the present unhappy ways those energies are employed, well, that would be a tremendous overall gain for everyone: the gang members, the poor community, and the city as a whole, which obviously would benefit in seeing a redirection of those efforts."

Speaking in his mannered way, his voice still slowed by Southern cadences, Eddgar seems to have scored over in the press box. His answer, carefully spun for public consumption, is being dutifully scribbled into a number of spiral-topped notebooks. Glancing over, I allow myself to look reluctantly at Seth. But for the first time since this trial started, I am beside the point. He is focused on Eddgar with an intensity suddenly reminiscent of the man I knew decades ago.

Tommy moves on to the meeting between Hardcore, T-Roc, and Nile. Eddgar has given the state a page from his Day-Timer fixing the meeting at June 11, earlier than Hardcore seemed to recall it. In bare strokes, Eddgar describes the irritation and disbelief T-Roc and Core showed for his proposal to turn the gang into a political organization.

"How did you leave it?" Tommy asks.

"That they would get back to me, through Nile."

"All right, sir," says Tommy. Rudy waves him to the prosecution table, where he hands Molto a note. Tommy reads it, then leans down to his colleague. The two confer briefly, debating something, then Molto straightens up, drawing himself to full height in his frumpy suit. "During that meeting in T-Roc's limousine, sir, did T-Roc or Hardcore, did either one of them offer you a bribe?"

"No," says Eddgar. Tommy turns to Hobie to preen, and is still faced that way when Eddgar clears his throat and adds, "They didn't actually offer me money." Molto's head shoots around toward the witness, then he looks down to Rudy's note and shoves it back crossly to his trial partner. The PAs were taking a chance, having apparently forgotten, during the frantic rush of the lunch hour, to go over this subject with Eddgar when he arrived. Behind them, Hobie peeks up from his notes with a quick, cutthroat grin.

Tommy begins again. "Calling your attention to the first week of September 1995, did you and Nile again have occasion to speak about Hardcore?"

"Yes, sir, we did."

"Can you tell us where you were?"

"We spoke by telephone. I was at my home in Greenwood."

"All right. And please tell us what was said and by whom."

"He merely told me that Core wanted to talk to me again."

"And how did you react?"

"I told him that was very good news, that I'd be pleased to meet him wherever he liked."

"And how were the time and place of the meeting set?"

"Well, as I recollect, I was taking the approach that I'd go anywhere, anytime. Core wanted to meet at Grace Street, and Nile suggested that the very early morning would be the wisest time for me to go down there."

"Nile suggested it?"

"That's correct."

Score for the prosecution. Nile set up Dad. At the defense table both Hobie and his client appear calm. Tommy travels along a bit, beneath the courtroom lights. In the same stoical tone he has maintained, he asks, "And who, sir, was June Eddgar?"

"My wife." Eddgar takes a beat. "My former wife." Once again, he does not make it through his response and goes on, handkerchief in hand. Tommy politely sorts through the history of Eddgar's relationship with June: separation in 1971, an amicable divorce in 1973, continuing contacts and friendship. June remarried in 1975 to William Chaikos, a veterinarian in Marston, Wisconsin. That marriage ended in 1979. Thereafter, she periodically visited Greenwood County to help Eddgar in his political campaigns—in 1980, when he ran for city council, in 1982, when he was elected Mayor of Easton, and several times after that for his senatorial campaigns. Eddgar answers quietly, ignoring the occasional tears as best he can. I find his inability to fully contain himself touching. Twenty-five years ago he was committed to accepting the inevitable harsh mechanics of history. I think what I never expected to: He's changed.

"And did Ms. Eddgar visit you or Nile from time to time?"

"She did."

"When did she visit Kindle County last?"

He blows his nose and lifts his head to say she had come over Labor Day and had remained for a few days to shop in the city.

"Had Mrs. Eddgar remained involved in your political career?"

"Her home was in Wisconsin. She preferred the country. But I always depended on her advice. She was up-to-date with most of my activities."

"Did you discuss this anticipated meeting with Hardcore?"

Hobie objects—correctly—that the question calls for hearsay. Tommy moves then to the events of September 6 and 7, with Hobie making persistent hearsay objections, most of them well-founded. The reporters and onlookers seem baffled by the arcana of the rule which allows a witness to testify about what someone said she would be doing in the future but not what she said she'd done in the past. Eddgar is allowed to say he was needed by his State Senate office staff on the morning of September 7, but he may not relate his conversations with his staffers, nor may he testify that he asked June to meet Hardcore in his place. I do admit in evidence the note found in her purse in which she recorded Eddgar's directions. Stained at the corner with a rusty brown I know to be blood, the slip of paper is handed up in its plastic jacket. There is a sloppy line drawing of the streets and the words "Hardcore. Ordell Trent. 6:15" in a somewhat erratic hand. Finally, because a witness is allowed to testify about his own state of mind, I let Eddgar explain why he asked June to meet with Hardcore, even though he can't relay his actual conversation with her.

"I believed," says Eddgar, "that she would recognize the potential importance of the meeting with Core and would understand it was critical that someone see him personally."

"And why was it critical?"

"I didn't want to insult him," Eddgar answers. He rolls his lips into his mouth in a further effort at self-control.

"And this meeting you had with Mrs. Eddgar at about 5:30 the morning of September 7—was that the last time you saw her?"

"The last."

Tommy waits an appropriate interval to allow the solemnity of death again to fill the courtroom.

"Now, on that day, on September 7, you were interviewed by Detective Lieutenant Montague. Do you recall that?"

"I do."

"And, sir"—Tommy puts his file down and folds his arms—"were you fully candid with Lieutenant Montague when you spoke to him?"

"I was not."

"And in what manner were you not fully candid?"

Hobie objects. "Mr. Molto's impeaching his own witness," he says. Lawyers in this country have been allowed to question the credibility of their own witnesses for forty years now. Hobie is simply trying to break Molto's collected rhythm, and I point him to his seat.

"He asked me," Eddgar answers, "if I knew why June had gone to Grace Street and at first I told him I didn't know."

"And why did you tell him that?"

Hobie objects again. "Now he's rehabilitating his own witness."

"Do you intend to cross on this subject, Mr. Tuttle?"

Hobie averts his face, looking for a dodge he can't find. "Sure," he finally says.

"Then you may as well hear the rehabilitation. Go ahead, Dr. Eddgar."

"I was very reluctant to disclose my political involvement with Hardcore. I realized it was likely to be controversial. And I didn't think it had any relationship to June's death."

I'm sure Molto and he have worked on this answer for some time, but it's a good one. Political self-preservation, Eddgar is saying. He didn't want to be publicly allied with BSD. But no matter how artfully packaged, this is the first trace of the Eddgar of old. He was instantly capable of a coldhearted decision: June was dead, anyway, why soil his skirts? Tommy walks along a moment, studying his shoes.

"Senator, let me cover one final subject with you. I'm sure Mr. Tuttle will bring this out, sir, but I believe you have told the police that you don't know of any motive for your son to do you harm—is that fair?"

"That's my view."

Tommy nods equably, as if this is all right with him. "Senator, let me take you back to the meeting with the gang leaders and Nile in the limo. Had you informed your son that you were going to suggest this plan to T-Roc and Hardcore for BSD to become involved in politics?"

"He claimed I hadn't. As I said, I've mentioned the subject to him often through the years, but I suppose he paid less attention than I imagined."

"He told you afterwards you took him by surprise?"

"Right."

"And what was his emotional state as he told you this?"

"He was put out."

"Do you recall what he said?"

Eddgar has stiffened slightly. Apparently, Tommy didn't give him a preview on this line of questioning.

"I believe he said I was using Hardcore."

"Did you and your son argue?"

"Nile and I have always had our moments. We had a somewhat heated exchange standing there on the street, and then within a day or two we both calmed down."

"But he was very angry at the time?"

"At first."

"At first," repeats Tommy. Hobie has ceased the note-taking and is watching Molto intently. Like Eddgar, he has seemingly been taken unawares. Beside him, Nile has lowered his face to the defense table as he twiddles with a rubber band. It's impossible to know if he's even listening.

"Now, you told us, Senator, that Nile introduced you to Hardcore. Correct?"

"Yes."

"And whose idea was that?"

"Mine, I think. We were having one of these discussions about what Nile was doing, his work, how it was going, a father-son talk, I guess, and he mentioned this concern about Kan-el's parole and I said, 'Nile, well, why don't you have him talk to me, I might be able to help.' Something like that."

"And how did he respond to that suggestion?"

"I don't recall."

"Did you bring up the subject again?"

Eddgar looks to the ceiling. "I believe so."

"So you had to suggest more than once that it would be a good idea for you to meet Hardcore?"

"Yes. I'm sure I did. I had this notion about the gangs, that— Well, I've testified to that."

Tommy takes a step closer. "Did Nile talk to you about his work often?"

"All the time. As I said, the subject interested me."

"Did Nile tell you he'd requested assignment to Grace Street cases?"

"Oh yes."

"Do you happen to remember, Senator, whether you suggested that assignment to him?"

"I might have." Eddgar nods serenely, but a certain calculating light has come over him. He's trying to recollect everything he may have unwisely admitted to Tommy in their many interviews. "I believe I did."

"Now, his job as a probation officer, Senator—do you remember who suggested that line of work to Nile?"

"I'm sure I did."

"You did?"

"Yes. Nile was at a point—Well, he was like many younger folks, he was casting about, and I suggested it, I said, 'Go on back to school in social work, you like all that.'"

"And how long did it take him to do the school work?"

"Eighteen months, as I remember."

"Did he do a thesis?"

"He did."

"What was the subject?"

"Street gangs."

Molto looks at Eddgar.

"Yes, I suggested that to him," Eddgar says.

"And you helped him get his job, too, didn't you?"

"I made some calls."

Tommy assesses Eddgar, straight on. "And can I ask, Senator—did you ever feel, sir, that Nile was undertaking these activities—school, the job, the assignment, arranging the meeting with Hardcore—in any way because he was pleased by your interest in him?"

As Eddgar is deliberating, Hobie rumbles to his feet. "Your Honor, I'm sittin here just wonderin whose side he's on anyway?" His hand, big as a paving stone, is directed at Tommy.

"Is that an objection, Mr. Tuttle?" Hobie, of all people, is hoping to cue Eddgar, who still seems to have little idea all this is coming at his expense.

"I'd say it's an observation, Your Honor. My objection is that Senator Eddgar can't testify to what the defendant felt."

"Well, Mr. Tuttle, I'd say, Keep your observations to yourself. The question is what the Senator believed. And I find the line of questioning directed at impeaching earlier testimony. Proceed, Mr. Molto."

Eddgar speaks enough of the lingo to catch the drift. Accustomed to being in charge, he swivels my way in the witness chair, looking both stumped and somewhat imperious. The question is read back.

"I'm not sure I ever thought about it in those terms."

Tommy eyes him briefly before he nods in the same sage manner.

"Now, let me see if I get this, Senator. Your son had spent more than three and a half years following your suggestions about his education, his thesis, his job, his cases. And then, according to what he said to you, he suddenly found out as he sat in the back of that limousine that in everything you'd suggested to him, you had a political agenda of your own?" Tommy utters this question in a placid tone. He might even be said to sound somewhat respectful, but everything else in his manner is stone-cold. I see what's going on now. Molto is one of those grey men of the bureaucratic world whose whole life has been spent in service to the likes of Eddgar, the savvy pols with the winning public manner and the unrestrained private appetite for glory. For such men, Tommy has risen and fallen, with few of them bothering to look back to him in the dust. And now he has the opportunity to call one to account. In what may be the most bizarre moment yet in an entirely unorthodox case, Tommy Molto, prosecutor for life, stands before the bar, advocating the defendant's point of view and lacerating the crime's intended victim with the professional calm of a surgeon. In his emotional funk, Eddgar seems to be the last person in the room to recognize what has taken place.

"Oh, please," he says suddenly, with a distinct echo of old-fashioned Southern hauteur, "please. You are mixing apples and oranges. Nile was as interested in all of this as I was."

"You said he became angry—*very* angry after you left the limo?"

"Briefly. For a day or two."

"He said someone was being used?"

"*Hard*-core, he said. He said Hardcore was being used." Eddgar shakes his shoulders to straighten his jacket. "You really don't see this clearly at all," he tells Molto.

"*I* don't?" asks Tommy, and with that takes his seat.

May 4, 1970

SETH

June and I spoke very little in the intervals between her calls to my father. Because my parents never vacationed, I had been in motels only three or four times before in my life, that is, if you did not count the U. Inn back home, the site of innumerable bar mitzvahs and sweet sixteens. I still experienced a childish thrill at the sight of the little free soap bars, the protective paper cap over the glasses, and the sanitary band on the toilet seat. Just for me. The odd environment of this tiny chamber and its purchased privacy seemed to heighten even more the peculiarity of what was occurring. Threadbare chenille spreads covered both beds. The floor was asbestos tile, while the dressers were strictly

1950s, with glass tops and a creamy lacquered finish. The owners, you could tell, still took some pride, but it would be swept away soon enough, and they would be renting by the hour.

There was a narrow balcony, no more than a yard wide, with a single aluminum-framed beach chair overlooking the Alameda Freeway. June had brought along some fruit for lunch and I sat out in the sun, eating my pear, watching the traffic race by, all these happy Californians on their way to who knows where. I decided that when I got to Canada I was going to get drunk. I would have liked to score some dope, but that of course was out of the question. Misdemeanors of any kind, anything that could lead to deportation, were now to be dreaded. I sat there abstractly, making plans I did not fully believe I'd ever carry out.

We were in Damon's poorer neighborhood, the black patch, as Eddgar would have it, abutting Oakland, and I surveyed all over again the diminished look of poverty. The military had come and gone in this part of town decades before, leaving a lot of unsound construction, light stucco buildings now seamed with tar. The stores on the commercial strip below compared dismally to what was only a mile or so east. They had painted signs above the doors, rather than neon, and merchandise was sparse in their windows beside the foldback grates. Watching the traffic, I noted for the thousandth time how black people still drove these terrible American cars, the big heaps meant to rust out and die within five years. Knowledge always comes hardest to the oppressed. That was what Eddgar would say. In glimpses between the crowded buildings, you could see the salt flats nearby, a terrain of marsh and mud beside the brackish waters of the Bay. Seabirds still nested there, although you could see the network of white pipelines and tanks from the refineries a mile off in Richmond, smell their grotty effluvium on a wayward wind.

Below us, a portly black man with a spirited walk went by. He was wearing a large cloche hat. I thought it was Hobie and my heart unpredictably lifted. I actually stood to wave, until I realized my mistake.

"Do you think you can find out where Hobie Tuttle is?" I asked June. I stood on the threshold to the balcony. They had to have known, I realized, given the connections to Cleveland. "It'd mean a lot to me to see him before I go."

June leveled a hand over her eyes to protect them from the afternoon sun. She was wearing a simple shirtwaist dress, meant to be unobtrusive. Two barrettes were in her light hair. She used a few fingers to motion me inside.

"We don't think you should be out on the street. You can never tell what happens if someone sees you. Control the random element," June repeated. It must have been from one of their revolutionary manuals, something said by Stalin or Giap, whoever it was they read on tactics. I knew better than to overtly quarrel with the notion of discipline. It was part of the revolution.

"Look, I'll be careful. Real careful. Like I said, it would mean a lot."

She said she would see. I was encouraged that she didn't deny the possibility outright. She looked at me intently until I realized I was expected to return to the balcony before she would lift the phone to have whatever furtive, coded conversation she was going to undertake with whomever — Eddgar or someone else.

When I came back in later, she was sitting in the room's one straight-back chair, her feet propped on the bed as she read. The book she'd brought along was a hardbound copy of *Mr. Sammler's Planet*, unlikely reading, I thought, but you could never tell with June. She had never fully renounced fashion. She told me she had no word yet regarding Hobie, then lifted her healthy arms, the book still in hand, and groaned a bit as she stretched. I had another sudden, forceful intimation, which seemed to broil off June like heat from a sun-soaked stone, of how easy it would be for us, if we were only just a little different, to fill this time with sex. It could be abandoned — crazy, happy fun, a reminder that life only became complicated when the human population exceeded two.

I sat for quite some time, adjusting to the change of light. There was a single picture on the wall, turned to an angle of ten degrees. A woodland scene. Something restful for those who could not find slumber as the freeway thrummed. I wanted to read, too. The Gideon Bible was in a drawer of the crummy, chipped dresser. I paged through Deuteronomy trying to find the words that had been in my mezuzah, as if they were a message in a bottle. I read: "Now therefore hearken, O Israel, unto the statutes and unto the ordinances and judgments, the law I teach you, for to do *them*, that ye may live and go in and possess the land which the Lord God of your fathers giveth you." Jehovah's line. It meant nothing to me. It was the rumble of the rhetoric, the weight of the words that seemed connected to the world of unchosen obligation and duty that I was seeking to shirk.

"Patriarchy," I said.

June smiled. She was the wife of a theologian.

Around noon, June called my father back to describe the ransom plan. She instructed him to phone immediately one of the major casinos in

Las Vegas—the Roman Coin—and to inform them that he wanted to open a betting line for his son, in preparation for an upcoming trip. People did it all the time. He would fund the line with a wire from his bank direct to the casino.

"Tomorrow, Seth is going to the cashier there to draw the $20,000 in chips," June told him. "He'll have his driver's license for ID. Don't think about any heroes from the FBI rescuing him, because he's also going to have some plastique taped to his belly and a detonator on a remote-control switch. Do you know what that is?"

"No." As my father answered, I was standing beside her, my head close to the telephone earpiece.

"It's a high-powered explosive," she said.

"Oh my God."

"Very safe," said June as my father said, 'Oh my God,' again. "Very stable. Just as long as nobody hits the button. Which they won't. Because we are going to get the money. Right?"

"Without question."

"Sure. Without question."

I would mail the chips Special Delivery to a post office box in San Francisco. I was free to go at that point. Someone would then drive back and redeem them, not at the Roman Coin casino in Las Vegas, but at the one in Lake Tahoe, as a precaution in case the chips had been marked in some way. Eddgar, I was sure, had been on the verge of delirium in plotting all of this. It meant something that this whole scheme had flung him as far as possible from Maoist drab into worlds he never entered. Gambling. Casinos. How did Eddgar even know about such crap? How was it that he had absorbed so many of the rules and customs of the life he abjured? Envy, I decided, was a motive force of revolution.

"Now, when we get the money, Seth is free to go. He'll give you a call. Only one condition. He's on parole."

"Parole?"

"Right. Parole. Like parole. Like, he's okay if he's a good boy. See? See, now this whole thing is fucked up, right? We're thinking this guy's like the son of Rockefeller or something and he's not. But we're not sitting in any pig slammer because we made a mistake and are dumb enough to say so. Do you understand me? We get covered for our expenses, bygones are bygones, blah blah blah. But not if it's us instead of him. Understand?"

"You wish to go free as well."

"Exactly."

"This desire is not surprising," my father said.

"Irony, right?" June asked. "That's just what we want. No surprises. We don't want Seth here giving physical descriptions. Or making sketches. Or you opening up your mouth."

My father pondered. Static sizzled on the line. It was, I realized suddenly, a great match, Eddgar against my father.

At last he said, "I give you my word of honor that we shall disclose nothing."

"Thanks. Well, that's great. That's outta sight. No, I think we need to do a little better than that. Just a little." She laughed, meanly. She was, like any actor, in love with the part. "And don't treat me like I'm a fucking moron. Because I'm not. Have I treated you like that?"

He didn't answer.

"See, we have a problem. And it gets worse. Because the way I get this, okay, your son — your son was supposed to show up and get his ass drafted sometime today, last week, whenever. And he ain't there, and so the boys in the blue suits and shiny shoes are gonna be looking for him. You following?"

"I believe so." He paused again to calculate. "Under the circumstances, I would think that Seth is no more eager than you to speak to the FBI."

"Now you're getting close, mister. What's that thing about great minds? The only thing is he plans to see the northern lights. Isn't that his gig? He's going to run away. And once he's up there he won't be afraid to take a call from the Bureau. And neither will you. Now it's 'Hi, how are you, let me tell you about these douche bags who ransomed my kid.' So that's how come he's on parole. Remember parole?"

"Yes."

"Okay, I'm talking fast because I'm running out of time. Don't want to break the rules. Here's the scoop: For the next six months, he goes where we say. We'll pick a place. Somewhere in America the beautiful, okay? Somewhere from sea to shining sea. Somewhere we can watch him. He can live there, work there. Whatever he likes. We'll get him some papers, a social security card, that kind of thing. He can be underground. Just so long as he keeps in mind that we got a ton of people who can check on him. He knows just what we expect. He doesn't disappear, not for ten minutes, without we know where he is. And he never, repeat never, talks to any kind of police. No pigs or any other farm animals. Local cops. FBI. Old Mother Hubbard. Same for you. Absolutely. Bureau comes around, you don't have the foggiest idea where he went. We get hinky in the least, Seth so much as has a cup of coffee with a meter maid, we call the FBI and tell them just where they can find little Seth. We bolt for Algeria and he heads for slam city to do eighteen months to three. Are you following me?"

"I have the entire picture," my father said.

"Goodbye."

She called back in forty minutes.

"Any questions?"

"None," my father said.

"The money cool?"

"I have spoken directly to the banker. The funds will be wired before the end of the day. The casino is on alert and will oblige Seth whenever he arrives."

"No problems?"

"None whatsoever. The banker was somewhat curious, but I explained that for some time, as a hobby, I have been studying the laws of probability and blackjack. He was quite interested and recommended a book."

"Far out. Here's your son."

"Dad, I'm sorry." I meant it, of course. In triumph, I was wretched and remorseful.

He didn't answer. He was, I was sure, torn by unbearable emotions— insane with rage and washed clean by the relief of hearing my voice.

"I want to be sure you understand what happens afterwards," I said.

"You will call us."

"I meant after that. The FBI will be looking for me. Within a few weeks. You won't be able to call me, to write me. Do you understand? Nothing that will trace."

"Your mother will not endure that."

"I'll call every few days. A pay phone. Just so you know I'm okay. That's all I can do."

"Will we know where you are?"

"It will be a lot safer for you if you don't. Really. If you can just say 'I don't know' when those people show up. I don't want you guys to get in trouble."

"Trouble," my father repeated. "My Lord, Seth." But as the shape of what was ahead settled in, he voiced no further complaint. This fit my father's needs too well. He would never see through it. Were it not for the pain of surrendering the money, he would regard all of this as perfect.

"Is Mom okay?"

"She knows nothing."

"Great. Look. It'll be all right."

"I pray," my father answered.

Afterwards, I sat with my hand still on the phone, while I wrung myself out one more time. It was over now. In all practical respects. I'd done the worst, and everybody had survived. No one had had a coronary. No one knew they'd been betrayed. I waited now to experience the uncertain mood of freedom. The traffic fumes, the whine from the road, flapped in with the curtains as they were tossed by the wind.

"You know, there's a lot of cruelty in life, Seth," June said, behind me. "That surgeon who saves your life—there's a little part of him that likes the blood when he cuts."

"Which one of us are we talking about?" I asked, although I had no doubts. I was dangerous and neurotic. I would have to accept that about myself. But I took no pleasure from the fact. I already sensed the bilious weight that would fall over me whenever I thought about this episode for the rest of my life. But for June, I could see, epic events were an essential measure: the heat of the spotlight, the rush of applause. Things that go boom. Change. Catastrophe. A new lover at night. She was turning out to be easier to comprehend than I'd imagined.

"I was trying to let you know how I look at this," she said. "You're helping something important. I know this riles you up. I can see it's painful. But we all make sacrifices for the revolution."

The phone rang then. June listened and said nothing, before she put down the handset.

"You might find Tuttle at Africa House," she said. "And be careful. There's a lot of irresponsible behavior with Cleveland inside. He kept his entire cell in line. That's another reason we need him out. Let's say one hour." She looked at her watch. I rooted in my pocket for my car key, then turned back.

"What's Eddgar's sacrifice?" I asked. "For the revolution?"

She studied me for some time. "His faith," she said

A clock clicked, a horn on the highway tore off in a Dopplering wail. She knew, somehow, that her remark was harder on me than her.

"And what's yours?" I asked.

"I stay with Eddgar," she answered at once and, without looking further at me, reached out for her book, which still lay on the bed.

Crossing the Damon campus, I encountered a festival atmosphere. This morning the faculty had voted to declare the university on strike. Classes had been suspended indefinitely, so that students could engage in letter-writing campaigns and community organizing. But they seemed impressed to have accomplished their own liberation, and in spite of a certain freneticness, the campus held some of the joyous air of the weekend. Stereos boomed from windows and people milled in the plazas and green spaces. Bedsheet banners hung from the windows of the dormitories. A closed fist of a brilliant, urgent red was stenciled on each sheet, beneath which a single word was set forth:
STRIKE.
Walking toward the quad, I was handed a mimeoed flyer:

STOP NIXON'S WAR MACHINE

Ohio State   Laos   New Haven   Cambodia   Vietnam
Nationwide Student Strike

Strike before it's too late!
Strike for knowledge!
Strike for sanity!
Strike for yourself!
Strike for peace!
Strike! Strike!!! STRIKE!!!

In the main quad, an open-mike speechathon was underway, one anti-war speaker after another, faculty and students reviling Richard Nixon to the celebration of enormous applause. Huge rock amps boomed out the message, which resounded off the buildings, echoing over a huge crowd. "We have declared an end to business as usual," a woolly-looking prof was shouting, "an end to standing by while our leaders continue this despicable war." He was an officer of the Faculty Senate, one of the guys who'd been happy two nights ago about booting Eddgar. He cried out for peace and the crowd shouted back to him. "The whole world is watching!" they chorused spontaneously at the end of his address. For a moment I let myself believe it. I fondled my passion and my hope like a precious toy—I clutched them, embraced them — then looked at my watch and put them all aside. I had only forty minutes left.

Africa House was located in one of the old red-brick dorms. The Afro-American students, as they recently had begun calling themselves, had swapped and cajoled and intimidated their way into a block of thirty rooms. Residency in Africa House was limited solely to members of the Negro race. It was intended as a separate paradise where everybody wore dashikis and called each other 'brother' and could debate issues of politics and culture of unique concern to the residents. Whenever I passed by, the music blaring from the windows was great — Miriam Makeba, Junior Walker, the Miracles — the sound track of my high-school years. The campus daily carried competing editorials regularly, debating whether this kind of separation was desirable. Having accepted from an early age that there was no more stupid way to judge a human than by skin color, I regarded the formation of Africa House as irrational and deeply destructive. But its existence was by now an accepted fact. A portrait of Malcolm X in Day-Glo shades had been painted on the doorway, over which the Ghanaian flag fluttered. Here too the strike banners hung from the windows, in an unexpected showing of solidarity.

In the corridor, a soul sister in shades and a high natural took her time when I asked for Hobie Tuttle. She was reading *Cane* at an old school desk, hauled in from a classroom. There were slogans from Frederick Douglass and Martin Luther King, Jr., inscribed on the walls.

"Who you?"

I told her. Friend. Roommate.

"You a narc?"

"You want to search me, search me." I lifted my hands from my sides.

The room where I found Hobie about ten minutes later was tiled entirely in black and white — large squares, eighteen inches on a side. They covered not only the floor but the walls and ceilings as well. The first impression was of looking into a kaleidoscope. When I pushed open the door, Hobie sat across the room, slumped in a corner, beside a simple dresser of university issue which had been refinished in dull black contact paper. He was wearing a long leather coat. My initial thought was that he was sick or drunk, but he smiled with enough sureness that I knew he had his bearings. There was a large silver pistol on the tile beside him, a few inches from his hand. I had never seen a gun before in my life, except in the holster of a cop, and I stared at it for quite some time.

"You gonna shoot me?"

He issued a wan smile and motioned me inside. I lifted a hand to the walls.

"Psychedelic."

"It works."

"If you passed through the looking glass. I got night sweats and it's 4:15. How you hanging, dude?"

"Feelin groovy," he answered. He looked bad. Through his color, his nose was reddened at the bridge and on the nostrils. His scruple against coke appeared to have eroded at a time of distress. He told me this was once Cleveland's pad, one of his locations.

"Cleveland's in pretty deep, huh?"

"Oh, you know, man. The pigs planted that shit. You know that. Pigs just can't *han*-dle this nasty colored boy in law school." That was the story the Panthers had put out. Whoever had replaced Eldridge Cleaver as Minister of Information had been on the radio calling Cleveland's arrest a setup. But we'd all heard this tune too many times now. Between Hobie and me the gloom of all our differences settled in his spirited rendition of this sad little lie.

"I'm heading to Canada," I told him.

"Yeah," he said. "Old Loopy Lucy Loo says she's gonna truck on with you."

"That's what she tells me. She needs to get away. She's been doing this heartbreak thing?"

"That's how it is," Hobie said.

"That's how it is," I answered. "So if you hear the Mounties are saying 'Groovy' instead of 'We always get our man,' you'll know why." I wanted badly to amuse him. I wanted him to be what he had always been — my friend. He smiled somewhat. "I was kind of hoping you'd have come around to say farewell."

"Well, you know how it is, man. I got a few serious problems here. Kind of layin low."

"Somebody looking for you?"

"Could be yes. Sort of hoping no." I wasn't sure how much I could ask. With his unfaltering ear for language, Hobie had mastered the urban accent that had never been his. His father, I knew, would slap him if he heard him talking like that. That was the point, I guess. Hobie'd taken everything his father had wanted him to care about and put it in another generation's wrapper. Two thousand miles away, removed from the vast penumbra of Gurney's influence, he was going about the business of being a man on his own terms. As was so often the case with Hobie, I found no comfort in any comparisons to myself.

From far away on the quad, a cheer went up. The strikers were making noise. Hobie, with weary immobility, looked back toward the window, where a black shade was drawn, and made an elderly sound.

"These kids got Tricky in a tight spot, man. He just gone *have* to stop that war, or else they ain't never gonna go back to school." Hobie was tickled by the thought.

"They're doing what they can, Hobie."

He lifted a hand. He didn't really care. We waited.

"We talking ARC?" I asked. "Is that your problem?"

He didn't stir, as he mulled answering. "I didn't do shit but what you know about, if that's what you're asking. Then again, seems as how that may be enough. Been hearin about a fingerprint on that piece of a can they picked up."

"Oh, Hobie. Jesus Christ." After the first wave of distress, I realized this was what June must have meant.

"I get all this from one of Cleveland's fucked-up comrades. These dudes, you know, could just be blowin my mind. On the other hand"— Hobie actually lifted the gun and put it to his temple—"sucker might come in handy." He smiled. "Or shoot the pig comes through the door for me." Very briefly, he pointed the pistol in my direction.

"Let's do a retake on that one."

Hobie shrugged. I could be right about that.

"So what's your bad dream here?" I asked. "Is Cleveland talking? Is that it?" If Cleveland was strung out, he would be easy to roll. He might even have turned over by now, although the Eddgars claimed that Cleveland's weekend visitors had bucked him up. Hobie denied there was any cause for concern.

"Cleveland, man—Cleveland's the baddest mother ever shit between two shoes."

"So he's not talking?"

"He ain talkin, less he wants to talk. You know, maybe he said some things. Maybe he's tryin to catch a few fools' attention." I could hear in the steady drumbeat with which these assurances rolled that Hobie had uttered them often in the last few days. "See, man, this is just, you know, a little internal struggle. Eldridge and Huey, man— Huey is kind of a strange motherfucker. Can be very abstract about stuff. Very cold. He's gone be comin out any day now. Cleveland was more in with Eldridge and them. Now Huey's saying, you know, like peddling dope and all, that isn't any kind of revolutionary act. You know? And all the fucker's really meanin is that the party didn't get a righteous enough piece."

I nodded.

"So you know, Cleveland, man, he's feelin a distinct lack of solidarity. I mean there 20,000 people in the streets of New Haven for Bobby and back here nobody can't even be bothered to throw Cleveland's bail. Maybe the brother said something to attract some attention. But that's dialogue, man. Dialectics. This is an ideological debate, you know? Stalin and Lenin."

"And which one's going to tell on you, Hobie? Stalin or Lenin?"

He gave me a sick smile to show he did not enjoy being mocked. He never had.

"If Cleveland turns, that's your ass, right?"

"Cleveland ain turnin. Not on no brothers. That's for sure." I knew he was persuading himself. But even with what he admitted—that Cleveland might give up a few ofays—I could see what worried the Eddgars.

"You could turn first, Hobe. You know, you didn't do anything. You could explain."

"Ain no snitch." He lowered his voice. He gestured with the gun. "They-all'd kill my ass anyway." That was what Bobby was on trial for in New Haven—killing an informer.

I could have chided Hobie, pointed out what a mess he'd made for himself, but today it would have been hypocritical. If I told him what I was doing with the Eddgars, there'd be no end to the names he'd call me. We'd both been overcome by something that still seemed to me to have started out so right. It was like a party where the good times—the music, the dancing, the girls, the excitement—had unaccountably led to disaster. I felt sorry for us both.

"For your information, the Eddgars seem to have a plan for Cleveland's bail. So maybe you can holster your weapon. He should be on the street soon."

"The Eddgars," said Hobie. "Fuck. Ain nothing come free with them."

"But you'll be okay then, right?"

He moved his shoulders in the same inconclusive way he'd done a number of times already. He didn't really know. It might be better. A moment passed.

"Are you scared?" I asked him.

He considered that, the sorrowful brown eyes dead still on me. The Panthers didn't know fear.

"This here, man, is Vietnam. It's like a bad trip wide awake, and you ain't got that little edge to hold to, tellin yourself that it's bound to wear off. I haven't slept but an hour, two hours in two days. The wrong dude comes through that door? 'These are the days of our lives, bubba.'"

"So get the hell out of here. Put on your PF Flyers and jump higher and run faster than anybody else. Come to Canada. How about that? Hope and Crosby do another road movie?"

A familiar whimsy shot through his face, then wore away. He shook his head no, decisively.

"I'm cool here. Bros be lookin out for me."

When I left, he roused himself and, after an instant of deliberation in which he pretended to be staggering around, raised his arms and returned my embrace. He kept the pistol in his hand for the instant we were connected. When I turned for the door, he spoke a few words to me in French, one of his typically stylish gestures, although he knew it was a language I didn't speak. I caught the words "*mon ami.*" I was sure it was a movie line, but I couldn't recall the picture.

When I got back to the Campus Travel Motel, Eddgar was there. I had taken the key, and when I came in I had an odd sense I was intruding on some intimacy, although there was nothing lewd about the pose in which I found June and him. They were seated on the facing sides of the twin beds, their heads drawn close. Clearly they'd been whispering, defeating some unknown surveillant, controlling the random element. As I entered, Eddgar's face shot around, the intense blue eyes riveted, as always, by anger and suspicion.

"My Lord, Seth. We've been sitting here hoping like hell, just hoping they didn't run into you."

"Who's that?"

Eddgar looked at June. From the thick smell of her cigarettes and the butts in the ashtray I could see they had been talking quite some time—probably as long as I'd been gone.

"Apparently we've had visitors at the apartment building, asking questions," she said.

What kind of questions? I asked.

"I didn't see them," Eddgar said. "Michael talked to them. I spoke to him over the phone. He said they were asking about you: How long since you were last seen? Who was with you then? Any signs of struggle, unusual sounds last night?"

"Bullshit," I said.

"I wish it were," said Eddgar.

"What did he tell them?"

"Nothing," said Eddgar. "He didn't know anything. He was on his way to look over his lab, so he didn't have time. You know how hard it is to get a word out of him normally. But it's damn clear to me they thought you'd been kidnapped."

"God. Who? Who was it?"

"Michael said they showed him credentials." Eddgar looked briefly to June, before me. "It was the FBI," he said.

December 11, 1995

SONNY

Often, there are evenings out, unavoidable occasions. On these nights, I race home to fetch Nikki from aftercare, feed her, and, with luck, get her in her pjs. Then Marta Stern's live-in nanny, Everarda, an effervescent Nicaraguan immigrant, takes over. She has been filling in for me for years now, when Marta has no plans herself. Early to bed, Everarda prefers to stay over in the small first-floor guest room behind the kitchen, walking the three blocks back to Marta's at dawn. It's a wonderful arrangement for me. Nikki loves Everarda and her accent, which she imitates with uncanny accuracy, even, in her most pettish moments, to the woman's face. Everarda pays no mind. She is one of those women who know that the real purpose of the world, unaffected by couturier dresses, rap albums, or political payoffs in the men's room of the Club Delancey, is the nurturance of children, and that in that critical field, no one exceeds her wisdom. She calls Nikki "Niña" and moves her through her evening routine as smoothly as if my daughter were a puppet on strings.

With her overnight bag, Everarda comes in, shaking off the snow, which has just begun falling and lies thick on the false-fur collar of her coat. She is full of gossip. Marta, pregnant with her third baby, is varicose and swollen, and put out with her husband, Solomon, a management consultant. "Solomon, he gone all de time? She war yellin, you know? He god to come home. He gib her kisses. He send her flowers. He just smile." Everarda smiles too at Solomon's patience. He is a thin dark man. His family are expats, Jews from Cuba who arrived there in the seventeenth century. He's as dark as someone Maltese or Sri Lankan, a person bred of the blood of many nations.

Tonight's event is a retirement dinner for Cyrus Ringler, former Chief Justice of the Supreme Court, for whom I clerked for a couple of years right after law school. Law clerks spend their first year or two as lawyers, an intensely formative period, at a judge's side, seeing firsthand how the flesh of real life hangs on the raw bones of law-school learning. Much as racehorses are always identified by sire and dam, clerks are forever known by their judges, and it is perhaps my proudest heritage in the law to be a "Ringler clerk."

Accordingly, I must go tonight. I drive faster than I should through the pelting snow to the Center City, parking in the indoor lot at the Hotel Gresham. I walk across the street to the Parker, where Justice Ringler is being saluted by the City of Hope. It's the end of cocktails, just as the five hundred lawyers and pols and judges are moving to their seats, making their last efforts to work the room. I hold a number of conversations at bay, so I can get close enough to the elevated dais to make sure Cy Ringler sees me—he blows a kiss and waves. From his color, I can tell he's already a little drunk, enjoying his last hurrah. A former Kindle County PA, the Justice, as I will forever call him to his face, is one of those redoubtable men of the law who gathered respect as he rose by refusing to break the rules for political purpose. He was not inflexible or unrealistic; but he always knew the outer limits. Even so, he was a fabulous compromiser around the court. He hated dissents, felt they diminished the authority of decisions, and loved to find procedural gimmicks allowing divisive issues to be passed back to the lower courts. Marjoe, who's had cancer twice in the last five years, is beside him, wasted-looking, but bearing up. She must fly a hairdresser in from the corn belt. Where else could she even find somebody to do her hair like that, tightly curled and flattened down around her ears like a bonnet?

Oddly, in this environment, surrounded by most of the Tri-Cities legal notables, I feel more than anywhere else the extraordinary attention Nile Eddgar's trial has generated. My neighbors in U. Park are too circumspect to speak to me about my job, and it has been no task, given my schedule, to avoid the papers and the news. I've caught sight of headlines now and then, but it's only tonight I fully sense how closely the case is being watched. Everyone passes a word about it. "Ooh, you got a hot one," Manny Escobedo, another of the Supreme Court Justices, tells me. Cal Taft, a bar president, remarks, "I don't have to ask what you've been doing, do I?" I glow with the neon of celebrity. The judges all quietly inquire how the bastard cornered me into a bench trial. I smile and keep my answers nondescript, which, in the strange ballet of accepted mannerisms at work here, is taken as a perfect response.

Seated at a table of former Ringler clerks and their spouses, I endure the usual struggle getting a vegetarian meal. The waiters in their cutaways look at me as if I'm a heathen. Who wouldn't want that baked chicken, rigid as a hockey puck? I have asked to sit next to Milan Dornich, who was my co-clerk for a year. When I split with Charlie, Mike Dornich was one of those guys who came to my mind, mild, angular, witty. With Marta one night, watching Nikki play with Clara, Marta's older daughter, I confessed these thoughts. Marta was alarmed. 'Jesus, Sonny,' she whispered, 'he's gay.' I realized instantly she was right, and felt amazed by myself, the way we forever see others through the lens of our own needs. Always happy for one another's company, Mike and I whisper together, conspiring over the absurdity of the event. The $200 I spent for two tickets, one of them unused, is a mild extravagance. Many lawyers from our era have rounded the bend into plum law-firm partnerships. Daniella Grizzi, my immediate predecessor in Ringler's chambers, makes millions every year in her P.I. practice and is listed as a $10,000 patron of the event. Only Mike Dornich, now second in command at the State Appellate Defenders, and I remain in the public sector, the poor mice at a banquet of fat rats.

The dessert and speeches come together. It's a work night and everybody wants to be gone by 9:30. I kiss Mike and slip out before the crowd. In the vast, carpeted reception room where cocktails were served and name tags applied, I catch sight of Chief Judge Brendan Tuohey. Three highballs along, he is glad-handing and waving to other early escapees, as he returns from the men's room. He greets me in a mood of après-work geniality, his nose red as sunburn from the lick of whiskey. He seems so happy I'm afraid he might even kiss me.

"Sonny, Sonny," he says, "how are you this evening?" He takes my hand and with the other grips me near the shoulder in an impressively neutral way. "I've been meaning to give ya a call. So your trial is going on, Sonny?"

"Yes, Chief," I answer, despairing, as ever, over the ludicrous salutation. Which tribe did I join? The judges all call each other by first names. Old-boy stuff. But I could never bring myself to 'Brendan' with this man.

"Seems to be quite a Donnybrook mess."

"Yes, sir."

He shakes his head in wonder at the tirelessness of human disputes. With a jolly smile, I beg off and hurry into the little corridor where the cloakroom and the johns are secreted. In the full-length mirror, beside the coat check, I look myself over. Good enough. Black sheath and pearls. All those years of looking for a style of my own—not camp, not trite, not hippie or yippie or yuppie or commercial—have resolved themselves in a sort of residue of fashion that says I don't have the time to fuss too much with hair or makeup, a look of having let go gratefully of a little of the heat and glory of the past.

Just as the young girl hands back my coat, I hear my name once more from behind. Tuohey again. Something slipped his mind. I have one of those instants of alarm the Chief Judge always provokes. Brendan Tuohey can turn a corridor, even a well-lit one, into a sinister enclave. He comes one step too close.

"Glad I caught you." His voice is lowered and he speaks between his teeth. "Happen to see Matt Galiakos tonight?"

I've nearly asked 'Who?' when I recollect: Galiakos is the state chair of the Democratic Farmers & Union Party. The people who count with Brendan Tuohey would no more fail to recognize Galiakos's name than John XXIII's.

"Interested in your trial," says Tuohey. "I guess he'd been lookin at tonight's news. Loves Lloyd Eddgar. Course we all do." Lloyd? I marvel. *Lloyd!* Tuohey's tongue actually appears as he wets his lips. "Says to me, he says, 'What's that gal doing? Don't she know we're in the same party? I thought she was a friend of his.' "

Tuohey laughs—oh, he's merry. He shivers in glee and is gone at once, his step spry with power and feigned delight, never again meeting my eye. Not because he's afraid of what he's done; he can tiptoe down the line as precisely as Nijinsky. Or because he hopes to mute his message, invisible and awful as the odor of plague. No, he wants to give me time. So I recognize it's in my interests to comply. He's some kind of genius, this man, with his narrow, crafty, wizened face. He couldn't have done this better if he'd staged rehearsals. All the phony confidentiality. *We love Lloyd Eddgar. We're in the same party. Thought you were a friend of his.* I've been at the law a dozen years—a clerk, a prosecutor, a judge—in each role wearing the borrowed mantle of public power, and have never faced anything like this. I stand here in the hall, alone in the bank of deep shadow between the sconces, weakened by rage.

Despite repeated tries, I can get only one arm into my coat. Half-frantic, I give up and ride down the escalator clutching the free sleeve against my side under my purse. But like the victim always, I feel cheapened and shamed. A few weeks ago, Brendan Tuohey was the one giving me all that malarkey: 'You're the right judge for this case, Sonny. Tricky situation, but it comes with the robes.' All the stuff I wanted to hear. And now he tells me the real reason: so I can smooth things out for my 'friend' Eddgar. For Godsake! I'm sick, as ill as if I'd stepped from a rocking boat, when I catch my reflection in the Parker's revolving doors and see the truth: I've compromised myself. I stayed on a case I should have given up, and now must stand still while a mangy alley cat like Brendan Tuohey rubs his flanks against me.

I rush across the street, high heels clacking on the glistening pavement of Mercer Avenue, which is rimed with salt and snow. By the time I reach the lobby of the Gresham, I'm actually shaking. I lay my hand over my chest and grip the pearls at my throat. In the old days, a judge who complied with a communication like this received a visit—and an envelope—a few weeks later from somebody connected, a lawyer, a councilman. Now discipline is a matter of negative reinforcement. Brendan Tuohey can send me to Housing Court, to listen to the endless lament of deadbeat tenants, or to Night Narcotics Court, so I'll never see Nikki during the week. Send me for the 'good of the court,' with no other explanation. That's what I'm supposed to think about, while he slides off to let Galiakos know the word has been delivered.

Can I even drive? I'm desperate, as so often, frantic for someone to talk to. I can't call Cy Ringler tonight. Sandy Stern! He'll know what to do. In fact, he already foresaw the very situation. There were a dozen friends, colleagues who were jealous when word leaked that Ray Horgan had called to sound me about the bench. Stern, alone among the persons whose advice I cared for, warned me against it.

'Pay no attention,' he told me. 'Dismiss what Raymond Horgan and his Reform Commission promise you.' Stern's soft face, with the tiny dark eyes surmounted in plump flesh, was suddenly reproachful, as I recited Horgan's commitments: A felony court assignment within two years. Complete independence. I must have sounded to him like Shirley Temple. Stein leaned across the linen cloth at the Matchbook, where we were eating, probably stifling the impulse to wag a finger. 'For today, Brendan Tuohey needs you and your spotless reputation. Two years from now the Commission will be an amusing part of history, one more toothless sop of briefly agitated public opinion, and they will force you to choose between your fine assignment or succumbing to their ways. You are not the first, Sonia. This, I remind you, is Kindle County, where great capacities of human invention have been set for a century on devising systems utterly invulnerable to reform.'

At the bank of telephones in an alcove, I probe the recesses of my purse. Nearby, the lobby of the Gresham, a towering space constructed in the Gilded Age, churns with sound and motion. Dramatic marble columns, the size of sequoias, offset by long curtains of green velvet, extend the entire height of the room. Five floors above, the ceiling is encrusted with gilt and cherubim and a poor Italianate mural of Venus and Cupid. On the marble shelf before the phones, I begin removing items. Kleenex. Lipstick. Where's the damned address book? When I was younger, I could have remembered the bloody number! Stern is not at home. I could call Marta, but she tends to show a tough, inflexible side on matters like this. She'll badger me to report it. To whom, for Godsake? And how do I keep these events from turning against me? Tuohey is too cagey to catch. He'll change a word or two and portray his remarks as innocuous and me as hypersensitive and unfit. Within a week, his minions will be clamoring for my resignation.

And then I realize that Seth is staying here, in this hotel. Seth! The thought of him—reliable, open, happy to help—is an inspiration. "Mr. Weissman," I tell the operator when I move down two bays to the house phone. There is no Weissman. "Frain," I say.

It's rung twice, when I suddenly slam the handset down. *Seth?* I think. Am I crazy? Tell Seth? Hobie's friend? I lay my fingertips, bloodless, frigid, against my forehead. Leaning over the small shelf beneath the house phones, awaiting my composure, I catch, incongruously, a sudden pleasant scent of my own perfume. If I phone Stern's office, I'll get his service. A criminal defense lawyer is like a doctor, always on call, available for midnight bailings, visits to a crime scene. They'll locate him. He'll remonstrate mildly, say he told me so, then figure out what to do.

And then — naturally, isn't that life? — I spot Seth across the lobby. He's dressed casually, in the white dress shirt he wore to court and a pair of khakis. He has magazines in one hand and, I think, a candy bar. Observed from one hundred feet, he appears humble and appealing: a tall, slender man, blondish, bald, pleasant-looking. He is chatting with a desk clerk. After a week and a half in the hotel, he has acquaintances. He's being himself, wholesome and engaging. He laughs, and then, by whatever magic there is in this, feels the weight of my glance from a distance and actually jolts a bit at the sight of me. He comes my way so quickly that he's gone several yards before he recollects the clerk, to whom he tosses a departing wave. Arriving in front of me, he is perfectly still.

"Hi," I answer. "I was at a dinner here. Across the street actually."

"Jeez, you look fantastic." He does a real routine, mouth open, ending by quickly touching his heart. As if makeup and hair spray turned me into Helen of Troy. I manage an expression of pleasant tolerance.

"I'm not feeling fantastic at the moment. I had something really, really rotten happen to me just now."

Beneath the fair brows, his greenish eyes search me. I hold up my hand. It quakes involuntarily, as if I'd been struck by palsy. The display nonpluses us both.

"You want a drink?"

God, do I! We set off together for the saloon across the lobby and actually reach its swinging doors. Mingled voices and the jazz piano well out of the dark room. Before my eyes adjust, I can make out only a large illuminated aquarium behind the bar, through which angel fish and other bright tropical creatures travel amid the bubbles. A quarter of the lawyers in Kindle County will be in here shortly, pausing for a nightcap before they ride up the parking elevator to collect their cars. Brendan Tuohey, who has watered himself in this place for years, is among the likely arrivals. Not the company I want to keep right now.

"Forget it," I say. "Bad idea."

"What?"

"Appearances," I answer.

"So come upstairs. We'll raid the mini-bar in my room. Come on."

When I issue a prim look, he makes a face. "Don't be ridiculous."

With my elbow in hand, he steers me into the old gilded elevator, a gorgeous cage of brass and mirrors. "So what happened?" he asks as we are rising.

"I don't know, Seth," I answer, which is almost true. "I had an unpleasant encounter with another judge. Something about this case."

"Uh-oh." His mouth narrows in a discreet pucker and he says no more until we reach his rooms. There, I fall into a barrel chair with a cane backing which is just inside the door. Seth's suite is the real thing, a relic of the grand era when suites were the refuge of the rich and not a promotional toy, offered like a free breakfast. There are mock-heirloom pieces with Queen Anne feet and satin-sheened wallpaper with a classic green stripe. Seth is at home here. He has a laptop computer open on the desk in the corner and the walnut doors of the armoire, which holds the mini-bar where he's bending, have been thrown back, revealing the dead eye of the TV. Newspapers from many different cities litter the room. In the bedroom, I can see a four-poster with those carved wooden pineapples atop the posts. Another pair of khakis has been heaved over one of them.

"I just need to settle down for a second." I bolt half the Chardonnay he gives me.

"You don't want to talk about this, right?"

"I shouldn't, Seth. I just need some company. Somebody passed a remark about Eddgar. It's smarter not to get into it."

"Yeah," says Seth, "that he belongs in the seventh circle of hell, right?" He laughs bitterly. "*God*, I despise him. What a heinous creep he is."

I do not answer, do not dare. What am I supposed to do for Eddgar? I wonder suddenly. I don't even know. A momentary fear takes hold that I might conform to Tuohey's wishes by accident. Considering that prospect, I emit a brief moan. But I have no choices now. With a few minutes to absorb all this, I can see that there's no backpedaling, no sidesteps. The only direction to go is forward. I have to finish as well as I can what I should never have started. As I cycle through these calculations, Seth watches, his eyes watery with uncertainty. I can't talk to him about this, I realize. Not him or anybody else. That's the only true thing Tuohey said to me. 'Comes with the robes.' It's my problem. Alone.

"I'm going to go, Seth."

"Wow," he says. "Is this the Guinness record for brief visits?"

"I just needed a second. I appreciate your being the port in the storm." I stand, taking hold of the ornate brass doorknob. I drain the rest of the wine. "Really," I add. "Thanks."

"Just a second," he says, "I'll kiss you good night." He makes no move to rise. He's in a wooden armchair, upholstered in satin to match the wallpaper, laughing at me, at both of us actually.

"I think the last time will hold me for a while."

"Well, that'll make a fella feel like Prince Charming."

"Oh, don't do your wounded thing, Seth."

"No, I'm not wounded." He turns to the glass table beside him and pours himself more wine. "By the time I got back here, I actually was pretty encouraged. You wanna know why?"

A person—a woman—who was going to remain aloof or at least unentangled would say goodbye right now. I know that, but I'm curious, of course. He takes a sip to steady himself and I feel myself make a measured nod.

"When I thought about it," he says, "really considered everything, I wasn't sure you ever found anybody better. You know, than me."

In shock, I laugh, a shot of sound that rebounds off the grand old walls. The gall or something! And he *means* it.

"You don't understand," he says.

"I don't. I certainly don't. I mean, Seth, really, some of the stuff you come out with."

"Look," he says.

"No, you look," I say, feeling an intense flare of the anger that I suddenly see I've been holding at bay. "I'm forty-seven years old. And I'm like you. I'm unhappy just like you are, Seth. I don't always enjoy the way my life turned out. I look back and wonder what happened to all the promise, just like you do. I envy people who are young and envision the future as something great. You're not the only one with angst. I'm tired of fucking up. I'm tired of making the same mistakes. At the worst moments, I'm sick of myself. And this, us, this isn't kidding around. And I'm running out of time for stupid things. I thought all weekend about how this would turn out and I can just see it: 'Auld lang syne' and 'Isn't it thrilling'; then, 'Hey, I have a life.'"

"Sonny."

"It's stupid," I repeat.

"It's not." He puts down his glass and stands to calm me. "I mean, I'm glad you're here. But you looked pretty damned happy to see *me* a minute ago."

"Yes, I was relieved. I needed — *need* — a friend. But that doesn't mean it's not dumb to retread a childhood love affair."

"It wasn't childhood," he answers at once, "and it's not dumb. One thing I've learned: I will *not* treat the rest of my life like it's meaningless, just because it's past." In conviction, he briefly makes a fist, then takes a step forward and grips both of my shoulders. "Look. I want you to take a deep breath. Okay? You know me. I'm maybe a quarter less crazy than I used to be. But I'm the same sincere dope. I think I know what I'm doing. I think I'm taking stock. Some things have mattered more than others. Some people have mattered more. You can fuck up with me like you can with anybody else. And maybe you will. But you're playing with a bigger bankroll if you get in the game with me. I knew Zora. I saw that whole scene. I saw your collection of black peasant blouses, so you wouldn't have to worry about what to wear, and how scared you'd get when you were afraid your skin was going to break out. And I've seen what you've accomplished off that start, which is a hell of a lot. There are maybe three billion men on this planet. Some are smarter. Some are better-looking. And most of them have more hair. But I've got one advantage over every single one of them: I know how great you are. And I'm not sure you've ever met another man who does."

He takes the wine glass, which unconsciously I've continued holding, and gazes at me in a fixed way. The Look. All mating primates, I learned once, utilize this dilated, dead-on stare.

"You know what happens now?" he asks.

"You kiss me good night?"

"Not good night," he says.

When he leans down, a trace of exasperated sound escapes me. But I do not resist. That great creature hunger begins to stir. In the cascades of longing, I will lose track of myself. And who will be here afterwards? I wonder. Who?

So, it happens. Outside, fresh snow clings to the city streets and within the bedroom of the suite the exterior light is softly refracted so the air seems enhanced by the glow, which includes darker, purplish shades from the lee end of the visible spectrum. Between us, it is surprisingly smooth. Memory, knowledge — the past brings its comforts. In the living room, urgently embracing, we shed our clothes. Some wary, calculating portion of me continues to stand guard, but I'm a slave now to sensation.

Even that awful moment, the one I have numbed myself to with so many half-conscious mental rehearsals, when my bra slides off and the lopsided work of modern surgery is disclosed, sluices by in the currents of desire. This is one promise Seth has kept: he is not afraid, not of anything about me, or that the present is not the past. God, sex is great! The body made servant to the spirit. His tongue is everywhere. Finally, he bodies me down on the four-poster, my feet still on the floor, and stands before me, erect, pointing north by northwest, as he fiddles with the condom wrapping. Then the slow opening, enveloping, the pressure and pleasure of merger.

"Slow, baby," I whisper, "slow," unable to recall if it's an honest memory or merely fantasy that I whispered this to him long ago.

I come last, throbbing by the end on the wilted heap of him. Afterwards, we lie together in the bed. He grabs the quilted spread, which we did not bother to remove, and wraps it around us. We are surrounded by the smells of hotel linen.

"That didn't take long," I finally say. "To get back there."

"I'd say I was right about everything."

"I'd say I was horny."

We laugh. Just giddiness. Life can be all right.

"What do you think the biological function is of female orgasm?" I ask.

"You mean how it happens?"

"From a Darwinian perspective. Men have to come to spill their seed. It's directly related to reproduction. But what do you think nature gets out of letting women feel so good?"

"I think it's what they call an incentive. Remember Green Stamps?"

"But as long as men were so inclined, and women had this profound desire to be mothers—" Considering, I pause. "Sex isn't pleasurable for all species. Aren't there cats—panthers, I think—the male has a barb at the end of his business and as he withdraws, she actually snarls and screams. It's the barb that causes ovulation. I learned that ages ago. Wasn't it with you?"

"Wrong boyfriend."

"No! I'm sure we used to go to the zoo and watch those large cats make it."

He laughs. He was putting me on.

"I didn't realize voyeurism was the motive," Seth says. "My recollection, Judge, is that we were taking Nile."

"Jesus," I mutter. He's right. My heart, in reflex, freezes over and I grow silent with the complications. Beneath the coverlet, his fingers trace and retrace the grooved stretch marks left years ago on the good breast by the period of explosive growth I went through at ten, eleven, twelve. I have asked all the doctors if there could be a relationship between that hormonal surge and cancer. They only shrug.

Seth sits up now swinging his legs over the edge of the bed. The sight of the older man remains marginally surprising. He is still lean, but his skin holds less color, less tone. There is the inevitable fleshy gathering at the waist, and his back, as he slumps, shows the slightest bow. He is pensive, as we both are, in the aftermath.

"I don't think much of this Darwin stuff," he says. "What would Darwin say about music? What's the survival function of that? And it exists in every culture."

"It makes me happy."

"Like your orgasm."

"Maybe nature wants us to be happy after all, Seth. Do you think that's possible?"

He doesn't take an instant. "Nope."

"Don't happy people live longer? Isn't there research? Isn't there something tonic to the organism in enjoying the whole grand show?"

"Then I'm doomed," he says. "I'm on borrowed time." His delivery is good and I feel lighthearted and laugh as he intends. "You still think you can achieve Nirvana?" he asks me.

"Not Nirvana."

"But you're happy?"

"Happier than when we were young. Like you said, I feel I've accomplished things. I love my child. I'm *proud* I'm a good parent. I'm a good judge." I wait then to see if I believe what I have said, if some internal truth meter will buzz in disbelief, but it goes down without a tremor. Seth, in reply, is quietly shaking his head.

"I don't know many happy anythings, Sonny. Not lawyers. Not journalists. Not Indian chiefs."

"You're in no position to assess that, Seth. After what you've been through. It's too soon."

"Two years? I would have thought—" He lifts a hand. "When it happened"—he takes a breath—"when he died, there was so much of that disconnected feeling from nightmares, you know, where you're reaching inside to grab hold of whatever part of your soul provides reassurance the terror isn't real? But, of course, what I recognized four times a day was that I wasn't getting out of this one, there was nothing better to wake to. I walked through months like that, and there are times now when I realize that period has never really ended."

Even now, back in Seattle, he cannot walk north from the house, he says. Down the block a few doors there's a house where they poured a new walk four years ago and Isaac, in a typically ungovernable mood, wrote his name with a stick, carving the ragged letters half an inch deep with his own special mix of strength and fury. The neighbors were so angry they stopped speaking to Seth, even to Lucy. Now the boy is dead and the name is still there. He has gone by once or twice, Seth says, and just dissolved. What a sight: a man in a trench coat, standing on an empty walk before a house where the occupants still hate him, weeping so fiercely that you know he feels he will never remember how to stop.

"I comfort myself in the most ridiculous ways. I mean, this is nothing compared to the legendary blows of history. I think about what my parents went through. But, you know"—he looks at me—"there's no relativity to suffering."

I hold him for quite some time, something I have yearned to do since he first told me. Then he goes out to the living room. He brings wine back for both of us.

"Have you tried therapy, Seth? Was that a joke the other day, about treatment?"

"I've been in therapy longer than Woody Allen. What about you?"

"Surgery? Divorce? I took my turn. It helps."

"It helps," he says, but shakes his head. Then he puts the glass down somewhat precipitously on the Louis-something night table, saying he knows what he needs. When he returns, he stands naked before the bed, that fox amid the bushes still red and glistening. He sings a few bars from Steely Dan: " 'The Cuervo gold, the fine Colombian, make tonight a wonderful night.' " He opens his palm, displaying a joint. I actually jolt a bit.

"Where did that come from? Is this a habit?"

"Hobie," he says. The one word is explanation enough. "How about it? Old times' sake?"

"You're kidding."

"Sure, I'll get my guitar. We can have a hootenanny."

"Don't forget the red lightbulb and the towel to stuff under the door."

I fear he's gone to get them, but when he returns from the living room again it's merely a pack of matches he's brought. He surrounds himself in a bouquet of smoke. I haven't been this close to the odor in years. Occasionally, there's an amusing fugitive whiff as some teenaged goof passes on the street, or a single breath taken in as something wafts in from the distance in a park or at a concert.

"I don't," I say, when he offers it. "I haven't since I got my law license."

"Oh bullshit," he answers in disapproval, not doubt. I'm being conformist, still a generational sin.

"Something has to count, Seth."

"I suppose," he answers and picks up the pillows and seats himself behind me on the bed, pulling me back so that I lounge against him as he smokes, snug within the warmth of his legs and the leisure of our nakedness. And what is it that counts, I wonder suddenly, what great absolute can I name? In the land of laws, the one thing I promised myself would not occur has happened. In the great new age, I have found a way to bring myself to shame like the heroines of old-time novels, fucked my way to ignominy like Hester Prynne and Anna Karenina. And for just this moment it does not seem to matter. No, that's not right. It matters even now that I'm not better or more honorable. It matters that I've tried and failed by some measure all my life. It will always matter. But it is, right now, just a fact like many others. Like the glow of the moon or the paths of the migrating birds. When he brings the joint back to my lips, I take it from him. The pungence and the raw taste of the smoke, more or less forgotten, for some reason make me laugh.

"Seduced you," he says.

"You seem to be an expert."

"Oh, please."

"Have you fucked around a lot, Seth?"

He answers that he doesn't think of this as fucking around.

"I meant before."

He takes another hit and peeks cutely around my shoulder. "Is this an AIDS check or character assessment?"

"The latter. I hope."

"What do you think?" he asks.

"I don't know. I suppose I think yes. But maybe I'm trading in stereotypes. You know, sort of famous, sort of rich. I always think people like that get loose. Were you?"

The ember of the joint brightens like a lightning bug. "You first," he says.

"I don't have anything to tell. Once, when I was a prosecutor, I fell half in love with the defense counsel in one of my cases, but that was temporary insanity. It only lasted a couple of days. And nothing came of it. He's fat and a lot older, and I was pregnant." Even telling the story, though, it occurs to me that what's going on right now fits my pattern. I only fall for men at the most unlikely moments—as if I need a time when my own security systems are not on high alert.

"That's it?"

"That's it."

He tokes again.

"Tell," I say.

"Among the many sad ways I've spent time in the last twenty years have been a couple of really hopeless affairs with women who offered me very little except an admiring audience and the usual animal thrill. And what I discovered is that life offers nothing more depressing than a relationship conducted solely within the wallpapered dimensions of an expensive hotel room."

"Did Lucy know?"

"Yeah, but it was complicated. This was all before Isaac was born. We had a pretty rough spell then."

"Like this one?"

"This isn't the same. Not at all. We're not angry. We just seem to be out of gas."

"Why were you angry then?"

"Why was I angry?" he repeats. "Lots of reasons. But let's just say that Lucy's arms aren't her only limbs that have been open to humanity."

"Ah." Their problems are getting clearer to me all the time. "That makes people angry."

"I suppose. But I didn't start wandering to get even. I loved the idea of it. Of falling. For someone. I still think it's the most thrilling thing in life. Does that sound corny? Or just weak?"

"Weak."

"Yeah." He knows it. He looks down between his knees. "That was the lesson I learned from you, though. The thrill."

"Right."

"I mean it," he says and touches the joint to my lips again. "It sounds like the song. What was his name. Something, something 'the thrill of it all/I'll tell them I remember you.' "

"Frank Ifield."

He rolls back. "I would. You know, say that. 'When the angels ask me to recall—' "

I turn away—I will not let him. What is this old fear? I still don't know, but I feel suddenly the presence of all the men—Seth and Charlie and a number in between—whom I turned from with the same morbid fluttering of the heart. I look at him squarely.

"I don't know a man who believes less in angels."

"But I believe in you, Sonny," he answers, and draws my hand down between his ruddy thighs to appraise the transitory emblem of his faith.

I had forgotten the aphrodisiac magic of marijuana, the forging sensation, like a river current, rippling outward, ever outward to the fingertips. Afterwards, I am sore and spent; the dope makes me sleepy. I wake in a flush of immediate embarrassment. I am laid out amid the rumpled bedding, thick with our musk, without a stitch of clothing, legs wide, oblivious, like somebody on a bender. The overhead fixture, old-fashioned milk glass festooned with silky cobwebs, burns blindingly.

"Two-fifteen," he says, when I ask the time. I groan and cover myself with the top sheet, then sit up. I always try to check with Everarda.

Seth is seated at the foot of the bed, still naked, his legs crossed. My purse has been emptied onto the spread and he is looking through it, all the telltale detritus of my life. My credit cards are laid out. Photographs. Business cards I've forgotten to throw away. My checkbook. He is eating an apple, a glossy Red Delicious, which looks to be one he bought the other day at Green Earth. Staring at him, I find that I'm no longer stoned. My mouth is stale, dry as a withered leaf.

"May I ask?"

"I'm amusing myself," he says. "I was alone."

I could tell him he's intruding. But that would be hypocritical. I knew he meant to intrude all along.

"And? Are you amused?"

"A little." He offers the apple and I take a bite.

"Did you do this when we lived together?"

"Of course not."

"Any surprises?"

"I have cards from two different travel agents and a brochure on the Philippines from a third. I thought that was interesting. Are you traveling?"

"Not with a six-year-old."

"But you'd want to go?"

"I'd love to go back. I'd love to go everywhere. Someday." I shudder with the thought: Travel. Free. Freed of custom, language, everything known. For me, the thought has always brought with it some delicious, unpronounceable fantasy that lurks in me, a tantalizing secret not fully known by anyone, even me. Another life!

"That's where you ended up when we split, wasn't it? The Philippines?"

"With the Peace Corps. I hoped they'd send me to some village, but I taught birth control to women in Olangapo City, near Subic Bay. It was disillusioning at times. I was basically helping a lot of them be whores. But I loved the country and the people. They have tremendous self-respect, in spite of all the colonization. The revolution didn't surprise me." I recall momentarily the English-language movie houses, the dampness, the fish, the sleek dark boys.

"I was flabbergasted, you know."

"Were you?"

"When you joined? I had no idea you'd want to do that."

"I also applied to be an astronaut."

"Come on!"

"No, I wanted to go to the planets. Venus, Mars. I'm dead serious. And I was sure it was going to happen. Somehow. In the future. It's strange to realize I'm never going to get there. I really thought I would."

How had that changed? When I was twenty-two, that destiny had seemed so real. The wish, the *need* to be a parent, to leave the species better off by one, and everything that came with it—house and things, job and schedule—had blown it all away. That's how it is for everyone. But did I ever really say goodbye to the girl in space who was going to make something spectacular of her desire to get a million miles from her mother? It doesn't matter, I suppose. I'm going home now. Not to the stars.

Seth hugs me as I dress, a silly burlesque of being unwilling to let me go. As I gather the last things, he waits by the door. Suddenly, inexplicably, the future is upon us. There is now a next move. I tell him to come for dinner tomorrow, Nikki will be thrilled. Then he catches me in one final embrace, and in the sheer delirium of weariness I am nearly knocked cold by the unexpected surge of passion, his and my own.

"How do you feel about this?" he asks as he finally lets me go.

After a second, I answer, "Better than I thought I would."

Smiles. God, he smiles.

"Great," he says. Then I'm gone.

May 4, 1970

SETH

I wanted to call my father for reassurance, but Eddgar insisted there was no point.

"He's going to deny it," Eddgar said. "Either way. If he's gone to the Feds, they'll tell him to lie."

"They'd *never* go." I'd been saying this for days, of course. Even I had to recognize some likelihood that my father, in his desperation over the money or my situation, might have made such an uncharacteristic move. But on balance, I continued to regard it as impossible.

"So where does it come from, Seth?" Eddgar asked me. "How does the FBI know? They seem to think you were abducted. You had to have told someone. Lucy?" Eddgar asked. "What does she know?" Both June and he had been put out that I'd taken a traveling companion. It showed a lack of discipline to allow whim to influence my plans. They had no choice, though, but to accept my terms. I insisted, truthfully, that Lucy knew nothing.

"So who?" Eddgar asked. He peered at me, sallowed by the cheap lamplight. I had settled heavily on one of the beds, weighing it all.

"Maybe it's because I didn't show for induction. Maybe they're after me already." It was possible I'd made a special target of myself with my anti-draft activities on campus. Maybe one of the Selective Service System's snitches had reported on my plan to flee and the Bureau had swung into action. But that didn't seem convincing to any of us.

"I went over the conversation with Michael three times," Eddgar said. "He called me because the way they were talking made him afraid something had happened to you."

Michael, of course, could have gotten the wrong drift. And there were other possibilities. I recollected my conversation with Graeme on Saturday. I'd told him enough to make it clear I knew more than I was saying about the bombing. Graeme could have law-enforcement contacts. It would fit his polymorphous view of the world to be living outside conventional boundaries. But that wasn't the prospect that really troubled me as I sat there.

"What?" June demanded. She'd detected something. Perhaps in my posture. Perhaps I'd slumped a bit. Eddgar too was staring.

"Damn it all," said Eddgar. "At a time like this he's holding out on us. Lord. Lord! We're in this *deep*! Who'd you talk to, Seth?"

When I told them what I'd said to Sonny, Eddgar groaned and held his head. June, too, had an excruciated expression.

"I didn't say anything about you guys. I didn't tell her the plan. She just wanted to know how I was handling my parents. So I said the word, you know? I said, 'Kidnapping.' But it's not her. It's not possible. She'd never sell me out. Christ, her mother is Zora Milkowski. She grew up with nightmares of the FBI."

"Half those old Commies are Bureau agents now," Eddgar said. "Hoover keeps the CP in business."

"It's *not* Sonny."

Eddgar refused to accept that. And his doubts of course dented, if only slightly, my confidence in her. Maybe I'd scared her by seeming so far gone. Maybe she'd done what she thought was best for my sake.

Eddgar paced to think. He and June talked a bit.

"We aren't going to know," he said at last. "Not for certain. Perhaps it's your parents. Maybe it's Sonny or someone else. Or just the draft. But if we assume the worst," Eddgar said, "then the FBI will be right there when you pick up the money. They'll surveil the whole thing. They'll follow you until they're sure there's no explosive device, or that it's been deactivated, and then they'll take you down."

Eddgar described this prospect with arrogant certainty about the predictability of the police. I was sure there was a saying somewhere in *The Little Red Book* about knowing the enemy. In the meanwhile, I thought through what he'd said. I was trying to calm myself, to remain rational. The memory of Hobie, with his puffy, drugged-out look, up against the wall in that checkerboard hellhole, remained with me. And I was guilty about being indiscreet with Sonny. I felt obliged to find a way to go ahead.

"So then I'll have to admit I was scamming, right? I'll say I needed the money to get to Canada. They're not going to bust me for kidnapping myself, right?"

Eddgar considered me briefly. "They *will* prosecute you for evading the draft. If the Bureau grabs you, you'll end up in the army. Or the slammer."

I had been oddly free of fear until that moment. Guilt and shame abounded, but I had, with certain obvious yearnings, followed the model of June and Eddgar, coldly working through the practicalities. Now I felt plain panic.

"I'm out," I said.

"Wait," said June. "Wait. Are we looking at this the right way? We're overstating the risks. Seth, you've said from the start your parents wouldn't contact the law. So it's probably something else that brought the Effin' BI around. Even if we assume it's Sonny, they don't have any hard information. Right? Isn't that what you said? The guys who came out tonight have already gone home for the day. They'll work on it in the morning, if they have time. And even on the odd chance your parents did go to the FBI, we told them you'd pick up the money tomorrow. That's when the Bureau will set up." June turned to Eddgar. "Seth should fly to Las Vegas tonight."

"Fly? How am I going to afford that?"

"Can you get hold of a credit card?" June asked me.

"You mean someone else's?" At some point I was going to have to stop being easily shocked by June.

"Too risky," Eddgar said. "Much too risky for Seth."

"Then suppose Seth doesn't pick up the money," said June. "What if it's someone else?"

"We said I'd present my driver's license."

"So we get someone who fits your description," she said. Photo IDs were still in their inception.

"Like?"

"How about Michael?" She looked to Eddgar for approval.

"Michael?" I asked. "What does Michael want to get involved with this for?"

"He needs a distraction," said June dryly. I didn't have the courage to see how Eddgar absorbed that.

"And what happens if they grab Michael?" I asked.

"They won't draft him," June said.

"They'll hold him for kidnapping," Eddgar said.

No one said anything. June and I both watched Eddgar as the digits tumbled in his mind.

"First," said Eddgar, "I agree with June. The risk is minimal. Minimal. But we want none." Between them, they began to debate how that could be accomplished. As they responded to each other, I was visited again by the sensation I'd had when I entered the room, that I was seeing something charged and private and vaguely perverse in actually witnessing the Eddgars in their moment of collaboration. Anyone else remained to some degree an intruder.

The plan emerged by turns between them, traded back and forth. Michael would be told that the FBI was looking for me because of the draft and that the money in Las Vegas was needed to support me in Canada. He would know no more, and could say nothing if questioned. To protect him from kidnapping charges, in the unexpected event that anything went awry, I would go to Las Vegas with him. I would be seen in his company, a happy volunteer, on the same plane, at the same motel, the rental car counter. For my safety, though, I would observe the pickup from a distance, part of the giddy gambling throng in the Roman Coin's mammoth casino. If anything misfired, if the Bureau or hotel security or the Las Vegas police stepped in as he received the money, I would depart instantly, mix into the crowd, and go North. If worst came to worst, if Michael was held, I could call the FBI and my parents and explain what I needed to explain when I reached Canada.

Even after this scheme was fully described, deliberated, quilted together between them, a strangled voice reared up in me. Crazy, it said, this is crazy.

"It's an insane thing for Michael," I said.

"He'll do it," said June. She stood up and ran her hands down her thighs to smooth her dress. Her face was harshly contained. "I'll talk to him," she said.

When I got back to Robson's, the dinner rush was beginning. Sonny was behind the lunch counter, holding a coffeepot and flirting in a harmless way with an old guy in a flannel shirt, a heavyset man with rough skin. The hour and the needy way he savored her attention, like a flower turning toward the sun, made me think he was a widower. She touched his hand to still him when she saw me. My look appeared to alarm her.

"You fucked up," I told her.

"What? What did I do?" She placed the coffeepot back on the Bunn machine behind her. She was a little pale with weariness—she'd been on her feet for twelve hours now—and, as ever, in no mood to contend with criticism. She asked why I wasn't gone.

"You told someone what I told you this morning. And now I'm in shit up to my eyeballs."

"Told what? What are you talking about?"

"You know what I mean."

The old man at the counter had stopped stirring his coffee to watch.

"What is *wrong* with you?" she asked. Her full brows were drawn into her eyes in a pained way. She clearly hoped for better from me.

We went out back again, but now stood at a distance in the graveled alley. June and Eddgar had warned me repeatedly that it was a bad idea to come back here. But I had insisted Sonny was the logical choice. She would come through, I said. If she'd made a mistake, she'd be eager to correct it. They capitulated only because they were desperate for the credit card and had no other sources for the money, Eddgar's hearings having left them and their organization broke. I, of course, had other motives. I needed to know for myself.

"What kind of shit are you in?"

"Deep." I told her she must have mentioned my kidnapping to somebody.

"No one. No. One."

"What about Graeme?"

"Graeme? He left last night. He'll be in San Rafael all week. Have you ever heard of Primal Scream therapy?"

Eddgar had warned me. 'She'll lie to you,' he said. 'She'll deny every-thing. Watch,' he'd said. I had girded myself, but now I was helpless not to believe her.

"Well, the FBI is on me."

"Already? Oh Jesus." She naturally assumed that the FBI was pursuing me for draft evasion and could not comprehend what kidnapping would have to do with that. I shook my head repeatedly rather than explain: I was not going to make the same error twice. Down the alley, she crossed her arms over the white uniform to protect herself from the evening chill. She remained peeved.

"So what do you need, Seth? Is there something I'm supposed to do to help, or did you just come back to accuse me of selling you out?"

"I need a credit card."

"A credit card?"

"Just go inside. When somebody pays with a credit card, bring it out here. I'll be back in five minutes. Less." June was parked around the corner, at the end of the alley, in the car. She wore a headscarf and dark glasses, something in the nature of a disguise. The travel agency where she'd booked the tickets was right there on Campus Boul, ready to close. She'd called ahead explaining she would have to leave her children home alone and they'd promised that June would be in and out in five minutes. The plan, by which we'd pay with this hijacked credit card, seemed almost sensible to me. I had not calculated beforehand the subtle psychological effects of declaring myself an outlaw. I already cared less about anyone's judgments of me, including my own.

"You're crazy," she said.

"I need this. I'm telling you, I need this."

"Why?"

"Don't ask why. You're always telling me you care for me. You have to save your life, but you care for me. Well, now my life needs saving."

"You can't explain? You're going to charge something on someone else's credit card?"

"I need to get on an airplane, Sonny. I have to get away." I was going to offer more, but I stopped. The skein of tenuous connections—Cleveland and Hobie, my parents and the army and my freedom—could not be tied together in my mind. Instead, again, it was simply she and I. I had fomented, with barely any masking of my intentions, one more scene between us, one more insistent demand that she show that she cared for me. I might as well have been some guy in the back seat of a Chevy saying, 'Prove it.'

"Look, I'll fade this," I said. "If it goes to shit, you tell them I must have picked your apron pocket when you came back here to talk to me. You'll be protected."

"Protecting me's not the point, Seth."

"Well, what is?"

"This is *crazy*." A wind came up then and snatched the little paper tiara off the top of her head. She watched it skitter down the pavement, then let her abundant dark hair down and shook it out. A minute passed while she bundled it back into the net. When she finished, I could feel the remoteness that had settled upon her. I had finally, fully destroyed myself with her. Looking down the alley, with the crisp white apron rising on the breeze, was the dark gorgeous girl I'd met on the bus a year before, who'd been reluctant at first to have anything to do with me and who now knew she'd been right. She'd always been intrigued by the mad, imperfect piece of me, the fact that I could let go of more than she could. But now she had witnessed the havoc that wreaked. Her rejection set a siren of regret singing in me. In spite of everything I had done to my parents, it was the first time I realized I was out of control, that the untamed parts of me were destroying what the saner self really wanted.

"Look, I'll give you the money," she said finally.

"It's too much. You can't afford it. There are other people."

"Other people? God, Seth, what are you into?"

"It's almost four hundred bucks. So I need the credit card."

She stood there, frowning deeply. "I have it. Most of it. I've been saving a lot. I wanted to give Zora something before I left. She can wait."

"I need it now."

"I have it now. Gus will cash a check. Just wait."

When she handed over the lump of bills, I knew we had settled accounts. So far as she was concerned, everything was complete.

"I'll pay you back."

"Someday," she said. "Look, I've got to get inside. I have half a dozen orders up. Gus is ready to kill me." She kissed me somewhat officiously on the cheek. "I'm worried about you."

"You probably should be."

She pulled the grate closed behind her as she returned to the restaurant, a slip of white closed off from me by the hard sound of iron. She was gone now for good.

"Control the random element," June said.

Lucy waited outside in the car while June went over it all again. Michael and I sat beside each other on one bed in the motel room and June stood, facing us. Eddgar, of course, was gone, present only in the commands which June relayed in her domineering, efficient way.

"For the next twelve hours you are Seth. You are Michael. Be rigorous about it. Be serious. What's your name?"

"Seth Weissman," Michael answered.

She pointed at me. I frowned, but she pointed again.

"Michael Frain," I said.

"Now switch IDs. Right here." We swapped wallets; Michael's was a worn lump, with Western tooling. June gave me Michael's air ticket.

She went over the rest of it. Timing. Surveillance. How to handle the money. In his intense, focused way, Eddgar had envisioned every detail. He was like an architect, building the entire structure in his imagination.

"There won't be any trouble, Seth," she said to Michael. "But if there is, remember: not a word. Don't hassle with them. Don't give them an excuse to trump something up, or to smack you around. Just keep silent. When you get your phone call, we'll figure out how to handle it. Michael," she said to me, "you listen to this, too."

I'd heard, but looked away, disturbed by her command, her aplomb. Colonel June. How many off-sites—basements, warehouses, cousin's apartments—had she stood in giving orders to her commandos? Union actions. Work stoppages. Soledad. The ARC. There was no trace of nerves, no sign of doubt. Her shoulders were square, her lithe frame hardened. It would have been better, I knew, if she enjoyed this less.

"Let's get this over with," I said.

Down in the Bug, Lucy waited. The cool night was settling in as always. It occurred to me—a thought heretofore lost in so much else—that I was leaving this landscape, too. The hills, the fog, the California majesty that always seemed like magic to a flatlander. I pined a bit.

"I am completely weirded out," said Lucy in the car. "This is the *weirdest* thing. Nobody tells me like *any*-thing."

"Michael and I are doing something," I said. "That's all. He's helping me with something. Just be cool."

We headed for the airport, where Lucy would drop us. Money was tight for a third ticket and, more important, I would need the car in Canada. We'd agreed, therefore, that she would drive to Las Vegas. She'd arrive by morning. We would meet her at the motel, a cheap place the travel agent had found down the Las Vegas strip. This plan, of hasty origin, had taken no account of the fact that Lucy had never driven a stick shift. In the motel parking lot, I'd given her a half-hour lesson, actually applauding every time she brought the machine through the pressure point without stalling it out. She seemed to feel immensely rewarded by my confidence that she could do it. Hobie had always refused to let her drive Nellybelle.

"Just get it in fourth and keep going," I told her, leaning into the car from the walk at the airport. A jet was screaming by at just that moment. The air was full of sound and engine fumes.

"Right." She bit down on her lip. "I'm already telling myself that I can't pee till Las Vegas."

I clapped Michael on the shoulder to make sure he was still all right. June had chosen to say goodbye to us at the motel room door, as we headed out. She was wary of Lucy, of raising curiosity about her role. June was just here to bid farewell to me, we'd said.

'Come here, Seth,' June had called as we passed out the motel room door. Still not in the drill, I turned around as well, and as result was left gawking as she flowed sinuously into Michael's arms and drew him to her. For all my imagining, the sight of the two of them together was astonishing. Eddgar's wife. Silent Michael. He had come to her willingly, and clutched her with evident desperation. As her head was gripped to his chest, her eyes were wide open and caught some of the light. She looked at me directly, coolly I thought, enduring the moment and seeming, if only for the instant, more interested in my reaction than her own.

Lucy's route took her down the Central Valley to Tulare, Bakersfield, and Barstow, then in the cool of darkness, across the desert, between the far-off hulking crags of the foothills and the mountains. She has told me the story many times. Occasionally she could see the lights of other cars approaching from miles off and felt comfort in the notion of company. It took longer than she could imagine for these vehicles to arrive, and then they flashed past in a tremendous snapping break of wind and were entirely gone. For quite some time she was convinced she was seeing things in the terror of the desert night, odd shapes gripped to the front grilles of the passing autos, forms which for all the world looked like bodies strapped above the bumpers. They were ice bags, she realized finally, secured across the front grilles as a precaution against engines overheating in the desert.

For the most part, she was alone. She heard the wind, the sound of her own speed; she smelled the dry, dusty odor of what was outside. She tried to control her mind, not to think of what might happen if she broke down, questions we should have asked before we sent her out there. There was no music that reached the radio in those days when cars were equipped to receive solely AM. From the speakers came only spitting static and occasional voices, clear then gone, as she spun the dial while she tried to watch the road. She hurtled on, amid the vast acres of the great open flatland between the mountains, where little blowing tendrils of scrub grass, weed, and sage skated by and where what life there was took place beneath the rocks, at the level of the taproots. Cacti with spiny arms and flowers like dracaena rose up periodically, as did the huge robotic forms of power-line towers. When dawn came, she could almost see every shaft of light accumulate in the open spaces like snow.

In her weary state, and after hours of the hallucinogenic sameness of the landscape, she was unprepared for Las Vegas. It was not far from the A-bomb testing ranges only recently abandoned during the Kennedy years. Suddenly, it was there on the horizon, its lights pinking the sky for fifty miles, like some radioactive miscreant that had slouched in from the desert. I saw it many hours before, from the air. Our plane swooped overhead before we landed, above a landscape of signs towering over the low casinos. The entire garish spectrum that could be emitted by neon raged at the eyes, a wild combination like dissonant music.

"God," said Michael, with his face at the plane window, "who gets the electric bill?"

Our mission was to pick up the money as soon as possible. For that reason, we headed straight to the Roman Coin from the airport. After arithmetic, it had made the most sense to rent a car, something I'd never done in my life. The reservation was in my name. I stood beside Michael as he presented my driver's license.

"I grew up in DuSable," the rent-a-car clerk told us. "But I don't know Shadydale." She nodded to the license. "Where is it exactly?"

I thought Michael would quit at that point. If a return flight were departing at that moment, he would have left the counter and climbed aboard.

"U. Park," I said. "On the Stony side. We grew up together."

An Italian girl from the South End, named DiBella, she barely knew where U. Park was. She had a long face and straight dark hair. Very attractive. You had to wonder if she'd come here to be a showgirl.

"Jeez," Michael said, wilting in the car. I drove. "Jeez. What else can somebody ask me?"

I tried to imagine questions my driver's license would prompt when he showed it at the cashier's cage. No, he was not that Weissman. Just in town for one day. He was playing blackjack. I told him about U. High so he might have something to say about the weird social circles of the well-to-do, the children of intellectuals, and the black kids who, in my day, only wanted to fit in with someone. We made the short trip down Paradise and traveled south along the strip on Las Vegas Boulevard, which some of the signs still referred to as U.S. 91. The avenue was lined with tropical-shaded buildings of exotic architecture — parabolas and cones. Before them, gargantuan signs of astonishing brightness announced hotel names and their resident stars — Paul Anka and Vic Damone were both here, singers whose homogenized American sounds I found as bland as Purina, music that I more or less took as the anthem of the enemy. A number of places gaudily advertised bare-breasted French showgirls, decadence of a kind I found more intriguing.

We drove past the Roman Coin so we could see it. It was big as an arena, a huge concave of stressed concrete that suggested some huge-winged fowl. It was set back from the road behind a lawn of thick-leaved Bermuda grasses that had been cultivated in the midst of the desert. Aloft a huge reader board sign boasted Jerry Vale's name in four-foot letters. I dropped Michael half a block away, as the Eddgars had suggested, in order to foil any snooper. Michael seemed relatively composed. I still had no idea what June had said to get him to do this, except that his manner suggested he knew it was dangerous.

"I'll say this for the last time," I told him. "You don't have to do this for me." I received the same stoical shrug I'd gotten on the airplane. He was powerless to resist June anyway. He was in jeans and a Western shirt of a yellow plaid, with imitation mother-of-pearl snaps. The blondish hair snaked about him, but just the dry air of the desert somehow made him look more at home than he did in Damon, living on the edge of the volcano. He stared at me in the rental car, stuck for words, as usual. It was a Chevy Bel Air with bucket seats, a car five times the size of my VW. I felt as if I were operating a tank.

"I figure," he said, "I figure you'd do it for me, if we'd traded places."

It was a confident testimonial to our friendship which I'd never have made, but he was gone with that and on his way to meet his fate, striding down the broad walk toward the hotel.

I drove past him and pulled into the Roman Coin, following the circular drive beyond the doormen and bellboys, in their red vests and bow ties, and followed the signs around the back where the desert had been paved over in an endless parking lot. My body rattled with fear. I had to do this, I told myself. It was a test of courage: I wouldn't think I'd avoided Nam out of sheer cowardice, I'd know I could make myself do anything. I found that this idea, which I hadn't quite pronounced before, had been circulating, like some advertising slogan, in the intervals of thought all day. I walked into the back of the vast hotel, jiggling the car keys.

The casino, when I reached it, was vast. Beneath the intense illumination, the stainless-steel corps of electrified slot machines, the wooden tables, the bettors, the intermittent islands of green felt were all set down on the flamboyant carpeting on which golden Caesar's heads repeated endlessly on a field of blood maroon. I had arrived humming some harmless tune I'd picked up from the lobby Muzak, but that was lost in the tumult of the casino: the outcry of a thousand voices—a number always reaching a raucous crescendo in the fortunes of a game—and the bells and occasional sirens screaming up from the slots where the old dolls, with change in paper cups, banged away at the machines. I had heard about this world from friends at home, guys whose fathers had grown up in the North End and liked to come out here so they could talk tough about losing money. No windows. No clocks. The quality of the light never varied with the hour, but about now, as the night was waning, there was nonetheless a certain soiled feeling. Some of the gamblers stood with their ties loosened and collars opened. Dressed in the Roman theme, the waitresses danced by in little toga getups, their tushes projected into tempting visibility on the stilts of their high heels. At odd moments, the sounds of the brass section of a tired band carried in from one of the lounge shows.

So here was lumpen America, everybody I felt better than. The women paraded by in their Capri pants and stiff hairdos. East met West here, North and South. There were probably two thousand people in the casino and they all felt great. After nine months in Damon, California, these Americans—the people Nixon had been talking to while he ignored me—seemed as strange as creatures from another planet. Big-bellied guys with belt buckles the size of my fist and slick dudes from L.A. in Nehru jackets. Painted women of a kind I had not seen for months on the streets of Damon — models or showgirls or high-priced hookers — glided by in long gowns. With my hair well past my shoulders, and my outfit of sandals and standard-issue denim, jeans and jacket, I was the odd duck now. Not that anyone cared to notice. They were given over to their own intense preoccupations. That was the worst part. Here they were, Americans with permission. And what was it they craved? Not guns and bombs, not race wars or killing in the jungles. Just cheap thrills and lounge acts — they wanted to see Elvis in their best duds and get a chance to risk more than they could really afford. It was June, I speculated suddenly, who'd thought of Vegas, who'd been here in the past and who privately enjoyed the recollection of it like some forsworn perversion.

At the side of the room, the lights glimmered on the domes of the chafing dishes of an enormous buffet piled with pink and yellow foods. It was cordoned off by the loops of a red velvet rope, strung between shining stainless-steel standards. Hunger came upon me with the intensity of lust. I watched some good-sized cowpoke, wobbling on the hob heels of his boots, fill a plate and I followed, but a security man in a maroon coat eyed me narrowly and I backed off with a lingering sniff, feeling like some Dickensian waif.

Across the casino, I finally caught sight of Michael. He was loitering nervously, walking here and back about one of the plaster pillars, which was dressed up with climbing circles of vine. The bank of cashier's cages, done in the heavy brass of old-fashioned banks, waited just beyond him. When he saw me, Michael did his best, as we had been instructed, to remain circumspect. Give the FBI no clues. I was perhaps 200 feet away. I nodded once. He waited a few more seconds and then pushed off toward the windows. He seemed to have chosen the one he wanted to approach in advance. I couldn't imagine how he'd made that selection — a lucky number, or had he actually assessed which teller seemed the most casual or worn down by the hour?

I tried not to stare, shifting location every now and then to preserve my sight line, and glancing about occasionally to be certain no one was watching me or Michael. I was near a crap table, where an enormous fellow with lizard boots and a rhinestone bolo on his string tie was having a spell of good luck. The pit boss came by to ask him to take his cowboy hat off the table, while a stout woman in a rayon dress a bit too tight for her bulk stood silently beside him, her dyed high heels swinging from her finger. Looking back to Michael, I could see a dark-haired woman nodding to him through the brass bars. Then he reached back for his wallet.

I knew it would be a wait. The signal could be going out right now. If the Bureau was poised, she would have had to do no more than meet somebody's eye. And there were watchers anyway: pit bosses and bouncers; guys who, according to legend, looked down from portholes above with shotguns to make sure no employees surrendered to the temptation of grand theft. I prepared myself to push off, to walk at no particular speed back to the Chevy. June had warned me: Just go. They would take care of the rest. But I felt no special peril. It was as anonymous as watching an event in a large stadium. In the interval, Michael turned away from the cage and peered into the smoke of the casino, catching my eye for an instant and heaving an enormous breath for my benefit. Beside me, a great cry went up again. The Texan at the crap table had made his point.

When I looked back a moment later, Michael had left the cage. I was afraid he'd been refused, but I saw then he was cradling two stacks of chips in his large hand. At the side of the casino he passed into a men's room labeled "Satyrs" in gilt. In there, he would enter a stall and pour the chips into an envelope preaddressed to the San Francisco post office box, already affixed with the postage and Special Delivery stickers. If the FBI was going to intercept him, Eddgar had predicted it would be in this interval. The money, Eddgar said, would be important to the government. But Michael was out in a moment, the manila envelope now beneath his arm.

According to June, the FBI tail would not be conducted as in a thirties movie—one dumb s.o.b. riding along the curb as Michael walked away. They would use a number of cars, passing him up, lagging far behind, crossing directions. My assignment was countersurveillance. Memorize license plates. Watch. Michael's job was to find a mailbox. He would be walking south. There was to be no contact of any kind between us until we were certain he was safe. I circled out of the parking lot and saw him walking calmly in the thick evening foot traffic of the strip, where couples lingered. Beneath the marquee of one of the hotels, a man with his wallet in his hand counted what was left, while his wife beside him refused to look. Michael disappeared into another hotel. I drove around the block, and when I caught sight of him again, he was still ambling peacefully, the envelope now gone. Tomorrow, the money would be in San Francisco. Cleveland would make bail. Hobie would be safe. I would be safe. We could recover from what we had done in the name of freedom.

At moments, Michael on foot made better progress than I did in the heavy traffic. Eventually though, as we moved farther north, it loosened up and I pushed on ahead. I'd seen nothing that merited alarm. Not one car had reappeared. None of the pedestrians, whom I'd scrutinized repeatedly, were noteworthy. There were a lot of powder-blue suits and white shoes, a striking prevalence of the new miracle fiber, polyester, but no one who seemed to have the markings of the FBI. At the Eden's Garden Spa Motel, I parked in the rear and edged back to Las Vegas Boulevard to watch Michael make his approach. There was a faced slate retaining wall that bounded the property and I sat atop it, checking the scene. We were well past the point of any danger. I wanted to tell Michael to knock it off, but he walked past me without glancing my way. "In the back on the right," I told him. "Key's under the mat."

He walked down the long drive, and in a moment the Bel Air appeared beside me. He nodded to me vaguely and pulled into the traffic. No cars had followed him in. There was a man walking a German shepherd who'd watched the dog lift his leg on a parking sign, but he was gone now and never returned to sight. If anyone was on Michael, they could not let him just drive away. Ten minutes later, he pulled back in. We both knew now that we were okay.

I met him in back. Floodlights from the third-story roof illuminated the lot. The night was still. He hugged me then, a rare effusiveness but no surprise under the circumstances. He was leaner and harder than I might have imagined, and smelled of several days' sweat. It occurred to me that he had learned something from the more outgoing styles of Lucy and Sonny and Hobie and me. He'd had his own breakthroughs.

"God, oh mighty," I said. "You okay?"

"Little shaky."

The motel reservation had been made in Michael's name. By June's rules, it was my job to claim the room.

"This is so stupid," I said. He nodded sadly as I left, but was still without any apparent inclination to disobey.

The motel room was inexpensive—$19 a night. In those days the casinos underwrote the room charges, even at a place like Eden's Spa. I stood in line, waiting my turn at the reception desk, too exhausted to feel much yet in the way of relief. I remembered Lucy driving the desert. Questions I'd never bothered with now surged at me. What if she got lost? What if the FBI had some bulletin out about my car? I realized again that I would never understand these few hours in my life.

The motel was a poor compromise between the hobbled architectural imagination of the fifties and Las Vegas's Italianate excess. A tree — a fully leafed deciduous variety — grew in the lobby. It mashed itself against the ceiling, three floors above. At its base, various igneous rocks had been piled in a grotto arrangement through which recirculated water splashed. From across the room, I could spot goldfish, swishing their tails to remain still in the current, and coins, black against the concrete. Two weary guys, businessmen by the looks of them, with the lost, dejected appearance of men on the road, were seated on a round circular sofa that circumscribed the tree, absorbed in conversation and pointing to the fish.

A group of New Yorkers emerged from the adjoining lounge and entered the lobby like a brass band. They were determined to have a grand time, calling each other's names at top volume. "Paulie. Joey. Joanie. Lookit here." Showy clothes and the reek of department store fragrances. They were making sly jokes — about sex, no doubt, from the way the women screamed together and smacked their manicures on the men's arms. I'd seen Vikki Carr's name in lights as we drove in, and all of them were gabbling about her by first name, as if they knew her, which I tended to doubt. Each man had the dimensions of a freezer and the women, no matter how sturdily built, wore skirts cut far up their thighs. Americans, I thought again. There was, after all, a lot I wasn't going to miss. One of the men, in a persimmon-colored jacket, was carrying a highball glass, which he left on the corner of one of the unoccupied reception counters as he went out the door.

When I got to the head of the line, I gave Michael's name. "Okay," the receptionist said. She walked away and returned with a painfully thin man in a sport coat, who had thick glasses and a sloppy mustache. He made a slight gesture toward someone behind me.

When I looked back, the two men by the fountain seemed to snap awake. In a crystalline moment, I watched them cross the carpeting, knowing that this was precisely what I had envisioned back at the Roman Coin. One fellow reached inside his pocket and I could read the words on his lips even before he spoke: FBI.

They were still thirty feet away. I held up one finger, asking for a second, and slid off, walking deliberately to the doors, faster than I should have but still not in full flight. That waited until I pushed through the glass vestibule and reached the parking lot. I flew. It was a few seconds before I heard a voice crying out, "Stop! You there, son. Stop." Amazingly, I had gained as much as fifty yards on them. I tore back through the parking lot to where I'd left the car. Michael would be waiting. I was going to be all right. I forced myself to remain cool. We had enough time.

When I got to the space where we'd parked, the car was gone. I was briefly too shocked to move. Then after a panicked instant, I realized I must have turned myself around. With the agent still yelling behind me, I headed for the other side of the building. I ran in my sandals. When I came around the rear corner, there was a wall where five or six cars were parked. A high cyclone fence adjoined the desert.

"Stop him!" the agent yelled this time. "FBI. Stop him!" He seemed farther behind than before. Apparently he had lost me when I surged around the building.

"Who? Dis one?" I heard. Suddenly, through the night, someone was reaching for me, standing now in the breach between a Ford and a car nearby. It was one of the New Yorkers.

"Tony, be careful," a woman called. He came to me through the night, his group nearby. The woman's bleached hair glowed under the parking-lot lights.

"Where you going, bud?" Tony asked me. He was wearing a sand-colored leisure suit and a shirt marked by colored shapes like lightning bolts.

"Tony, for Godsake," the woman yelled, "he might have a gun." I heard her as she turned to speak to her friends. "Always on the job," she said.

"This don't god no gun," Tony said. "Come on here. This gentleman back here wants to have a word with you. Whatsa matter?" he said. "You don't like to talk wit the FBI?"

I said nothing. I made no move. The time—the few precious seconds I had unconsciously counted—whittled away while this man and I stared at each other. He had a massive face with walrus jowls, set with a confidence that was not particularly malevolent. It simply said, I am a man and you are not. I have been alive long enough to know what to do here and you do not. I was immobilized by the sheer force of his experience. I had been caught. Busted. I was completely bewildered by the thought. The agent arrived then, blowing hard.

"You are one dumb son of a bitch. Do you know that's how people

get shot? Do you know what kind of trouble you can get yourself in?"
He shoved my shoulder roughly. "Lie down on the ground. Lie down
there. Go on, damn it all."

He ran his hands along my legs, inside and out, as I was prostrate on
the asphalt with its strange worldly scent. He pulled Michael's wallet
from my pocket and tugged on my hair.

"What am I supposed to call you? 'Jesus?' You smell bad," he said to
me. I'd bathed last night. I remembered June. I was not going to say
anything. They told me to get up.

I had been caught, I kept thinking. I realized I had walked into a
new plane, another reality. Each instant now would be a piece of fresh
time. One of them pushed me from behind and they walked me toward
the front of the motel, leading me along by the shirt collar. Tony introduced himself to the agent. From the Two Two One in Newark.

"You know Jack Burk? In the RA in West Orange?"

"Jack? Jack was in my class in Quantico."

"No shit? He's my brother-in-law."

"How do you like that? How is old Jack?"

"Pig in shit, that one. He god Hoover's picture on the wall next to
the Sacred Heart."

The second agent watched us coming, looking out the window of a
blue Ford Fairlane with black-walled tires. He'd turned the dome light
on inside the car. He wore a straw fedora and let his arm dangle out
the open window, an unfiltered cigarette, which he idly raised to his
mouth on occasion, between his fingers. He was parked in the front of
the motel, blocking the driveway. He'd been waiting for me, of course.
I'd never had a chance. The one who'd caught up to me introduced
Tony, and the two agents fawned over him for a while. A siren keened
down the strip.

"Cavalry's on the way," the second agent said. "Tammy's 10–1'd half
the county."

"Oh brother," said the agent who held me.

"You take him in. I'll stay to explain. Fourteen's coming. You sure
you got who you want?"

The agent flipped open the wallet he'd taken from my pocket.

"Michael Frain," he said.

"He's the one."

The agent grabbed me by the collar again and jerked me around to
face him for the first time.

"We been looking for you, Michael," he said.

December 12, 1995

S O N N Y

Tuesday-morning status call. Open house in the chamber of horrors. I've had perhaps two hours' sleep. My blood is hot tar; wakefulness at instants feels like an out-of-body experience. And I have lost that convenient armor on my emotions. Words and events strike straight at my viscera with nothing in between. I'm in no condition for the sad procession taking place before me.

The courtroom teems. Clients and families huddle with attorneys. Cops and PAs, probation officers, the State Defenders, all the felony court regulars greet each other in the corridors and the adjacent lawyers' and witness rooms. They agree on dates for the next appearance or talk out the plea deals, by which most of these cases are finally resolved. Annie polices the spectators' rows, directs defendants to the front, points out the lawyers or court personnel they need to see, while Marietta goes on crying out case numbers, passing up files, and reminding me why they're on the call—for arraignment or guilty plea, status report or ruling on motions. Her memory is phenomenal, her notes precise. This guy was supposed to bring in proof of employment; that lady has to make a urine drop this week, per prior order of Judge Simone.

Some of the morning's crimes have a touch of bathos. One hapless schmo paid a policewoman posing as a hooker $50 to suck her toes. When she badged him, he begged her, tear-struck, to take $400 to let him go. Wired to avoid entrapment claims, she had no choice but to charge the bribery. But for the most part we wallow in sadness.

"You're old for this line of work," the transport deputy says, muscling a white-whiskered defendant, a drunk or junkie by the depleted looks of him, out of the lockup toward the bench. He is charged with armed robbery: razor to the throat.

"Don't I know," the defendant answers and arrives before me with a wistful look.

Scanning his rap sheet and its cryptic notations—nine convictions by my count—I do the math. "How many days ago, Mr. Johnson, were you released from the penitentiary?"

There is no type that has not arrived before me: a senior vice-president of First Kindle arrested in the North End for scoring smack. A seventy-two-year-old grandmother, a valued employee for forty-four years at a garden store, who began a few months ago, for reasons no one can explain, to jigger the receipts, making off with almost $32,000. Often, I imagine, if I remain here long enough, every creature that rode with Noah will appear, charged with something.

But usually when I lift my eyes it's a young black man who's there, his story, told in his bail or pre-sentence report, numbingly the same—poverty, violence, a shattered fatherless family, little schooling, nobody to care. There is often a special sulkiness that grips them when they face the bench to find another woman. Women have been trying to tame them all their lives, at home, in school, mothers and caseworkers and truant officers whose remonstrations and example never answered the one question that seems to be boiling away in so many: What's this thing they call a man, does he have a peaceful, rightful place in this world? I want to lecture occasionally. 'There was no father in my home, either. I understand, I do.'

That's never said. It's enough to move ahead. Some come before me defiant, making little effort to hide their hatred for the entire apparatus. But most are simply terrified and clueless. A nineteen-year-old, here for sentencing on a jewelry store–window smash-and-grab, a boy with a head of curls as disorganized as rubbish, wears a jeans company's T-shirt that reads UNBUTTON MY FLY, a message not calculated to impress the court. The battle-hardened, on the other hand, are often disarmingly familiar.

"Judge, she sayin I got to take six on this." The lank defendant, with a sleeveless T that reveals arms scored by tattoos and scars, gestures without respect at Gina, the PD beside him. "Judge, man, I's just hidin in that store when they cracked me, Judge, I din't even take nothin, Judge, six, that's cold."

"You're on probation, Mr. Williams, for another armed burglary."

"Oh, Judge, that's just a little ol knife, that ain't but a can opener. Six is cold, Judge."

"Yes or no," I say. We both know it will be ten years after trial. Even I, who swore before taking the bench to remember a trial is a constitutional right, have found myself whacking defendants who rack twelve out of sport or in defiance of overwhelming proof. There is no alternative. I will dispose of a thousand cases this year and have time to try no more than fifty.

Called to justice, no one stakes a proud claim to their crimes; no one believes these events define them. Their misdeeds, even if only hours old, seem remote as legends. Here at the time of judgment, everyone is mystified by what occurred. Their anger, their isolation, their need for whatever self-respect they were striking toward is, for the time being, wholly forgotten. Most cannot explain. They pensively murmur, "Don't know, Judge," when I ask, as I do often, "Why?" As they stand here, almost everyone knows better.

This morning I sentence Leon McCandless. Six weeks ago, Leon met a lady, Shaneetha Edison, who was at the Evening Shade Tavern with her three-year-old. By now, I know all about this kind of place. The fact that people have no money is everywhere. There are only a few lights that work, including the reflecting beer sign behind the bar, and what they reveal is filthy and broken. The paneling in the room is so old it has started to fray. The toilet in the back is stained, with a seat that's been cracked in half and a cistern that leaks and is always running. The whole tavern smells of rot. The people here are poor and drunk. There are customers all day, little groups of men standing around, talking stuff nobody believes and now and then dealing little bits of dope in coveys in the corners.

After a drink or two, Shaneetha asked Leon for a smoke and he went to the corner for some loosies—individual cigarettes the Korean grocers sell from the pack for two bits apiece. When he returned, another fellow had his hand inside Shaneetha's dress. A classic tale: Frankie and Johnny. A moment later, the three-year-old, still at his mother's side, was dead. In Area 7, through whatever mysterious means they seem to employ there, by which almost three-quarters of the black defendants seem to speak freely in spite of Miranda warnings and a lifetime knowledge that confessing seldom makes anything easier—in the police station, Leon, the defendant who stands before me, explained about the gun he'd drawn. 'Damn thing just went off,' he said.

"Thing just went off," his lawyer, Billy Witt, repeats now for my benefit. None of us can tell in how many layers of his psyche Leon meant to shoot. I give him fifty years.

'People just can't imagine. They don't get it.' That's what the coppers and the prosecutors are always saying. I scoffed when I arrived here and now hear myself making similar remarks. People think they understand this. They see it reenacted on TV, and in the privacy of their homes, in the dopey glow of the television, thinking whatever dreamy thought they have, figure they have the picture—they know what it's like to be scared, to see violence, to feel the antagonism of black and white. But that does nothing to convey the shock of foreignness, the distance between their world and mine which I feel in every glance, or the dismal truth that the average citizens of Düsseldorf or Kyoto, people whom my mother regarded as enemies, now share more of my life than four-fifths of the young men who stand before me, my supposed countrymen. I revert all the time to the structuralist stuff I studied in graduate school, about thought and culture and custom being one, and think, again and again, *We have to change it all.*

After a brief lunch, as the call is winding to an end, we reach the Crime of the Day. Four members of the Five Street Diggers, a Gangster Outlaw set, stand before me for arraignment on a newly filed complaint. Rudy Singh has stepped up for the state. Two cops, Tic-Tacs, are beside him with their beerpots, sweaters, and running shoes. Gina Devore, the PD, takes the lead for the defense.

Singh explains the background. As she was leaving the jail where she had visited her brother, a Five Street homegirl, Rooty-Too, was snatched — kidnapped — by other Goobers, the Hanging Hipsters, a rival group within the gang. I decline Singh's invitation to describe Rooty-Too's injuries in greater detail than saying she is hospitalized with contusions, missing teeth, and lacerations in the vaginal area. The Five Streets were desperate for revenge. They captured a Hipster, a ghetto star known as Romey Tuck, beat him, and then chopped off both his arms with machetes. The defendants were arrested in an apartment at Fielder's Green. There one forearm sat bleeding onto newspaper on the linoleum kitchen table, as it was being displayed to other Five Streets as a trophy.

"Is the issue bond?" I ask.

"Judge," says Gina, "the defendants are juveniles. The state's petitioned to try them as adults."

Good, I almost say.

"Judge, they're being held in the jail. You know what that's like." In for violence within the gang, they may not be protected by the usual strict codes. None of these boys is full-grown — two are rangy but not filled out, the smallest is still not much over five feet. I understand. "Judge, if you'd consider bail. They can't go to school. Their visiting privileges are limited. One of these young men, Marcus — my client Marcus Twitchell —" Gina's eyes cheat southward to her file to be 100 percent certain she has got the name. "Marcus is an honor student. He was selected last summer for Project Restore. He was —"

Marcus, the last arrested, has been brought straight here from the station and has not yet been processed. He's still 'G-down' or 'Gangster down,' dressed in gang attire, which includes a satiny Starter jacket in the glistening aquamarine of the Miami Dolphins and gangsta baggies hiked down so his belt line's at pubic level, revealing several inches of his striped briefs. His Brownies — brown garden gloves worn for scuffling, shooting, and leaving no fingerprints — still hang out of his side pocket. His eyes never reach above a spot two or three feet below me. He is slowly chewing gum. I ask about his record.

"Three station adjustments," Rudy reads. Marcus has two thefts, which count for little with me. The poor will steal. Then the third. Agg Battery. Another revenge beating. Someone was stomped.

"How long ago?"

"Two weeks, Yaw Onah."

I shake my head. Bond at $100,000 full cash. So much for Marcus. So much for his chance. Even on a sleepless morning, with my loins sore from loving and my heart pregnant with what I figure for false hope, I cannot stretch this far. The other lawyers do not even bother with similar motions.

During this hearing, Loyell Eddgar has found his way into the court-room. He appears irretrievably somber, dressed in the same wool sport coat as yesterday. His face, like mine, looks ruined by lack of sleep. I would have expected a powerful pol, even a reformer, to travel with a retinue, but he's alone. Being a judge and being a state senator are probably the same, finding you are now the Great Oz, just some weary individual pulling the whistles and levers behind the fearsome mask of great authority. Eddgar has taken the lone chair behind the prosecution table, which Jackson Aires had periodically occupied. In the wake of yesterday's ending, Eddgar and Molto noticeably avoid one another. For the time being, the Crime of the Day appears to have Eddgar's attention. As he absorbs my ruling, and the last of the prisoners are being herded off, he frowns harshly. It brings to mind the disdainful scowl Zora always had for her enemies, the rebuke of a superior spirit. I find myself piqued, even as Eddgar, with his message smugly delivered, looks away.

Don't you dare turn away, I want to say, especially not you, you who waited for these communities to rise up in the simpleminded fantasy it would change the world. The war that began in 1965—the war on the streets which you and Zora promoted, rooted for, and helped cause— that war has never stopped. The terrible violence that was released, the expression of an overwhelming grievance, has proved to be a demon genie, never to be forced back into his bottle.

Yet were they wrong? I think suddenly. Eddgar? My mother? Am I prepared to renounce their commitments? I have been through it a million times in my own mind. I judge both of them dimly. Long ago, I learned their dirtiest, most crabbed secret, that their passion to change the world derived from the fact they could not change themselves. But that confuses the messenger with the clarion she sounds. What my mother shrilled out about, carried on for—the desolating circumstances of Americans of color; the routine abuse of females; the heartless ex-ploitation of the weak; the arrogance of privilege and the corruptions of power; the persistent childishness of greed and the redeeming value of mutual concern and sharing—she was not wrong about any of that. In the ledger book of this century, our greatest achievements are the hu-man ones made in response to those concerns. I will always think of that as Nikki's truest heritage.

Just as the call is winding to a close, as a transvestite hooker in an orange dress pilfered from a Goodwill box is explaining why she sliced her john, a formidable presence blows into the courtroom. Raymond Horgan, former Prosecuting Attorney for Kindle County and head of the Judicial Reform Commission which recruited me for the bench, tosses a wave to the deputies at the door and moves to the front of the courtroom, trailed by two younger lawyers, a fair-skinned African-American woman and a tall, thin man with an Adam's apple prominent enough to make me wonder about goiter. Raymond hands Marietta a half-sheet notice of motion while he turns back to the door, awaiting someone else. Grown stout in the land of corporate excess—his face is now little more than a rubbery mask—Horgan retains an impressive public bearing. He wears his money: a handmade shirt, dark grey with white cuffs and collar, a fancy grey suit, a mohair overcoat squashed beneath the same arm that totes his briefcase. His cologne and hair tonic can almost be sniffed from the bench. Finally, the stragglers he is awaiting arrive—Tommy Molto, hurrying, and last, Hobie, with a harassed expression. Molto and Horgan, well acquainted from Raymond's years as Tommy's boss, confer briefly. Raymond has him by more than half a foot and there is a fleeting impression of parent and child. Then Marietta calls out Nile's case.

"Raymond Horgan for an unnamed intervenor," Raymond says as the lawyers circle before me. "I have a motion, Your Honor, which I would like to make in chambers and under seal."

Not in front of the press, in other words. Hobie steps forward to object, which, these days, is sign enough for me that I should grant Horgan the opportunity he wants. I wave everyone back to chambers, while in the jury box Dubinsky, the lone early arrival from the media, glowers furiously and heads out, probably to phone the *Tribune*'s lawyers. Nothing is more important to the press than what they are not allowed to know.

We wait some time for Suzanne, the court reporter, who has gone to renew her paper. A tall, slender, quiet woman, she carries in her stenograph machine and takes a seat. There are not enough chairs for everyone, and so only she and I sit. The others—Raymond and his minions, Tommy, Rudy, Hobie, Marietta, Annie—stand, circling the round side table that occupies the corner of my chambers. Nile has elected to remain in the courtroom. Raymond's male associate draws from his briefcase a mass of papers that are handed to Marietta, while Raymond, in stentorian baritone, reviews the circumstances for me.

In our lengthy dealings before I agreed to take this job, I found Raymond wily, wise, a slick former politico, beguiling with self-deprecating

Gaelic charm. His white hair, slightly yellowed now, crinkles back above the brow in waves that seemed to have been stamped from the forge of age and wisdom. Yesterday, Raymond says, late in the day, the River National Bank was served with a forthwith subpoena demanding production of certain banking records relating to a $10,000 check. He is here to ask that the subpoena be quashed.

"Who issued the subpoena?" I ask.

"Me," says Hobie.

"He's doing it again, Judge," Tommy says. "He's going to pull another end run around the discovery rules."

"Mr. Tuttle, let me say right now that better not be true."

"Judge, I gave Molto here a copy of the subpoena."

"After Mr. Horgan notified me of it."

"Your Honor, I just became aware of this evidence," says Hobie in that ridiculous blank-faced way he has when he's lying. I don't even bother to reply.

"Judge," Tommy whines, "Judge, I mean, look how unfair this is. He turns up a new document for cross-examination, I can't talk to the witness—"

"Go talk to him," says Hobie. "I don't care."

"He's not very eager to talk to me today."

"Not my fault," says Hobie.

"On the contrary, Mr. Tuttle," I intervene. "It *is* your fault. Mr. Molto made tactical decisions based on the available evidence, as he understood it. If you had some eleventh-hour discovery, then you should have notified the court and Mr. Molto before his direct. I warned you. I told you no more, and I meant it." I push my hair back, using the instant to reassure myself it's not my nerves, stripped bare by lack of sleep, that are speaking. "Mr. Horgan's motion will be allowed."

"Judge!" Hobie actually jumps. Two hundred fifty pounds if he's an ounce, he lands a foot behind where he started. "Judge Klonsky. This is my whole defense, this is the crux of my case."

"Which you just discovered yesterday." I give him what you would call a dirty look, which brings Hobie to a rare silence. He looks on with the wrenching vulnerability that falls over a bully out of bluffs.

"Your Honor, I'm begging you. I'll beg you, Judge." He reaches toward a metal file cabinet for support and on old football player's creaky knees begins sinking toward the floor.

"Don't you dare, Mr. Tuttle."

"Your Honor, take it out on me. Hold me in contempt. But don't take it out on my client. Your Honor, if I can explain about this check—"

"Look, Hobie"—I use his first name advisedly, a sign my wrath goes beyond role-playing—"I told you I would not put up with another episode. I won't hear explanations."

"Judge—"

"Not another word."

"At least look at the check, Your Honor. All you have to do is *look* at it. Please. Just look. This is the entire defense. You're gonna see what's at stake here. Please, Your Honor. Judge, *please!*" He has both hands clasped; his knees are weakening again. Despite the beard and today's fancy double-breasted suit, he is—like every man in extremis—a desperate boy. I heave a breath or two and close my eyes, as if I cannot stand the sight of him, which is just about the truth.

"Give me the check."

Molto's voice leaps into his agonized falsetto, but I've already held out a hand toward Horgan, who eventually turns to the two young lawyers behind him. When the pink draft finally reaches me, I find that it's on business stock, eight inches long. The check is drawn on the account of the Democratic Farmers & Union Party in the amount of $10,000, made payable to "Loyal Citizens for Eddgar." Dated June 27, 1995, it's signed in a clear hand by Matthew Galiakos.

At sight of the name, the harp string in my chest resounds. Brendan Tuohey is the slyest fox. Matthew Galiakos. My hands are cold. I wonder if I might have groaned. I have revealed something. They are all staring.

"Mr. Horgan," I say, hoping against hope, "you'd better name your client for the record. Are you here for the bank?"

"I am here in behalf of Matthew Galiakos, chair of the state Democratic Farmers & Union Party."

So this is how the game is played. Brendan Tuohey tees it up. Then they bring in the all-star to hit the ball. It's exactly as I feared. Purely by accident, I've already done what they wanted. And the record could not be better. Given all of Hobie's horsing around, there's not an appellate court in the world that would reverse me. And I see nothing on the face of this check that will change this trial. It's the kind of contribution the central party routinely makes to campaign organizations. All I have to do is shake my head and repeat, 'Motion allowed,' and I'll secure my felony division seat for years, perhaps even take my first step on the journey to a higher court. But about the imperatives here, even in my fragile state, I feel not so much as a tremor of doubt. As I have already noted to myself once this morning, I am Zora Klonsky's daughter.

"Mr. Tuttle?"

"Yes, Your Honor." He snaps to. Hobie's tongue—his renegade feature—briefly appears between his lips.

"At your request, Mr. Tuttle, I have examined this draft." I describe it for the record. "You're representing as a member of the bar, Mr. Tuttle, that this check and the other documents you subpoenaed are essential to your defense?"

Shock radiates off every other person in the room at my apparent change in direction. Hobie reacts first.

"I am, Judge Klonsky. I am."

"Well, given this is a bench trial, and that I will disregard anything inflammatory or irrelevant, I'll accept that representation, reconsider my ruling, and deny the motion to quash. Mr. Horgan, give Mr. Tuttle the records. Mr. Tuttle, share the records with Mr. Molto. I'll take objections when the documents are offered."

Horgan slowly settles into the one available chair beside me. He opens his fat, freckled hand my way.

"Your Honor," he says.

"I've ruled, Mr. Horgan." I stand up. Horgan is so astonished it takes him a moment to come back to his feet.

"Judge, I would think, I would *hope* I'd get the chance at least—This is nothing more than an attempt to embarrass parties who have no relationship to this matter, to inject politics into a garden-variety murder case."

"We're done, Mr. Horgan. I've ruled. It's nice to see you." If I investigate further, ask what the check has to do with this case, I'll only make it harder on myself.

"Judge, can the transcript at least—of these proceedings—can it remain sealed?"

"I think that would just inflame the press, Mr. Horgan. There's no need to keep secrets here." I smile at him wanly. I'd like to think he's just a cat's-paw, not fully filled in, but there's no telling about that.

"Mr. Tuttle," I say, "I'm trusting you, against my better judgment. I expect you to deliver fully on your promises. If you do not, sir, it will be a sad day for us both."

Marietta peers my way. She rarely sees much she doesn't understand.

As I pass, she hums beneath her breath, marveling at my authority or my daring.

"Comes with the robes," I murmur to her.

"Seems to me, Senator, you and Molto don't get on?"

Arranged somewhat fragilely beside me on the witness stand, Eddgar takes an instant to ponder Hobie's first question to him before he agrees. He wears the same heavy grey tweed sport coat and squarish gold-framed glasses that were not on his face yesterday.

"Was it the fact you lied to the police? Is that when you and the prosecutors seemed to fall out?"

"Frankly, I think it was when I agreed with you that I'd secure my son's bond with my home."

"Molto was angry?"

"Incredulous," says Eddgar. "Apparently, he doesn't have children." This shot, understandably, brings Molto to his feet. No mutual-admiration society there. Tommy has one of those cloistered lives of suppressed desire. No Mrs. Tommy. No girlfriends. A former seminarian, he is known behind his back as the Mad Monk. I strike Eddgar's last remark and Hobie starts again.

"My question, Dr. Eddgar, is whether the prosecutors and the police and you have discussed the evidence."

"I suppose not. I suppose we've all been somewhat wary."

"Because you lied to them to start, right?"

"They told me I was a witness and we shouldn't talk about other persons' testimony." Molto, rising to object again, smiles at Eddgar's answer and reverts to his seat.

"All right," says Hobie, "but just to get us all straight: you did lie to the police, didn't you?"

"As I told Mr. Molto yesterday, I wasn't completely candid when I first spoke to Lieutenant Montague." Eddgar, wrung out after yesterday, after being handballed by the prosecutor, after enduring whatever the papers and TV stations wrought from his performance, sits here in quiet command of himself. He is neat, if subdued. He has answered most questions thus far with almost no visible movement—not a hand raised, not a tic of feeling in his face.

"Well, as a matter of fact, Senator, as I read the reports, what you told them the first day—September 7—was that your wife had gone out, and you couldn't account for it. Right? Isn't that what you told them, Senator?"

"That's what I told them."

"And that was a lie?"

Asked and answered, says Tommy. I overrule. The cross-examiner has the right, in my view, to test the sincerity of a witness's *mea culpas*.

"It was a lie," Eddgar says at last. He cannot constrain a quick glance at the jury box and the press row.

"Okay," says Hobie, "and if I understand your testimony yesterday, you lied in the first place because you felt admitting that someone like *you* knew someone like Hardcore would be embarrassing, right?"

"That was one factor. I'd also say I didn't realize that my projected presence had anything to do with the incident. It was being presented to me at that stage as a drive-by."

"Well, let's talk about the embarrassment part, Senator. You didn't think it was wrong to be trying to help the poor community, did you?"

"Everybody knows where I stand on that, Mr. Tuttle."

"So what's the problem?" Hobie lifts his round face and lets the question linger a second. "Was it embarrassing that you'd tried to involve BSD in politics, or were there specific steps you'd taken you didn't care to talk about?"

For the first time, Eddgar moves around in his seat. "The latter, I suppose."

"The latter," says Hobie. He walks a few steps, looking at his feet, then stops to abruptly face the witness. "Senator, fact is, you haven't told the whole truth yet about what went on between you and BSD, isn't that so?"

"I've answered the questions that have been asked, Mr. Tuttle."

"And the questions, you well know, have been based on what Hardcore said, correct?"

"I don't know what they've been based on exactly. I suppose that's one basis."

"Well, let's get specific, Senator. This meeting. You remember that? Last summer? Nile. Core. T-Roc. Just the four of you, sittin round cozy in the back of T-Roc's armored limousine? Remember?"

"I've seen the scene reconstructed on all three local channels, Mr. Tuttle. It's firmly in my mind." The reporters' laughter rings out. Eddgar manages the trace of a smile.

"And there in that limo, you preached at them, right? You're a preacher by training, Senator, aren't you?"

"I am."

"And you preached, didn't you? You tried to explain that if they would organize voters, support campaigns, they would have legitimate power. Right?"

"Right."

"They could be leaders like other political leaders. With influence. Because they had the same source. Votes and money. Am I correct?"

"That's the gist of what I suggested."

"Now, were these suggestions to get BSD involved in mobilizing poor voters—was that completely altruistic on your part?"

"I'm sorry?" replies Eddgar.

"Well, what were you gonna get out of this, Senator?"

"Me? Nothing."

"Just bein progressive, huh?"

"I believe so."

"When you ran four years ago, for state controller, you lost by 50,000 votes, didn't you?"

"That's right."

"Would increased turnout in the African-American community help you, especially if BSD's organizing effort became the model for other gangs?"

Molto's on his feet. "Judge, you can see the irrelevancy of this. This is just what I was afraid of when we were in chambers."

I'm curious myself about what Hobie thinks he's doing. I point to him.

"Your Honor, the state's theory, what they've been sayin, is that Dr. Eddgar was the intended target of this shooting. Isn't that their theory?"

"I believe that was printed in the papers first," I say coolly. The non sequitur has its intended effect. Hobie's eyes skitter away and a half-spoken word briefly rattles in his throat before he dares look my way again.

"Well, okay," he says, "but Dr. Eddgar has admitted he knows no motive for his son to do that. So shouldn't I be entitled to show there was another motive for this shooting, one which has nothing to do with Nile Eddgar?"

"Is that what you're doing?"

"That's what I'm doing."

"Is he entitled to do that, Mr. Molto?"

"Judge, I don't know anything about this other motive."

"That's why each side gets a turn, Mr. Molto." I don't find this line particularly funny, but the room, reacting to the lapse in tension, explodes in laughter. Tommy often deserves what he gets, but I had no intention of showing him up. He accepts my apology desultorily. "Let's hear a few more questions," I say. Hobie retreats to the podium, where he probes his beard while he examines his notes.

"Senator, set me straight on one thing. Core and T-Roc, they did offer you a bribe to get Kan-el out, didn't they?"

Eddgar mulls. "Not in so many words."

"Did the words they spoke, Senator, sound like somebody offering a bribe?"

"They seemed to be approaching the subject, talking about what I could get out of this. And I cut off the discussion. I told them they could do something for themselves, for their community, *and* help Kan-el's situation."

"And then what did you tell them, Senator?" Hobie pauses to lift his face toward Eddgar as he did a minute ago, with the same dead-cool air, knowing he's going to like what's coming next better than the witness. "Let me help you, can I? You explained to Hardcore and T-Roc that they should understand how really powerful people approached such things, didn't you? Didn't you tell them that the way the world, your world, worked, not only could they secure Kan-el's release, but they could get money, not have to give it? Am I right?"

Eddgar briefly closes his eyes. "Yes," he says.

"And you became quite enthusiastic, didn't you? You told them if they would commit to organize their community, you could get them seed money for the effort from the state central committee of the Democratic Farmers & Union Party? Right? And that once they were political players, their ability to influence the decision-makers who controlled Kan-el's release would be much, much greater."

"Judge!" screams Tommy. "My God. What *is* this!" Behind him, as if I needed the hint, Raymond Horgan, whom I hadn't noticed back beyond the glass, has also come to his feet. Fearing the array against him, Hobie steps right before the bench.

"For one thing, Your Honor, it's called impeachment. Hardcore said he never talked about money with Senator Eddgar. And that's just for one."

"We were supposed to be hearing motive testimony," I remind Hobie. He gives me his bad-dog look, caught again. Meanwhile, I leaf in the bench book for my notes of yesterday: 'Hard denies offering bribe. Never disc'd with Edd give/rec $.' I tell Hobie to be quick.

He repeats his question: "Did you tell Hardcore and T-Roc you could get money from the party? Yes or no?"

"Yes," says Eddgar, with resignation. The reporters are writing furiously.

"And they scoffed, did they not?"

"I suppose. I suppose you'd call their reaction scoffing. Basically, they said when they saw the money they'd believe it."

"And so, Senator, did you make a request to the DFU for seed money to get this street gang involved in politics?"

Like a spotlight coming on again, Raymond stands once more. Seeing him, Tommy follows suit.

"Judge, this is getting ridiculous," says Tommy.

Hobie's before the bench, hands lifted prayerfully. "Two more questions."

On the witness stand, Loyell Eddgar has pivoted to observe my ruling. He probes his forehead unconsciously, while the blue eyes, mysterious as moonstones, glow with some faint appeal by which I'm immediately determined to be unmoved. '*Thought she was a friend of his.*'

"Two more," I say. Molto slaps his thighs, and turns first to Rudy, then to Horgan, in exasperation. There is a ruffle in the room now, the sibilance of whispers. Annie smacks her gavel. "Let's proceed," I say.

Suzanne reads back the question: Did Eddgar ask the DFU for money?

"Yes. But I was vague—I didn't really say what it was for. I said it was an organizing project I was working on for my own campaign."

"And did you receive the money?"

"Yes."

"How much?"

"Ten thousand dollars." Hobie turns his broad face to me to see how he's doing. The check, I realize. But I'm still missing something. Molto has made no new objection. Instead, Rudy and he are huddled whispering.

"And did you make a plan about how you would get the money to BSD?"

Eddgar's head is down and rests on his open hand. He is just getting himself through this. He cannot see the courtroom now. It's merely voices.

"Since the check was to my campaign, it was necessary to cash the check and to deliver cash to BSD."

"And who did you ask to do that?"

"My son."

"The defendant here on trial, Nile Eddgar?"

"The defendant, yes."

At the defense table, Hobie has the envelope Horgan gave him. He applies a stick-on marker to the check. Defendant's Exhibit 7. He slaps it down on the rail of the jury box and Eddgar identifies it as the $10,000 check he received from the DFU. Hobie asks if it's endorsed. Eddgar slowly changes glasses, reaching into an inner jacket pocket for his little half-frames, then turns the check over.

"It is endorsed."

"Whose signatures appear there?"

"Mine, and below that Nile's."

"Is there a teller stamp there to note cash received?"

"Yes."

"Are there any initials in the cash-received block?"

"Yes."

"Whose?"

"Nile's."

"Is there a date on the stamp?"

"July 7."

Hobie's at the prosecution table, pointing to their cardboard evidence box. Singh hands him People's 1, the blue plastic bag, the two packets of money.

"And did you have a conversation with Nile on July 7 in which you-all agreed he'd cash this check, as you'd discussed?"

Tommy, visibly subdued now, objects that it's hearsay. I overrule, since the conversation concerned Nile's future acts.

"We did."

"Have you ever seen Nile with a blue plastic bag like this one, People's 1A?"

"The *Tribune* comes in it. I know he gets the *Tribune*."

"Did he have a bag like this with him when you gave him the check on July 7?"

Eddgar briefly lowers his head again. "I want to say yes," he says, "but I can't completely recall."

"Well, sir, did Nile ever tell you he'd delivered this money to Hard-core?"

"Judge," Tommy says lamely. This time the question calls for hearsay. Hobie sees that, too, and withdraws it.

"Well, let's get this far, Senator. Did Nile ever have $10,000 in any bank account you knew of?"

"No."

"In fact, did he borrow money from you at times?"

"In the past. Especially before he got this job. Less so recently."

"And when he borrowed, what kind of amounts are we talking about?"

"Fifty. One hundred. Five hundred for the security on his apartment."

"Okay." Hobie strolls. He's doing it. The highwire he's on is the nerve of victory. This has come so quickly now, with so little preparation, that I want to call a halt to the proceedings just so I can think. But Hobie is rolling on.

"By the way, what did you do about Kan-el? Did you ever do anything?"

"I made some calls."

"And did you make any progress? Could you help?"

"I don't know if I was helpful or not. It was a very complicated situation, requiring a lot of research and attention over time."

"Did you ever inform BSD that you had made this start?"

"I did."

"When, and who did you speak to?"

"Hardcore. Right before Labor Day."

"Was that conversation in person or by phone?"

"I called him from my office and arranged to see him in person."

"And where did you meet?"

"We had a brief meeting at Grace Street."

"Now, at that time, Senator, had BSD engaged in any of the political organizing that was supposed to follow this payment?"

"None that I had heard of or could see."

"And did you discuss that with Hardcore—the DFU money for BSD, the money you'd promised and which you'd asked Nile to deliver?"

"Yes."

"You were pretty angry in that conversation, weren't you, Senator?"

"Very, very put out."

"Did you tell Hardcore he had taken advantage of the situation?"

"I told him I felt he was dishonest, yes."

"Didn't you in fact threaten to turn him in to the prosecutor's office?"

"Yes."

"And did you tell Nile you'd made that threat to go to the PAs?"

"No. I didn't regard it as a safe subject. As I told Mr. Molto yesterday,

Nile and I'd had words about my intentions toward Ordell from the start."

"But, at any rate, sir, a few days later, when Nile delivered a message that Hardcore wanted to speak to you again, you weren't surprised?"

"No, I wasn't."

The pace between them, lawyer and witness, is emotionless, almost mechanical. The truth in all its homely plainness steps into the courtroom like an orphaned child. But there is no minimizing the impact on me and everyone else. In the ten years I've been around criminal courtrooms, as a prosecutor, as a judge, I'm not sure this has occurred before. A defense lawyer in the course of a cross-examination has persuaded me his client is probably innocent. Nile's fingerprints on the bag and on the bills which Hardcore produced now have a source. And Hardcore's motive to kill Eddgar on his own is established — the threat to go to the PAs, a challenge to Core's ego as much as his well-being. I have a jangling feeling that the details may not completely work out. But they seldom do. It's close enough, and more than sufficient to raise a reasonable doubt. In the jury box, the news is rolling through. Dubinsky, for the benefit of Stanley Rosenberg, is gesticulating at the money, which Hobie has just tossed down on the prosecution table, as if it's refuse.

In the meantime, I steal a look at Nile. A few days ago, while Kratzus was on the stand, I glanced over there and saw Nile with his chin on the defense table blowing paper balls into a goal he'd made by placing a foam cup on its side. He has seemed so isolated from the proceedings at moments, I've wondered if there are headphones beneath the unmanageable ruff of hair over his ears. Only now, at the instant of his exculpation, has he shown much emotion, and as usual, it seems inappropriate. Facing the wall, rather than the witness, he has thrown his face into his hands. Always live to the focus of my attention, Hobie saunters that way, and, while pretending to fiddle with his notes, elbows Nile's shoulder so hard his client gasps. Nile straightens up and his arms drop to the table, but he refuses to look in his father's direction, even as Hobie prepares to face Eddgar again.

"Judge." It's Molto. His dried-up hair is mussed. His dark-ringed eyes open and close, as he briefly loses his train of thought. He's too deflated now to bother to rise. "Judge, can I get a foundation here? Was Nile present for this conversation? The one where the Senator was arguing with Hardcore?"

Watching Tommy, Hobie displays a benign smile. "Do you understand what Mr. Molto's really asking, Dr. Eddgar? He wants to know
how come I know about all this and he doesn't?" Hobie faces the witness. "He's right, isn't he, Senator? Let's be clear. You didn't mention
any of this to Mr. Molto, did you?"

"I answered the questions he asked. As you pointed out, we were very
guarded with one another."

"But you knew the significance of money going from your son to
Hardcore, didn't you?"

"Neither the prosecutors nor the police ever talked to me about the
money. And even when I began to learn the details of the case, it didn't
dawn on me at first, Mr. Tuttle, what the connection might be. By then,
Nile had been indicted and I raised the subject with you—as you
know—and you told me to leave the defense to you and that—" Eddgar
stops cold.

"Go on."

"You told me you might not even have to get into it."

"Fooled you, didn't I?" Hobie asks. He has the nerve to issue a luminous smile, and then, as if that were not enough, he takes a single
step toward the witness and actually bows fully from the waist. It's an
astonishing moment. When he straightens up, he boils Eddgar, for
just a second, in a look of absolute hatred. Eddgar absorbs this with
more composure than I might have imagined. He touches a finger to
the notch above his lip and studies Hobie in silence. Somewhere, a
few seconds ago, we stopped trying this lawsuit and entered another
realm, something quite beyond me which is wholly between these two
men.

"Mr. Tuttle, are you finished?" I ask. He's about nailed the coffin lid
shut on the prosecution. And probably on Eddgar's political career. The
newshounds will run Eddgar till he drops. But Hobie's preening over
the remains does not sit well.

In response, Hobie looks up at me for quite some time. It's another
striking gesture, the large brown face inscrutable, the eyes solemn and
complex. Fleetingly, he seems, if not gentle, at least humane. Then he
says, mildly, "No, Your Honor, I'm not done." I tell him coolly to get
on with whatever he has left, and he walks a bit, considering his subject,
before pausing in front of Eddgar.

"You told Molto here yesterday you know of no motive for your son
to kill you, right, Senator?"

"Not as far as I was concerned."

"In fact, sir, since he learned to speak, has Nile Eddgar ever threatened or carried out physical violence of any kind against you?"

"No."

"How about his mother?"

"He wouldn't hurt a fly, Mr. Tuttle."

Singh prods Molto's shoulder. Tommy waves a hand: who cares? Singh moves to strike Eddgar's answer as non-responsive, which I allow.

"Indeed, Senator, as you mentioned, you agreed to pay your son's bail?"

"I did."

"Mr. Tuttle," I interject, "I think I see where you're going. If I'm right, don't even consider it." He's about to ask whether Eddgar believes Nile is guilty. Deciding that is my job, not Eddgar's.

"Your Honor, I was going one better." He faces Eddgar. "Isn't it a fact, Senator, that you *know*—have personal knowledge—that Nile Eddgar did not commit this crime?" Over his shoulder, he looks back to me, as if to say, How's that? This man, this Hobie! Now what?

"You may answer," I instruct Eddgar, "but based only on your personal knowledge."

"How would I know?" he asks me. "I have opinions."

"No opinions. I don't want your opinions."

"Let me withdraw the question and start again more slowly," Hobie offers. Standing still in the brightest spot of courtroom light, Hobie momentarily considers his manicure. "Senator, let's go back to Montague. He came to see you again on September 11 and you told him that what you said on September 7 wasn't true, didn't you?"

"I did."

"On September 11, you told Montague *you* had intended to be at Grace Street the morning Ms. Eddgar was killed. You told him how you had tried to involve BSD in politics, correct?"

"That's right."

"So how'd he get you to change your mind?"

Eddgar shakes his shoulders in equivocal fashion. "Conscience, I suppose, Mr. Tuttle. Obviously, I could tell from the fact that he was asking the same questions again, he was somewhat skeptical."

"Skeptical? Well, let's set the scene now, Senator. You're the chair of the State Senate's Committee on Criminal Justice?"

"Yes."

"Your committee helps decide on funding for police programs all over the state?"

"Yes."

"So Montague, he's a lieutenant on that police force, he knew better than to take a rubber hose to the likes of you, didn't he? He was polite to you, wasn't he?"

"Always."

"Did he tell you, Senator, they had a witness who contradicted you?"

"I don't recall that."

"But you changed your story anyway?"

"That's what happened."

Hobie moves one way, then back, his tongue tucked meditatively in the corner of his mouth. "Well, Senator, here's what I'm wondering. If he didn't tell you what Hardcore had said—if Montague didn't—had you received that information, Senator, from some other source, say from one of these police connections you have around the state?"

Eddgar takes a long moment. His upper body rises and falls as he sighs.

"I had an idea of the substance. Someone had called me. A friend from the state capitol. I really would prefer not to give a name."

"Don't need it, Senator," says Hobie with a magnanimous wave. "But your friend—did he describe the report?"

"In a fashion."

"Did he read it to you?"

"Yes. Portions."

"So you knew on September 11 that Hardcore had implicated Nile?"

"Yes."

"You knew Hardcore had produced some money to the police, which he claimed Nile gave him?"

"Right."

"You knew that Hardcore had talked about meeting you in T-Roc's vehicle?"

"I did."

"And you knew, Senator, that the plan supposedly had been to murder you?"

"I knew all of that."

"And that's why you changed your story, isn't it?"

"Learning what I had, Mr. Tuttle, I could see that the circumstances of my planned meeting with Hardcore on September 7 were obviously material to what the police were looking into, and when Montague repeated his questions, I answered them correctly this time."

"So you decided to tell them what they had already heard from Hardcore?"

"I told them the truth."

Hobie's rambling again, striding briskly over the carpet. "Well, you didn't tell them about the money from the DFU, did you? Even though, Senator, you knew as early as September 11, whenever that report was read to you, that Hardcore was claiming he'd gotten $10,000 from Nile for this shooting? You still kept that information about the DFU $10,000 to yourself, right?"

"We've covered that, Mr. Tuttle."

"Have we? You said you didn't see a connection at first, because Molto and the police weren't giving you information about the case. But you *did* have information."

Mostly for the sport of hindering him, Molto objects that Hobie's badgering. Tommy should probably just let him go. Hobie's exhibiting symptoms of the trial lawyer's chronic ailment, overtrying his case. Having proved enough, he's trying to prove some more. Now he wants to show that Eddgar won't be named Father of the Year, something Molto established yesterday. But even after I tell him to move on to another topic, Hobie continues in a personal vein.

"Wasn't it you, Senator, who suggested the police contact Nile? Didn't you do that on September 7?"

"I don't think I was suggesting that. Once I said I didn't know why June had gone to Grace Street, in that first interview, Montague asked me to speculate. Could I imagine any reason she would go down there? I didn't know how to answer. I told him my son was a probation officer and had cases down there and perhaps they were going to meet there for some reason. Mr. Tuttle, what can I say? I was lying. It's that tangled web Shakespeare warned us of."

"Well, okay, Senator, but there's something about that interview on September 7 I've never understood. I've read the police reports a number of times, but they don't seem to have asked you about this. When you first spoke to Montague, on September 7, that was at your home in Greenwood County. True?"

"True."

"But I thought you had an important meeting in your State Senate office that morning? Isn't that what you testified on direct? That an emergency came up. Isn't that why Ms. Eddgar went in your place to meet Hardcore?"

"I think I said I was needed by my office."

"For what?"

Eddgar sits back in his chair. His eyes close and his brow is furrowed.

"I believe there was a conference call scheduled. I have to confess, Mr. Tuttle, my memory on this may not be perfect."

"A conference call? You never left your house?"

"No."

"And who did you talk to, Senator? Who was on that conference call?"

Eddgar shakes his head repeatedly. "Again, my recollection isn't clear. I think there was a mix-up at the last minute. Maybe everybody who was supposed to be on the phone couldn't be rounded up. I don't recall why exactly. But it didn't happen."

"No call. No meeting. No actual emergency. But June went to Grace Street anyway. Right? Have I got the picture?"

"The words are right, but you don't seem to have the picture."

"Not the picture," says Hobie, rhetorically, and nods as if he actually stood corrected. "Well, tell me this, Senator—did your former wife, did June Eddgar, did she have any history of substance abuse?"

Tommy, who'll never stop being his own worst enemy in the courtroom, asks about relevance.

"Judge, I'll tie it up," Hobie answers. That is the trial lawyer's equivalent of 'the check's in the mail.' At this point, though, it seems to me Hobie's risking his own case, which is his right. I motion Molto down.

"I'm sure June was drug-free at the time of her death. If you're implying she was drunk or stoned or something when she went down there—"

"We have an autopsy, Senator. That's not disputed. What I'm asking you is if in the past she had problems with drugs or alcohol."

"At times."

"With drugs?"

"When she went through her divorce—from her second husband— yes, I think she had a cocaine habit."

"Was she treated?"

"She was in support groups. There are records, I imagine, if it's that important."

"That's my point," says Hobie. "There are people who know, who would say June's had problems in the past with cocaine."

Dumbfounded, Eddgar doesn't bother to answer.

"What about you, Senator? Have you ever had any problem with chemical dependency?"

"I'm the son of an alcoholic father. You'll find, Mr. Tuttle, many of us don't care to become intoxicated."

"No drugs?"

"Judge," says Tommy. "Really."

"Mr. Tuttle, I'm going to have to sustain the objection. I'm lost."

Hobie's face shoots up at me in pure astonishment. He's not questioning my ruling. I've amazed him by being thick. He adjusts himself and turns back to Eddgar.

"Well, let's make it clear then, Senator. If someone was going to plant drugs on you, it would be pretty suspicious, wouldn't it? There would be no objective basis to believe that at the age of sixty-six you developed a drug habit, would there?"

Eddgar and I both get it now. This is where we were the other day. Hobie's saying clearly that June, not Eddgar, was the actual target of the shooting. And it finally clicks. That's why Hobie leaked the state's theory to Dubinsky in the first place. To emphasize it. To misdirect. Because in the end he was going to dispute the notion, anyway. Absorbing Hobie's suggestion, the reporters ruffle. The buffs squirm. Eddgar under the track lights is motionless.

"June?" he finally asks. "Hardcore didn't know June. What are you thinking? He was trying to get even with me?" Eddgar has taken hold of the front rail of the witness stand. In his confusion, he briefly glances over his shoulder toward me. Hobie now is standing just a few feet before him.

"Well, certainly you've read the papers, Senator, as the case has gone on. You know both Hardcore and Lovinia testified that when the shooter, this Gorgo, arrived on the scene, Hardcore hit the pavement and acted as if he knew in advance June was going to be shot. Have you read that?"

"Why would Hardcore want to kill June?" Eddgar responds. "And Lord knows, Nile had no reason. No one did." He has done this a number of times, asked his own questions. Under stress, he assumes he's in charge, here as elsewhere. But Hobie does not bother to object. Instead, he offers an answer of sorts.

"Senator, we don't need the details, but isn't it a fact there are acts, events, occurrences, things you did years ago during the period of your marriage, that *you* wanted your former wife, June Eddgar, not to disclose?"

In the courtroom, the only sound at first is an elderly buff, caught short of breath, who dispenses several phlegmy eruptions behind the glass.

"Oh God," Eddgar says at last. "Oh Lord. Sweet baby Jesus," he says. Fifteen feet from the witness, Hobie is calm and, in this modulated mood, especially imposing.

"While June Eddgar was alive, Senator, your political career, in fact, even your liberty remained in peril, did they not?"

"Lord, Hobie, what in *hell* are you doin? This is horrifying." As Eddgar has lost track of himself, his accent has become julepy and full. "This is not a de-fense. You know what happened here. Who's to believe this? Everyone who knows me, if they know anything—Nile knows, you know, I felt June was the most sacred soul on this planet."

"You're a lot safer now, Senator, aren't you, than when she was alive?"

"After twenty-five years? After twenty-five years could anyone believe I would concern myself about this?"

"We don't have her here, do we, to tell us what was going on between you two—why she came to town? All we know is you sent her down to Grace Street because you claimed you had an emergency that never actually materialized."

"Oh Lord," says Eddgar again.

"In that meeting you had with Hardcore before Labor Day, the meeting where you threatened him, did you reach any other agreement with him? Did you agree with him, Senator, that he could keep the $10,000 and you would secure Kan-el's parole if BSD would kill your former wife?"

There it is. We have all known for a minute what was coming, but even so, with the question, my heart nearly leaps out of my chest. In the press row, one of the reporters squeezes out of the jury box, scrambling over her colleagues' knees so she can go running for the phone. One, then another follow. Annie, who places order above the First Amendment, approaches to shush them even as they hustle by. Seth is leaning on the front rail of the jury box. He is watching with an intensity so complete he could not have even a remote awareness that I, a woman he made love to a few hours ago, am seated in this room. Eddgar has turned about completely to face me. His mouth is parted and it moves once or twice before he speaks.

"Do I actually have to answer these questions?"

As near as I can reason, he does. I nod minutely and Eddgar pivots erratically, tossing a hand Hobie's way.

"This is Perry Mason," he says, "this is absurd. Why," he says, "why, this is senseless. This is drug-induced, Hobie. You know the truth here. If I had done such a thing, can you explain for a *moment* why Hardcore would not have been sitting on this witness stand pointing his finger at me?"

"What sense would that make, Senator, if the goal was to secure Kan-el's release? Core couldn't have made a better deal, could he, than the one he got for blaming Nile? One Eddgar is just as tasty as another to a hungry prosecutor. And this way, Senator, they can hold your feet to the fire, make sure you deliver on your promise about Kan-el. I bet he's out six months from now."

"And I would sacrifice my son? Is that your theory? You *know* that isn't true. My God. This is evil, Hobie, what you're doing. This is the very *face* of evil!" His outcry resounds in the silent courtroom. Beside himself, Eddgar grabs hold of the lapels of his coat, he looks all around the witness stand, as if something that might help him is concealed there. Then he points at Hobie. "I understand this," he says. "I understand just what you're doing to me."

"It's called justice, Eddgar," Hobie whispers. His eyes never leave the witness as he lumbers back to his seat. Next to him, Nile has laid his face down on the defense table with both hands over his head.

After court, a fragile foreboding air grips my chambers. Judgment is near. Annie and Marietta both keep their distance. Tomorrow, the state will rest. Hobie, if he's smart, will not offer much evidence for the defense. He'll capitalize on today's events and let the trial move quickly to conclusion.

I have motions to review on a number of other cases, but in the few minutes before I must go, I find myself stuck on the trial. It was like watching a car wreck today. Something awful. Destructive. Yet it's no longer possible to find Nile guilty. My assessment of the case has reversed so quickly I doubt myself at first. I still feel light-headed from sleeplessness and slightly poisoned, as if my heart is pumping battery acid, not blood. But my conclusion appears firm. Hardcore has been proven a liar about too much that's essential. Something about the money, the $10,000 he said Nile gave him, is simply wrong. The cocaine residue. The campaign check Nile cashed. There is real doubt. I ruminate on whether to rule from the bench at once or to make a show of some period of deliberation.

But that's only the formalities. I'm still wrapped heart and soul around The Questions. Who wanted to kill whom? Is it really possible, I keep wondering as I sift the facts, could it really be that Eddgar has engaged in a monstrousness on the order of Medea's, killed his wife and blamed his son? I could almost believe it about the man I knew so many years ago. And his silence about that $10,000 seems awfully telling. He probably went to Matt Galiakos and Brendan Tuohey, in hopes of keeping the DFU money out of the case. So he could save himself. Pondering all of this, I'm gripped by the profound elusiveness of the truth, as it drifts like smoke through every courtroom. Something happened. Something objective but no longer verifiable. When I was a child, they used to claim all history was knowable, if you could catch up with the light emitted by the body and traveling eternally in space. 'Light prints,' they talked about, better evidence than fingerprints. An intriguing idea. But Einstein said that wasn't possible. The past is always gone, retrieved only, ultimately, in the filaments of memory.

Near five, with her hat and coat on to leave, Marietta knocks. One look at the smirk tautening her cheeks and I realize Seth is here. She scouts my countenance for any telltale sign. Oh, and isn't there a part of me which would love to boast? 'We had a fabulous night,' I want to say, 'he is a fine, sweet man, he loves every inch of my skin, just as you said.' Instead, I greet her with my frostiest judicial demeanor.

"Show him in."

He slides past Marietta, thanking her effusively, making jokes — they are pals already. I signal discreetly and he gently closes the door, then comes around to my side of the desk and leans against it. He takes my hand.

"Okay?" he asks.

"Sore," I say.

"I take it as a compliment." He peeks back over his shoulder, then leans down for a quick, sweet kiss. A lovely silent second passes. "I didn't want to bother you, but I need a rain check tonight. I forgot Sarah's coming up. I'm taking her to dinner and she's staying over at my dad's to help him with some stuff tomorrow."

We agree on tomorrow night instead. I shake his wrist.

"How about you? Are you okay?"

"Me?" He straightens up. He stretches. He beams. "I've had the best twenty-four hours in years. Years," he repeats. "I mean it." Like me, he's pale with sleeplessness, but he's clearly inhabited by a tonic air. "I've taken the cure," he says. "Like the Count of Monte Cristo: love and revenge."

"Revenge?" I ask, but dampen the question in my voice, even as I'm speaking, for I understand. Eddgar, he means. "You really hate him that much? After all this time?"

"You don't know the whole story."

"And I don't want to hear it. Not now."

"I understand. But it does my heart good to see somebody finally catch up with him. Believe me. He's a bad, bad dude." His eyes have sparked with an incendiary light. "Now I finally get why Nile told me he didn't want a lawyer from around here. No one Eddgar could fix."

There is something jarring in the remark. I rerun it several times before I catch hold of what bothers me.

"He told *you*?" Seth looks my way at length and I repeat myself. "Nile told you? You said the other day you don't even talk to him."

"Not during the trial. Hobie won't let me. But I'm the one who hooked them up."

"Wait, Seth." I stand. "You? Are you still close with Nile?"

"Close?" He shrugs. "I've stayed in touch. You know me. The Sentimental Heart. What did you think?"

"Think? I thought he was a little boy you baby-sat for a century ago. My God, Seth! The defendant? You're close to the defendant? Why didn't I know this? Why didn't you say something to me?"

" 'Say something'? Jesus. Shit, that's exactly what you keep telling me not to do."

"Oh God." I feel polluted. The defendant! Seth's allied not just with the defense lawyer, an advocate with a limited stake, but with the man on trial. I've slept with Nile's friend, his crony, his guardian angel. "Oh God," I say again. "What else don't I know?" And then, with this question, a connection whirls in place, possible only in the dizzy ether of little sleep. I search Seth for reassurance.

"What?" he says.

"Hobie's trick-bagging me." I'm battling something now—the paranoid center, the injured child. "Tell me you're not in this with him."

"In what?"

"Tell me you weren't part of this from the start."

"Jesus Christ. Of course not. I don't even know what you're talking about."

But I've finally seen it all: why Hobie wanted a bench so I'd decide this case, why he took his mischievous steps to arrange that, and worst, perhaps, why Seth insinuated himself again into my life. A jury, another judge, would recognize Eddgar only as a solid citizen: respected legislator, grieving father, loyal ex. They would have scoffed at Hobie's ultimate suggestion that Eddgar was responsible for June's murder. They would never allow it to inspire any doubts. But I'm susceptible, willing. I have my griefs with Zora. I know Eddgar's past. And now I've heard more from Seth. *Bad, bad dude. Heinous creep.* That's the hellish thought. Because it seems so plausible that the two of them, Seth and Hobie, friends for life, could have engineered this together. And if that were so, then all of this, the sweet romance, the tireless if unbelievable claims of passion, are just part of a scheme molded against me. It makes sense—except when I look again to Seth, take in his confusion, the aura of sincerity always surrounding him, the solidness of his presence.

"Just tell me you're not in this with him."

"With Hobie? Are you crazy? He's barely talked to me for two weeks. He works at Nile's all night and goes to sleep at his parents'. You know him. He *loves* the fact I don't know which end is up. I mean, Jesus, what's the trick?"

True—or an act? He would say the same thing either way. I am so tired, so unbelievably confused. I have an instant more intense than the one before—something from dreams: the world collapses and shows itself as a monstrous scam, a stage set where the paper walls fall in, revealing a director back there with a megaphone and people you've believed in now wiping off their makeup. I'm full of a terror as old as I am. It's all these men, Tuohey and Hobie and Seth, able to play me, because they see what I can't recognize in myself. I sit here tormented again, feeling so vulnerable and incomplete I could almost reach inside myself and find the place where there's a missing piece. No father. That's what I always think at the ultimate moment. I blame Zora for too much. Half-orphaned, I simply can't be whole.

"What?" he asks. "Now you don't believe me? Christ!" He tears around the desk, but wheels back in my direction when he's halfway across the room. "I'm sorry I broke your rules, Sonny. But you've got so fucking many it's hard to keep track. And, frankly, it's what you're waiting for anyway. That's your deal, right, Judge? Let's keep everybody six feet below you and safely remote."

He's right: he knows me. And how to hurt me, too. His anger literally takes away my breath.

"Go to hell, Seth."

He thrusts a dismissing hand in my direction and rushes through the doorway, nearly crashing into Marietta, who, in her coat and hat, has been lurking there.

May 5, 1970

SETH

Another car arrived. Another Fairlane. The agent who'd caught me shoved me in the back seat and fell in beside me.

"Hey, Rudolph, you collared Frank Zappa." The driver was looking in the rearview and smiling.

"Lucky for me he runs like Frank Zappa. Some dick from Jersey wandered by and stopped him."

"Hard time? You give Special Agent Rudolph a hard time, Frank? What's his name?"

"Michael."

"Michael, you give SA Rudolph a hard time? He's not as young as he used to be. He keels over from a hard attack, then it's murder."

"All right, Dolens. You're supposed to be busting his chops, not mine."

We were making our way slowly down the strip. It was well past midnight by now and goodtime America was still thick along the broad walks, beneath the signs. Dolens lifted the radio microphone and told someone they had the subject on the lead out of San Francisco. The agent in back, Rudolph, pushed himself up so he faced me. There were spots of sweat visible on the front of his white rayon shirt. I hadn't run that far. I must have scared him, thinking he'd let me get away.

"You don't got as many friends as you think you do, goodbuddy. Somebody dropped a dime on you. You understand? We didn't turn up just by accident. You oughta think about that." He watched me to see what effect the information had. "Did you know there was a grand-jury subpoena out for you?"

"For me?"

He grimaced to show he didn't appreciate my act. "Agents in Frisco tried to serve you today." He looked at his watch. "Yesterday actually."

I vaguely recollected my instructions. Say nothing.

"See, I think you must have known that, Mike. Otherwise I have a hard time figuring why you were skedaddling through that parking lot."

Rudolph wasn't particularly good-looking, a big guy with the close haircut that Hoover demanded—'white sidewalls,' as they said. You could see the skin and the sweat at the sides of his head. His sideburns had crawled down past his ear, in an allowable concession to style. Assessing myself, I found I was not as fully terrified as I might have expected. The presence of the second agent relieved me a little bit. He had a sense of humor. I'd never heard of the FBI hitting. Local cops did it. Not the FBI.

"Where am I going?" I asked.

"Wait, Mike," Rudolph said. "Wait. Did you answer my question?"

"He answered your question, Rudolph," said Dolens. "You just didn't like what he said." Dolens was a smaller guy, very happy. Either he liked driving around, or having a prisoner, or giving it to Rudolph. He wore a cheap blue sport coat and a tie. "We're taking you to the FBI Field Office, Mike. For processing."

"Am I under arrest?"

Neither of them answered at first.

"I told you, Mike," said Rudolph. "There's a subpoena out."

None of us said anything for a while. Dolens had turned the radio down after calling in, and at this hour there was little broadcast: sleepy voices and static. Eventually, we turned into a hulking squarish structure. By now we had left the land of glitz. It was just a Western downtown, the buildings sprawling rather than rising in this region where land was cheap. From the shapes, it all looked to have been constructed in the last few years. At the bottom of a subterranean driveway, Dolens hung out the window and inserted a key card. A segmented metal door rose with much creaking. I thought of a mouth opening, of Jonah and the Whale, a story which had paralyzed me with fright as a child. They parked and walked me through a maze of concrete corridors.

"Is this the record case?" Dolens asked. "The guy who was duping records?"

"No, no. This is a possible UFAP." Yew Fap.

"Christ, I got it mixed up. That's why I was calling him Frank Zappa. What's the violation?"

"Nine twenty-one," said Rudolph.

"Christ," he said. "Kid just looks like a hippie."

The lights were out when we got off the elevator. We were in a small carpeted reception room, furnished with a few cheap chairs. On a wall before me, I recognized the crest of the FBI, an eagle screaming, with the banner of justice in its talons. It surprised me to find that their office closed for the night. I would have imagined this as a twenty-four-hour operation, men in grey suits and glasses who never slept. Rudolph seemed more like a gym teacher. One of them hit some lights and they pushed me through another door.

Down the corridor was a horrible government room—grey asbestos floor tile, with those grained flecks of white and black and blue so that the grime of daily use didn't show, and ranks of green metal desks topped in Formica and stewing under painful fluorescence. There was not a thing that anyone could consider beautiful, except an American flag in the remote corner. Photos of Richard Nixon and his Attorney General, John Mitchell, hung askew on one of the sheet-metal partitions. Rudolph's desk was in the middle of the room.

"Have a seat here, bub. Michael. Okay. Let's see what Frisco says. Biddie-bee, biddie-bum," he said as he read to himself. "Okay. Okay. 'Expected to arrive Eden's Garden Spa, approximately 2300 hours P.S.T.' That part was right, wasn't it?" He smiled. "City by the Bay," he said. "Great place. That was my OP, Office of preference? Only then my wife got rheumatoid arthritis. So here I am. Life can turn out strange, can't it? Where you live out there, Mike?"

He was shuffling the few papers on his desk, but I knew it wasn't an innocent question.

"Damon," I said.

"Girls with no bras. Must get kind of distracting."

I dipped a shoulder. Us guys.

"Whatta you have to do with that bombing, Mike?" He plunged the full weight of his meaty face onto his hand as he considered me.

I wasn't speaking. Whatever little lick of terror was left in me, after the depletion of my adrenal systems, flitted across my thorax. Rudolph had light eyes, a feature that seemed somewhat disarming.

" 'What bomb?' Right? That lab where you work blew up four days ago. Did you know that? Or were you out of town for that, too?"

I murmured that I knew about it.

"What?"

"I said, 'I know.' "

"Oh. Just wanted to be sure. Well, here's what it is, Mike. Guys in Frisco think headquarters ought to get a look at your prints. Cause if they match anything we got on any of those little bitty pieces of what went boom, your ass is grass, and I'm not referring to anything you smoke. Follow me?"

"Yes, sir."

"See now, my guess—I been doing this sixteen years next month, and I've gotten to be a pretty good guesser—I think you may have taken flight when you heard about that subpoena. I think you think your fingerprints are all over that device. I think you smuggled in the pieces. That's what Frisco thinks." He held the paper he'd read from beside his face.

"No, sir," I said.

"Will you take a lie detector?"

I shrugged, as if I didn't care. I knew I should ask for a lawyer. That or shut up. But I had the feeling I was doing all right.

"What are you doing out here, Mike?"

I shrugged again. Rudolph sighed in manifest disgust and looked down to an open space on his desk where there was absolutely nothing to see.

"What's the subpoena for?" I asked.

"Told you. Grand jury wants to see your fingerprints, Mike."

"You can subpoena somebody's fingerprints?"

"Yessiree, Bob. There's one with your name on it. You go back to Frisco, you'll get a chance to see it."

"Do I have to go along with it?"

"I'm not your lawyer, Mike. Far as I know, you gotta go along with it." He let his guard down a little. "Some Commie took it to the Supreme Court years ago and they said you gotta." He read the paper again. We were the only people in this vast area. Across the way, there was a large interior window revealing a brightly lit room banked with radios and electrical equipment. An older blond woman was speaking disinterestedly into a microphone suspended a few feet before her. She caught me staring at her and looked me off with malevolence.

Rudolph was laughing. He had picked up another piece of paper, a yellow pulpy sheet ragged at the bottom.

"Know who finked on you? I love this. Guess."

I decided not to oblige him. I realized by now I was getting the treatment.

"Your mom."

I didn't answer.

"Yep. Good old Mom. Apparently one of your neighbors reached her after the agents came out. Mom was real upset. Agent here in his teletype says he cut a deal with her. She tells us where you are, we take your prints. You clear, you go. You don't"—he lifted a hand—"you don't. Standard deal," he said. The greenish eyes lingered again, trying to measure my pain. "Don't be mad at Mom. Sounds to me like she tried to bring you up right."

Michael's mom was buried in Idaho. I was getting the entire picture now.

"So here's the deal, Mike. You wanna do like Mom said? Gimme your prints and see if we can clear this right now? Or you wanna go back to Frisco and face the music there?"

"You mean I can just go back to San Francisco?"

"No. Not exactly. Look, here's what I'm saying. You gimme your prints right here, I'll send them to D.C. See what comes out in the wash. Maybe it all straightens itself out. Otherwise, I'm gonna wake up an Assistant U.S. Attorney and tell him how you decided to play Bob Hayes in that parking lot and that I think I oughta arrest you. Unlawful Flight. Then I'll take your prints anyway. You'll probably get bail within a couple days. Clark County jail isn't too bad at all." He scratched his cheek as he watched me, without blinking.

"You're telling me I have no choice."

"You make your own bed, bub. Can give Mom a call if you like."

"What if I want a lawyer?"

He took a while with that.

"Do what you want. You play your card, I'll play mine. You call your lawyer, I call mine. That's the AUSA. You'll have to go to jail overnight. I'm being straight with you, Mike. Believe it or not. This is just how it is. You're three times seven. You figure it out."

I thought with some meager confidence about calling my parents for bail money. Then I realized everything that meant—what I'd have to tell them and maybe the FBI—and I felt my soul sink. I continued trying to deliberate, but I got nowhere. Eddgar had calculated all of this coolly, perfectly, shifting the chess pieces eight and nine moves ahead. I seemed to be able to get no further than gut instinct. All I wanted to know was what he'd been thinking. But his intentions, as ever, were unfathomable to me.

Rudolph took me to another area, a smaller room, more government issue, white walls and grey filing cabinets, to do the printing. He got a blue card and made me sign it. Michael hand-lettered his signature— he said he'd decided as a child that he didn't want to have a name he couldn't actually read, an early manifestation to my mind of the kind of pure-minded logic he always followed. I did my best imitation, then Rudolph inked my fingers with a stamp pad and rolled them across. He bore down on each digit somewhat painfully. One finger smudged and he threw the card out and started again. When we were done with that, he inked each palm and made me press them to the bottom of the card. He took me to the john, so I could wash my hands, then I followed him back to his desk, where he began to fill out papers. He spoke to me as he worked.

"Frisco says you live in the same apartment building with the chief suspect. Isn't that a funny coincidence?"

"A lot of people live in that building."

"Didn't think anybody'd notice, I bet. Six hundred employees. Lots of names. Lots of suspects. Computers, you know. Great things. Pigs aren't always as dumb as you guys think." He'd looked up again, the way he'd been doing, stabbing a little and hoping to see me bleed. "Funny thing," he said. "All you great revolutionary heroes ain't so great or revolutionary when you see the inside of a cell." Cleveland had rolled over. I knew what that meant. He'd rolled over and pointed at a white guy. Rudolph grinned, big as the Cheshire. This was one of the parts of his job he really liked—you could see that much.

After he finished his paperwork, he explained the next step. The pouch would go to D.C. on the first plane out in the morning. He would send a teletype ahead. If I was lucky, they'd do the comparison before the end of the day.

"We got a cot room, Mike, if you want to try to close your eyes."

"You mean I have to hang around here?"

"Well, look who's surprised. If you were me, son, and we'd begun our acquaintance—let's call it that—with you chasing me through a parking lot, would you be lettin go of my tail feathers so fast? I think not."

"You said I wasn't busted."

"Look, Mike. We can do this your way, or we can do this my way. I thought we already had this discussion. Didn't we? Now you get some rest. And maybe if you're lucky, this'll work out."

The cot room, so called, was really a closet. I lay there, on a coarse blanket fitted over a narrow army cot which betrayed every spring. I felt lost in my life. To my amazement, I fell into an enduring sleep, broken only by dreams of a man in a long dark coat. I thought it might be my father. Perhaps it was Eddgar. When I awoke, the vast room, formerly empty, was full. Purposeful people slipped back and forth, gossiping with each other. Phones pealed randomly, ten, twelve rings, often unanswered. A few men walked about in white shirts without their jackets. They were wearing pistols, shiny chrome most of them, peeking out from worn leather shoulder holsters. I could have gotten shot last night, I thought. That was what Rudolph had said.

A woman in her fifties was typing near where I stood. "Coffee's over there if you like. Just feed the kitty."

There were vending machines next to the pot. I bought cigarettes to have something to do and a package of Twinkies for food.

"You Rudolph's?" A man stood in the doorway. I'd just shoved a snack cake whole into my mouth and I could only nod. "He said to tell you that he'd be back around five to figure out where you stand. He left some money to get you something to eat. Hamburger okay?" It was about 9:30 according to a clock I had seen.

I spent the day there in what was called the witness interview room, a small, plastered space without a window. There was a 13-inch TV, a black-and-white, with a cream-colored chassis coated in grime. One of the rabbit ears was broken and mended with a fantail of aluminum foil. I watched soaps until I finally found someone's discarded newspaper in the john. I was stupefied by the headline: "4 KENT STATE STUDENTS

KILLED BY U.S. TROOPS. Nine Others Wounded." National Guardsmen at Kent State University in Ohio had opened fire on unarmed student protesters. The Guardsmen claimed they had heard sniper fire. The war had come home.

I tried to get what details I could from the TV. I watched intermittently. Somehow this treachery seemed more important, more reprehensible than what the Eddgars had done to me. From that I felt entirely remote. Perhaps I'd always recognized a chance this was coming. For the moment, I couldn't do any more than wait to find out what was going to happen to my life. Each hour that passed, I figured out more of it. Michael and the bomb. Michael and June. The elaborate plan June and Eddgar had made in that motel room while I was with Hobie. He'd come to tell her about the subpoena, no doubt, that the FBI was after Michael. I didn't know if they'd ever needed my father's money. But with me they had a perfect foil. Someone who was better off being Michael than himself. Jailbait now, I could never just spill to the FBI. I had no choice but to give up my fingerprints and endure this charade.

At five, the first thorough news reports were broadcast. America was in turmoil, coast to coast. Congressmen were making angry speeches about killing our own children, and thirty-seven college and university presidents had called on Nixon to end the war. At Kent State, no evidence could be found of any sniper fire at the Guardsmen. Twenty-eight hundred students had congregated in what the reporters called a near-riot in Madison, Wisconsin. Nixon had responded to all of this by promising our troops would be out of Cambodia in three to seven weeks. More than eighty colleges were closed now; at least two hundred others were expected to take up the issue in the next forty-eight hours. A clip was on, showing students eagerly working phone banks and canvassing in Dorchester for signatures on antiwar petitions.

Behind me, I noticed Rudolph. He was dressed in a grey suit now, rather than blue. He watched the TV for some time with a fierce, pained look.

"You really think all this helps?"

I didn't know what I thought about that. I didn't know if it helped. I didn't know if the bomb helped either. But I thought there was a chance there might be more of them this week. If the ghettos rose up all over the country, if the students fought back, then who knew? Maybe it was going to be a revolution. Or just another civil war. I had no idea where I stood either. I felt alternate periods of remorse and relief I was leaving.

"My little brother's over there right now," said Rudolph. "Near Chu Lai. This kind of stuff—it isn't helping a whole hell of lot. I can tell you that. You know, they don't have a free society over there. They take this stuff at face value. Charlie sees what you guys are up to. It encourages him. What do you say to that?"

"The war is wrong," I answered. It remained one of the few truths I knew.

He fixed his face to contain himself. Then he threw his stuff— papers, a leather folder, and a huge ring of keys—down on an old table there.

"What'd you do about the service, Mike?"

"Asthma," I said.

"Tough luck."

I smiled, even though I knew that was not a particularly good idea. Rudolph popped out his lips in exasperation.

"You cleared," he said. He ripped open an envelope and handed me Michael's wallet.

I'd figured I would clear. That was the point, of course. That was why the Eddgars had needed me. At one point, I had worried about the signature. What if somebody noticed that my handwriting didn't match Michael Frain's? But Eddgar, I was certain, had mastered the details, and must have known somehow—from a book, from some radicalized vet who'd worked army intelligence—what was likely to occur. At moments, I'd felt other shifting anxieties. What if the point of all of this was to set me up, to blame the bombing on me? I could make no sense of that. But in my present state, I had been prepared to put up with virtually anything.

"I can go?"

"With God," he said. "Or without. You know," he said, "if I was the kind of asshole you think I am, I'd bust you anyway. For running on me. You oughta think about that. But I'm gonna keep my word." He moved out of the doorway. I pushed my cigarettes down into the pocket of my jeans. "Why *did* you run?" he asked quietly as I brushed past him.

I was going to say something smart—I must not have been myself— but I finally did what I'd been told and kept my mouth shut. I shrugged as if I didn't have a clue. I started away, then looked back to tell him I hoped his brother was home soon.

———

It didn't occur to me until I was outside that I had no transportation. The sun was sinking but the air was still fierce with heat. I removed my denim jacket as I walked. I had no idea where I was going, but I saw the strip across a stretch of scrubby lawns and desert. When I reached Las Vegas Boulevard, I stopped in one of those dim, clanging hotel lobbies and called my parents. At this hour, I'd find my father at home. I hated to place the call with my mother around, but I knew by now he'd be in a state. He picked up on the first ring.

"I'm all right. I'm okay. It worked out just as you agreed."

My father gave forth an intense groan. Behind him, I heard my mother at once. She questioned him intensely. What is wrong? she asked repeatedly. My father told my mother that it was me, but that did not seem to calm her. Why was I calling?

"Later, Dena," he finally told her sternly, then returned to me. "I am very relieved. Very relieved. You are unharmed?"

"I'm just fine. I'm tired and I don't have enough change for the pay phone. So I'll call you again in a few hours. But I wanted you to know I'm okay."

The electrical sounds of the filaments and wires that connected us popped along for an instant. My father did not ask any of the questions someone else might have. What was it like? What did they do? Because he was a survivor, I realized. He knew better than that.

"I'm really, really sorry," I said. My father did not answer. He may have been crying or gathering himself or concerning himself with my mother. Before replacing the phone, I repeated that I would call again soon.

It was Happy Hour here and the hotel habitués seemed just that, happy. They gabbled over the noise of a band playing country music. I walked up to the buffet and speared eight little wieners out of the oily water with the same toothpick, gulping them down before anyone could say anything. It dawned on me that I should call the motel and I went back to the phone. I asked for Seth Weissman or Lucy McMartin. Amazingly, she was registered. They rang the room, but there was no answer and I thought better than to leave a message.

The last stretch to Eden's Spa took me across military land, an open alley of desert scrub. The sun, even this late, had some intensity, and I felt parched. Approaching the motel, I had no idea how to find Lucy. I figured I'd wait in the Bug if it was there. Instead, as I prowled the lot, I saw her. She was at the pool, in a loose-waisted granny gown of some greenish floral print. Her shoes were off, her small freckled face toward the waning sun. I knelt next to her.

"Don't say my name," I said when she opened her eyes. I asked where the room was. She picked up a book—a manual on the *I Ching*—and showed me inside. Neither of us spoke as we padded through the motel corridors. Inside the room, the air conditioning had been turned up too high, so that there was a shock in coming in out of the heat. I was briefly light-headed. My skin prickled and my ears seemed to ring from suddenly escaping the noise of the traffic. The air-conditioner fan and a newspaper rattling on the register were the only sounds. There was a sense of the silence of the desert, the heat of struggle, the passing of time.

When I sat down on the bed next to Lucy, I knew my childhood was over. I had stopped thinking of my life as something my parents had done to me. My horror with myself, which had finally, fully settled—and which has never really left me since—had taught me that much. In that moment, I thought, for no reason I could understand, of Sonny. I wondered, as I long would, if I might have done better with her knowing what I did now.

"Is he gone?" I asked.

"Michael? He left when I got here."

"What did he tell you?"

"Just—" She shrugged. "Nothing. He said you can keep his wallet."

"Great," I said, "thanks a lot." I shook my head in wonder, then told Lucy that I believed Michael had set the bomb at the ARC.

Lucy's eyes are tiny and dark, with the occasional glassy look of a babydoll's, but within I saw something fast, immobile disks of light planted on her contacts. I encountered no enlarging look of amazement, just a stoical settled straightforward stare, a depth of knowledge I'd only begun to recognize recently.

"Am I that dumb?" I asked.

"He didn't *say* anything," she answered. It was merely apparent to those less oblivious than I. Michael's grief, his loss, was not over his colleague or June but himself.

"She talked him into it?"

"I suppose," Lucy said. It was some test of love, we both imagined. But Lucy had no better idea than I did. Only that June had required it and Michael had complied.

"Shit," I said.

"Where were you? Michael just told me if you weren't here by to-morrow, I should call this number." She went to her pocketbook. The phone number, written on an Eden's Spa notepad, was in the Bay Area. I didn't recognize it otherwise. I told her about being held at the FBI, about Rudolph and the fingerprint switch.

"I get the scare of my life and he leaves his wallet." I took it out and together we peered into the long pocket of the billfold. There were three worn singles and a five. I laughed out loud as I counted them, but Lucy took the wallet from me and wormed a finger behind the windowed card section. Michael's driver's license, social security card, and draft card were there along with his university ID.

"I think what he means by his wallet," she said, "is his name. You know? You get his lottery number. You can keep on being him. You don't have to go to Canada."

The notion took hold slowly. I realized he really had no choice about abandoning his name. He didn't want to be Michael Frain in case the FBI ever came back for more prints. After an initial hopeful spurt, I saw that the advantages of this arrangement were limited. I still could not go where I was known, or any place Michael was present. I would be more or less living the life the Eddgars had promised my father on the telephone.

"If I'm him, who's he going to be? Me?"

"He can't be you."

"No," I said. "That's true." The FBI would be looking for Seth Weiss-man, the draft dodger. "So where's he going?"

Neither of us could figure that out either.

"These fucking people," I said. A TV went on too loudly in an ad-joining room. "And you were just sitting here all this time?" I asked. "You must have been scared to death."

She shrugged, with her usual indifference to herself. At long last, I focused on Lucy. If you asked either of us, we would say many months passed before we recognized the slightest prospect of falling in love. We had been living together in Seattle for nearly six months before we became lovers, and even at that we weren't sure at first how seriously to take it. But constancy, friendship—the high virtues Lucy has always embodied for me—were marked in those moments in that motel room as perhaps the most important in the world. Looking at her tiny, pretty, earnest face, I was overwhelmed to think I knew anyone still worth believing in.

"Do you know how brave you are?"

"I didn't do anything. I just stayed."

"You know how many other people would have run away? You know how many people would never have driven across the desert all night? You're fabulous. Do you know that?"

She blushed. The crimson reached every point on her face but her nose. She took my hand as we sat there and closed her eyes, trying to fight off the pure pleasure of my—of anyone's—admiration.

My parents never knew. Nor did they ever ask for details, even my mother, who for years could not stop thanking God for my survival. Occasionally, by allusion, I suggested to my father that things might not have been as he thought, but he clearly preferred not to pursue the subject, since neither that, nor anything else, seemed likely to alter our discontent with one another. To this day, I remain horrified that I tested him so cruelly. But I have also come to accept that I had my reasons. And God knows, I received my comeuppance. In 1978, a year after Jimmy Carter's draft amnesty, when I was able to reclaim the name I was born with and which I no longer fully thought of as my own, I gave my father a check for $32,659, my debt plus interest at prevailing rates. He took the money with a grave nod, so I knew it had never left his mind, all these years.

For the first few months in Seattle, after I had taken Michael's name, I lived as June had provided. I called my parents twice a week from a pay phone to assure them I was fine and did not disclose my location. We chose Seattle because it was close to the border. If something went bad, we could be in B.C. in an hour. Those initial months, of course, were ravaged by fear. I went over a number of times to look at Vancouver. But I was soon established in Seattle and everything seemed to fall into place. So far as I could tell, the FBI search for Seth Weissman lasted no longer than one week in August. My parents—and surely everyone who knew me in Damon—reported I had gone to Canada. A warrant was issued, but no indictment was ever returned. I often feared that the FBI would somehow retrace their steps with Michael Frain, realize they'd been fooled in Las Vegas, but the Bay Area papers, which I read whenever I could, always referred to the ARC bombing as unsolved, and still do to this day.

Within the first months in Seattle, I was hired at *Seattle Weekly*, an alternative paper, full of ads for paraphernalia shops and macramé makers and of course every record store in town. I was the janitor. It was a blow that I couldn't submit my 'movies' for publication, but I was too fearful that kind of signature detail would tie me to Seth Weissman. Instead, when the opportunity opened up, as I'd been promised when I was hired, I began to do lightweight reportage and little opinion items. I seemed to have a talent for mixing sly insights with whimsy and a number of Michael Frain's pieces were syndicated by the Liberation News Service.

The following March, as I grew more confident in the foolproof nature of my false identity, I allowed my mother to visit. My father, as I'd imagined, remained at home. By then, I wanted my mom to meet Lucy.

"This girl?" she asked me the first night. "Her last name?"

"Goy, Ma. Her name is goy." On the whole, my mother behaved with greater aplomb than I would have guessed.

When I remembered many months along that the VW was still titled to Seth Weissman, I arranged for someone heading East to drive it back to Kindle. She left it with Sonny's Aunt Hen, to await Sonny's return from the Philippines. My only message was that Sonny would know what it was for, referring to the money I'd borrowed. I was never certain if I was evincing mettle or loyalty to Lucy or caution of the authorities by leaving no other word or any way to get in touch. But at the age of twenty-three I had begun to think of myself as a realist. Like many other Americans, I had become one in Las Vegas.

Surprisingly, Lucy and I saw a lot of Hobie. We first spent an evening with him in early September 1970 in a cabin in Humboldt, California, halfway between Seattle and the Bay Area. He told us repeatedly he was happy Lucy and I were together and predicted great things for our relationship. He had passed the summer working for a well-known criminal defense lawyer in Kindle County, Jackson Aires, who at the time was representing a number of Black Muslims. Hobie was now going by the name of Tariq and was considering joining the Muslims himself.

We had gotten together not so much to make amends as to discuss something we preferred not to talk about over the phone — the death of Cleveland Marsh the previous June. Less than a month after he had been released on bail, Cleveland had been found dead one morning in a private 'sleeping room' at Ciardi's, a gay bathhouse on Castro Street. He was unclothed, and beside him was a pocket mirror on which rested a scalpel, traces of white powder, and a gram of rock cocaine which the medical examiner determined had been cured in strychnine. Cleveland's fame, the lurid circumstances, and the prospect of bad coke on the street all combined to keep the case in the Bay Area papers for days.

The medical examiner had found the cause of death to be accidental self-poisoning.

"Murder, man, straight up," Hobie said. "Ain no question." A summer in a criminal-law firm had imbued him with his usual authoritative voice concerning matters about which I'd heretofore assumed he knew next to nothing. Hobie had even been to the medical examiner's office to look at the records. "You know, lividity got Cleveland dyin face-down but po-lice find him layin face-up. Body temperature, digestive enzymes, they say man's dead no more'n two hours and Ciardi's close up at 4 a.m. And you tell me how they coulda shut down in the first place with him layin in there? None of this makes any damn sense anyway. Every fool on the street knows somebody just dumped that body in there. But thing is, man, po-lice figure, why sweat it? They're all bent out of shape about Cleveland to begin with, man, cause they think when they busted his ass back in May, he handed them a whole long line of shit bout that bomb and how they had just got to be this white boy's fingerprints on the pieces of the thing. They done their nationwide manhunt and come up with diddly-squat, then Eddgar and his lawyers went truckin in there laughin and scratchin and bail Cleveland out. Po-lice figure Cleveland was just mindfucking them all along. So hell with his dead ass. That's what the coppers are thinkin. Uppity nigger anyway."

With the reference to Michael and the fingerprints, a sober moment passed between us. Hobie had heard my story by then and we both seemed to feel bound together by fortune and the sheer glee of undeserved escape. I finally asked if he knew who it was. He remained at the perimeters of Panther circles and was likely to have asked the question himself.

"Who what?" Hobie demanded.

"Who offed Cleveland?"

"You know same as I do. Feature this: Cleveland snitched out Michael, then Eddgar bails his ass anyway? Only one reason to do that. Eddgar wanted him back on the street so he could deal with him. What white dude you think it was Cleveland was tryin to give the pigs anyway when he dimed Michael? Think Eddgar didn't figure that? Oh, they all made like Cleveland was a hero of the revolution when he come out. And Cleveland, poor motherfucker, he'd believe just about anything so long as somebody was standing there applaudin. But I rapped to Josita, Cleveland's old lady? She told me after they found Cleveland, Huey and them did all kinda head-trips on her, 'Don't say nothin,' party discipline, that shit, and she's a stone sister anyway. But here's what she was puttin down, dude: was Eddgar what called Cleveland in the middle of the night, was Eddgar Cleveland was leavin out to see last time he left their pad. This was Eddgar's thing all the way, man. Makin it look like it some kind of accident went down with a dude who was scorin? You know, Eddgar's done that ten times before, man, this here's his m.o."

When we returned to Seattle, I called the Eddgars. I'd had notions of doing it before, but there was nothing for me to say then, other than to demand explanations that would never be made. Now this news, the dark mess of guilt about this death and my role in it, left me anguished. I wanted to do to Eddgar something of what he had done to me. I would not give my name, would speak only a few words: "I know about Cleveland. I know why you wanted the bail money." A declaration that would paralyze him with fright.

Instead, Nile answered the phone. His wee voice united me at once with the suggestion of perilous loss he always waked in me. When I finally spoke, he knew immediately who it was, even though I'd merely asked for Eddgar.

"Hi," he said. He sounded certain I'd called for him. "Are you someplace?" he asked.

I tried to say everything I would have wanted said to me. I miss you, Nile. Be a good boy. We all love you. I'm far away but I think about you and I'm going to write. Nearby, I heard June repeatedly asking who it was.

"Is Michael there?" Nile asked.

"Michael? No, not right now."

"Oh." He deliberated only an instant and then, without a further word, put down the phone.

December 13, 1995

SONNY

Every month or so, Raymen and Marietta vow to start again. There's always a new plan. This summer, she was slipping a chemical her sister-in-law gave her into his coffee, so he'd retch whenever he drank. Last week, they swore off credit cards and cigarettes. They're going to pay down their debts, she tells me. They're going to get out from under. She is ardent about this, even as she admits it's tough. Without the ciggies, he's drinking too much, maybe they both are.

"Are you getting on each other's nerves?"

"No, no," she insists. "He's sayin this here's the best it's been in years.

He's happy. My daughter was on the phone with him a whole hour last night? She's thinkin he's a changed man."

Leaving yesterday, I had every intention of reading-out Marietta this morning. Call her a busybody, a snoop, tell her to cease meddling. With a night's sleep, though, I was put out mostly with myself. Late last night, I thought of phoning Seth, then recalled he was out with Sarah. Yet listening to Marietta's proclamation of renewal, I'm nearly moved to tears. There's hope, I think, hope. Everyone wants hope.

"It's terrific," I say, as we start into the courtroom. "I want to know how this turns out."

By the chambers door, Fred Lubitsch is lurking, several yellow sheets—a search warrant—in hand. "Quickie, Judge, I swear." I'm glad to see him here, pleased he understands his honest testimony cost him nothing in my esteem. Wells and he want to toss the apartment of a mugger whom they took down an hour ago, on the street. They expect to find the booty of a number of recent armed robberies.

" 'Subject apprehended at G&G's Pizza Parlor, 4577 North Greeley,' " I read aloud. "Why do you always get them at pizza parlors, Fred?"

"I guess they get hungry, Judge." He looks on as I read. "Trial's still going, huh?"

"Yep."

"So, good guys winning?"

"Whoever they are."

I eye him without further comment, initial the warrant, and go on my way. I will have to follow Marietta's example. Learn from my mistakes.

Hobie this morning is splendidly turned out—a corner of his silk braces can be seen through his open jacket; a yellow pocket hankie accents his dark suit. He's dressed for victory, a walking celebration. Approaching the bench, a man of many courtroom voices, he adopts his most grandiloquent mode. Beneath the lights, the hankie looks bright as a flower.

"As the court may have noted, my client is late." He dips his chin to the defense table, where I had not yet noticed Nile's absence. "I've asked someone to give him a call. In the meanwhile, Mr. Molto tells me he intends to rest. Perhaps we can go on to the motions for directed verdict, while my client's gone. Then proceed to the defense case when he gets here. Should we have to." With the last phrase, the large reddened eyes, rheumy and mysterious, rise to the bench and meet mine ever so briefly, only to transmit the message that Hobie believes he deserves to win right now. He'd like me to declare a TKO, finding that no reasonable person should convict on the basis of the evidence the state has offered.

Even Molto sees little reason to object to Hobie's proposed agenda. Tommy reoffers his exhibits, then gathers himself to his feet and announces, "The People rest." With Montague and Rudy beside him, I have a momentary vision of the revolutionary trio, the fife and drum and flag bearer, bandaged, gimping along to their own marching tune.

"The People rest," I repeat. "You have a motion, Mr. Tuttle?"

He takes some time adjusting himself behind the straight-lined oak podium. He is wearing little octagonal reading glasses that have appeared occasionally during the trial.

"First of all, Judge Klonsky, I recognize the standard here at the end of the state's case. I know you're not giving us your judgment now. You're just deciding whether the state's evidence, taken most favorably to the state, could ever be sufficient to convict. So I'm not going to bother myself to tell you now what we think really happened here. You got a good taste of that yesterday, but I realize you can't decide the case on that basis right now.

"What you can decide, Your Honor, and should decide, is that the state's case has failed. And it has failed for one reason, one huge reason: namely, they have chosen to rely on a human being who has been proved to be a terrible liar, a fellow whom we've all met here, named Ordell Hardcore Trent.

"Now I realize that ordinarily judgments of credibility don't come into play at the time of a motion for a directed verdict. But we all know of cases where they do, where the undisputed facts, the objective truth, show that a witness cannot be believed, and I tell you this is exactly such a case. Exactly.

"Let us be clear: the state's case rests completely on Hardcore. This Miss Bug, Miss Lovinia, she adds nothin to this case, not a thing, because, Your Honor, as we learned from Detective Lubitsch, she didn't do any more'n repeat what the po-lice had told her. Shot-caller said roll, she rolled. Po-lice sang 'A, B, C,' she picked up the tune. As she said herself in her own truthful way, she ain never said nothin gainst Nile." He rolls the phrase, just so we all know that when he wants, the accent, the words can be his completely.

"So all we have in the end is this fellow Core. And I won't bother you now to tell you what a terrible, hardened person he is. I won't spend a lot of time telling you he has no respect, no *need* for the truth, that as far as he's concerned, he shouldn't have any regard for this system —

I won't bother with that, because, Your Honor, we proved, we *proved* he's lying." At the podium, his eyes tilt up through the watery lower regions of his lenses. 'We' is solely euphemistic. 'I' is the right word. 'Me.' Hobie took Core down on his own. He briefly savors the achievement.

"He says, Your Honor, my client gave him $10,000 to kill his father. Well, Judge, we know now my client did give him $10,000. We finally found that out yesterday. But not in August. In July. And not to kill his father, but rather at his father's request. And it's not the defense witnesses who say that. It's the state's witness, its *star* witness, in a phrase, Senator Eddgar. The state's star witness tells us that Hardcore's a liar." Hobie waves the check around. He again recounts the trail of funds from the State Democratic Party to the Senator's campaign fund and then out and into Nile Eddgar's hands in cash. "Where else does a probation officer get $10,000? Your Honor, his salary is $38,000 a year, his bank accounts show less than $3,000." Tommy properly objects that those documents are not yet in evidence. "Well, his father said he had to borrow money for his rent, his security. So Mr. Trent is lying. My Lord, Your Honor, there's *dope* on that money."

"Why?" I ask. "I've been wondering."

"He saved this bag, sure, he saved a few bills so he'd have Nile Eddgar's fingerprints. Judge, a dope peddler like Hardcore—the risk of apprehension and planning for what he'll do, that's as much a part of his profession as you conferring with Ms. Raines to decide what case you'll be trying next week." Marietta's woolly head rises and she sits up straighter at mention of her name. "Core saved the bag, the bills, so he'd have a sacrifice if he ever got himself in trouble again, and when, sure as night follows day, he got in trouble, he filled this bag, Your Honor, with the money from his own stash. He's a dope-peddling liar, Judge, and this money is a dope peddler's lie. That's obvious." He spends a few more minutes on other points, then yields to Molto.

Tommy and Rudy have waited tensely throughout, scribbling notes. If I follow the law, take Core's word for the moment, the case should go on. But there are many judges who would just call it quits, especially since a ruling against the state at this point is not appealable. Fittingly, Molto devotes a lengthy preamble to the legal standard applicable here, before talking about the proof.

"Judge, I know you've followed the evidence closely, so I won't go over it *ad nauseam*. Let me just say I think we fulfilled our promises in opening statement. There's no dispute that Mrs. Eddgar was murdered, no doubt that Mr. Trent ordered it. Mr. Trent says he was paid to do this by Mr. Eddgar, his probation officer. Mr. Trent— Of course, the People know Mr. Trent is not a letter from home. Mr. Trent is a criminal. Mr. Trent is a murderer. But you know the line, Judge, and it's true: we didn't choose Mr. Trent, Nile Eddgar did.

"And Mr. Trent is corroborated, Judge. Mr. Trent is corroborated first by Bug, by Lovinia Campbell, who says Mr. Trent told her this murder—which was intended to be of Nile's father—this murder was being set up 'on account of Nile.' I know there are disputes about aspects of that testimony, but for purposes of this motion, Judge, you have to consider it most favorably to the state. And that means Core's corroborated.

"Secondly, Judge, the circumstances corroborate Mr. Trent. He says he had no choice but to do what his probation officer demanded, because his probation officer in essence held the keys to the jailhouse. And that makes sense. It makes sense he'd want to keep Nile Eddgar happy. More important, Judge, Mr. Trent says he got $10,000 from the defendant Eddgar, and, in fact, Judge, he has produced bills with Nile Eddgar's fingerprints on them. Three of Nile Eddgar's prints. And, Judge, we know Senator Eddgar was told by the defendant to come to this meeting. We know the defendant was aware of it. And we know from telephone records that he called Mr. Trent within minutes of the murder. Finally, Judge—and I notice Mr. Tuttle doesn't mention this— we know Nile Eddgar told Al Kratzus, when he heard of his mother's murder, 'my *father* was supposed to be there.' So we know, just as Hardcore told us, that Nile Eddgar had prior knowledge of this plan.

"Now that, Judge, leaves Senator Eddgar—" That's a lot, of course. Even Molto pauses, contemplating what lies ahead for him. He brings his fingertips, the bitten nails, halfway to his mouth, then catches himself and lets his hand fall again. "Judge, I've been thinking all night about what I can say. And let me just say this: I was surprised. The Senator admitted he never told the People anything about this $10,000 check. And of course I wonder why. And this is hard to say, but let me say it. He's a skillful, powerful politician, and perhaps, Judge—I mean no disrespect—but perhaps, Judge, he's been manipulating this system in the ways someone in his position can." He looks at me once, starkly: a laser of absolute truth. Tommy knows Ray Horgan didn't arrive in this courtroom yesterday on a whim, that the resistance to this case from higher-ups in the PA's office, which Montague mentioned, which Dubinsky suggested, may well have had an outside source. But why not infer Eddgar was protecting himself? That Hobie is right?

"I'm not really following, Mr. Molto."

"Judge, I can't tell you what Senator Eddgar's agenda is. And I know we put him on the stand. But, Judge, he lied to the police at the start. So maybe you should hesitate before taking all of this stuff he came up with yesterday at face value. I'd say he lied on September 7 to protect his son. And maybe that's what he's doing now. Maybe, Judge, he finds the People's justice harsh. He may even feel, Judge, that because he was the intended victim, he may feel it's up to him to forgive and forget. I don't know, Judge. I can't give you chapter and verse."

This is a desperate tactic, assailing your own witness in this fashion. Yet in a way I respect Tommy for it, for not giving up, for not abandoning his own view of the truth. Throughout his presentation, I've felt the force of a personal appeal: Don't direct me out. Don't say the case was a stinker. Let me lose on the merits—say the evidence raised too many questions to travel to the land beyond reasonable doubt. But don't say we never should have been here in the first place. Don't let the pols in the PA's office cover themselves with told-you-so's. He's urging this for pride, and also because he knows that technically, legally, adhering to the rules he adores, the very sticks and bones of his character, he's correct. Tommy is a lawyer to the core. It's both his glory and his weakness that he believes so potently in the rules.

"But here's one thing, Judge," says Tommy, "about that $10,000 check from the state party. Now, I saw the check. I know it's a real check. But we still haven't heard testimony that Nile actually delivered any cash from that check to Hardcore. We haven't heard that."

"Your Honor!" Hobie's on his feet. "I tried to ask that very question."

"Sit down, Mr. Tuttle." As usual, Hobie's being diversionary. He'd prefer I not notice what Tommy's doing, which is challenging him to put Nile on the stand. Down to his last dollar, Tommy's betting he can turn his case around with Nile's cross. A good move, in these circumstances. But not bait I expect Hobie to rise to. I interrupt Tommy.

"As long as we're on the money, Mr. Molto, I've heard Mr. Tuttle's theory—why don't you tell me yours for the cocaine traces on those bills."

"Judge, again, that's not in evidence yet. And I'd argue, given the discovery violation, the way Mr. Tuttle hid those lab results, that proof never should be received. But since you've asked, let me just say this: I think if you get paid to kill someone, you'd store the money in the same place, in the same way, you'd store other contraband. That's what I would suggest. I don't think you take it to the bank. If you have a floorboard, or a stash pad, or a medicine cabinet you pull out of the wall to hide your dope, Judge, I'd think that's where this money would go."

"Except your witness, Hardcore, said he kept those funds carefully segregated."

"And he must have made a mistake in saying that, I concede that," says Tommy, although he can't quite force his glance to meet mine, as he makes this gallant admission. "He's not the FBI, Judge. He doesn't keep an evidence log. And again, Judge. Right now, as the case stands, the defense has not actually established there was cocaine on the currency."

He's right about that. If I end the case now, I'd reward Hobie for his miserable behavior. With that in mind, I eventually deny the motion, careful to say that my ruling reflects no evaluation of credibility and is, accordingly, no prediction of my ultimate judgment in the case. The lawyers are seated at their tables as I rule, and I eye each of them to make sure the message is clear. I have given Tommy the latitude he deserves, and the last he's getting. Singh actually grips Molto's arm in mild delight.

"Now, Mr. Tuttle, where's your client?"

He asks for a recess so he can check. When I return to the bench, perhaps a quarter of an hour later, Seth, improbably, is seated beside Hobie at the defense table, drawn close to him in urgent, hushed conversation. My heart does another of those ballet jumps at the sight of him within the well of the court and comes down crashing when I take in the significance of the two of them in league. By this morning, I had put yesterday's suspicions aside to sleep-deprived paranoia.

With my appearance, Seth jumps to his feet. He parts from Hobie, with a pointed finger and a sharp downstroke of his head, leaving the impression they're cross with one another. Seth walks to the jury box, but does not step inside, waiting there in his rumpled khakis and his blazer. His tie knot is pulled down several inches from his open collar.

"Your Honor," Hobie says. He stands but for some time says nothing. The light makes two bright balls on the open regions over his forehead. "We'll have to adjourn, if the court please. My client cannot be located."

We all take a moment with that.

"He's on my bond, Mr. Tuttle. Don't you think I'm entitled to a little fuller account?"

"Your Honor, I called him three times this morning. When he didn't appear, I asked a friend of his to go to his apartment, but he's not around. Your Honor," he says, "I would speculate, estimate, if I have to—I would think, Judge Klonsky, he might, unwisely, have been doing some premature celebrating after yesterday. That's a guess."

"I see." It strikes me at once that Hobie's up to something again. Briefly, I look at Seth. He's watching both Hobie and me tensely.

"Judge," says Tommy, "I'm not going to agree to an adjournment. The defendant knows our schedule. I'm not agreeing at all. He's absented himself voluntarily, we should go ahead."

"Your Honor, I don't know where Nile Eddgar is. And neither does Molto. He can't just say he's voluntarily absent. Maybe there's a car wreck. Maybe my client picked a fight in a barroom. Maybe he's in a hospital or a police station. Lord, he could be a victim of some kind of foul play. His face has been all over the TV. Who knows what's happened?"

But it's Seth and his knitted expression that has my attention. Recollecting what he told me yesterday about his continued relationship with Nile, I finally catch on.

"Mr. Tuttle, whom did you send to look for your client?" Caught short, Hobie doesn't answer. "I think I should hear from him directly. Don't you, Mr. Tuttle?"

Hobie looks as big and empty as a kettledrum. A hand, glistening with his manicure, loiters midair. "Well" is all he finally brings out. Seth's already started forward.

"Mr. Molto," I say, "Mr. Weissman has been a personal friend of mine for twenty-five years. I'm sure he can help inform the court, but only if that doesn't present a problem to you."

Tommy shrugs. "Suit yourself, Judge."

And so the moment. Oh, it's mad! I think. Is this every woman's dream, to swear him under oath and make him speak the truth? To see if he will place her above others? Beleaguered, Seth shuffles to the center of the courtroom. What did he say? Everyone six feet below me and remote? Not remote. My heart races. As he addresses me, his eyes are deep and even. With the first word, I know he's telling me the truth.

He recites the story in a few strokes. The janitor let him into Nile's apartment. The bedroom was a mess. There were two soft-sided bags on the bed, the drawers were empty.

"It looked to me like he left town," Seth adds. Hobie has just lifted a hand in hopes of dashing that remark. Now we all are silent.

"He's fled?" The words, like so many before them, leap from me impulsively. They sail into the courtroom causing a sudden hushed consternation among the smaller group of spectators behind the glass today.

"Well, 'fled,' " says Hobie. "He had an emotional reaction to yesterday's testimony, probably. That's how I'd assess it."

"I thought your assessment was your client was out celebrating."

Gunned down, Hobie pulls a mouth, but otherwise looks up without apology, or resentment. We both know the score now. He takes the constant fooling around as his job, his duty. Tommy raises a hand.

"Judge, I want to proceed," he says.

"Come on," Hobie answers.

"Judge, we should go ahead." Molto has not had much opportunity to ponder. All he knows is that something is different, and given where things were going, that can't be bad for him.

"I'm sure he'll turn up," says Hobie. "Why don't you give him a day, Your Honor?"

Tommy is on his drumbeat now. The defense should be forced to proceed.

"For Godsake, Your Honor," answers Hobie. "He's my only witness. I have a few stipulations, a few exhibits, and Nile. I can't proceed."

"Two o'clock. You find your client, Mr. Tuttle. Otherwise, we're going on without him."

Seth has shrunk back in the courtroom and watches somberly from the rear wall, awaiting my reaction, my judgment.

Lunch in chambers, signing orders. Annie is still clearing files from yesterday's call. Out the door, Marietta, who has brought in carryout, has skillfully deployed a napkin between her pizza slice and her TV. I remain agitated.

"He's up to something," I say to Marietta from my desk.

She cocks one earphone. "Who?"

"Hobie. Tuttle. What's he doing, Marietta?"

She shakes her head for some time. "You know, the boy is not-right, Judge. The defendant? He's crazy as a coot." We all know that. Watching Nile day in and out you can't escape that impression. Functional, but not a mainstream personality. Eccentric.

"It's another trick. Like Dubinsky. Like the chemist's report or the check. Hobie can't walk a straight line. If Nile's run, who do you think told him to do it?" I check Annie, who, as always, listens carefully, attempting to learn from our assessments, while she continues loading files into the steel carts from the chief clerk's office.

"Probably. Only thing is, Judge," says Marietta, "what's he get? Molto's gonna kick and carry on. He's gotta know that."

That's the clue: Hobie knew Tommy would demand that the case go forward.

"Don't you see, Marietta? It's an excuse for not putting Nile on. Did you hear that malarkey just now how Nile's his only witness?"

"He's just tryin to slow you down, Judge. No way that young fella's gettin up there. Uh-uh," adds Marietta, envisioning Nile on cross.

But perhaps that's the point. Nile surely is under no obligation to take the stand, and the law forbids me from making anything of his failure to testify. But Molto's already thrown down the gauntlet; he'll point out every detail of the defense which is unsupported. This way, Hobie's got an excuse. Whatever he's up to, I'm hellbound that Hobie won't get away with more smelly antics.

When I resume the bench, the courtroom is tense. Before, without the defendant present, many of the journalists didn't even bother to come in from the corridor. Now word has circulated that something of consequence is at hand. The jury box is full, all the familiar faces, except for Seth, who is probably on the street, a one-man posse. The sketchers have their pads open. Hobie and the large white cardboard boxes are by themselves at the defense table.

"Mr. Tuttle?"

"Your Honor, I have to move for a further continuance."

"You haven't found him?"

"Not yet, Your Honor." He turns his large head to the corners of the courtroom, as if he might find Nile here. He'd rather not look at me.

"And, Mr. Molto, you still desire to proceed?"

Tommy comes to the podium. "The People move to reopen their case," he says. "I want to offer Mr. Eddgar's non-appearance as evidence of flight, of consciousness of guilt." He and Rudy have cooked this one up in the interval and it's clever. The law has always reasoned that an innocent person would stay to defend himself. Only the guilty run away. Privately, the logic of this rule has eluded me. Who, having been falsely accused, would have enough faith in the system to stick around for trial? It's an assumption from a more formal era, when people lived by concepts like Honor and Obedience. But rule it is, age-old. Hobie explodes.

"Consciousness of guilt! Any person with eyes in his head could see what went on in this courtroom yesterday. That's ridiculous, Your Honor."

"Mr. Tuttle, you know the law as well as I do. Tell me why the state is not entitled to urge the traditional inference from the defendant's absence?"

"Because it makes no sense. Judge Klonsky, this case is going well from the defendant's perspective. Your Honor knows that. He has no reason to flee. None."

"Then why's he gone, Mr. Tuttle?"

Hobie gasps and blusters; he might as well be a landed fish. For the first time in the trial, Tommy appears to have outflanked him. After all of Hobie's tricks, it's hard not to relish his comeuppance. He tries again.

"Your Honor, with all respect, you have to think about the emotional aspects of this case. This is pretty hard on the defendant. His mother's gone. And then he had to confront yesterday. That had to be a terrible moment. He had an emotional reaction. But that's not a guilty reaction. His reaction, I guess, it would appear, was 'I can't stand this, I can't handle this.' Your Honor, how hard is it for you, for any of us, to understand his feeling that way?" Very eloquent—and very much what my reflections in chambers led me to suspect. Hobie wouldn't have sent Nile away without cooking up a compelling explanation, one that would make me willing to recall the bond forfeiture warrant when Nile appears an hour or so after the case has come to a close. I tell Hobie he can argue that at the end of the case.

"Judge," says Tommy, "let me suggest that the defendant didn't like watching his father take the blame for a crime he knew he committed himself. I think that makes a lot more sense than what Tuttle's saying."

"Mr. Tuttle, why isn't the prosecution entitled to make that point? Tell me why not." I motion toward Tommy. Hobie again looks around the courtroom for help.

"Your Honor, you can't," he finally says. "You just can't do this."

"Mr. Tuttle, in my first years out of law school, I was law clerk to Justice Ringler, and one of the things he taught me, which I have never forgotten, is that the three most dangerous words in the English language are 'Judge, you can't.' I can and I will."

"Judge Klonsky. Please!"

"Mr. Tuttle, I'll give you until tomorrow morning to find your client. If he doesn't appear, we're going to proceed. And at that point, I'm going to allow the People to reopen. I will take notice that the defendant is absent, and I will allow the parties to argue the inferences that flow from that non-appearance, including availing the state of the traditional presumption that flight implies a consciousness of guilt. That's my ruling." I drop my head decisively. No more bullshit. No more playing chicken.

Furious with me, Hobie stands before the bench, rowdily tossing his head. "Your Honor, if you allow them to reopen—"

"Mr. Tuttle, there is no 'if.' I've ruled."

"Judge, I'm going to have no choice but to move for a mistrial."

It's as if the world has divided, right in front of me. What did Seth say about Hobie? He can't get over himself? Intent on having his way, he seems not to have noticed how angry I am. And of course he'd never sense how welcome the opportunity is which he's presented. Without a mistrial motion by the defendant, double jeopardy requires the trial to proceed to conclusion. But Hobie is claiming that by allowing the state to make hay from Nile's absence, I've so prejudiced the defense that he'd rather call the trial a washout and start over from scratch whenever Nile turns up. I can feel the courtroom trained on me, aware I've grown unusually still.

"Your motion is allowed, Mr. Tuttle."

Utter stillness. Across the entire floor, in all eight courtrooms, it seems to be one of those breathless moments in which no one even moves. Hobie stares up at me, searching for a clue as to what he must do now.

"Judge, I'll withdraw my motion."

"I just granted it."

"Your Honor, I said—I said I was going to make the motion. It was what I was contemplating for tomorrow morning. I didn't make the motion."

"Your motion is deemed made and granted."

"Then I move you to reconsider. I move you reconsider and take a day to think about it. I offended Your Honor. I can see that. I apologize. Humbly. Humbly, Judge Klonsky. But please reconsider."

And so I reconsider—but only momentarily. In some part of me, I will always be sitting up here in judgment of myself, speaking out for my beliefs, fearing my own weaknesses, struggling with my past. Objectivity is, at best, a matter of degree. But after all the strange outside forces that have buffeted me—after Brendan Tuohey and Seth, after Hobie himself and his antics with Dubinsky—I'm no longer in the comfort zone that passes for impartiality. Probably, I should have known to start I'd end up here. I would go on if I had to. But I won't—I *can't*— let this opportunity pass. It's the saddest thing in life to make the same mistake twice.

"Mr. Tuttle, this case is over. And because I have presided as the finder of fact, it would be inappropriate for me to hear the case again. I'm going to send it back to Chief Judge Tuohey for reassignment. That will be the order of the court."

"Your Honor," says Hobie, in final desperation, "please, don't be like this."

I don't bother with a response. Molto looks dazed. As I stand, he finally wakes and comes to the podium to make a motion.

"People move to forfeit bond."

Sallow little man, always lit by the eternal candle of one unending hatred or another. He is asking for Loyell Eddgar's house.

I retreat to chambers. For an hour the phone rings constantly, distracting me from the silence of my two court officers, who both clearly believe I lost my temper or my mind. Marietta handles each of the calls the same way. "Judge don't give interviews." She bangs the phone down. Any moment now Brendan Tuohey will be on the line. But as I busy myself I am jubilant. Free! Not of responsibility, but what greater gratitude can there be than to have been accidentally saved from our errors?

Near four, I decide to call it a day. In the spirit of the season, the court deputies have hung a wreath over each of the metal detectors. As I am passing on the outer side, I catch sight of the haggard figure of Tommy Molto, also heading out. We arrive at the single exit at virtually the same moment.

He apologizes for the bond motion. I did not even rule, only glowered before stalking off the bench.

"I didn't mean to put you on the spot," he says.

"We were all in quite a state."

"So what do you figure, Judge? Think Tuttle sent him to the woods so he'd have a reason not to put him on? That's one of the guesses downstairs."

Proprieties, judiciousness survive the case. I reply with an inscrutable fanning of my fingers, as if such a thought had never crossed my mind.

"Rudy thinks he did himself."

"Really?" This alarms me. "Any reason?"

"He's a screwy kid. Hell, 'kid,' " Tommy snorts. "Past thirty. He'll turn up. That's my bet."

"We'll see, Tommy. It's a strange development."

"I'll say."

"You did a good job with what you had." I tell him his direct of Eddgar was classic. With the compliment, he lights up like a little boy. Poor Molto. So seldom praised. "The case was well tried on both sides. I'd tell Hobie that, too, but I don't expect he'll ever speak to me again." Tommy looks off, rather than show much.

"He got *under* my skin," he says and shakes his tight, tired face about. When he looks back, he's gripped by a different thought. "Why'd you do it, Judge?"

"The mistrial? It was the right thing," I say. "Given all the circumstances."

"Sort of made my day." He laughs at his willingness to settle for a tie. "I thought I was going to win this case when we started."

"Maybe next time."

He laughs at that thought, too, the same self-deprecating little huffing sound.

"It won't be me. They can play monkey in the middle with somebody else," he says and again considers the distance. After a second, he says, "Probably not anybody. Can't put Hardcore on again. Or the father. Not that I believe all of Tuttle's stuff. I don't. I think the kid is wrong, Judge."

"You didn't prove it, Tommy." We've arrived at the moment of candor we both wanted. He hitches a shoulder.

"I got out with my boots on. I appreciate that."

I've been so focused on my own fortunes, I haven't considered anybody else's. They're all winners: the PA's office, even Nile, who apparently will not be retried. Maybe Hobie, too. A fear strikes me: Brendan Tuohey may like this, may compliment my diplomatic style. Then, of course, there's Eddgar. He's still as ruined as he was at the start of the day.

"I'm glad for your sake, Tommy. It's nice somebody's a hero."

Tommy in an ironical, reflective mood just shakes his head. It's a bitter thing for him, I guess, this system. I understand. Practicing, I had days when it did not seem there were rules at all, just random results and rationales composed after the fact.

"Hero," he says. "You know what I am? I'm the chump. I'm the poor so-and-so who just does his job, who goes down to the factory every day and busts his butt and then comes home and gets sassed by the kids and nagged by the wife. I'm just doing my job. That's all I've ever done. 'Try this case, Tommy.' Okay, I'll try it. I read the reports, I talk to the witnesses. I come up to court. What they're doing or thinking downstairs, I don't begin to fathom. I never was a politician. That's my problem. I don't think their way. These guys have got wheels inside of wheels. You know, they're sitting in the back room with the PA, having skull sessions, drinking single-malt Scotch after hours and getting excited trying to figure what everybody else is really up to, and how much of what people say they ought to believe. I don't know. I don't know about that stuff. I'm just up there trying the case. They think I don't know I'm the burnt offering. They sent me up there to lose that case. I know that. I've known it all along. But I was up there anyway. Trying to win." He gives me one further penetrating look—someone who knows he'll never be rescued from himself—and moves ahead of me, into the air growing brittle with the touch of winter.

Then I go on with my life. I bring Nikki home. Near six, the phone rings. Seth. He sounds as if he's in an airport or a train station. There is clatter thrown down from some huge space, drowning his voice.

"I'm not going to make it."

"Oh?" Don't think it, I tell myself. I want to reach inside my chest and grab my heart.

"I'm at the hospital." He takes a breath. Nile? That's my next thought. "My father had a stroke," he says.

"Oh God."

"Sarah was with him. They'd finished their stuff. She went to make him some soup for lunch and when she came in, he was on the floor. He was actually grey when we got him here."

"How is he?"

"Not good. He's not quite dead. The word I keep hearing is 'linger.' "

"Seth, I'm sorry."

Nikki, at the mention of his name, runs in from the den. "I want to talk." I spend a second shushing her, but Seth tells me to put her on and a minute passes with them gabbing about the teeth he sent her.

"The trial's over," I say, when she hands back the phone.

"I saw it on a TV in the ER."

The prerecorded, robotic voice of commerce interrupts, demanding more change. A coin rings through. Afterwards, there is no more about the trial from either of us. I realize there never will be. There's only one real question.

"Are we okay?" he asks.

"I think so."

" 'Cause, look, I'm a straight guy. It's a pretty short list, you know, what I can say for myself. But that's on there."

"I'm sorry, Seth. You caught me by surprise, but I know you didn't deserve that."

"I want you to trust me."

"I'm going to try, Seth."

"All right. Well. I have to get back to Sarah."

We both wait, trying to figure out if there is any more to say. But there isn't, not right now. We have time.

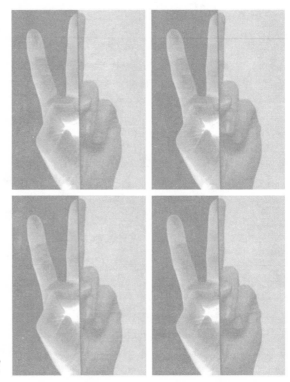

Part Three

JUDGMENT

*T*HE SIXTIES ARE OFTEN REGARDED AS A STORM that came and passed, a cyclone that blew through, its damage long repaired. But among the era's more enduring legacies was establishing a style of youth, of being young, that's been passed on for thirty years now by example in an endless chain of kids. Whether it's matters of speech—using the word "like" as an article, or the omnipresent "man"—or the torn jeans, the shoulder-length hair like Spanish moss, or the hazards of sex, drugs, and rock'n'roll, we developed rites of passage of a surprisingly enduring nature. Listening to my daughter, I often feel a little like the American natives who puzzled as Columbus told them he'd discovered a New World.

Which only goes to augment the fundamental Boomer dilemma. Unable to reform the world, many of us decided to have families in hopes of creating a more perfect order at home. We didn't want children so much as allies. Thus, the sixties became the nineties tied together by the motif of child worship. And as a result there can be no generation more thoroughly unprepared for the inevitable discovery that we've become our parents.

— MICHAEL FRAIN
"The Survivor's Guide,"
May 16, 1990

April 1, 1996

SONNY

On a spring morning, so fragrant and perfect that winter, ferociously present only a few days ago, seems a stark impossibility, Bernhard Weissman is laid to rest. Gathered for the graveside service is a small party, no more than thirty or thirty-five persons, on the rows of folding chairs placed over the soft lawn. Mr. Weissman had no siblings or cousins, none that survived, and he has outlasted his contemporaries. He was like Ishmael. But the people whom Sonny knows Seth and Sarah want are here. Lucy has flown in from Seattle; Hobie from D.C. Lucy and Sarah both stayed at the old man's house last night, preparing for the visitation, the *shiva*, which will take place there after the ceremony. Seth was with them past midnight, cleaning, pushing around the furniture, looking through his father's papers, remembering if not reminiscing. This morning, so that the three of them had a final, private moment at the funeral parlor, Sonny took over, stopping at Mr. Weissman's to plug in the coffee urns and receive delivery of some trays. Then she raced through traffic to the service, only to find it had commenced seconds before, without her.

The casket, a plain pine box with a Jewish star—'the economy model,' Seth called it, sure this much would meet his father's eternal approval—stands on a steel contraption over the bleak opening in the earth. On either side, the grass has been peeled back and the mounded soil heaped over the small granite stone that carries Dena Weissman's name. A few clods have tumbled down and touch the shoes of the front-row mourners, Seth and Hobie sitting stiffly, Sarah weeping with her mother's narrow arm about her. From the distance, Lucy appears as Seth has described her, still very much the figure of a girl, small and slender in a black sheath and flat shoes. Her tiny, freckled face, observed at various angles, is chafed at the nose and puffy with tears.

Officiating at the graveside ceremony is Rabbi Herschel Yenker of Temple Beth Shalom, who Seth says presided at his bar mitzvah. Seth portrayed him as a cranky, fulsome character, but Sonny finds the rabbi's round tones and eyes-clenched transport in prayer to be somewhat soothing. Eulogies are offered by Seth and Hobie. Each talk is heartrending, forthrightly emotional and honest to the core. Neither man pretends the old man was sweet or kindly. He was fierce, brilliant, immeasurably and inarticulately anguished by the evil he had survived and the incomprehensible conspiracy of forces which had allowed that to occur. More clearly than ever, some sense of the way torment has traveled between generations invades Sonny, and throughout the eulogies, she, like a number of those present, finds herself in tears. She thinks alternately of her mother, and also of Seth, a good person, she feels, truly a good man, yet, for all his privileges and success, tortured at moments. As the ceremony ends, he makes his way to her, palpably uncomfortable in his dress-up clothes—his blue suit and his white shirt, his tie a bit too narrow for current fashion. The new beard he's grown, which adds an element of conviction to his appearance, has filled in everywhere now but the hollows of his cheeks. He holds Sonny at length.

"What I'm trying to figure out," he whispers, "is if I'm free now, or damned forever." Some of both, that's what she knows, but he'll find out on his own. He moves off then to the funeral home limo that will take Sarah and Lucy and him to his parents'. At the curb, Lucy, still weeping fiercely, is hugging Hobie's parents, whom she's known forever. Seth takes his wife's elbow to help her into the car.

Sonny has yet to speak a word to Lucy and isn't looking forward to it either. No matter how sage or life-rumpled they pretend to be, it will be awkward. She doesn't know exactly what Seth has said to his wife about their relationship. 'Seeing each other,' probably, that wonderfully vague nineties locution. Of course, she doesn't know precisely what she'd say herself. Often, at the smallest moments, Sonny feels as if Seth and she sprang from the same soil. The twenty-five years—an entire adult life in which they did not really exist to one another—occasionally seem to have inexplicably steered both of them into the same estuaries of habit. They each subscribe to *The Nation* and *Scientific American*, both crave strawberry frozen yogurt and pad thai. Often some forgotten fashion or event of the bygone decades comes up—the Chrysler bailout, pet rocks, Wilbur Mills, quarry tile on kitchen floors—and they will respond with identical remarks. 'Exactly,' they are always saying to each other.

Yet overall, there's a distance to travel. 'Guarded' is the word she'd use in assessing the present temper of their relationship, certainly on her side. She's heard that about the second time around. Either you make the same mistakes all over again or at every moment labor not to repeat them. Last month, Seth did a column on two tightrope walkers. They made it sound like Zen: You keep your eyes forward. You believe the rope will be where you place your foot. That's their life together at the moment. Counting the trial, Seth has remained in Kindle County for more than sixteen weeks, but his father's condition, which seesawed dramatically for four months, has allowed both of them to avoid any clear declarations. He sleeps at Sonny's usually, and made a point of being there last night, but his clothing's at the Gresham, where he goes each day to write his column. The paper pays for the room anyway, he says. Yet she suspects he'd move in lock, stock, and barrel if she suggested it, which she won't until she's really sure he'd stay, and that she wants him to.

Shining black, the mortuary's stretch Cadillac lumbers off, trailing exhaust. Sonny's heels stick in the soft lawn, as she makes her way to the minivan, alone. Outside the old man's house, at the top of the concrete stoop, Sonny finds a pitcher and bowl placed on an old-fashioned TV table with foldaway aluminum legs. "To wash away the soil of the graveyard," Stew Dubinsky explains, as he comes wheezing up the stairs. His belly, the size of a large globe, parts both his suit jacket and his overcoat.

Inside, taking her wrap to Seth's old bedroom, Sonny spies Sarah. She's in her grandfather's study, where old Mr. Weissman privately surveyed his account statements and brokerage confirmations, locking the door, even when he was alone. Sonny, who has not had a moment with Sarah yet today, enters. Turning from her grandfather's desk, Sarah throws her arms wide to Sonny, her face again a mask of grief. She is a terrific girl, possessed of all the gifts, sincere, sober, if sometimes frenetic with her many commitments, everything from varsity volleyball to teaching English to Russian immigrants. Often, when she has shown up at Sonny's on Saturdays after visiting her grandfather, she confesses she hasn't slept. In private, Sonny wonders if Sarah somehow feels obliged to accomplish everything two children might.

On the desk, where Sarah was occupied, a toy of some kind stands, not fully constructed. A castle?

"It's a three-dimensional puzzle." Sarah displays the box cover. "We worked on it last night. My folks and I? Whenever we're together the Weissmans do puzzles," Sarah offers with a somewhat helpless smile. "Isaac was awesome." She turns and fits a piece into a jigsawed opening along the parapet. The image of the three of them—Lucy, Sarah, Seth—working here at the rolltop comes to Sonny clearly. The metal desk lamp, with its old-fashioned beetle-shell head and flexible coiled arm, was burning. They seldom spoke. But each of them knew what they were doing and did not care—they needed the union, the memory, the way Isaac lives when they are together. Sarah offers a handful of the foam-plastic puzzle pieces to Sonny, but she has a strong reaction. She could no more touch them than the dead boy's bones.

In the kitchen now, Lucy has taken charge, giving directions to Seth and Hobie and Dubinsky, who've all removed their jackets, rolled their sleeves. She addresses Seth as "Michael," a habit born in their paranoid, terrified dodger days in the early 1970s, when Seth's freedom depended on making no slips. Seth married with that name; Sarah's birth certificate still reads "Sarah Frain." The practice seems a little precious now, a boast about the excitement of the past, and yet Sonny has heard herself occasionally calling Seth 'baby.' What's in a name? That old question. She will have to be sure to call him Seth today.

Sonny asks for an assignment, and Lucy, busy at the sink, says it's all done. She turns only as an afterthought and, when she sees it's Sonny, cries out, "Oh!" and instantly rises to her toes to embrace her, tugging at Sonny's neck and saying how wonderful she looks. Lucy smells of various herbal scents and feels much stronger than Sonny imagined, given either her size or Sonny's memories of her as a girl.

The house fills. Several neighbors filter in, a few elderly friends of Seth's mom. Lucy's brothers and their families arrive. Sarah's boyfriend has led a group up from their residential house at Easton. Alert young people, they stand about together, the girls noticeably better dressed than the boys, all somewhat at a loss for the proper gestures. Sonny spends time with Hobie's parents. They are spectacular—warm and funny, wise with age, one of those perfect couples everyone dreams of being a part of. Now well into their seventies, they are each overweight and arthritic, but still sharp. They tease one another constantly. Then Solomon Auguro and Marta Stern, who have both taken to Seth, come in, and Sonny passes time with them. Across the room, Sonny catches sight of Jackson Aires. What's *he* doing here? She never gets the chance to ask, because the publisher of the *Tribune*, Mas Fortunato, arrives, joining Dubinsky and a group of his executives, who've been here for a while. They've been courting Seth for weeks, hoping he'll make the *Tribune* his home paper, now that his contract in Seattle with the *Post-Intelligencer* is about to expire. In the last two weeks, Seth has had interminable phone conversations with his lawyer in Seattle, Mike Moritz, every night.

Across the living room, Sarah, who's been summoned to receive Fortunato's condolences, casts Sonny a desperate look and Sonny begins searching around the house for Seth. Through the dining room's bay window, she finally spots him, touring the perimeter of the small back yard with Lucy on his arm. Seth and his wife arrive at the far corner where his father's narrow barnwood shed stands. From somewhere, Seth produces a key and for a moment the two slip inside. In the fissures between the planks, Sonny can detect motion, like figures glimpsed through the trees. She has the wildest association. Long ago, one Sunday afternoon in California, when they'd gone apricot picking, Seth wanted to screw in the woods. From the grove a hundred yards away Hobie, stoned as always, singing 'Sunny Afternoon' at top volume along with a phonograph booming from a window, suddenly spotted them, naked as creation. He cried out, 'Nymph! Satyr!' Grabbing her clothes off the twigs and leaves, she ran away, shamed and angry. She wonders if it would work to cry out the same thing now. Instead, when Seth emerges from the shed, he's wearing a plastic watering can on his head and Lucy's laughing. For her amusement, Seth tries it on again with the spout over the other ear. He has almost none of that frivolity with Sonny.

It's there all the time with Nikki, but she wouldn't have even known he could share it with a grown-up, let alone another woman.

"How you doin?" She marks the voice behind her as welcome before she turns. It's Hobie.

"I've had better moments. We all have." His tie is dragged down and he looks even bigger without his jacket, the white shirt stretched across his upper body reminiscent of the skin over a large drum. She can smell his cologne, the same scent that traveled with him when he came to the sidebar during the trial. "Are we on speaking terms?"

"Hell, yeah. I'm off duty. You do your job, I do mine, that's how I look at it."

"Me, too."

"Mind," he says, in the same intonation she heard half an hour ago from his father, "I didn't say I don't care. I do. Or that I agree. I don't."

"I heard what you said. I can pick on you, too, you know. I had my reasons and I'm not apologizing." Sonny has spent little time reflecting on the trial. The principal sensation in memory is one of grateful escape. Nile Eddgar by now is one of the thousands of younger people who pass before her, headed for moral oblivion. There is no figuring, anyway, what really happened. Everybody was lying. She knows that much. Once that starts, you can never tell. For her, the trial is one more conquered portion of the past. In some ways, she feels it was only a prelude to other things: to something firmer in herself, to this time with Seth, and also, of course, to the cautionary tale he finally related to her so abjectly about the crazy events of twenty-five years ago—the 'kidnapping,' Cleveland's death, Michael Frain's disappearance. He says he's tried at times to write it all down for Sarah, as if that might abate his anger at himself and Eddgar, both of which somehow remain alive to him, despite the years.

She glances back to be certain Hobie has been subdued, then tells him how touched she was by his eulogy. His large shoulders move.

"I talk," he says.

"It was more than talk."

"I suppose. You know, I always figure if my momma was just your average black Baptist lady, I'd a been a preacher, maybe better off than I am with law. Being Catholic, however, I found clerical life lacked a certain fundamental appeal." He clears his throat and they laugh together. Sonny has no religion. It was another of Zora's subjects. 'The great swindle,' she called it. 'Human beings on bended knee before pieces of wood. Using their last potato to hold the candles, even as they starved.' The Inquisition, the Crusades, war upon war. More evil, Zora maintained, had been done in the name of religion than any other force in human history. But today, in that gathering at the cemetery, standing, sitting, listening as many chanted with the rabbi in that ancient tongue, a language which to Sonny has always sounded like the voice of mystery itself, she had some sense of the majesty of spirit which the ritual is meant to inspire. Not that she could ever yield to it. In her own terms, she can think only of woodland moments, mountain views. But she would like to leave this door open for Nikki. Until the old man's death threw things into commotion, Sonny had been talking with Sarah about holding a seder at Sonny's house this week. She wanted Nikki to be exposed to a religious ceremony of some kind, and Passover, the festival of liberation, is the sole Jewish observance Seth seems to enjoy.

Meanwhile, Hobie emits a ruminative sound. He's finally caught sight of what attracted her outside.

"So what do you think, Hobie?"

"I don't think he stands much chance in the Easter Parade."

"And what about me?" she asks with sudden daring, "what kind of chance do I stand?" She's a bit shocked by herself, not by the pained tone, which is genuine, but because she knows there's an element of folly. Seth would ask exactly the same question about her: What chance do I have? Then, too, this could be taken as prying. Seth and Hobie are on the phone every week or so, having those weird guy-talks, half an hour on basketball, and then out of the blue, almost as if they hope neither notices, the most heartfelt intimacies. But Hobie turns from the window, looking as puzzled as she is. Large and solemn, he places one hand on her shoulder.

"Only thing I know," he says, "is there ain't a tougher guess in life than love."

SETH

"Eddgar's got brass clackers, but I don't see even him pulling this off." Coming down the hall, Seth recognizes Dubinsky's penetrating nasal tone. "Turn a fucking street gang into a political organization?" Stew asks. "That shit went out with Hobsbawm." Seth has just spent a minute with Sarah in his father's study. She was suffering intensely, revisiting all the losses of the recent years. His daughter is learning the hard lessons of a giving nature, that great passion means great pain. Entering the light and noise of the gathering, Seth is amazed to see that Stew's addressing Jackson Aires.

"My condolences, my condolences," says Jackson and falls forward for Seth's hand. "It didn't even *strike* me Bernhard was your father. You see how doggone funny these things are?" It turns out Hobie's father had introduced Aires and Mr. Weissman long ago. Jackson received investment advice from Bernhard for decades and speaks warmly of him, which, Seth supposes, means Jackson made money. The last time Aires and Seth met, they were in their own professional modes, during Nile's trial. Introducing himself as Michael Frain, Seth had proposed an interview with Hardcore. Aires had stared with unapologetic hostility and walked away.

"I told you I remembered you," Seth says. "You lived on the other side of U. Park."

"I lived on the black folks' side," Aires replies, a piece of revisionism that neither of them fully believes. In the 1950s, the Negro professionals in U. Park simply thought they'd finally crossed the river to the real America. "You were always in Gurney's kitchen. That's what I remember. I remember you fine." Limber in spite of his age, Aires, with his snowball pomp, draws back, the better to eye Seth and to reflect on whether he's gained any advantage with this display of potent memory. He wears his burgundy sport coat, shiny at the shoulders, and an old paisley tie. "See, what got me confused's the name, you know. You weren't Michael Frain when I knew you. Can't have been too happy to be your daddy's son. Not if you lived your life with someone else's name. Guess you just got sick and tired of bein Jewish, huh?"

Startled, Seth actually laughs out loud. In all these years, no one has ever suggested that motive before. He is tempted, in his present melancholy, to surrender to a mood of self-accusation, but he finally screws up his face to disagree. Aires goes on, though, certain he's right.

"I've known a couple Jewish fellas over the years who done that. One bird I went to law school with—what was this rascal's name? Abel Epstein. He became Archibald van Epps. Can you imagine? Envied him, too, I must say. Now and then. Don't you look at me like that. Hell yes, I'd change my name and be done with it. You damn right, I would, I'm not afraid to say it. Only thing is, black man can't do it. You see? Whether I call myself Tyrone or Malcolm X or Steppin Fetchit, still some white fella gonna see me comin three blocks away, half of them afraid I'm what I am and the other half afraid I'm one of them hoodlums I represent. Ain't gonna change for centuries. Centuries." There really is no arguing with him, Seth knows. Jackson's been thinking about this one subject, race, his entire life.

It's Dubinsky who rescues Seth. Always on the beat, Stew wants to talk about the trial, hoping to catch Aires in an unguarded moment. It wouldn't occur to Stew this is out of place. Ordinary lives, even in their tragic instants, are second-tier events to him, inherently less worthy than the news.

"It doesn't make sense *politically*," he tells Aires, returning to their quarrel about Eddgar. "Is the Governor gonna release Kan-el from the pokey one morning and meet him for breakfast the next? It's not possible. It never was."

"Can't say about that. You see. All you journal-ists"—Jackson gives the word a derisive turn—"you-all are just professional Monday-morning quarterbacks." In his humorless, confrontational mode, Jackson rises to the balls of his feet, looming over Dubinsky. With its abrupt and unsatisfactory ending, the trial remains the subject of gossip. Everyone has theories—about where Nile went and whether he is alive or dead and who might have killed him, about Eddgar's role in the crime and his future in politics. One piece—Dubinsky's, Seth thinks—said Eddgar would not run again. Oddly, however, what Seth hears about the case, he overhears almost as background noise, much like this conversation he's happened upon. No one speaks to him directly. Sonny, Hobie, Dubinsky—they all have secrets, ruminations they won't disclose. On his own, he has occasional fantasies of encountering Eddgar on the streets of DuSable. Perhaps they'll stare each other down, or Seth will resort to violence, or they'll have a terse but complete exchange in which they finally finish their business after all these years. He thinks less elaborately about Nile, but wonders often if he's safe.

"So you think Eddgar was on the level?" Dubinsky asks. "See, to me, this whole case, something's wrong. My editor's like, Give it a rest, but you know, there's just that basic Kindle County aroma here."

Dubinsky, Seth thinks. He lays down the best dish in this burg. You read it, you think, Holy smokes, maybe it really *is* like that. But it isn't. Seth would love to live in Stew Dubinsky's world, believing all evil is the result of bad old men hatching plans in back rooms and corner taverns. It would be wonderful if people were actually that powerful, if chaos was not the predominant force in the universe. But Seth's learned otherwise. You stop on a street corner and thirty seconds later the little boy beside you is dead. Listening to Stew now, Jackson Aires chortles in audible disbelief.

"No?" asks Stew. "So then how was it?" He takes a step closer. But Jackson has played dice on too many corners; he's been hustled by better than Dubinsky. He simply shakes his head.

"I tell you how it was. Same as it always is. My client's in the penitentiary servin twenty years for murder and the white fella's runnin round loose. That's how it is." Jackson again briefly flexes upward to his toes and then, to dispel any doubt about the injustice of all this, adds, "If that boy wudn't guilty, you gonna have to tell me why he run."

With that, Jackson breaks off and Seth goes too. He briefly joins Sonny with her friends, Solomon and Marta. Marta is enormous with child and radiant about it. Even in the spring, the heat of a crowded room is too much for her. When she embraces Seth her cheek is damp. Seth receives their condolences, then moves around the living room thanking others. Dick Burr, one of the honchos from the *Tribune*, is here, a decent guy, out to woo Seth, but earnest in his consolations. Burr says Dubinsky gave him copies of their eulogies, which they're going to have typeset for Seth at the paper. Together, Burr and his assistant, Fortune Reil, have been speaking with Lucy's older brothers, Douglass—known as Deek—a banker, and Gifford, a manager of pension funds. Both live in Greenwood County and are members of an endangered life-form—the high-born WASP. Seth is enormously fond of each. They have shown unflagging loyalty and good humor through the years, in the face of Seth's columns about their lime-green slacks, their boats and exclusive clubs, and their slavish, sensual attraction to alcohol, which each man experiences as the 'open sesame' to the universe of emotion.

As Hobie's parents make ready to depart, Seth crosses the room to embrace them again, then stands outside on the stoop seeing them off. Afterwards, he faces his father's small brick house alone. What a strange business this is, he thinks, inheritance, owning the walls you once wanted to escape. He looks through the poor glass of the storm door to the tiny entry. The dim, fusty halls, which his father, in his penny-pinching foolishness, did not repaint in forty years, have now acquired a museum quality, as if some special meaning arises from the simple fact they were preserved.

He comes down the stairs, feeling a sudden urge to make a proprietary survey. Daffodils are sprouting in the weedy bed on the south side, next to the tiny cellar windows, which in childhood reminded him of his own mouth, with its gapped teeth. It is that magic time in the Middle West. In the distance, the trees are stark and bare, but up close one sees the branches heavy with sensuous buds. A day or two of warmth and the green explosion will occur, the air will be sweet with chlorophyll.

Across the small back yard, he spies Lucy. Her straight skirt has been hiked fetchingly to allow her to take a seat on the worn steps of the grey wooden porch behind the house. Her eyes are closed and her face raised adoringly to the sky. She looks like a young girl waiting to be kissed.

"A Seattleite struck dumb by the sight of sun," Seth remarks.

Waking to him, she smiles wordlessly and lifts her far hand to reveal a cigarette. After Isaac, she lapsed, secretly. He didn't suspect until she started wheezing after their evening runs. Embarrassed to be caught now, she crushes the butt carefully under heel and, as Lucy would, folds it into her palm for later disposal. Seth takes the step below her. They marvel momentarily about the day, the promise of blue skies.

"I never said how wonderful your talk was, Seth. Your eulogy."

"Yeah." Words. The fundamental medium of human exchange. They're great. And then what? "I worried about Sarah. I was afraid she'd think I was profaning the sacred."

"Sarah understands."

"As much as I do."

"Are you really all right with her plans?" Lucy asks. "I wouldn't be shocked if she stays with this." Last night, Sarah, who has talked of grad school, even the rabbinate, told them that she and her boyfriend, Phil, have enrolled in an Americorps program to train teachers for inner-city schools. They expect to stay here or somewhere else in the Middle West.

"Great by me. I'm proud of her. That she's that kind of person. I never expected her to become a columnist."

"You seemed to like the idea of her as a professor."

"I've always loved intellectuals. They seem so distant and admirable to me." He thinks fleetingly of Sonny twenty-five years ago, his thrall with all that philosophy he couldn't really comprehend.

"Your father was a professor," Lucy says.

This is Lucy, always on the nerve. How did he ever miss that? How? He stands to continue his inspection of the back yard. He offers Lucy his arm and she takes it, accompanying Seth as he ambles. This is always there: they like each other so much. Even as their life together has seemed in the last two years unfathomable, impossible, she remains the nicest human being he knows.

In her mothering years, he lived in undying amazement of Lucy. She looked at every paper, bored in until she'd heard every question the teacher asked at school. She knew by heart what was on the lunch menu, the name of every friend and whether she or he was a good influence, even if the kid had never set foot inside their home. She'd memorized every trumpet note or ballet turn. She hit the laundry room at 6 a.m., because she knew what clothes they'd want to wear, right down to the undies. Her children's lives were so thoroughly understood, digested, *imagined*, so thoroughly her own, that other women often seemed to freeze over in shame.

But all of that allowed Lucy to avoid wondering about herself. Coming here, seeing Sonny up there on the bench, so positive about what's right, sure about the fate of others, he realized again that was one of the things he wanted, someone whose desires were less frightening to her than they are to Lucy, who is always somewhat oppressed by her need to please, and even past the age of forty can look primitively pained by the question What do you want? Isaac's death somehow fit in with that and drove him often to the point of rage. Didn't she know there was no accepting this, that it was not part of some universal harmonic? It made him crazy, crazy because he was not enough, not big enough, positive enough, to give her what she required. He has often predicted to himself, in solitary moments when he thinks he's given up, that Lucy's next husband will be an oracle of some kind—a clergyman, a visionary. It was no accident she started out hooked up with the likes of Hobie.

"Are you holding up?" he asks her, as they turn the outer boundary of the small yard. An old hedge here is gnarled at its joints with an arthritic thickness that brings to mind his father at the end.

"I guess. I still find death amazing, don't you? It seems so contrary to all of my assumptions."

He smiles toughly. For him, it's always present now. You build a foothold in the world in the first half of life, and then watch it slip away. But he didn't mean to exchange philosophies. He was daring to ask about her life at present. Shortly after he left, Lucy took up with a twenty-six-year-old, the associate director of the soup kitchen. But that fizzled. People—other women, especially—were unbearably cruel. One neighbor asked Lucy if she was going to give Moe a graduation party when he finished school. She's lonely now, Sarah says. To that observation Seth made no reply, even though he'll always feel the impulse to tell Sarah everything will be all right. He really didn't want his kids growing up in one of those screwed-up American *fin de siècle* families, where Dad's married to his former secretary, a great gal for a transsexual, and Mom is taking dope and sleeping with the bishop on the sly, and Brother gets off handling snakes and robbing convenience stores, and everybody joins hands at Thanksgiving and says, Thank God we have our family. He wanted his daughter and his son to know there was a true center, that some things are enduring, and healing. And then Isaac died.

As they walk, as Seth thinks about these things, his mind turns to the piece he'll write tomorrow. His work is always with him, a part of him forever lodged in that mainframe in Seattle where the man known in 167 daily papers as Michael Frain seems to exist. That Michael, in Seth's mind's eye, has a somewhat distinct physical appearance, shorter than Seth, fuller in body, perpetually young, with a wry, unflappable expression, probably the physical self he idealized when he was, say, a freshman in high school and still thought anything was possible for him.

The column he'll take up tomorrow is one of half a dozen he dredged from his months visiting his father in hospitals and rehab facilities. It's about marriage. The piece concerns a lean bald-headed man from Kewahnee who donated a kidney to his wife. Seth didn't know that was possible. He thought it was like bone-marrow transplants, where you faced problems unless you were born with a twin. This man, an engineer at Dunning, a defense outfit, is not particularly articulate, not the kind of fellow who can say much about motives. But this couple now lies together in the same room in Sinai-Cedars Hospital, getting different IVS drugs and the same painkillers, with matching fourteen-inch incisions on their left sides. It seems like an act from mythology, reaching inside yourself, an organ from him now an organ in her, an echo of Adam's aboriginal rib.

The magic of what Seth does is the interviews, asking people to account for things like that. He can be 1,500 miles away, no more than a voice on the phone, someone whom they know at best by reputation, and usually not at all, merely somebody trying to let his soul crawl down the line, saying 'I want to know you, would like to tell your story,' and folks, in their hunger to be understood, will say almost anything. In his hospital bed, his hand bruised by the IV's, this man took a sip of water first. 'Well,' he told Seth, in that slow Midwestern drawl, 'well, it didn't really occur to me there was anything else I'd like to do.' The line was a killer. Lucy and he once had that kind of autonomic commitment, and would still do anything for one another, he thinks, whether out of habit, or gratitude or admiration. But listening to that man he was suddenly unsure that what's growing up between Sonny and him will flower that fully. There's been peace, humor, sensitivity—and amazing sensuality. But he doubts Sonny, in the face of sacrifice, could ever really convince him there's nothing else she'd like to do.

At Seth's feet lies the little corner of the lawn his mother ripped away a generation ago to form a vegetable garden. She tilled this fifteen square feet of soil relentlessly and made it yield remarkable things: leaf lettuce first, then tomatoes, peas, pole beans. A huge zucchini somehow sprang up in the adjoining privet and was mistaken by the entire family, when they spotted it, for a raccoon. He can recall his father, terrified, edging up like a fencer with a rake extended. Seth remembers many Sundays out here, hoeing, weeding, being the man his mother needed, doing her gentle bidding while he tried to keep up with the Trappers game on his transistor. Lucy has wonderful vegetable gardens and he's always adored her for them.

His mother's gardening equipment was housed in the narrow barnwood shed his father positioned in the rear corner of this lot. Bernhard feared thieves, of course. A heavy rusted padlock hangs there. Seth would love to look inside. What has my father left me? he thinks again. He heaves on the old wooden door, then recalls the key, still hidden under the same piece of loose walk. The interior is dark, smelling of rotted wood, of rancid fertilizers and loam. The old tools lie in disarray, the metal parts rough with rust. The spiders have choked each other in bleak, silky competition.

"Jeez-o Pete," he says suddenly, "what a horrible day this is." Behind the open door, safe from the wind and prying eyes, actually alone with Lucy for the first instant in months, he wordlessly accepts her comfort. Here she is in the crook of his arm, this woman, this tiny female person whom he was with longer than he lived without her. Here she is.

SONNY

"You aren't leaving? I hoped we'd get a chance to talk," Lucy says as Sonny, carrying her purse, approaches the front door. It's a few minutes past 4:30 and most of the afternoon visitors have departed. Attempting to sound casual, Sonny explains she has to pick up Nikki from day care, a few minutes away, and expects to return with her. Unmentioned is the fact that Seth performs this task many afternoons now.

"I'd love to get away for a second," says Lucy. "How about I come along?" As Lucy rushes off for her coat, Sonny indulges in an instant of stark assessment. Lucy is one of those women born in the right age. In the era of Botticelli and Rubens her looks would have been disregarded. Yet at the end of the twentieth century her slender waifishness is right. She has intense black eyes, a tangle of dark hair, a narrow, fragile face. Her size and apparent vulnerability always made Sonny feel like half a cow, even a quarter of a century ago, and watching her slip around the house, she's been unable to contain her amazement that any woman after two children can actually have a waist that small. Seth's side-of-the-mouth descriptions of Lucy have tended to portray her youthfulness as a failing, a sign of continuing childishness, but avoided mentioning that she's retained a lot of sensual pizzazz. Dating a twenty-six-year-old no longer seems pathological. Lucy's one of those women whom men — on the sidewalk, across a revolving door — still turn to watch in that idiot way, as if there's actually some hope you might commit a carnal act right here on the street. Is Sonny envious? Only slightly. There are other aspects of youth — bending from the waist without back pain or the ability to remember seven-digit-number strings — she'd rather recover.

In the car, heading off, Lucy chatters. People remain so fundamentally themselves, so recognizable. Seth insists Lucy is brilliant, but hamstrung by self-doubt, something Sonny can hear in the urgent way she gushes about the fact that Sonny is a judge. How exciting! How difficult! Support and flattery, the rhetoric of women of our age, Sonny thinks, but she knows Lucy is sincere. She answers that her job is far less lofty than it sounds.

"But it's important in the lives of other people," Lucy answers. "And you did that. As a woman. I know what that means, how *hard* that was. When Michael told me you were a judge, I actually felt proud. Does that sound ridiculous? But I'm very proud of all of you, the women I knew who did all these things that their grandmothers or even their moms couldn't even dare to consider. When we started college, if you think about it, we were so vague. So many women were. I was. We didn't have any sense of what we could do. And what you did, you, all our women friends, they did for themselves. Together, I mean, hand in hand. I don't think Sarah can really understand the imagination that required."

The reaching trees rush by in reflection on the windshield. Sonny tips her head.

"I can't take credit," she says. "My mother gave me that."

"Really?"

"It was very unusual for the time, but a wonderful gift. I owe her so much for that." 'You are great,' Zora whispered. 'You are a treasure of the world.' Day in, day out, the message was repeated, with a passion that left no doubt it was true. At instants, that unrestrained praise of her abilities seemed more a burden than a benediction, but in the end, Sonny thinks, it's a lot to have, to reach back to.

They park at Drees, a small brick building, retooled three or four times for various municipal uses. Rush hour, sometimes madness on University Avenue, is light today and they are early. At Sonny's suggestion they walk down the block to a gourmet coffee shop, the Seattle franchise which has America mainlining caffeine. A native, Lucy knows all the code words. "Grande, macchiato, double shot." They sit on brushed-steel stools across a granite table. Shoppers, mostly female, pass on the street. A woman with a baguette from the French bakery across the way turns in the midst of conversation and nearly knocks Lucy from her seat. There is a brief scene, much laughter, and a flurry of apologies. When they are alone once more, Lucy hunches over her coffee cup and lets her tongue slide forth kittenishly to lick the foam.

"So, is it love?" she asks. Sonny, who had not contemplated such directness, feels her chest rock when she attempts to draw a breath.

"I know Seth's in love with my daughter. I'm not as sure about me."

"Oh, I think he's always been hung up on you. What's the term? With the torch? As a child it made me think of the Statue of Liberty. But it means love is never finished. Don't you think that's right? I think love is never finished."

Sonny sees how this will be, one of those oblique, neurotic dialogues, saying one thing and, in some lost recess, meaning something else. If love does not quit, where does that leave Lucy and Seth? Registering Sonny's discontent, Lucy apologizes. She didn't mean to pry, she says.

"It's hardly prying," Sonny says. "It's natural. You wonder about Seth and me, I wonder about you and Seth."

In response, Lucy stirs her coffee, her eyes nowhere in the room. "Life is messy," she says suddenly. "Isn't it? People have these messy little corners that you can't get to with one another." Is it Seth and her, she means? Or is she talking about the fact that even decades ago Sonny and she were not especially close?

"I don't need explanations," Sonny finally says, then, after an instant's reflection, murmurs Isaac's name. Lucy cannot contain a small, tense reflex.

"Naturally," Lucy says. "I mean, that's the biggest piece of it. Isaac. Michael won't give it up. Resolve. Let go. God, I don't know the word.

But he won't. The sadness won't leave him. And I empathize, I think I'm a sympathetic person—"

"Of course you are," offers Sonny, realizing it's foolish to reassure someone she hasn't seen for twenty-five years, but still certain she's right.

"But it's me, too. He was my child, too. I can't live with this silent accusation that I've forgotten Isaac and he hasn't, that he suffers and I don't. I can't *bear* that." She has started crying now. The liner goes at once, and settles on her cheek, a trail of greying sludge. Lucy stares at the traces on the paper napkin grabbed from the stainless dispenser and shakes her head. Why did she bother with makeup? she asks. She's been crying and redoing it all day.

Having touched this great pain so quickly leaves Sonny uneasy. It's like digging in a garden and inadvertently exposing the root of a plant, a white, awkward thing never meant for light. As she watches Lucy regather herself, the day presses in on her amid the hubbub of the store. The place is filling. Women and men, on the way home, with time to grant themselves a few minutes of relief, queue before the bright chrome-and-brass fittings at the counter. A few little ones grind against their mothers' thighs. The steam machines whir, spilling out sensational aromas, while the young clerks bustle about, enjoying the frenzy and performance of the rush hour. For a moment, it seems to Sonny that she can recover some recollected kinship to every person in this store: young and unknown to herself; at loose ends with spare moments; mom with babe in arms. She surmounted all that. Why can she see the arc backward so clearly, but nothing ahead?

"I mean, Isaac's not our whole thing," Lucy says. "We're like any other married couple. We've done some bad stuff to each other over the years."

"I was married," Sonny says.

"Right," says Lucy, and smiles quickly, tentatively, not certain it's polite to agree. "But for Michael, for me—you know, the issue is how much disappointment you can embrace before you say, 'I have to start again.' I mean," Lucy says, "it turns out there are some things you can't say. In a marriage? You can mess up a relationship in a sentence. You don't know it for sure until ten years later. But that's how it turns out." Lucy, whose dark eyes are flighty, seldom loitering, now land directly on Sonny. "He's never told you, has he?"

Trying to find the thread, Sonny does not answer. Lucy leans on the tiny hand she has brought to her forehead, the nails short but carefully trimmed in red.

"God, I need a cigarette," she declares. Lucy takes her paper cup and moves to a table in the corner. She has lit up, wreathed in smoke, by the time Sonny arrives. And her mother died of emphysema. Sonny recalls Seth's stories of this woman, with a ruined face like Lillian Hellman's, smoking behind the oxygen mask, and her family screaming, begging her to consider the fire hazard, if nothing else.

"This, you know, period, whatever you call it," Lucy says, "this is like our second Big Crisis. We had a first Big Crisis. About ten years ago. Did you know that?"

A little, Sonny says.

"Michael's mother was dying. And he was having a hard time with that. Alzheimer's. They just disappear right in front of you, it eats the soul before the body. And he was becoming very successful at the same time. And he was having a hard time with that, too, you know, people were different with him now that he wasn't just some weird guy ventilating a lot of crazed private thoughts. It was like the commercials that were on then about 'Everybody listens'? That was his life all of a sudden. The room would go silent. Everybody listened. And so he was pretty nuts with all of it, and he started sleeping with some girl around the paper. He was traveling with her and telling me nothing was going on. His assistant. But you could just about see sparks when they even said hello. And men never will get it, will they, that women *know*? And I put up with stuff, that's one of my problems, I always take way too much—but this? Finally, after a party, I threw a fit. I realized I was entitled. I was *so* hurt, savagely hurt. And he was kind of a skunk about it. He said all of the usual incredibly dumb things, but the one that got me was 'You don't understand this doesn't mean anything,' and I said, 'No, I do understand, and don't say it doesn't mean anything,' and, I don't know, I just said, I said, 'For Godsake, I was still sleeping with Hobie a year after we were married.' So I'd said it." She waits an instant, considering only the ember at the end of her cigarette.

"Even when that was going on," Lucy says, "I didn't understand much of it, but I told myself, 'If you do this, this is for yourself and only yourself and he can never know.' And he hadn't. They were two completely different spheres, like sleeping and waking, or stoned and straight, it seemed completely implausible they could even touch. But they did. They had.

"I mean, the whole thing was like ancient history. It had been over years and years before, Hobie and I had both seen it was crazy and absurd. And one of the problems—I mean, now I was a mom, we had a home; we had, you know, our customs, our things, furniture and breakfast cereal, and honestly, one huge problem was I couldn't even understand it any- more myself. I looked back and it seemed like being with the Moonies. I mean, how can I even explain what I used to think when I was twenty- one? We forget what we used to be like, what everything was like. It seems like there weren't the same *categories*, you know? I mean, everything wasn't in this sort of *place*. Who understands what an adult commitment is when you're twenty-one? I thought I could sleep with Hobie and be Mi- chael's wife. It sort of made sense, and then eventually it didn't. I mean, that's life, that's reality, I can't apologize for that.

"And you know, the shrinks, the counselors, they pointed out the right stuff, about how complicated it is between Michael and Hobie anyway, and why did Michael—Seth—why did he want to hook up with Hobie's girlfriend in the first place, and we all played a part. But it was still a major mess. Not that he ever wagged a finger, because he's done more than his share of shitty things and he knows it. But he couldn't even talk to Hobie for a couple of years. And I mean Hobie prostrated himself, he absolutely begged forgiveness, which I frankly didn't even think Hobie would know how to do. And you know, I forgave Michael and Michael forgave us. He's a forgiving person. Except for his father. I'd had trouble getting pregnant again, secondary infertility, and we did in vitro and we had Isaac. And we went on. But there's that term 'sadder but wiser'? That's a terrible phrase, don't you think? When you really hear the words? And he was sadder but wiser after that. And our marriage was sadder but wiser. And with Isaac suddenly, maybe it was too sad and too wise. And what's the way out, you know? Is there one?"

Lucy, boiling in shame, closes her eyes and crushes out her cigarette. The store is emptying out. As the customers pass through the doorway, a touch of cooler air, swifter movement, the simpler smells of sundown and spring cross the café. Through her bleared eyes, Lucy dares to look again at Sonny. She says, "So now you know."

SETH

The day, like some lingering sweet lament, lolls toward a close. Seth and Nikki sit on the grey stairs of the back porch, facing the failing stockade fence his father years ago erected along the property line of the tiny city lot. The birds twitter urgently, and a block or two away a power mower thrums, as some citizen tries to liberate the weekend with an hour's labor after work, rushing through the first cutting of the year. In magnificent hue, the sky loses light about them. Lucy and Sonny have gone together to pick up takeout for dinner. Inside, Sarah, who just led a *minyan* in reciting the mourners' prayer, is whiling with the last of her friends. Nikki watched in awe as Sarah chanted and now has asked Seth to hold a conversation in a foreign language, albeit one of her own invention. They have gone on quacking and gargling at each other for some time.

"You know what I was saying?" the little girl asks. She is in jeans and a pilled turtleneck adorned with corny, small flowers and two smears of fingerpaint. "I was saying, 'Yes, I want to go on a horse ride.'"

"Oh, I misunderstood. I thought you were saying, 'Thank you, Seth, for hanging out with me, you're such a swell fella.' I could swear that was what you meant."

"No-o-o!" she exclaims and in mock-reproof squeezes his cheeks, stopping to comb her fingers through his new beard, which all three of them—Seth, Sonny, and Nikki—privately refer to as 'Nikki's Whiskers.' Her laughter rollicks momentarily, then her dark eyes grow serious again, reverting to what was on her mind. "Why was she talking Spanish, anyway?"

"Spanish? Who?"

Nikki waves a tiny hand desperately toward the living room. She cannot recall Sarah's name or otherwise describe her. He has told her a thousand times Sarah is his daughter, but Nikki seems to find it impossible that a daughter is not someone her age.

"You mean when Sarah was praying?" he asks. "That was Hebrew. *Span*-ish," he mocks and grabs Nikki about the waist momentarily, jostling her in delight. She throws herself deep into his arms, and the compact feel of the little girl, with her mysteriously sweet aroma and innocent seductiveness, enters the core of him. Isaac was such a handful, so haunted and inconsolable, that Seth had half-forgotten the spectacular buoyant pleasures normally part of this age. Around Nikki he has often been called back with a throb to those times, when he was in his late twenties and Sarah was little. She'd been a surprise in every aspect, her conception first, and then, upon arrival, the way her needs dominated Lucy and him. Every meal, for instance, was a task. She was allergic to milk products and worse, for years, would only take her food disguised in baked beans. Each day was a thicket, planning for her, working, scheduling. Lucy was trying to finish college. He had been hired at a daily in Pawtucket, and one day one of his columns was picked up by a real syndicate, fifty papers, which kept asking for more. He'd write. Research. Do interviews. He'd keep endless notes on different ideas and work on them with no particular consistency, free-form, a renegade enemy of order in his writerly role. But with all the pulling and heaving, at home, in the office, he found suddenly there was no activity in the course of the day which did not feel imbued with deep purpose — Lucy, Sarah, what he wrote. And where it all was going, who knew, who knew, but he was laboring toward something, if only perhaps the creation of the self he was, after long wondering, seemingly meant to discover all along. Good years, he thinks now. Good times.

In this mood, he clings to Nikki. Her long dark hair, pigtailed today, spins around as he lolls her back and forth. He is always self-conscious about handling her. Welcome to our era. But a six-year-old needs to be hugged. When his children were little, he enjoyed, nothing more than lying down with them for a nap, clinging to their small hands, losing track in sleep of where exactly their bodies and his began and ended. He finally lets her go so he can explain what Sarah was doing.

"Sometimes people feel that they have to try to talk to God. That's praying. And Sarah was praying about her grandfather. Remember that real, real old man? I showed you his picture? I used to go visit him? We're remembering him."

"Did he get dead?" Seth knows Sonny has gone over this at length, but no doubt they'll be repeating it for days.

"He was more than ninety. He was almost ninety years older than you." He was the century, this benighted, amazing century, Seth thinks. He has not cried yet, but he's been on the verge once or twice, and with this new thought, he stifles a sob. It would upset Nikki. If she was his kid, it would be all right if he upset her. He would just cry. He'd be willing to say this is life, too. No truckling before the altar of tiny vulnerabilities. But she's not his.

"Is he in the ground already?"

He tells her what he can. That it's all right, the way it's supposed to be. Yet that is no comfort. Lurking here, Seth suspects, is the fact that neither Sonny nor he has ever told Nikki that Seth had a little boy, not much older than Nikki is now, who passed. Even if Nikki were only a third as bright as she is, only partially possessed of that remarkable insinuating intelligence in which she is forever assessing the adult world, she would sense, would know. Who after all does she think this person is to whom Sarah and he are always referring? If things go on, he thinks, they will have to deal with this forthrightly. He will not do what was done to him, create a home poisoned by a secret terror, never to be mentioned.

"So that's what Sarah was doing. She was praying. And when Jewish people pray, they talk in Hebrew. See? Sarah and I are Jewish people, so she talked in Hebrew."

"Am I a Jewish people?"

He ponders this. Her grandfather, Jack Klonsky, according to family legend, was Jewish. Among the Reform that might be sufficient.

"I don't think so, Nikki. Your mom isn't. Usually, people are what their moms are. Or their dads. And Charlie and your mom don't really like to go to church. Some people don't like to pray. I'm not crazy about it, to be honest."

"Jennifer 2 goes to CDC." In Nikki's kindergarten class, there are three Jennifers, all of whose last names start with G.

"Right. So she probably likes praying. And Sarah likes it."

"Well, how do I tell?"

"What?"

"If *I* like it. Duh," she adds, with noble six-year-old contempt.

"I'm sure your mom will help you. Maybe you can go with Jennifer 2 sometime. Or, you know, you could go with Sarah. Then you and Charlie and your mom can talk about it. Maybe you'll want to be Catholic like your Aunt Hen, or you could be Jewish like me. Probably you'll decide you want to be like Charlie and your mom. That's what most people do. But whatever it is, you don't have to worry about it now."

"I do."

"What?"

"Want to be a Jewish." She laps her hand over Seth's. And moves a trifle closer on the stair.

SONNY

"Well, we're all together again," says Hobie with an ironic glimmer, as he glances about the old mahogany dining table to Sonny and Nikki, Lucy, Seth and Sarah. The visitors have departed. A few may look in later, but given the spare connections in Mr. Weissman's life, the family decided to limit visitation to the afternoon and early evening. Lucy has a late plane to Seattle. On the table, the cartons of Chinese—the food of Jewish anguish, as Seth puts it, one of those jokes of his Sonny will never really get—leave the room savored of foreign spices and fried oil.

How can anybody be hungry again? she thinks. The Jews are like the Poles, chewing their way through any meaningful event. But the energy of high emotion and the drain of the crowd this afternoon seem to have had a ravening effect. They eat speedily, on paper plates. Large foaming bottles of soda pop, dimpled from being grasped, stand amid the cartons. Nikki picks at an egg roll, then draws her hands inside her sleeves and tours the table telling everyone a pair of chopsticks are her fingers.

Sonny sits beside Sarah, discussing Sarah's plans for next year. Teaching was Sonny's final career before she lit on the law, and she recounts some of her experiences. Everything was wonderful until she got to the classroom, where she was done in by thirty-eight third-graders, all of whom wore their deprivations as visibly as wounds. She laughs now at the memory of a girl of eight with a variety of behavioral disorders.

"I hated her, and not because she was out of control. But when she got upset she ate Crayolas. Bit them *and* swallowed. Supplies were always so short, and she ate *all* the good colors. At the end of the year, the only ones left were black and white."

Listening, Nikki is momentarily amused by the notion of eating crayons, but she soon turns whiny, pulling on Sonny's sleeve. "This is *boring*," she moans, a lament that has been steadier since she discovered the black-and-white TV in Mr. Weissman's study, which her mother will not let her turn on. In the living room, Sonny digs out the markers and books stowed in Nikki's backpack this morning. They read *The Pain and the Great One* together, then start a book of pencilpoint mazes, which Nikki churlishly insists she can do on her own. When Sonny returns to the table, Seth and Lucy are complimenting Sarah's friends — their kindness, their maturity.

"God, don't sound so amazed," says Sarah. "We're the same age the four of you were when you started hanging out together."

There is silence until Seth says, "Gulp," to considerable laughter.

"So is this what you guys used to do when you hung out together?" Sarah asks. "Eat Chinese and tell cool stories?"

"We'd get ripped and listen to your father," Hobie says.

Listen to what? Sarah wants to know. Lucy explains about Seth's movies, the science-fiction tales he once composed.

"Cool," she says. "So why'd you stop making them up, Dad?"

"Who says I stopped? My computer's full of them."

"I didn't know that," says Lucy. Her declaration is a substantial relief to Sonny, who had no idea either.

"Whenever I get blocked doing a column, I fiddle with one of them.

This is the halcyon era of science fiction. Recombinant engineering? Computer science? There's no end to weird little thoughts."

"Like what? Come on. Let me hear one." Sarah reaches across Sonny to drag on her father's hand.

"It's just stupid, private stuff. They're like topical parables or something. I don't know."

"Go ahead," says Hobie. "Let Sarah see how wigged-out you really are. I bet you got some twisted shit on that hard drive. Don't say no, cause I know you do. You got some tales about black folks?"

"Naturally. Nobody is spared."

"Okay." Hobie throws his broad arms out, then folds them: Do me something. The age-old challenge between them. He gave Seth ten minutes before about the inadequacies of his new beard. Seth requires additional encouragement from both Lucy and Sonny, but at last he scrapes his chair back and spreads his hands. Even Nikki comes to Sonny's lap to listen.

"Soon," he says, as the stories always started, "soon, as we know, cloning will be possible. From a single cell—from dandruff or a piece of fingernail—an entire being can be created. When writers speculate on this, they talk about cloning geniuses—a whole league of Michael Jordans or another de Kooning. But I suspect that people will be most interested in cloning themselves. We'll be like paramecia, reproducing ourselves in an endless chain. You'll literally be the parent of yourself. The kid won't have your bad trips and nightmares and squirrelly parents, but otherwise it's you, someone who'll grow up to look exactly like you, who has your same insane predilection for peach ice cream and, regrettably, the same genetic defects."

"Like baldness?" asks Sarah. Around the table, there is a thunderous laughter. On Sonny's lap, Nikki roars, too, for the sheer joy of participating. Seth levels a finger at Hobie and tells him to take note of what you get when the last tuition bill is paid.

"So what's the rest?" asks Sarah. "This is cool. I want to hear more."

"Okay," Seth answers. "Well, naturally the next impulse is people want to *improve* upon themselves through genetic engineering. They don't want their kid to be stuck being them exactly. He'll be like me, but with my grandfather's talent for music, my mother's for math. And on the other hand, aberrant genes can be repaired. No one need have sickle cell or Tay-Sachs. Of course, there is a potential for horrible mischief, people experimenting, or creating geeks or Hitlers from their own DNA. And so all gene choice and repair is conducted under the auspices of a federal agency, the Biomedical Genetic Engineering Administration, which must consider all applications for genetic alterations. And here our story begins.

"It is one of the legacies of slavery that virtually all African-Americans carry some white genes. Not long after BGEA has been opened, word leaks out that an unknown number of black parents have applied to have white children. This causes tremendous agitation around the country. Racist whites don't want blacks 'passing' this way—even though they'll be white in every real sense—while many African-Americans feel these parents are turning their back on their heritage. Some white leaders, including a few generally regarded as progressive, urge *all* African-Americans to take this step and thus, in a single generation, to put race behind us as a national issue. They are denounced by most blacks and many whites, a few of whom, in defiance, apply to have black-skinned children. Pressure is brought on Congress to prevent race-crossing. A law is enacted, but the Supreme Court strikes it down, ruling that the Constitution guarantees Americans the right to be whatever color they want. Now the nation is in turmoil. The Biomedical Genetic Engineering Administration is looted and the names of the black parents who have applied are discovered; around the nation four of them are lynched. Facilities doing gene alteration are sabotaged. Civil war erupts, with racist whites fighting beside the Nation of Islam. The cities burn again." Seth rattles his fingers down like rain. "Fade scene. So?" he asks. The silence is prolonged.

"I liked the stories you used to tell a lot better," Sonny says.

"Uncle Hobie's right," says Sarah. "You're twisted."

"Hey," says Seth. "You guys asked for it."

"It's upsetting, Seth," says Sonny. "It's provocative."

Hobie, who has been fumbling with his beard for some time, says, "I think it's a righteous story."

"My pal," says Seth.

"God," says Lucy in reply. "The two of you never understand the way you sound to anybody else. That's a terrible story."

"Sure it is," says Hobie. "But true. Fact is, nobody in this country, black or white, knows how they wanna feel about difference. There plenty of white folks in this country, maybe even most of them these days, tellin themselves they ain't so hung up. You give them one of those nice-type black people they see on TV to move in next door—Clint Huxtable or Whoopi Goldberg or Michael Jordan—somebody, you know, who lives and talks like them, fine by them. Only whoever it is, don't you dare marry my daughter and hand me no darkie grandchild. And *we* aren't a damn bit better. We-all are *proud* of being different, we wanna be different, 'cept when white folks say we are. Don't nobody mention the number of black players in the NBA. Cause then we feel it's a curse, as if that difference runs straight from the skin right through the soul. We're all fucked up, all of us, and not gettin *any* better."

Lucy looks to Sonny. "They both believe we're doomed."

"Not doomed," says Seth. "Just in deep, deep trouble." His wife makes a face and Seth repeats himself: Deep trouble. Still in her black dress, Lucy pulls in obvious agitation at each of the sleeves and leans across the table toward Seth.

"I won't listen to this. Not tonight. I don't want to hear how bad it is, how hopeless, how urban life is going to be roving bands of murderous hoodlums fighting it out with armed militias, while the rest of us cower from both."

"Maybe you should drive down to Grace Street, Luce. Or spend time sitting beside Sonny and hear what passes in front of her on the average day."

Sonny shoots him a severe look and mouths quite clearly, Leave me out.

"It's not just one way, Seth. Why won't you *ever* see it? Years ago, you committed yourself to making things being better. And they are better. We—all of us in this country—we've accomplished an enormous amount. Why doesn't anybody *ever* say that? Why doesn't anybody give themselves just a minute of joy? You tell me another century when so many people made so many advances against the kinds of tyranny human beings have always imposed on each other."

She is reaching toward him, imploring, Sonny sees, near tears. This is the heart of what Lucy knows she can offer him. Himself. Who he was and longs for, if he will just reestablish his courage and his faith. It's too private, too unsettling to Sonny to witness this appeal. Nikki has edged over to Seth's knee, and muttering that she'll be right back, Sonny heads into the kitchen, where she withdraws a bottle of spring water from the refrigerator, a chugging Shelvador, forty years old if a day. The whole kitchen is a relic, with white metal cabinets so old the runners have fallen out of the drawers, and a floor of black and white linoleum squares. Sonny finds a glass—they are all, as Seth long claimed, food-store giveaways—and gulps the water down.

Whoever said we could name our feelings? It's an old riddle, left over from the foregone life of a *philosophe* at Miller Damon. The way any individual sees the color green can be measured now; a probe to the optic nerve would find the same chemicals annealing in the neurons of almost all of us. But this contorted stirring, the sensation that someone has driven rivets through her heart, the twisting fore and back, is simply what it is, the massive accumulation of a day, a life, and is wholly unique to her. Who has the right to call it by any known word, whether it's 'love' or 'regret' or 'pain'?

From the dining room Hobie's voice booms out. He's telling a story about a Fourth of July years ago, when he was still married to his second wife. Seth, a second later, peeks in from the doorway.

"Don't kill me, okay, but I turned on the TV for Nikki. 'God, Seth, this is *so* cool. There's *no* color.' I mean, is this the next wave?"

She returns his smile wanly. Sonny keeps telling him he has to learn to say no to Nikki, to stop acting like a doting aunt. But there's not much point in that discussion right now.

"What's the matter?" He edges in. "My story get to you?"

"I suppose. There's a lot to talk about. It's been a hard day for all of us."

He looks behind him, then crosses the kitchen and takes her in his arms. He asks if she's okay. She does not answer, but falls against him. Beside them, the window, opened for the cross-draft when the house was crowded, remains unclosed in spite of the growing nighttime chill. The wind kicks up, transmitting the sound of a cat a few houses down, squalling in some act of overheated masculinity. The air, the sound, Seth's presence raises within her the first faint throb of sexual need. Amid all the uncertainty between them, their lovemaking has been a spectacular success. She has had these periods before with a couple of other men — Charlie was one — and when you're into it, sex, having great sex, it seems to be the center of the world. All other connections grow slightly more remote. In the last hour of the day, when Nikki is in bed, Sonny turns to him, as formerly she turned to herself. He brings her a glass of wine. They drink. They make love. Sometimes it goes on. He roams. He approaches from behind. The side. He leaves. He caresses her ankles, knees, the vulva, then mounts her again reeking with her strong female scent. It feels always, as the minutes pass, as if they are going deeper and deeper into one another. The twined fingertips. The pleasure points. The outbreak of exulting sound. As if they were twins, separate selves swimming toward the retained memory of how they issued from the same core. The flooding recollection of this now is moving, disturbing. She will hate herself if she comes to tears.

"How are *you* doing?" she asks.

Confused, he says. Numb.

"I nearly wrote you a letter last night."

"Did you? Was it a love letter?" He rears back with that puckish smile. Always the jokes, the hapless defenses.

"It was condolences, Seth."

"Oh."

"And I tore it up because I didn't know exactly what to say."

"I'm not sure I would, either."

"No, I mean about us. I didn't know what to say about us. I didn't know what right or role I'd have comforting you tomorrow or the day after."

"Oh." He lets her go. "Is that what we have to talk about?" His innocence is such a complete show she has to stifle an urge to pinch him. His eyes, in fact, are watery with fear.

"This may be the wrong time."

He looks back to the dining room. Hobie is talking about fireworks, imitating his wife, Khaleeda, as she begged him not to set them off around the girls. His mimicry, always perfect, has Lucy and Sarah in the heat of laughter.

"Go on," Seth says. "It's working on you. Let's hear it."

"Well, Seth. I already said it. What are you doing? Say, tomorrow. Are you staying? Going?"

"Tomorrow? Look, you know I've been promising Moritz for two weeks I'll come out to Seattle so I can meet with the people at the *PI* face to face. I said I'd leave as soon as the funeral is over. You know that. And it's Passover anyway. Sarah wants to have it with Lucy now. She asked if we could all be together. So I'll probably fly out tomorrow."

"And then? How long will you be there?"

His mouth parts vaguely. He slumps a bit, backed up against the old black counter on which the linoleum's secured by steel borders.

"I'm entitled to ask, Seth, aren't I?"

"Of course," he says, but averts himself somewhat. "Look, I have to get down to it. I know we're there. Only, I want to be sure you realize it's not only me. Do you know that?"

In the four years since Charlie fell out of the picture, she never seemed to recall his most fundamental complaints, that she was cold at the core, elusive. At his angriest, he wrote a poem: *Humans have four-chambered hearts/You keep three for yourself.* She was crushed by those lines and happily forgot them until Seth cautiously began to hint at the same thing.

"I know that," she says.

"Because," he says, "there's a way we've never gone one step beyond where we were last December—when you were calling this a childhood romance? There's a level where you don't believe me. Or won't take me seriously."

"I take you seriously, Seth. But I'm afraid."

"Of?"

"I don't know. It's hard to say."

He runs down a list of possibilities and she says no each time. She's not afraid of being hurt. Or being abandoned again. Or the mess of another breakup.

"So?" he asks.

She has her arms about herself in the cool air. The kitchen light is bright.

"Seth, I don't know. I hear Hobie call you 'Proust' sometimes and I guess—I quiver. It scares me. That you remember every detail about your friends from college. That you're still hung up on what Loyell Eddgar did to you twenty-five years ago, as if it happened yesterday. Because I can't help thinking that's the same reason you're here with me, trying to pick up where we left off."

"And the reason is? I'm not following."

"I think what I'm afraid of is that beneath it all, Seth, you've been trying to figure out one thing, which is, basically, how you might have been happier. If you'd stayed with me, if you'd faced down Eddgar, would your life have turned out differently? Would you be more complete? Would it have turned out, if you'd been tougher or luckier, something—Would it have turned out he didn't have to die, Seth?"

She stops for a second, to see if she's gone too far. Across the kitchen his eyes are flat, his jaw turns a bit. But he seems to be taking it.

"That's why it scares me," she says. "Because in the end, Seth, sooner or later, you're going to get a grip, you're going to see what everybody has to see. You're going to say, 'I can't disrespect the life I've lived. I can't pretend I don't have these connections. I could have had a different life, but I didn't.' I think you're thinking those things right now."

"Look," he says, but says no more for quite some time. In his white shirt, he too has crossed his arms in the chill. "This is really complicated. Maybe we should save this. Why don't you take Nikki home? And then I'll swing by whenever we're done here." His approach seals off the window, so she unexpectedly catches a swirling breath of the warm air still hovering in the house, which carries the stimulating current of his presence. He wants to sleep with her, she realizes. When all this anguish is expressed, when they have pulverized themselves with this raw cavalcade of doubt and high emotion, that ardor will fuse itself in motion, contact, pleasure, and connection, so that something will be left. When he goes in the morning, there will be a wake of tenderness as well as pain, something to return to. "We'll talk, okay?"

"We have to."

In the dining room, Hobie's voice booms out: "I light the first sparklin devil and it spins around shootin sparks and whatnot, and all the sudden, the sucker rolls right under my car, my brand-new Mercedes 560 SEL, and I swear to God, *swear*, the whole fucking car, man, goes like ka-boom—there's a flash of light, you'd have thought God, man, was behind the wheel." Lucy's and Sarah's laughter, the identical high-pitched squeal from mother and daughter, peals from the dining room. Hobie's wheezing too hard to continue.

"Funny story," Sonny says.

"Hysterical," says Seth. "Funnier if it was true."

She looks at him soberly, briefly reflecting on the depths between the two men. Neither of them, Seth nor she, seems disposed to move.

"Look," he says again, "I don't want to fight about whether you're right or wrong. Because in some ways you are, I'm sure you are. And I have to think about that a lot. But there's also a self-fulfilling element to what you're saying. You're using what you think you see in me as an excuse to avoid dealing with yourself. It's fair to worry about whether my commitment's transitory. I dig it. But I'm not sure I'm getting even that much. Really, Sonny. Listen to you. All this worry about what Seth's gonna do. But not once have you actually asked me to come back here next week, or made me any promises about how it'll be if I do. I've spent months trying to find the magic word that'll let you feel secure enough to come across. I've made a hell of an effort here. You've had all of me. Do you really think you can say the same thing?"

"Seth, I'm who I am. You know that. I'm not going to write you love letters."

"And I accept that. However reluctantly. I know that. But I'm entitled to more. It's just that simple. Right now, if I call you up from Seattle, if I say, 'I'm staying here' or 'I'm not coming back,' I'm afraid I know just how you'll feel."

"God, Seth, how would you want me to feel?"

"What would I *want?* I'd want you to feel devastated. I'd want you to feel torn away from something vital." From the dining room there's the sound of movement, chairs creaking. They're clearing the cartons, their voices are coming this way. She waits in the full force of Seth's gaze, his light eyes intent between those funny, frail brows. She feels somewhat overpowered because of what she's invited. She will have to bear the invasion of that vast terrain where Zora's daughter, the determinedly normal child of an unconventional and impulsive woman, has dwelled in shuttered privacy throughout her life, in dread of being known not merely to others but to herself. "And what I'm most afraid of, Sonny, is that secretly, in a large part of yourself, you'll be happiest to avoid all of this and to be left alone." He points to her from the doorway. "I'm afraid you'll be relieved," he says.

SETH

Mrs. Beuttler, Seth's father's secretary for the last twenty years, a dry woman who held a distant and somewhat charitable view of Mr. Weissman, returns after dinner so that her husband, Ike, can pay his respects. A few neighbors also appear. For the most part, they are older folks who co-existed with his father in the perfunctory amity of a familiar wave and remarks about the brute nature of recent ice storms or the insanity of the county's creation of no-parking zones in the middle of the block. A younger couple, the Cotilles from two houses down, arrive, and the missus, a well-intended straitlaced blonde, insists that Bernhard was the sweetest old thing.

By nine o'clock, the ceremonial aspect of mourning is over. Sonny has gone to put Nikki to sleep. Hobie loads as many of the folding chairs borrowed from the Tuttles as fit into his parents' car and drives down the street to pass the remainder of the night with Gurney and Loretta. Lucy and Sarah and Seth undo the work of the night before, push the elderly divan back into the center of the living room, dry and stack the dishes, study odd objects that are suddenly outlined with the striking clarity death provides. In the living room, beneath the glass of a corner table, his mother laid out a mosaic of photographs over the years, single instants in the march through time, the early Kodachromes bleeding green into the other hues. Seth is the principal subject: gleeful, at the beach, with sailor cap and shovel; a solemn cowpoke at his seventh birthday party, incapable of much levity, because the guns and chaps he received were in line with his father's wonts, second-rate, plastic, possessing none of the substance leather and metal would have lent Seth's fantasies. The years go forward: here he is in mortarboard at Easton. Then Lucy begins appearing. Sarah in infancy frolics in a tub. Seth, Lucy, Sarah, age seven, and both his parents, all outfitted with walking sticks and rucksacks, stare at the camera in the Olympic rain forest. There are also a couple of snaps of Isaac which his father added, maintaining Dena's shrine: the infant swaddled and then, Seth's lost boy, at three in his He-Man outfit.

The plan is for Sarah to drop Lucy at Kindle International on the way down 843 to Easton. At the curbside, beneath the weird purplish tones and penumbral shadows which the mercury vapor lights cast through the bare trees, Seth heaves her small case into the back of Sarah's Saturn. Leaving, Lucy allows herself a full embrace. She rises to her toes and throws her slender, solid arms around him. Squeezing her small form to him, she quickly kisses his lips, then her cheek appears beside his and in the smallest voice possible, with their daughter some unaccountable distance from them in the dark, Lucy whispers, as he has known for hours she would, "Come home." She breaks from him before he can answer. The pale side of her palm, lifted to the window, catches some of the light as the car zips into the dark.

He stands at the curbside watching this departure, locks the door to his father's house, and loads the last of the folding chairs borrowed from Hobie's parents into the Camry. At the Tuttles' bungalow, a close replica of his father's, Hobie's mom, Loretta, fumbles through the many bolts, then throws her arms open and comforts Seth in her familiar abundance for what seems the tenth time today. "Oh, how you doin now, baby?" she asks. Waddling with the folding chairs, he clatters down the stairs to the basement, where Hobie has established himself for the night.

Throughout the trial, Hobie was in tenancy here, in the knotty-pined domain which was the kingdom of their youth. Here, at the age of fourteen, Hobie opened what he called his 'office.' They hung *Playboy* Playmates on the wall, set up his hi-fi, with the tweed speaker covers, and his aquarium with the grow light and the bubbler, which imparted a chill, dank smell to the basement air. With other friends, Seth would take the bus to downtown DuSable, see a movie, run up and down the streets, dodge into alleys in flocks when they saw a cop even a block away, as if they had done anything that merited fleeing. Hobie would seldom come along. He never said why, although Seth knew. There was always somebody who stared, snarled a little, pushed him, wouldn't respond. Once a trip. Just for a moment. But it was enough to keep Hobie at home in U. Park. Here in this basement he was the exalted ruler. Seth can still clearly recollect the cold kiss of the floor, can see without looking the precise pattern in which the variegated asbestos tiles have been cut to fit the hummock of cement at the foot of the central I-beam. He would listen to Hobie go on, an exotic, spectacular young man, with a mind full of thoughts like shooting stars, a personality of unlimited art and promise, before the world brought him to heel.

During the trial, Hobie, a restless sleeper, preferred to bed down here rather than pad through the house all night and wake his parents. He slept on the davenport, with its tartan bolsters, which has been here since their childhood. He would arrive late, 11 p.m. or even midnight, and Seth often met him for a beer, or, as Hobie preferred, a joint. Hobie never discussed the case. He'd spent his evenings at Nile's apartment, supposedly preparing for the next day of trial, although from idle references it sounded like Hobie passed most of the time on the phone, trying to keep up with the rest of his law practice in D.C. Descending now, Seth spies four banker's boxes full of the records of the case—the reports, exhibits—on two pallets near the furnace. They're stored here, rather than D.C., in the event of Nile's apprehension, even though Hobie calls the prospect of a retrial remote.

In greeting, Hobie sticks his head out of his paneled enclave and makes a low noise. He has on an old button-down shirt, open over an olive-green T, both garments splattered with bright gobs of acrylics. He is holding a brush. For years, he's painted as a pastime. He is at work on a small canvas set on a large easel, a Pollockesque piece he started during the trial and apparently did not complete. On the same spattered box where smeared tubes of pigment rest, a tiny TV glows. Seth admires the artwork, but Hobie remains dissatisfied.

"Sometimes I think, Man, if I'd only started earlier. But you can buy a lot of jive, talkin like that." He tosses his head sadly and briefly considers the TV.

"Professional wrestling?"

"Greatest Show on Earth."

"Hobe, they're still using the same script they were when we'd put Buddy Rogers's Figure Four grapevine on each other thirty-five years ago."

"Eternal as the rock," answers Hobie. "This here is opera for the working class. Big-time ballad of good and evil." He has an open jar of dry roasted nuts nearby and pops a whole handful in his mouth. In this low-rise room, the acoustical ceiling is close to the spongy mass of his hair. Seth sniffs twice, noticeably, at the basement air, in which the predominating odor of the paint doesn't fully mask other scents.

"Hell yeah, I'm stoned," says Hobie. "That a problem?" It is actually. The volume of intoxicants in this man's body still remains stupendous. Hobie takes note of his equivocal look. "Hey, man," Hobie says, "substance abuse has got a bright future — it's a growth industry. People will take chemicals to improve their mood just as long as human unhappiness persists. That's word. May as well face facts. Fuck, we all grew up junkies anyway. You ever watch a kid in front of a TV set?"

"Often, unfortunately."

"Tell me it don't look like someone tripping." Seth laughs, but Hobie insists. "Am I right? I know I am. Sure," he agrees with himself. "This here's gonna be the liberty of the twenty-first century," he says. "Gotta let folks journey to their inner self, come to grips with the primordial mind, the pre-rational head that exists and is supreme over the world of rationalist signs and symbols. That's where folks reside. And that's the world that's beyond true governance. People gotta realize that. Let freedom ring, baby."

"Listen to this," says Seth, laughing at the gusto with which Hobie goes on. He grabs both Hobie's hands. "Hobie T. Tuttle," he says, "you are still a trip."

In answer, Hobie gives a brimming look, wise and regretful, half a life in it. He tips his head a bit.

"I ain't just talkin shit, you know."

"You never have," says Seth.

Satisfied by that, Hobie grunts again and turns away. "So I hope you didn't come round here to ask me somethin dumb, like can a man love two women."

"Can he?"

"Folks keep tellin me no. I'm paying a piss-pot full of alimony for tryin." Hobie's adult years have been a mixed bag at best. The law is its own universe and he reigns in every courtroom, but given the wreckage in his personal life, Seth never hears him claim to be a success. Seth loved Hobie's second wife, Khaleeda; she was a follower of W. D. Muhammad, a serious complex person who, unlike most of Hobie's women, had some sense of the immensity of his spirit. But he philandered his way out of that marriage. It's been hard for him since and will probably remain that way.

"Does it violate a biological law," Seth asks, "or is it just psychologically impossible, like grasping your own death?"

"Good, man," says Hobie, "good. Let's hear all your crazy shit. That's what you come to do, right? Tell me how tormented you are?"

"I'm too blown out to be tormented. I'll be tormented tomorrow. I wanted to drop off the chairs and thank you for your eulogy. It was great."

Hobie acknowledges him with another low rumble, a sound of mild pleasure, and dries a brush on the bottom of his shirt. This is hardly a novelty, telling him he made a deep impression in his public portrayal of himself.

"Yeah, I was on today. Think maybe I oughta become Jewish? I's a sorry-ass Catholic, and a worse Muslim. Maybe third time be the charm." Hobie's fascination with religion remains obscure to Seth. He explained it once in terms borrowed from the Grand Inquisitor. If everything is permitted, he said, then belief is permitted, too. So why not do it, since in existential terms, it requires the same effort? The logic was lost on Seth. But he smiles at the thought of Hobie undergoing another conversion.

"Now that would *really* get Jackson Aires going," says Seth. "Did you hear him ripping on me about my name?"

"Jackson, man, I've heard his shit all my life. Sometimes, it's how the impoverished young black man ain't got nothin but his anger and his self to blame for that, since every crime, every stickup and robbery, makes life harder for other black folks. Then next sentence he's gone tell you how the black male's been in deep trouble in America since the first slave on the dock got told to drop his shorts, seein as how no white man was gonna set loose a fella with a dong that size. Jackson, man, he's goofy, he's just as confused as everybody else." Hobie picks up a rag and lifts his chin to remove a dab of green paint that has landed on his beard. "Don't pay no mind to Jackson. He's gonna rip-all on everyone. He was rippin the living hell out of me during that trial bout how I was treating that sack-of-shit gangbanging client of his, and he knew better than me the fool was up there tellin tales."

"What kind of tales?" asks Seth quietly.

"Don't start." Hobie points the paint-smeared rag. "Now don't you start." They have never talked about the trial, even after it was over. Hobie shut down every conversation once Seth told Hobie about Sonny and him.

"But it *was* a lie, right? Through and through? Nile didn't want to do anybody?"

"You were there. You heard the evidence."

"There was a lot of bullshit in that courtroom, Hobie."

"Yeah, but you're considering the source." Hobie's eyes twinkle at the thought of his own devilment.

"The whole thing with the money Nile gave Hardcore? That was all fairy tales."

"Music to my ears."

"One day it was dope money. Then it was campaign money."

"Okay."

"Well, which was it?"

"Hey." Hobie briefly turns. "I'm the question man. Him, Moldo, whatever his name was, the prosecutor, he's the answer person. I'm the this-don't-make-sense guy."

"But look. Like the bank books? You were going to put in all Nile's financial stuff to show Nile couldn't have given Core $10,000 of his own, right?"

"Pretty slick, huh?"

"But Nile paid your fee. You told me that. So where'd *that* money come from?"

Hobie stops now. He looks around for a sheet of newspaper and lays it on a beaten wooden chair, where he takes a seat.

"And here's the real thing," says Seth. "Nile told me straight up—he *never* handed Hardcore any goddamn $10,000. Campaign or no campaign. He said it was a stone lie. Remember? I told you that the day in the jail." Hobie has watched him, holding his whiskered chin.

"Listen," he says, "listen, I'm gonna tell you something. 'He said.' *The defendant said.* Shit. Listen, when I got hired as a PD in D.C., 1972? I got into a prelim courtroom right away, cause they wanted brothers moving up fast as possible? And, man, I didn't know what the fuck I was doin. First preliminary I had, I remember, I'm representing a guy named Shorty Rojas. You know, as it is, you get about two minutes in advance to confer with your client and this dude, no fuckin lie, he can't talk. He's some kind of calypso spade, but I couldn't suss out what blood this dude had in him. I mean, he starts in, it's like, What motherfuckin language is this? This idn't street, this isn't island, this ain't Puerto Rico, this is just like fuckin glossolalia or somethin. And the case is a knifing, okay? Shorty, he performed a splenectomy out on the avenue. And thank God, the victim made it, and he's up there on the witness stand,

and the prosecutor gets the victim down, 'Show the judge just what Shorty done to you.' So here's this motherfucker, he's stabbin away with the actual knife, about two inches from the judge's nose, you'd think you're watching Zorro. And Shorty, who I've understood maybe two words he's ever said, pipes up, 'That's a lie. All lie. No right. No right.'

"And I hear this and I'm like, Holy smokes! Hold on, heart! I got myself an innocent client! I got so fuckin excited. I cross-examined like some ferocious motherfucker. And lost. Naturally. Never win a prelim if the victim says that's the guy. But I'm blue, I'm whale-shit low. So I go over to the jail that night, I walk up on the tiers to see my client. 'Hey, man, Shorty, I'm sorry, we'll beat it at trial.' He starts in again. 'No right. No right. No right.' And somehow, I'm walkin away and it dawns on me, he's still shaking one hand at me. And I go back, I say, 'You mean, he's lying cause you didn't stab him with the right hand, it was the left?' Seen the fucker smile, you wouldn't believe it. 'Left, left, left. No right.' So don't tell me that the defendant said it was a lie, all right?"

"Well, what does all that mean?"

"It means what it means." Hobie stands again to ponder his painting.

"Nile was lying to me? Nile really paid him? What?"

"See, this is why I didn't want you involved. This is why I was telling you, stay away from him. Cause you can't handle this. Man, I knew you, Jack, when you cried cause you found out Mary Martin was flying with strings. And you ain't changed. So leave it be. Scat."

"Hobie. Something happened there. Someone was murdered. I've known this boy almost his entire life."

"Look, I ain't gonna tell you what he said to me. I can't. Privilege holds unless he's dead. And he ain't dead."

"You sure?"

"Pretty sure." Hobie smacks the canvas with his brush. "Why, you afraid Eddgar murdered him, too?"

"It's crossed my mind."

A rankling snuffle shoots from Hobie's nose. "You the only fucker on Planet Reebok who hates Eddgar worse than I do."

"Maybe I've got more reason."

"You know your problem with him?"

"I have a feeling you're about to tell me. Sock it to me, bro."

"You envy him."

"Say what!"

"Yep, I think that's what it is. See, man, I hate him for the shit he did. But you hate him for that *and* what he is now. You look back to all that stuff you were going through twenty-five years ago and you say, 'Wow, that was exciting, that's when I was political, idealistic, committed. But I quit that nonsense.' And you blame him because you think he's basically the one what forced you to give it up. Yet here he is, that dog, talkin all that shit you'd still *love* to believe, doin it too, and you find that infuriating."

"No," says Seth. "I mean, yeah, I see it. And I know I still believe it. I mean, not all of it. I can't. It was a children's crusade and some of it was childish. But I recycle my bottles. I vote for the good guys. But it's the wild hopefulness I really miss. All that time, it didn't seem there was any difference between love and justice. You could have them both, without conflict. We were going to revise life, down to the essence. We were going to abolish unhappiness. It was glorious."

"Right," says Hobie. "We asked the essential questions: How many roads must a man walk down, before you call him a cab?"

"Thank you for your support."

"Shit," says Hobie. Momentarily, neither speaks.

"How about just a yes or no on one thing, Hobe? Did Eddgar get Hardcore to off June?"

Hobie's sole response is to draw his mouth down into an irked little pouch.

"Goddamn," says Seth. "You just want to be Captain Marvel."

"Oh, fuck you, motherfucker. All you're doin is lookin after yourself. This is the single thing in this life I am any good at, leastwise that means something to anybody else. And I'll be goddamned if I will treat it with disrespect, just cause you got the blues or some Holy Grail about some boy you looked after when he used to wet his pants. It's in the books, man: I can't tell."

They are within a few feet of one another in poses that would look combative to an outsider, staring each other down. Seth turns away first, wandering from Hobie's room, and takes a seat on the basement stairs, picking at the metal runner. The cellar is a collection of musty smells. Glancing menacingly over his shoulder, Hobie emerges but stalks off in the opposite direction. In the darkness, beside the glimmering sheet-metal venting of the furnace, Hobie rummages in the banker's boxes where the trial records are stored. Swearing in all the romance languages, he throws the top two aside to reach the herniated carton below. When he returns to Seth, he is holding a sheet of paper.

"Not so fast," he says, turning the paper to his chest. "Not so fast."

He sits on the step below Seth, his bulk occupying the entire space of the stairwell. "Now look, you're such a journalistic hotshot," Hobie says, "maybe you can figure this much out. See this prosecutor, what's he called? Moldo?"

"Molto."

"I got onto him right from the start. You gonna be a PA for life, man, you gotta be an angry fella, you gotta be lookin to see the right people kick the shit out of the wrong people, you gotta get off on that, day in and day out. So I'm hip, and I start runnin some changes on him, and pretty soon he's so sore at me, he ain't even *thinkin* bout Nile, cause he figures I'm the evilest, most deceptive bastard ever walked into a courtroom. Which is just fine with me. All right?"

"Are you going to say anything plainly?"

"Lookee here," he says, "just listen up. Now here I am at the end of this trial, and I pull the rabbit out of the hat. State says my client brought $10,000 to this gangbanger to get him to commit murder, and lo and behold, I go and show Nile give him $10,000 cash okay, but it was from the DFU. You remember that part?"

"Are you looking for applause?"

"You be fresh, I can just go back to paintin on my picture."

"Fine, I apologize. So what's the point?"

"Now, if I know from day one, from before that trial starts, that skunk Hardcore is lying through his gangbanging booty about what that $10,000 is and where it came from—and I do, I surely do know those things for fact—then why wouldn't I go in and say, 'Now now, Mr. Prosecutor, you done made one hell of a mistake, here's the check, go see the folks at DFU'? Why wouldn't I do that? How does Moldo answer that question?"

"Because you're the evilest, most deceptive bastard that ever walked into a courtroom?"

"Right on. I just get my jollies pullin his chain. That's what he thinks."

"And what's the truth?"

"You supposed to tell me."

Seth thinks. "It's a smoke screen, right? I would say you waited because you didn't want him to have time to look into this. Something about the money was wrong."

"Doin good, bro. Now I'll tell you the truth, man: There's a *lot* about that money, a *whole lot,* that's wrong, and I can't tell you but a little tiny part of it."

"You didn't want Molto to ask Hardcore about it?"

"No. Hardcore, he had to tell the lies he told before. Jackson gave him a script—that whole thing was so Jackson, man—and Core stuck right to it. Wasn't worried about Hardcore. See, what I didn't want Moldo and them to do was go out to that bank and talk to the teller who cashed that check. Cause she might tell them what-all she told me."

"Which was? Is that privileged too?"

"Not really."

"So what'd she say?"

"She remembered Nile. She remembered him cause he acted like his usual dumbbell self. She handed him $10,000 in cash—100 one-hundred-dollar bills, by the way, no fifties or twenties. And he stuck them in an overnight delivery envelope. And she says, 'You shouldn't oughta do that, it says right on the form, like, Don't send cash,' and he says, 'Neh, we've done it before,' and 'fore he leaves out, asks her is FedEx around the corner."

"So he didn't give money to Core? That's the point?"

"No."

"He did give the money to Hardcore?"

"I'm saying that's not the point."

"Well, who'd he send the money to?"

"That's the point."

The paper which Hobie's been holding is a printout from microfiche, white on black and heavy with toner, reflecting the data about a FedEx delivery last July. Nile is listed on one side of the form as the sender. On the other is the destination:

> Michael Frane
> RR 24
> Marston, Wisconsin   53715

When Seth looks back, Hobie is studying his reaction abstractly, waiting to see how long it takes to sink in.

"April Fools?" Seth asks.

"This here's no foolin."

"It's him, right?"

"Be a funny coincidence if it wasn't."

Seth stares at the paper again. His arms feel weak.

"How long were you going to wait to tell me this?"

"Probably forever. I'm probably doin somethin I shouldn't, as it is. Only you're breakin my heart with that hangdog shit, fuckin Oliver Twist or something, waitin for more. And this is a goddamn secret, Jack. The judge doesn't hear word one about this. I had enough lectures from her about withholding evidence to last a lifetime." Hobie nods. "You forgot to ask me when I got that from FedEx."

"When?"

"Night before Nile run off. One hell of a surprise, too. I'd asked them to dig it up weeks before. I opened the mail. It's like 'Ee-yow!'"

"He hadn't told you?"

He shakes his head again, not a reply, but a sign he cannot respond.

"He couldn't have told you," Seth says. "You just said you were surprised."

Hobie merely looks: a great stone face, which in fact it is, a face that would be worthy of some sculptor's efforts.

"What else did I miss?" Seth asks.

"Name of the town familiar?"

Marston. "Is that where June lived?"

"Bingo."

"He's been living there with her?"

"Not with. Not so far as I can tell. But he'd been in those parts twenty-five years, same as her. Ran a little TV/radio/stereo kind of store since the eighties. Big chains, volume discounts finally put him out of business. Left him with some heavy debts."

"Is that what the money was for?"

Hobie points. Bingo again.

"Apparently, bankruptcy wasn't an option. Some folks didn't like the notion of a credit check on Michael or anything like that. You know, he'd sort of kept the name, case he ever ran across somebody he used to know, but he changed the spelling so he didn't step on your toes. Remember, you had his social security number. So his must have been a phony. Which meant they didn't want anybody pokin round about his background. That's how I figure it. Seems he's kind of a sensitive guy, anyway, not too good with stress. Had some kind of breakdown years back. He was working around there as a farmhand originally and cut off half of one foot in a threshing machine. That's like 1971. I think that's when June showed up. June and Nile. Kind of nursed him back to health."

"Where the hell do you get all of this?" he asks Hobie. "Not from Nile, right?"

"Nope, else I wouldn't be telling you. No, I spent quite a bit of time on the telephone, starting with lunch the last day of the trial. While you were beatin the streets? I talked to the banker, realtor, chamber of commerce. Everybody liked Michael. Sweet, peaceful fella. Kind of strange. The boy we knew. I guess he stayed pretty close to my client over the years. Kind of like you and my client? Anyway, that's who I was trying to rustle up—my client. I've always figured this is where he bolted. Wanted to warn Michael his cover was blown."

"*That's* why he took off?"

"Partly, I'd guess. In part. I'd say, overall—strictly an estimate, not a confidence—Nile wasn't very pleased by the direction of the defense. He was ripshit with me already, by the time I showed him that piece of paper. But I think this here's a secret he'd always sworn to Mom he'd keep. I'm damn sure he didn't want me to go into all of this in court. Which, of course, I'd be obliged to do, if he would have let me. And then again, I think he might have worried I'd let word slip to you."

"To me? What would I do?"

"Hey, dude, way I remember this one, Michael set you up big-time. Only logical to think you'd want to trash him, if you ever got a bead on where he was."

"I never held him to blame. You know that. I'd actually like to see him."

"Proust," says Hobie.

"Right," says Seth. His imagination, anchored in the past, already is crawling toward some usable image of Michael. Seth has been to towns like Marston. Several years ago, he did a few columns on a girl up in Podunk, Minnesota, who wanted to play the tuba in the all-boys marching band. He spent a week out there. Everybody has strange hair: girls with dos like woodpecker's combs, guys whose fathers ragged the hippies now with greasy locks dripping to their shoulders. All of them get drunk on Friday nights and tear down the county roads, picking off the rural-delivery post boxes with their bumpers. Their parents, farmers mostly, are utterly confused by the viral spread of urban life. Their kids take drugs and hang out at the malls down on the interstate, wear their seed caps backwards, and call each other 'motherfucker.' What the hell? the adults always seemed to be asking.

And here, where people once thought they were the real America, Michael Frain has remained. Seth envisions him on the main street peering discontentedly into the window of his store. An unlit neon sign, too small for the frontage it decorates, mentions a popular brand, Sony or G.E. Behind it, the shop is gloomily, grimly out of business. Some disused something, two cardboard boxes, and a few stray kinks of wire are piled meaninglessly on a ledge blanketed with acrid dust, which has gathered at places into hairy wisps. The fixtures and display shelves have been removed. The man himself remains angular, still slender, though his gut has taken on some slope. He wears a washed-out plaid shirt, with the tails hanging outside his twill trousers. He looks a bit wasted, gawky, with a knobby weight at the elbows and the knees. He still has some hair, ragged but not quite as wild, not quite as bright of course. And he would take considerable pain in stepping down into the street. To walk, Michael wheels his upper body to the left and stiffly hurls the opposite leg, an elaborate, painful-looking motion which he has thoughtlessly mastered. Down the way, the unpainted clapboard church and corrugated Farm Bureau building stand beside a new brick restaurant, prefab construction from the looks of it, insubstantial as a cereal box. As he moves along, Michael's eyes, still glossy and uncertain, would flash this way and avoid Seth, as they avoid all strangers, with no hint of recognition. That's him. Seth gathers himself around the picture.

"And did you find him?"

"Which one?"

"Either. Nile?"

"Nope. Course not."

"How about Michael?"

"Nope. That's how come I ended up talking to everybody in town. Man's just gone. Nobody could find him that day. Or since."

"They're together?"

"Doing their fugitive thing. My guess. Michael's had practice slipping his name, his past. I figure he's showing Nile how."

In the silence of the basement, the voice of one of the wrestlers, at the same pitch as an engine exhaust, rumbles across the room from the TV. "I'll crush the Mighty Welder's butt," he declares to an interviewer.

"And you're not going to tell me the rest. How we get to this point?"

"Can't, man."

"Who can?" Seth asks. "Who will?"

Hobie lays his heavy hand on Seth's knee. He smells of paint, his eyes are bleary. He looks at Seth, as they look at each other, with what's been imbued over a lifetime.

"You'll figure," he says.

Summer 1995

NILE

Weak, Nile always thought when he entered the jail. The damn guards were so weak, just in a total snooze. Their whole deal was papers and forms. 'Captain wants them forms to be right.' Here they were, with all these bad actors and tough customers, killers and heartless slobs two hundred feet away, and the realest thing to these tools was whether every visitor put down a sign-in time and the inmate's pen number. Probation was the same way. Jesus. Nile sighed and thought about the girl.

Nile was in love. He was always in love, but this was different. It was always different, because he didn't love the girls other men did. He didn't think Julia Roberts was so beautiful. In high school, he wasn't like every guy who thought about boning the whole pom squad. He liked sweet girls, gentle girls, girls who had something special—girls who maybe some way reminded him of himself. Right now he was really in love. Better than ever. He was like the dude in the song who loved being in love. He loved Lovinia.

"Nile, my man, my man," said the lieutenant. He said that each week. Nile timed it so this sphincter-brain named Eddie was on the desk, because he barely searched him. "It rainin out there?"

"A little," Nile said. "Kind of misting."

"Shit. That damn pizza boy get slow. Any doggone excuse. Step into my office. Kind of mistin," said Eddie, as he extended a slightly arthritic finger to the examination room. "Shit, you know, it been mistin all damn month. That pollution and all's what done it. You think I'm kiddin? I'm not kidding. Mistin. Shit, I'll be havin this damn cough all year." He ran his arms along the outside of Nile's torso, inside each leg until he reached the thigh. "Okay, you done. Which one you want?"

"Henry Downs. Sly Bolt."

"Mr. Sly Bolt. Yessir, we gonna tell another gangbanger this week how he got to be a good boy when we let him out. You make sure he listen up." Eddie laughed and stamped Nile's hand. He said he'd call to have them bring Bolt down.

Nile walked on. At the gatehouse, he stuck his hand under the ultraviolet and the guards inside discharged the lock, admitting him. Nile could feel it there behind him. It reminded him of Bug; every step, every twitch, brought her to mind. She was always with him, like magic. He saw some skinny girl on the street and he remembered her. He saw stocking caps or grey twills; he felt the package in his can. It was like a town where all the roads ran to one place. Lovinia.

Girls always got Nile like that. He was always waking up and trying to remember first thing who he was in love with. His heart was always flying along, airborne with secret love. He was crazy all the time about someone who didn't even know it. There was Emme Perez, a receptionist at Main Probation who had two little babies from two different men. He'd loved her secretly for a long time, with her thin little legs and her kind of attitude. There was Marjorie in his father's campaign office, who had a limp from something she'd had as a kid. There was another black girl named Namba Gates he met at college who seemed to like him, too. Nile thought she was waiting for him to ask her out, and he almost did it, until he realized he couldn't bear to. When he was a freshman in high school, there was a girl in Geometry, Nancy

Franz, chubby really, but kind of sweet on him, she used to bump him in the hallways and stuff, steal his books; it was fifteen years later and he still thought of her sometime. There were so many.

Bug was the best. She was so sweet. That was just the word for her was sweet. And shy. She got so she could barely stand to let those huge eyes of hers get near yours, that had to be why they called her Bug, those eyes. It drove Nile crazy when she did that, like she wasn't even fifteen but seven.

'Do you suppose you'd say you were my girl?' he asked this morning, when they were doing the package.

'Not to none of them, I wouldn't. No how.'

'Would you say it to me?'

And she got that look. She batted him on the arm.

'You psychin,' she said.

'No, I'm not. I think you're my girl, man. That's what I think.'

'Well, you gone think what you think, then. Ain you? Ain gone matter none what I say.' And she skirted away from him, the way she did usually. Not in person. But like her spirit. It was like a ghost. Something you couldn't catch. A part of her was shy. Or hidden. Or something. He didn't have the words. He was inside Department 2 now and he sighed aloud thinking of her.

"What's got you down, men?" asked Runculez, the guard at the desk.

"I'm not down," said Nile. "I'm up. I'm happy." He lifted his arms to show he was free. Then he smiled stupidly. "Henry Downs," he said, and the guard shouted. "Downs." Two tiers up you could hear them shouting "Downs."

"You got the Henry Downs," said Runculez. They both laughed so that it actually seemed funny.

"Interview room," said Nile.

"Got some lawyers in there, men. How bout the cafeteria? We don' start in with lunch till e-leben."

"Got to have an interview room, man. Bureau regs. Got to read the rules of the road in a one-on-one interview room." Ordell had told him to say that. And he told Core that was strictly crazy. Who'd believe that? Who'd believe there was a rule so dumb? 'Shit,' said Ordell in reply. 'Where you been?'

The Mexican guard shook his head, but he was smiling. They all liked Nile. He was easy. Runculez spoke to another uniform a few feet away.

"Go tell that PD down there we got to hab that room, men. Tell her go by the cafeteria."

The PD came out with her briefcase in a minute. The guard went to explain, but she was cool. She was done anyway.

The interview room was a little cinder-block square with a folding table and those old-fashioned plastic bucket chairs. Graffitied gang signs on one of them had been scoured off with steel wool, leaving a spot where most of the color was gone from the plastic. A blast of overhead fluorescence interrupted the usual jailhouse gloom and leaked into the hall through a narrow plate-glass panel in the door meant to allow observation by patrolling guards.

Bolt arrived in cuffs and leg irons, accompanied by two solemn correctional officers. Here in the jail, half the guards had something going with one gang or another and they'd kid around a lot, especially with a Top Rank Saint like Bolt, downtalk him or make jokes about the weather. But Bolt presented himself as above that. Hard case. In seg. There was a chain around his belt that attached the manacles and ankle irons. As the correctional officers closed the door, Bolt took a seat. Nile immediately wandered to the near corner, where he could not be seen from the viewing panel, and began speaking.

"Now I gotta give you this pre-probationary briefing thing, Henry, okay? I want you to understand the rules of the road, once you get out of here. You've done eighteen months here, DOC, jail time. You have another year's probation. Okay?"

Sly Bolt was a cousin of Hardcore's. He wore a beard and he was tremendous across the shoulders and belly. Somewhere, Nile had heard he had played good b-ball in school, but it was hard to believe looking at him now. He had the mass of a boulder and an ill-mannered glower.

"Now, I know we've gone over this three times already, but you sign the form today. That's a contract, man, me and you. You keep this contract, you're on the street. You break it, you're not just back here, you're at the Yard in a blink, okay? Are you listening, Henry?"

As Nile spoke, he'd opened his belt. He stuck his hand under the elastic of his briefs and reached behind him and tore the line of tape off. He had shaved his ass. Bug had done it actually, one morning about three weeks ago. God, they both thought that was funny. Fun, he thought and reached back for the package. It was a rubber, tied off at the end, so it was about four inches long. Core made jokes about white guys. Nile just reached back to the crack in his butt and drew the condom out and held it close to himself as he approached Bolt and dropped it on the table.

"Now I'm going through this one by one. Okay? No guns. I don't care what you call it. 'Gat.' 'Strap.' 'T–9.' Any firearm, you're back inside."

In a single motion, Bolt had the rubber in his lap, beneath the table, the chain that ran from his cuffs barely clinking on the table top. Nile kept talking. Once he had his trousers hitched, he stood with his back against the glass panel in the door. No leaving the state without court approval, he said. No felonies or misdemeanors. Bolt would go back in, even for DUI.

"And no gang association," Nile said. "I know they're your homies. But you see them, you better go the other way. I catch you out there with those guys, then it's back inside. No way around it. If you're straight, I'm straight. You understand?"

Beneath the table, Bolt pumped his hands around the condom like it was a bat handle, gradually thinning and extending it. Then he suddenly reared his head back, lifted his chained hands, and dropped the rubber straight down his throat. Gone. Like stories June told about college dudes eating goldfish. Bolt, rarely happy, smiled as Nile spoke.

"You understand me, Henry?" Nile asked again. "I don't want any b.s. about you didn't hear this part or that part. This is serious shit I'm talking here."

"Mmm-hmm," said Bolt, both hands on his stomach. His eyes were closed. He was concentrating to make sure he kept it down. If that balloon—that's what Ordell called the rubbers, the balloons—if that balloon broke in Bolt's gut, full of straight stuff, pure white, they couldn't get him to emergency fast enough. He'd be dead. He wouldn't call for a doctor either. Bolt was Top Rank, bar none for his. He'd just smile. They all laughed about it. 'Fuck man, that'd be motherfuckin kickin, man. That'd be a rush. Whoo-ee.'

Whoooe, thought Nile. From inside his jumpsuit, Bolt took a wad of bills, loot he'd collected in here for the dope. Nile couldn't believe there was cash in here, but anything small enough to pass between hands—pills, razor blades, currency—made its way inside if it was useful. On a chair, there was a blue plastic bag, the delivery sleeve from a local paper one of the guards must have been reading. Nile put the bills in there and just stuffed all of it down his trousers. No one searched him on the way out.

He kept speaking the same way ten more minutes, then stepped out-

side to let the COs know they could take Bolt back. He was led off with his ankle irons clanking. Bolt didn't bother with even a backward look at Nile. In his cell, he'd take a box of Ex-Lax and wait.

Nile dropped dope with somebody new each week. A few whispered, 'You all right, man, you okay.' Nile represented to them by hand: B, S, D, b, 4, me. It was a quick code, sign language, concluding with his index finger jabbed like a dagger toward his heart. They were startled by that, a white guy down for his. Fuck you doin? their looks would say, and inevitably his head rang in a customary instant of shame. Question of his life. People always acted like he was strange. He wouldn't drive his car in the rain. That was one thing people thought was strange. Not that he wouldn't travel. But he thought the rain was bad for the finish. And he got all weird around strangers, not looking people in the eye, but lots of people were like that. Michael was the same. But around Core, around Bug, it was different. I got carried away, he wanted to explain to the Saints who'd give him that look. I just got carried away. I'm in love, he'd say. I love being in love. He thought about Bug as he came back into the jail corridor.

How this started, bringing shit into the jail, was strange — Eddgar's fault, Nile would say, though how much could you fade that way? He'd fucked up, too. He had got himself in a bad place with Hardcore, straight off. Nile knew that. Ordell was powerful. Right from the giddyap, Nile felt his strength, this vitality that reached through Core, like the force of nature that drove through a plant from root to leaf. He almost said to Eddgar half a dozen times, 'This guy, Ordell, Hardcore, he reminds me of you.'

He wrote his reports about Core each month, and somehow he started letting Hardcore tell him what to say. Sitting in Nile's cubicle down at Probation in the Central Courthouse, Core would whisper so his raspy voice would not carry beyond the rimpled plastic partitions. 'What-all you scribblin bout me?' Core would clown around, laughing, reaching for the sheet, and finally Nile let him turn it over, like what's the dif, no secrets here. Hardcore read, scratching his long evil fingernails through his scraggly goatee. "Don't be sayin that, man, don't be gone on bout what a loose motherfucker I is, you be worryin bout my gangbangin."

"No, what should I say?"

"You know, bro. Be cool. Put down I got me a good job and shit."

"What job is that, man?"

"Commu'ty organizin." He laughed, because Nile had mentioned Eddgar. Eddgar was already in a heat. This is an opportunity, Nile, he'd say, this is a tremendous opportunity. "Say I'm like doin that commun'ty organizin shit."

He had. Oh well. When Nile went out to the IV Tower for the home visits, Ordell was always there to greet him, standing on the street, waving his arm around in huge swooping gestures, making fun of somebody, probably both of them.

"Park right here, thass good, thass good." He saved the best spot for blocks for Nile. Hardcore put on a good show. His artillery, his musclemen were all stuffed in one black Lincoln half a block down. There was nobody around to wait on Hardcore, just a few neighborhood kids— 'shorties'—he couldn't keep away, and this skinny little smooth-skinned girl, Lovinia, who carried messages. "Go tell Bolt, done said get wit it," Core said to her one day.

"What's that about?" Nile asked.

"Oh, that." Hardcore laughed. His mouth was wide and on one side he had several teeth crowned in gold. He never answered. He had the decency not to lie. Of course, each time Nile came he saw more. The guns were out, the Tec-9s and AK-47s. The pagers. Kids running and flying whenever Hardcore walked around. "You the man," Hardcore would tell Nile. "You the man, you tell me when I'm bustin on folks or somethin, you say, 'Be done, man,' I gone quit. This here is jus some bidness, man, got to have some bidness."

"You oughta listen to my father. You oughta talk to him," Nile said. Why would he say that? Especially when, most days, the last thing in the world he wanted to do himself was talk to Eddgar? Kind of swap, Nile supposed. You talk to him, then I don't have to.

Eddgar always had projects for Nile. In college, when Nile was sort of cutting up, doing t's and blues a lot and watching a shitload of MTV, Nile had his favorite job: he was a messenger. The whole shot, the whole thing, Nile loved it. He had the bike, the tights, the optic safety vests, the weak little Styrofoam crash helmet. He went around ripped half the time, with his Walkman blasting, and a walkie-talkie on his waist turned up full volume. He couldn't really hear it, but it vibrated when Jack started yelling in dispatch. That job was the tits. What Nile liked best was the way you were in the scene and not. All these characters are ricocheting off the walls, like, Man, where's the messenger, Jesus, where's the messenger? And you bop in there, Okay, here's the messenger, take a pill.

Eddgar hated that job. Nile could just tell Eddgar was waiting him out. He was waiting for Nile to see the job was frostbite city in the winter and stroke city in July. What jacked Eddgar was not so much that Nile was a flunky but that he liked it. Maybe that was part of why it was a great job. Then the second summer Nile was getting fucking prickly heat between his legs from the bicycle seat, and he said something about how they ought to have a union, all the messengers. Eddgar got very intense. He must have asked Nile sixty times if he talked to anybody else, until Nile spent hours wondering what kind of embolism he'd had to even say something like that out loud to Eddgar. Nile quit the job soon after that. He went back to Kindle Community College, he took social-work courses like Eddgar was always saying. It was just easier that way.

Now and then, Core would go off to do his business. He'd put his hand on Nile's shoulder. "You cool, man. You okay. Back atcha." Usually he left Nile on one of those broken benches behind T-4, the IV Tower, facing a sealed-off portion called The Chute, or The Shoot; nobody ever spelled it, so you never knew. It was fenced on one side and bounded by the bricks of the IV Tower on the other. This was the domain of the T-4 Rollers, Core's set. They were all kickin here, wallbanging, drinking Eight Ball, shooting dice. Nile sat and watched, with Core's blessings, but it was as if he wasn't there, some white nothing, no more noticeable than the lid from a paper cup amid the trash moldering at the buildingsides. He saw shit, though. One afternoon, late, Gorgo, a long rawboned cavalryman, pulled his '86 Blazer with deep-dish tires right up on the walk, N.W.A. blastin through the open windows. Gorgo flew out, G-down, black t-shirt trailing, hard leg jeans sagging. For reasons Nile could not understand, the Saints around knew he'd been rippin.

"Yo, Saint, 't's 'up?" they all demanded.

Gorgo indulged a moment of macho bashfulness. "Ain no thang." But soon he was persuaded to share his exploits. "Just jacked some lames for ten large."

"In you ride?" There were a lot of shorties—Unborns and Tiny Gangsters—around now, listening, inquiring. They were incredulous that Gorgo had pulled the stickup in his own truck. It would make him identifiable, open to reprisal.

"Yay, foo', I ain hidin from no Goobers. Name is Gorgo."

"Fat," these kids all said. But they were flying in a minute. Two

Goobers rolled down in different cars, shooting between the buildings from the avenue a hundred yards away. For an instant, as the birds rose, as the kids shouted "Incomin" and "Dustin" and dashed for cover, Nile was by himself on the bench, stumped by the resonating sound, which in the open air was somewhat less dramatic than he would have imagined. Eventually, he heard Gorgo screaming, "Get yo'self down." War! he thought, huddled behind the bench. Insane, he thought. The gunfire lasted only a few minutes. From high above, up in T–4, he heard the answering shots as the cars out on Grace Street roared off.

"Ain gone light up no one from so far. Punk asses!" Gesturing in defiance at the departing cars, Gorgo strode back and forth across the bench in splendid white hightops with fancy laces. He was thumping his chest, rallying his fist, screaming. His satin jacket flew around him and a solid gold .45, four inches across with a diamond in the barrel, swung from his neck. On the bench, one corner was newly splintered by gunfire. He looked below to explain to Nile. "They-all just trippin. Now they gone tell they homes how they ripped the Sissies, but I got all they loot." Gorgo reached into a bulging pocket and pulled out the bills which he had taken at gunpoint from the Gangster Outlaws. His smile disclosed that he was missing a front tooth. "It's on now," he said, meaning there would be shooting for weeks afterwards, which there was. Gorgo was sixteen, seventeen, by Nile's estimate, and crazy. His Tec–9 had come from somewhere and he wore it upside down, slung from the shoulder, like a soldier in a war flick. They said he would kill anyone. The crazy life! That's what they called it, the bangers. The crazy life. Nile loved it. These kids were ex-treme.

War, Nile thought for days afterwards. When he was little, a shorty whizzing in his bed every night, war was what terrified him. There was a war out there which he somehow envisioned: artillery fire and the smoke of bombs, the percussive flashes of light and magnesium flares, the sick odors of smoke trailing on the air. War would take him, break his tiny body. War could not be held at bay, could not be kept outside the door. Eddgar wanted war. And Nile was terrified. And now here, amid the guns, these brave warriors, Nile was thinking, Yeah. He was thinking, Cool. It was way weird. But still. So cool for Gorgo to be standing there pounding his chest, like, 'I don't care, live or die, I don't care, I'm here screamin.' Nothing made any more sense than that. No future. That's what Gorgo was screaming, No! to the future. For him it did not even exist. Cool, Nile thought for days. Cool.

After Nile nearly got snuffed that day, Hardcore had Lovinia look after him when Core went off to do his stuff. She was like Hardcore's secretary is what you'd say. Carrying messages. Keeping things straight. She was just so cute and shy. Nile always talked to her, tried at least. At first he could barely get her to say her name. She had one of those dos, a lot of straighteners and stuff, the front plastered out into bangs that looked like sheet metal, and the back formed into a high roll with a little white bow. They'd sit there on one of those broken benches in front of the IV Tower like two frogs on a stone. Not a damn thing to say. This was one of the things in life Nile was purely worst at, making conversation. With girls, he was a lost cause. But even on the job he was like constipated. Some POs were pretty good with clients. Ninety-nine percent of these kids didn't want to tell you shit to start, afraid you'd jam them with it later, knowing they couldn't make themselves sound right anyway. With Nile, they all sat there, chewing gum, or looking at their fingers, slouched over in the chair, sort of tip-tapping their Nikes and hoping to figure out what little they had to do to get it over with. Nile kept the radio on, just so the silence wasn't so bad. He'd read questions off the form. Health? School? Have you looked for work? 'Talk sports. Ask them about the Traps, the Hands. Ask them about songs on the radio.' There was all kinds of advice. None of it did Nile much good. With Bug, he was stuck with the dumb and obvious.

"School?" he asked. "You go to school?"

"Nn-uh, not hardly. I don't dis my teachers none. Some fool be crackin up, I turn round and tell him, 'Shut yo mouth, punk, we all learnin somethin here.' But you know, I get tired with it, man. Cause they all the time just tryin to turn me out. On account there all them Goobers round." He didn't understand what Bug meant. "You know, they in my face, man, bout how I can't bring no strap with me to school." A gun, she meant. "Now I don't have no weight, how I gone get one block from that school without my ass gone be smoked? All them Goobers waitin for me. On account of my big brother Clyde?"

"Clyde around? He BSD?"

"Top Rank BSD, uh-huh," she said. "He slammin. He on vacation."

"The Yard?"

"Uh-huh. Doin twenty-forty. Some damn Goobers come right up here, representing and carryin on. Right here, be standin twenty feet from where you be. Shit. Clyde popped they ass. I begged him when I saw him takin off with that gat, say, 'Whatchoo doin foo'. This Goober's dusted, man, he flyin on some shit.' He say, 'Leave me be, girl, I cain't let this sucker do that shit right here in my house. True Saint, man, he don't bar none.' So what kin I say? I go down there see him lots. Ride time on them weekends? All us g-girls goin. He doin okay, seem like. But I sure miss him. He out in twenty oh seven, man, make me cry, he talk bout twenty oh seven like it be tomorrow. Anyway, thass how come them Goobers be lookin for me."

He didn't even bother with the obvious: Get out of BSD. They all said the same thing. 'BSD, man, that's me, man.' And Nile understood. This gang-thing, people didn't get it, white people, grown-ups, however you'd say. But like Bug, man, he could see she needed BSD. It was food to the hungry, someone to look at her and say, You cool. All the time: 'You cool. We be for you, girl, homegirl. You be silly, you be crazy, girl, we be for you.' People didn't see that. They said 'Gang' and like freaked. Gats and Blood. Dope. Holy shit! But it was like sweet at the center, like candy.

Nile didn't know when he started in thinking about Bug. It was sort of an accident almost. He talked about her at work. She was on a juvie probation. Nile knew the guardian's PO, Mary Lehr. Bug had gotten busted selling. Cop named Lubitsch pinched her and then didn't come down on her because she wasn't really a case. Juvie pro. That was like nothing.

One day they were there on the benches and Bug was telling him about her father. He'd spotted her on Lawrence yesterday and took her down to Betty's Buy-Rite, bought a ribbon for her hair. He always did like that, Bug said, getting her things.

"Who-all Eddgar anyway, man?" she asked then. "That you daddy? You ravin bout Eddgar all the time."

"Bullshit. I do not talk about him all the time."

"Uh-huh," she answered.

Who was Eddgar? God, man. That was another question Nile could never answer.

"Yeah, he's my father," Nile said eventually.

"He somebody big-time?"

"He's big-time. He's sort of a politician, you'd say. He was a preacher to start."

"Preacher?"

"He was trained that way. He never preached."

"My auntie, she a preacher."

"Really?"

"Uh-huh. Over there at Evangelical Baptist. Sister Serita? You done heard of her?"

"Maybe."

"Yeah, lots of folks heard her, man. She powerful. Powerful. She start preachin and screech—Hoo!" said Lovinia and shook her head. "She, you know, all the time wantin me to come to that church. Keep me off these mean streets, keep me from slammin and jammin. Back in the days when I's little and shit, you know, I singed in the choir, man." She closed her eyes momentarily and felt the power of song.

Sometimes Nile wondered about religion. He liked churches, Catholic churches especially, with their mysterious dark murals, the Virgin Mary with that humble, innocent look, a little like Lovinia's, too shy and holy to even look all these grungy mortals in the eye, or else the incredible gore that was on the walls of these places, Jesus getting nailed, or Saint Sebastian with more arrows in him than a porcupine had quills, or some of these horrifying panels of John the Baptist with his head on the plate and his tongue gorking out. But here was the point: people worshipped that. It filled them with some great sense of spirit.

His father, Nile knew, was into all this stuff. June wouldn't hear of it. To her it was a bunch of stories, important stories, stories she loved to hear told, but stories—what people wished was so, not what was. Religion was some big part of what didn't click in the end between Eddgar and June. When they'd gone freedom-riding, she'd like decided that God, faith, Bible-thumping, it was all just a piece of that whole cornpone tradition that had its foot on the throat of everybody underneath. She just quit on it, and sort of made Eddgar choose almost between God and her. Nile wondered sometimes if his life would have been different if he really was a preacher's kid, instead of the son of whatever it was Eddgar thought he might be. There was a thought and a half: what Eddgar was.

When Hardcore met Eddgar, Core was trippin. He had heard he was a senator and he asked questions about Washington.

"You flied in for this here meet? Where-all in D.C. you hang, man? I got kin there."

Nile told him, as they were about to get into the limousine with T-Roc, "You know, he's not that kind of senator."

"You mean he ain elected and shit?"

"He's elected. But he's a state senator. There're two different kinds of senators, man."

"Yeah," said Hardcore, then after a moment added, "but don't be sayin nothin to T-Roc."

Eddgar talked that day. He was hot-wired. He was so fucking goggle-eyed excited with himself, waving his lean hands around, Nile thought the windows were going to pop out of the car. Eddgar loved these guys, Hardcore and T-Roc, they were like his poster children or something. Sitting there, shrunk back into the corner of the seat, amid the walnut paneling, the crystal liquor decanters, the velvety leather, Nile thought again that there was some fury in Eddgar he would never understand. This was a scene and a half: T-Roc, Core, Nile, Eddgar in back, and two artillerymen in the front seat, one of them rank, just an unbelievable unbathed hard-sweat odor hanging on him. Eddgar talked. The future, he kept saying, the future. Here is the future, I see the future. They didn't want to hear it.

"Brother Kan-el, mon," T-Roc kept saying. "We here kind of seein bout arrangements. Somethin maybe we can be doin?"

Eddgar had said, You think I want money? No, it's not like that. Money, if anything, you'll get money. T-Roc sat forward then. He was a very stylized character. He wore a full beard, a derby, a silk vest with dice and roulette wheels on it, and impenetrably dark glasses, Murder Ones, they called them. Core laughed at him behind his back, but not to his face. T-Roc was one of those guys, dude who knew every bad thing and had it all swimming in him, like some septic pool, could grab hold of the meanest piece of himself any time he needed it. And smart, too. Look you in the eye and suck your brains out. He was short, with thick legs that strained the seams of his black trousers. And a slight Bimini accent. He hiked himself forward on the ribbed black leather seats of the limousine. He figured Eddgar for a psych now.

"Money? How we all gettin motherfuckin money from dis, mon?"

So Eddgar slid into it. It could be arranged. This was what politics really was about.

"Well, you get him dat motherfuckin money, we see bout dat," said T-Roc and waved them out.

Core was in Nile's shit then, all the time. "That all was just bogus, that motherfucker was just playin us, man." Nile couldn't say anything but no, he didn't think so. "I ain down for that. I go head up any motherfucker, man, play me like that, daddy or no. I'd cap that mother soon as look at him. T-Roc, man. T-Roc rip-all on me. 'Lame mother-fuck.' They wasn't shit he ain call me." Core was deep.

What could he say? Eddgar would do it. That was the truth. Eddgar loved this kind of shit. He loved to 'move the system,' make the walls come down. And sure enough, two weeks later, no more, Eddgar told him he had the money coming and Nile told Core. And then June was on the phone three nights in a row. Nile could tell it was about Michael. There was always a certain tone Eddgar took on. Like he'd gotten some icy fluorocarbon up the heinie. Like, 'Hold tight, team, I am in charge, Comrade General of the Revolution, ready to die for the cause.' After the third night, Eddgar, who was on the way to the state capitol, handed Nile the check from the DFU and told him to cash it and send the money to Michael, overnight mail.

"Michael?" Nile had asked. Were other people raised like this? With secrets? Not like Aunt Nelly nips the strawberry wine or Uncle Herman has the hots for the summer girl. But fucking secrets. Like: Don't Tell! Like, if you tell, the Black Hole of Calcutta will open, we'll fall in, we'll die, we'll fucking worse than die. That's how Nile was raised. When he was seven or eight, when they moved to Wisconsin, June had taken him by both arms, gripping him hard enough to hurt. 'Listen to me,' she said for the third or fourth time. 'Listen. You may never tell anyone about Michael, Nile. Do you hear? Never. This is important, Nile. This is critical. You should never say that you knew him before. If anyone makes a mistake, if you do, or I do, if Michael does, if Eddgar does, we will all be apart for a long time. Do you understand? This is important!' That was how he grew up. Jesus.

"He's in some trouble, Nile," Eddgar said.

"What do I tell Core?"

"We'll take care of Core. We'll take care of everybody. It's just a matter of time." Eddgar was in that mood—the democracy of problems, each one solved as well as it could be in five minutes, and then put on hold. The legislative session was drawing to a close and Eddgar was on the phone all night; the fax machine upstairs was curling out paper in what seemed to be a single message. Every time Nile answered the phone it was somebody else, asking urgently for Eddgar—constituents, legislators from around the state, reporters, downstate staffers. Eddgar took each call and allowed himself an instant of reflection before making a terse response. "We'll take care of it," he said again, and left with his small overnight bag.

One day Bug and he were doing what they usually did, just hanging on the benches by the IV Tower.

"Don't be listenin to him, man," she said quietly. "He sell you out."

"Hardcore?"

"Dude gone sell you out."

Nile shrugged. He already knew that, he supposed, was afraid of it at least, but it felt bad to have some skinny little girl say so.

"I don't think so, man."

"Uh-huh. I seed him, man."

"He's cool."

"Okay." She did that girl-thing, flapped a loose wrist, and started to walk away. Nile followed her. "Don't pay no mind to me, man. No man got to listen to no bitch."

"I didn't say that, man. Did I say that?"

"Girl can see what you thinkin too easy, man." She turned, her huge eyes full of the world. "'Ts just tryin to help you, man."

"I know."

She stepped back his way. "Don't say nothin to him, man. Hurt me bad."

"No," he said.

It was all too late by then anyway. By then, Nile had started thinking about her. She was fifteen. Sometimes he'd hit on that number, he'd think, Whoa. He'd shake his finger at himself. Fifteen. Cradle robber, he'd think. Jailbait. It didn't really matter, though. He was swept. It was in his head. Like it always was. Captain Sex in the Head. Even when he got with a girl, that was where it was mostly. Not that he was like a virgin or anything. Nile had fucked four girls. He remembered their names and everything about it. Before Bug, he would count them up each day, as if there might be a surprise. He thought about each time at least once a day, except for one girl, Lana Ramirez. That was a total thing for Nile, it had gone on months and he could only remember the sort of general idea of being with her. She was a big girl, redheaded, she worked in the place where Nile was a messenger. They'd have a few pops after work, she had her own place, they would fuck. That was love for Nile, that was definitely total love. She moved to Miami. He wrote her and tried calling once or twice. But what the fuck? He'd wonder, How'd she get away from me? It seemed impossible. He'd been her slave. Slave.

Sometimes in the middle of the night, when everybody gets weird thoughts, Nile would think, Eddgar doesn't. Like that. That clear, man. Eddgar doesn't. Who ever told Nile that? Well, who had to? He'd been around the guy for nearly twenty years now, and so far as Nile knew, Eddgar'd never been interested — not girls, not boys, not mountain goats. The guy was like immune. Well, that was Eddgar's problem. Not his.

His problem was the money. Hardcore would never let up about it. It was like this circle. Nile would explain what Eddgar had explained to him. First, BSD gets a political organization going, a legitimate presence. Then they have a voice. Then Eddgar can help them be heard. On Kan-el. So it always came back to the money.

"Where that fuckin loot, Jack?" In Core's head it was like a job he'd do when he got ten large. You couldn't tell him the money wasn't for him, it was for organizing, because he already had the organization. He could snap his fingers tomorrow and say, 'Yeah, you-all, better do this registering-to-vote thang.' But until they saw the money, they weren't going to start. Core was always giving face. No letup. If Nile said he'd make changes in a report for Core or some other Saint, if he said he'd talk to somebody about a pending beef, Core would give him a big 'hmpf' and say, 'Same as you gone get us money.'

So one day Nile — he was crazy, he knew he was crazy — but one day Nile said, "It's going to take a while for the money, because we had to spend it on something else, so why don't you do this other part, you know, you and T-Roc, work on this voter thing, there's an election in the fall, then you'll be started, you'll be going good, and I'm sure the money will come through." Core just stared, that look, his street cred, which boasted he was a stone killer.

"No," said Hardcore. He said "No-o-o" many times. "You spent my money? Now idn't that somethin? You spent my money. Ain nobody spend my money but me."

Nile tried to reason with him. It wasn't his money. It was political money. It was walking-around money. It was for political organizing and Core hadn't organized and Eddgar hadn't given him the money. But Core was like a tracking dog, or a mosquito, or a shark. Something that smelled blood. "Where all hell my money gone to?" He must have asked that seventy times.

"Ordell — you want the money, I'll get the money back." This was maybe the most ridiculous thing Nile Eddgar had said in his entire life and Hardcore knew it, like he knew everything else.

"Damn motherfuckin right, you get my loot back. Get out my face, man. Just stop comin round here till you got me that money in you dogs. Gone get me a new PO. I ain down for no more this friendly shit, like you some homie. You ain no homie. Get you ass far away, mother-fucker, 'fore I do somethin I ain s'pose."

So where was that going? When Nile came back a few days later, Core ripped him up again.

"What you doin here, no money in you hand, told you go."

"I don't want to go," said Nile.

They were in front of T-4, where Core held court. All the little Un-borns with their close haircuts, looking like pebbly sandpaper, watched this exchange; a covey of Rollers, hats turned three-quarters, kept an eye on them too. Hardcore was looking straight at Nile now, his brown eyes overfull. Hardcore had a face. He had wrinkles and little brown marks. He had a scar over his nose, and the teardrop beneath his eye. Hard-core's face said Time.

"Mmm-hmm," said Core. And Nile knew he'd told him way too much now.

"How it is," Hardcore said a few days later, "is I got this little thang I need for you to be doin. Need you to take me somethin over in the jail." Ordell had a way, when there was something he wanted—he low-ered his face so his eyes rose to you like dark suns. Eddgar did it, too, funny as that was. Core was up on 17. Central, he called it, like it was some military command or police headquarters. It was really just some old lady's apartment that BSD like essentially stole.

"Just this here one time," Core said. "We tight, you know. Then, you know, this whole money thang, man, that be back in the days, we go do our commu'ty organizin shit, vote for you daddy and who-all. Right?"

Core never said what Nile was supposed to do. But Nile knew, he wasn't that out of it, he knew it wasn't good. And he took a pass. The first time. Just made a face like, 'Get a grip,' and walked out. But of course Hardcore was back at it the next week.

"Bug gone show you," Core said this time, when Nile finally asked what he had in mind. Hardcore scratched his face and looked away, down to the street, where he could see his trade at work. From this apartment on 17, he looked right down on the intersection of Grace and Lawrence, a one-way street where he could observe Tic-Tac coming from every direction. Core was a genius, Nile thought suddenly as he saw the point of being up here.

Finally, Nile said, "Show me."

"Homegirl gone show you, I said."

"I'm not saying I'll do it. I just want to, you know, kind of see."

"See if you gone get gaffled?"

"The whole thing. How I'll feel. I want to kind of figure the whole thing."

"You ain gone get cracked. You get cracked, man, first word out you mouth gone be Hardcore, ain that right? Ain that how it is? You gone lighten the load, man. So, I ain gone let you get cracked."

"I just want to see."

"Lovinia show you."

So she walked him down the street, to one of the crummy buildings on Lawrence, broken-down three-flats, brick buildings with boarded windows and lawns scuffled away to dirt. This was one of Core's stash pads. Lovinia led him along, three steps ahead of him, talking to herself.

"I done tol' you," she said. "You think you way past cool, and I done tol' you." She shook her head sorrowfully.

The building was empty. On the first floor, one door was broken in, just smashed in half, the wood veneer broken off in crazy pieces. This was a crackhouse. Tic-Tac was in and out of here once a month. The acerbic reek of the smoke remained, even though this week, with the last raid only days past, the place was deserted. There was no electricity and the broad old stairwell in the walk-up was lit solely by a window on the fourth floor which wasn't boarded. They moved upward through the cone of falling light. The railings had been ripped off the walls, the light fixtures stolen, the carpet runners, even some of the hardwood from the flooring, had been scavenged. Gang signs were written in paint and marker on the walls. At the fourth floor, Bug stood with her finger across her lip. She wanted to see if they'd been followed. After quite some time, she led Nile back down to the second floor. There were heavy padlocks installed on each front door of the four apartments. Bug opened one of the middle ones with a key.

The place was cold and empty. The linoleum floor had been picked up in places and was soiled in huge spots, which had lain under built-in units, now removed. Bug piled through the cabinets in the kitchen till she found the balloon. Someone had left it there, hours before. Probably Hardcore. They both stood looking at it in her hand. About half a pound of straight coke in the condom, Nile figured. Ten years, minimum mandatory.

"Where do I carry it?"

"Didn't he tell you nothin? You got to put it where they ain gone feel. Them suckers shake you down."

"Barely."

"Yeah, man, you cain't be gettin cracked with this shit."

"I know that." He actually laughed at that point.

"Got to put it where they ain gone feel."

"Which is where, man?"

Lovinia got shy. Her eyes shot away like fish in water.

"Oh man," she said, "how come I got do everything?" She had the tape and some extra condoms in her pocket. She laid them down on a small wooden table in the kitchen, beside the package. "This got to go in you little booty. Okay?"

"No."

"Uh-huh. Don't you be sayin no. Here."

"I'll do it. That's okay."

"Come on, man. I gone do it. Just that damn Hardcore get me some-time. Okay, boy. Come on."

"Come on, what?"

"Leave down you damn pants, man."

"Jesus."

She took the balloon and massaged it. She took it in her two thin hands, working on it with her long fingers, squeezing it out. Just that was enough to get him started.

"Come on, dude. Get wit' it."

He loosened his belt. He worked the pants down his thighs. She got behind him and pulled the elastic on his briefs down herself.

Wait a minute, he thought. Wait a minute. He remembered then he had told Hardcore he just wanted to see. But there was nothing to say now. Bug had told him that on the way over. Core'd be ripping her if Nile didn't go ahead.

"Okay now, bend you over. Thass right. Come on. Put you hands on you cheeks. Okay." Her fingers were chill and startling, but she started laughing. "You know, I don't think I ever seed a white one. Like for-real and all."

"Really?"

"Nn-uh. Weird, you know. Man, you pale, man. Be kind of frightnin."

"Yeah, well, that's nice," he said.

"Oh, you know, you okay." She touched him soothingly. "Only I ain used to it is all. You seed a black girl?"

"Yeah." He wasn't lying. In high school, there was one girl.

"What her name? Now hold 'em apart. Go right there." She ran her fingernail along. "Now it go like that. Now you cain't put no tape over it, or it tear and burstes itself apart. You get that powder over that in- terview room, man, that's big-time shit. So you put some threads and we tape over them threads. Okay?" She told him what he would have to do, who he'd be going to see. Core had planned it all. "So you been gettin busy wit some black chick, huh? You think that's right, huh? Black is best, huh?"

It hadn't come to that, but he didn't say so now. She had her cool, thin fingers all over. She was playing, he knew it, she did too, and he started getting hard. Shit, he thought, shit. But something told him. He really had no will to stop it. His briefs were still up in front, but he was sure she'd notice.

"So you was likin that chick, huh?" She rubbed his ass with both hands. He had no idea what she thought she was doing.

"It was a long time ago."

"Cain't barely 'member, huh?"

"Man, you're playin me."

"You don't seem to mind none." She said it and he didn't say any- thing. "Yeah, you don't seem to mind." She came around the side, looked down, and then, shy as she was, dared his eyes. "What you got there? What you hidin?" She poked it, and he flinched. She laughed, laughed. "I knowed you be likin me."

He didn't move. He didn't say anything either.

"You think I ain never seen that? You don't wanna know what I seen. I seen that." She skirted her hand inside his briefs. "You gettin scared now?" She laughed. She touched him. Just touched and drew her hand back, and laughed some more. "Ain you got nothin to say?"

He was up now, stiff as steel.

"Don't that feel good?" she asked.

"Yes."

They both looked, her hand wrapped all around him.

She sucked. That had never happened to Nile. That had never hap- pened. She went around him in that cold apartment and took him in her mouth and dug her hands into his backside and pushed him back and forth the first few times. It didn't take long for him to be done. She went to one of the back rooms and spat.

"Some girls say it make you sick. You think?"

There was the virus, but he was clean. All county employees got screened each year.

"I don't think so. I learned something about it. Health class or something. I don't think it makes you sick."

Health class. She loved that.

"Don't say nothin to none of them," she said when she reached the door.

"God, no."

Then she smiled. "I knowed you be likin me."

After that, it happened each week. He brought the dope in; the second or third time, he started bringing money out. Core handed him half back and Nile returned it. "Oh, man," said Core with disgust. He stuffed it into the pockets of Nile's trousers. "Damn, man. You too much," he said. Nile kept the money in a carton in his closet. He figured he'd send it to Michael sometime. Or buy something for Bug.

Sometimes Lovinia and he fucked. There was a mattress there and Bug rode him. She had tiny little pouchy breasts and her ribs showed. She was so thin it was frightening. There never seemed to be much in it for her. She was working. He was a man and this was what men wanted. One thing Bug knew about was the world. She liked it when he said it felt good. She liked it when he said stuff afterwards. There were a hundred things Nile wanted to ask her. Did Hardcore know? But Nile was pretty sure he didn't. Was it because he was white? But that was crude. Was it because he was nice? Which is what she was always saying. Had she ever done it for money? Had she done this for Hardcore?

"Ain you gone touch me?" she asked him the next time, once they were in the apartment.

He wanted to ask her a hundred things. But nothing so much as this: What does it mean to you? Do you think about me all the time, the way I think of you? Do you feel your skin surge, do your hips and heart ache? What does it mean to you?

He never really knew.

"Dang," Eddgar said. He stood by the refrigerator, a hand planted on his forehead. This was how Eddgar spoke in the privacy of his home, when Nile was around, as if Nile were still three years old. Imagine a person, a human being, ripping out a 'Dang' like he was Gomer Pyle or something. At moments, his father could do things—sniffle, pick his *teeth, scratch—display a sign he was just as fucking dumb as everybody else, and Nile would hate him worse than any other person in his life. Because he couldn't get past him, couldn't get away. Sometimes, Nile felt like some poor yapping mutt, a dog in the yard running this way and that, barking at you, charging in your direction, and never remembering till he was jerked back so powerfully his forepaws left the lawn, never recalling, Hey, I'm tied to this goddamn stake in the ground. That was Nile. That was Eddgar.*

"I keep forgetting about this," Eddgar said. He was holding the wad of notes he carried in his shirt pocket. It was strange to Nile how his father had turned into an old man. He was one of those strange old birds now with everything he had to remember written on a paper in his pocket.

"What?"

"The money. Make sure you tell Ordell I'm going to get to it. I just don't know where it's supposed to come from."

"He's okay about it."

"You didn't tell *him*?"

"No. You mean where it went? No. I just said, you know, it'd be a little longer than we expected. He's cool, though. You know, I've been giving him some help."

"Help?"

"Yeah, you know."

"What kind of help?"

"Help. H,e,l,p."

"As his probation officer?"

"Sort of. It's not important."

"Wait, wait. Nile. Pay attention. Look at me." His father was at the kitchen table. "What are you doing?"

"Eddgar—"

"Wait. What are you doing, Nile?"

Fuck you doing? He stood in the fiery furnace. Fuck you doing? The question of his life.

EDDGAR

You could never really judge Eddgar without seeing this. That's what he told himself. Those who scorned him—there were many, the reporters, the statehouse guttersnipes, the ugly claque tittering about Loy-

ell Eddgar and his life of endless plotting—they could never really take account of him without seeing him as he lived here, in a three-room apartment carved out of the large house. He'd bought this house for June twenty-five years ago in the most grandiose gesture he could conceive of to reflect personal reform. It never mattered to her. She left anyhow, and over time he cut away the space. He had student roomers during the term, and in the winter a flophouse in the basement for homeless men. But privacy, solitude remained precious. Those parts of the house where others dwelled were sealed off from the smaller area Eddgar and Nile occupied.

Eddgar's rooms were spartan. He never bothered with carpets. The hardwood was chilly. He still fell wearily upon the same Danish Modern sofa which had traveled from their place in Damon, its orange cushions covered with Guatemalan prints. There was nothing on the walls, only a single picture in a frame on an old maple coffee table: Nile, June, Eddgar in the late sixties, the boy with flossy curls, a hand upraised in childish jubilance. Bulwarks of books and papers were piled neatly. In his bedroom, the spread was tucked precisely beneath the outline of the pillow, leaving no sign of the man who was here in the middle of the night with the covers in turmoil.

What did he think then? Did he wake with longing? And for whom? That is what people wanted to know, he realized. But he could not fully say himself. He recalled coming to in that state and instantly feeling somehow thwarted and ashamed, his mind quickly diverted. He spoke then to God, as he had done in moments of utter privacy all his life. For years—the bad years as Eddgar thought of them, when so much seemed beyond his control—in those years he would hide from himself the fact he did this, so that the disarming knowledge that he was still secretly conducting this conversation with Him would come flying at Eddgar out of nowhere, like a levitating object at a séance. He would think, How can it be? But he never stopped. For one reason. He listened. At that age of four or five or six, somewhere far back there, one thick summery Southern night, with the locusts sawing themselves in shrieks of desiccated passion, the intimation came to Eddgar of the vast presence above who heard with welcome Eddgar's inner thoughts. God listened. Not always with patience or admiration. At times, Eddgar grappled with God, as Jacob wrestled the angel. Sometimes in his dreams, Eddgar saw them locked together, tussling, their naked flanks sweat-glistered and etched in shadow. He felt the overheated breath, the ferocious violent embrace of God nearly squeezing life from him, a sort of ecstasy arising amid the pain.

Now fresh from bed, he imagined everything he must do today, how he would be in the world. He recollected meetings, a staff lunch, committee members he needed to persuade, calls to Farmers Alliance members downstate, a constituent requiring help at the U. Tonight he would speak at a dinner in the South End in DuSable at a Legal Aid Center function. Eddgar had gone for years—good folk, Irish, Italians, and Mexicans, organized around one of those parish priests, Father Halloran, still lean and energetic at sixty-four, who'd been there thirty years, full of hope, kindling kindness amid the lives that would stand parched and lonely without him. Halloran kept his parishioners supporting this little clinic where the poor received free advice about overbearing landlords, their sad divorces, the kids in trouble on the street. Eddgar loved these events, finding people, ordinary people, secretaries and shop floor managers, who cared to see the world made better, whose feelings ran beyond the boundaries of their lives. Their kids came, too, half of them grown, moved off to the far-flung corners of the suburbs, but still drawn back to this, to the flame of their beliefs.

He would talk about the pure good of this enterprise. No sentiment. But he'd say that good faith and caring are not government responsibilities alone. And they'd ask: 'Senator Eddgar,' they'd ask, 'what else can we do? What can we do?' And for a minute, this hall, a basement room in a K. of C. Hall, a place with cheap paneling and magenta carpeting worn to a number of blackened spots, would be quiet. What can we do? The whole place would throb with the pained life of the poor. He did not know exactly what he'd say, but he savored the moment in prospect. In the statehouse, they could laugh at him all they liked, the staffers and media thugs could be smug, but this was still his work, still where he knew just who he was, when he felt both the torment of people warring all their lives against the dim weight of poverty and scorn, and the furious strength of his dedication to them.

They never understood, men like Hardcore, men like Huey, they never recognized that it was a thrill to Eddgar to see them—black men, powerful, rigid with anger. It thrilled him to think these men were the heirs, the successors of the beaten, woebegone souls he'd watched chop tobacco during his childhood, men and women who grasped the spiny stems Eddgar could not even touch, migrants, moving listlessly, hopelessly up the dusty roads, carrying with them the odor of the thick aromatic sap. He had loved those people, so cruelly thwarted by the likes of his father, adored them with a mighty, towering, limitless love. He did not love Hardcore or Huey. They did not want his love, which was one reason they frightened Eddgar, much as they frightened everybody else. But he was thrilled, because their strength, their anger equipped them to move forward in the world. *Now we must move beyond anger. That is what he would say tonight. We must move on to gratitude, participation, responsibility.* Wide-awake, at the lee end of the night, he stared toward the ceiling fixture, the textured glass that captured the glaring light of two bulbs, and saw the brightness only as a tangible sign of his own commitments.

Downstairs, at this hour, past 5 a.m., he heard the ruckus of Nile readying himself for departure. He was gone early on these days to avoid the traffic. It was an hour and a half sometimes from Greenwood into Kindle Probation. *He has been getting better,* Eddgar thought, knowing he had told himself this nearly Nile's entire life. But it seemed to be true. He was less edgy, more responsive, holding this job, a real job, with which he seemed legitimately involved. Yes, all right, he was still under his father's guidance, still hovered over at moments like a small child. But he was working where there was so much good to be done. Eddgar proceeded downstairs to find his son in a denim shirt and a leather tie, eating cereal and watching the TV.

"Hey," said Nile. His son still slept here two or three nights during the work week, if Eddgar was not downstate. Nile's place in town was a lonely closet. Nile also passed the weekends here. The boy, the man Nile had become, six foot one, sloppy with loose flesh, sprawled on the sofa, unshaved, unwashed, drinking name-brand beer in the living room downstairs and watching TV. They did not speak much. He was not sure what Nile wanted. Free food? A place to lounge and be looked after? There were a hundred sarcastic answers. But he welcomed the boy's presence. Eddgar liked to have him here, in sight. They both felt better that way. Eddgar had put on yesterday's shirt and found his notes in the pocket.

"Dang," he said. He touched his forehead. "I keep forgetting. The money. Make sure you tell Ordell I'm going to get it. I just don't know where it's supposed to come from."

"He's okay about it," Nile had offered, fixed on the TV. But the alarm had started faintly clanging. It was experience, nothing else. Eddgar began to pursue him, until Nile said he had given Hardcore some form of help.

"Wait, wait. Nile. Pay attention. Look at me." His father was at the kitchen table. "What are you doing?" How did he know? There was a look Nile had, a sly, shamed, hound-dog look, confronting the fact that the internal realm where he resided did not mesh with the one recognized at large. It was always frightening to observe this, and Eddgar was petrified now.

"I'm just helping out."

"Helping what? On probation beefs? Are you throwing files away?"

"Nothing like that. I do my job."

"Where? What are you doing?"

"In the jail," Nile said finally.

It had come out in pieces. Eddgar, who thought of himself as stoical and strong, had his head down on the table by the time the discussion was through. He wrapped himself in his own arms. He asked Nile many times, many times to say it was a joke. As a boy, a teenager, Eddgar thought every day of Jesus on the cross, as the nails drove through the flesh of His hands first, then His feet. Even as the nerve and bone was crushed He must have welcomed his pain, knowing it would soon bring the world salvation. All his life, Eddgar had tried to welcome pain, but he could not welcome this.

"It's cool," said Nile, actually hoping to comfort him.

"No, it's not cool. It is the most uncool, stupid, dangerous thing you could possibly be doing. It's crazy."

"You think someone else wouldn't do this, Eddgar? There's so much shit in there. Just money, for Godsake. They're not supposed to have a nickel, and I bring out 5,000 bucks a week."

"Oh, Nile." In the rising biliousness, in the sense of delirium taking over the moment, the most sickening thought to Eddgar was that he was going to have to call June. He was going to have to say, 'This is the worst yet.' He was going to have to give her news which would only drive her down further. He was going to have to say what they had been saying for years: 'We have a problem. A crisis. You need to come here. We have to straighten this out.' He was going to have to ask her again to rise, memorably, to the occasion, to closet her own suffering and to focus on the desperate task of salvaging Nile.

"Lord, Nile," he said. He was sick.

There was a fantasy Eddgar had, a grisly impossible vision that had come to him once and repeatedly beckoned him back, the cruel Lorelei of the sickest kind of self-punishment. He was eighty-five and terminal. And trying to figure out what to do with Nile, how to protect him from the savagery of the world, much as he tried when Nile was twelve and thirteen to protect him from the insolent, heavy-lidded-looking boys at school who beat Nile and stole from him with utterly no fear of reprisal. Cowering, so desperately in need of his father's protection, Nile could seem precious to Eddgar. But in this fantasy Eddgar realized there was no way to save Nile, he would not grow wiser or stronger. In mercy, Eddgar would have no choice but to kill them both. It was a dream, actually, that was how these thoughts had started, but it had been enough to make him weep, seeing the gun in the dream and waiting, hoping his son would turn his head, because there was no way to do this if he had to face him. Shoot fast, he always thought, when he tried to turn the vision away and could not, shoot fast so you don't have to live for that instant in between.

"We have to fix this, Nile. We have a chance to make this right before any real damage is done. I want to know how I can get in touch with Hardcore. And your career as a drug courier is over. It's done. Right now."

"No," said Nile. He stood up. He actually seemed horrified by Eddgar's declaration.

"Right now."

"Fuck you," he answered. He was gone from the house in a few minutes and did not return.

HARDCORE

They was some motherfuckers, some white motherfuckers, who knowed they owned the motherfuckin world. You could tighten up on these motherfuckers, jam them up, put you a strap right in they motherfuckin face, and it don't matter none, cause this motherfucker, till the minute he be motherfuckin dead, he still thinkin, Damn, nigger, I am the motherfuckin owner of this motherfuckin world. And what-all you gone do with a motherfucker like that?

One o'clock, bright in the daytime, Nile daddy rolled in. Homies get up under him, soon pop his ass as see his face, and he still goin, Where-all Hardcore at, man? Damn, I a senator and shit, I want to talk to his ass.

Core told Bug, "Bring that fool up here, motherfucker make me laugh."

And then he come through the door up at Central on 17, not so much as 't's'up, not so much as How you do, he just rainin on Core how he can't be havin none this shit.

"I'm sorry you think I've shortchanged you, or misled you somehow, but what Nile is doing for you, that has to stop, that cannot and will not continue, I'm sorry."

He sorry. Core just shook his head at the thought.

"Damn, man, you in my crib." He pointed to the cement floor, where there was nothing but three telephones and their cords. "You don' be tellin me where I sit, where I stand, in my crib. Cause it's my crib. This son of you, he a growed-up man, idn't he?"

"You know Nile."

"Yeah, he my PO." Hardcore could not suppress a minute smile, a moment of pure whimsy at the notion of the state, in its bureaucratic ineptitude, allowing such a pitiful mismatch. "He can decide for his own self."

"I've decided. This is done, Ordell. I'm in this now. I know, so I'm implicated. I can't take that chance myself. And I certainly can't take it for Nile."

"Damn, man, so what you aimin for me to do here? Just gone say, 'Hey, homes, ain gone be no shit this week, you-all just get yo'self strung out and shit, cause Nile daddy say No, cause he complicated?' That how I s'pose to do all mine? No, motherfuck. When I say 'Cool,' then it be motherfuckin cool. And it ain now."

Nile's daddy just stood and did him a minute with his eyes. This mother, just some lumpy little white man, but he got him eyes like a spook, goin like, 'It's on, motherfucker, cause ain no nigger gone work on me.'

"Ordell, if I hear you're trying to involve him in any more, I'm going with Nile and the best lawyer I can find straight to the PA."

Core laughed then. Core came right up in his face.

"You gone tell the PA what a dope-peddlin fool he been? I don't think so, motherfucker. You gone turn on yo own kin? I don't think so. Damn motherfuck, he may as well plead guilty to murder. Kind of quantities that boy carried? Pounds of that shit. He a damn organizer, don't you know? He a drug kingpin. He gone be on the wall for life, Jack."

Nile's daddy, he be shakin his head the whole time Core spoke. "Not if he talks, Ordell. Not if he gives them you."

Core very nearly busted a cap in Eddgar right here. Like to took his own dogs and beat the motherfucker dead. Only he needed time for that. He needed to think.

"No," Hardcore said, "you sure enough right about that. He beef me out, ain gone be life, no parole. Only gone be fifteen, no parole. That all the minimum mandatory. He could kill somebody's ass and get out sooner. Ain you one them mothers thought that shit up? That be the law, man."

"Ordell, for Godsake, do you know who I am? If I get on that telephone, the PA himself will be on the other end. You really think I can't work this out? It's not the same for me as it is for you. You know it, Ordell, and I know it. So let's not kid ourselves. Because we're both too intelligent for that."

That was it. Too much! He told Bug to get him out. He sighted Eddgar down the length of his finger.

"Head up, motherfucker: Yo ass here any more, you gone have a dead ass. I ain talkin no shit here. Word up." Motherfucker come in his crib and do him like that. Be a dead motherfucker now, and he don't know it. Motherfuckin owner of the motherfuckin world!

Core had Bug call Nile at Probation. Took him three whole days to get hisself there, but he come. Hardcore knew he would. He jumped in his shit soon as Nile was out his ride. Ripped him right there on the street.

"Man, what the fuck you done and done?" he asked. And Nile, this silly Opie motherfucker, with all that greasy hair and shit, hippie motherfucker or somethin, he like he got whooped in the gut, he can't even talk.

"Core," he said. "I just told him, man. I had to."

"Had to what? So he kick yo butt? Man, I don't fall to none of this shit. I don't compre-hend it. You know? My daddy, man, he just some fool on the corner, man. I see him, I book. What kind of shit you puttin down here? 'Had to tell him.'" Core worked his mouth around to spit, then did it, a long glob to the dirty, broken walk. This was just some unbelievable shit, Nile and his daddy, like to make him wanna smoke them both. "That daddy yourn, man, he piss off the Good Humor Man. You hear me? He one of them uptight motherfuckers think he always runnin changes on you. See? You know, like he be fuckin Charlie Chan or somethin, you know? Number-one son, all that shit. He a cold, deadly motherfucker. Stand right up on me and say he gone snitch me out. Ain't no motherfucker on the street down me like that. I kill they ass soon as look at them." Core walked a few paces in pure agitation and turned back to Nile. "So you gone beef me out, motherfucker?"

"Of course not."

"So what-all gone jump off here then, huh? You hate this mother-fucker or what?"

"Eddgar?"

"Fuck yeah. Charlie Chan. You hate him? You gone let him do you like that?"

"No," Nile said mildly. "But I mean—" He got dumb like he do, can't even think to talk or move. "I mean, what choice do I have?"

On the street, man, standin round chillin, every dude say he a man. Every bro is down for his. But it ain but half strap up. And in the joint, you see the same. All these proud, tough motherfuckers claimin Goo-bers, whoop them some and they be beggin, 'Don't do me like that, I ain representin no one.' But Nile, man, he was the lamest, the weakest. Like to think he was a punk, but the stiff-dick motherfucker busy now with this skinny little ho, she suck you dick, man, ain no better than she polishin you shoes, but Nile, he like that too.

"Straight down, man. You tell that daddy of yourn this. You tell him, Core say you be here 6:15, tomorrow mornin. Gone meet in the street, man."

"For what? What are you going to do?"

"Gone tell him the word, man: Ain no foo'. He ain even think, that motherfucker. He think he the owner of the motherfuckin world, man, and he don't even know I got plans of my own. What kind of dumb motherfucker he think I bein? Man, you in-surance now. I got you fingerprints and all over all that dope money, man. I been savin that shit up like in the bank. I dime on you, man, PA gone call me 'Sir.' Best do like I say. And he be sayin, you gone beef on me? Bullshit. What proof he got?"

Nile made a face. "Don't be an asshole, man. I've been cool. You don't have to dis me like that."

"I ain dissin. I ain hissin or dissin. I ain fuckin you momma. This just how it be, man. It cold, man. Thass all I'm gone tell yo daddy. Tell him, 'Daddy, man, it's too late. Too late. Trust me or bust me, man, and you ain gone bust me.' Hear?"

Nile looked at him, those lame eyes, skittering like bugs. Hardcore could hardly stand it.

"Listen up, dude. You hate this motherfucker worse than I do. Ain that straight shit, now? Ain nothin gone happen here you wudn't done

youself. You do like I'm sayin. Ain nothin for you to do after that. Hear?"
Core took Nile's chin. He made him look at him, like he hated to do.
"Listen here," he said. "I be you daddy now."

J U N E

Fear and danger. Well, she'd been here before. Driving, June felt her
pulse stirring in unlikely places—above her elbows, in her neck beneath
the points of her chin. Anxiety, danger always had divided her. A fat old
woman, cheerful and controlled, gripped the wheel of Eddgar's Nova,
careful not to let the needle of the speedometer drift even a mile over
the limit. Shrunken down inside her was someone else, ready to sing
out in terror. She'd been here before, her hair roots, her nipples, her
fingertips juiced with adrenal output. She tuned in Dusty radio for a
second, hoping for some great old tune, and then thought, No, no, too
much, way too much, and laughing at herself drove on, into DuSable
toward Grace Street. The large forms were somehow shocking after the
low, soft shapes of the prairie. How could humans live like this, exist at
such close quarters, with the sacred, saving earth, from which life sprang,
paved over beneath their feet? A kid who looked to have been up all
night gunned by in an old jacked-up blue deuce and a quarter, mouthing dirty words in Spanish, the decorative fringe of an old bedspread
shimmying in his rear window.

　　Were those the best years, she wondered suddenly, those years of
danger? How could they be? She had been so miserable by the end—
frightened of everything, of Eddgar and of herself, of what she had done.
She was the one who demanded they look after Michael. She parted
from Eddgar to do it, insisting they could not simply leave wreckage in
their wake. How could it seem so wonderful now? She asked Eddgar a
few years ago, when she was in town, apropos of absolutely nothing, she
asked, 'Do you ever think about that time?' He answered, 'No.' Not an
instant's hesitation. No. It was gone. It could not be reclaimed. It was
gone, like his childhood, like their marriage, like the many events of
everyone's past that meant something when they were happening but
would never return.

　　When she looked back to those years, the years with Eddgar—from
the start to the end—there was always a universe of stalled feelings inside
her. At the planetarium here in the city, you could sit and watch the
stars turn about you as the earth moved through a season, a year. Living

with Eddgar was like that. It always seemed as if he were the single point around which the whole moving panorama of the sky turned—him, and her because she was beside him. She never spoke to anyone about Eddgar. There was never anyone else who understood. Not now. Not then. Perhaps she did not understand herself. In bed with various men years ago, she sometimes mentioned his problems, as if trying to save somebody's opinion. It was always the same routine, lying there, smoking cigarettes, watching the ceiling, because she did not want to think about who in particular was next to her. And in this mood of celestial detachment, she would remark how Eddgar had been more or less incapable since Nile's birth. Did she want them to know she needed less than they might think? Of course, in those days, she would have laughed at the word 'unfaithful.' Doctrine forbade chattelizing any relationship. She was not Eddgar's possession. It was a piece of regressive patrimony to say that her pleasure was not her own business. But she remembered all of that, sleeping with his colleagues, stretching her body against a dozen men she did not know well, allowing them inside her—she remembered it with shame, because Eddgar was there anyway, and they both knew it.

She had never loved anyone the same way. Not before or since. Thank God. Thank God. He was a divine, beautiful thing when he started out; she loved him in the illusion-haloed manner of a teen, this beautiful young man with incredible eyes who spoke about God with an unnerving intimacy. She'd been raised in a religious home. Her mother passed hours on the veranda, with an iced tea and the Bible on her lap. She died rocking and trying to decipher the same verses she'd read her whole life. Secretly, from childhood forward, June had believed none of it. And yet when Eddgar spoke, she believed she had met the man—there had to be a man—to take her to the greater life out there. It was some variant, she supposed, on the idea of heaven, that there was a better life here on earth, too. He was inspired, on fire with the rage to make that better life. Teach me! she thought. Share it! She was so jealous of his faith, the more so when she realized years on that the only real expression of Eddgar's passion was for the people who were not close to him. He loved the poor like puppets, like dolls, a love that left him in complete control. For Nile, for her—'impotent' was the right word. But his passion was like the heat of the sun. She always knew it was really the love he wanted to feel for them.

In the years since, Eddgar and she had both come to assume, without ever saying it, that their demise was her fault. She'd wanted his faith and could not have it. She could not believe what he believed and so she took it from him. Believe something else, she said, something I can share. Rev-o-lution! Oh, she had believed in that. Sanctified by revolution. Reformed by revolution. Everything errant in her life would be corrected. She challenged poor Eddgar. Because he was always her example. How much can you believe? she wanted to know. How much faith can you have? Are you still pure? If I let other men inside me? That was her challenge. And he took it up in his own way and eventually invited himself into those beds. Not in the lurid sense that he ever wanted details. But her love affairs, her animal needs, had to serve the revolution somehow. And in that way, Eddgar, with his stillborn loving, remained, in the way he always had to be, supreme.

"I think this could be dangerous," Eddgar had said holding the car keys this morning.

"He's my son, too."

"I'm not questioning your devotion, June. I don't think it's safe. I know it's not safe. Ego and self-esteem are what really move the folks down there. I think we should do what I told Ordell we were going to do. We should take Nile and go to the PA. I know him."

"Eddgar, stop. Stop the heroism. And the scheming. It's no answer. That's a disaster. For you. And especially for Nile. Even Michael will be jeopardized if you're not careful. That's asking to destroy everyone. You should speak to a lawyer before you do anything, and you shouldn't do that until I've talked to this fellow now."

"June. It's dangerous. I wouldn't be surprised if he's got half a mind to kill me. Maybe more than half. This is too dangerous for anyone."

"It's not as dangerous for me as it is for you. I'm a fat old woman. I'm not going to threaten anyone. Give me the keys. I'll call as soon as we're through."

So here she was again, on one of Eddgar's missions. God, the places she had gone in this life. She thought about the Panther safe houses to which Eddgar used to send her. What a crazy scene. With the guns all over. The automatic weapons, fully loaded, leaning against the wall, much as a farmer would lean his hoe, bandoliers of rounds in full metal jacket looped over the rifle barrels. The windows were newspapered so the cops and FBI could not see inside. Near the end, after the Oakland Armory raid, there was military issue about: M–16s and M–79s, ammunition boxes, blasting caps piled into a green duffel marked by stencil COMPANY A, 92D ENGINEERS and the M–18 smoke grenades and C–4 plastic explosives. Sometimes there was cocaine piled up on a table like flour. And always women, and babies crawling under foot, among the men in berets and boots.

Eddgar had nearly been shot half a dozen times in those places. Someone was always pulling a gun on him, angered not so much by his opinions as by his manner. He looked down the barrel of the gun, implacable. She—everybody there, everyone but Eddgar—saw the same thing in him, a Southern boy refusing to bend to their rage. But Eddgar would not flinch. He thought about his death, the need to die for the revolution every day. And he never let those incidents pass. He believed in discipline. When poor Cleveland was released from the Alameda County jail, when they bailed him after he had snitched out Michael, Eddgar could barely wait to get to the inevitable denouement. He made a show of good cheer, but the last time they saw Cleveland, the morning he was killed, Eddgar took a .44 and fired off a round and laid the muzzle, hot enough to burn, right against Cleveland's temple. He left a mark and didn't say a word, even as Martin Kellett and two Panthers grabbed Cleveland. The mark of Cain, she thought now. It was all so crazy.

About much of it, about Cleveland's death, for example, she had been too sorry since to live much of a life. She had gone down, fallen help-lessly into the chasm. She had made a silly marriage to a handsome, empty man, a man who was even somewhat cruel. He gave her drugs, and she took that for love. They broke up. She took the cure, but started drinking again seven years ago, and now she drank too much every day. She sat up nights, lapping up cheap Bordeaux by the liter and playing computer solitaire.

Now she made a right and came closer to the projects. She could see the blunt towers looming over the rows of industrial buildings, the final structures before the blocks of wasteland around Grace Street. There were old foundries with smokestacks, like arms raised in warning, ware-houses with huge gantry doors, all the buildings guarded by razor wire atop their fences. What was in there to steal? The few faces on the streets now, as the early-morning dark was starting to dissolve, were black, and in her present mood of recollection she thought of Mississippi in the old days and the God-fearing simple people they wanted to help, people who were so good, so radiantly good they seemed almost angelic, suffering their life of deprivation and toil. Lord, she loved to leave the churches, the meetings on Sunday nights in summer. The Southern air hung like a damp sock and the broken light of the moon silvered the trees and the bosks of the heavy landscape. She loved to hear the singing voices rising, gathered together and holding, like the voice of history, to a single note. How could we have gone from there to here with so little gained? she wondered. How could we have raised up these despairing children, dispossessed, who felt from their first moments there was no place on earth for them, who were untouched, unsaved by any tradition of human nobility? How could this have occurred? We were right! she thought, suddenly, desperately. We were right. That was why she was here now, in the cold hand of danger. She was doing what she'd done a hundred times before, saving him, saving Eddgar, this beautiful passionate boy, because she had to save everything he believed in, because she had no faith herself. But oh, oh, she had believed in him, in revolution, and she claimed some fragment of that surging feeling now as she swung onto the street. She rolled the window down and smiled absurdly.

"Lady," a young woman said, a perfectly beautiful young woman with flawless chocolaty skin. She had a stocking cap tugged down over most of her face. "Lady," she said, "you in the wrong damn place."

April 2, 1996

SETH

So this is how it happens, Seth thinks. You hassle the guy inside your head for twenty-five years and then you walk up to his door on a Tuesday morning and knock and here he is, holding his half-frame glasses and today's newspaper. Eddgar is stock-still behind the screen door.

"Is this about Nile?" he finally asks. "Is he in more trouble?"

"I hope not."

Eddgar undertakes another instant of visible deliberation, his face obscured in the deep shadows of early morning. Seth waits on the tongue-and-groove porch that wraps around the front of the old frame house.

"I was about to make a cup of tea," Eddgar finally offers and nudges the door open a few inches. The interior architecture is baffling. The corridor goes on forever, and the air is heavy with the scent of frying oil and gathered human smells, a little like a barracks. "Have you heard from him?" Eddgar asks when they reach the small kitchen.

Seth removes the paper Hobie gave him last night, the microfiche from the delivery company showing Michael's address. Eddgar puts the kettle on to boil and replaces his glasses before taking up the record.

"Am I being threatened?" he asks then.

"I'm trying to put some things together, Eddgar. It's not a threat."

"Quite certain? Not planning any reunions with the FBI? No *confessional* in your column? You see, I want to be sure we aren't going to have another act in that morality play in the courtroom. *The Revenger's Tragedy?* Isn't there a drama of that name? I believe June studied it." Eddgar coughs at that moment, a rattling attack on his lungs. He holds a fist before his mouth. "But I suppose your impulse for vengeance is well satisfied at this point." Eddgar smiles solely for his own benefit. "What is it you want to know, Seth?"

"The truth? There was a lot of lying in that courtroom."

"Surely not by me," says Eddgar. "It was your friend Tuttle who distorted the facts." He stands somewhat stiffly and returns to the whistling kettle, casting about the kitchen to find a second cup. When he opens the refrigerator for milk, it is largely bare, holding only a dairy carton, a gallon jug of water, and a single green olive and a red pimento, separated and floating in half a jar of greenish juice. "Is he crazy or melodramatic?" Eddgar asks.

"Hobie? More a performance artist. That's how I think of him. The word as gesture."

"He's a treacherous person." Eddgar shakes his head at the thought and places both cups, curling steam, on the table. "I'm sure you had a good time watching Hobie play with my life. I assume you felt it was appropriate. Because you think I played with yours."

"Didn't you?"

Eddgar takes his time with that. Across the table, he folds his hands carefully.

"I took advantage of a circumstance, Seth. There were careful plans and they went awry. Someone was arrested, quite accidentally. He started blabbing. So I seized an opportunity, yes I did. Unkind? Probably. Yet I was confident — and correct as it turned out — it would work out for all of us."

"The greatest good for the greatest number, Eddgar? Including number one?"

"It was a *long* time ago, Seth."

"Are you invoking the statute of limitations? I thought there wasn't one on murder." Eddgar's eyes squeeze shut then and Seth eases forward in the beaten old kitchen chair. The maple table between them is small, stained with berry juice in one place, a relic of many decades' use in Eddgar's household. "I want you to understand something, Eddgar. I'm as old now as you were then. Older, I guess. And I blame myself. First and foremost. The things I did, *I* did. Not you. But if I was czar of the universe, or the Lord High Executioner, you'd be punished. You escaped. And it bothers me, man, it kills me. How come everyone suffered but you, Eddgar? Don't you ask yourself? Do you think about them, Eddgar? The lives you took? The ones you ruined?" Seth stabs a finger down on the paper he brought. "How do you sleep at night, for Godsake?"

Eddgar takes the question with a taut, slightly whimsical expression. Well, he doesn't sleep at night. Seth can read that thought. There is a small window at Eddgar's back and in the early-morning light his face is haggard. A day's growth clings to his cheeks, like a sugared topping.

"Do you know people who fought wars, Seth? I fought a war. Yes, there were casualties, and I rue them, I mourn for them. But I certainly didn't turn my back on Michael. That should be obvious." His face dips toward the paper on the table. "I gave him every kind of support imaginable. For years. My wife—and my son—essentially abandoned me to see after him. With my consent. Yet it wasn't in repentance. Because I don't repent." Eddgar's face is raised at that characteristic angle of willful invulnerability. But this much no doubt is true. Seth thought about it all night and realized it wasn't charity or grief that motivated Eddgar to care for Michael from this distance all this time. No. Michael was the man Eddgar could not be: to June a lover, to Nile a gentle guiding hand. He was Eddgar's own lost fragment. He could no more let go of Michael than himself. But Eddgar doesn't see that part. His justification, as ever, lies in history.

"I had something to fight against," says Eddgar, "and I fought. And the war I fought still makes more sense to me than many of the wars waged in this country: the Indian Wars. The Spanish-American War. The Mexican-American War. Vietnam. I believe—as I believed even then and was afraid to say to myself—I believe I shall be judged. And

I don't fear it. But don't you dare think I did not suffer. Then or now. Because I have, I *have*. I have paid prices you cannot *imagine*." Red creeps up to Eddgar's scalp, and he winds himself away in a momentary effort to contain his anguish. "And don't think I'm speaking about what you and your friend did to me in that courtroom. I care much less than you might suppose for my reputation."

That wasn't what he thought. June, is what Seth guesses. June was Eddgar's anguish, a whirlwind of torment right up to the terrible end.

"What did we do to you in the courtroom?" Seth asks.

"Oh, please, Seth. I'm old, I'm not addled. You had to have been part of that."

"Of what?"

"You know this story. You must." And Eddgar begins to serve out the details as a challenge. You must know, he says. About the dope. The jail. About Nile and Hardcore. "You must know," he repeats.

No, Seth says. His reaction—the pallor, the faltering—brings Eddgar up short, and he responds more sparingly as Seth begins to question him. But he answers. The story is told—about sending the DFU money to Michael, about this young girl, Lovinia, and, most despairingly, about Eddgar's confrontations with Hardcore. Only at the end does Eddgar permit his full glance to fall again on Seth. Even in age, his eyes have remained remarkable. Seth does not remember where he developed the impression that wolves have eyes this color, glacial blue, an outward aspect of beauty and tranquillity concealing a teeming, unmanaged spirit.

"This was all unknown to you?" Eddgar asks again.

"Unknown," says Seth.

Still in doubt, Eddgar stands arthritically for a second cup of tea and speaks as he's standing at the stove, describing the game of prisoner's dilemma that Core and whoever advised him played. They were mutual hostages—Nile and Hardcore. When June was killed, Eddgar understood at once that it was not an accident. But what was he to say? The truth would put Nile in the penitentiary. He remained silent, never guessing that the police would be able to build a case on Hardcore, or what Ordell would do as a result. But there was not a lawyer Eddgar spoke to after Core had implicated Nile who did not say the same thing: Nile would do less time for a crime of family passion than for distributing pounds of narcotics in the course of abusing a public trust. Not to mention that Nile stood a chance at trial this way. They were trapped.

"And I've thought about this, naturally," says Eddgar, "I've thought at great length about what Hardcore did, and I doubt his motive was to punish Nile—I doubt that entered his mind—or only to minimize his position in a very bad situation. What he wanted, also, was to make a point to me. To let me know I was not the only shrewd operator, that for all my grand proclamations, all my ill-considered threats, I still couldn't protect Nile." Eddgar glances briefly, balefully toward Seth, before staring down again into his teacup, which bears the blue seal of some state agency. "Somehow, I had made myself the one true enemy.

"Which is why I told Hobie from the start: Blame me. I actually said that to him. 'Blame me.' And not as an act of misplaced valor. You know, I see that look in your eye—I saw it in court—I think you've regarded me for decades as a monster. People—way back when, back in California—people believed I was not self-aware. Perhaps I wasn't. Not sufficiently. But I think, I believe, I see some of myself. And I mean that when I say I am to blame. I am. For thinking I could control what I couldn't control. For bearding Hardcore. For not accepting my child's limitations. For pushing my own wants on him. I saw that. I'd seen that. People, some people, do see these things. Insight isn't everything, you know. You make mistakes anyway.

"And I made those mistakes, and a dozen more. I was pleased that Sonny was the judge. I suppose that was where it really started. Well, this will fit, I thought. I saw the opportunity immediately. I told Tuttle that. The first time we spoke. 'She never liked me. Blame me. Contrive some other reason Core on his own would want to kill me. She'll believe it.' I started this. I know. And Hobie twisted it, of course. He took advantage of me. He said, 'Will you say yes if I ask the questions the right way?' I told him, 'I won't lie. I just can't. I can't swear an oath to God and lie.' But the right questions, the right way—I could say yes. And he told me before it started, he said very little to me, just 'Listen to my questions, very carefully, because I'm going to be doing something. You don't have to lie, just be careful,' and I agreed to that in advance. I knew he'd use that money, the $10,000 from the DFU, and make it look like that was the money Nile had given Ordell. Because after all, that *was* the plan. And yes, Nile *had* cashed the check. And no one had any reason to know where the money actually had gone. And, of course, of *course*, Hardcore was lying, there never was a $10,000 payment. So what Hobie was doing—it was a lie to combat a lie, and not my lie. And, naturally, I agreed. He's very shrewd about people, your friend Tuttle, isn't he?"

"Very shrewd."

"Yes," says Eddgar. His feet—in his old penny loafers—are tapping on the floor now, but thought has otherwise stilled him. He is somewhat nattily dressed, in a stylish plaid shirt, and he pulls momentarily at the collar. He thought he was being noble, he says, not merely toward Nile, but toward the party people, Galiakos and his crowd. They were after him from the minute Nile was arrested, and Eddgar had promised he'd do everything in his power to keep that $10,000 out of the case, out of the news. They were terrified, understandably. Imagine what it's like, Eddgar says, trying to convince people to make contributions when they've read on the front page of the *Tribune* about party money going to a street gang. He was willing to take the blame for all of it. For the money. For Nile.

" 'Blame me,' I said. And Hobie pulled the rug out, turned the tables. Made day night, night day. Now *I*—I who loved June Eddgar better and longer than any soul on earth—now I was her murderer. And this is where you come into it, Seth, or where I've always imagined you came into it. Because I could see you having the last laugh. Both of you. As I was sitting there, I understood. I could see the parallels. I had agreed to something, to be used in something, a deception for the ben-efit of someone I cared about—as you agreed many years ago, Seth, and then were changed up, misled. Tit for tat. I understood. This strange theatrical revenge. You said it before: You regard me as a man who got away with murder. So why not let me take the blame in public for one I did not commit? I was quite sure you two believed it was entirely appropriate."

"It's entirely appropriate," Seth answers. "But he never told me."

"No?" Eddgar again considers Seth askance. "Well, it was a gleeful experience for him. I'll say that. Because he had me. I could see in the courtroom, Hobie was laughing at me in a thousand different ways, most of all because he was saying, 'What for your child? This much? More? How about this much? How much, you bastard? How much?' And he relished it. It was sadistic."

"No," says Seth. "He's not a sadist."

"It surely appeared that way."

"No," says Seth again. He ponders the curve of events. The vast im-ponderable enigma of Hobie T. Tuttle looms here—like the Buddha emerging from the mists. Impetuous, yes. Complex. Brilliant. But Hobie would never have permitted such a twisted sport for his own sake. He'd have laughed to think of it; the notion would have kept him up all night chuckling. But he carried through only for one reason.

"He did it *for* me, Eddgar," Seth says, "not with me. He did it because he's my friend. And was Cleveland's friend. In his heart of hearts, he was taking our revenge. As well as helping Nile, of course. I'm sure he meant to do that, too."

Eddgar holds the thought, then lets his head bow with the weight of that possibility. Out on the gravel drive, Seth hears the crunching of someone's approach. It's Nile, Seth thinks. It's Michael. That would be perfect. They'll shuffle in, unshaven, weary from the road. But when Eddgar returns from the front door he's merely holding an overnight delivery envelope, papers parceled off from the state capitol for the senator's inspection.

"Have you talked to Nile?" Seth asks.

Eddgar, sadly, futilely, flexes his hands. "No way to reach him. I know they're together, Michael and he. You realized that much, I take it?" says Eddgar, and again casts a glance at the paper Hobie gave Seth last night. "I heard from Michael once. In the immediate aftermath. A day or two later. Sounded like he was at a pay phone by a highway. I was quite relieved. I have every confidence that Michael won't let Nile come to grief. They're very capable together. What's the word? 'Syntonic.' I suppose, they always have been. They'll look after one another. And I'm certain that in a desperate case Michael could get word to me.

"You should understand," says Eddgar. "I could find them. They have to be within a day's drive. Michael wouldn't have much appetite for change. He's not good with it. He's still probably going by the same name, the same social-security number we dug up for him when he gave his to you. I have no doubt they're settled in another little town."

Sipping the tea, Seth takes an instant to imagine Nile and Michael together as Eddgar described them. Probably living on some rented farmette with a tiny frame house which the wind blows through in winter. Working day jobs in town, clerks or something, tilling the earth as weekends and summer light allow. They probably speak little. Michael these days surfs the Internet, instead of the shortwave bands. Nile watches TV. But they make allowances for each other. And to the world they are father and son, one of those odd pairs families often create, attuned to each other and hardly anybody else. Nile has become the man he always wanted to be: Michael, another erratic fugitive, the best example he had.

"I could find them," Eddgar repeats. "But I'm not going to trail Nile as if I were a bounty hunter. When he wants to see me, he will. I understand how it is. He's likely to keep running, isn't he? If I pursue him?"

"I think that's right."

"I think it's shame," says Eddgar. "His reason for fleeing? That's more or less how I explain it to myself."

"Sounds more like anger to me."

"Anger?" asks Eddgar. He shows the first open surprise since the moment he saw Seth on his porch this morning.

"I bet the sight of you on the witness stand lying your ass off to save him — playing along with Hobie, whatever you want to call it — was probably more than he could stomach. I take it neither one of you bothered to fill in Nile in advance." They're both too high-handed to have troubled with that, Seth knows. Eddgar was right before, he thinks. Insight isn't everything. Because it's seldom complete. Eddgar might see himself as meddlesome, overly protective, but he'll never recognize the message he delivered to Nile on every possible occasion, that his son would always be beholden, incapable, incomplete.

"But isn't it puzzling?" Eddgar asks. "I think about it every day. For hours. And I'm baffled. Perhaps he was angry, as you say, at the end of the trial. I surely meant well. But we could have misunderstood one another. That's an old story. But what could he have been thinking to start? Getting mixed up that way? With Core? In that kind of business? What did he want?"

Seth takes his time, although he's known the answer from the moment Eddgar told him the story.

"I imagine he wanted to be one of the people you cared about, Eddgar." This observation, leveled with no more mercy than a hammer blow, provokes little visible reaction at first. Eddgar brings his hand to his mouth momentarily. On the wall, there's a large white clock. It buzzes faintly, clicking slightly whenever the second hand moves. Ten after eight. He may miss his plane, Seth thinks. But he has no desire to go.

"It's so complex," Eddgar says finally. He circles a finger through a little puddle of gathered moisture left on the table by the bottom of his cup. "I'm not one to dwell on the past, Seth. But whenever I think back, what seems bleakest and most confused to me is Nile. I loved him so truly, so deeply. I still think of his birth as a moment like no other. I can describe the hospital waiting room — it was the days when men were not involved." He permits himself the wee, reflective smile Seth recollects, as if neither of them should make much of the oddity that Eddgar, the great suspect of institutional power, lost his radar at a moment so essential. "I recall the other fathers sitting around, a sandwich one of these men was eating. It was peanut butter and bacon, which he'd brought from home in used-looking silver foil. I can remember everything. I can smell the smoke from everybody's cigarettes.

"It seemed such a perfect recompense that a son should have been born to me who so suffered his own father, who was still wrestling him, the way Jacob in that wonderful passage in the Scripture wrestled the Angel of Death all night. I thought—" He gropes, staring to the distance and the past. "It seemed very important," Eddgar says.

"It was," says Seth.

"Yes, it was. It was, of course it was. I mean merely that the path seemed clear. The way seemed certain—everything I should do and shouldn't do. And of course, it wasn't. I was terribly afraid of him, terribly scared of him, almost at once. Terrified. Of this little tiny child. Of course, I couldn't say to myself that it was fear I felt. I just seemed frozen up somehow. I seemed commanded by some kind of learned response, instead of my own inmost impulses. Oh God." And there is another of those improbable moments Seth first witnessed in the courtroom. Loyell Eddgar is crying. He is probably entitled to comfort, Seth realizes. As a father, Seth has comfort to give. But not to this man. He sits on the other side of the table, in silence, as Eddgar sobs a second, then recovers.

"And I would watch him with you and Michael. You recall how he was with Michael, Seth? I would just watch the two of them, out there in that tree, pounding, sawing, laughing at one another—I'd feel terrible. Just terrible. Because I still loved him so. So much. I was brimming with feeling. Looking back, I think I felt more honest emotion toward Nile than any other person in my life.

"And I would worry and worry and worry about one thing, one question all the time. It sounds like madness now, but I was haunted by this question, maddened by it, absolutely obsessed. If I had to give him up, I kept thinking, if I had to give him up, could I?"

"Give him up?" asks Seth.

"Yes. To the revolution. If the day came. If I had to let him fight. Do things that would endanger him. It never seemed—you can take this as you like, I'm sure you're doubtful, question motives, I'd do the same probably—but it never seemed awful to be placing ourselves in danger. June. Me. I could imagine—I *had* imagined that. You know all the prison literature that's been created by captured leaders. I'd read that. Torture. Isolation. I'd imagined that."

And gloried probably in the prospect, Seth thinks. Eddgar's greyish hair has fallen forward, over his brow, as he looks down to his folded hands.

"But I was riven," he says, "agonized, by the total quandary of being a parent. How could I show Nile everything I treasured and believed, which I seemed impelled to do, how could I do that and then confront the moment decades on when that led to his sacrifice? Would I be able to pay that price, I kept asking, would I be able let him go, my son, my love, my life, my future? I avoided thinking about it for months, and then the question would strike me, more powerfully than any fear I've ever felt for myself, and I found no comfort really, but was led back again and again, by some distraught impulse, to the words of the Scripture, that God's greatest love was shown by this, that He gave us the life of His only son. As if that thought could really be any help, as if it could do anything but deepen the mystery."

He stands, draining the last from his cup. He claps his shirt pockets and, not finding what he's seeking, removes his glasses and wipes his eyes on his sleeve. On the worn heels of his loafers, he crosses into the brilliant path of light that emerges from the window, an elongated parallelogram divided by the shadowed mullions, and nods from the doorway, older and littler than he was in Seth's memory. With one hand, he attempts some heartless gesture, a farewell and a direction to Seth to show himself out.

He goes. It will take pure luck now to make his plane to Seattle. Traveling far too fast, he dodges traffic on 843 in the morning rush. So are you done now? he finally asks himself. In part, he still valiantly resists everything pulling on him in the wake of this visit. It wasn't genuine, Seth keeps thinking. The tears. The torment. Like all great actors, Eddgar will always become exactly who his audience wishes him to be. But there is no turning away from his vulnerability to Eddgar. That was fixed long ago, in the stars, in the genes, in nature. So what's the point? Seth asks himself. Everybody has his story? His grief? He knew that. Already. He knew it. Maybe it's what he said to Hobie last night. About love and justice. Maybe there is no difference. In the ideal, at least. Maybe love and justice are one.

He drives on.

Are you done now?

April 4, 1996

Seth—

Who writes letters anymore? This is probably an act of craziness. But Dubinsky dropped off the copies of the eulogies the *Trib* people had printed. (Beautiful, aren't they? This was a touching gesture, Seth.) I'm a little too hard-headed to hold on to them on the assumption you're coming back. And I can't simply slide them into this envelope without a word of my own. It's 9:30 now. Hot Time, as you say. The hour we have spent together most nights. I miss you. The laughter, the connection. I have nasty thoughts. The body yearns.

Which means what? I've been running all the what-ifs in my

mind, watching each clip to see the different endings to our movie. Nothing is exactly right. But I thought I'd take you at your word and speak my mind, at least the part I know. We're both relatively honest. I regard that as one of our pluses.

When I left Charlie, at the age of forty-four, I had to recognize that I'm one of those people who may never come to rest, never find the opening in the world where I am going to squarely fit. My life, in its current shape, will tumble on for a while, and then I'll feel the way I always do, that it's not quite right, that maybe there's something better, or not quite as bad, over the next hill and I'll be gone in that direction. There are times I think almost abstractly about my lifetime of shifting obsessions and feel washed away by a pounding wave of shame. Four different graduate programs. All my jobs. And men. And a thousand pastimes undertaken with unflagging ardor, each intended to save my spirit at night while my body slaved in obeisance to the future during the day. The relics are in that horrible Fibber's closet of a basement where I won't let you roam: an enormous loom; plastic jugs and curing vats (I was going to culture my own wine); bridles, bits, and saddle from the period I decided to retake my squandered childhood by riding. Not to mention the boxes of Y-Me literature and the books on various dietary obsessions. Each of these phases passed away, lifted like fog, traceless, if you do not count the accessories that mildew in the cellar or a single blanket I wove which Nikki still clutches for comfort when she sleeps. At my worst moments, I suspect I bore Nikki simply to have an anchor.

And even having done that, I'm never right, never fully at ease. I know there's a chance I'll be here by myself at the end, on the other side of something I'm still longing to get over. There's a lot of pain in that. Not just the recognition, but the fact. Yet there are moments, like now, when I'm more or less at peace and willing to say, Maybe that's me. If this thing—us—if it doesn't work out, I'm going to be okay. I know that. It's one of the best lessons I learned from Zora: I know how to wrap my arms around myself. And I don't mean that as a sop. It may even be a warning.

Which is not to deny I'm angry. I am. I'm aggravated that

you're gone and that you let it come to this, with two women reaching after you. I ask myself questions I heard in my head all the time with Charlie: Why does it seem to be women who have to stand up for everything of real value in the world? For children, first of all; for nurturance. For homes. And, yes, even love. I know that's not entirely fair. I sometimes watch you with Nikki in mild amazement—unloading her backpack, making snacks. I leave you a lot more room to be that person than Lucy ever did. But it's your confidence and contentment that are striking, the way you *see* a household. Not a war zone. Not a field of mutual striving. Not some prolonged adolescence in which the partners travel, each for themselves. But a family. You can show me how to do that, as Charlie, of course, never did. And even so, that's hard for me, because it leaves me wrestling with the hardest question of all, whether it's me you need or Nikki. In the end, we both have to deal with the fact that it's loss that brings you to me.

History. Circumstances and events. They still stand between us. I never would have suspected the degree to which I'm haunted by our past together. Twenty-five years, you think. We were only children. And yet it feels like it could be fatal. What's the difference now? I wonder. Why won't we fail the same way we did a quarter-century ago? I suspect these are the furthest questions from your mind, Seth. What's the saying? *Within the body of every cynic beats the broken heart of a romantic.* You still believe in the transforming power of Will and Love. It's so endearing. I want to let you win, to triumph at this quest. I know how important it is for you.

But I worry I may let you down the way I did decades ago. Back then, you needed my devotion, probably so you had the strength to stand apart from your parents. And I couldn't provide it. Not, as I think you feared then, because I didn't believe in or admire you. You do not know ten people, Seth, who feel more vindicated or less surprised by the way the world has embraced your talent. No. What troubled me was your celestial devotion to *me*. To the girl philosophy student who was supposed to light up the skies at Miller Damon. Because I knew she was a fake. Oh, I had certain gifts. I've never sold myself short. I read Plato while I was still in high school. And believed what

Socrates said about knowledge as life's highest quest. To the thought of replacing passion with reason, some singing (passionate?) chord in me responded. Instead, over time, I learned that the differing endpoints of various philosophical excursions were due largely to the places they'd begun. The zero points. The irreducible assumptions. It's who you are to start that makes the difference. And in that light, Plato was, if not wrong, at least deserving of correction. All knowledge derives from passion. And what my passions were was largely a mystery. Certainly not philosophy. I read the texts in a bloodless way, like an inspector on a tour. I was, I suddenly decided, leading someone else's life. Whose? I didn't have a clue then. But my mother knew like Holy Writ those heavyweight German philosophers I studied. To this day, I can hear her shrilling at meetings, 'That is *not* what Engels meant! Never!' So I fled, mystified about my motives.

All my life I've been afraid I lack common sense. My mother, shrewd as she was, had none. I mean that she seemed to forget that people would be hurt if she called them names, that a small child might need a meal now and then, that she couldn't work in South Carolina and be a mother to me here. It wasn't just that she seemed at times to feel overpowered by her own needs—the truth is that we all do—but she had no recognition when it was occurring. And even now I'm afraid she left the same traits in me, the way an unhappy spirit is supposed to remain in a woodland tree. 'You're acting just like Zora' is something I can unleash against myself with the primitive anger of a curse, as I prime myself not to act or speak or feel in given ways. It turns out that one of the passageways to my adulthood was this vow, this secret I didn't even tell myself out loud, not to be like her.

Don't misunderstand. I loved—love—my mother. Yet it was years—not until the end of that trial was nearing—since I felt free to embrace the best of her. I believe Zora would be proud of me. And I know she would adore Nikki. Both thoughts mean a lot. But throughout my younger years I wanted a lot more. I wanted her to be my salvation, my ideal. God, I *needed* that. I would feel fifty times a day how much I could utilize the strength born of knowing I could simply form myself to her example. And it's my task, the stone I've been rolling up the hill forever, to recognize that can't take place, to see—even though I couldn't bear to say it most of my life—that she was, at moments, a selfish lunatic, that there were times when all her passions, her anxieties, all her towering concerns made me beside the point. Here I am in the shadow of fifty and there still are mornings I wake to happy dreams of the *total*, devoted, desperate way I loved her when I was young. And when it comes to me that's no longer right, possible, *real*, I'm crushed. My spirit's broken for hours.

She loved me. Passionately. When it suited her. In response, I learned how to hold some distance. (Big surprise!) And resolved, with the same desperation of my love for her, that I would try not to be as unhappy as she was. Because I knew that for certain, too, that nutsy Zora, with her rages, speeches, scraps of quotes, with her warm whispers for me, her smell of lotion, her walleye, her midnight pacing, meetings, and constant grumbling at the way of the world—that she was swirling like some nebula around a livid core of pain.

The project of my life is to cherish what I can of her, and yet to be neither her mindless imitator nor her willing victim. I will always worship her ferocious independence. But I would rather be dungeon-condemned for all eternity than consign myself to her isolation. I want you to understand how hard this is for me. To be the one writing this letter. To be the one speaking first. To be the one asking. It seems almost cruel to have to say Yes, knowing you may say No. But I heard what you said the other night and I know this won't happen any other way. You are entitled to be told that you are needed. More—essential. Not only to Nikki, but to me. You are. It has taken my whole life for me to say this, but I deserve someone I can rely on. Through and through. I know you can be that person, Seth. If I let you. I want to try.

This is a love letter.

Sonny

Eulogy for Bernhard Weissman
by Seth Daniel Weissman
April 1, 1996

I always return to the story of Abraham and Isaac when I think about my father. Some of that springs from the legacy which gave our son his name. But there is more to it, of course. No doubt, we all recall the story. Abraham was the founder of the Western faiths, the first Jew, the first person to know the God to whom most peoples in the world now pray. He was a visionary, a prophet, and, surely, an iconoclast capable of cleaving to his beliefs in the face of universal scorn.

But despite this, Abraham's God decided to test him. He asked Abraham to make a sacrifice of his and Sarah's only child, Isaac, their miracle, who had been born to them when Sarah was already ninety years old and Abraham one hundred. And according to the story, Abraham complied. He did not say what we would hope a father of today might: I am hearing ugly voices, I need help. He did not ask what was wrong with a God who would demand such a thing, or question whether He was worth worshipping. He did not, so far as the Bible tells us, even beg for Isaac's life, as he had done for the people of Sodom. Abraham simply walked his child up Mount Moriah—I imagine he even made the boy carry the wood for the fire. When Isaac asked where the lamb might be for the religious sacrifice they were undertaking, Abraham told him God was bringing the lamb.

In candor, I've regarded this for some years now as a strange story, a grim tale of how a father would sacrifice his son to his own faith, his own visions. What kind of starting point is this for us anyway, for all the Western faiths? Celebrating the twisted dynamic between the first Jewish father and the first Jewish son? Why do we retell this story? Is it to remind us that every parent since has done better?

I initially asked these questions in an anguished state. It was the last time I ever entered a synagogue. The occasion was the New Year. The other congregants were there to express their commitments to what is referred to now and again in the writings as the God, the faith, and the laws of our fathers. I was there to say the Mourner's Prayer, inasmuch as not much time had passed since my own boy named Isaac had died. For us—Lucy and Sarah, and certainly for me—it's probably the case that every funeral we go to for the rest of our lives will be Isaac's. I apologize for having to share this. But in order to speak of my father, I also have to talk about my children—our wonderful, extraordinary daughter, for whose presence I thank God and all else in the universe every day, and the son we lost.

I don't know how many of you here know the story of how our Isaac came to be given that name. But it is, fittingly, my father's story, and the one we all shudder to recall. In March 1938, the German Army marched into Austria and brought with them their war against the Jews. Jewish businesses were emblazoned with signs and vandalized or confiscated, while 12,000 Jewish families were thrown out of their homes. The Nazis turned synagogues into smoking parlors and beat at random Jews found on the streets. On April 23, a Saturday, in Vienna, that most genteel of cities, the home of Sigmund Freud and Gustav Mahler, a group of Jews was taken to the Prater, Vienna's amusement park, and there, in the presence of the usual weekend crowd, the SS forced the Jews to their knees and made them eat the lawn. By June, more than 500 Viennese Jews had committed suicide. On the sixteenth of that month, my father, his young wife, and their four-year-old son, who had been out together for a hasty visit to a shop, were accosted by storm troops. They were informed that their home was now state property.

In the next three years they moved half a dozen times as more and more of the city was closed to Jewish residency. Jews were removed from their jobs and forced to wear the yellow star when they walked down the street. But my father remained. His mother-in-law had had a stroke and was not transportable. And emigration became increasingly difficult as time went on and the nations throughout Eastern Europe closed their borders for fear of being overrun by Austria's 180,000 Jews. More to the point, flight would have shattered some essential vision of himself. He was, very much, the man he had planned to be, the son of a shopkeeper, a silversmith, who, as I understand it, had longed to have a son who would be, as my father had become, a scholar, broadly respected at the university.

The deportation to the camps of Vienna's Jewish population came slowly at first, but by October 1941 was fully under way. With the assistance of the leaders of the Jewish community under the direction of Rabbi Murmelstein, Jews were sent off to the 'East' in batches of 1,000 in closed freight cars. My father, his wife, and his son were among the first to go. He was pleased to be sent to the concentration camp at Buchenwald, where many noted Viennese had preceded him.

The boy, now seven, developed a painful ear infection on the trip. By the time they were herded off the cattle car in Buchenwald, the boy was crying nearly constantly, whimpering and moaning in pain. His mother begged the guards for medical treatment. Finally, after three days, a guard agreed, took the child from the barracks by the hand, and immediately outside the door shot him, where the boy, my brother Isaac, died.

These events, which my father never once mentioned to me during his lifetime, defined him. They were with him every day. They transformed him—forgive me—deformed him, as a tree can be misshapen by tethering it as a sapling. He needed no injunction never to forget. It was from my mother that I learned what transpired, in short, unbearable conversations over the years. One of the great agonies of her Alzheimer's was that the horrible recollection of the camps survived with her far longer than anything else except, probably, her memories of me. During the stage when she could still speak of things with clarity she repeated a phrase I had heard from her from time to time. 'The best did not survive,' she said. 'Those who would not wheedle or cheat, who shared with the sick—I think they were admired to a degree, but admiration in such circumstances is a very fleeting feeling.' Then my mother, frail and enfeebled, her flesh loose, her eyes dull, but her very look still deeply familiar and precious to me, made certain to face me. 'I have lived the rest of my life recalling them,' she said. She cleared her throat. 'They are my heroes.'

Death deepens my wonder at her. She was surely wrong, for my heart allows no doubt that she was among the best. But I realize that in her usual deep and delicate way she meant to communicate to me some exculpation of my father. For no matter who they were when they entered those horrible facilities, neither she nor he nor any other human being could be subjected on a prolonged basis to such confinement, such humiliation, such intense and repeated brutality, such incessant privation, fear, and constant debasement, and emerge with their humanity fully intact. I accept this. It seems obvious to me, although you can travel to corners of this city—to the towers of Grace Street or Fielder's Green—and see the lesson is not yet learned.

One of the thousand morals of the story of Abraham and Isaac is that the parents' ordeal—and we all have ours—will inevitably become the child's, as my father and mother's ordeal became mine, and mine no doubt became Sarah's and Isaac's. But it is also a tale of survival and of mercy. In the end, Abraham heard his God instruct him not to set his hand against his son. Isaac was spared. He survived and surmounted. He became a parent, blind to Jacob's defects, but one who, pointedly, attempted no sacrifices of his own.

I bear my father the intense gratitude I ought to. Lame and halting, he still went on. But surely we could have both done better. Here at the end, things can be put simply. My father and I often treated each other cruelly. I am sore with shame at the memory of my craziest antics—and would have been more at peace if I had seen in my father any trace of a similar regret. I wish we had negotiated some truce, some settlement. It would have been hard bargaining. No doubt, he trumped me in the category of suffering, particularly since much of mine has been self-inflicted, which, generally speaking, people of his age and experience refused to recognize as pain. But couldn't we have matched up, soul for soul, those two dead little boys, his son and mine, the Isaacs whose fathers could not save them? Isn't there a point of absolute equality in futility and despair? Yet we learn, we grow, we gain. Sarah, surely you and I have already done much better. There's a great deal in that.

So I think about Isaac—my son, my brother, my father's son, the first son of the Western faiths—and I think about the story that is told again and again. We hear it first as children, and repeat it throughout our lives.

We tell it by way of apology. And warning. We tell it with some measure of hope. We tell it because we have all been the child, we have all been Isaac, and we know the part of the story that is never mentioned. For the Bible does not record Isaac's responses. We do not know if he, like Jesus, asked, Father, why have you forsaken me? We do not know if he begged, the way most of us would, for his life. We know only this: that he obeyed. That he was a child. That because he knew nothing else, he did as his father required. We know he allowed himself to be bound in rope. We know he let his father lay him on the altar of pyramided firewood which together they had raised to God. We know he watched his father on the mountaintop raise the gleaming knife above his breastbone. We know he was a child, the son of a man with a Big Idea, who in his longing and confusion, even in his final instants, could only look to his father with that eternal if foundering hope for love.

Eulogy for Bernhard Weissman
by Hobart Tariq Tuttle
April 1, 1996

Allah, Yahweh, sweet Jesus—by whatever name we know You, Lord—take the soul of Bernhard Weissman. You caused him in his life to confront terrible wickedness. He now deserves Your eternal peace.

Were we all—all of us here—to share our memories of Bernhard Weissman, You'd hear a lot of different things. There'd be many voices. There are folks here who can tell You he was a genius in his work. Winners of the Nobel Prize in Economics invited him to their table and treated him as a peer. His granddaughter, our sweet Sarah, would tell You he was a great old guy who responded to her kindness. And You've heard Seth say he was a tough father, and I tell You, I was around to see that, and it is word.

I can speak only for myself. I *liked* the dude. I'm here as his friend. Soundin goofy, I know, sayin I was friends with a fella twice my age. But we *were* friends. When I was a little kid, he scared the livin hell out of me. I remember him wearing those nasty glasses that looked like they pinched your nose—pince-nez?—and talking with that funky Viennese accent? Half the time to start, I couldn't tell if he was speaking to me or clearing his throat. I wanted no part of this cat.

But by high school, I had gotten into him. I can tell You a lot of good things about Mr. Weissman. He was funny. Kind of sneaky funny. He'd catch you. I remember a few years ago, I was visiting, and we were talking about the things we talked about often, politics, race, America, and I said I saw how the government had finally relented and was going to let a group of black and Jewish leaders go together to visit various capitals in the Middle East, hoping to make peace. "Zere is no kvestion, Hopie, zat ze government vants zem to go," he told me. "Zey vould razzer, however, zat zey not come back."

And something else I always appreciated about the man—he liked me. Part of that, I always knew, was for Seth's sake. Bernhard was doin the best he could, takin to Seth's main man, even if he couldn't always do the same for Seth. But he was into me for me, too. I had no doubt about that. I could make him laugh. And he had no trouble with a Negro kid being smart. He was not born American and he did not have a trace of our color-thing, not even a speck of it, on his soul. I appreciated that, I must say. And I have to allow, on my side, that it was easier for me to accept him than many other white folks, because he had paid the price. I couldn't ever say to him, 'You don't know what it's like.' He knew. He understood how it felt to be stuck in this situation, to be labeled and judged, always and constantly under the weight of something you never really fully chose.

You know, I'm like everybody else on the planet: I am deeply struck by the suffering of my own. It's a terrible truth that identity is steeped in the blood of martyrs, a phenomenon you can see clear round the world, people everywhere grouped under ethnic banners and all of them beefin about the way their kin were treated in times past. The Armenians, the Kurds. The Igbo. The Rom. The list is damn near endless. Everybody recalls their oppressors. Even the Pilgrims, WASPs, who I grew up thinking had everything, celebrated Thanksgiving to recollect how bad folks back in England had been to them. And the fact is, nobody's makin this stuff up. We cannot bear homage to those who made us without recognizing their suffering. But it's a sad lesson, nonetheless, that we all so often lay claim to our heritage out of fear of those who once hated us and thus may do so again.

But I'm like the rest: I have always known the pain of black folks. All my life. I've felt it in my bones. We had it good in my home, no complaint about that, but it didn't take me very long, even as a little kid, to notice how hard it was for so many others, and to see that a whole lot of those folks had the same skin on them as I did. I'm the first to tell you that I did not have a clue what to do with that. As a young man, I didn't want the burden. And then I discovered I'd never know myself, never accept myself, unless I took it up. And the absolutely amazing part, as I look back, is that the person who taught me more about dealing with that—*the* man in my life—is Bernhard Weissman. I'm sure, if there had been some cagey old ex-slave who lived down the block, I'd have sat at his feet instead. But there wasn't. I guess Bernhard was the closest thing I could find, a firsthand victim of unbearable oppression, someone I could ask what I see now I was always askin him, even though I never once said it out loud, namely, How do you come to terms?

The last time I saw him, I was asking that again. I was truly in a state.

Upset. I was trying a lawsuit, a very confusing lawsuit. It was confusing to me, because I saw what I see every day in a new light. Usually, I view the life of the ghettoized as a professional. I see it case by case: one crime, one rousting, this thieving client, that dishonest cop. I render what aid I can on that basis, one at a time. But being home, I somehow lost my grip on my professional perspective. I saw the larger picture again, and it was, at moments, heartrending. A terrible thing is happening here. In our midst. And I saw how hatred and desperation may yet engulf us all.

And I talked to Bernhard about this. We walked. We went out there, not far away, and inched along the Midway, that beautiful tree-lined esplanade, with its benches, on the west side of U. Park. It was one of those mysterious late-autumn days in the Midwest, the pewter sky losing the hope of light, the big trees stretching black and stark, the walks slick with moldering yellow leaves. Bernhard listened to me as I confided my anguish, and he confronted me with an odd question.

"Do you know, Hopie," he asked, "vere zis Mid-vay comes from?"

I didn't of course. So he told me the story. During the Civil War, after the Yanks had freed the Mississippi River, they used to freight Confederate prisoners up here, far from the front lines. These rebs—20,000 of them—ended up imprisoned here on the land that now stands beneath the Midway. The city was pretty much a wreck by then. There were no provisions. Everything was being commandeered for the front. There wasn't food to spare, nor coats nor blankets. And in the dead of winter, these prisoners, Southern boys, some who'd barely seen a frost, just basically stood out here on the Midway and died. Froze to death. More than 12,000 of them. They buried those Confederate soldiers right there. And after Dixie was subdued, the city fathers, embittered by war and eager to forget its horrors, plowed the ground over and planted grass and trees, rather than raise gravestones.

You think about that, though. Those lovely stone mansions, up on Grand Boulevard, they were there by the 1850s. It was a fashionable street. Ladies in their hoop skirts went perambulating up and down every day. They walked their babies. And yonder, behind a mess of wire and fences, stood the rebs, huddling under the trees for cover in the snow, freezing and screaming and carrying on, crying out for mercy, and dying. Every day a couple got shot trying to escape.

It was something for me to think about, of course, because it called up all of an African-American's complicated feelings about the Civil War. I still cleave to a schoolboy's understanding of those events, because I think it is fundamentally correct. In the minds of many of those fighting—probably most—it was the War to Free the Slaves. Oh sure, it had a thousand other motives, too, Genovese and them-all, I've read the books. But for the most part there were Americans, who, no matter how they varnished it over with talk of states' rights or the cotton economy, were willing to die for the right to own a nigger, and other Americans, hundreds of thousands of them, white Americans, prepared to lay down their lives because God wanted all his children, including the black ones, to be free. I often think we'd do well in this country to bear both facts in mind. Surely I had them in mind at that moment. And although a part of me listened to Bernhard's story in shock, to think that I had walked a thousand times across the unmarked graves of young soldiers who died so pitifully in their own country, another part of me—the greater part, I confess—heard this with the parched thirst of a people who have never had a full measure of revenge. For it occurred to me at once that those men, cruelly imprisoned, were slaveholders and their supporters. And I thought to myself, Good, this was good, this was as it had to be. Well, there was a look we shared then, Bernhard and me, he the survivor of a similar captivity and I the great-grandson of slaves. He read the thought passing behind my eyes as surely as if I had spoken it, and I do not believe we exchanged another word as we walked slowly home.

Bernhard made his mistakes. But we cannot lay him to rest without admiring his strength of character. He had the courage to tell me what he meant to out on the Midway, which was that this would never end. He could hardly be faulted for that view, not only because of his own experience, but given what has gone on since, dozens of hideous episodes that seem to show that humankind has not learned a damn thing from all that suffering. Pol Pot's killing fields. Idi Amin. The Chinese slaughters in Tibet. The Ayatollah's annihilation of the Baha'i. The Hutus' dismemberment of the Tutsis. The disappeared in Argentina. The carnage in Bangladesh. In Biafra. In Bosnia. We may only pray it does not happen here.

We cannot blame Bernhard for his pessimism. There are days—many, many days—when I know in my bones he was right. But perhaps there is another way to accept his legacy. Perhaps there is meaning in these millions of seemingly meaningless deaths. Perhaps Darwin—or God—is sending the species signs so large we cannot fail to heed them. Perhaps our survival depends on recognizing that we can be monsters, so that self-awareness reinforces our commitment to what is more noble in us. For in his lifetime, Bernhard also saw freedom in South Africa, the enfranchisement of women in the West, the withering of colonialism, the blooming of democracy in nation after nation, and the growth of a million varieties of the fruit of human cunning which have immeasurably advanced knowledge and well-being across the planet. Perhaps that was what Bernhard meant to tell me, after all: we are both. We are the tyrant *and* the democrat, the captor *and* the survivor, the slaveholder *and* the slave. We are blood heirs to each heritage. On the best days—his and mine—that is what I hope Bernhard would admonish all of us never to forget.

September 7, 1996

SONNY

Sonny is sick. As she envisions it, the cancer is a fire, an errant spark that smolders and is never out, an ember no larger than an atom that somehow licks itself to life and burns through her flesh, with ghoulish smells and unbearable heat she somehow does not feel. It grows. The cancer burns. In the dream, the light of fire magnifies itself until her breast is glowing like E. T.'s heart in the movie Nikki is always watching, until the blaze shows the palpitating strength of life, so that life resembles death, and the fire suddenly blooms in a monstrous explosion of light, the dreaded atomic flashpoint of her childhood, ending all the world.

"No!" she screams into the dark, and Seth, struggling awake, claps his hand over her mouth, then holds her from behind. For a long moment, their bodies move together in the labored breath of terror. She has warned him. The dreams come every six months or so and the fear is plundering. It hangs in her bones, like the ache of an ailment, until she has a mammogram. She will call Gwen in the morning. With luck they can take her today. Embracing her, Seth kisses her neck, then her mouth, stale with sleep.

"Oh, I hate this, I hate this," Sonny declares in the dark. "And even when Gwendolyn's called and told me everything's all right, I'll still worry. Because what do I do the day it isn't all right?"

"That won't happen."

"Don't treat me like a child, Seth. You can't make promises."

"Sonny, look, we go on. Okay? You don't know and I don't know. But we go on. It hasn't happened, and I trust it won't."

"It's Nikki," she says. "It's deserting her, failing her that way. That's the worst part. It's torture. To think that for everything, everything I've done and tried to do—that she'll be alone."

"Nikki will be okay. That I *can* promise you."

Sonny sits up. Damp with sweat, she has started to grow cold. She grabs the satin binding of the blanket which her thrashing wrested from the mattress and draws it around herself.

"To leave her with *Char*-lie! God," says Sonny.

"Over my dead fucking body will she be with Charlie. Forget that."

"He's her father."

"When was the last time he called? A cottonwood has more feeling for its lint than Charlie has for his children." She actually laughs. It's terrible. Does Seth delight her any more than at the moments he speaks of Charlie, riled by contempt and wrath? "If I tell Charlie I'm taking care of her, that I'm adopting her, he'll be relieved. You know that."

Adopt her. Seth could do that. The law. Thank God for the law. Charlie can consent and Seth can adopt her.

"Would you really adopt her?"

"Today."

"Do you mean it?"

She feels him move from her and is blinded then by the bedside light. When she removes her hand, Seth is staring at her.

"Look into my eyes," he intones. "I mean it. If you'll have it, if she'll have it, we'll start whenever. She's precious to me. You know that."

She thinks out loud. What if Charlie won't go along?

"You tell Charlie he doesn't have to pay child support anymore," says Seth, "and he'll crawl here from Cincinnati to sign."

In the absolute quiet of night, Sonny laughs. A pure bubble of delight. He's right.

"You really mean it?"

"Of course, I mean it."

Seth can adopt her.

"I want to know you understand how important this is to me," Sonny says. "Right now I'm here, and whatever happens between us happens. But if I'm gone—Promise," she says. "Promise me you really understand and really mean this."

"You're going to be fine."

"I need your promise. I don't want to think of her in someone's home and not being a part of it. I don't want her feeling she's in between, like I did whenever I was with my aunt and uncle, that I didn't really have a place there, that I was sweet and nice but not fully tied to them. I don't want that. Bring her into your life. Completely. Will you promise? Promise that."

"Fine," he says. "Okay."

"Don't humor me, Seth. This is the most serious thing in my life."

"Sonny, I'm as serious as you are."

"Because if you promise this and don't do it, I will haunt you. I will be a mean ghost. I really will. You have to take her in. Let her feel she belongs to you. As she belongs to me. I want you to promise you'll be her father. Not a stranger. Not just somebody who thinks she's wonderful. But someone committed to her life as his legacy, someone who wants her to understand everything that is deepest in you. That's what you have to promise. Give her what you know most purely is yourself. I'm serious."

"Of course, I promise that. I know what it means to be somebody's father, Sonny. Right now—here, today—she's my daughter."

"I want to *know* you mean it."

Forlornly, he looks into the brightness of the bedside lamp for quite some time.

"What would you say—" His face, in the harsh light, swims in feeling. He starts again. "If it's all right with both of you—" He gets no further.

"Say it, Seth. I need to hear this."

When he turns, his look contains all his familiar skepticism about himself.

"I think I'd like to raise her as a Jew," he says.